POLAR
STAR
&
ROSE

Also by Martin Cruz Smith

THE INDIANS WON

GYPSY IN AMBER

CANTO FOR A GYPSY

NIGHTWING

STALLION GATE

GORKY PARK

RED SQUARE

HAVANA BAY

MARTIN CRUZ SMITH

POLAR STAR & ROSE

PAN BOOKS

Polar Star first published 1989
by Collins Harvill and first published by Pan Books 1996
Rose first published 1996
by Macmillan and first published by Pan Books 1997

This omnibus edition published 2002 by Pan Books
an imprint of Pan Macmillan Ltd
Pan Macmillan, 20 New Wharf Road, London N1 9RR
Basingstoke and Oxford
Associated companies throughout the world
www.panmacmillan.com

ISBN 0 330 41824 6

1 3 5 7 9 8 6 4 2

A CIP catalogue record for this book is available from
the British Library.

Phototypeset by Intype L:ondon Ltd
Printed and bound in Great Britain by
Mackays of Chatham plc, Chatham, Kent

POLAR
STAR

Contents

POLAR STAR

Officers' quarters

Americans' quarters

Workshops

Bridge

4 below decks

Bow

Fish hold

Fish hold

Freezing rooms

Fish hold

Inspection tables

Processing line

Trawl deck

Fish hold

Aft house contains
crew's mess, galley,
infirmary, library

3 decks on bridge
and aft house

Lifeboats

Well

Stern

Ramp

Crew's quarters

Engine room

571 feet

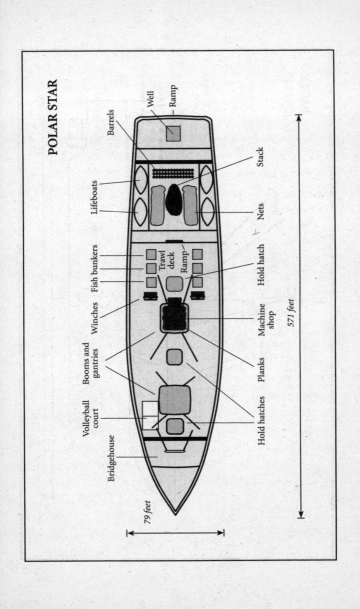

POLAR STAR

Barrels

Well

Ramp

Lifeboats

Stack

Nets

Fish bunkers

Trawl deck

Winches

Ramp

Hold hatch

Booms and gantries

Machine shop

Volleyball court

Planks

Bridgehouse

Hold hatches

571 feet

79 feet

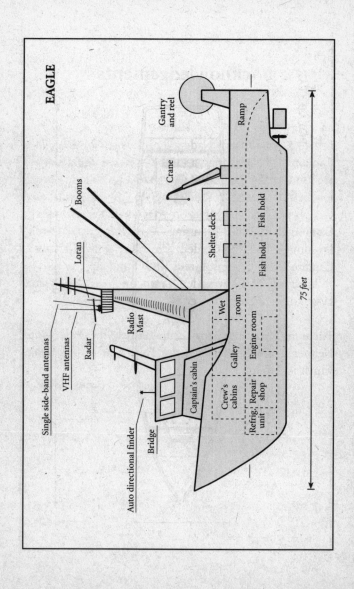

EAGLE

Gantry and reel

Ramp

Crane

Booms

Shelter deck

Fish hold

Fish hold

Loran

Radio Mast

Wet room

75 feet

Single side-band antennas

VHF antennas

Radar

Galley

Engine room

Captain's cabin

Crew's cabins

Refrig, Repair unit shop

Auto directional finder

Bridge

Acknowledgements

I thank Captain Boris Nadein and the crew of the *Sulak*; Captain Mike Hastings and the crew of the *Oceanic*; Sharon Gordon, Dennis McLaughlin and William Turner for their hospitality in the Bering Sea. Valuable assistance was also provided by Martin Arnold, Kathy Blumberg, Captain D. J. (Jack) Branning, Knox Burger, Dr Gerald Freedman, Beatrice Golden, Professor Robert Hughes, Captain James Robinson and Kitty Sprague.

Most of all I owe Alex Levin and Captain Vladil Lysenko for their patience.

There is a Soviet factory ship named the *Polar Star*. Neither it nor the *Sulak* is the *Polar Star* of this book, which is fiction.

Part One

WATER

Chapter One

Like a beast, the net came steaming up the ramp and into the sodium lamps of the trawl deck. Like a gleaming pelt, mats of red, blue, orange strips covered the mesh: plastic 'chafing hair' designed to ease the net's way over the rocks of the sea bottom. Like rank breath, the exhalation of the sea's cold enveloped the hair in a halo of its own colours, brilliant in the weepy night.

Water hissed from the net's plastic hair onto the wooden boards that provided footing on the deck. Smaller fish, smelts and herring, fell free. Starfish dropped like stones. Uprooted crabs, even dead, landed on tiptoe. Overhead, gulls and shearwaters hovered at the outer glow of the lamps. As the wind shifted the birds broke into a swirl of white wings.

Usually the net was tipped and disgorged headfirst into the forward chutes to begin with, then ass-end into the rear. Either end could be opened by releasing the knot of a 'zipper', a nylon cord braided through the mesh. Though the men stood by with shovels ready for work, the trawlmaster waved them off and stepped into the water raining from the net's plastic 'hair' and stared straight up, removing his helmet the better to see. The coloured strips dipped like running paint. He reached and spread the 'hair' from the mesh, then looked into

3

the dark to find the other, smaller light riding the ocean swells, but already fog hid the catcherboat the net had come from. From his belt the trawlmaster took a double-edged knife, reached through the dripping plastic hair and sawed the belly of the net down and across. Fish began dropping by ones and twos. He gave the knife a last furious tug and stepped back quickly.

Out of the net and into the light spilled a flood of silver pollock, a whole school which had been caught *en masse* and dredged up like bright coins. There were thick, bruised-looking bullheads; overlapping waves of flatfish, blood-red on the eyed side, pale on the blind side; sculpin with heads like dragons; cod, some bloated like balloons by their air bladders, some exploded into soft tissue and pink slime; coral crabs as hairy as tarantulas. The bounty of the night-time sea.

And a girl. She slid loose-limbed like a swimmer as the fish poured from the net. On the deck she rolled lazily, arms awry, against a mound of sole, a bare foot tangled in crabs. A young woman, not a girl. Her hair was short and her blouse and jeans were sodden and twisted, heavy with water and sand, unprepared for any return to the world of air. The trawlmaster lifted a strand of hair that had wrapped itself across her eyes, revealing the open surprise in them, as if the ship's lamplit fog were golden clouds, as if she had risen in a boat sailing towards heaven itself.

Chapter Two

Originally when it came down the rails in Gdansk, the *Polar Star*'s four superstructures had been a dazzling white and the gantries and booms a candy yellow. The decks were clear; silver chains wound round the winches; the facing on the deckhouses was stylishly raked. In fact the *Polar Star* had looked like a ship.

Twenty years of saltwater had repainted it with rust. The top decks had accumulated wooden planks, full barrels of lubricating oil and empty barrels for fish oil, the refuse of piled nets and floats. From the black stack with its red Soviet band drifted the dark smoke of a diesel in poor condition. Now, seen from a distance with a good view of the hull battered by unloading side trawlers in bad weather, the *Polar Star* resembled not so much a factory ship as a combination factory-and-junkyard cast into the sea and making improbable headway through the waves.

Yet day and night the *Polar Star* efficiently caught fish. Not caught, that was wrong; smaller trawlers caught the fish and transferred their nets to the factory ship to be processed: headed, gutted, frozen.

For four months now, the *Polar Star* had followed American catcherboats in American waters from Siberia to Alaska, from the Bering Straits to the Aleutian Islands. It was a joint venture. Simply put, the Soviets provided processing ships and took the fish, while the Americans provided trawlers and translators and took the money, all of this managed by a Seattle-based company that was half Soviet, half American. The crew of the *Polar Star* had seen the sun perhaps two days in that time, but then the Bering Sea was known as 'The Grey Zone'.

Third Mate Slava Bukovsky walked the processing line while workers sorted the catch: pollock on a conveyor belt to the saws, mackerel and rays into the fishmeal hatch. Some of the fish had literally exploded as their air bladders expanded on the way from the bottom of the sea and soft bits of them clung like mucus to caps, oilskin aprons, lashes, lips.

He passed the rotary saws to the 'slime line', where workers stood in slots on either side of the belt. Like automatons, the first pair slit fish bellies open to the anus; the second pair sucked out livers and guts with vacuum hoses; the third pair washed slime from the skin, gills and cavities with saltwater jets; the last pair vacuumed the fish a final time and laid the trimmed and dressed result on a belt moving towards the freezers. In the course of an eight-hour watch the gutting and spraying spread a mist of blood and wet pulp over the belt, workers and walkway. They were not the usual Hero Workers, least of all the pale man with dark hair loading the dressed fish at the end of the line.

'Renko!'

Arkady vacuumed pinkish water from one eviscerated

belly, slapped the fish on the freezer belt and picked up the next. Pollock was not firm-fleshed. If it wasn't cleaned and frozen quickly it would be unfit for human consumption and be fed to minks; if unfit for them, it would go to Africa as foreign aid. His hands were numb from handling fish little warmer than ice, but at least he wasn't working the saw like Kolya. In bad weather when the ship began to roll it took concentration to handle a frozen, slippery pollock around a blade. Arkady had learned to dig the toes of his boots under the table so that he wouldn't slide on the duckboards. At the beginning of the voyage and at the end, the entire factory was hosed down and scrubbed with ammonia, but meanwhile the fish room had a dank, organic slickness and smell. Even the clicking of the belt, the whining of the saw, the deep rhythmic moan of the hull were the sounds of a leviathan that was resolutely swallowing the sea.

The belt stopped.

'You're Seaman Renko, aren't you?'

It took Arkady a moment to recognize the third mate, who was not a frequent visitor belowdecks. Izrail, the factory manager, stood at the power switch. He wore layers of sweaters and a black stubble almost to his eyes, which rolled with impatience. Natasha Chaikovskaya, a huge young woman in oilskin armour but with a feminine touch of lipstick, listed discreetly better to see the third mate's Reeboks and unstained jeans.

'Aren't you?' Slava repeated.

'It's not a secret,' Arkady said.

7

'This is not a dance class of Young Komsomolets,' Izrail told Slava. 'If you want him, take him.'

The belt started moving again as Arkady followed Slava aft, stepping over sluices where liquid slime and fish-liver oil ran through bilge holes directly out the side of the ship.

Slava stopped to scrutinize Arkady, as if trying to penetrate a disguise. 'You are Renko the investigator?'

'Not any more.'

'But you were,' Slava said. 'That's good enough.'

They climbed the stairs to the main deck. Arkady assumed the third mate was leading him to the political officer or to a search of his cabin, although that could have been done without him. They walked by the galley and the steamy smell of macaroni, turned left at a sign that promised 'Increase Production in the Agro-Industrial Complex! Strive for a Decisive Upswing in the Supply of Fish Protein!' and halted at the infirmary door.

The door was guarded by a pair of mechanics wearing the red armbands of 'Public Order Volunteers'. Skiba and Slezko were two informers – 'slugs' to the rest of the crew. Even as Arkady and Slava went through the door, Skiba pulled out a notebook.

The *Polar Star* had a clinic bigger than most small towns could boast of: a doctor's office, an examining room, an infirmary with three beds, a quarantine room and an operating room, to which Slava led Arkady. Along the walls were white cupboards with glass cannisters of instruments in alcohol, a locked red cupboard with cigarettes and drugs, a cart with a green tank of oxygen and a red tank of nitrous oxide, a standing ashtray and a brass spittoon. There were anatomical charts on the wall, an astringent tang to the air. A dentist's chair sat in one corner. In the middle of the room was a steel operating table covered by a sheet. Soaked through, the cloth clung to the form of a woman underneath. Below the edge of the sheet dangled restraining straps.

The room's portholes were bright mirrors because it was black outside. 0600, another hour's work to go before dawn, and as usual at this point in his shift Arkady was stupefied by the number of fish in the sea. His eyes felt like those portholes. 'What do you want?' he asked.

'Someone has died,' Slava announced.

'I can see that.'

'One of the girls from the galley. She fell overboard.'

Arkady glanced at the door, picturing Skiba and Slezko on the other side. 'What has this got to do with me?'

'It's obvious. Our trade union committee must make a report on all deaths, and I am the union representative. You're the only one on board with experience in violent death.'

'And resurrection,' Arkady said. Slava blinked. 'It's like rehabilitation, but it's supposed to last longer. Never mind.' Arkady eyed the cigarettes inside the cabinet; they were papirosi, cardboard tubes with tobacco wads. But the cabinet was locked. 'Where's the doctor?'

'Look at the body.'

'Cigarette?'

Caught off-stride, Slava fumbled in his shirt before coming up with a pack of Marlboros. Arkady was impressed. 'In that case, I'll wash my hands.'

The water from the sink tap was brown, but it rinsed the slime and scales off Arkady's fingers. A mark of veteran seamen was discoloured teeth from drinking water from rusting tanks. Over the sink was the first clean mirror he'd looked into for a year. 'Resurrection' was a good word. 'Dug up,' he decided, described him better. The night shift on a factory ship had drained what colour his skin had ever had. A permanent shadow seemed to lie across his eyes. Even the towels were clean. He considered getting sick sometime.

'Where were you an investigator?' Slava asked as he lit the cigarette for Arkady, who filled his lungs.

'They have cigarettes in Dutch Harbor?'

'For what sort of crimes?'

'I understand that in the store in Dutch Harbor the cigarettes are stacked to the ceiling. And fresh fruit. And stereos.'

Slava lost patience. 'What sort of investigator?'

'Moscow.' Arkady exhaled. For the first time he delivered his whole attention to the table. 'And not for accidents. If she fell overboard, how did you get her back? I never heard the engines stop to pick her up. How did the body get here?'

'It is not necessary for you to know.'

Arkady said, 'When I was an investigator I had to look at dead people. Now that I am a simple Soviet worker I only have to look at dead fish. Good luck.'

He took a step towards the door. It was like pressing a button. 'She came up in the net,' Slava said quickly.

'Really?' Arkady was interested in spite of himself. 'That is unusual.'

'Please.'

Arkady returned and pulled the sheet off.

Even with her arms stretched back over her head, the woman was small. Very white, as if bleached. Still cold. Her shirt and pants were wrenched around her like a wet shroud. One foot wore a red plastic shoe. Slack brown eyes looked up from a triangular face. Her hair was short and blonde, but black at the roots. A mole, a beauty mark by the mouth. He lifted her head, let it drop limply onto the table. Felt her neck, arms. The elbows were broken, but not particularly bruised. Her legs were stiff. More than from any fish, the reek of the sea came from her. There was sand in her shoe; she'd touched bottom. Skin was scraped from her forearms and palms, probably by the net on the way back up.

'Zina Patiashvili,' Arkady said. She'd worked in the cafeteria ladling out potatoes, cabbage, compote.

'She looks different,' Slava said analytically. 'I mean, from when she was alive.'

A double difference, Arkady thought. A death change and a sea change. 'When did she go over?'

'A couple of hours ago,' Slava said. He took an executive stance at the head of the table. 'She must have been at the rail and fell over when the net was pulled in.'

'Someone saw her?'

'No. It was dark. Heavy fog. She probably drowned as soon as she hit the water. Or died from shock. Or couldn't swim.'

11

Arkady squeezed the flaccid neck again and said, 'More like twenty-four hours. Rigor mortis starts from head to foot and it leaves the same way.'

Slava rocked slightly on his heels, not from the motion of the ship.

Arkady glanced at the door and lowered his voice. 'How many Americans are on board?'

'Four. Three are representatives of the company, one is an American Fisheries observer.'

'Do they know?'

'No,' Slava said. 'Two were still in their bunks. The other representative was at the stern rail. That's a long walk to the deck. The observer was inside having tea. Fortunately, the trawlmaster was intelligent and covered the body before any Americans could see.'

'The net came from an American boat. Didn't *they* see?'

'They never know what's in the net until we tell them.' Slava pondered. 'We should prepare a proper explanation, in case.'

'Ah, an explanation. She worked in the galley.'

'Yes.'

'Food poisoning?'

'That's not what I meant.' Slava's face turned red. 'Anyway, the doctor examined her when we brought her in and he said she is only two hours dead. If you were such a good investigator you would still be in Moscow.'

'True.'

*

Arkady's shift was over, so he went to the cabin he shared with Obidin, Kolya Mer and an electrician named Gury Gladky. No model seamen here. Gury was on the bottom bunk thumbing through a Sears catalogue. Obidin had hung his overcoat in the closet and was washing slime that clung to his beard like webs on a feather duster. An oversized Orthodox cross swayed on his chest. His voice emanated as a rumble; if a man could speak comfortably from the grave, he would sound like Obidin. 'That is the anti-Bible,' he told Kolya as he looked at Gury. 'That is the work of an anti-Christ.'

'And he hasn't even seen The Sharper Image,' Gury said as Arkady climbed to the upper bunk. In his leisure time, Gury always wore dark glasses and a black leather jacket, like a lounging aviator. 'You know what he wants to do in Dutch Harbor? Go to church.'

'The people have maintained one,' Obidin said. 'It is the last vestige of Holy Russia.'

'Holy Russia? People? You're talking about Aleuts, fucking savages!'

Kolya counted pots. He had fifty cardboard pots, each five centimetres wide. He had trained as a botanist and to hear him talk about the port of Dutch Harbor and the island of Unalaska was to imagine that the ship was going to put in at Paradise and he would have his choice of the Garden.

'Fishmeal in the soil will help,' he said.

'You really think they're going to make it all the way back to Vladivostok?' A thought occurred to Gury. 'What kind of flowers?'

13

'Orchids. They're more hardy than you think.'

'American orchids? They'd go over big, you'd need some help selling them.'

'They're the same as Siberian bog orchids,' Kolya said. 'That's the point.'

'This was all Holy Russia,' Obidin said, as if nature agreed.

Gury pleaded, 'Arkady, help me. "That's the point"? We have one day in an American port. Men here will spend it looking for fucking Siberian flowers, and Obidin wants to pray with cannibals! Explain to them; they listen to you. We spend five months on this ocean-going shitcan for that one day in port. I have room under my bunk for five stereos and maybe a hundred tapes. Or computer disks. All the schools in Vladivostok are supposed to get Yamahas. Supposed to, at least. Someday. So anything compatible is worth a fortune. When we get home I'm not going to go down the gangplank and say, "Look what I got in America" and hold up pots of Siberian flowers.'

Kolya cleared his throat. He was the smallest man in the cabin and had the unease of the smallest fish in an aquarium. 'What did Bukovsky want?' he asked Arkady.

'That Bukovsky gives me such a pain in the ass.' Gury studied the picture of a colour television. 'Look at this: "nineteen inches". How big is that? I had a Foton colour set in my flat. It blew up like a bomb.'

'There's something wrong with the tubes,' Kolya said meekly. 'Everyone knows that.'

'That's why I had a bucket of sand by the set, thank

14

God.' Gury leaned out to look up at Arkady. 'So what did the third mate want from you?'

There was just enough room between the overhead and the bunk for Arkady to wedge himself into a semi-sitting position. The porthole was open to a faint line of grey. Sunrise in the Bering Sea.

'You know Zina in the galley?'

'The blonde,' Gury said.

'From Vladivostok.' Kolya stacked his pots.

Gury grinned. His incisors were porcelain and gold, decoration as much as dental work. 'Bukovsky likes Zina? She'd tie his cock in a knot and ask if he liked pretzels. He might.'

Arkady turned to Obidin, who could be counted on for a judgment from the Old Testament.

'A slut,' Obidin said and examined the jars that lined the bottom of the wardrobe, the lid of each one plugged with a cork and a rubber pipe. He unscrewed one, releasing the sweet exhaust of fermenting raisins. He examined a jar of potatoes.

'Is this dangerous?' Gury asked Kolya. 'You're the scientist. These fumes, can they explode? Is there any vegetable or fruit he can't make alcohol from? Remember the bananas?'

Arkady remembered. The closet had smelled like a rotting tropical jungle.

'With yeast and sugar, almost anything can ferment,' Kolya said.

'Women should not be on a ship,' said Obidin. On a nail in the back of the closet was a small icon of

15

St Vladimir. His thumb to two fingers, Obidin touched his forehead, chest, right shoulder, left shoulder, heart, then hung a shirt on the nail. 'I pray for our delivery.'

Curious, Arkady asked, 'From who?'

'Baptists, Jews, Freemasons.'

'Although it's hard to see Bukovsky and Zina together,' Gury said.

'I liked her bathing suit,' Kolya said. 'That day off Sakhalin?' A warm-core ring of water had wandered north from the equator, making a false few hours of summer. 'That string bathing suit?'

'A just man covers his face with a beard,' Obidin told Arkady. 'A modest woman keeps herself from public view.'

'She's modest now,' Arkady said. 'She's dead.'

'Zina?' Gury sat up, then removed his dark glasses and stood to be at eye level with Arkady.

'Dead?' Kolya looked aside.

Obidin crossed himself again.

Arkady thought that probably all three of them knew more about Zina Patiashvili than he did. Mostly he recalled that freak day off Sakhalin when she had paraded on the volleyball deck in her bathing suit. Russians loved the sun. Everyone wore the skimpiest possible bathing suit in order to apply the greatest amount of sunshine to their pale skins. Zina, though, had more than a meagre bathing suit. She had a Western body, a bony voluptuosity. On the infirmary table she looked more like a damp rag, nothing like the Zina walking up and down the deck, posing against the gunwale, her sunglasses black as a mask.

'She fell overboard. The net brought her back up.'

The other three stared at him. It was Gury who broke the silence. 'So why did Bukovsky want you?'

Arkady didn't know how to explain. Each man had his past. Gury had always been a *bizness* man, dealing inside and outside the law. Kolya had gone from academe to labour camp, and Obidin zigzagged from drunk tank to church. Arkady had lived with men like them ever since Moscow; nothing broadened acquaintanceship like internal exile. Moscow was a drab hive of *apparatchiks* compared to the diverse society of Siberia. All the same, he was relieved to hear a brusque knock on the cabin door and to see Slava Bukovsky's face again, even if the third mate did step in with a mock bow and address him with scorn.

'Comrade Investigator, the captain wants to see you.'

Chapter Three

Viktor Sergeivich Marchuk needed no uniform or gold braid to announce he was a captain. Outside the Seaman's Hall in Vladivostok Arkady had seen his face among the giant portraits of the leading captains of the Far East fishing fleet. But the picture had softened Marchuk's face and propped it on a jacket and tie so that he looked as if he sailed a desk. The live Marchuk had a face with angles of rough-hewn wood sharpened by the trim black beard of an individualist, and he commanded his ship wearing the wool sweater and jeans of an outdoorsman. Somewhere in his past was an Asian, somewhere a Cossack. The whole country was being led by a fresh breed of men from Siberia – economists from Novosibirsk, writers from Irkutsk and modern mariners from Vladivostok.

The captain seemed at a loss, though, as he pondered the confusion on his desk: a seaman's dossier, a codebook and cipher table, scrap paper covered with rows of numbers, some circled in red, and a second page of letters. Marchuk looked up from them as if trying to get Arkady into focus. Slava Bukovsky took a tactful step away from the object of the captain's attention.

'It is always interesting to meet members of the crew.' Marchuk nodded at the dossier. ' "Former investigator." '

I radioed home for details. Seaman Renko, these are some details.' A heavy finger thudded on the deciphered letters. 'A senior investigator for the Moscow prosecutor's office dismissed for lack of political reliability. Next seen in the lesser metropolis of Norilsk on the run. No great shame, many of our finest citizens came east in chains. As long as they reform. In Norilsk you were a night watchman. As a former Muscovite, you found the nights brisk?'

'I'd burn three oil cans of tar and sit in the middle of them. I looked like a human sacrifice.'

While Marchuk lit a cigarette, Arkady glanced around. There was a Persian carpet on the floor, a sofa built into the corner, a nautical library on railed shelves, television, radio, and an antique desk the size of a lifeboat. Over the sofa was a photo of Lenin addressing sailors and cadets. Three clocks told local Vladivostok and Greenwich Mean Time. The ship ran on Vladivostok time; the log was kept on GMT. Altogether, the captain's dayroom had the look of a private study that merely happened to have lime-green bulkheads for walls.

'Dismissed for destruction of state property, it says here. The tar, I assume. Then you managed to sign on at a slaughterhouse.'

'I dragged reindeer on a killfloor.'

'But again it says you were dismissed for political instigation.'

'I worked with two Buryats. Neither of them understood Russian. Maybe the reindeer talked.'

'Next you show up on a coastal trawler in Sakhalin.

Now this, Seaman Renko, really amazed me. To work one of those old trawlers is to be on the moon. The worst work for the worst pay. The crews are men on the run from their wives, from child support, from petty crimes, maybe even manslaughter. No one cares, because we need crews on the Pacific coast. Yet here it is again: "Dismissed for lack of political reliability." Please tell us, what did you do in Moscow?'

'My job.'

Marchuk brusquely waved blue smoke aside. 'Renko, you've been on the *Polar Star* almost ten months. You didn't even leave the ship when we returned to Vladivostok.'

When a seaman disembarked he had to pass the Border Guard, frontier troops of the KGB.

'I like the sea,' Arkady said.

'I am the leading captain of the Far East fleet,' said Marchuk. 'I am a decorated Hero of Socialist Labour, and not even *I* like the sea that much. Anyway, I wanted to congratulate you. The doctor has revised his estimate. The girl Zina Patiashvili died the night before, not last night. In his capacity of trade union representative, Comrade Bukovsky will naturally be responsible for preparing the report on the matter.'

'Comrade Bukovsky is no doubt equal to the task.'

'He's very willing. However, a third mate is not an investigator. Besides yourself, no one on board is.'

'He seems a young man of initiative. He already found the factory. I wish him luck.'

'Let's be grown men. The *Polar Star* has a crew of two

hundred and seventy deckhands, mechanics and factory workers like you. Fifty of the crew are women. We are like a Soviet village in American waters. News of an unusual death on the *Polar Star* will always find an interested ear. It is vital there be no suggestion of either a cover-up or a lack of concern.'

'So the Americans already know,' Arkady guessed.

Marchuk conceded the point. 'Their head representative has visited me. The situation is even more complicated by the fact that this unfortunate girl died two nights ago. You speak English?'

'Not for a long time. Anyway, the Americans on board speak Russian.'

'But you don't dance.'

'Not recently.'

'Two nights ago we had a dance,' Slava reminded Arkady. 'In honour of fishermen of all nations.'

'I was still cleaning fish. I just glanced in on the way to my shift.' The dance had been held in the cafeteria. All Arkady had seen from the door were figures bouncing in the lights reflected from a ball of mirrors. 'You played the saxophone,' he said to Slava.

'We had guests,' Marchuk said. 'We had two American catcherboats tied up to the *Polar Star* and American fishermen at the dance. It's possible you might want to speak to them. They do not speak Russian. Of course this is not an investigation; that will, as you say, be carried out by the appropriate authorities when we return to Vladivostok. Information should be gathered now, however, while memories are fresh. Bukovsky needs

the assistance of someone with experience in such matters and with a command of English. Just for today.'

'With all respect,' Slava said, 'I can ask questions with
complete correctness and no help from Renko at all. We
must keep in mind that this report will be studied by
the fleet, by departments of the Ministry, by—'

'Remember,' Marchuk said, 'Lenin's thought:
"Bureaucracy is shit!"' To Arkady he said, 'Seaman
Patiashvili was at the dance, which was held about the
time you say she died. We count ourselves fortunate in
having someone with your skills on the *Polar Star*, and
we assume that you count yourself fortunate to have an
opportunity to serve your ship.'

Arkady looked at the litter of papers on the desk.
'What about my political reliability?'

Marchuk's smile was all the more startling in contrast
to his beard. 'We do have an expert in your reliability.
Slava, some interest in Seaman Renko has been expressed
by our friend Comrade Volovoi. We would not want to
start any enterprise without Volovoi.'

Films were presented twice a day in the cafeteria. All
Arkady could see from the hall were murky images on
a screen set up on the stage where Slava and his band
had performed two nights before. A plane was landing
at an airport with modern architecture: a foreign locale.
Cars swung to the terminal kerb: limousines, maybe a
few years old and a little dented but definitely American.
In American accents voices addressed each other as

'Mister This' or 'Mister That'. The cameras focused on foreign wingtip shoes.

'*Vigilance Abroad*,' said someone wandering out. 'All about the CIA.'

It was Karp Korobetz. Barrel-chested, with a hairline that started within a millimetre of his brows, the trawlmaster resembled those massive statues erected after the war, the soldier hoisting his rifle, the sailor firing his cannon, as if victory had been gained by primitive man. He was the model worker of the *Polar Star*.

In fact, on display in the hall was a board that kept count of the competition between the three watches, the winner each week being awarded a gold pennant. So many points were awarded for the quantity of fish caught, for the quality of fish processed, for the percentage of the all-important quota. Karp's team won the pennant month after month. Because Arkady's factory team had the same shift, they won too. 'You Are Building Communism by Feeding the Soviet People!' said the banner over the board. That was him and Karp!

The trawlmaster idly shook out a cigarette. Deckhands didn't take much notice of crew that worked below. He hardly glanced at Slava. On the screen, white packets were being passed from one secret agent to another.

'Heroin,' Karp said.

'Or sugar,' said Arkady. That was hard to get too.

'Trawlmaster Korobetz was the one who found Zina,' Slava changed the subject.

'What time was that?' Arkady asked.

'About 0300,' Karp said.

'Was there anything else in the net?'

'No. Why are *you* asking questions?' Karp demanded in turn. The quality of his gaze had changed, as if a statue had opened its eyes.

'Supposedly, Seaman Renko has experience in matters like this,' Slava said.

'In falling overboard?' Karp asked.

'Did you know her?'

'I only saw her around here. She served food.' Karp's interest was growing all the time. He tried Arkady's name like a bell. 'Renko, Renko. Where are you from?'

'Moscow,' Slava answered for Arkady.

'Moscow?' Karp whistled appreciatively. 'You must have really fucked up to end up here.'

'But here we are, all of us proud workers of the Far East fleet,' Volovoi said as he joined them, and with an eye to another newcomer, an American boy with freckles and a bush of springy hair who was coming warily down the hall. 'Bernie, go in, please,' Volovoi urged him. 'It's a spy story. Very exciting.'

'You mean we're the villains, right?' Bernie had a sheepish grin and only a slight accent.

'How could it be a spy story otherwise?' Volovoi laughed.

'Think of it as a comedy,' Arkady suggested.

'Yeah.' Bernie liked that.

'Please, enjoy yourself,' Volovoi said, although he had stopped laughing. 'Comrade Bukovsky will find you a good seat.'

The first mate took Arkady down the hall to the ship's

library, a room where a reader had to slip sideways between the stacks. In such a limited collection it was interesting to see who was represented. Jack London was popular, as were war stories, science fiction and a field of literature called tractor romances. Volovoi dismissed the librarian and sat himself at her desk, pushing to one side her tea cosy, pots of glue and books with broken spines to make room for a dossier he had brought in his briefcase. Arkady had tried to stay out of the political officer's way, hanging back at meetings and avoiding entertainments. It was the first time the two of them had ever been alone.

Although Volovoi was the ship's first mate and habitually wore a canvas fishing jacket and boots, he never touched the helm or a net or a navigational chart. The reason was that a first mate was the political officer. There was a chief mate for more mundane matters having to do with fishing and seamanship. Very confusing. First Mate Volovoi was responsible for discipline and morale; for hand-painted signs in the corridor that proclaimed 'Third Shift Wins Gold Pennant for Socialist Competition!'; for announcing the news every noon on the ship's radio, mixing telegrams to proud crew members about babies born in Vladivostok with items from revolutionary Mozambique; for running movies and volleyball tournaments; and most important, for writing a work and political evaluation of every member of the crew from the captain on down, and delivering that judgment to the maritime section of the KGB.

Not that Volovoi was a weakling. He was the ship's

champion weightlifter, the kind of redhead whose eyes were always pink, whose eyelids and lips had a crust of eczema, whose meaty, well-kept hands had golden hair. Crewmen called political officers 'invalids' for their lack of real work, but Fedor Volovoi was the healthiest 'invalid' Arkady had ever seen.

'Renko,' Volovoi read, as if familiarizing himself with a problem. 'Chief Investigator. Dismissed. Expelled from the Party. Psychiatric rehabilitation. You see, I have the same file as the captain has. Assigned to labour in the eastern section of the Russian Republic.'

'Siberia.'

'I know where the eastern section is. I notice also that you have a sense of humour.'

'That's basically what I've been working on for the last few years.'

'Good, because I also have a more complete report.' Volovoi placed a thicker dossier on the desk. 'There was a murder case in Moscow. Somehow it ended with you killing the city prosecutor, an unexpected twist. Who is Colonel Pribluda?'

'An officer of the KGB. He spoke for me at the inquiry, which decided not to charge me.'

'You were also expelled from the Party and kept for psychiatric observation. Is that the fate of an innocent man?'

'Innocence had nothing to do with it.'

'And who is Irina Asanova?' Volovoi read the name.

'A former Soviet citizen.'

'You mean a woman whom you helped to defect and

who has since been a source of slanderous rumours about your fate.'

'What are the rumours?' Arkady asked. 'How far off?'

'Have you been in contact with her?'

'From here?'

'You've been questioned before.'

'Many times.'

Volovoi flipped the pages of the dossier. ' "Political unreliability" . . . "political unreliability". Let me tell you what is humorous to me as first mate. In a few days we will be in Dutch Harbor. Everyone on this ship will go into port for shopping with one exception: you. Because everyone on this ship has a No. 1 seaman's visa with one exception: you. I must assume you have only a No. 2 visa because those people who should know believe you cannot be trusted with foreigners or in a foreign port. Yet you are the man the captain wants to assist Bukovsky, even to help him speak to the Americans on board or to those on the trawlers. That's either humorous or very odd.'

Arkady shrugged. 'Humour is such a personal thing.'

'But to be expelled from the Party . . .' The Invalid liked hitting that nail, Arkady thought. Never mind dismissal and exile; the real punishment, the fear of every *apparatchik*, was losing his Party card. Molotov, for example, was denounced for writing up the murder lists of thousands of Stalin's victims. He wasn't in real trouble, though, until they took away his card.

'Membership in the Party was too great an honour. I could not bear it.'

'So it seems.' Volovoi pondered the file again. Perhaps the words were too painful. He lifted his eyes to the bookshelves, as if no story there could be so tawdry. 'The captain, of course, is a Party member. Like many sea captains, however, he has a decisive nature, a personality that enjoys risk. He's astute about fishing, about avoiding icebergs, simply going to starboard or port. But politics and human personality are more complicated, more dangerous. Of course he wants to know what happened to the dead girl. We all do. Nothing is more important. That's why the proper control of any inquiry is vital.'

'I've heard that before,' Arkady admitted.

'And didn't listen. Then you were a Party member, a high official, a man with a title. I see by your file that you haven't been on shore for almost a year. Renko, you're a prisoner on this ship. When we return to Vladivostock, while your cabinmates return to their girlfriends or families, you will be met by the Border Guard, an arm of State Security. You know that or you would have left the ship the last time we were home. You have no home, you have no place to go. Your only hope is a strongly positive evaluation from the *Polar Star*. I am the officer who writes that evaluation.'

'What do you want?'

'I expect', Volovoi said, 'to be closely and quietly informed before any report is made to the captain.'

'Ah.' Arkady bowed his head. 'Well, it's not an investigation, it's only asking questions for a day. I'm not in charge.'

'Since Slava Bukovsky speaks little English, it's obvious you will do some of the questioning. Questions have to be asked, the truth ascertained, before any proper conclusion can be reached. It's important that no information be given to the Americans.'

'I can only do my best. Would you like accidental death? We've considered food poisoning. Homicide?'

'It's also important to protect the name of the ship.'

'Suicide comes in many forms.'

'And the reputation of the unfortunate worker.'

'We could declare her still alive and name her the Queen of Fisherman's Day. Whatever you want. Write it out and I'll sign it right now.'

Volovoi slowly closed the dossier, dropped it into his briefcase, pushed back his chair and stood. His pinkish eyes became a little redder and more fixed, the instinctive reaction of a man sighting a natural enemy.

Arkady gazed back. *I know you too.*

'Do I have permission to leave?'

'Yes.' Volovoi's voice had gone dry. 'Renko,' he added as Arkady turned to go.

'Yes?'

'Suicide, I think, is what you're best at.'

Chapter Four

Zina Patiashvili lay on the table, her head resting on a wooden block. She had been pretty, with the nearly Grecian profile that Georgian girls sometimes possessed. Full lips, a graceful neck and limbs, a black pubic stripe and a head of blonde hair. What had she wanted to be, a Scandinavian? She had gone into the sea, touched bottom and returned with no apparent signs of corruption aside from the stillness of death. After the tension of rigor mortis all flesh became slack on the bone: breasts sagged on the ribs, mouth and jaw were loose, eyes flattened under half-open lids, the skin bore a luminous pallor. And the smell. The operating room was no morgue, with a morgue's investments of formaldehyde, and the body was enough to fill the room with an odour like the stench of soured milk.

Arkady lit a second Belomor straight from the first and filled his lungs again. Russian tobacco, the stronger the better. On a medical chart he drew four silhouettes: front, back, right side, left.

Zina seemed to levitate in the flash of Slava's camera, then settle back on the table as her shadow faded. At first the third mate had resisted attending the autopsy, but Arkady insisted so that Slava, already hostile, couldn't later claim any findings were prejudiced or incomplete. If this was a last twinge of professional pride on Arkady's part he didn't know whether to be amused at himself or disgusted. The adventures of a fish gutter! At this point, Slava was snapping pictures like a combat-hardened photo-journalist from *Tass*, while Arkady felt ill.

'Altogether,' Dr Vainu was saying, 'this trip has been a great disappointment. Back on land I had a good trade in sedatives. Valeryanka, Pentalginum, even foreign pills. But the women on this boat are a group of Amazons. Not even many abortions.'

Vainu was a young consumptive who generally received patients in his leisure suit and slippers, but for the autopsy he wore a lab coat with an ink-stained pocket. As always, he chainsmoked cigarettes laced with anti-stormine for seasickness. He held the cigarette between his fourth and little finger so that every time he took a puff his hand covered his face like a mask. On a side table were his surgical tools: scalpels, protractors, clamps, a small rotary saw for amputations. On the table's lower shelf was a steel pan holding Zina's clothes.

'Sorry about the time of death,' Vainu added airily, 'but who in their right mind would believe a trawl would pick her up more than a day after she went over?'

Arkady tried to smoke and draw at the same time. In Moscow a pathologist did the actual work and the investigator only walked in and out. There were laboratories, teams of forensic specialists, a professional apparatus and the steadying hand of routine. One comfort of the past few years had been the idea that he would never have to deal with victims again. Certainly not a girl out of the sea. A salty rankness underlay the smell of death. It was the smell of all the fish that had come down the factory line, and now of this girl from the same net, her hair matted, her arms, legs, and breasts mottled purple.

'Besides, estimating a time of death from rigor mortis is very chancy, especially in cold conditions,' Vainu went on. 'It's only a contraction caused by chemical reactions after death. Did you know that if you cut a fish fillet before rigor mortis the flesh will shrink and get tough?'

The pen slipped from Arkady's hand and his boot kicked it when he stooped for it.

'You'd think this was your first autopsy.' Slava picked the pen up and surveyed the table clinically. He turned to the doctor. 'She seems pretty bruised. Think she hit the propeller?'

'But her clothes weren't torn. Fists, not a propeller, from my experience,' Vainu said.

Vainu's experience? He was trained in broken bones and appendectomies. Everything else was handled with green liniment or aspirin because, as he said, the infirmary dealt primarily in alcohol and drugs. That was why the table had restraining straps. The *Polar Star* had run out of morphine a month ago.

Arkady read the top of the chart: 'Patiashvili, Zinaida Petrovna. Born 28/8/61, Tbilisi, G.S.S.R. Height: 1.6m. Weight: 48k. Hair: black (dyed blond). Eyes: Brown.' He handed the clipboard to Vainu and started walking around the table. Just as a man who is terrified of heights will concentrate on one rung at a time, Arkady spoke slowly and moved from detail to detail.

'Doctor, will you indicate the elbows are broken. The small amount of bruising suggests they were broken after death and at low body temperature.' He took a deep breath and flexed her legs. 'Indicate the same for her knees.'

Slava stepped forward, focused, took another shot, picking angles like a movie director on his first film.

'Are you using colour or black-and-white?' Vainu asked.

'Colour,' Slava said.

'On the forearms and calves,' Arkady continued, 'indicate a pooling of blood, not bruising, probably from the position she was in after death. Indicate the same on the breasts.' On the breasts the pooled blood looked like a second, liverish pair of aureoles. He wasn't up to this, Arkady thought; he should have refused. 'On the left shoulder, left side of the rib cage and hip some faint bruises evenly spaced.' He used a ruler from the lab table. 'Ten apparent bruises in all, about five centimetres apart.'

'Could you hold the ruler a little steadier?' Slava complained and took another shot.

'I think our former investigator needs a drink,' Vainu said.

Silently Arkady agreed. The girl's hands had the feel of cool, soft clay. 'No signs of broken nails or any tissue under them. The doctor will take scrapings and examine them under a microscope.'

'A drink or a crutch,' Slava said.

Arkady took a deep pull on the Belomor before he opened Zina's mouth wide.

'Lips and tongue do not appear bruised or cut.' He closed her mouth and tilted her head to look down her nostrils. He squeezed the bridge of her nose, then pulled the eyelids up from elliptical irises. 'Indicate discolouration in the white of the left eye.'

'Meaning what?' Slava asked.

'There are no signs of a direct blow,' Arkady went on. 'Possibly shock from a blow on the back of the skull.' He rolled Zina on to her shoulder and pulled brine-stiffened hair from the nape of her neck. The skin there was bruised black. He took the clipboard from Vainu and said, 'Cut her.'

The doctor selected a scalpel and, still smoking a cigarette with a long ash, made a slice the length of the cervical vertebrae. Arkady cradled the head as Vainu probed.

'This is your lucky day,' the doctor said drily. 'Indicate a crushed first vertebra and base of the skull. This must be a little triumph for you.' He glanced at Arkady and then at the saw. 'We could bring the brain out to make sure. Or crack the chest and examine the air passages for sea water.'

Slava snapped a picture of the neck and straightened up, swaying a little as he stood.

'No.' Arkady let her head settle on the block and closed her eyes. He rubbed his hands on his jacket and lit a second Belomor from the first, sucking fiercely, then sorted through the clothes in the pan. If she had drowned there would have been ruptures in her nose and mouth; there would have been water in her stomach as well as in her lungs, and when she was moved she'd still be seeping like a sponge. Besides, Vladivostok had enough investigators and technicians who'd be happy to carve her up and analyse her down to atomic elements. The pan held a red plastic shoe of Soviet manufacture, loose blue exercise pants, panties, white cotton blouse with a Hong Kong label and a pin that said, 'I ♡ L.A.' An international girl. In a pocket of the pants was some sodden blue pasteboard that had been a pack of Gauloises. Also a playing card, the queen of hearts. A romantic girl, Zina Patiashvili. Also a sturdy Soviet condom. But a practical one too. He looked at her waxy face again, at the scalp already withdrawing from the black roots of her blonde hair. The girl was dead, leaving her fantasy life behind. He always got mad at autopsies – at the victims as well as the murderers. Why didn't some people just shoot themselves in the head the day they were born?

The *Polar Star* was in a turn, trailing after its catcher-boats. Arkady steadied himself unconsciously. Slava braced himself at the table while trying not to touch it.

'Losing your sea legs?' Vainu asked.

The third mate stared back. 'I'm fine.'

Vainu smirked. 'At least we should remove the viscera,' he told Arkady.

Arkady took the clothes from the pan. They were daubed with fish blood, torn here and there by fish spines, no more than you'd expect from a ride in a net.

There might have been an oil smudge on a pants knee. Spreading the blouse, Arkady noticed a different sort of rustiness on the front flap, not a rip but a cut.

He returned to the body. There was a maroon discolouration on the limbs, breasts and around the navel. Maybe it wasn't all blood pooling; maybe he'd been too quick to say that just to get away from her. Sure enough, as he spread the belly from the navel he saw a puncture, a narrow stab wound about two centimetres long. Just what a fisherman's knife would leave. Everyone on the *Polar Star* had a knife with a white plastic handle and a 20cm double-edged blade for gutting fish or cutting net. Signs throughout the ship advised: 'Be ready for emergencies. Carry your knife at all times.' Arkady's was in his locker.

'Let me do that.' Vainu elbowed Arkady aside.

'You found a bump and a scratch,' Slava said. 'So what?'

Arkady said, 'It's more than the usual wear and tear, even for a high dive.'

Vainu staggered from the table. Arkady thought he must have opened the wound more because a short length of intestine, purplish-grey and slick, stood out of it. More of it rose with a life of its own, and continued to emerge from the girl's belly through a bubbling collar of salt water and pearly ooze.

'Slime eel!'

Slime eel or hagfish. By either name, a primitive but efficient form of life. Sometimes the net brought in a halibut two metres long, a beast that should have weighed a quarter-ton and was nothing but a sack of skin and bones and a nest of slime eels. The outside of the fish could be untouched; the eels entered through the mouth or anus and forced their way into the belly. When an eel appeared in the factory the women scattered until the men had hammered it to death with shovels.

The eel's head, an eyeless stump with fleshy horns and a puckered mouth, whipped from side to side against Zina Patiashvili's stomach; then the entire eel, as long as an arm, slid seemingly forever out of her, twisted in mid-air and landed at Vainu's feet. The doctor stabbed, snapping the scalpel in two against the deck. He kicked, then grabbed another knife from the table. The eel thrashed wildly, rolling across the room. Its main defence was a glutinous, pearly ooze that made it impossible to hold. One eel could fill a bucket with slime; a feeding eel could cover bait in a cocoon of slime that not even a shark would touch. The tip of the knife broke off and flew up, cutting Vainu's cheek. He tripped, landed on his back and watched the eel squirm towards him.

Arkady stepped into the passage and returned with a fire axe which he swung, blunt-end down, on the eel. With each blow the eel thrashed, smearing the deck. Arkady lost his balance on the slime, caught himself, turned the hatchet edge down and cut the eel in half. The two halves went on twisting separately until he had chopped each of them in two. The four divided parts twitched in pools of slime and blood.

Vainu staggered to the cabinet, pulled the instruments from the sterilizing jar and poured the alcohol into two glasses for Arkady and himself. Slava Bukovsky was gone. Arkady had a fleeting memory of the third mate bolting for the door a moment after the eel appeared.

'This is my last trip,' Vainu muttered.

'Why didn't anyone notice she was missing from work?' Arkady asked. 'Was she chronically ill?'

'Zina?' Vainu steadied his glass with both hands. 'Not her.'

Arkady drained his own glass in a swallow. A little antiseptic, but not bad.

What sort of doctor, he considered, did factory ships generally have? Certainly not one with curiosity about the whole range of physical dysfunction, of deliveries, childhood diseases, geriatrics. On the *Polar Star* there wasn't even the usual maritime hazard of tropical diseases. Medical duty on the waters of the North Pacific was pretty boring, which was why it drew drunks and medical-school graduates assigned against their will. Vainu was neither. He was Estonian, from a Baltic republic where Russians were treated like occupying troops. Not a man with a great deal of sympathy for the crew of the *Polar Star*.

'No problems of dizziness, headaches, fainting? No problems with drugs? You didn't treat her for anything?'

'You saw her records. Absolutely clean.'

'Then how is it that no one was surprised by the absence of this able-bodied worker?'

'Renko, I have the impression that you are the only man on board who didn't know Zina.'

Arkady nodded. He was getting that impression, too.

'Don't forget your axe,' Vainu said as Arkady started for the door.

'I'd like you to examine the body for signs of sexual activity. Get her fingerprints and enough blood for typing. I'm afraid you'll have to clean out the abdomen.'

'What if . . .?' The doctor stared at the eel.

'Right,' Arkady said. 'Keep the axe.'

Slava Bukovsky was bent over the rail outside. Arkady stood beside him as if they were taking the air. On the trawl deck mounds of yellow sole waited to be shovelled down the chute to the factory. An American nylon net was strung between two booms, and a net needle – a shuttle with a split tip – hung from an ongoing repair. Arkady wondered if that was the net Zina had come up in. Slava studied the sea.

Sometimes fog acted like oil on water. The surface was dead calm, black, a few gulls hovering over a trawler he could make out only because American boats were so bright, like fishing lures. This one was red and white, with a crew in yellow slickers. It swung in and out behind the *Polar Star*'s stern, the factory ship's rusty hull looming forty feet above the trawler. Of course the Americans went out only for weeks at a time, whereas the *Polar Star* was out for half a year. The American boat was a toy in the water; the *Polar Star* was a world to itself.

'That doesn't usually happen at autopsies,' Arkady said softly.

Slava wiped his mouth with a handkerchief. 'Why would anyone stab her if she was already dead?'

'The stomach has bacteria. The puncture was to let the gasses out, to keep her from floating. I can carry on alone for a while; why don't you catch up when you feel better?'

Slava stiffened up from the rail and folded his handkerchief. 'I'm still in charge. We will do everything like a normal investigation.'

Arkady shrugged. 'In a normal homicide investigation when you find the body you go over the ground with a magnifying glass and metal detectors. Look around you. Is there any particular wave you want to examine?'

'Stop saying homicide. That's rumour-mongering.'

'Not with those wounds.'

'It could have been the propeller,' Slava said.

'If someone hit her over the head with it.'

'There were no signs of a struggle – you said so yourself. It's your attitude that is the greatest problem. I'm not going to let your antisocial posturing compromise me.'

'Comrade Bukovsky, I'm just a worker off the factory line. You are an emblem of the radiant Soviet future. How can I compromise you?'

'Don't play the worker with me. Volovoi told me about you. You made a big mess back in Moscow. Captain Marchuk was crazy to let you off the line.'

'Why did he?' Arkady was genuinely curious.

'I don't know.' Slava seemed as confused as Arkady.

*

Zina Patiashvili's cabin was the same as Arkady's in space and layout, four people living in what could pass for a fairly comfortable decompression chamber: four bunks, table and bench, closet and sink. The atmosphere itself was different. Instead of male sweat, the air contained a powerful mix of competing perfumes. Rather than Gury's pin ups and Obidin's icon, the closet door was decorated with Cuban postcards, sappy International Women's Day greeting cards, snapshots of children in Pioneer scarves, magazine pictures of movie stars and musicians. There was a smiling picture of the roly poly Soviet rock star Stas Namin. There was a scowling photo of Mick Jagger.

'That was Zina's.' Natasha Chaikovskaya pointed to Jagger.

The other cabinmates were 'Madame' Malzeva, the oldest worker from Arkady's factory line, and a little Uzbek girl named Dynama in honour of the electrification of Uzbekistan. Her family had done the innocent girl no favour, because in more sophisticated parts of the Soviet Union a 'dynama' is a flirt who wines and dines on a man's money, then goes to the rest room and disappears. Mercifully, her friends called her Dynka. Her black eyes balanced anxiously on enormous cheekbones. Her hair was done up in two ponytails that looked like black wings.

For such a sombre occasion, Natasha had eschewed lipstick, compromising with a tall haircomb. Behind her back she was called 'Chaika', for the broad-shouldered limousine of that name. She could have smothered Stas

41

Namin with one squeeze; Jagger wouldn't have had a chance. She was a shotputter with the soul of Carmen.

'Zina was a good girl, a popular girl, the life of the ship,' Madame Malzeva said. As if holding court in her parlour, she wore a tasselled shawl and darned a sateen pillow with stitched waves and the invitation 'Visit Odessa'. 'Wherever there was laughter, there was our Zina.'

'Zina was nice to me,' Dynka said. 'She'd come down to the laundry and bring me a sandwich.' Like most Uzbeks, she couldn't pronounce 'zch'; she just dropped it.

'She was an honest Soviet worker who will be badly missed.' Natasha was a Party member with the Party member's ability to sound like a tape recording.

'Those are valuable testimonials,' Slava said.

A top bunk was stripped. In a cardboard box designed for holding thirty kilos of frozen fish were clothes, shoes, stereo and cassettes, hair rollers and brushes, grey notebook, a snapshot of Zina in her bathing suit, another of her and Dynka, and an East Indian jewellery box covered with coloured cloth and bits of mirror. Over the bunk a framed panel screwed into the bulkhead gave the occupant's assignment in case of emergency. Zina's post was the fire brigade in the galley.

Arkady could tell immediately who the other bunks were occupied by. An older woman always had a lower, in this case one lined with pillows from other ports – Sochi, Tripoli, Tangiers – so that Madame Malzeva could repose on a soft atlas. Natasha's bunk held a selection of pamphlets like 'Understanding the Consequences of Social Democratic Deviationism' and 'Towards a Cleaner Complexion'. Perhaps one led to the other; that would be a propaganda breakthrough. On Dynka's upper bunk was a toy camel. More than men did, they had made a real home out of their cabin, enough for him to feel like an intruder.

'What interests us,' Arkady said, 'is how Zina's disappearance went unnoticed. You shared this cabin with her. How could you not notice that she was gone for a day and a night?'

'She was such an active girl,' Malzeva said. 'And we have different shifts. You know, Arkasha, we work at night. She worked during the day. Sometimes days would pass without our seeing Zina. It's hard to believe we will never see her again.'

'You must be upset.' Arkady had seen Madame Malzeva cry in war movies when the Germans got shot. Everyone else would be screaming, 'Take that, you fucking Fritz!' but Malzeva would be sobbing into her babushka.

'She borrowed my shower cap and never returned it.' The old woman raised dry eyes.

'It would be good to gather testimonials from her other mates,' Slava suggested.

'What about her enemies?' Arkady asked. 'Would anyone want to hurt her?'

'No!' the three women said as a chorus.

'There's no call for such a question,' Slava warned.

'Forget I asked. And what else was Zina's?' Arkady scanned the photo montage on the closet door.

'Her nephew.' Dynka's finger went tentatively to a snapshot of a dark-haired boy holding a bunch of grapes as big as figs.

'Her actress.' Natasha pointed to a picture of Melina Mercouri looking pouty and wreathed in cigarette smoke. Had Zina seen herself as a sultry Greek?

'Any boyfriend?' Arkady asked.

The three women looked at each other as if they were consulting; then Natasha answered, 'Not any one man especially that we were aware of.'

'No one man,' said Malzeva.

Dynka giggled. 'No.'

'Fraternization with all your mates is the best course,' Slava said.

'Did you see her at the dance? Were you at the dance?' Arkady asked them.

'No, Arkasha, not at my age,' Malzeva said, dusting off some coyness. 'And you forget that the factory line still processed fish during the dance. Natasha, weren't you sick?'

'Yes.' When Slava, erstwhile musician, gave a start, Natasha added, 'I may have looked in at the dance.' In a dress, Arkady guessed.

'Were you at the dance?' Arkady asked Dynka.

'Yes. The Americans dance like monkeys,' she said. 'Zina's the only one who could dance like them.'

'With them?' Arkady asked her.

44

'It seems to me there is a certain unhealthy sexuality when Americans dance,' Madame Malzeva said.

'The dance was meant to encourage friendship between workers of both nations,' Slava answered. 'What does it matter who she danced with if she had an accident later that night?'

Arkady poured the box of effects onto Zina's bunk. The clothes were foreign and worn to the last thread. Nothing in the pockets. The tapes were of the Rolling Stones and Dire Straits variety; the player was a Sanyo. There was no ID, nor had he expected any; her paybook and visa would be in the ship's safe. Lipsticks and perfumes lay in the hollow of the bunk; how long would the scent of Zina Patiashvili linger in the cabin? Her jewellery box had a string of fake pearls and half a deck of playing cards, all the queen of hearts. Also a roll of 'pinkies', ten-ruble notes, held together by a rubber band. It would take more time to go through the effects than he had at this moment. He put everything back into the box.

'Everything's here?' he asked. 'All her tapes?'

Natasha sniffed. 'Her precious tapes. She always used her headphones. She never shared them.'

'What are you trying to find?' Slava demanded. 'I'm tired of being ignored.'

'I'm not ignoring you,' Arkady said, 'but you already know what happened. I'm more slow-witted; I have to go step by step. Thank you,' he told the three women.

'That's all, comrades,' Slava said decisively. He picked up the box. 'I'll take care of this.'

At the door, Arkady paused to ask, 'Did she have fun at the dance?'

'It's possible,' Natasha said. 'Comrade Renko, maybe you should go to a dance sometime. The intelligentsia should mix with workers.'

How Natasha had settled on this label for him Arkady didn't know; the slime line was not an avenue of philosophers. There was something ominous in Natasha's expression he wanted to avoid, so he asked Dynka, 'Did she seem dizzy? Sick?'

Dynka shook her head, so that her ponytails rode back and forth. 'She was happy when she left the dance.'

'At what time? Where was she going?'

'To the stern. I can't say what time it was; people were still dancing.'

'Who was she with?'

'She was alone, but she was happy, like a princess in a fairytale.'

It was a fantasy far better than men put together. These women believed they were sailing the seas with all the ordinary intrigues of a women's apartment, as if you couldn't step outside into the wide sea and simply disappear. During the ten months that Arkady had spent on board, he was feeling more and more that the ocean was a void, a vacuum into which people could be drawn at any moment. They should hang on to their bunks, and hold on for their lives if they stepped on deck.

When Slava and Arkady reached the deck, they found Vainu jackknifed over the rail, his lab coat smeared with blood and slime. The axe lay at his feet. He held up two fingers.

'. . . more,' he blurted and turned his face back into the wind.

A void or a well of too much life. Take your pick.

Chapter Five

Arkady happily followed Slava towards the stern. He could almost breathe in the view: a lone figure at the rail, a catcherboat in the middle distance, black sea folding into grey fog. It was a change from claustrophobia.

'Look around,' Slava said. 'You're supposed to be an expert.'

'Right.' Arkady stopped on command and turned, not that there was much to see: winches and cleats lit by three lamps that even at midday glowed like poisonous moons. In the middle of the deck was an open stairwell that led to a landing directly over the stern ramp. Stern ramps were a feature of modern trawling: the *Polar Star*'s ramp began at the waterline and tunnelled up to the trawl deck on the other side of the aft house. All he could see of the ramp was the part below the well, and all he could see of the trawl deck were the tops of the booms and gantries beyond the smoke stack. Around the stack were oil barrels, spare cables and hawsers. On the boat deck, lifeboats hung on davits. On one side was emergency gear: fire axes, a pike, gaff and spade, as if fire could be fought like foreign troops.

'Well?' Slava demanded. 'According to the girl this is where Zina was headed. Like someone in a fairytale.'

He stopped in mid-stride and whispered to Arkady, 'Susan.'

'Soo-san?' Arkady asked. There was a name that lent itself to Russian pronunciation.

'Shh!' Slava blushed.

The figure at the rail wore a hooded canvas jacket, shapeless pants and gumboots. Arkady had always avoided the Americans. They rarely came down to the factory, and above deck he felt he was watched, that he was expected to try to make contact with them, that he would compromise them, if not himself.

'She's taking a net.' Slava stopped Arkady at a respectful distance.

Susan Hightower's back was to them as she talked into a hand-held radio. It sounded as if she were alternately answering the *Eagle* in English and giving instructions to the bridge of the *Polar Star* in Russian. The catcherboat approached, putting its shoulder to the waves. A rattling came from below. Arkady looked down the well to see a cable of scarred red and white buoys spill down the grooved, rust-brown slope of the ramp. 'If she's working,' he said, 'we can talk to the other Americans.'

'She's the head representative. As a courtesy, we must speak to her first,' Slava insisted.

Courtesy? Here they were shivering and ignored, but Slava was in the throes of social embarrassment.

On the water, the cable straightened as it played out twenty-five, fifty, a hundred metres, each buoy riding its own crest. As the line spread to its full length, the

American boat approached on the port side and kept pace.

'This is very interesting,' Slava announced heartily.

'Yes.' Arkady turned his back to the wind. At this longitude there was no land between the North and South Poles and breezes built quickly.

'You know how in our Soviet fleet we come so close to transfer fish,' Slava went on. 'There are battered hulls—'

'Battered hulls are a signature of the Soviet fleet,' Arkady agreed.

'This system that the Americans taught us, the "no-contact" system, is cleaner, but it is more intricate and demands more skill.'

'Like sex between spiders,' Susan said without turning her head.

Arkady admired the technique demanded. From the American trawler a fisherman with a strong arm threw a gaff over the trailing line. Another fisherman ran the line along the gunwale to the stern, where a full net of fish covered the trawler's narrow deck. 'They're connecting,' Susan told the radio in Russian.

Like spiders having sex? An interesting comparison, Arkady thought. A buoy line was a relatively fine thread. Not only were the boats at a distance, but they were moving up and down in relation to each other. If the ships separated too much, the line would snap from the pressure; too little and the net wouldn't leave the trawler or would drop towards the bottom, where vertical drag could break the line and lose gear and fish worth $100,000 in American money.

'Coming in,' Susan said as the net slipped off the trawler's deck. At once the weight of the bag made the *Polar Star* slow half a knot. The catcherboat veered off, while winches far back on the factory ship's trawl deck started hauling the line in.

Susan gave Arkady no more than a glance as he stepped to the rail beside her. He thought she must be wearing layers of sweaters and pants to appear so shapeless, because her face was thin. She had brown eyes and the kind of concentration you see in a girl on a balance beam who doesn't give a damn about the rest of the world.

'Fifty metres,' she was saying in Russian.

Gulls started to gather. It was always a mystery how there could be not a bird in sight; then suddenly by the tens they would appear, as if the fog were a magician's cape.

Behind its vanguard of buoys, the incoming net, its orange-and-black plastic hair glimmering wet, surged towards the *Polar Star*. Behind them a trawlmaster crossed the deck and ran down the stairs of the stairwell, taking his position on the landing over the ramp. The slim cable rose taut and dripping. Buoys bounced up the ramp. Dragged by its steel bridle, the bag surged out of the water and onto the ramp's lower lip.

'Ease off!' Susan ordered in Russian.

The *Polar Star* slowed almost to the point of wallowing. There was a necessary caution to hauling in thirty tons of fish which lost buoyancy and doubled in weight as it left the water. Any more tension on the winch of forward motion to the ship and the line could part. On the other hand, a dead stop could force the bag into the propeller screws. Patiently the cable eased the bag half on to the ramp as the ship coasted at dead slow. There the bag paused as if exhausted, water pouring out, crabs and starfish dripping out.

Susan asked Arkady, 'You're from the factory?'

'Yes.'

'The mystery man from the Lower Depths.'

Slava pulled Arkady to the stair-well rail. 'Don't bother her now.'

At the well they looked down at the trawlmaster as the ramp's steel-mesh safety gate swung up and two men in hard hats, lifejackets and lifelines around their waists dragged heavy messenger cables down the ramp to the bag. The closer they came to the net the more steeply the chute curved down to the water. A floodlight in the well showed where, at the belly of the waiting bag, the ramp dropped dead away.

The lead man shouted, slipped and clung to his lifeline. It was a deckhand named Pavel; his eyes had gone white with fright.

From the landing the trawlmaster encouraged him. 'You look like a drunk on a dance floor. Maybe you'd like a pair of skates.'

'Karp,' Slava said with admiration.

Karp's shoulders stretched his sweater. He turned his broad head up to them and grinned, displaying golden dental work. He and his team were taking an extra shift, another reason they were the favourites of the first mate.

'Wait until we reach the ice sheet,' he yelled up. 'Pavel will do some real skating on the ramp then.'

Arkady remembered the half-mended net he had seen earlier on the trawl deck.

'Did you cut Zina out?' he called down to Karp.

'Yeah.' The gold left the smile. 'So?'

'Nothing.' It was simply interesting to Arkady that Karp Korobetz, that exemplar among the trawlmasters, had taken the chance of ruining expensive American mesh rather than pour the fish out and wait for her body to emerge.

Below, Pavel was struggling to untangle the bridle of this net so that his teammate could attach the G-hooks of the messenger cables and relieve the weight on the buoy line. It was one thing for a cable to snap and fly wildly on an open deck; in the close tunnel of the ramp, a broken cable would be a whip in a barrel.

'Were you at the dance?' Arkady called to Karp.

'No,' Karp yelled. 'Hey, Renko, you never answered my question. What did they nail you for?'

Arkady detected the faint imprint of a Moscow accent.

Susan turned around. 'Is there a problem?'

Pavel fell again, this time to midway down the net before his lifeline saved him. A wave flowed up the ramp and lifted the net, so that it rolled indolently over the fisherman. Arkady had seen men die like this before. The weight of the bag wouldn't let the lungs breathe, and half the time the bag was in the water. Pavel's teammate shouted and pulled on the rope, but with Pavel beneath twenty tons of fish and net the line didn't budge. Yells didn't help. As another wave broke over the bag, it rolled some more, like a walrus crushing a pup. Receding, the wave tried to suck the bag back to the sea, and the lifeline broke.

Karp jumped down from the landing onto the net – what was another hundred kilos compared to tons? With the next wave, he was up to his waist in freezing water, holding onto the net by one hand and by the other dragging Pavel from a kelp-like mass of plastic chafing hair. Karp was laughing. As Pavel sputtered and climbed onto the back of the bag, the trawlmaster pulled himself up to the bridle and helped connect the G-hooks. It was all over in a second. What struck Arkady was that Karp had never hesitated; the trawlmaster had moved with such speed that saving another man's life seemed less an act of courage than a gymnast's spin around a bar.

The catcherboat swung back into the *Polar Star*'s wake, waiting for the call on the net's catch – so many tons, so much sole, crabs, mud. Gulls hovered at the mouth of the ramp, watching for any fish slipping through the net.

'Someone from the slime line is the last thing we need here now,' Susan told Slava. 'Take him to my cabin.'

As soon as the G-hooks snapped shut, Karp and his deckhands moved quickly up the ramp, hauling themselves in step by step on one lifeline. The net began stirring behind them. The *Polar Star* had a 'Trip Plan', a quota of fifty thousand tons of fish. So many frozen fillets, so much fishmeal, so much liver oil for a nation starved for protein to build the muscles that were building Communism. Say ten per cent was lost on board to freezer burn, ten per cent spoiled on shore, ten per cent was split between the port manager and the fleet director, ten per cent was spilled on unpaved roads to villages where there might or might not be a working refrigerator to save the last well-travelled fillets. No wonder the net rushed eagerly to the trawl deck.

Slava led Arkady forward past the trawl deck and midships by the white hangar of the machinists' shop. 'Can you believe her accent? It's so good,' he said. 'Susan is a fantastic woman. That she can speak so much better than that Uzbek girl – what's her name?'

'Dynka.'

'Dynka, right. No one speaks Russian any more.'

True. Upwardly mobile Russians in particular spoke the increasingly popular 'Politburo Ukrainian'. Ever since Khrushchev, the Ukrainian-born leaders of the country had spoken in crude, halting Russian, substituting w's for v's, until sooner or later everyone in the Kremlin, whether from Samarkand or Siberia, started sounding like a son of Kiev.

'Say your name,' Arkady asked.

'Slawa.' Slava eyed Arkady suspiciously. 'I don't know what it is, but you always seem to be getting at something.'

On the dark seam where fog met the horizon was the glow of another catcherboat working a trawl.

Arkady asked, 'How many boats do we have with us?'

'We usually have a fleet of four: the *Alaska Miss*, the *Merry Jane*, the *Aurora* and the *Eagle*.'

'They were all at the dance?'

'No. The *Alaska Miss* had a crew change coming and the *Aurora* had a steering-gear problem. Since we'd stopped fishing for the night and since we're about to go to Dutch Harbor, they decided to leave for port early. We only had two boats at the dance, the same two we have now.'

'You have a good band?'

Carefully Slava said, 'Not the worst.'

The forward deck was divided between a volleyball court on one side and a loading deck which Arkady and Slava walked across. Netting covered the court. Despite this, sometimes a ball escaped into the water; then the captain would turn the *Polar Star* around right to the bobbing dot, a task equivalent to steering a giant sow through heavy mud. Volleyballs were scarce in the Bering Sea.

The Americans on board lived in the forward house, on the deck below the officers' cabins and the bridge. Susan had yet to arrive but the three others had assembled in her cabin. Bernie was the freckled boy Arkady had met outside the cafeteria with Volovoi. His friend Day wore steel-rimmed glasses that emphasized a scholar's doll-like earnestness. Both reps wore jeans and sweaters that were at once shabby and superior to any Russian clothing. Lantz was a National Fisheries observer charged with making sure the *Polar Star* didn't take fish of an illegal type, sex or size. As he was about to go on duty, he wore oiled coveralls, a plaid shirt with rubber sleeves, a rubber glove on one hand and a surgical one hanging like a handkerchief from his shirt pocket. Acting half-asleep, he lounged on the built-in bench, curling up because he was so tall, a cigarette stuck in his mouth. While they waited for Susan, Slava talked with the three of them in Russian with the enthusiastic ease of friends, contemporaries, soul-mates.

Susan's cabin was no great step up from crew quarters. Two bunks instead of four, which she had to herself as the lone American woman. There was a waist-high ZIL refrigerator and the metallic aroma of instant coffee. A typewriter and manuscript boxes on the upper bunk and, stacked in cartons, books – Pasternak, Nabokov, Blok. Arkady saw Russian-language editions that would have sold in seconds at any Soviet bookstore or for hundreds of rubles on a Moscow back street. It was like coming upon cartons of gold. Susan could read these?

'Explain again, please,' Day asked Slava. 'Who is he?'

'Our workers have many talents. Seaman Renko is a worker from the factory, but he has experience with the investigation of accidents.'

'It's terrible about Zina,' Bernie said. 'She was great.'

Lantz blew a ring of smoke and asked lazily in English, 'How would you know?'

'What happened to her?' Day asked.

Arkady groaned inwardly as Slava answered, 'It seems Zina became ill, went out on deck and perhaps lost her balance.'

'And perhaps came up in the net?' Lantz asked.

'Exactly.'

'Did anyone see her fall over?' Bernie asked.

'No,' Slava said. This was the primal error of first-time investigators, the tendency to answer questions rather than ask them. 'It was dark, you know, and foggy after the dance and she was alone. These things happen at sea. This is the information we have so far, but if you know anything . . .'

Assisting Slava was like following a lemming. The three Americans shrugged and said in unison, 'No.'

'We were supposed to wait for Susan, but I don't think we have any more questions,' Slava told Arkady.

'I don't have any,' Arkady said, and then switched to English. 'I am impressed with your Russian.'

'We're all graduate students,' Day said. 'We signed on to improve our Russian.'

'And I'm struck by how well you knew our crew.'

'Everyone knew Zina,' Bernie said.

Day said, 'Zina was a popular girl.'

Arkady could see Slava mentally translating, trying to keep up.

'She worked in the crew's galley,' Arkady said to Day. 'She served you food?'

'No, we eat in the officers' mess. She worked in the officers' mess at the start of the trip, but then she transferred.'

'We did see Zina on deck – at the stern rail, in fact,' Bernie said.

'Where your station is?'

'Right. There's always a company rep at the stern

during the transfer of the fish. Zina would come out and watch with us.'

'Often?'

'Sure.'

'Your station is . . . ?' Arkady turned apologetically to Lantz.

'The trawl deck.'

'You were on watch when the net bearing Zina came on deck?'

Lantz brushed cigarette ash from his sweater and sat up. For such a tall boy he had a small skull and the raked hair of a narcissist. 'It was cold. I was inside having some tea. The deckhands know they're supposed to tell me when a bag is coming up the ramp.'

Even below deck in the din of the factory line, Arkady knew when a net was coming by the high whine of the hydraulic winch and the shift in the ship's engines from 'half speed' to 'dead slow' as the net cleared the water, followed by the return to 'half speed' as it came up the ramp. In his sleep, he knew when fish were coming on board. Nobody had needed to call Lantz from a glass of tea.

'You enjoyed the dance?' Arkady asked.

'Terrific dance,' Bernie said.

'Especially Slava's band,' said Day.

'You danced with Zina?' Arkady asked.

'Zina had more interest in the motorcycle gang,' Lantz said.

'Gang?' Arkady asked.

'Fishermen,' Bernie explained. 'American fishermen, not yours.'

'Boy, your English is really good,' said Day. 'You're from the factory?'

'The slime line,' Susan said as she entered and threw her jacket on a bunk. She pulled off a wool cap, releasing thick blond hair cut short. 'You started without me,' she told Slava. 'I'm the head rep. You know you don't talk to my boys without me.'

'I'm sorry, Susan.' Slava was contrite.

'As long as it's clear.'

'Yes.'

Susan had taken command, that was obvious, with the imperious manner small people sometimes have of inserting themselves into the centre of a situation. Her eyes darted around the cabin, taking roll call.

'It's about Zina and the dance,' Bernie said. 'This Seaman Renko with Slava said he didn't have any questions, but I think he does.'

'In English,' she said. 'I heard.' She turned to Arkady. 'You want to know who danced with Zina? Who knows? It was dark and everyone was bobbing up and down. One second you're dancing with one person and the next you're dancing with three. You dance with men and women or both. It's like water polo without the water. Now let's talk about you. Slava told me you have experience with accidents.'

'Comrade Renko served as an investigator for the Moscow Prosecutor's Office,' Slava said.

'And what did you investigate?' she asked Arkady.

'Very bad accidents.'

She studied him as if he were auditioning for a part and not doing well. 'How convenient that you happened to be cleaning fish on the factory line of this ship. An investigator all the way from Moscow? Fluent in English? Cleaning fish?'

'Employment is guaranteed in the Soviet Union,' Arkady said.

'Fine,' Susan said. 'I would suggest that you save all your other questions for Soviet citizens. Zina is a Soviet problem. If I hear you've approached any American stationed on this ship again, I'm going straight to Captain Marchuk.'

'No more questions,' Slava said and pushed Arkady to the door.

'I have a last question,' Arkady said. He asked the men, 'You're looking forward to Dutch Harbor?'

This broke the tension a little.

'Two more days,' Bernie said. 'I'm going to the hotel, get the best room, sit in a hot shower and drink an ice-cold six pack of beer.'

'Soo-san?' Arkady liked saying it that way, making her name Russian.

'Two more days and I'm gone,' she said. 'You'll get a new head rep in Dutch and I'll be flying out of the fog to California. So you can say goodbye to me now.'

'The rest of us are coming back,' Day assured Slava. 'We have two more months of fishing.'

'Just fishing,' Slava promised. 'No more questions. We

61

should always keep in mind that we are shipmates and friends.'

Arkady remembered that on the way from Vladivostok the *Polar Star* had staged exercises in camouflage and radiation cleansing. Every Soviet seaman knew that in his captain's safe was a sealed packet to be opened upon receipt of a coded signal of war; inside were instructions on how to avoid enemy submarines, where to make friendly contact, what to do with prisoners.

Chapter Six

Arkady usually didn't enjoy amusement rides, but he liked this one. Nothing fancy. The transport cage had a chain for a gate and a tyre on the base to cushion its landings, but it lifted off the deck of the *Polar Star* with a satisfying taut jerk of the crane cable, swaying as it rose, and for a moment, in midflight, felt like an over-sized birdcage that had taken wing. Then they cleared the side and began dropping towards the *Merry Jane*. Next to the looming hull of the factory ship any catcher-boat looked diminutive, even though the *Merry Jane* was forty metres long. It sported the characteristic high bow of a Bering Sea trawler, a forward wheelhouse and stack, a mast hung with antennae and lamps, a wooden deck with a side crane of its own, and a stern ramp and gantry with three neatly reeled nets. The hull was blue trimmed white, the wheelhouse white trimmed blue, and the boat looked bright as a toy as it rubbed against the black sea fender of the *Polar Star*. Three fishermen in slickers steadied the cage as it descended to the deck. Slava unhooked the chain and stepped out first. Arkady followed; for the first time in almost a year he was off the factory ship. Off the *Polar Star* and onto an American boat. The fishermen vied with each other to pump his hand and to ask enthusiastically, 'Falha Portugues?'

There were two Diegos and one Marco, all short, dark men with the soulful eyes of castaways. None of them spoke any Russian or much English. Slava hurried Arkady up the wheelhouse stairs to meet Captain Thorwald, a pink-faced, bear-sized Norwegian.

'Crazy, isn't it,' Thorwald said. 'It's American-owned, that's all. The Portuguese, they spend ten months of the year fishing here, but they have families in Portugal. Just, they make a fortune here compared to what they could at home. Same with me. Well, I go home to shovel snow off the walk, they go home to fry sardines. But two months on land is enough for us.'

The captain of the *Merry Jane* wore pyjamas open to gold chains nesting on a chest of red hair. Russians supposedly traced their ancestry back to Viking raiders; 'Russ' meant red, for the hair of the invaders. Thorwald looked as if nothing less than Viking pillage would wake him up.

'They don't seem to speak English,' Arkady said.

'That way they don't get into trouble. They know their jobs, so there's not much need for conversation. They may be little fuckers, but next to Norwegians they're the best.'

'High praise,' Arkady said. 'Beautiful boat.'

The luxurious bridge alone was a revelation. The chart desk was teak-lacquered to an agate gleam; the deck bore a carpet thick enough for a member of the Central Committee; and at each end of the wide, padded console was a wheel with its own high, upholstered swivel chair. The chair on the starboard side was surrounded by the colour monitors of fish-finders, radar screens and the digital read-outs of radios.

Thorwald reached inside his pyjama pants to scratch. 'Yah, this is built solid for the Bering. Wait till you see us in the ice sheet. To bring a boat like the *Eagle* up here, to me that's really crazy. Or to bring women.'

'You knew Zina Patiashvili?' Slava asked.

'When I fish, I fish. When I fuck, I fuck. I don't mix them up.'

'Wise,' Arkady said.

Impervious, Thorwald went on, 'I didn't know Zina and I didn't go to any dance because I was in the ward-room with Marchuk and Morgan trying to show them where to trawl. Sometimes I don't think the Russians and Americans are after fish at all.'

Slava and Arkady descended to the galley, where the crew had assembled for a meal of salt cod and wine, hardly the mid-day fare on a Soviet ship. Fishing was arduous work, but again Arkady was struck by the amenities on the *Merry Jane*: the big range with sliding bars to keep food from flying in heavy seas, the table covered by anti-skid pads, the cushioned banquette, the coffee machine with its pot strapped in place. There were homey touches: hanging from a lamp cord, a wooden model of a sailing boat with eyes painted on the bow; a poster of a whitewashed village on a beach. Very different from the galley of the inland trawler Arkady had served on off the coast of Sakhalin. There the crew ate with no room to take off their coats, and everything – groats, potatoes, cabbage, tea – tasted of mildew and fish.

As they ate, the Portuguese watched a videotape. Aside from a polite nod, all interest in their guests was gone. Arkady understood. If someone was coming to ask them questions, that someone should speak their language. After all, when Russians were mucking around in rowboats the Portuguese had an empire that circled the world. On the screen was the hysterical narration and languid action of a soccer match.

'Zina Patiashvili?' Slava asked. 'Does anyone here know Zina? Does . . . do you . . . have you?' He turned to Arkady. 'This is a waste of time.'

'Football,' Arkady said as he sat down.

The Diego next to Arkady poured him a tumbler of red wine. 'Campeonato do Mundo. You?'

'Goalie.' Twenty years ago, Arkady realized.

'Forward.' The fisherman pointed to himself, then to the other Diego and Marco. 'Forward. Back.' He aimed his finger at the television. 'Portugal white, Ingles stripe. Bad.'

As all three fishermen winced, a figure in a striped jersey broke away and scored. How many times had they already seen the tape of this game, Arkady wondered – ten times, a hundred? Over a long voyage, men tend to tell the same tale over and over. This was the more refined torture of high technology.

While Diego averted his eyes from the television, Arkady showed him the snapshot of Zina and Dynka.

'You stole that,' Slava said.

'Zina.' Arkady watched the fisherman's eyes slide from woman to woman equally. He shrugged. Arkady showed the picture to the other two crewmen and got the same reaction, but then the first Diego asked to see the photo again.

'No baile,' he told Arkady. 'A loura da Russia. A mulher com os americanos.' He became passionate. 'Entende? Com americanos.'

'She danced with the Americans. That's what I thought,' Arkady said.

'Beba, beba,' Diego refilled his glass.

'Thank you.'

'Muito obrigado,' Diego instructed him.

'Muito obrigado.'

'Meo pracer.'

Arkady held onto the centre bar as the transport cage swung down to the second trawler. Slava was looking more and more miserable, like a bird caged with a cat.

'This is upsetting the work schedule.'

'Look on it as a holiday,' Arkady said.

'Ha!' Slava soberly regarded a gull hovering outside a bilge hole of the *Polar Star* waiting for slops to drop. 'I know what you're thinking.'

'What?' Arkady was mystified.

'That since I was on stage I could see who Zina was with. Well, you're wrong. When you're on stage playing, the lights are right in your eyes. Ask the other members of the band; they'll tell you the same thing. We couldn't see anyone.'

'You ask,' Arkady said. 'You're in charge.'

The *Eagle* was smaller than the *Merry Jane*, red and white, lower to the water, a side crane and a gantry with a single reel. Another difference was that not a single fisherman was on deck to greet them. They stepped out onto wooden planks empty except for the dregs of the boat's last tow: limp flatfish, skeletal crabs.

'I don't understand,' Slava said. 'Usually they're so friendly.'

'You feel something, too?' Arkady asked. 'A certain coolness. What language will we be speaking, by the way? Swedish? Spanish? What kind of Americans will these be?'

'You're going to embarrass me, aren't you?'

Arkady looked Slava over. 'You have your jogging shoes on, your jeans. You're the picture of a Young Communist. I think we're ready to face the captain.'

'Some assistant I have, a regular fugitive.'

'Worse, someone with nothing to lose. After you.'

The *Eagle*'s bridge was smaller than the *Merry Jane*'s and had no carpeting or teak, but otherwise was more what Arkady had supposed an American bridge would be like: a veritable space capsule's array of colour monitors banked around and behind the captain's chair; a circle of radar screens and the cathode green of fishfinders that targeted schools of fish as shifting orange clouds. Radios hung from the overhead, their ruby numbers floating in the static of open channels. The chrome hoods of the compass and repeater were polished to shine like crystal. In all, glitter without clutter.

The man in the captain's chair fitted in. Fishermen

were usually scarred by exposure to knives, spines and frayed ropes, and coarsened by cold air and brine, but Morgan seemed to have been abraded by something sharper. He was lean to the point of gaunt, with prematurely grey hair. Although he wore a cap and a sweatshirt there was about him and his ship's bridge a sense of monkish order, of a man who was happiest alone and in control. As he unwound from his chair Slava gave him a nod of obeisance, and it occurred to Arkady that the third mate would have made a good dog.

'George, this is Seaman Renko. Or you can call him Arkady.' To Arkady, Slava said, 'Captain Morgan.'

The captain gave Arkady's hand a brief squeeze. 'We're sorry about Zina Pishvili.'

'Patiashvili.' Slava shrugged as if the name were ridiculous or didn't really matter.

'Pashvili? Sorry.' Morgan said to Arkady, 'I don't speak Russian. Ship-to-ship communications go through the company reps on the *Polar Star*. Perhaps you should ask a rep to join us, because right now we're losing trawling time and that means we're losing money. Can I offer you a drink?' On the chart chest was a tray with three tumblers and a bottle of Soviet vodka. Better than what the Soviets drank at home: export-quality vodka. He lifted the vodka a millimetre off the tray, as if measuring the minimum of hospitality. 'Or are you in a rush?'

'No, thank you.' Slava could take a hint.

'Why not?' Arkady asked.

Slava hissed, 'First wine, now vodka?'

'It's like New Year's Eve, isn't it?' Arkady said.

Morgan poured Arkady half a glass and, bemused, one for himself. Slava abstained.

'Nazdrovya,' Morgan said. 'Isn't that it?'

'Cheers,' said Arkady.

Arkady drank his in three swallows, Morgan in one that he followed with an even smile of excellent teeth. 'You don't want a company rep,' he said.

'We'll try to do without.' The last thing Arkady wanted was Susan joining their conversation.

'Well, Arkady, ask away.'

Morgan was so assured, Arkady wondered what would faze him.

'Is this boat safe?'

Slava started. 'Renko, that's—'

'It's OK,' Morgan said. 'This is a seventy-five-foot Gulf boat with a North Sea rig. That means it was originally built to tend oil platforms in the Gulf of Mexico and then was refitted to come up here for the crabbing boom. When crabs went bust, they put on the gantry for trawling and some extra plating for hitting the ice. The real money went where it counts, into electronics. We don't have all the tradition of our round-headed friend and his three dwarfs over on the *Merry Jane*, but we do catch more fish.'

'Did you know Zina?'

'Just to see. She was always friendly, waving.'

'And dancing?'

'I didn't have the pleasure of dancing with her myself. I was in the wardroom going over charts with my good friends, Captains Marchuk and Thorwald.'

'Do you like the joint fishery?'

'It's exciting.'

'Exciting?' Arkady had never thought of it that way. 'How so?'

'After Dutch we're going up to the ice sheet. Soviet captains are intrepid. Last year you people got a whole fishing fleet, fifty boats, iced in off Siberia and almost lost them all. You did lose a factory ship and the only reason the whole crew didn't go down with it was because they were able to cross the ice.'

'Those were Soviet boats,' Arkady said.

'Right, and I don't want to end up like a Soviet boat. Don't get the wrong idea, I like Russians. It's the best joint fishery. Koreans will steal half of every bag. The Japanese are too proud to cheat but they're colder than the fish.' Morgan was the sort of man who smiled while he reassessed a situation. 'Arkady, how is it I don't recall ever meeting you on the *Polar Star*? You're a fleet officer or from the Ministry or what?'

'I work in the factory.'

'The slime line,' Slava said.

'And you speak fluent English and investigate accidents? I'd say you're overqualified for cleaning fish.' There was a candid, glass-blue quality to Morgan's eyes that told Slava and Arkady what liars he thought they were. 'It was an accident?'

'There's no doubt of it,' Slava said.

Morgan had kept his eyes steadily on Arkady. His gaze moved to the net now idle on the gantry, then to two crewmen in oilskin coveralls coming up the outside stairs from the deck, and then back to Arkady. 'Okay. It's been a delightful social call. Just remember, these are American waters.'

The narrow bridge became crowded as the fishermen entered. These were the Americans he had been curious about since he heard Lantz describe them as a 'motorcycle gang'. In the Soviet Union, where two wheels chained to an internal combustion engine were the symbol of personal freedom, bikers were called 'Rockers'. The authorities were always trying to channel Rockers into approved motordromes, but the gangs slipped away like Mongols on the loose, took over whole villages, then vanished before a state motor patrol could arrive.

The larger fisherman had a sallow face, hooded eyes and the strong, hanging arms of someone who has spent time shoving crab pots and nets. Not a smooth man. He looked Arkady up and down. 'What is this shit?'

'This, Coletti,' Morgan explained, 'is the joint venture. The man with our old friend Slava speaks English well enough to teach you. We'll make it fast but clean.'

'Renko, this is Mike.' Slava introduced the younger fisherman, an Aleut with fine Asian features on a broad face. 'Mike is short for Mikhail.'

'A Russian name?' Arkady asked.

'Up here there are a lot of Russian names.' Mike had a soft, hesitant voice. 'There were a lot of crazy Cossacks around here way back.'

'At one time the Aleutians and Alaska all belonged to the tsars,' Morgan told Arkady. 'You ought to know that.'

'Do you speak Russian?' Here was someone who could have talked to Zina.

'No. I mean, we use expressions,' Mike said, 'without, you know, really knowing what they mean. Like if you hit your thumb with a hammer, right? Or when we go to church, some of that's in Russian.'

'There's still a Russian church in Dutch Harbor,' Slava said.

The Aleut dared a glance at Coletti before saying, 'We're really sorry about Zina. It's hard to believe. Every time we brought in a bag of fish she'd be at the stern rail giving us a big wave. Rain or shine, night or day, she was there.'

'You danced with her?' Arkady asked.

Coletti cut in. 'We all did.'

'And after the dance?'

'When we left, the dance was still going on.' Coletti held his head at an angle, getting a fix on Arkady.

'Zina was still dancing?'

'She left before us.'

'Did she seem ill in any way? Drunk, dizzy, light-headed? Nervous, preoccupied, afraid?'

'No.' Coletti answered questions like a Moscow militiaman, the type that volunteered nothing.

'Who did she leave with?' Arkady asked.

'Who knows?' answered a late arrival as he came up the galley stairs onto the bridge. This third crewman raised peaked brows in mock concern, as if the party had started without him. A gold ring decorated his left ear; a leather thong tied his long hair into a ponytail.

His beard was wispy, almost feminine, like that of a young actor. He didn't offer to shake hands because he was wiping his own on a greasy rag. He said, 'I'm Ridley, the engineer. I wanted to add my own condolences. Zina was a great kid.'

'Then you talked to her at the dance?' Arkady asked.

'Well . . .' Ridley paused apologetically. 'Your captain laid out a generous spread for us as soon as we got on board. Sausages, beer, brandy. Then we visited with the Americans, Susan and her boys. Old friends, so there was more beer and vodka. As I understand it, it's against your regulations to have liquor on board, but it runs like a gusher every time I've been on the *Star*. Plus there's the time factor. The *Star* runs on Vladivostok time, which is three hours earlier than ours. You start a dance at 9 p.m. That's midnight to us. At that hour we relax real fast.'

'It was a good dance?'

'Best rock and roll band in the Bering Sea.'

Slava shook his head under the force of flattery.

'The truth is', Ridley added in a confessional tone, 'I think we're an embarrassment when we get on the *Polar Star*. We get drunk and try to live up to the reputation of being wild Americans.'

'No, no,' said Slava.

'Yes, yes,' said Ridley. 'The Russians are so hospitable. We get stoned and you go on smiling, picking us off the floor. I got so drunk I had to come back early.'

Every crew had a natural leader. Even in the tight

quarters of the *Eagle*'s bridge, Coletti and Mike had taken a perceptible step towards the engineer.

'Do I recognize you?' Arkady asked.

'Ridley spent two weeks on the *Polar Star*,' Slava said.

Ridley nodded. 'The voyage before this. The company wants us to be familiar with Soviet techniques. I can tell you that after working with Soviet gear my opinion of Soviet fishermen was higher than ever.'

Arkady remembered Ridley being pointed out. 'You speak Russian?'

'No, there was a whole lot of sign language. Language is not one of my talents. Look, I had an uncle who lived with us. He studied Esperanto, the new international language. Finally he finds a woman who also studies Esperanto. In Washington State there had to be about five people. Anyway, she comes over and we're all in the parlour waiting for this big moment, two people speaking Esperanto, like a glimpse of the future. It takes about ten seconds to see that they don't understand each other at all. She's asking for the wine, he's telling her the time. That was Russians and me. Sorry. Just out of curiosity, did you serve in Afghanistan?'

'I was too old to do my "internationalist duty",' Arkady said. 'Did you serve in Vietnam?'

'Too young. Anyway, I don't even remember saying goodnight to Zina. What happened? Did she disappear?'

'No, she came back.'

Ridley enjoyed the answer, as if he'd found someone worth talking to. 'Came back from where?'

'As I understand it,' Morgan said, trying to put the

conversation back on conventional rails, 'her body was picked up by our net and was found when the bag was opened on the *Polar Star*.'

'Jesus,' Ridley said, 'that must have been a moment. She fell over?'

'Yes,' Slava said.

Coletti pointed at Arkady. 'I want to hear him say it.'

'It's too soon for that,' Arkady answered.

'Fuck that!' Coletti exploded. 'We don't know what happened to Zina. We don't know if she took a swan dive or what, but we were off that fucking boat before anything happened.'

'Coletti.' Morgan stepped in front of him. 'Some day I'm going to open up your head just to see how small your brain is.'

Ridley eased Coletti back with a touch. 'Hey, we're all friends. Take it easy like Arkady. See how he watches.'

'Yes.' Morgan noticed; he told Arkady, 'We apologize. Whatever happened to Zina was a tragedy, but we hope it doesn't affect the joint venture. We all believe in it.'

'We'd be shit out of work if we didn't have it,' Ridley said. 'And we like making new friends, having Slava play his sax or explain all about perestroika and how the Soviet Union from top to bottom is thinking in new ways.'

'Thinking in New Ways' was a catchphrase of the new men in the Kremlin, as if Soviet brains could be rewired like circuit boards.

'Are you thinking in new ways?' Ridley asked Arkady.

'I try.'

'A senior man like you has to keep up,' Ridley said.

Slava said, 'He just works at the factory.'

'No.' Coletti disagreed as if he had special information. 'I used to be a cop and I can smell another cop.
He's a cop.'

Being lifted by cage up the *Polar Star*'s hull was like
floating across a great curtain of suppurating steel.

Slava was furious. 'We made fools of ourselves. This
is a Soviet affair, it has nothing to do with them.'

'It doesn't seem to,' Arkady agreed.

'Then what is there to be cheerful about?'

'Oh, I think of all the fish I didn't see today.'

'That's all?'

Arkady looked down through the open bars of the
cage at the catcherboat below. 'The *Eagle* has a low hull.
I wouldn't take it into the ice.'

'What do you know about trawlers?' Slava demanded.

There had been the Sakhalin trawler. Captured from
the Japanese during the war, it was a little drift trawler,
a porous wooden hull around an ancient diesel.
Wherever paint peeled, ghostly Japanese markings
emerged. There was no trouble getting a berth on a
vessel overdue to sink, especially when the captain had
a simple quota: cram the hold with salmon until the
boat shipped water. As the new man, Arkady was stuffed
into the warp hole; when the net was pulled in he had
to run in a crouch around and around, coiling a hawser
spiked with frayed metal threads. As the hawser filled

the hole he circled on all fours like a rat in a coffin, then climbed out to help shake the net. By the second day he could barely raise his hands, though once he got the knack he developed the first shoulders he'd had since the army.

Of course, the lesson of that foul little boat was that fishermen had to be able to get along in a confined space for long periods of time. All the rest – knowing how to gaff wind or mend – meant nothing if one man set his shipmates on edge. Arkady had never seen as much antagonism on the troller as he had witnessed on the glittering bridge of the *Eagle*.

The cage swayed with Slava's agitation. 'You had a day off, that's all you wanted.'

'It was interesting,' Arkady granted. 'Americans are a change.'

'Well, I can promise you that you're not getting off the *Polar Star* again. What are you going to do now?'

Arkady shrugged. 'There were many people on special duty during the dance. I'll ask whether any of them saw Zina on deck or below. Try to find out when the Americans actually left the ship. Talk to people who were at the dance. Talk to women she worked with in the galley. I want to talk to Karp again.'

'After we talk to the women we'll split up,' Slava said. 'I'll take Karp. You take the crew below decks, that's more your style.'

The cage cleared the side and began its descent toward the familiar, scrofulous deck and the barrels heaped like a high-tide line of sea trash around the stack.

'You set them off,' Slava said. 'The crew on the *Eagle* are usually great guys. Susan is generally an angel. Why is everyone nervous? We're in American waters.'

'A Soviet boat is Soviet territory,' Arkady said. 'They should be nervous.'

Chapter Seven

To a fanfare of trumpets white lines emanated from a red star. Natasha pushed the fast forward button to the image of a white clock-face on a blue background. Fast forward again to the slanted log of *Novosti News*, then the silent picture of a man reading accounts of stale events into two microphones, then fast forward again until finally a slim girl in a skin-tight vicro warm-up outfit appeared on the television screen. She had a dappling of freckles across her nose, hoop earrings and braided hair the colour of brass. She began stretching like a willow bending in a strong wind.

In the ship's cafeteria, facing the glow of the connected television and VCR, outfitted in sweatsuits and aerobic gear, twenty women of the *Polar Star* tilted grudgingly like sturdy oaks. When the girl bent forward and touched her nose to her knees, they took only slight bows, and when she ran lightly in place, the women sounded like an enthusiastic, thundering herd. Though Factory Worker Natasha Chaikovskaya was in the lead, not far behind her was Olimpiada Bovina, the massive chief cook of the crew's galley. Like a little ribbon on an oversized box, a powder-blue sweatband decorated Olimpiada's brow. Sweat leaked from the band, welled around her small eyes and flowed poignantly like tears down her cheeks as she pursued the graceful, tireless acrobat on the screen.

When Slava called her name, Olimpiada abandoned the trotting and puffing with the wistful reluctance of a masochist. They talked to her at the back of the cafeteria. She had the fruity voice of a mezzosoprano.

'Poor Zina. A smile is gone from the galley.'

'She was a hard worker?' Slava asked.

'And cheerful. So full of life. A tease. She hated to stir the macaroni. We have macaroni often, you know.'

'I know,' Arkady said.

'So she would say, "Here, Olimpiada, is some more good exercise for you." We will miss her.'

Slava said, 'Thank you, Comrade Bovina, you can—'

'An active girl?' Arkady asked.

'Certainly,' Olimpiada said.

'Young and attractive. A little restless?'

'It was impossible to keep her in one place.'

Arkady said, 'The day after the dance she didn't come to work. Did you send someone for her?'

'I needed everyone in the galley. I can't have all my girls wandering around the ship. I run a responsible kitchen. Poor Zina, I was afraid she was sick or over-tired from the night before. Women are different, you know.'

'Speaking of men . . .' Arkady said.

'She kept them in line.'

'Who was at the head of the line?'

Olimpiada blushed and giggled into her hand. 'You will think this is disrespectful. I shouldn't say.'

'Please,' Arkady said.

'It's what she said, not what I said.'

'Please.'

'She said that in the spirit of the Party Congress she was going to democratize her relationship with men. She called it "Restructuring the Males".'

'There weren't one or two men in particular?' Arkady asked.

'On the *Polar Star*?'

'Where else?'

'I don't know.' Olimpiada suddenly became discreet.

Slava said, 'You've been very helpful, Comrade Bovina.'

The chief cook chugged back to her position in the class. The girl on the screen spread her arms and rotated them; she seemed light enough to fly. Through the power of television, all across the Soviet Union this young dancer had become the new ideal of Soviet women, a shining, bobbing icon. Sleek Latvian women, Asiatics in felt tents and settlers in the Virgin Lands all watched the show and copied her every move. Thanks to the VCR, the ladies of the *Polar Star* could follow suit, though looking at their broad backs and outstretched, powerful arms, Arkady was put less in mind of birds than of a squadron of bombers lifting off.

The VCR was a Panasonic, a prize of the ship's last visit to Dutch Harbor, and had been adapted to Soviet frequencies. There was a flourishing black market for Japanese VCRs in Vladivostok. Not that Soviet VCRs like a top-of-the-line Voronezh weren't good – they were fine for Soviet videotapes – it was just that Soviet machines lacked the ability to tape shows. Also, just as Soviet railroad tracks are a wider gauge than foreign ones in order to prevent an invasion by train, Soviet VCRs took a larger tape to prevent an influx of foreign pornography.

'Women!' Slava was disgusted. 'To reduce a subject of such importance as restructuring to so trivial a level. And I'm sick of you asking questions and going off in different directions. I have my own ideas and I don't need assistance from you.'

Olimpiada looked over her shoulder to see Slava storm out of the cafeteria. Natasha half-turned from the television and fixed her black gaze on Arkady.

When he'd been a boy Arkady had little lead soldiers, the heroic General Davydov's sabre-wielding cavalry-men, the sly Field Marshal Kutuzov's artillerymen and the scowling grenadiers of Napoleon's Grand Army, all kept in a box beneath his bed, where they rolled together in a mêlée as he took the box out, played with the pieces and then slid them back home. Like casualties, they soon lost their original coats and faces of paint and he daubed them afresh, less expertly each time.

Skiba and Slezko looked like a pair of those grenadiers toward the end of their careers: fierce, with mottled pink-and-grey chins, spots of gold in their teeth, ident-ical except that Skiba had black hair and Slezko grey. They were on the midship deck, the same place they had been during the dance when their duty had been to watch the transport cage that carried the American fishermen from and to their boats.

'The *Merry Jane* was tied up to the *Eagle*, which was tied up to our starboard side?' Arkady asked.

'We prefer answering the third mate,' Skiba said.

'I can tell the captain that you refused to answer questions.'

Skiba and Slezko looked around the deck and then at each other until a telepathic decision was made.

'More private,' Slezko said. He led the way inside, downstairs, around a machine shop and through a door into a dank, badly lit room with sinks and stalls. The sinks were brown from the ship's water; the stalls had concrete benches with holes. In Moscow, informers always wanted to meet in public toilets; in a desert, an informer would unearth a toilet to talk in.

Skiba folded his arms and leaned against the door as if he were temporarily in the hands of the enemy. 'We will answer a question or two.'

'The arrangement of boats was as I described?' Arkady asked.

'Yes.' Slezko closed the porthole.

'Chronologically, by our time, when did the Americans leave?' Arkady opened the porthole.

Skiba consulted a notebook. 'The captain and crew of the *Merry Jane* returned to their boat at 2300 and immediately cast off. One crewman of the *Eagle* returned to his boat at 2329; then two others and the captain returned at 2354. The *Eagle* cast off at 0010.'

'When the trawlers cast off, how far did they go?' Arkady asked. 'A hundred metres? Out of sight?'

'It was too foggy to tell,' Slezko said after much consideration.

'When the Americans left, did any Soviets see them off?' Arkady asked.

While Skiba referred to his notebook Arkady's eye fell on the newspapers stuffed in baskets by the stalls; crumpled headlines on top announced, 'Bold Refor—' and 'New Age o—'. Skiba cleared his throat. 'The head rep Susan came out on deck with them. Captain Marchuk shook hands with Captain Morgan and wished him good fishing.'

'No undue fraternization,' Arkady said. 'There was no one else?'

'Correct,' Skiba said.

'From 2230 on, who else did you see on deck?'

'Oh.' Skiba thumbed through his notebook, flustered but also angry, as if he'd known there would be a surprise question. 'The captain I said already. At 2240, the Americans Lantz and Day headed aft.' He pivoted to be sure. 'At 2315, Comrade Taratuta.' She was in charge of the captain's quarters and galley.

'Which direction?'

As Slezko held up his left hand and then his right, Skiba faced the door and then away.

'From aft—' Slezko began.

'To forward,' Skiba finished.

*

85

'Thinking in new ways. What does this mean?' Gury asked. 'The old ways meant Brezhnev—'

'No,' Arkady corrected him. 'They may mean Brezhnev, but you don't say his name. Brezhnev no longer exists, only the problems of old ways, obstructionism and foot-dragging.'

'It's confusing.'

'All the better. A good leader mystifies people at least half the time.'

Gury had spent a month reading two American books, *In Pursuit of Excellence* and *The One-Minute Manager*, a feat of concentration that was religious considering how little English he understood. Arkady had translated much of these chronicles of business greed, and the collaboration had, at least in Gury's mind, made them fast friends.

Now Arkady watched Gury test condoms in a tub. Users called them 'galoshes', and they came rolled in talc, two to a paper envelope. Powder exploded as he inflated each condom, tied it and plunged it under water. A film of talc covered his leather jacket.

The site Gury had chosen for this consumer review was an empty fuel bunker. Although the bunker had supposedly been flushed there was an acrid edge to the air and the promise of a petroleum-based headache. In the absence of vodka, a lot of sailors sniffed fumes; they would be found laughing or crying uncontrollably or dancing off the walls. Or Thinking in New Ways, Arkady guessed.

As champagne-sized bubbles worked their way to the

surface of the tub and broke through a scum of talc, Gury fumed. 'Lack of quality control. Basic lack of management commitment and product integrity.'

He tossed the condom on to a growing pile of tested and rejected ones, unwrapped another one, blew it up and held it under water. His plan was not only to buy radios and cassette players in Dutch Harbor, but also to smuggle out as many batteries as possible in elastic, watertight containers that could be secreted in an oil drum.

Getting condoms was no problem; Gury ran the ship's store. The problem was that the KGB had informers that not even Volovoi knew about. Someone always seemed to know about the book in the sand bucket or the nylon stockings in the anchor well. Unless, of course, Gury was himself one of those extra ears of the Committee for State Security. Everywhere Arkady had gone a different informer had appeared – in Irkutsk, at the slaughterhouse, even in Sakhalin. Setting out from Vladivostok on the *Polar Star* he had simply assumed that one of his cabinmates was an informer, but whether it was Gury, Kolya or Obidin, paranoia could fight friendship just so long. Now they all seemed comrades.

'How will you get the batteries on board?' Arkady asked. 'They're going to search everyone coming back to the ship. Some they'll stripsearch.'

'I'll come up with an idea.'

Gury was always coming up with ideas. The latest was a book that would teach anyone to Think in New Ways in a minute. 'The crazy thing', he went on, 'is that I was convicted of Restructuring. I was doing away with state planning, offering initiatives—'

'You were convicted of illegally buying a state-owned coffee roaster, selling coffee privately, and doctoring the beans with fifty per cent grain.'

'I was just a premature entrepreneur.'

Bubbles trailed to the surface and popped. 'You sold condoms to Zina,' Arkady said.

'Zina was not a girl to take chances.' Gury threw the latest failure on the pile, picked up another and sneezed. 'At least, not that kind.'

'She bought them regularly?'

'She was an active girl.'

'Who with?'

'Who not? She wasn't a slut necessarily; she didn't take money; she didn't like to be obligated. *She* did the choosing. A modern woman. Aha!' He tossed a condom on the good pile. 'Quality is on the up-swing.'

'Is this really where the country is headed?' Arkady asked. 'A nation of entrepreneurs happily sorting out condoms, cars, designer furniture?'

'What's wrong with that?'

'Gogol's great vision of Russia was of a troika madly dashing through the snow, sparks flying, the other nations of the earth watching in awe. Yours is of a car trunk stuffed with stereo equipment.'

Gury sniffed. 'I'm thinking in new ways. Clearly you're not.'

'Who were Zina's friends?' Arkady asked.

'Men. She slept with you; then she wouldn't sleep with you again, but she didn't hurt your feelings.'

'Women?'

'She got along with Susan. You've talked to her?'

'Yes.'

'Fantastic, isn't she?'

'Okay.'

'She's beautiful. You know how sometimes after a ship passes, the wake will glow with a bioluminescence? Sometimes when I've just missed seeing her on the ship there will be that glow.'

' "Bioluminescence"? Maybe you could bottle it and sell it.'

'You know,' Gury said, 'there's a hardness in you I worry about. Finding out you were an investigator has made me see you with new eyes. Like there's someone else inside you. Look, I just want to make money. The Soviet Union is about to leave the nineteenth century, and there are going to be—' He found he was waving a condom as he spoke, laid it down and sighed. 'Everything's going to be different. You were such a help to me with those books. If we could combine them with the inspirational words of the Party . . .'

In spite of himself, Arkady knew the clichés. They had poured from the Party like a rain of stones, rising to the ankles, to the knees. 'Working class, vanguard of restructuring, scientific analysis, both broadening and deepening ideological and moral victory?'

'Exactly. But not the *way* you said it. I believe in restructuring.' Gury found he was waving a condom again. 'Anyway, don't you think we should leave stagnation and corruption behind?' He caught Arkady's glance at the tub. 'Well, I wouldn't call this corruption – not real corruption. Brezhnev's daughter was smuggling diamonds, having orgies, fucking a gypsy. *That*'s corruption.'

'Zina had no special man?'

'You're starting to sound like an investigator, that's the scary part.' Gury tested another condom. 'I told you, she was very democratic. She was different from other women. Let me give you some advice. Find out what they want to hear and then give it to them. If you get serious, Arkady, they'll nail you like Obidin's Christ on a cross. Lighten up.'

Gury seemed sincerely concerned. They were cabinmates and comrades, both with troubled pasts. Now that Arkady thought about it, who was he to sneer at another man's aspirations, given the lack of any on his part except to lie low and survive? Where did this righteousness come from? He thought he'd killed it long ago. 'Okay, you're right,' he said. 'I'll think in New Ways.'

'Good.' Relieved, Gury dunked another condom. 'New and profitable ways, if possible.'

As an experiment, Arkady gave it a try. 'Say you don't just mask the smell from the Border Guard. Take another approach. When we get back to Vladivostok, misdirect the dogs by getting them to sniff something else. Collect some dog or cat urine and smear it on some crates.'

'I like that,' Gury said. 'The new Arkady. There's still hope for you.'

Chapter Eight

It was evening when Arkady returned to the captain's cabin. The sea-green walls gave the room a proper underwater aspect. Around the desk's glittering collection of glasses and bottles of mineral water sat Marchuk, First Mate Volovoi and a third man who was not much larger than a child. He had eyelids dark from lack of sleep, hair wild as straw and an unlit navigator's pipe drooping from his mouth. What made him remarkable was that Arkady had never seen him before.

Slava had already begun. At his feet was a canvas sack. 'After my visit to the *Eagle*, I conferred with First Mate Volovoi. We agreed that with the aid of the ship's Party activists and volunteers, we would be able to canvass the crew of the *Polar Star* and determine the location of every crew member on the night of Zina Patiashvili's disappearance. This enormous task was completed in two hours. We learned that no one saw Seaman Patiashvili after the dance, and that no one was with her when she fell overboard. We made special inquiries among the co-workers of Comrade Patiashvili, as much to lay rumour to rest as to find answers. There are those whose first instinct is to turn accident into scandal.'

'Also,' said Volovoi, 'we had to take into account our unusual situation, working with foreign nationals in foreign waters. Was undue fraternization with these nationals a factor in the tragic death of this citizen? Facts had to be faced. Hard questions had to be asked.'

This was good, Arkady thought. Here he'd been running around the ship while Slava and The Invalid were polishing a speech.

'Again and again,' Slava said, 'these suspicions were put to rest. Comrades, there is no testimony with more weight in any socialist court than the thoughts of those workers who toiled side by side with the deceased. In the galley I heard it time after time. "Patiashvili was an unstinting cook's assistant," "Patiashvili never missed a day," and, Slava lowered his voice out of respect, ' "Zina was a good girl." Similar sentiments were echoed by her cabinmates; I quote, "She was an honest Soviet worker who will be badly missed." That from Natasha Chaikovskaya, a Party member and herself a decorated worker.'

'They will all be commended for their forthright statements,' Volovoi said.

No one had greeted Arkady yet. He wondered whether he should disappear or become part of the furniture. Another chair would be useful.

'I again enlisted the aid of Comrade Volovoi,' Slava told the captain. 'I asked Fedor Fedorovich, "What kind of girl was Zina Patiashvili?" He said, "Young, full of life, but politically mature." '

'Typical of Soviet youth,' Volovoi said. For the occasion he wore a shiny running suit typical of political officers. It hadn't occurred to Arkady before that the first mate's cropped red hair looked like the stubble on a pig's snout.

Slava said, 'The trawlmaster who first found her body was badly shaken.'

'Korobetz,' Volovoi reminded the others. 'His deck team leads the ship's socialist competition.'

'I questioned him and his team. Although he had only ever seen her in the cafeteria, he too remembered a worker who gave unstintingly.'

Of mashed potatoes? Arkady wondered.

As if he could read minds, The Invalid slipped Arkady a brief, malevolent glance before holding up his end of the duet. 'Still, we must face the mystery of what happened to her on the night of her death. Not only for her sake, but for all her comrades, that they may move past this unhappy event and again put their full effort into productive ends.'

'Just so.' Slava couldn't agree more. 'And that is what we have accomplished today. We established that Zina Patiashvili was at the dance held at the cafeteria that night. I myself was in the band, and I can attest to the heat generated within a closed space by active dancers. This led me to inquire among the female crew members who attended whether at any time they felt uncomfortable because of the heat. Yes, a number of them answered; they had to leave the cafeteria and go out on deck for fresh air. I then returned to the infirmary and asked the ship's doctor whether Zina Patiashvili had ever complained of dizziness or headaches. His answer was affirmative. Earlier Dr Vainu had performed an autopsy on the deceased. I asked him whether there were any signs of violence that could not possibly be accidental. "No," he said. Were there any signs he found difficult to explain? I asked. Yes, there was discolouration on the torso and limbs, and there were evenly spaced bruises along the ribs and hips that he could not explain. Also, there was a small puncture of the abdomen.

'Comrades, there is no mystery. I myself retraced the steps of Zina Patiashvili the night of her disappearance. She was not seen in the passageways leading to her cabin, nor on the trawl deck. The only place she could have gone was to the stern. If she had fallen over the side directly into the water, yes, the marks on her body would be difficult to explain. However, alone and in the dark, Zina Patiashvili did not fall over the side rail but over the rail that surrounds the open stair-well above the stern ramp, hitting the back of her head as she fell on the stairs. Sliding down the steps she also bruised her front and limbs.'

A rather handy 'also', Arkady thought. Marchuk earnestly studied the autopsy report on his desk. Arkady felt for him. Viktor Marchuk wouldn't be a captain without a Party card, and he wouldn't be trusted to fish with Americans unless he were a Party activist. An ambitious man, but still a 'sailor's captain'. The anonymous guest in the third chair rested his head on his hand. He wore the enlightened expression of a person who actually enjoyed the wrong notes in an amateur piano recital.

'There's a landing on those stairs,' Marchuk said.

'Exactly,' Slava agreed, 'and there the body of Zina

Patiashvili rested while the dance went on. She lay with her body pressed against the outer rail of the landing, which explains the bruising of the ribs and hips. Then, when the dance was over and the *Polar Star*'s work began again, her body rolled as the ship moved. As you know, our designers bend their efforts to build the safest ships in the world for our Soviet seamen. Unfortunately, not every freak event can be foreseen. There is no protective rail on the inner side of the landing. Zina Patiashvili rolled free and fell onto the ramp. There is a safety gate further up the ramp to protect anyone falling down from the trawl deck, but not anyone falling from the well. Unconscious and unable to cry out, Zina Patiashvili slid down the ramp and into the water.'

Slava related his conclusion as if it were a radio play. In spite of himself, Arkady saw it: the girl from Georgia in her jeans and bleached hair leaving the smoke and heat of the dance; feeling lightheaded, staring into the soft oblivion of the fog, stepping carelessly back towards the rail of the well . . . No, frankly, he couldn't see it. Not Zina, not the girl with the queen of hearts in her pocket, not alone, not that way.

Unexpectedly Captain Marchuk asked, 'What do you think of this theory, Comrade Renko?'

'Very exciting.'

Slava went on. 'I do not have to explain to veteran seamen how briefly Zina Patiashvili could have survived in such near-freezing waters. Five minutes? Ten at the most. The only question left is the puncture wound in the abdomen, a wound brought to our attention by

Seaman Renko. Renko, however, is not a fisherman and is not trained or familiar with trawling gear. Has he ever handled a cable frayed from dragging forty tons of fish over the rocks of the sea floor?'

Well, yes, Arkady thought, but he didn't want to interrupt when the third mate was building to a climax, or at least to an end. Slava opened the sack on the floor, brought out a loop of 1cm steel cable and held it up triumphantly. In a few places steel threads fanned out like spikes.

'Cable like this, frayed like this,' Slava said. 'It's a fact that the body of Zina Patiashvili came up in the net. We seamen know that the net is drawn by worn cables. We know that as the net is drawn through the water the cables vibrate, making any frayed threads into virtual saws. That's what cut Zina Patiashvili. End of mystery. A girl went to a dance, became overheated, went out on deck alone for air, fell overboard and, I am sorry to say, died. But that is *all* that happened.'

Slava displayed the section of cable to Volovoi, who affected great interest in it, and to the stranger, who waved it aside, and to Marchuk, who was busy reading a new document. The captain had a feline manner of stroking his trim black beard as he concentrated on the page.

'According to your report, you recommend no further inquiry on board, and that any outstanding questions be left to the proper authorities in Vladivostok.'

'Yes,' Slava said. 'Of course the decision is yours.'

'There were some other recommendations, as I

remember,' Volovoi suggested. 'I saw the report only for a moment.'

'That is correct,' Slava answered dutifully. It was really wonderful, Arkady thought, almost as good as table tennis. 'If there is one lesson to be learned from this tragic incident it is that safety can never be taken for granted. I propose two firm recommendations. First, that during evening social events volunteers be placed on watch at either side of the stern deck. Second, that social events be held as much as possible during the daytime.'

'Those are useful recommendations that I'm sure will be discussed with great interest at the next all-ship meeting,' Volovoi said. 'The entire ship owes you their thanks for your labour, for the completeness and speed of your inquiry, and for the factual, clear-sighted nature of your conclusion.'

Tolstoy's aristocrats spoke effervescent French. The grandsons of the Revolution spoke plodding, measured Russian, as if each word were so many centimetres that, when carefully laid end to end, would inevitably lead to consensus, and spoken politely and soberly because it was the genius of Soviet democracy that all meetings should reach comradely unanimity. Say a worker came before a factory committee and pointed out that they were turning out cars with three wheels, or told a farm committee they were turning out calves with two heads. Such news never stopped a calm, experienced committee from marching in single formation.

Marchuk sipped from a glass, lit another cigarette, a

Player's with rich, foreign smoke, and studied the report, his head down. The angle accentuated the Asiatic cast to his cheeks. The captain looked like a man made for subduing the taiga, not for nosing through bureaucratic jargon. The stranger in the oatmeal sweater smiled patiently, as if he'd wandered by chance into this meeting, but was in no great hurry to leave.

Marchuk looked up. 'You conducted this inquiry with Seaman Renko?'

'Yes,' Slava said.

'I see only your signature at the bottom.'

'Because we did not have an opportunity to speak before this meeting.'

Marchuk motioned Arkady closer. 'Renko, do you have anything to add?'

Arkady thought for a moment and said, 'No.'

'Then do you want to sign it?' Marchuk offered a thick fountain pen, a Monte Cristo, right for a captain.

'No.'

Marchuk screwed the cap back on the pen. This was going to be more complicated.

The Invalid poured himself more water and said, 'As Seaman Renko did not do the bulk of the work, and as the recommendations are purely those of the third mate, there's no need for Renko's signature.'

'Let's see.' Marchuk turned back to Arkady. 'You disagree with the conclusion that we leave the loose ends for the boys in Vladivostok?'

'No.'

'Then with what?'

'Only . . .' Arkady searched for precision, 'the facts.'

'Ah.' For the first time the man in the oatmeal sweater sat up, as if he had finally heard a word in a language he understood.

'Excuse me,' said Marchuk. 'Seaman Renko, this is Fleet Electrical Engineer Hess. I have asked Comrade Hess to contribute his able mind to our meeting tonight. Explain to him and to me how you can disagree about the facts and agree with the conclusion.'

The *Polar Star* hadn't seen the fleet in six weeks and wouldn't see it again for another four. Arkady wondered where Hess had been hiding, but he concentrated on the question at hand.

'Zina Patiashvili died on the night of the dance,' Arkady said. 'Since she was not seen below decks on her way to her cabin, she probably either went to some other compartment in the aft house or, as the third mate says, onto the stern deck. However, when someone faints they drop, they do not take a running start so that they can flip over a rail that would have come up to Zina's ribs. There are characteristic marks to drowning, none of them present with Zina, and when they open her lungs in Vladivostok they'll find no saltwater. The characteristic marks present on the body – the lividity on the forearms, calves, breasts and belly – only result *after* death, from being on all fours for a period of time, and the bruises on the ribs and hips could not come from resting against a rail, but from being packed viciously against hard protuberances. She was killed on the *Polar Star* and stowed on board. As for the puncture of the belly, it was done with the single stab of a sharp knife. There were no scratches or sawing, and there was little bleeding. The facts are that before being thrown over she was stabbed to prevent her from floating to the surface. Another proof that the cut was not made by a net bringing her up was that she was thirty fathoms down on the sea bottom, long enough for slime eels to penetrate the puncture wound, enter her, and nest in her.'

'There's nothing in your report about eels,' Marchuk said to Slava. Fishermen hated slime eels.

'More?' Arkady asked.

'Please.'

'Her co-workers state that Zina Patiashvili was a ceaseless toiler, yet the Americans say that she appeared at the stern rail every time, day or night, that the catcher-boat *Eagle* delivered a net. Often that coincided with Zina's watch, which meant that she dropped her work whenever she cared to and was gone for half an hour at a time.'

'You say Soviets lie and Americans tell the truth?' Volovoi asked as if uncertain about a distinction.

'No. Zina spent the entire dance in the company of the Americans from the *Eagle*, dancing with them and talking to them. I do not think a woman runs to a stern rail in the middle of the night or in the rain to wave to a boat of men; she runs to wave to one man. The Americans are certainly lying as to who that might be.'

'You mean one of our boys was jealous?' Marchuk asked.

'That would be slander,' Volovoi stated, as if this

disposed of the question. 'Of course, if there were dere-
lictions in the galley, if any worker gave less than her
full time, there will be a stern rebuke.'

'Water?' Marchuk lifted a bottle to Volovoi.

'Please.'

Bubbles danced in The Invalid's glass. There was an
ominous curve to Marchuk's smile, but the words would
stay Soviet, level and businesslike.

'The problem,' Marchuk defined it, 'is the Americans.
They will watch to see whether we conduct an open and
forthright investigation.'

'We will,' Volovoi said. 'In Vladivostok.'

'Naturally,' Marchuk said. 'However, this is a unique
situation and may require a more immediate effort.' He
offered The Invalid a cigarette. All this was still within
the bounds of Soviet discussion. Sometimes there were
immediate crises, such as at the end of each month when
the month's quota could be fulfilled only by turning out
cars with three wheels. The equivalent on a fishing boat
was to meet the tonnage quota by turning the entire
catch, foul or fresh, into fishmeal.

'The doctor agreed with Comrade Bukovsky,' Volovoi
pointed out.

'The doctor,' Marchuk said, trying to take the suggestion seriously. 'The doctor was even wrong about the
time of death as I remember. A good doctor for the
healthy, not so good with the ailing or dead.'

'The report may have some flaws,' Volovoi conceded.

Full of regret, Marchuk addressed himself to Slava.

'Excuse me, the report is shit.' To Volovoi he added, 'I'm sure he did his best.'

The last Russian ship the *Polar Star* had seen was an off-loader that had taken three thousand tons of sole, five thousand tons of pollock, eight thousand tons of fishmeal and fifty tons of liver oil in exchange for flour, hams, cabbage, cans of film, personal mail and magazines. Arkady had been part of the crowd on deck that day. He hadn't noticed any tiny fleet electrical engineer riding the block and tackle.

Under his muff of hair Anton Hess's face was half forehead, the other features squeezed into a southern hemisphere of rounded brows, sharp nose, broad upper lip and dimpled chin, all lit by two amiable blue eyes. He looked like a German choirmaster, someone who had collaborated with Brahms.

Still using the measured tones of Soviet authority, of facts reluctantly stated, the first mate had decided to take the offensive.

'Seaman Renko, for our information, is it true you were dismissed from the Moscow Prosecutor's Office?'

'Yes.'

'Is it also true that you were expelled from the Party?'

'Yes.'

There was a sombre pause suitable for a man who had confessed to two incurable diseases.

'May I be blunt?' Volovoi begged Marchuk.

'Please.'

'From the start I was against the involvement of this worker in any inquiry, especially one involving our

American colleagues. I already had a dossier of negative information on Seaman Renko. Today I radioed the KGB in Vladivostok for more information, not wanting to judge this seaman unfairly. Comrades, we have a man with a shady past. Exactly what happened in Moscow no one will say, except that he was involved in the death of the prosecutor and in the defection of a former citizen. Murder and treason, that is the history of the man before you. That's why he runs from job to job across Siberia. Take a look – he has not thrived.'

True, Arkady admitted. His boots, crusted with scales and laced with dried slime, were not the footwear of a thriving man.

'In fact,' Volovoi went on, as if only the greatest pressure could bring the words to his lips, 'they were looking for him in Sakhalin when he signed on the *Polar Star*. For what, they don't say. With his kind, it could be any of a million things. May I be candid?'

'Absolutely,' said Marchuk.

'Comrades, Vladivostok will examine not what happened to a silly girl named Zina Patiashvili but whether we as a ship have maintained political discipline. Vladivostok will not understand why we involve in such a sensitive inquiry anyone like Renko, a man politically so unreliable that we don't let him ashore in an American port.'

'An excellent point,' Marchuk agreed.

'In fact,' Volovoi said, 'it might be wise not to let any of the crew ashore. We reach Dutch Harbor in two days. It might be best not to give them port call.'

At this suggestion, Marchuk's face darkened. He poured more water for himself, studying the silvery string of liquid. 'After four months' sailing?' he asked. 'That's what they've been sailing for, that one day in port. Besides, our crew is not the problem; we can't stop the Americans from going ashore.'

Volovoi shrugged. 'The representatives will report to the company, yes, but the company is half Soviet-owned. The company will do nothing.'

Marchuk screwed out his cigarette and produced a smile that had more irony than humour. Etiquette seemed to be wearing thin. 'The observers will report to the government, which is American, and the fishermen will spread tales to everyone. The tale will be that I hid a murder on my ship.'

'A death is a tragedy,' Volovoi said, 'but an investigation is a political decision. Any further on-board investigation would be a mistake. On this I must speak for the Party.'

In a thousand communes, factories, universities and courtrooms, the same words could have been spoken at that same instant because no serious meeting of managers or prosecutors was ever complete without someone finally speaking for the Party, at which point the niceties of debate would come to an end and the cigarette smoke would be cleared by that decisive, ineluctable word.

Only this time, Marchuk turned to the man on his right. 'Comrade Hess, do you have anything to say?'

'Well,' the fleet electrical engineer said, as if he had just thought of something. His voice had a timbre like a woodwind with a cracked reed, and he talked directly to Volovoi. 'In the past, comrade, everything you say would have been correct. It seems to me, however, that the situation has changed. We have a new leadership that has called for more initiative and a more candid examination of our mistakes. Captain Marchuk is symbolic of this young, forthright leadership. I think he should be supported. As for Seaman Renko, I also radioed for information. He was not charged with either murder or treason. In fact, there is a record of him being vouched for by a Colonel Pribluda of the KGB. Renko may be politically reckless, but there has never been a question of his professional abilities. Also, there is an overriding consideration. This is a unique joint programme we have undertaken with the Americans. Not everyone is happy that Soviets and Americans are working together. What will happen to our mission? What will happen to international cooperation if a story spreads that any Soviets who fraternize with Americans will have their bellies slit and be thrown overboard? We should show a sincere and genuine effort now, not only in Vladivostok. Third Mate Bukovsky has great energy, but he has no expertise in this area. None of us do except for Seaman Renko. Let us proceed with more confidence; let's find out what happened.'

For Arkady this was curious, like watching the dead rise. For once The Invalid hadn't ended the debate.

Volovoi said, 'Sometimes the ugly rumour of the moment has to be overlooked. This is a situation to be contained, not stirred up or publicized. Consider: if the

Patiashvili girl was murdered, as Seaman Renko insists, then we have a murderer on board our ship. If we do encourage an investigation on board, whether run intelligently or ineptly, what will be this person's natural reaction? Anxiety and fear – in fact, a desire to escape. Once in Vladivostok that will do him no good at all; a proper investigation in our own port will find him already in our hands. Here, however, the situation is different. The open sea, American boats and, most dangerous of all, an American port. Premature zeal here will prompt desperate acts. Wouldn't it be possible, even logical, that a criminal fearing exposure would abandon his group during its turn in Dutch Harbor and try to escape Soviet justice with the claim that he was seeking political asylum? Isn't this what prompts so many so-called defectors? Americans are unpredictable. As soon as a situation becomes political it gets out of hand, a circus, the truth vying with lies. Of course in time we would get the man back, but is this the right line for a Soviet ship? Murder? Scandal? Comrades, no one would argue that this crew does not, under normal circumstances, deserve a port call after four months' hard work at sea. However, I would not want to be the captain who risked the prestige and mission of an entire fleet so that his crew could buy foreign running shoes and watches.'

After such immaculate spadework by The Invalid, Arkady thought the issue was buried again. Hess, however, answered immediately.

'Let's separate your concerns. An investigation on board creates an abnormal situation, and an abnormal situation prevents a port call. It seems to me that one concern can resolve the other. We're a day and a half from Dutch Harbor, which is time enough for us to reach more definite conclusions about this poor girl's death. If it still seems suspicious in thirty-six hours, we can then decide not to allow the crew a port call. If not, let them have their well-earned day on shore. Either way, no one escapes and there will still be a full investigation waiting when we return to Vladivostok.'

'What about suicide?' Slava asked. 'What if she threw herself overboard, down the well, or wherever?'

'What about that?' Hess asked Arkady.

'Suicide is always a borderline issue,' Arkady said. 'There's the suicide who names fellow criminals before locking the garage door and starting the car. Or the suicide who paints "Fuck the Soviet Writers Union" on the kitchen wall before putting his head in the oven. Or the soldier who says, "Consider me a good Communist" before he charges a machine gun.'

'You are saying that the political element is always different,' Hess said.

'*I* will determine the political element,' Volovoi said. 'I am still the political officer.'

'Yes,' Marchuk said coolly. 'But not the captain.'

'On such a delicate mission—'

Hess cut Volovoi off. 'There's more than one mission.'

There was a pause, as if the entire ship had veered in a new direction.

When Marchuk offered Volovoi a cigarette, the lighter's flame lit a fan of capillaries spreading in the first mate's eyes. Exhaling, Volovoi said, 'Bukovsky can do another report.'

'Bukovsky and Renko strike a good balance, don't you think?' Hess asked.

Volovoi hunched forward as consensus, the goal of Soviet decision-making, rolled over him.

Marchuk changed the subject. 'I keep thinking about that girl being on the bottom, about the eels. Renko, what were the odds a net would find her? A million to one?'

Arkady's participation in the meeting had been an order, but also an honour, as if a toe had been invited to the deliberations of the brain. Marchuk's question was a gesture of that inclusion.

'A million to one is about the odds that Comrade Bukovsky and I will find anything,' Arkady said. 'Vladivostok has real investigators and real laboratories, and they know what to find.'

'The inquiry here and now is what matters,' Marchuk said. 'Report the facts as you find them.'

'No,' Arkady said. 'I agree with Comrade Volovoi; leave this for Vladivostok.'

'You're reluctant, I understand,' Marchuk sympathized. 'The important thing is you can redeem yourself—'

'I don't need to redeem myself. I agreed to spend a day asking questions. The day is over.' Arkady started for the door. 'Comrades, goodnight.'

Marchuk got to his feet, stunned. Stupefaction turned into the rage of a powerful man whose good intentions had been betrayed. Meanwhile, Volovoi sat back, scarcely believing this turn of fortune.

'Renko, you say someone killed this girl and you won't find out who?' Hess asked.

'I don't think I could – and I'm not interested.'

Marchuk said, 'I'm ordering you.'

'I'm refusing.'

'You forget you're speaking to your captain.'

'You forget you're speaking to a man who has spent a year on your slime line.' Arkady opened the door. 'What can you do to me? What could be worse?'

Chapter Nine

Wind had rolled the fog back into one dense bank. Arkady was crossing the deck intent on bed when he saw his cabinmate Kolya at the rail. A clear night always brought Kolya on deck, as if the moon were lit only for him. His hair curled up around a wool cap while his long nose pointed towards phenomena.

'Arkasha, I saw a whale. Just its tail, but it went straight down, so it was a humpback.'

What Arkady admired about Kolya was that even though the botanist had been chased off land he went on collecting scientific data. He had the courage of a monk willing, in spite of his meekness, to be tortured for his beliefs. Shining in his hands like a little French horn was his prize, a highly polished, old-fashioned brass sextant.

'Are you done with the captain?' he asked.

'Yes.'

Kolya had the delicacy not to ask any more questions, such as, Why didn't you tell your friends you were an investigator? Why aren't you an investigator now? What did you find out about the dead girl? Cheerfully he said, 'Good. Then you can help me.' He gave Arkady a watch. It was plastic, digital, Japanese. 'The top button lights the read-out.'

'Why are you doing this?' Arkady asked.

'It keeps the mind alive. Ready?'

'Okay.'

Kolya put his eye to the sextant telescope and sighted on the moon, swinging the index arm along the arc. As he had once explained to Arkady, sextants had the charm of being archaic, simple and complicated all at the same time. In essence, a pair of mirrors mounted on the arc brought an image of the moon down to the horizon, and the arc marked how many degrees off a right angle with the horizon the moon was at that precise instant.

'Mark.'

'10:15.31.'

'22:15.31.' Kolya corrected to nautical hours.

As a Young Pioneer, Arkady had once performed celestial navigation. He remembered being surrounded by nautical almanacs, sight-reduction tables, scratch paper, charts and parallel rules. Kolya did it all in his head.

'How many almanacs have you memorized?' Arkady asked.

'Sun, moon and Ursa Major.'

Arkady looked up. The stars seemed immensely bright and far away, with colours and depth, like a blazing night.

'There's the Little Bear,' Arkady looked straight up.

'You'll always see the Little Bear here,' Kolya said. 'At this latitude we're always under the Little Bear.'

When Kolya did calculations his eyes took on a fixed, inward look, a kind of bliss. Arkady could tell he was

111

subtracting the moon's refraction, adding the parallax, moving to the moon's declination.

'You've been under the Little Bear too long. You're round the bend,' Arkady said.

'It's no harder than blindfold chess.' Kolya even smiled to prove he could talk while he thought.

'Does it ever bother you that the sextant is based on the idea that the sun goes around the earth?'

Kolya faltered for a second. 'Unlike some systems, it works.'

Once declination was fixed, Kolya's brain would review its memorized tables. It was the sort of endeavour only a quietly manic personality would pursue, like looking for whales in the dark. Not so dark. As the swells lifted the moon's reflection, the sea seemed to be breathing slowly and steadily.

During his first months at sea, Arkady had spent a lot of time on deck watching for dolphins, sea lions and whales, just to see them moving. The sea gave the illusion of escape. But after a time he realized that what all these creatures of the sea had, as they swam this way and that, was a sense of purpose. That was what he didn't have.

He peered back at the Little Bear and its long tail ending in Polaris, the North Star. A Russian folk tale said Polaris was actually a maddened dog tied by an iron chain to the Little Bear, and that if the chain ever broke it would be the end of the world.

'Don't you get angry, Kolya? Here you are, a botanist, hundreds of kilometres from land.'

'Only a hundred fathoms from the sea floor. And

there's more land all the time. The Aleutian Islands are still building.'

'I think I would call that the long view,' Arkady said. He could feel his friend's anxiety; Kolya always became anxious when Arkady was depressed.

'Have you ever considered how much the Volovois of the world cost us?' Kolya was changing the subject, as if a good riddle was always balm. 'What are we paid?'

'I thought you were shooting the moon.'

'I can do both. What are we paid?'

That was complicated. The *Polar Star*'s pay was shared on a coefficient from 2.55 shares for the captain to 0.8 shares for a second-class seaman. Then there was a polar coefficient of 1.5 for fishing in Arctic seas, a ten per cent bonus for one year's service, a ten per cent bonus for meeting the ship's quota, and a bonus as high as forty per cent for over-fulfilling the plan. The quota was everything. It could be raised or lowered after the ship left dock, but was usually raised because the fleet manager drew his bonus from saving on seamen's wages. Transit time to the fishing grounds was set as so many days, and the whole crew lost money when the captain ran into a storm, which was why Soviet ships sometimes went full steam ahead through fog and heavy seas. Altogether, the wage scale of a Soviet fisherman was only a little less intricate than astronomy.

Arkady guessed, 'Around three hundred rubles a month for me.'

'Not bad. But did you factor in the Americans?' Kolya reminded him.

Because there were Americans on board, the work rules were different: a lower quota and a slower pace to impress the visitors with the humaneness of the Soviet fishing industry.

'Say three hundred and twenty-five rubles?'

'For a first-class seaman three hundred and forty rubles. For you two hundred and seventy-five. For a first mate like Volovoi, four hundred and seventy-five.'

'This is cheery,' Arkady said. But he was amused by his cabinmate's virtuosity, and Kolya grinned fiercely, like a juggler demanding the test of one more ball added to the ones already in the air.

'There are almost twenty thousand Soviet trawlers and factory ships with political officers, right? Giving them an average salary of only four hundred rubles a month we come to a total outlay for these entirely useless Invalids of eight million rubles a year. That's just the fishing fleet; imagine for the whole Soviet Union—'

'Fish! We're here for fish, not mathematics, Comrade Mer!'

Volovoi stepped out of the shadow of a companion-way, his running suit iridescent in the moonlight. There was something particularly gloating about his saunter, and Arkady realized that the first mate had followed him in triumph from the captain's cabin. As usual, Kolya automatically looked away.

Volovoi's hand reached out and took the sextant. 'What's this?'

Kolya said, 'It's mine. I was taking a reading from the moon.'

Volovoi glanced at the moon suspiciously. 'What for?'

'Finding our position.'

'You clean fish. What do you need to know our position for?'

'Just curiosity. It's an old sextant, an antique.'

'Where are your charts?'

'I don't have any charts.'

'You want to know how far we are from America?'

'No. I just wanted to know where we are.'

Volovoi unzipped the jacket of his running suit and slipped the sextant inside. 'The captain knows where we are. That should be enough.'

Walking away, The Invalid didn't say a word to Arkady; he didn't need to.

And so to bed.

The cabin was black as a grave, a proper abode. Kolya curled up with his flower pots while Arkady pulled off his boots and climbed into his bunk, pulling a sheet tight around his shoulders. A vinegary scent from Obidin's homemade brew tinged the air. Before he drew his second breath, he was asleep. It was sleep like a lightless void, one he knew well.

On Moscow's Garden Ring, near the Children's Library and the Ministry of Education, stood a three-storey building with a grey fence, the Serbsky Institute of Forensic Psychiatry. The fence was topped by thin wires invisible from the street. Between the fence and the building guards patrolled with dogs trained not to bark. On the second floor of the institute was Section Four. Along the parquet hall were three general wards that Arkady saw only on the day he arrived and the day he left, because he was held at the end of the hall in an 'isolator', with a bed, toilet and one dim bulb. On arrival, he was bathed by orderlies, two old women in white, and shaved by a fellow patient, head, armpits and pubis so that he would be as clean and hairless as a babe for the doctors, then dressed in striped pyjamas and a belt-less robe. There was no window, no day or night. His diagnosis was 'pre-schizophrenic syndrome', as if the doctors could confidently predict.

They injected caffeine under the skin to make him talkative, followed by a needle of barbital sodium into the vein of his arm to depress his will. Sitting on white stools, full of concern, the doctors asked, 'Where is Irina? You loved her, you must miss her. You made plans to meet? What do you think she's doing now? Where do you think she is?' They moved from arm to arm to the veins of his legs, but the questions were always the same, as was the humour of his situation. Since he had no idea where Irina was or what she was doing he answered everything in full, and since the doctors were convinced he knew more, they thought he was holding out. 'You're suffering under a delusion,' he told them. It didn't help his case.

Frustration naturally led to punishment. The favourite was the lumbar puncture. They strapped him to the bed, swabbed his spine with iodine, and with one vigorous push inserted the needle. The puncture was a two-fold experience, the agony of the probing needle and, for hours afterwards, spasms exactly like the comical reaction of a frog's leg to an electric current.

It was hard work for everyone. After a while they dressed him only in a bathrobe, the easier to get at veins. The doctors removed their lab coats and laboured in their uniforms, dark blue with the red shoulder boards of the militia.

Between sessions they kept him quiet with aminazin. So quiet that he could hear through two sets of closed, sound-proofed doors the scuffing of slippers in the hall during the day, the squeak of the guard's shoes at night. The light was never off. The door's peephole would blink: doctor's rounds.

'Better to talk to us and let go of this paranoia. Otherwise there will always be more questions, another interrogator when you least expect it. You really will go crazy.'

True, he felt himself losing control. From the street he could hear the occasional siren of a police car or fire engine, klaxons muffled in concrete, and he pouted like a dead man whose grave has been transgressed. *Leave me alone.*

Arkady squirmed in his straps. 'Just what is "pre-schizophrenic syndrome"?'

The doctor beamed, encouraged. 'It is also called "sluggish schizophrenia".'

'It sounds terrible,' Arkady had to admit. 'What are the signs?'

'A wide variety. Suspicion and uncommunicativeness – you recognize those? Listlessness? Rudeness?'

'After injections, yes,' Arkady confessed.

'Argumentativeness and arrogance. An abnormal interest in philosophy, religion or art.'

'What about hope?'

'In some cases,' the doctor said, 'absolutely.'

The truth was that the interrogators gave him hope simply because they wouldn't have brought him here if Irina weren't well. The KGB liked nothing more than to write off a defector as 'another émigré waiting on tables'; or 'The West wasn't such a soft bed after all, even for whores' or 'They squeezed her dry and then threw her out, and now she wants to come back, but of course it's too late.' When they demanded whether he was trying to reach her, his hope soared. Was she trying to reach him?

To protect Irina he changed his tack. He wanted to babble nothing, not even in his most feeble condition, so he thought about her as little as he could in order to purge her from his mind. In a sense, the doctors did achieve the schizophrenia they had predicted. Even as he took heart that Irina had survived, he tried to wipe her face from his memory, to make her a blank.

Besides the robe, Arkady had a green enamel jug, the perfect gift, something you couldn't swallow, cut or hang yourself with. Sometimes he would put the jug in front of the door so that the doctors would knock it over when they came in. Then not for a week, just enough to create the smallest uncertainty in the staff. One day they marched in as a group and took the jug away.

This time they used insulin. Insulin was the most primitive tranquillizer; in fact, it induced coma.

'Then let us tell you. She's married. Yes, this woman you're shielding is not only living in the luxury afforded traitors, but she's living with another man. She's forgotten you.'

'He's not even listening.'

'He hears us.'

'Try digitalis.'

'He could go into shock. Then we'd have nothing.'

'Look at his colour. Another minute you'll be pounding on his chest.'

'He's faking. Renko, you're faking.'

'He's white as snow. That's not faking.'

'Shit.'

'Better give it to him right away.'

'Okay, okay. Fuck.'

'Look at his eyes.'

'I'm giving it to him.'

'Ones like him can slip away on you, you know.'

'Bloody bastard.'

'Still no pulse.'

'He'll be fine by tomorrow. We'll start again, that's all.'

'Still no pulse.'

'He'll be babbling like a parakeet tomorrow, you'll see.'

'No pulse.'

'I still think he's faking.'

'I think he's dead.'

No, just hiding in the deep faraway.

'Only half-dead,' judged a visitor. His squat nose wrinkled as he sniffed the astringent air of the isolator. 'I'm taking you to more rigorous accommodations, away from this health spa.'

Because Arkady recognized the voice he made an effort to focus on a heavy Slavic head with piggish eyes and jowls that seemed to ooze out of a brown-and-red uniform with the star-and-dagger patch of the KGB.

'Major Pribluda?'

'Colonel Pribluda.' The visitor pointed to new epaulettes, then tossed a paper bag at the orderly who rushed in. 'Get him dressed.'

It was always bracing to see the effect that a brute in the right uniform could have, even on the medical community. Arkady had thought he was lost for ever, like a larva in the centre of a hive, yet in ten minutes Pribluda had him out on the street. Wrapped in pants and a coat admittedly two sizes too large, but out and shivering in the snow until Pribluda contemptuously shoved him into a car.

The car was a badly dented Moskvitch missing its wipers and rearview mirror, not a Volga with official plates. Pribluda pulled away from the kerb quickly, looking forward and back through his open window, then pulled his head back and erupted with a laugh. 'Not a bad actor, eh? By the way, you look terrible.'

Arkady felt ridiculous. Giddy with freedom and exhausted by the short walk, he slumped against the door. 'Didn't you have papers for my release?'

'Not with my name on it; I'm not dumb enough for that, Renko. By the time they find out, you'll be out of Moscow.'

Arkady took another look at Pribluda's shoulder boards. 'Did they promote you? Congratulations.'

'Thanks to you.' Pribluda had to pull his head in and out both to drive and hold a conversation. 'You made me look very smart when you came back. Let the girl run off and sell herself on the streets in New York; what state secrets did she have? You were a good Russian; you did what you had to and then came back.'

Flakes caught on Pribluda's hair and brows, making him the picture of a coachman. 'The problem is the prosecutor. He had many friends.'

'He was KGB, too.'

For a block, Pribluda acted offended. 'So you see my point,' he said finally. 'People think you know more than you do. For their own safety, they have to wring you like a rag until they get every last drop, and I don't mean of water.'

'Where is Irina?' Arkady asked.

Pribluda reached around and pushed snow off the windshield as he drove. Ahead, an East German Warburg sedan, built like an inverted bathtub, made a complete three sixty-degree turn on the trolley tracks.

'Fascist!' The colonel stuck a cigarette in his mouth and lit it. 'Forget her. For you she's as good as dead – worse than dead.'

'That means she's either very sick or very healthy.'

'For you it doesn't matter.'

The car swung through a gate and bounced over what at first seemed unlikely ruts in the centre of Moscow, but Arkady dimly saw a railroad switching yard with ramps built over rails so that trucks could cross. A field of trains like so many armoured hosts were standing in the snow, with flatcars of cable reels, tractors, pre-fab walls half-erased by white. In the distance, appearing to rise in the falling snow, were the gothic spires of Yaroslavl Station, the gateway to the East. Pribluda stopped the car between two passenger trains, one with the short, helmeted locomotive of a commuter line, the other with the long red coaches of the Rossiya, the Trans-Siberian Express. Through the windows Arkady could see travellers taking their seats.

'You're joking.'

'In Moscow you're surrounded by enemies,' Pribluda said. 'You're in no condition to protect yourself, and I won't be able to rescue you twice – not here. The same would be true in Leningrad, Kiev, Vladimir – anywhere near. You need to go where no one wants to follow you.'

'They'll follow me.'

'But they'll be one or two instead of twenty, and you'll be able to keep moving. You don't understand; you're dead here already.'

'Out there I'll be as good as dead.'

'That's what will save you. Believe me, I know how their minds work.'

Arkady couldn't deny the truth of that; the line between 'them' and Pribluda was fine enough.

'Just two or three years,' the colonel said. 'With the new regime, everything is changing – though not all for the best as far as I'm concerned. Anyway, give them a chance to forget you and then come back.'

'Well, it was a good act,' Arkady said, 'but you got me out too easily. You made a deal.'

Pribluda killed the engine, and for a moment there was no sound except the settling of snow, all those tons of flakes gently blanketing the city.

'To keep you alive.' The colonel was exasperated. 'What's wrong with that?'

'What did you promise?'

'No contact, not even the possibility of contact between you and her.'

'There's only one way you could promise "not even the possibility of contact". '

'Stop playing the interrogator with me. You always make everything so difficult.' Under his cap Pribluda had little eyes driven deep as nails. It was a strange place to find embarrassment. 'Am I your friend or not? Come on.'

Each red railroad care bore a golden hammer and sickle and a plaque that read 'Moscow–Vladivostok'. Pribluda had to carry Arkady up the high steps of the platform to a 'hard class' section. Exotic families in skullcaps and brilliant scarves camped on bedrolls, their berths occupied by new appliances still in packing cases – goods they could buy only in Moscow. Brown children peeked through curtains rolled up like bunting. Women opened bundles, releasing a buffet's smell of cold lamb, kefir, cheese. Students heading to the Ural Mountains stacked skis and guitars. Pribluda talked to the conductress, a top-heavy woman wearing what looked like an airline captain's cap and a short skirt. Returning, he stuffed into Arkady's overcoat a through ticket, an envelope of rubles and a blue workpass.

'I've made arrangements,' Pribluda said. 'Friends will take you off in Krasnoyarsk and put you on a plane for Norilsk. You'll have a job as a watchman, but you'd better not stay too long. The main thing is, once you're above the Arctic Circle you'll be too much trouble to bring back. It's just for a few years, it's not a lifetime.'

Arkady had never hated anyone as much as he once had Pribluda, and he knew Pribluda had loathed him in return. Yet here they were, as close to friends as each other had alive. It was as if everyone travelled the world in the dark, never knowing where he was going, blindly following a road that twisted, rose and fell. The hand that pushed you down one day helped you up the next. The only straight road was . . . what? The train!

'I meant it about the promotion,' Arkady said. 'That's good.'

On the platform a row of conductresses were raising batons, signalling that the express was ready to leave. Ahead, the locomotive released its air brakes and a tremor ran the length of the cars. Still the colonel lingered.

'You know what they say?' He smiled.

'What do they say?' Arkady wondered. Pribluda was not known for humour.

'They say some waters are too cold even for sharks.'

If the hospital had left him dazed, the motor yard in Norilsk made him numb. To keep from freezing, trucks were left running all night on Siberian diesel fuel, the cheapest on earth. Or else fires had to be carefully set under the engine block but away from the fuel line. The problem was that the surface was actually a thin cover of moss and dirt over permafrost, and as the frost around the fires melted and re-froze, the grounds became an icy swamp.

One night in his second month on the job, Arkady was building a fire in the black space under a Belarus earth-mover, a ten-wheeler the size of an iron house, when he saw figures approaching from opposite sides of the yard. Truck drivers wore boots, quilted jackets, caps. These two were in overcoats and hats and stepped daintily across the rutted ice. The one skirting a coal pile picked up a pick axe and carried it with him. Theft of construction equipment, the sacred property of the state, was not unusual, that's why there were watchmen like Arkady. If you want it, take it, he thought. The two men stood in the shadows and waited. The temperature was ten degrees below zero and Arkady began to freeze. It felt like burning on a spit. He stuffed a glove in his mouth to keep his teeth from chattering. In the dark he saw the two men shivering, arms folded, hopping in place, their breath crystallizing and drifting to the ground. Finally, on wooden legs, they gave up and gathered at the fire in the oil can. The one with the pick axe held it up and carefully peeled his fingers back; when the axe dropped and bounced smartly off his knee he didn't seem to feel a thing. The other was so cold he cried tears that froze in waxy stripes down his face. He tried to smoke, but his hands were shaking too hard to get out one cigarette, and half the pack spilled into the can and onto the ice. Finally, slowly, as bent and unsteady as if they were walking into violent wind, they moved away. Arkady heard one fall: a muffled impact and an agonized curse. A minutes later he heard car doors shut and an engine start.

Arkady dragged himself on his elbows to the burning can. He emptied kerosene into the fire and vodka into himself, and in the morning he didn't return to his hostel. He went to the airport and boarded a plane east, further into Siberia, like a fox heading for deeper woods.

He was pretty safe. With the Siberian labour shortage, any strong back got double pay for laying railroad ties, sawing ice or slaughtering reindeer with no questions asked, because Siberian managers had their quotas too. A man carving ice with a chainsaw, his own face encased with frost, might be an alcoholic, a criminal, a bum or a saint. What were the odds? Once the quotas was fulfilled, then a local *apparatchik* would check names against a list of persons in whom the militia or the KGB had an interest. But each of these work camps was a minuscule dot in a land mass twice the size of China. That was why workers were so prized, when Siberia's mere fifteen million inhabitants faced an envious one billion Chinese! By the time any agent of State Security arrived, Arkady was gone.

The interesting thing was that although Irina was Siberian he never saw a woman like her, not in all the villages and work camps that he passed through. Certainly not among the Uzbeks or Buryats, nor among the women who tended cement mixers like so many milkmaids around a cow. Nor among the Young Komsomol princesses who came to pose on tractors for six months and then flew home having fulfilled their lifetime quota of volunteer labour.

Yet when he cared to, he could stand on the duck-boards of a work camp and be sure that the next woman to jump from a truck to the mud, jacket open, scarf around her hair, lunch pail in hand, would be Irina. Somehow she had returned, and through a trail of incredible coincidences had arrived at the very same place he was. His heart would stop until she landed and looked up. Then he would be sure Irina was the next one. It was like a children's game.

So he didn't think of her.

At the end of his second year, escaping the Border Guard on Sakhalin, he crossed to the mainland and boarded a southbound train, re-connecting with the red Trans-Siberian Express after all this while. But this time he rode the platform because he smelled like a fish net. At dusk he arrived at Vladivostok, the 'Lord of the Ocean', the major Pacific port of the Soviet Union. Under tall, fluted streetlamps well-fed, well-dressed people filled the sidewalks. Motorcycles raced buses. Across from the terminal a statue of Lenin pointed to the Golden Horn, Vladivostok's bay, and on the rooftop above Lenin's steel brow glowed a welcome in neon script: 'Forward to the Victory of Communism!'

Forward? After two years of exile, Arkady had ten rubles in his pocket; the rest of his money was back on the island. A seaman's hostel was only ten kopeks a night, but he had to eat. He followed the buses to the Shipping Administration, where a board displayed the status of every civil vessel that claimed Vladivostok as its home port. According to the board, the factory ship *Polar Star* had put to sea that day, but when Arkady wandered to the docks he saw it still taking cargo and fuel. Floodlit gantries lifted barrels that had passed inspection by the Border Guard. Army veterans outfitted by the KGB in navy-blue uniforms. Their dogs sniffed each barrel, although how the animals could smell anything over the dockside odours of diesel fuel and the ammoniated steam of refrigeration plants was hard to understand.

In the morning, Arkady was the first man into the Seaman's Hall, where a clerk admitted that the *Polar Star* was still in port and still needed a worker on the factory line. He took his workpass behind a steel door to be stamped by the Maritime Section of the KGB, where he also signed a statement that defection by a Soviet seaman was treason. On the desk were two black phones for local offices and a direct red phone to Moscow. Arkady was surprised because for coastal fishing there were no such precautions. The black phones were no danger, he felt, unless they called Sakhalin. If anyone bothered to check his name on the red phone, this would be as far as he got.

'There are Americans,' warned the captain in charge.

'What?' Arkady had been watching the phones.

'There are Americans on the boat. Just be natural, friendly but not over-friendly. Better to say nothing at all, in fact.' He stamped the workpass without even reading the name on it. 'I'm not necessarily saying hide.'

But isn't this what Arkady did, hide? First in the deep faraway of the psycho ward. Then, after Pribluda revived him, in Siberia and on the ship, carrying on inert and semi-dead?

Now, asleep in his narrow bunk, he asked himself, *Wouldn't it be good to be alive again?*

Zina Patiashvili had swum back. Maybe he could, too.

Chapter Ten

In the morning, showered and shaved, Arkady took the long walk to the *Polar Star*'s white wheelhouse and the cabin of the fleet electrical engineer for advice.

'You're lucky,' Anton Hess said. 'You caught me between going off duty and coming on. I was just making tea.'

His accommodations were no larger than a crew cabin, except that they were for one man rather than four, leaving room for a desk and a wall map that appeared to show every Soviet fishing fleet in the North Pacific. On a rubber pad on the desk was, instead of a samovar, a coffee maker, the sort that might grace a Moscow apartment.

Hess had the sort of look Arkady had once seen on submariners returning from a polar voyage. Eyes red and sprung. Step shuffling and uncertain. The little man's hair was stiff and wild, as if attacked by a cat, and his sweater reeked of pipe tobacco. The coffee dripped in greasy black drops. He poured out two mugs, added a generous amount from a cognac bottle, and gave a mug to Arkady. 'Confusion to the French,' he said.

'Why not?' Arkady agreed.

The coffee delivered a kick to his heart, which started beating anxiously. Hess sighed and allowed himself to sink in slow motion into a chair, where his eyes fixed wearily across the room on a waist-high vertical glass tube with a stand and cord for the radiation of ultraviolet rays. Sunlight. Vitamin D. During winter in Siberia they would ring children around tubes like this.

Hess's pale face smiled. 'My wife insisted I bring it. I think she wants to believe I'm in the South Pacific. Good tea?'

Tea for coffee, French for Americans. Hess had an ease for misleading that struck Arkady as appropriate.

There was no such thing as a fleet electrical engineer, it was a title of convenience that allowed an officer of the KGB or of Naval Intelligence to move from ship to ship. The question was which of these agencies the amiable Anton Hess belonged to. The best indicator was Volovoi, who was the political officer and who regarded Hess with both respect and animosity. Also, these days the KGB tended to be a strictly Russian club, where a name like Hess was a liability. The Navy tended to promote competence, with the exception of Jews.

On the map Alaska yearned towards Siberia. Or was it the other way around? Either way, Soviet trawlers dotted the sea from Kamchatka, across the island arc of the Aleutians and down to Oregon. Arkady hadn't appreciated before how well the American coast was covered. Of course, in Soviet-American joint ventures Soviet trawlers functioned as processors; each fleet shared its company of American catcherboats. Only a great factory ship like the *Polar Star* could operate independently with its own family of American boats. The red dot for the *Polar Star* was about two days north of Dutch Harbor and nowhere near other fleets.

'Comrade Hess, I apologize for bothering you.'

Hess shook his head, exhausted but indulgent. 'Not at all. Whatever I can do.'

'Very well,' Arkady said. 'Let's say that Zina Patiashvili did not accidentally stab, beat and throw herself overboard.'

'You've changed your mind.' Hess was delighted.

'And let's say we investigate. Not a real investigation with detectives and laboratories, but with the meagre resources we have on hand.'

'You.'

'Then we must consider the slim possibility of actually finding something out. Or of discovering a great many things, some of which we did not set out to find. This is where I need your counsel.'

'Really?' Hess sat forward, his whole attitude suggesting rapport.

'See, my vision – which is that of a man who cuts fish in the hold of a ship – is very limited. You, however, think in terms of the entire ship, even of the entire fleet. The work of a fleet electrical engineer must be difficult.' Especially so far from the fleet, Arkady thought. 'You would be aware of factors and considerations I know nothing of. Perhaps of factors I *should* know nothing of.'

Hess frowned as if he couldn't imagine what these could be. 'You mean there might be some reason not to ask questions? And if there were such a reason, that it would be better to ask no questions at all rather than to stop questions once you've begun asking them?'

'You've expressed it better than I could,' Arkady said.

Hess rubbed his eyes, fumbled with a tobacco pouch, filled and tamped his pipe. It was a navigator's pipe designed to hang out of the way while its smoker studied charts. He lit it with short sucks of air, sounding like a radiator.

'I can't think of any such reason. The girl seems to have been ordinary, young, a little loose. But I have a solution for your concern. If you come across anything especially unusual, anything that bothers you, then please feel free to come to me first.'

'Sometimes you might be hard to find.' After all, I didn't even know you existed until last night, Arkady thought.

'The *Polar Star* is a large ship, but it's still only a ship. Captain Marchuk or his chief mate always know where I am.'

'His chief mate, not his first mate?'

'Not Comrade Volovoi, no.' Hess smiled at the idea.

Arkady wished he knew more about the man. German communities had been invited to settle in, cultivate and tone up the Volga for hundreds of years, until the Great Patriotic War, when Stalin ripped them out in advance of the Fascist invasion and shipped them overnight to Asia.

Hess scrutinized Arkady in the same way. 'Your father was General Renko, is that right?'

'Yes.'

'Where did you do your service?'

'Berlin.'

'Really? Doing what?'

'Sitting in a radio shed, listening to Americans.'

'Intelligence work!'

'Hardly so grand.'

'But you monitored enemy movements. You didn't make any mistakes.'

'I didn't set off a war accidentally.'

'That's the best test of intelligence.' Hess pushed his hair back, but it rose again, like a stiff beard. 'Just tell me what you need.'

'I'll need to be released from my usual duties.'

'Of course.'

Arkady kept his voice level, but the truth was that every word brought blood rushing through his veins in a sensation that was shameful and intoxicating. 'I can work with Slava Bukovsky, but I'll need an assistant of my own choice. I'll have to question crew members, including officers.'

'All reasonable, if done quietly.'

'And question Americans, if necessary.'

'Why not? There's no reason for them not to cooperate. After all, this is just a fact-finding preliminary to the official investigation in Vladivostok.'

'I don't seem to get along with them.'

'I believe the head representative's cabin is directly below mine. You could talk to her now.'

'Anything I say seems to annoy her.'

'We're all out here together peacefully fishing. Talk about the sea.'

'The Bering Sea?'

'Why not?'

Hess sat with his hands on his belly like a little German Buddha. He looked too comfortable. Was he KGB? Sometimes it took a sharp stick to find out.

Arkady said, 'The first time I heard of the Bering Sea I was eight years old. We had the encyclopedia. One day we received in the mail a new page. All the subscribers to the encyclopedia were mailed the same insert, along with instructions how to cut out Beria so that we could tape in vital new information about the Bering Sea. Of course Beria had been shot by then and was no longer a Hero of the Soviet Union. It was one of the rare times I ever saw my father truly happy, because it gave him so much pleasure to cut off the head of the secret police.'

If Hess were with the KGB the inquiry would be over now. Even so, his smile wore the strain of a man whose new dog has proven to be a biter. 'You killed the Moscow Prosecutor, your boss. Volovoi was right about that.'

'In self-defence.'

'A number of others died too.'

'Not by my hand.'

'A German and an American.'

'Them, yes.'

'A messy business. You also helped a woman defect.'

'Not really.' Arkady shrugged. 'I had the chance to wave goodbye.'

'But you didn't go yourself. When all was said and

done, you were still a Russian. That's what we count on. You know seals?'

'Seals?'

'In the winter. How they hide under the ice sheet near a hole, just coming up to breathe? Is that a little bit like you right now?'

When Arkady didn't answer, Hess said, 'You shouldn't confuse the KGB and us. I confess that sometimes we seem hard. When I was a cadet, far back in the days of Khrushchev, we set off a hydrogen device in the Arctic Sea. It was a hundred-megaton bomb, the largest ever detonated then or since. Actually, it was a fifty-megaton warhead wrapped in a uranium case to double the yield. A very dirty bomb. We didn't warn the Swedes or the Finns and we certainly didn't tell our own people who were drinking milk under this rain of fall-out a thousand times worse than Chernobyl. We didn't tell our fishermen who sailed in the Arctic Sea. I signed on as a third mate, and my mission was to take a Geiger counter without telling anyone else on board. We caught one shark that measured four hundred roentgens. What could I say to the captain – to throw his quota overboard? His crew would ask questions, and then the cry would spread. But we let the Americans know, and the result was that Kennedy was frightened enough to come to the table and sign a test-ban treaty.'

Hess let his smile fade and held Arkady's eyes, the way an executioner might briefly show his professional face to a son. Then he brightened. 'Anyway, for most of the crew, sailing on the *Polar Star* is no different from working in a factory anywhere, with the positive aspect of visiting a foreign port and the negative one of seasickness. For some, however, there is the attraction of freedom. It's the aura of the wide sea. We are far from port. The Border Guard is on the other side of the earth and we are in the world of the Pacific Fleet.'

'Does this mean I have your support or not?'

'Oh, definitely,' said Hess. 'Support and growing interest.'

As he left the cabin, Arkady saw the informers Skiba and Slezko slip around the end of the passageway. Walk, don't run, don't trip, Arkady thought. Don't bust your lips before you tell The Invalid what seaman visited the fleet electrical engineer's accommodations. Carry the news as if it were a mug of tea from Hess himself. Don't spill a drop.

Susan was at her cabin table, resting her head on one hand and letting cigarette smoke curl in the mop of her hair. It was actually a very Russian pose, poetic, tragic. Slava was with her and they were dining on soup and bread which Arkady suspected the third mate had brought straight from the galley.

'I'm not interrupting?' Arkady asked. 'I wouldn't have stopped, but your door was open.'

'It's my rule to keep my door open when Soviet men come to call,' Susan said. 'Even when they come bearing strange breakfasts.'

Out of her jacket and boots she was practically a girl.

Brown eyes and blond hair made an interesting contrast but were hardly unique. She had neither the complete ovalness nor the Slavic cheekbones of Russian women. The cigarette marked a fuller mouth, and etched around her eyes were those first lines that made a woman more real. But she was too thin, as if Soviet food wouldn't take. Admittedly, the soup was a pasty liquid dappled with grease. She idly dredged bones which she dropped back in the stew.

'It's sweet butter,' Slava pointed out to her. 'I told Olimpiada, "No garlic cloves." Anyway, you must visit Lake Baikal. Sixteen per cent of the world's fresh water is contained in that lake.'

'How much is contained in this bowl?' Susan asked.

Arkady began, 'I was just wondering—'

Slava took a deep breath. If Arkady was going to ruin the intimacy of a civilized repast, the third mate would make him pay. 'Renko, if you have questions you should have asked them yesterday. I think I hear them calling you on the slime line.'

'I've noticed,' Susan said. 'You're always "just wondering". Wondering what?'

'How do you like fishing?' Arkady asked.

'How do I like fishing? Christ, I must love it or I wouldn't be here, right?'

'Then do it like this.' Arkady took the spoon from her hand. 'Fish. If you want the bones, then do as you're doing and trawl the bottom. But everything is at a different level. Cabbage and potatoes are a little higher off the bottom.'

'Baikal has indigenous seals ... blind fish ...' Slava tried to hold the thread of his monologue. 'Many species of ...'

'To catch an onion is more difficult,' Arkady explained. 'You must use a mid-water pelagic trawl to hunt them down. Ah!' He scooped one up in triumph. A burnt pearl.

'What about meat?' Susan asked. 'This is a meat stew.'

'Theoretically.' Arkady gave her back her spoon.

Susan ate the onion.

Slava lost patience. 'Renko, your shift is on duty.'

'This may seem a silly question,' Arkady said to Susan, 'but I was wondering what you wore to the dance.'

She laughed in spite of herself. 'Not my prom dress, that's for sure.'

'Prom?'

'Crinoline and corsage. Never mind, let's say I wore my basic shirt and jeans.'

'A white shirt and blue jeans?'

'Yes. Why do you ask?'

'Did you leave the dance for fresh air? Perhaps went out on deck?'

Susan was silent. She sat back against the bulkhead and studied him with a flare of confirmed distrust. 'You're still asking about Zina.'

Slava was outraged, too. 'That's over; you said so last night.'

'Well,' Arkady said, 'I changed my mind this morning.'

Susan said, 'Why are you so fixated on Americans? On this factory ship with hundreds of Soviets, you keep coming back to us. You're like my radio; you work in reverse.' She pointed her cigarette to a speaker built into a corner of the cabin. 'In the beginning I wondered why it didn't work. Then I climbed up and found a microphone. See, it did work, just not the way I expected.' She tilted her head and blew smoke that drifted toward Arkady like an arrow. 'When I get off at Dutch Harbor, no more imitation radio or imitation detectives. Never again. Any more questions?'

'I didn't know anything about this,' Slava promised Susan.

'Are you taking your books with you?' Arkady asked.

On the upper bunk were the typewriter and cartons of books that Arkady had admired before. What Soviet poetry and toilet paper had in common was scarcity, due to the inadequacies, despite the largest forests in the world, of the Soviet paper industry.

Susan asked, 'You want one? Besides being a slime-line worker and an investigator, you're also a book lover?'

'Some books.'

'Who do you like?' she asked.

'Susan is a writer.' Slava said. 'I like Hemingway myself.'

'Russian writers,' Susan told Arkady. 'You're Russian and you have a Russian soul. Name one.'

'You have so many.' More good books than the library on board, he thought.

'Akhmatova?'

'Naturally.' Arkady shrugged.

Susan recited,

' "What do you want," I asked.
"To be with you in Hell," he said.'

Arkady picked up the next verse,

'He lifted his thin hand
and lightly stroked the flowers:
"Tell me how men kiss you,
Tell me how you kiss." '

Slava looked back and forth from Susan to Arkady.

'Everybody knows that one by heart,' Arkady said.
'People do when books can't be bought.'

Susan dropped her cigarette into her soup, rose, grabbed the first book she could reach on the upper bunk and threw it to Arkady. 'That's a goodbye gift,' she said. 'No more questions, no more "wondering". I was lucky you only surfaced at the end of the trip.'

'Well,' Arkady suggested, 'actually you may have been luckier than that.'

'Tell me.'

'You were dressed like Zina. If someone did throw her overboard, it's good they didn't throw you by mistake.'

Chapter Eleven

The cabin of the late Zina Patiashvili had the privacy of a dream; merely by turning on the lamp Arkady felt like a trespasser.

Dynka, for example, came from a race of Uzbeks and there was her own toy camel, a Bactrian from a miniature Samarkand standing on the pillow of her upper bunk. There were Madame Malzeva's embroidered cushions, each a sachet redolent of talcs and pomades. Her scrapbook of foreign postcards displayed minarets and crumbling temples. An embossed portrait of Lenin guarded Natasha Chaikovskaya's berth, but there was also a snapshot of a mother smiling timidly at giant sunflowers, as well as a glossy photo of Julio Iglesias.

The bulkheads of the cabin were dyed a romantic maroon by a glass wind chime that hung before the porthole. The room was a little dizzying, a nautilus shell of colours, of inner folds and cushions, of warring perfumes as powerful as incense, of life crammed into a steel compartment. There were more pictures in evidence than before, as if the removal of Zina had released the last constraint on the three cabinmates remaining. The wardrobe door was decorated with more Uzbeks and Siberian construction workers shimmering in the watery reflection of the chimes.

He was looking under Zina's stripped mattress when Natasha arrived. She was in a damp blue running suit, the universal outfit of Soviet sports. Sweat lay like the dew on her cheeks, but her lipstick was fresh.

'You remind me of a crow,' she told Arkady. 'A scavenger.'

'You're observant.' He didn't tell her what she reminded him of, which was her nickname 'Chaika' for the big limousine. An out-of-breath Chaika in a blue tarp.

'I was doing callisthenics on deck. They said you wanted to see me here.'

Because Arkady was wearing rubber gloves from the infirmary his sense of touch took all his concentration. When he pulled open a slit in the mattress, a tape cassette slid out. 'Van Halen', said the case. Rooting around inside the mattress he came out with three more tapes and a small English–Russian dictionary. Flipping through it, he noticed some words underlined in pencil. The lines had the heavy assertiveness of a schoolgirl's, as did the words, which all had to do with sex.

'A major breakthrough?' Natasha asked.

'Not quite.'

'Aren't there supposed to be two witnesses in a police search?'

'This is not a search by any official body; this is just me. Your cabinmate may have had an accident, maybe not. The captain has ordered me to find out.'

'Hah!'

143

'That's what I'm thinking too. I was once an investigator.'

'In Moscow. I heard all about it. You became involved in anti-Soviet intrigue.'

'Well, that's one story. The point is, for the last year I've been in the hold of this ship. It's been an honour, of course, to take part in the process of preparing fish for the great Soviet market.'

'We feed the Soviet Union.'

'And a wonderful slogan it is. However, not expecting this particular crisis, I have not maintained my skills as an investigator.'

Natasha frowned as if examining an object she didn't know quite how to handle. 'If the captain has ordered you to carry out a task, you should do so happily.'

'Yes. But there is another limitation. Natasha, we work together on the factory line. You've expressed the opinion that some men on the line are soft-bellied intellectuals.'

'They couldn't find their pricks if they weren't tied on.'

'Thank you. You come from different lineage yourself?'

'Two generations of hydroelectric construction workers. My mother was at the upper Bratsk Dam. I was brigade leader at Bochugany Hydroelectric Station.'

'And a decorated worker.'

'The Order of Labour, yes.' Natasha accepted compliments stiffly.

'And a Party member.'

'I hold that lofty honour.'

'And a person of underestimated intelligence and initiative.'

Arkady remembered that when Kolya lost a finger in the saw and blood was spraying from his hand over his face, the fish and everyone around him, it was Natasha who immediately tied her scarf tightly around his wrist, then made Kolya lie down with his feet up and guarded him fiercely until a stretcher was brought. When he was taken to the infirmary, she searched on her hands and knees for the missing finger so it could be sewn back on.

'The estimation of the Party is sufficient. Why did you ask me down here?'

'Why did you leave construction work for the cleaning of fish? You got double pay at the dams, plus an Arctic bonus for some of them. You worked outside in the healthy air instead of in the hold of a ship.'

Natasha crossed her arms. Her cheeks coloured.

A husband. Naturally. There were more men than women at a construction site, but not like a ship, where more than two hundred healthy men were trapped for months with perhaps fifty women, half of them grand-mothers, leaving a ratio of ten-to-one. Natasha was always touring the deck in her running suit or fox-trimmed coat or, on a day with the merest hint of balminess, in a flower-print sundress that made her resemble a large, threatening camellia. Arkady was embarrassed for being so obtuse.

'Travel,' she said.

'The same as me.'

'But you don't go into the foreign ports; you stay on the ship.'

'I'm a purist.'

'You have a second-class visa, that's why.'

'That too. What's worse, I have a second-class curiosity. I have been so content on the factory line that I have not participated in the full social and cultural life of the ship.'

'The dances.'

'Exactly. It's almost as if I haven't been here at all. I know nothing about the women or the Americans – or, to be more particular, about Zina Patiashvili.'

'She was an honest Soviet worker who will be badly missed.'

Arkady opened the wardrobe. The clothes were on hangers and in order of owner: Dynka's girl-sized apparel, Madame Malzeva's frowsy dresses, Natasha's giant red evening gown, sundresses, pastel running suits. He was disappointed in Dynka's clothes because he'd expected some colourful Uzbek embroidery or golden pants, but all he saw was a Chinese jacket.

'You took away Zina's clothes already,' Natasha said.

'Yes, they were laid out for us very nicely.'

Three wardrobe drawers held lingerie, stockings, scarves, pills, even a swimsuit in Natasha's drawer. The fourth was empty. He checked the backs and bottoms for anything taped to the drawers.

'What are you looking for?' Natasha demanded.

'I don't know.'

'Some kind of investigator you are.'

146

Arkady took a hand mirror from his pocket and looked under the sink and bench for anything taped to the underside.

'Aren't you going to dust for fingerprints?' Natasha asked.

'We'll get to that later.' He checked under the berths, leaving the mirror propped against the books on Zina's mattress. 'What I need is someone who knows the crew. Not another officer and not someone like me.'

'I'm a Party member but I'm not a slug. Go talk to Skiba or Slezko.'

'I need an assistant, not an informant.' Arkady opened the wardrobe again. 'There are only so many places to hide anything in a cabin like this.'

'Hide what?'

He felt Natasha tensing beside him. He thought he'd sensed her doing it before. She seemed to tilt as he opened her drawer a second time. It was the swimsuit, of course, a green-and-blue bikini that wouldn't get past her knee. It was the suit Zina had worn with the sunglasses on deck that warm day.

The moral code on a ship was like the code of prison. The worst crime – more heinous than murder – was theft. On the other hand, it was only natural to divide up the possessions of someone dead. Either way, though, having the swimsuit and concealing it could cost Natasha her sacred Party card.

'I bet your cabin's the same as mine,' Arkady said. 'Everybody's always lending and borrowing from

147

everyone else? Sometimes it's difficult to know whose is whose? I'm glad we found this.'

'It was for my niece.'

'I understand.'

Arkady laid the bikini on the bed. In the mirror he watched Natasha's eyes remain on the wardrobe. He did feel shameless about the mirror, but he didn't have the time or means for an ethical, scientific investigation. Returning to Natasha's side, he again perused the clothes rack. As a kind of generalization it could be said that adult Russian women went through a metamorphosis that provided them with a Rubensesque bulk against northern winters. Zina had been Georgian, a Southerner. The only one of her three cabinmates who could have worn any of her clothes was little Dynka, and the only piece of apparel with the sort of dash that seemed like Zina was Dynka's red quilted Chinese jacket. In most foreign ports there were shabby stores that specialized in the cheap goods that Soviet mariners and fishermen could afford. Often the shops were in poor neighbourhoods far from the dock, and groups of Soviets could be seen walking miles to save the cab fare. A prime souvenir was such a red jacket with golden Oriental dragons and snap pockets. The trouble was that this was Dynka's first voyage and they hadn't made any port calls yet. With a little thought he wouldn't have had to use the mirror at all. He really felt ashamed.

As Arkady removed the jacket from its hanger, Natasha's eyes grew like those of a girl watching her first magician. 'And this,' he said. 'Zina lent this to Dynka before the dance?'

'Yes.' More firmly she added, 'Dynka would never steal anything. Zina was always borrowing money and never paying it back, but Dynka would never steal.'

'That's what I said.'

'Zina never wore it. She was always fussing with it, but she never wore it on board. She said she was saving it for Vladivostok.' The words poured out of her with relief. There were no more glances at the wardrobe.

'Fussing?'

'Sewing it. Mending it.'

The jacket seemed new to Arkady. He kneaded the quilting and the padded edge of the front. The label said, "Hong Kong. Rayon".

'A knife?'

'One second.' Natasha found one in an apron hanging by the door.

'You should carry your knife at all times,' Arkady reminded her. 'Be ready for emergencies.'

He felt the quilting at the back and sleeves, then squeezed the edge at the neck and bottom hem. When he slit the hem at the centre, a stone the size of a candy lozenge dropped into the palm of his hand. As he pinched the hem, more stones dropped until the hollow of his palm was filled with the red, light purple and dark blue of polished but uncut amethysts, rubies and sapphires. Although they were pretty, they didn't look like high-quality gems.

He poured the stones into a pocket of the Chinese

jacket and snapped it shut, then pulled the rubber gloves off his hands.

'They could have come from Korea, the Philippines or India. No place we've been, so Zina got them from another ship. Let's just be happy that Dynka didn't try to wear this jacket past the Border Guard.'

'Poor Dynka,' Natasha muttered as she considered the prospect of her friend being caught for smuggling. 'How would Zina get the stones through?'

'She'd swallow them, sew the jacket and wear it down the gangplank just like she said. Then she'd collect the stones later.'

Natasha was disgusted. 'I knew Zina was brazen. I knew she was a Georgian. But this . . .'

Arkady struck while the Chaika was still awed by his elementary reasoning and good luck. 'See, I didn't know she was "brazen". I don't know anything about the crew. That's why I need you, Natasha.'

'You and me?'

'We've worked the same factory line for six months. You're methodical and you have nerve. I trust you, just as you can trust me.'

She glanced at the jacket and the swimsuit. 'Or else?'

'No. I'll report I found them under her mattress. The third mate and I should have found them before.'

Natasha pushed a damp curl away from her eyes. 'I'm not the sort who squeals.'

She had nice eyes, about as black as Stalin's but nice. Striking, in fact, with the blue running suit.

'You wouldn't be informing; you'd be asking questions. You'd be telling me what other people say.'

'I'm not sure.'

'The captain wants to know what happened to Zina before we reach Dutch Harbor. The first mate says we shouldn't have a port call at all.'

'That bastard! All Volovoi does is run the movie projector. We've cleaned fish for four months.'

'You only have one more shift in the factory. Skip it. You'll be working with me.'

Natasha studied Arkady as if really seeing him for the first time. 'No anti-Soviet agitation?'

'Everything according to Leninist norms,' he assured her.

She was good for one final hesitation. 'You really want me?'

Chapter Twelve

Arkady enjoyed the view from the crane operator's cabin, the top decks covered with nets and planks, the yellow gantries framing the fog, the gulls seesawing in the wind. Looking forward, around the gantries of the forward house was a spider's nest of wire antennas strung to catch low radio frequencies. An array of whip dipoles cast in the breeze for shorter frequencies. Two interlocked circles were a radio directional finder, and star-shaped antennas picked up passing satellites. Despite all appearances, the *Polar Star* was not alone.

'Bukovsky is happy about my selection?' Natasha asked.

'He will be.' Arkady was pleased because the book from Susan was by Mandelstam, a wonderful poet, very urban, dark and probably not Natasha's cup of socialist tea. Even if it was only a collection of letters, Arkady had already stashed it as tenderly as gold leaf under his mattress.

'Here he comes,' Natasha said.

Indeed, the third mate was fairly flying across the forward deck and around a group of mechanics who were lazily batting a volleyball back and forth over the net.

She added, 'He doesn't look happy.'

Slava disappeared below and Arkady thought he could hear the reverberations of his Reeboks as they ran up three flights. In Olympic time the third mate emerged on the top deck and pushed into the crane cabin. 'What is this about another assistant?' Slava gasped. 'And why are you calling me to meet you? Who's in charge?'

'You are,' Arkady said. 'I thought we might have some fresh air and privacy here. A rare combination.'

The crane cabin was the ultimate in privacy because the windows, broken and repaired with washers and pins like crockery, sloped in and forced intimacy whenever more than one person was inside. Still, the view could not be beaten.

Natasha said, 'Comrade Renko thinks I can be helpful.'

'I've cleared Comrade Chaikovskaya with the fleet electrical engineer and the captain,' Arkady said. 'But since you are in charge, I thought that you should know. Also, I have to make a list of Zina's effects.'

'We did that,' Slava said. 'We saw her old clothes, we examined the body. Why aren't you looking for a suicide note?'

'Victims rarely leave them. It will be very suspicious if that's the first thing we find.'

Natasha laughed, then cleared her throat. Since she took up half the cabin it was hard for her to be subtle.

'And what are you going to be doing?' Slava glared at her.

'Gathering information.'

Slava laughed bitterly. 'Great. Stirring up more trouble. I can't believe this. My first voyage as an officer and they make me trade union representative. What do I know about workers? What do I know about murder?'

'Everyone has to learn sometime,' Arkady said.

'I think Marchuk hates me.'

'He's entrusted a vital mission to you.'

The third mate slumped against the cabin side, his face sunk in misery, his curly hair limp with self-pity. 'And you two, a pair of deuces from the slime line. Renko, what is this pathological need of yours to lift every rock? I know Volovoi will write the final report on this; it's always a Volovoi who writes the final – Look out!'

The wall below the crane cabin resounded as the volleyball bounced off. The ball fell back down onto the deck and rolled by the mechanics, who glared up at the threesome in the cabin.

'See?' Slava said. 'The crew has already heard all about their port call depending on this so-called investigation of ours. We'll be lucky if we don't end up with knives in our backs.'

Gantries had another name, Arkady recalled: gallows. A succession of bright yellow gallows sailing through the mist.

'But you know what really gets me?' Slava asked. 'The worse our situation becomes, the happier you are. What difference does it make whether there are two of us or three of us? Do you really think we're going to find out anything about Zina?'

'No,' Arkady conceded. He couldn't help noticing that

Natasha was starting to be affected by Slava's pessimism, so he added, 'But we should take heart from Lenin.'

'Lenin?' She perked up. 'What did Lenin say about murder?'

'Nothing. But about hesitation he said, "First action, then see what happens." '

Wearing rubber gloves, Arkady laid out on the operating table jeans and blouses with foreign labels. Paybook. Dictionary. Snapshot of a boy amid grapes. Postcard of a Greek actress with racoon eyes. The intimate hardware of rollers and brushes still coiled with bleached hair. Sanyo cassette player with headphones and six assorted Western tapes. Bikini for a single sunny day. Spiral notebook. Jewellery box containing fake pearls, playing cards and pink ten-ruble notes. An embroidered Chinese jacket with a pocketful of gems.

The paybook: Patiashvili, Z.P. Born Tbilisi, Georgian Soviet Socialist Republic. Vocational-school training in food industries. Three years working galleys of the Black Sea Fleet out of Odessa. One month in Irkutsk. Two months working in a dining car on the Baikal–Amur main line. Eighteen months at the Golden Horn Restaurant in Vladivostok. The *Polar Star* was her first Pacific voyage.

Arkady lit a Belomor and drew in the raw fumes. This was his first time alone with Zina – not the cold corpse but the inanimate odds and ends that held whatever soul was left. Somehow smoking made it more social.

Odessa had always been too rich and worldly. They didn't settle for smuggling semi-precious stones there; they brought in bars of Indian gold for the locals and bags of Afghan hash for trucking north to Moscow. Odessa should have been a natural habitat for a girl like Zina.

Irkutsk? Rabid Young Communists volunteered to lay railroad ties and fry sausages in Siberia, not a girl like Zina. So something had happened in Odessa.

He broke the wad of pink ten-ruble notes: a thousand rubles, a lot to take to sea.

Vladivostok. Waiting tables at the Golden Horn was a clever move. Fishermen drank by the bottle to make up for their relatively dry months at sea, and they regarded their hard-won Arctic bonuses as onerous burdens to be shared with the first warm women they met. She should have done well.

Slut. Smuggler. Depending on politics or prejudice, it was easy to write off Zina as either a corrupted materialist or a typical Georgian. Except that usually it was Georgian men, not Georgian women, who were adept privateers. Somehow from the start Zina was different.

He fanned the playing cards. They were a collection, not a deck. A variety of cut-down Soviet cards, corners cracked, with bright-cheeked peasant girls on one side, the design of a star and sheaves of wheat on the other. Swedish cards with nudes. A British Queen Elizabeth on her Silver Jubilee. All of them the queen of hearts.

Arkady hadn't heard the Rolling Stones for a long time. He slipped the cassette into the tape deck and pushed "Play". From the speaker came a commotion like the sound of Jagger being dropped from a height onto a set of drums and then being pummelled by guitars; some things never changed. Fast forward. Stones in the middle of the tape. Fast forward. Stones at the end. He turned the tape over and listened to the other side.

Arkady tore a strip of electrocardiograph paper from a roll and sketched an outline of the ship, marking the cafeteria where the dance was held, Zina's cabin and every possible route between the two. He added the position of each crew member on watch and the transport cage on the trawl deck.

Out with the Stones, in with The Police. 'Her precious tapes,' Natasha had said. 'She always used her headphones. She never shared them.'

Fast forward. With a following sea the ship seemed to be gathering speed, as if plunging downhill and blind through the snow. He couldn't see it, but he could feel it.

Why did Zina ship on the *Polar Star*? The money? She could have made as much off sailors in the Golden Horn. Foreign goods? Fishermen could bring her whatever she wanted. Travel? To the Aleutians?

Out with The Police, in with Dire Straits.

He sketched the stern deck and the well to the ramp. There was room to kill her, but no place to hide her.

What had been in her pockets? Gauloises, a playing card, a condom. The three great pleasures in life? The card was a queen of hearts of a style unfamiliar to him. Fast forward. Below the *Polar Star* he drew the *Eagle*.

'Politically mature' was the label the Party applied to

any young person who was not a convict, dissident or outspoken defender of Western music, which by itself was a whole arena of subversion. There were over-age 'hippies' who still listened to the Beatles and migrated to the Altai Mountains to meditate and drop acid. Kids tended to be 'Breakers', who danced to rap, or 'Metallisty', who saturated themselves in heavy-metal music and leather gear. In spite of her taste in music, in spite of her absences from the galley, in spite of her casual sleeping around, Zina was still, according to as conservative an arbiter as Volovoi, an 'honest toiler and politically mature'.

Which only made sense given the first mate's task of watching foreign provocateurs.

Slut, smuggler, informer. A neat and simple total. A sliding of beads on an abacus; answer as addition. A girl from Georgia. Education limited to ladling soup. Expanded to smuggling in Odessa. Sleeping around in Vladivostok. Informing at sea. An abysmal life begun and ended in ignorance, without morals, soul or a single reflective thought. At least it seemed that way.

Arkady noticed that on the Van Halen cassette, the recording-proof tab had been punched. He put the tape into the player and heard a woman with a Georgian accent say, 'Sing to me, just sing.' It was Zina's voice; Arkady recognized it from the cafeteria. There was a microphone built into the corner of her player.

A man accompanied by a guitar answered,

'You can cut my throat,
You can cut my wrists,
But don't cut my guitar strings.
Let them tramp me in the mud,
Let them push me under water,
Only leave my silver strings alone.'

As Arkady listened he found spoons in a desk drawer and looked for iodine crystals. Not finding crystals, he searched for iodine pills. There was a padlocked metal cabinet for radiation medicine – in other words, for war. He broke the lock by twisting a screwdriver through the shank, but there was nothing inside except two bottles of Scotch, a booklet on the effective distribution of iodine and Vitamin E in case of nuclear explosions. He found the iodine itself in an open cabinet.

'Sing another,' Zina said. 'A thieves' song.'

The man on the tape laughed and whispered, 'That's the only kind I know.'

Arkady couldn't put a name to the man's voice but he did know the song. It wasn't Western at all, not rock or rap; it was by a Moscow actor named Vysotsky who had become famous underground throughout the Soviet Union by writing, in the most traditional Russian style, the plaintive and bitter songs of criminals and convicts, and by singing them accompanied by a seven-stringed Russian guitar, the most easily strummed instrument on earth. Magnatizdat, a tape version of samizdat, spread every song, and then Vysotsky had sealed his fame by drinking himself, while still young, into a fatal heart attack. The Soviet radio offered such mindless pap – 'I love life, I love it over and over again' – that you'd think people would caulk their ears; yet the truth was that no other country was so dependent on or vulnerable to music. After seventy years of socialism, thieves' songs had become the counter-anthem of the Soviet Union.

The singer on the tape wasn't Vysotsky, but he wasn't bad:

> 'The wolf hunt is on, the hunt is on!
> For grey prowlers, old ones and cubs;
> The beaters shout, the dogs run themselves until they
>   drop,
> There's blood on the snow and the red limits of flags.
> But our jaws are strong and our legs are swift,
> So why, pack leader, answer us,
> Do we always run towards the shooters,
> And never try to run beyond the flags?'

At the end of the tape all Zina said was, 'I know that's the only kind you know. That's the kind I like.' Arkady liked the fact that it was the kind she liked. But the next tape was completely different. Zina was suddenly speaking in a low, weary voice. 'Modigliani painted Akhmatova sixteen times. That's the way to know a man, to have him paint you. By the tenth time you must start to know how he really sees you.

'But I attract the wrong men. Not painters. They hold me like I'm a tube of paint they have to empty in one squeeze. But they're not painters.'

Zina's voice could sound honeyed or as tired as death, sometimes all in one sentence as if she were casually playing an instrument. 'There is a man on the factory line who looks interesting. Paler than a fish. Deep eyes, as if he were sleepwalking. He hasn't noticed me at all. It would be interesting to wake him up.

'But I don't need another man. One thinks he tells me what to do. A second thinks he tells me what to do. A third thinks he tells me what to do. A fourth thinks he tells me what to do. Only I know what I'm going to do.' There was a pause; then, 'They only see me, they can't hear me think. They have never heard me think.'

What would they do if they could hear you? Arkady wondered.

'He'd kill me if he could hear me think,' Zina said. 'He says wolves mate for life. I think he'd kill me and then he'd kill himself.'

On the fifth tape the tab had been removed and then taped over. The cassette began with a sibilant rustling of cloth and an occasional muffled thud. Then a man said, 'Zina.' It was a younger voice, not the singer.

'What kind of place is this?'

'Zinushka.'

'What if they catch us?'

'The chief's asleep. I say who comes and goes here. Stay still.'

'Take your time. You're like a boy. How did you get all this down here?'

'That's not for you to know.'

'That's a television?'

'Pull them down.'

'Gently.'

'Please.'

'I'm not going to get completely undressed.'

'It's warm. Twenty-one degrees Celsius, forty per cent humidity. It's the most comfortable place on the ship.'

'How do you have a place like this? My bed is so cold.'

'I'd climb into it any time, Zinushka, but this is more private.'

'Why is there a cot here? You sleep here?'

'We put in long hours.'

'Looking at television. That's work?'

'Mental work. Forget about that. Come on, Zinushka, help me.'

'You're sure you shouldn't be doing important mental work right now?'

'Not while we're taking a net.'

'A net! When I met you at the Golden Horn you were a handsome lieutenant. Now look at you, at the bottom of a fish hold. How do you know we're taking a net?'

'You talk too much and kiss too little.'

'How do you like that?'

'That's better.'

'And that?'

'That's much better.'

'And this?'

'Zinushka.'

The microphone was voice-activated and apparently she'd had no chance to turn it off. The recorder was probably in the pocket of her fisherman's jacket and either under her or hanging beside the cot. Arkady had two cigarettes left. On his match a flame bobbed toward his fingers.

He was five years old. It was summer south of Moscow, and in the warm nights everyone slept on the porch with doors and windows open. There was no electricity in the cottage. Luna moths flew in and danced above the lamps, and he always expected the insects to flare up like burning paper. Some of his father's friends, other officers, had come by for a buffet. The social pattern set by Stalin was of dinners starting at midnight and ending in a drunken stupor, and Arkady's father, one of the Leader of Humanity's favourite generals, followed this style, though while others got drunk he only got more angry. Then he would wind up the gramophone and always play the same record. The band was the Moldavian State Jazz Orchestra, an ensemble that had followed General Renko's troops on the Second Ukrainian Front, performing in their greatcoats in each town square the day after it had been liberated from the Germans. The tune was 'Chattanooga Choo-Choo'.

The other officers hadn't brought their wives, so the general had them dance with his. They were pleased; none of their wives were as slim and tall and beautiful. 'Katerina, get in the spirit!' the general would order. From the porch, the young Arkady felt the floor shake under the shuffling of heavy boots. He didn't hear his mother's feet at all; it was as if they were spinning her through the air.

When the guests had left was always the worst. Then his father and mother would go to their bed behind a screen at the far end of the porch. First the two sets of whispers, one soft and pleading, one through the teeth of a rage that made the heart shrink. The whole house swayed like a seesaw.

The next morning Arkady had a breakfast of raisin cakes and tea outside under the birches. His mother came out still in her nightshift, a gown of silk and lace his father had found in Berlin. She had a shawl over her shoulders against the morning cool. Her hair was black, loose, long.

Did he hear anything during the night? she asked. No, he promised, nothing.

As she turned back towards the house a branch reached out and plucked off the shawl. On her arms were the bruise marks of individual fingers. She lightly picked the shawl off the ground, replaced it on her shoulders and tied it tight by its end tassels. Anyway, she added, it was over. Her eyes were now so serene that he almost believed her.

He could hear it now. 'Chattanooga Choo-Choo'.

'Seriously, Zina, the chief would have my head and yours if he found out about this. You can't tell anyone.'

'About what? *This*?'

'Stop it, Zina, I'm trying to be serious.'

'About your little room here?'

'Yes.'

'Who would care? It's like a little boys' club in the bottom of the ship.'

'Be serious.'

Each tape was thirty minutes long. As the last narrow band of black unreeled there was no way for Zina to turn the recorder off. Her companion would hear the 'click' as the tape stopped.

'One moment it's all "Zinka, I love you"; the next it's "Zina, be serious." You're a confused man.'

'This is secret.'

'On the *Polar Star*? You want to spy on fish? On our Americans? They're dumber than the fish.'

'That's what you think!'

'Is that your hand?'

'Keep your eye on Susan.'

'Why?'

'That's all I'm saying. I'm not trying to impress you; I'm trying to help you. We should help each other. It's a long voyage. I'd go crazy without someone like you, Zinka.'

'Ah, we've stopped being serious.'

'Where are you going? We still have time.'

'You do, I don't. My shift is on and that bitch Lidia is looking for any reason to get me in trouble.'

'A little minute?'

There was a rasp of canvas over the microphone, the sigh of a cot as a body stood up.

'You go back to your mental work. I have some soup to stir.'

'Damn! At least wait until I look through the hole before you go.'

'Do you have any idea how silly you look right now?'

'Okay, the way is clear. Go.'

'Thank you.'

'Zinka, tell no one.'

'No one.'

'Zinka, tomorrow?'

A door shut reluctantly. Click.

The other side of the tape started as a blank. Fast forward. It was all blank.

Arkady studied the spiral notebook. On the first page was pasted a map of the Pacific. Zina had added eyes and lips so that Alaska leaned like a bearded man towards a shy and feminine Siberia. The Aleutians reached out to Russia like an arm.

The last cassette started as Duran Duran. Fast forward.

On the second page was a photo of the *Eagle* anchored in a bay surrounded by snowy mountains. On the third page, the *Eagle* wallowed in choppy water.

'Making a *baidarka*,' the tape said in English. 'It's like a kayak. You know what a kayak is? Well, this is longer, leaner, with a square stern. The old ones were made with skin and ivory, even with ivory joints so it just flowed through the waves. When Bering came with the first Russian boats, he couldn't believe how fast the *baidarkas* were. The best *baidarkas* have always come from Unalaska. You understand a word of this?'

'I know what a kayak is,' Zina answered in a slow and careful English.

'Well, I'll show you a *baidarka* and you'll see for yourself. I'll paddle it around the *Polar Star*.'

'I should have a camera when you do.'

'I wish we could do more than that. What I'd like to do is show you the world. Go all over – California, Mexico, Hawaii. There are so many great places. That would be a dream.'

'When I listen to him,' Zina said on the second side, 'I hear a first boyfriend. Men are like malicious children, but he is like a first boyfriend, the sweet one. Maybe he is a merman, a child of the sea. In a rough sea, on a big boat, I hold onto the rail. Down below, on his small deck, he stands with perfect balance, riding the waves. I listen to his innocent voice over and over again. It would be a dream, he says.'

The next dozen pages were photos of the same man with straight dark hair. Dark eyes with heavy lids. Broad cheekbones around a fine nose and mouth. The American. The Aleut with a Russian name. Mike. Mikhail. The pictures, all taken from above and at a distance, showed him on the deck of the *Eagle* working the crane, posing on the bow, mending a net, waving to the photographer.

Arkady smoked the last, intoxicating cigarette. He remembered Zina on the autopsy table in this same room. Her sodden flesh and bleached hair. The body was far removed from life as a shell on a beach. This voice, though – this was Zina, someone no one on the ship had known. It was as if she had walked in the door, sat across the desk in the shadow just outside the lamp's veil of light, lit her own phantom cigarette and, having finally found an understanding ear, confided all.

Naturally Arkady would have preferred to have the technical lab back in Moscow throwing an exciting array of solvents and reagents, or mortar-sized German microscopes and gas chromatographs into the fight. He used what he could. In front of the spiral notebook he laid out spoons, pills and the card of fingerprints Vainu had taken from the body. He crushed the pills between the spoons, wrapped his sleeve around the handle of the spoon that held the pulverized iodine, struck a match and held it to the spoon's bowl. He moved both close to the notebook so that the fumes from the heated iodine would flow up the page opposite the map. The hot-iodine method was supposed to employ iodine crystals over an alcohol burner in a glass box. He reminded himself that in the spirit of the 'New Way of Thinking' announced by the last Party Congress, all good Soviets were willing to bend theory to practical application.

Iodine fumes reacted quickly to the oils of perspiration in a latent print. First a ghostly outline appeared of a whole left hand, sepia brown, like an antique photograph. Palm, heel, thumb and four fingers spread out, as they would have been while she held the book flat to paste in a picture. Then the details: whorls, deltas, ridges, radial loops. He concentrated on the first finger and compared it with the card. A double loop, like yin and yang. An island at the loop's right delta. A cut at the left delta. Card and page were the same; this was Zina's book and the imprint of her hand as if she were reaching out to him. There were two other prints, male by the size of them; rough, hurried marks.

As the match burned down, the hand began to fade, and in a minute it had disappeared. He repacked all the effects neatly. He'd found Zina. Now to find the lieutenant who called her Zinushka.

Chapter Thirteen

Below decks everything was built around fish holds. Noah's Ark must have had a fish hold. When he called Peter a 'fisher of men', Christ must have appreciated the virtues of a tight fish hold. If cosmonauts ever sail on solar winds and collect specimens of galactic life, they will need a fish hold of sorts.

Yet, for ten months the *Polar Star* had sailed with a forward fish hold that was inoperative. Various explanations were offered for why the hold was out of commission: pipes kept cracking; there was an electrical short in the heat pump; the plastic insulation seeped some kind of poison. Whatever, the result was that off-loading ships had to make more frequent rendezvous to take the fish crammed into the *Polar Star*'s other two holds. Another result was that the area around the unused hold had been abandoned to stacks of barrel staves and steel plates. As the walkway became more crowded, the crew tended to take the longer but faster route on deck.

A line of bulbs lit the way between the bulkhead and the hold. Access to it was a watertight door with a ramp to carry carts of frozen fish over the coaming. The wheel on the door was chained with an impressively large padlock. On one side of the door was a heat pump, its hood open to display a convincing tangle of unattached wires. On the other was an oil can of tall capstan shafts. The bottom of the can stirred with rats. The ship hadn't been fumigated since Arkady had been on board. It was interesting that rats ate bread, cheese, paint, plastic pipes, wiring, mattresses and clothes – everything, in fact, but frozen fish.

There seemed to be two Zinas. There was Zina as the public slut; then there was this private woman who dwelt within a world of hidden photographs and secret tapes. One tape could only be called dangerous. The amorous lieutenant had boasted of the fish hold's bedroom temperature and forty per cent humidity. Arkady had heard someone bother to mention a humidity ratio only once before: in the computer room back in militia headquarters on Petrovka Street in Moscow.

All well and good. Arkady had no argument with naval intelligence. Every Soviet fisherman on the Pacific coast knew that American submarines constantly violated his country's waters. On dark nights periscopes would pop out of the Tatar Strait. The enemy even followed Soviet warships right into Vladivostok harbour. What he couldn't understand was how a listening station in a fish hold hoped to hear anything. An echosounder only told you what was directly below, and no submarine would venture under trawlers. As Arkady understood it, passive sonar like hydrophones could detect sound waves at a distance, but an old factory ship like the *Polar Star* had plating that was substandard, so thin that, pounding like a drum, it bowed in and out with each wave. It had been welded with the wrong beading, riveted with burned and undersized rivets, seamed with cement that wept, shored with timbers that creaked like bones. All of which made the ship more human, in a way, and even more trustworthy in the sense that a patched-up veteran, for all his complaints, was more to be trusted than a handsome recruit. Still, the *Polar Star* marched through the water like a brass band; its own noise would smother the whisper of any submarine.

Arkady had no interest in espionage. In the Army, sitting for hours in a radio shack on the roof of the Adler Hotel in Berlin, he used to hum – Presley, Prokofiev, anything. The others asked why he didn't want to take a turn on the binoculars, to study the American shack on the roof of the Sheraton in West Berlin. Perhaps he lacked imagination. He needed to see another human to get interested. The fact was that in spite of Zina's tape, from the outside the fish hold looked like a fish hold.

The lieutenant had told Zina about looking through a hole. There was no peephole that Arkady could see. The door had an ambient, clammy touch, nothing cosy about it. He pondered the shafts in the oil can, and after a moment's indecision selected one. It was like lifting a hundred pound crowbar; once he had it to his shoulders he wouldn't be able to casually brush off any rat that came with it. Sweat came just at the thought. But no rodent appeared, and when he inserted the shaft into the hasp of the padlock and gave it a twist the lock popped open like a spring: another black mark for State Quality Control. The wheel lock itself wouldn't give until he got a foot against the pump. Grudgingly, with short, metallic cries, it turned and he pushed the door open.

The interior of the hold rose through three decks of the *Polar Star*, a shaft of dark air lit by a dim bulb at Arkady's level. Ordinarily each level of a hold had its own deck, open in the middle to raise fish from below. This single, precipitous drop was odd, as if there was no intention of using the hold at all. A watertight hatch covered the main deck overhead, sealing in a stale smell of fish and brine. The sides were covered with spaced wooden planks over the grid of pipes that usually circulated coolant. A ladder ran from the hatch down to the bottom deck two levels below. He swung onto the rungs and closed the door behind him.

As Arkady descended his eyes adjusted. Once in a while he caught sight of rats climbing the pipes away from him. Rats never tried to enter an operating cold store, a sign of intelligence. It occurred to him that a flashlight would have been a sign of intelligence on his part. There were so many rats that the sound of their movement was like a wind in the trees.

There should have been decks, block and tackle, crates covered in hoarfrost. The packing of a cold store was a maritime art. Cases of frozen fish not only had to be stacked but separated by planks to allow torpid air colder than merely freezing to circulate. Here there was nothing. At each level he descended was a door, a light socket and a thermostat. Each level was darker, and when he stepped off the last rung onto the wider bottom deck of the hold he was almost blind, though he felt the pupils of his eyes expand to their rims. This is a pit, he thought, the centre of the earth.

He lit a match. The deck was more planking over a grid of pipes above a cement base. He saw orange peels, a piece of planking, empty paint cans and a blanket; someone had been using the hold to sniff fumes. There were comblike bones that explained what had happened to the ship's cat. What he did not see was a lieutenant of Naval Intelligence, a cot, a television or a computer terminal. Beneath the base was a double hull with tanks for fuel and water, enough space to smuggle contraband maybe, but hardly to hide an entire furnished room. He inserted the broken board between wall planks. No secret door swung open. When subtlety didn't succeed he swung the board against the planks. Through the booming echoes came high-pitched protests from the gallery of rats overhead, but no officers of Naval Intelligence emerged.

Climbing back up the ladder, Arkady felt like a man returning to the surface of the water, as if he were holding his breath and swimming up to the bulb. Zina's tape made no sense any more. Perhaps he'd misunderstood the conversation. Perhaps he could find some vodka in Vainu's office. A little vodka in a bright room would be nice. Back at the bulb, he pulled the door open and swung himself through to the deck. By now the barrel staves and heat pump had a homey, welcoming appearance. He slipped the broken padlock onto the wheel; Gury, the *biznessman*, would help him find another.

As Arkady started towards the factory the light over the cofferdam went out, then the one over the heat pump. A figure stepped out of the dark and hit him in the stomach. The pain was so sharp that at first he thought he must have been stabbed. While he bent and gagged, a ball of wet rags was stuffed in his mouth. Another rag was tied tightly over his mouth. A sack was pulled over his head and shoulders, all the way down to his feet. Something like a belt was pulled tight over the sack and around his arms and chest. He reacted the right way, breathing deeply and flexing his arms, and at once choked because the rags in his mouth had been soaked in gasoline. The cloths had pressed his tongue back into the soft palate, and he was close to swallowing his tongue. So he blew out, trying to clear his tongue, and as he did so, the belt was pulled tighter like a cinch.

He was carried – by three men, he thought. There would also be one man up ahead to clear the way or stall anyone coming, and possibly another man following to do the same. They were strong; they toted him as easily as a broomstick. He tried not to choke on the gasoline fumes. On long voyages, seamen got together to share fumes and get a little dizzy. A coil of acrid vapour teased its way down his throat.

They could have just thrown him down the fish hold; his body wouldn't have been found for days. So perhaps being hit, gagged and sacked was a good sign. He'd never been kidnapped before, not in all his years with the Prosecutor's Office, and he wasn't sure of the nuances of being beaten and seized, but it was clear they didn't want to kill him right away. Probably they were crew members irate about the possibility of losing their port call. Even if they kept him in the sack, he might recognize a voice if they whispered.

It was a short promenade. They stopped and a door wheel turned. Arkady was unaware of the men making any rights or lefts; had they returned to the fish hold? The only watertight entrances at this level were to the holds. The door opened with the clap of splitting ice. A furnace emits a fiery blast; a cold store, with a temperature of −40°C emits a more languid, frozen steam, but even within his sack Arkady could feel it, and he began kicking and twisting. Too late. They threw him in.

The impact of landing snapped the belt. Arkady rose, but before he could pull off the sack he heard the door shut, and the wheel lock turn. He found himself standing on a wooden case. When he untied his gag and unwound the rags from his mouth the first breath was a draught that burned the lungs. It was a joke, it had to be a joke. White, almost liquid steam seeped from the planking and rolled down the walls of the fish hold; within the planking he could see the cooling grid, the pipes cased in skeletal ice. Each of his feet stood in a separate pool of milky vapour. As he watched, the hairs of the back of his hands stood and turned white with frost. As it left his lips, his breath crystallized, glittered and snowed.

He stopped himself as he reached for the wheel of the door, because bare skin would adhere to the metal. He covered the wheel with the sack and then put his weight into it, but it wouldn't budge. The men outside must be holding it shut, and there was no chance he was going to overpower three or more of them. He shouted. Around the cold store were ten centimetres of fibreglass wool insulation; even the inside of the door was padded. No one was going to hear him unless they walked right by. For the last week, fish from the flash freezers had been stowed in the aft hold to balance the ship's trim. If this was the midships hold, there was no reason for anyone to hear. Overhead and out of reach was an insulated, watertight hatch. No one was going to hear him through that, either. Two cases below was the false deck and access to a lower level and another door. There was no way he could think of to lift two cases, each weighing a quarter of a ton. On one case was a rumpled tarp stiff with ice. The stamp on the cases said, 'Frozen Sole – Product of USSR'. Not a joke, but there was something comical about that.

Veterans of the north knew the stages of exposure. He was shivering; shivering was good. The body could actually maintain its temperature for a while by shaking to death. Still, he lost a degree every three minutes. When he lost two degrees he would stop shivering and his heart would start slowing and shutting off the flow to skin and limbs to maintain core heat; that was the cause of frostbite. When he lost eleven degrees his heart would stop. Coma came midway. He had fifteen minutes.

There was another problem. He had the classic first signs of poisoning he'd seen in sailors who had imbibed vapours: blinking, dizziness, intoxication. Sometimes they howled like hyenas; sometimes they danced off the walls. He couldn't help laughing. He'd gone to sea to die in this ice? That was funny.

His arms jerked spasmodically as if a maniac were bending his bones. He'd worked in this kind of cold before – granted in quilted coveralls, felt boots and fur-lined hood. Frost made its own white fur over his shoes and cuffs. He swayed, trying to keep his balance and not step into the narrow space between the cases; he was sure if he slipped he wouldn't get his leg out again.

At his chest level was a plate that covered the thermo-coupler, a coil of copper-constantan wire. He couldn't get the plate loose with his fingernails; it was another good example of the sort of emergency for which a fisherman should carry his knife at all times.

He jiggled the matches out of his pocket and dropped them. Since he was trying not to tip over, he picked up the book painfully with the sort of graceful bow a French dandy might execute as he swept a lady's handkerchief from the ground. Again he dropped the matches and this time went down on all fours to retrieve them. The flame was a tiny yellow ball overwhelmed by the cold, but a precious dew formed on the thermocoupler plate as it warmed. The problem was that his hands were jerking so badly he couldn't keep the flame to the plate for more than a second at a time.

There was a certain cunning to killing him this way. Freezing him and, he assumed in thinking it through, moving his body one place to thaw, then taking him to another site to be found. It was now well established that Vainu was not the most expert of pathologists, and the most obvious evidence he would find would be signs of sniffing fumes, the tragic vice of petroleum-age man. With official approval, they'd slap his body back in the same cold store until they reached Vladivostok. He saw himself riding a block of ice back home.

These were excellent matches, wood tipped with phosphorus and wax especially for the foul weather that seamen encountered. On the box cover was the design of a ship's prow splitting a curling wave. On the ship's stack was a hammer and sickle. His whole body was shaking so badly that it was hard to even aim the flame at the plate. For no reason he suddenly remembered an even better case of suicide than the ones he'd cited to Marchuk and Volovoi. A sailor had hung himself in Sakhalin. There was no investigation because the boy had secured the rope to the hammer and sickle on the smoke stack. He was put in paper slippers and buried in a day since no one even wanted to ask questions.

At least he'd stopped shivering and could hold the match steady. Looking down, he saw that both his pants legs were covered in fleecy frost. A big fish like a halibut could be frozen rock solid to the core in an hour and a half. The box squirted from his fingers. They were turning from white to blue and moved so slowly. When he knelt to pick the box up, his hands fumbled like a pair of hooks. As he struck another match, the box dropped, bounced off the crate and fell between it and the wall. He heard it ticking off crates on its way down to the deck.

With all his concentration he brought the cool, little

glow again to the thermocoupler, marvelling at how the dim heat spread visibly like breath upon the metal plate. It was his last match now. He held on while flames burned on his fingernails. There was still some gasoline left on his hands from taking the rags from his mouth. Secondary flames lit like candles on his palms. They didn't hurt. He stared because they were so remarkable, like a religious experience. Slowly his eyes moved to the rags. Was this how slowly fish thought? he wondered. As the match flame sank to a nub, he thrust it and his hands into the rags, which burst into a beautiful flowerlike fire. He kicked the burning rags closer to the planks beneath the plate.

The rags unfolded in hues of violet and blue that turned to rich black smoke. Around the fire, on the planks and on the crate, grew a ring of wet glaze, of ice melting, re-freezing and melting again. Arkady sat at the edge of the flames, arms out to cup the heat. He remembered a picnic he'd once had in Siberia of frozen fish whittled into shavings, frozen reindeer sliced into strips, frozen berries formed into patties and Siberian vodka that had to be constantly turned, first this side and then that, towards the fire. The year before, an Intourist guide had taken a group of Americans into the taiga and laid out an even more splendid lunch but had forgotten to turn the bottle. After many toasts with warm tea to international friendship, mutual respect and closer understanding, the guide poured glasses of nearly frozen, almost congealed vodka and showed his guests how to drink it in one go. 'Like this,' he said. He tipped the glass, drank it and fell over dead. What the guide had forgotten was that Siberian vodka was nearly two hundred proof, almost pure alcohol, and would still flow at a temperature that would freeze the gullet and stop the heart like a sword. Just the shock was enough to kill him. It was sad, of course, but it was also hilarious. Imagine the poor Americans sitting around their camp-fire, looking at their Russian guide and asking, 'This *is* a Siberian picnic?'

It was an unequal battle between a mere rag fire and the glacial cave of a fish hold. The flames subsided to eyes of light, to a nest of wrestling glow-worms, then to a last black gasp of smoke above a shell of ashes. The crate and planks were smudged, not even charred.

Gasoline was a bit like Siberian vodka. Moment by moment he felt more Siberian. Finally, sailing off the coast of America, he had achieved that blissful distinction. Frost advanced up his pants and sleeves again. He blinked to keep his eyes from icing shut and watched his breath explode into crystals that rose up, then eddied down in fine drifts. How else would a Siberian breathe? Wouldn't he have made a good guide? But who for?

Time to lie down. He tugged the tarp off the crate to use as a blanket. It slid off stiff with ice, revealing Zina Patiashvili in a clear plastic bag. Clear but covered within by wonderful patterns of crystalline frost like a coat of diamonds. She was white as snow and her hair was dusted with ice. One eye was open, as if she wondered who was joining her.

Arkady curled up in the corner farthest from Zina.

He didn't believe the wheel really was turning until the door cracked open. Natasha Chaikovskaya filled the doorway, eyes and mouth agape at the remains of the fire and at Zina and then at him. She rushed into the hold and lifted Arkady, gently at first so his skin on the ice wouldn't tear, then like a weightlifter starting a press. He'd never been lifted by a woman before. Probably Natasha wouldn't take that as a compliment.

'I made a fire,' he told her. Apparently it had actually worked. He had dropped the temperature at the thermocoupler and finely tuned monitors had sounded. 'You heard an alarm?'

'No, no. There aren't any alarms. I was just walking by when I heard you inside.'

'Shouting?' Arkady didn't remember.

'Laughing.' Natasha shifted, getting a better grip to angle him out the door. She was frightened, but also disgusted, as anyone is with a drunk. 'You were laughing your head off.'

Chapter Fourteen

While Izrail Izrailevich gently massaged Arkady's fingers and Natasha ministered to his bare toes their patient responded with hypothermic spasms. The factory manager looked with scorn and disappointment at Arkady's eyes, which were a brilliant pulpy red from gasoline fumes.

'Other men I expect to be drunkards or sniffers, not you,' Izrail said. 'It serves you right to wander into a fish hold and almost freeze to death.'

The trouble was, feeling returned as a sensation of skin burning, of capillaries bursting and waves of shakes. Fortunately none of his cabinmates were home when Izrail and Natasha laid him out on the lower bunk. Buried in blankets when touch itself was torture, he felt as if he were wrapped in broken glass.

Fish scales glittered on the factory manager's sweater and beard; he had run from the slime line to help carry Arkady to the cabin. 'Do we lock up all the gasoline, the paint and thinner as if they were expensive foreign liquors?'

'Men are weak,' Natasha reminded him.

Izrail gave his opinion. 'A Russian is like a sponge; you don't know his true shape until he's soaked. I thought Renko was different.'

Natasha blew her warm breath on each naked, individual toe and then tenderly kneaded it, which felt like having red-hot needles stuck under the nails. 'Maybe we should take him to Dr Vainu,' she suggested.

'No,' Arkady managed to say. His lips were rubbery, another effect of the fumes.

Izrail said, 'I let you off the line because you were going to perform some sort of investigation for the captain, not so you could go crazy.'

'Zina was in the hold,' Natasha told Izrail.

'Where else are we supposed to keep her? Did you say he started a fire?' Izrail was concerned. 'Did he thaw any fish?'

'He didn't even thaw himself.' Natasha attended to a toe that remained blue.

'If he damaged any fish—'

She said, 'Fuck your fish, excuse me.'

'All I'm saying is, if you want to kill yourself, don't do it in my fish hold,' Izrail told Arkady. Vigorously he rubbed Arkady's other hand.

A thought occurred to Natasha and spread on her brow like a furrow on virgin snow. 'Does this have to do with Zina?'

'No,' Arkady lied. Go away, he wanted to say, but he couldn't slip more than one word at a time through a chattering jaw.

'You were looking for something? Someone?' she asked.

'No.' How could he explain about a lieutenant who might or might not exist? He had to stop shaking and rest his traumatized nerve endings a little; then he could start asking questions again.

'Maybe I should get the captain,' Izrail said.

'No.' Arkady started to rise.

'Okay, okay, that seems to be the only word you remember,' Izrail said. 'But if this was an attack, I'm not surprised. I don't share their attitude, but I can tell you that the crew is unhappy about this rumour that you've put Dutch Harbor off limits. What do you think they come on this stinking barrel of shit for? Fish? You want to jeopardize all their months of work to find out what happened to Zina? This ship is full of silly women. Why do you care so much?'

As his shakes receded, Arkady burrowed into a comatose state. He saw that he had been changed from his frozen clothes into dry ones, a task that must have been performed by Izrail and Natasha, an act about as erotic as dressing a fish. He had a vision of himself on a conveyor belt moving towards the saw.

Obidin and Kolya came into the cabin, fumbled quietly for one thing or another and left without paying any attention to Arkady or the fact that he was in the wrong bunk. It was etiquette on a ship to let other men sleep.

When he surfaced again, Natasha was sitting on the opposite bunk. As soon as she saw he was awake, she said, 'Izrail Izrailevich wondered why you cared about Zina. Did you know her?'

He felt comically weak, as if his body had been beaten and badly sunburned while he dozed. At least he could talk now, in a rush of words between the shakes. 'You know I didn't.'

'I thought I knew you didn't, but then I wondered why you cared.' She looked at him, then away. 'I suppose it helps to care, in a professional manner.'

'Yes, it's a professional trick. Natasha, what are you doing here?'

'I thought they might come back.'

'Who?'

She crossed her arms as if to say she wouldn't play games. 'Your eyes are red slits.'

'Thank you.'

'Are all investigations like this?'

He burped in his sleep and the entire cabin reeked like a garageful of gasoline fumes. When Natasha opened the porthole to clear the air, a song mournfully crept in from outside.

'Where are you, wolves, ancient wild beasts?
Where are you, yellow-eyed tribe of mine?'

Another thieves' song, again about wolves, rendered in the most sentimental fashion by a hard-handed fisherman. Or, just as likely, by a mechanic in greasy coveralls, or even an officer as prim as Slava Bukovsky, because in private everyone sang thieves' songs. But especially workers sang. They strummed their guitars, always primitively tuned D-G-B-D-G-B-D.

'I'm surrounded by hounds, feeble relatives,
  We used to think of as our prey.'

Westerners thought of Russians as bears. Russian men saw themselves as wolves, lean and wild, barely restrained. To see them standing in line hours for a beer was hard to understand unless you saw the inner Soviet man. The song was another one by Vysotsky. To his countrymen much of Vysotsky's appeal lay in his vices, his drinking and wild driving. The story was that he'd had a 'torpedo' implanted in his ass. A 'torpedo' was a capsule of Antabuse that would make Vysotsky sick whenever he had alcohol. Yet still he drank!

'I smile at the enemy with my wolfish grin,
  Baring my teeth's rotten stumps,
  And blood-specked snow melts
  On the sign: "We're not wolves any more!"'

As Natasha closed the porthole, Arkady came fully awake. 'Open it,' he said.
'It's cold.'
'Open it.'
Too late. The song had ended; all he could hear through the open porthole was the heavy sigh of water as it slid by below. The singer had been the same as on Zina's tape. Maybe. If he sang again, he could tell. Arkady

started shaking, though, and Natasha closed the porthole tight.

As the cabin door opened, Arkady sat bolt upright, knife in hand. Natasha turned on the light and regarded him with worry. 'Who were you expecting?'

'No one.'

'Good, because in your condition you couldn't scare a doormouse.' She uncurled his fingers from the knife handle. 'Besides, you don't need to fight. You have a brain and you can out-think anyone else.'

'Can I think myself off this ship?'

'The brain is a wonderful thing.' She put the knife aside.

'I wish the brain were a ticket. How long have I been asleep?'

'One hour, maybe two. Tell me about Zina.' She wiped the sweat from his brow and eased him back on to his pillow. His hand was still cramped from holding the knife, and she began massaging the fingers. 'Even when you're wrong, I like to hear how you think.'

'Really?'

'It's like listening to someone play the piano. Why did she come on the *Polar Star*, to smuggle those stones?'

'No, they were too cheap. Natasha, I want the knife.'

'But just for herself the stones might have been enough.'

'A Soviet criminal rarely operates alone. You don't

find a Soviet criminal alone in the dock. There are five, ten, twenty in the dock at a time.'

'If it wasn't an accident, and not for one second am I saying that it was anything but, maybe it was a crime of passion.'

'It was too clean a murder. And planned. For her blood to pool the way it did she must have been stowed for at least half a day before she went into the water. That means moving her to hide her, then moving her again to throw her overboard. We were fishing harder then, people were on deck.'

Arkady stopped for breath. A therapeutic massage was not easy to distinguish from torture.

'Go on,' Natasha said.

'Zina fraternized with Americans, which she only could have done with the permission of Volovoi. She informed for Volovoi. There wouldn't be any reprimand from the galley staff because they were told to let her roam, and she probably kept Olimpiada happy by feeding her chocolates and brandy. But why did Zina always go to the stern deck when the *Eagle* delivered fish? And *only* when the *Eagle* delivered fish, not any other boat? To wave to a man she might dance with one night out of every two or three months? Is Slava's band that good? Maybe the question should be asked the other way. What were the Americans looking for when they delivered fish?'

Arkady didn't mention the possibility that there was an intelligence station on the *Polar Star*. On the tape the lieutenant invited Zina into the station when fish were coming on board. Did the station only operate between incoming nets? Was it a matter of nets or Americans?

'Anyway,' he said, 'Americans, various lovers, Volovoi – a lot of people used Zina or were used by her. We don't have to be brilliant, we just have to see the pattern.'

He remembered her voice on the tape: 'He thinks he tells me what to do. A second thinks he tells me what to do.' Arkady counted the 'He's. Four significant men, one of whom even she knew was a killer.

'What people?' Natasha asked.

'An officer, for one. He could be compromised.'

'Which?' She was alarmed.

He shook his head. His hands were pink, as if they'd come out of boiling water. They felt that way.

'What do you think?' he asked her.

'About First Mate Volovoi, I don't agree. About the Americans, they must answer for themselves. About Olimpiada and the chocolates, you may be right.'

When he awoke again Natasha had returned with a giant samovar, a silver urn with a spigot for a nose and cheeks shining with good-natured heat. While they took tea, each drinking from a steaming glass, Natasha sawed a round loaf of bread.

'My mother drove trucks. Remember how we built trucks then, when the factories fulfilled their plan according to gross weight? Each truck weighed twice as much as trucks anywhere else in the world. Try to steer one of those in the snow.

'The route was across a frozen lake. My mother was a shockworker of Communist Labour; she was always in the first truck. She was popular. She had a photo album and she showed me a picture of my father. He drove too. Maybe you wouldn't think it, but he looked surprisingly intellectual. He read anything, could argue with anybody. Wore glasses. His hair was light, but actually he looked a little like you. She said he was too romantic was his problem; he was always in trouble with the bosses. They were going to be married, but in the spring, in the thaw, his truck went through the ice.

'I grew up around dams. I always loved them. There's nothing on earth as beautiful and beneficial to mankind. Other students were interested in special institutes, but I got out of school as fast as I could and up on a scaffold with a mixer. A woman can mix cement as well as any man. The most exciting time is working at night under lights powered by the last dam you helped to build. Then you know you're someone. A lot of the men, though, are drifters because they make so much money. That's their dilemma. They make so much money that they have to drink it up or spend it going to the Black Sea or on the first girl like Zina. They don't make homes. It's not their fault. It's the site directors who are shameless, who offer anything to get their project finished first. Naturally the men say, why stay in one place when you can sell yourself for more money somewhere else? That's Siberia today.'

*

191

The net slid up the stern ramp into a circle of sodium lamps, rose on boom cables and swayed as if alive, sea water weeping from chafing hair and flowing over the deck in shallow waves. Forty tons or fifty tons of fish, maybe more! half a night's quota in one tow. Crabs danced over wooden planks. Taut cables moaned from the weight as the trawlmaster flashed his scalpel and on the run sliced the belly of the bag from one end to the other. The whole net seemed to split open at once, flooding the deck up to the gunwale rail and boat deck stairs in a rich, live, twisting mass of slime eels, milky blue in the light . . .

Arkady awoke with a start, heaved off his blankets, pulled on his boots, found his knife and fought the door to get out of his cabin. It wasn't just a claustrophobia but a sense of being buried alive; leaving the bed didn't help if he was still below steel decks.

Outside the lights were smothered in an underlit night fog, no worse than the smoke of a fire. He'd slept through the entire afternoon. It was now a day and a half since he'd first been introduced to Zina Patiashvili's dead body, and he was feeling rather that way himself. And he had less than twelve hours before he was supposed to uncover some startling revelation that would resolve to everyone's satisfaction the mysterious death of Zina Patiashvili and allow the ship's crew to go into port. He stumbled against the rail, inching away from the trawl deck towards the bow. The catcherboats had disappeared, so there were neither stars or other lights to lead the eye away from the dull glow of the *Polar Star*'s lamps.

The deck was empty, suggesting that it was dinner time. Everyone was falling into a single schedule now that the factory ship had stopped taking fish and was steaming to port. He hooked an elbow over the rail for support. This was not going to be the usual brisk perambulation around the deck. It would be a stroll with ample time to think about drowning, about fear that wrapped like a wet shroud around his heart. He marked his progress by the machine shop. The bridgehouse was a goal far in the distance, dissolving in the mist.

'The poetry lover.'

Arkady turned towards Susan's voice. He hadn't heard her approach.

'Taking a break?' she asked.

'I like the sea air.'

'You look it.' She leaned on the rail next to him, pushed her hood back and lit a cigarette, then held the match up to his eyes. 'Christ!'

'Still pink?'

'What happened to you?'

His muscles were still cramping, going from numb to hot to numb again. As casually as possible he gripped the handrail. He would have walked away if he could have trusted his legs to make a dignified exit. 'I was just trying to See in New Ways. It was a strain.'

'Oh, I get it,' Susan said as she glanced around the deck. 'This is the scene of the accident; that's why you're here. It's still an accident, isn't it?'

'Of the unexplained sort,' Arkady granted.

'I'm sure you'll come up with the right explanation.

They wouldn't have picked you unless they knew you would.'

'Thank you for your confidence.' He felt his knees sag treacherously. If she disdained him so much, why didn't she go?

'I wondered,' she said.

'Now you're wondering?'

'Well, you questioned the fishermen on the catcher-boats. Weren't they all off the *Polar Star* before anything happened to Zina?'

'It appears so.' She wants to know, he thought.

'You're almost for real, aren't you? I hear Slava is running everywhere looking for a suicide note, but you stagger around as if you actually want to know what happened. Why?'

'That's a mystery to us all.' Although his mouth tasted like a gas tank, he felt the urge for a smoke. He patted his pockets.

'Here.' Susan put her cigarette between his lips and then pulled back from the rail. At first he thought that it was from him; then he saw that the *Eagle* had come alongside out of the fog. As the trawler edged nearer, he could make out the form of George Morgan on the darkened bridge. In the lights of the deck, two fishermen in slickers were tying torn mesh and garbage to dump at sea. Arkady recognized Coletti's sullen glare and Mike's open grin. The Aleut's picture was the same as in Zina's photo: innocent and without shading.

The deck around the men was wet and littered with flatfish and crabs, and though the trawler was pitching more than the *Polar Star*, the Americans seemed rooted where they stood in forward-leaning, lock-kneed stances. Between the two boats was a shifting screen of birds that materialized out of habit. Perhaps a hundred birds hovered on outstretched wings: black-capped terns with swallow tails, masked petrels and milk-white gulls see-sawing overhead. They looked as if someone had emptied a basket of papers off the ship and the pages had flown and kept pace. The slightest dip of one bird created a ripple of adjustments, so the flock shimmered and squawked.

Mike waved again and it took Arkady a moment to realize that a third person had joined him and Susan at the rail. Natasha spoke into Arkady's ear. 'I found someone who wants to talk to you. I went to your cabin and you were gone. Why did you get out of bed?'

As he started to describe the benefits of fresh air, Arkady began to cough, which set off a chill that doubled him over. There seemed to be frozen bits inside of him which, as they melted, spread currents of debilitating cold.

With one eye on Susan, Natasha went on talking as if they were taking tea at the rail. 'Now it's time for my lecture. Afterwards, we'll go meet my friend.'

'Your lecture?' Susan made it clear she was trying not to smile.

'I am the ship's representative of the All-Union Knowledge Society.'

'How could I have forgotten?' Susan asked.

It would have been less cruel for her to laugh out

loud, because Natasha only had the sense that she was being mocked, the way a woman whose slip shows only at the rear is vaguely aware that she is the subject of humour without knowing why. Out of sheer nervousness she took the cigarette from Arkady's mouth. 'In your condition the last thing you need is this.' She turned to Susan. 'This is the most disgusting habit of Soviet men. Smoking is man's most unnatural act.'

She snapped the cigarette at the birds. A gull tipped its wings, caught it, then dropped it. A petrel slid forward, caught the tumbling cigarette, ate half and rejected the rest. The filter landed in the water, where it was studied by a tern.

'They must be Russian birds,' Susan said.

An idea struck Arkady while he coughed. Susan was wearing a fishing jacket and Natasha was wearing a fishing jacket; it was about all the two of them had in common. Where was Zina's fishing jacket? He hadn't thought about it before because no one took a jacket to the dance, and during intermissions when people went on deck they could stand a few minutes of sub-Arctic air. Soviet women especially wouldn't bother with any jacket that might encumber an embrace. In their stolid frames were souls so romantic that they lifted like doves on the slightest breeze.

As Arkady finished his last rasp and straightened up, Susan lit another cigarette and kept it for herself.

'Renko, are you the investigator or the victim?'

'He knows what he's doing,' Natasha said.

'That's why he looks like the shark's lunch?'

'He has a system.'

What is it? Arkady wondered.

Morgan's voice came from the radio in Susan's pocket: 'Ask Renko what happened to Zina. We all want to know.'

On the deck of the *Eagle*, Mike waved again and gestured to Natasha as if inviting her down for a visit. Her cheeks reddened, but she gave the fisherman her shoulder to indicate that fraternization was an item strictly in her past. 'We have to go to the lecture,' she said firmly.

'They want to know what happened to Zina,' Susan said.

Unsure of his legs, Arkady tested them with a casual shuffle.

'What do you want me to tell them?' Susan asked.

'Tell them,' Arkady stalled. 'Tell them they still know more than I do.'

Chapter Fifteen

The inspirational lecture on scientific atheism given in the cafeteria by Natasha Chaikovskaya, corresponding member of the All-Union Knowledge Society, was well attended by the off-duty crew because Volovoi stood at the back, his raw face scanning not only the presence but the enthusiasm of the audience. Skiba and Slezko were in the last row of benches, giving The Invalid an extra four eyes. The day before a port call was always the most anxious, when it could be cancelled for any number of reasons: time did not permit, money transfers had not been completed, the political climate wasn't right.

The anticipation of Dutch Harbor had gripped everyone. It was not only the first land in more than four months; it was the point of the entire voyage, those blessed few hours with foreign currency in an American store. If a man wanted to catch fish or a woman wanted simply to clean them, they could trawl the Soviet coast rather than spend half a year in the Bering Sea. The women were wearing freshly laundered blouses with flower prints coming into bloom, their hair spiked with pins. The men were more divided. The ship had gathered speed for the long run to the Aleutians, incidentally firing its boilers for showers, and half the men were scraped clean and sporting the knit shirts of men at ease. The other half, sceptics, still wore a crust of beard and dirt.

'Religion', Natasha read from a pamphlet, 'teaches that work is not a freely given contribution to the state, but an obligation imposed by God. A citizen who holds this view is unlikely to economize on materials.'

Obidin spoke up from the middle row of tables. 'Did God economize when He made heaven and earth? When He made the elephant? Maybe God doesn't care about economizing on materials.'

'Materials of the state?' Natasha was outraged.

'Why are you trying to subvert her?' Volovoi had sidled up to Arkady. 'She's a simple worker. Why drag her into this dirty work of yours?'

Natasha had dragged Arkady to the lecture. Not that he could have resisted; he was standing because he was afraid if he sat he wouldn't be able to rise. His arms were crossed over feverish tremors.

People shouted at Obidin, 'Shut up! Listen and learn!'

'Two days ago half the ship didn't know who you were,' Volovoi went on. 'Now you're the most hated man on board. You've outsmarted yourself. First you say Zina Patiashvili was murdered. Now you can't let these people, your own shipmates, have their port call without saying she wasn't.'

'Someone's been spreading the story that it's up to me,' Arkady said.

'Rumour always has a thousand tongues,' Volovoi observed. He looked at his watch. 'Well, you have eleven hours before your great decision: Dutch Harbor or no Dutch Harbor? Will you admit to error or put yourself above your entire ship? Others might say you will compromise. I don't know you in particular, but I know your type. I think you'd keep this whole crew anchored off Dutch Harbor and not let a single man on shore rather than confess that you're wrong.'

'Science has shown,' Natasha was saying, 'that the flame of a church candle induces an hypnotic effect. In comparison, science is the electrification of the mind.'

'After all,' Volovoi asked, 'what do you have to lose? You have no Party card, no family.'

'You have a family?' Arkady was interested. He saw The Invalid's apartment in a Vladivostok highrise, a spiritless wife, a litter of little Volovois in red Pioneer scarves gathered at the glow of a television set.

'My wife is second secretary of the City Soviet.'

Erase the spiritless wife, Arkady thought. Enter a match for Volovoi, the hammer and anvil from whom the next generation of Communists would be pounded out.

'And a boy,' Volovoi added. 'We have a stake in the future. You don't. You're the bad apple and I don't want you infecting Comrade Chaikovskaya.'

Natasha progressed from the electrification of the mind to the evolution of the flesh, from Homo Erectus to Socialist Man. Her refresher course in atheism had been ordered up because of the old Orthodox church in Dutch Harbor, pitting science against ghosts.

'What makes you think I can infect her?'

'You're glib,' Volovoi said. 'You had an important

father, went to special schools in Moscow, had everything the rest of us didn't. You may impress her – you may even impress the captain – but I see you for what you are. You're anti-Soviet. I can smell it on you.'

'There's no difference,' Natasha was saying, 'between belief in a "supreme intelligence" and the faddish interest in aliens from other galaxies.'

Someone protested. 'Statistically there has to be life in other galaxies.'

'But they're not visiting us,' Natasha said.

'How would we know?' It was Kolya; who else? 'If they have achieved intergalactic flight, then they certainly have the ability to disguise themselves.'

No one annoyed Natasha more than Kolya Mer. It didn't matter that they worked side by side on the factory line. Even the fact that she'd come to his aid when he sawed off his finger seemed to have made her more his enemy than his friend.

'Why would they come to visit us?' she demanded.

'To see scientific socialism in action,' Kolya said and drew some approving murmurs around the cafeteria, though to Arkady the idea was the equivalent of walking around the world to see an anthill.

'I notice you haven't visited me yet,' Volovoi said. 'You haven't cared to inform me of your progress.'

'I think you're sufficiently informed,' Arkady said, and thought of Slava. 'Anyway, I'd only ask to see your file on Zina Patiashvili, and you wouldn't show it to me.'

'That's right.'

'But I can guess what it says: "Reliable toiler, politically mature, cooperative". She didn't do her work, she was a giddy girl who slept with everyone, and you must have known all this, which means she was an informer – not a Skiba or a Slezko, but an informer. Either that or she was sleeping with you.'

'Have you read the Bible?' Obidin asked.

'It is not necessary to read the Bible. That's like saying you have to have a disease to be a doctor,' Natasha said. 'I know the structure of the Bible, the books, the authors.'

'The miracles?' Obidin asked.

'Shame! Shame!' The audience around Obidin rose to denounce him. 'She's the expert! There are no miracles!'

Obidin shouted in return, 'A woman is murdered, lies on the ocean floor and returns to the very ship where she was killed and you say there are no miracles!'

More people stood, infuriated, shaking their fists. 'Liar! Fanatic! That's the kind of talk that will keep us out of Dutch Harbor!'

Slezko rose and pointed at Arkady; it was like looking into the barrel of a sniper. 'There's the provocateur who's keeping us out of Dutch Harbor!'

'Miracles are real!' Obidin shouted.

'It will be a miracle if you get off this ship alive,' Volovoi told Arkady. 'I hope you do. I look forward to your return to Vladivostok and your walk down the ladder to the Border Guard.'

Lidia Taratuta poured Arkady a glass of fortified wine. A *bufetchitsa*, the woman in charge of the officers' mess, rated a two-berth cabin, but she seemed to have this one all to herself. Red was her favourite colour, he suspected. A maroon Oriental rug of intricate design was pinned like a huge butterfly to the bulkhead. Red candles sat in brass holders. Red felt boots stood by the bunk. The cabin had the aura of an actress who had become a touch too voluptuous with age. There was an overfullness to Lidia's hennaed hair and to her lips. An amber pendant hung in the warmth of a blouse that was half unbuttoned. The blouse expressed recklessness and generosity, as if it had unbuttoned itself. In the Soviet fishing fleet a captain did not choose – he was given his ship, his officers, his crew – with one exception: his *bufetchitsa*. Marchuk had used his option well.

'You want to know what officers Zina was sleeping with? You think she was a slut? Who are you to judge? It's good you have Natasha to work with because I see that you don't understand women. Maybe in Moscow you dealt with nothing but whores. I don't know what Moscow is like. I only went once as a union representative. On the other hand, you don't know what life on a ship is like. So which is worse, that you don't understand women or that you don't know this ship? Well, you may never want to be on another ship. More wine?'

Since Natasha was standing in front of the door in case Arkady tried to escape, he accepted the glass. He was the first to admit he didn't understand women. He certainly didn't know why Natasha had hauled him here.

'He can't leave the ship,' she said. 'He's an investigator, but he's in some kind of trouble.'

'A man with a past?' Lidia asked.

'A spell of political unreliability,' Arkady said.

'That sounds like a head cold, not a past. Men have no past. Men move on from place to place like leaves. Women have pasts. I have a past.' Lidia's eyes flicked to a framed wardrobe picture of two little girls sitting like a pair of cockatoos on a single chair, wearing white dresses, with white bows in their hair. 'That's a past.'

'Where's the father?' Arkady asked, to be polite.

'What a good question. I haven't seen him since he kicked me, six months pregnant, down the stairs. So now I have two children in a day-care centre in Magadan. There's a nurse and an aide for thirty kids. The nurse is an old woman with consumption; the aide is a thief. That's who's raising my angels. All winter the girls have coughs. Well, those women are paid ninety rubles a month, they're forced to steal, so I send extra every time I'm in port just to make sure my girls don't starve or die of pneumonia before I see them again. Thank God I can go to sea and make money for them, but if I ever saw their father again I'd cut off his prick and use it for bait. Let him dive for it, right, Natasha?'

A giggle rose like a bubble from the Chaika, who caught herself and stared soberly again at Arkady. 'Be careful, he's a mind reader.'

'Believe me,' Arkady said, 'I can't remember when I've understood a situation less.'

Lidia smoothed her lap. 'Well, what do you know

about your crew-mates? For example, what do you know about Dynka?'

He was taken by surprise again. 'A nice—' he began.

'Married at fourteen to an alcoholic,' Lidia said. 'A cab driver. But if her Mahmet goes to an alcohol clinic, as soon as he registers he loses his driver's licence for five years, so she has to get him Antabuse on the black market. She's not going to make that kind of money in Khazakhstan, so she has to come here. The old lady in Natasha's cabin, Elizavyeta Fedorovna Malzeva, sits and sews all day. Her husband used to be a purser on the Black Sea Fleet until his pecker wandered up a passenger who charged him with rape. He's been in a camp for fifteen years. She gets by with her daily dose of Valeryanka. Watch her in Dutch Harbor; she'll try to get some Valium. Same thing. So, comrade, you're surrounded by frailty, by women with pasts, by sluts.'

'I never said that.' Actually, it had been Natasha who had first called Zina a slut, but Arkady thought it probably wouldn't help to protest on grounds of consistency. Anyway, he wasn't fighting the situation any more. He'd always suspected that while men might make the best police, women would make the best investigators. Or at least a different kind of investigator, picking up different sorts of clues in a different manner, searching sideways or backwards, as compared to the straightforward, pig-in-a-rut method of men.

'He's more interested in Americans,' Natasha said. 'We left Susan smirking up on deck.'

'He's sick?' Lidia asked.

Arkady was so used to trembling that he no longer noticed it.

Natasha said, 'He doesn't take proper care of himself. He goes places he shouldn't go and asks questions he shouldn't ask. He wants to know about Zina and officers.'

'Which officers?' Lidia asked.

Defensively Arkady said, 'I only mentioned to Natasha the question of officers sleeping with crew.'

'That's a broad brush.' Lidia refilled his glass. 'On a ship we live together for six months at a time. We spend more time here than we do with our families. Of course relationships develop because we're human. We're normal. But if you start putting things like that in your report you can ruin people. A name gets written down in a report and never gets erased. From the outside it can look bad. An investigation about Zina suddenly becomes an investigation of the whole ship, of philanderers and sluts. See what I mean?'

'I'm starting to,' Arkady said.

'He is.' Natasha nodded.

'You mean your name,' Arkady said.

'Everyone knows what the *bufetchitsa* does,' Lidia said. 'I direct the officers' mess, I clean the captain's cabin, I keep the captain happy. It's custom. I knew it the day I applied. The Ministry of Fisheries knows it. His wife knows it. If I didn't take care of him on board ship, he'd rape her at the door, so she knows. Other senior officers have other arrangements. You see, it makes us human, but it doesn't make us criminal. If you put even a hint of that in your report, it forces the Ministry and all those wives back on shore, who would much rather kiss their husbands' pictures than come sail on the *Polar Star*, to demand our heads.'

Lidia took a ladylike sip of wine. 'Zina was different. It wasn't that she was a tramp, necessarily; it was just that sleeping with a man meant nothing to her. There was no affection in her. I don't think that she ever slept with anyone more than once; that was the way she was. Of course, once I was aware of what was going on, I took steps to remove the temptation.'

'Such as?' Arkady asked.

'She was working in the officers' mess. I moved her to the crew's.'

'That sounds more like spreading temptation.'

'Anyway,' Lidia said, 'she became obsessed with Americans, so you see that there's no need to even mention our good Soviet men at all.'

Arkady asked, 'Obsessed with Americans or one American in particular?'

'See how sharp he is!' Natasha said proudly.

Lidia answered evasively, 'With Zina, who could say?'

Arkady tapped his head as if it might stir an idea. He had received the message Lidia was sending – don't name the ship's officers in any report – but he didn't understand her reason for sending it.

'He's thinking,' Natasha said.

He seemed to have dislodged a new headache. 'Did you go to the dance?'

'No,' Lidia said. 'That night I had to prepare a buffet in the officers' wardroom for the Americans. Sausages, pickles, delicacies they don't have on their own boat. We were too busy to dance.'

' "We"?'

'Captain Marchuk, Captain Morgan, Captain Thorwald and myself. The American crews went on to the dance, but the captains were going over charts, and I was serving and cleaning.'

'All evening?'

'Yes. No, I did take one break, a cigarette on deck.'

Arkady remembered that Skiba saw her walking forward at midships at 1115. 'Someone saw you.'

Lidia put a lot of work into hesitating, batting her eyelashes, even delivering a sigh from the bosom. 'It doesn't mean anything, I'm sure. I saw Susan at the stern rail.'

'What was she wearing?'

The question took Lidia by surprise. 'Well, a white shirt and jeans, I suppose.'

'And Zina, what was she wearing?'

'A white shirt, I think, and blue pants.'

'So you saw Zina too.'

Lidia blinked, like a person walking off an unexpected step. 'Yes.'

'Where?'

'The stern deck.'

'Did they see you?'

'I didn't think so.'

'You were close enough at night to know what two different women were wearing and neither of them saw you?'

'I have excellent eyes. The captain often says he wishes he had an officer with eyes as good as mine.'

'How many times have you sailed with Captain Marchuk?'

Lidia's excellent eyes brightened like a pair of candles. 'This is my third voyage with Viktor Sergeivich. He became a leading captain of the fleet on our first trip. On the second, he overfulfilled the quota by forty per cent and was named a Hero of the Soviet Union. He was also named a delegate of the Party Congress. They know him in Moscow; they have big plans for him.'

Arkady finished the wine and got to his feet, which didn't feel excellent or even good, but serviceable. His brain was finally working. 'Thank you.'

'I can get us some smoked fish,' Lidia offered. 'We can have more wine, a little something to eat.'

He tried a tentative step or two. It looked like he'd make the door.

'Arkady,' Natasha said, 'be careful where you throw the first stone.'

The bridge was dark except for the green glow of radar and loran screens, of VHF and side-band radio displays, of the glass ball of the gyrocompass, of the lunar face of the engine telegraph. The twin figures of left- and right-rudder controls stood at either side of the deck. Marchuk was at the starboard window; a helmsman was at the wheel. Arkady realized how much the *Polar Star* ran itself. With meditative clicks the automatic pilot hewed to a course already set. The luminous numbers that seemed to hang in the air were largely information after the fact, dispensed by the factory ship as it ploughed into the night.

'Renko.' Marchuk noticed Arkady. 'Bukovsky is looking for you. He says you haven't reported.'

'I'll get to him. Comrade Captain, can we talk?'

Arkady could feel the helmsman stiffen. Factory workers did not come onto the bridge uninvited.

'Leave us,' Marchuk told the man.

'But . . .' Regulations were that two officers or an officer and a helmsman had to be on the bridge at all times.

'It's all right,' Marchuk assured him. 'I'll take over. Seaman Renko will scan the heavens and seas and keep us safe from harm.'

After closing the door behind the helmsman, Marchuk checked the navigation room to be sure no one was there, then took his position behind the wheel. The bulkhead behind him held a fire-control panel and a closed box of radiation metres; these were in case of war. Whenever the autopilot clicked, adjusting to a swell, the wheel made a barely perceptible turn.

'Did you sleep with Zina Patiashvili?' Arkady asked.

For a while Marchuk said nothing. Oversized wipers spread snow on the windshield, and through the streaks Arkady could see anchor winches riding the bow deck and little arabesques that were counter-clockwise coils of rope on either side of the winches. Beyond, in the wide beam of the searchlight, was a seemingly solid wall of snow. It was cold on the bridge, and his shakes started again. The radar monitor in the windshield counter was a Foruna – Japanese. Its ever-moving beam, a little fragmented by the snow, showed two blips keeping pace – the *Eagle* and the *Merry Jane*, he assumed. At least the echosounder was Soviet, a Kalmar; it said the *Polar Star* was making fourteen knots over the bottom, which meant that the old ship had the aid of a following sea. According to the terms of the joint fishery, Soviet ships weren't allowed to use their echosounders in American waters, but no captain would sail blindly while Americans were off the bridge.

'This is the way you run an investigation?' Marchuk asked. 'With wild accusations?'

'With the time limit I have, yes.'

'I hear you took Chaikovskaya as your assistant. A strange choice.'

'No stranger than your picking me.'

'There are cigarettes on the counter. Light one for me.'

Marlboros. As Arkady lit one for him, the captain stared across the flame at his face. It was an intimidation that strong men practised to catch a flinch. 'You have a fever?'

'A chill.'

'Slava calls you and Natasha his "pair of deuces". What do you think about that?'

'Slava could use a pair of deuces.'

'Natasha said something about me?'

'She introduced me to Lidia.'

'Lidia told you?' Marchuk was startled.

MARTIN CRUZ SMITH

'Not meaning to.' Arkady blew out the match and
wandered back to the windshield and the lethargic
rhythm of the wipers. The fog had been brooding up to
this snow. If fog was thought, snow was action. 'She
heard I was asking about Zina and officers. She was
concerned about your reputation and confided to me
that you already had a lover – herself. Why? As she says,
everyone, including your wife, knows that you sleep with
your *bufetchitsa*. Even I knew it. She was trying to stop
a line of questioning, to throw herself in front of a train
for you.'

'Then you're guessing.'

'I *was* guessing. When?'

The wheel clicked right, left, left, held course. On
the counter, the echo-sounder displayed the depth: ten
fathoms. Such a shallow sea.

Marchuk either cleared his throat or laughed. 'In port.
I was there for so long while the ship was hauled out.
Generally, you know, I'm busy during repairs because
the yards outfit you with such shit – inferior plates, bad
welding, cracked boiler mounts. The Navy gets the quality goods, so it's a full-time job to wheedle any decent
brass, copper, alternators. This time it was all taken
care of.

'In short, I was bored, and the wife had been in Kiev
for a month. Look, this is a typically maudlin story. I
took out some Navy men who wanted to eat at a real
sailor's restaurant. The Golden Horn. Zina was a waitress
there. We all made a pass at her. After my guests were
drunk enough to be put to bed, I went back. That was

the one and only time. I didn't even know her last name. You can imagine my surprise when I saw her on board.'

'Did she ask to sail on the *Polar Star*?'

'She asked, but a captain doesn't have that authority.'

It sounded like the truth, Arkady thought. Even if Marchuk had arranged her berth, he certainly wouldn't have placed her under the eye of Lidia Taratuta. 'Did you see Zina the night of the dance?'

'I was in the wardroom. I had a buffet set out for the American fishermen.'

'From?'

'From the *Eagle* and the *Merry Jane*. The crews went to the dance and the captains stayed to argue over sea charts.'

'Captains have different opinions?'

'Or they wouldn't be captains. Of course there are different qualifications. A Soviet captain must study six years in a maritime academy, then have two years as a coast mate, then two years as a deepwater mate to finally qualify as a deepwater captain. There are always a few, whom we shall not name, who think a father in the Ministry can make them an officer, but they're rare. A Soviet captain has degrees in navigation, electronics, construction and law. An American *buys* a boat, he becomes a captain. The point is, when we leave Dutch Harbor we're going to the ice sheet. That's good fishing, but you have to know what you're doing.'

'And Lidia was with you?'

'The entire time.'

Arkady didn't like the idea of the ice sheet. The sky

was already covered with fog. Covering the sea with ice, paving the water white, would remove what little dimension was left. Also, he hated the cold. 'How far is it from the wardroom to the stern?' he asked.

'About a hundred metres. You should know that by now.'

'It's just that I don't understand something. Lidia says she stepped out of the wardroom here in the wheelhouse and happened to see Zina on the stern deck. But you can't see the stern deck from here, not even with her keen eyes. You have to walk there. That's two hundred metres altogether, back and forth the length of the ship, that Lidia travelled in the cold to have a cigarette and happen to see a young rival who dies that same night. Why would Lidia do that?'

'Maybe she's stupid.'

'No, I think she loves you.'

Marchuk was silent. The snow impacted on the windshield into wet craters, so it wasn't freezing outside. The heavy snow settled the water too, and the *Polar Star* seemed to be easing through the night.

'She followed me,' Marchuk said. 'I got a note under my door that Zina wanted to talk to me. "Meet me at the stern at 11" was all it said.'

'It was from Zina?'

'I recognized the handwriting.'

'So you'd received other notes.'

'Yes, once or twice. Lidia caught on. Women sense these things; they just know. Lidia is more jealous than my own wife. Anyway, all that Zina wanted to know was who she was going into Dutch Harbor with. She didn't want to be stuck with any old women. I told her that Volovoi drew up the lists, not me.'

'In Vladivostok, the night you were with Zina, you went to her place?'

'I certainly wasn't going to take her to mine.'

'Describe it.'

'An apartment on Russkaya Street. Pretty nice, actually – African figures, Japanese prints, a lot of guns. She shared it with some guy who was away. I would have turned him in for the guns, but how could I explain how I'd seen them? It wouldn't sound good at Fleet Headquarters, a leading captain informing on a man whose woman he'd shared. I don't know why I'm telling you.'

'Because you can deny everything later. That's why you chose me in the first place, so you can dismiss everything I find if you don't like it. What I don't under-stand is why you wanted any investigation at all, knowing the stories that could come to the surface. Were you crazy or stupid?'

Marchuk was silent for so long that Arkady thought that he might not have heard the question. In any case, the captain wasn't the first with a sexual appetite.

When Marchuk finally spoke, his voice choked with self-disgust. 'I'll tell you why. Two years ago I had a trawler in the Sea of Japan. It was night, bad weather, a Force 9 wind. I was trying to fill the quota because I'd just been named a leading captain. Anyway, I put my men on deck. A wave hit us broadside. It happens. When it's past, you count heads. We were missing one man. His boots were on deck, but he was gone. The wave took him over the side? Down the ramp? I don't know. Naturally, we stopped fishing and looked. At night, in waves like that, in water that cold, he must have died of hypothermia in a matter of minutes. Or else he took a mouthful and went right to the bottom. We never saw him. I radioed Fleet Command in Vladivostok and reported the death. They ordered me to continue search-ing, and also to check the ship to be sure no lifevests or anything floatable was missing. We steamed back and forth for half a day searching the water, tearing the ship apart and counting vests, buoys, barrels. Only when we could declare nothing missing did Fleet Command say that we could go back to fishing. Fleet Command never said it directly, but everyone knew why; it was because Japan was only twenty nautical miles away. To the minds at Command, it was possible that this fisherman had conceived the idea of defection and had set out to cross near-freezing, heavy seas in the dark. How grotesque. I had to order this dead man's friends to search for him not to find him, not to return his body to his family, but as if he were a prisoner escaping, as if we were all prisoners. I did it, but I told myself that I would never again leave my crew to the mercy of Vladivostok. So Zina wasn't perfect? Neither am I. You find out what happened.'

'For your crew's sake?'

'Yes.'

There was something both confusing and suffocating

about the snow. The radar had buttons for brightness, colour, range. On the screen nothing lay ahead but the scattered green dots of wave return.

'How long to Dutch Harbor?'

'Ten hours.'

'If you want to do something for your crew, give them their port call. I'm not going to learn anything in ten hours.'

'You were my compromise with Volovoi. He's the first mate. You heard what he said.'

'You're the captain. If you want your crew to go ashore, do it.'

Marchuk fell silent again. The cigarette burned down to a coal between his lips. 'Keep looking,' he said finally. 'Maybe you'll find something.'

Arkady left by the outer bridge. Inside, Marchuk looked like a man chained to the wheel.

Chapter Sixteen

By the time Arkady reached his cabin he was shaking so hard he decided to confront the spasms and kill them. From his room he took a towel and descended one deck to a small shower room with pegs and a sign that said, 'A good citizen respects the property of others.' A handwritten sign advised, 'Take your valuables with you.'

With his knife tucked into the back of his towel, he entered the greatest luxury on the *Polar Star*, the sauna. It had been built by the crew and if not much larger than a stall, it was all of red cedar. A cedar box held smooth river stones heated by pipes that carried live steam from the laundry. A cedar bucket held water and a cedar ladle. A satisfactory mist already hung in the air. Two pairs of legs dangled from the upper bench, but they looked too spindly to be the legs of killers.

Whether at a palatial spa in Moscow or a cabin in Siberia, it was a Russian credo that nothing cured more ills than a sauna. Chills, arthritis, nervous and respiratory diseases, and especially hangovers were helped by the balm of steam, and since the *Polar Star*'s little sauna was in constant use it was always hot. The pores of Arkady's skin opened wide and he felt prickly sweat on his scalp and chest. Though his hands and feet stung, they hadn't turned white, the first warning sign of frostbite. Once he'd driven the shakes out, he'd be able to think straight. As he ladled more water on to them the stones turned a glossy black and then as quickly dried to grey. The super-heated mist became more dense. There was a birch lash in the corner for driving out the poisons of a bad drunk, but he had never believed in whipping himself, even under the guise of medical attention.

'You're going to pick up any stuff?' a voice asked in English from the cloud. It was the American fisheries observer, Lantz. 'Dust or shit, Dutch is on the route. A lot of those fishing boats make funny runs all the way to Colombia, to Baja.'

'I'll stick with beer.' The other voice was the rep called Day.

'Ever try rocks? Smoke it in a pipe. Very intense. That'll unwind you fast.'

'No, thanks.'

'Worried? I'll get you a cocktail, it looks like a regular cigarette.'

'I don't even smoke. After this, I'm going back to school. I'm not going to do crack in the Yukon. Lay off.'

'What a wimp,' Lantz said as Day stepped down from the mist and out the door. There was a sound like Lantz blowing his nose on his towel. Slowly he slid off the bench. He was skin and bones, like a pale, long-limbed salamander. His eyes finally took in who was sitting on the lower bench. 'Well, look who's sneaking around and listening to other people. How about you, Renko? Are you going to get your American dollars and run into Dutch Harbor?'

'I don't think I'll be going in,' Arkady said.

'No one will. They say you fucked it for everyone.'

'That could be.'

'And I hear that even if everyone else does, you won't. So what are you, Renko, a policeman or a prisoner?'

'This is coveted employment, to work on an ocean-going ship.'

'If you can make the port calls, not if you're trapped on board. Poor Comrade Renko.'

'It sounds like I'm missing a lot.'

'It looks like you need a lot. And you're just going to be walking up and down the deck hoping someone's going to bring you back a pack of smokes. Pathetic.'

'It is.'

'I'll bring you back a candy bar, a stick of gum. You wait, it'll be the fucking highlight of your trip.'

The door sucked steam out as Lantz left. Arkady threw more water in on the box and collapsed on the bench again. He was scared when even an American saw how much trouble he was in.

He was also scared by how little he understood. It didn't make sense that Zina would leave the dance just to ask Marchuk who her shopping companions in Dutch Harbor would be. And then she stayed on the stern deck. According to the notes kept by Skiba and Slezko, Lidia crossed the mid-ships deck at 1115, at which point Zina was still alive at the stern rail. That was fourteen minutes before Ridley returned to the *Eagle* and fifty-five minutes before the *Eagle* cast off. Zina was too smart to try defecting when an American boat was tied up to the factory ship. Vladivostok would demand and the company, half Soviet-owned, would agree that the *Eagle* and the *Merry Jane* be searched. The two conditions for a successful disappearance, from what Marchuk had said, were that the Americans be beyond conceivable swimming distance and that not a single item of lifesaving gear be missing from the *Polar Star*. If defection was impossible, what *did* Zina want?

The suggestion of a beer stuck in his throat. Sakhalin trawlers had made extra money by picking up cases of Japanese beer tied to crab pots and leaving in exchange sacks of salmon roe. He could use one of those beers, as cold as the sea, not the warm, liquid headache that Obidin brewed.

The sauna door opened, and in the thick steam the new arrival seemed to be wearing shoes. He was a large man, naked except for a towel tied at the waist, and he was not wearing shoes; his feet were dark blue, almost purple. They were tattooed in a design of florid curls, each toe standing out as a green claw. This leonine design reached up his legs to his knees, like a griffin. He was what a scientist would call a mesomorph, muscular and nearly as deep through the chest as he was broad. Some of the older tattoos had smudged and blurred, but Arkady could make out chained, buxom women climbing each thigh to the red flames that spread around the edge of the towel. The stomach was scalloped with blue clouds. On the right side of the ribcage was a bleeding

221

wound with the name of Christ, on the left side a vulture held a heart. The man's breast was smeared with scar tissue. Administrators did that in labour camps; if a prisoner tattooed something they didn't like, they burned it off with permanganate of potash. The man's arms were green sleeves, the right covered in fading dragons, the left with the names of prisons, labour camps, transit camps: Vladimir, Tashkent, Potma, Sosnovka, Kolyma, Magadan and more, a roster of wide personal experience. The tattoos stopped at the wrists and neck; the total effect was of a man wearing a tight dark suit, or of a pale head and hands levitating. Another effect was that a person knew just what this tribesman was: an *urka*, in Russia a professional criminal.

It was the trawlmaster, Karp Korobetz. He smiled at Arkady broadly and said, 'You look like shit.'

'I know you,' Arkady realized and said it at the same time.

Karp said, 'It was a dozen years ago. In the hall when you started asking questions, I said to myself, "Renko, Renko, I know that name." '

'Article 146, armed robbery.'

'You tried to hang me for murder,' Karp reminded him.

Now Arkady's memory worked fine. Twelve years before, Korobetz had been a big, soft kid who worked whores twice his age out of the tough Maria's Grove section of Moscow. Usually an arrangement was maintained between pimps and the militia, especially at that time, when prostitution was not supposed to exist, but the boy took to robbing victims when their pants were down. One old man, a veteran with a chest of medals, resisted, and Karp shut him up with a hammer. His hair had been lighter and longer then, with fanciful plaits around the ears. Arkady had appeared at the trial only to testify as the senior investigator for homicide. But there was another reason he hadn't recognized Korobetz. Karp's face had changed; his hairline actually was lower than before. If prisoners tattooed something on their brow like 'Slave of USSR', camps had the skin surgically removed. The whole scalp had shifted forward.

'What did you write there?' Arkady pointed to the trawlmaster's forehead.

'"Communists Drink the Blood of the People." '

'All that on your forehead?' Arkady was impressed. He looked at Karp's chest. 'And there?'

' "The Party = Death." They took that off with acid in Sosnovka. Then I wrote, "The Party is a Whore." After they burned that off the skin was too rough to use any more.'

'A short career. Well, Pushkin died young.'

Karp brushed away a wisp of steam. His slate-blue eyes lay in a crease that ran across the bridge of his nose. He combed his damp hair with his fingers. Now his hair was full at the top and short on the sides, Soviet-style, while the body had become Neanderthal. An inked Neanderthal.

'I ought to thank you,' Karp said. 'I learned a trade at Sosnovka.'

'Don't thank me. Thank the people you robbed and beat; they're the ones who identified you.'

'They taught us how to make television cabinets. Did you ever have a Melodya set? I might have made it. Of course, that was long ago, before my social rehabilitation took hold. See how strange life is? Now I'm a seaman first class and you're a seaman second class. And I'm on top of you.'

'The sea is a strange place.'

'You're the last person I ever expected to meet on the *Polar Star*. What happened to the high and mighty investigator?'

'The land is a strange place.'

'Everything's strange to you now. That's what happens when you lose your desk and your Party card. Tell me what you're doing for this so-called fleet electrical engineer.'

'I'm doing something for the captain.'

'Fuck the captain. Where do you think you are, the middle of Moscow? There are about ten officers on the *Polar Star*; the rest is crew. We have our own system; we sort things out between ourselves. I sort things out. Why are you asking about Zina Patiashvili?'

'She had an accident.'

'I know that, I found her. If it's just an accident, why bring you in?'

'My experience. You know my experience. What do you know about Zina?'

'She was an honest toiler. The ship is poorer for her

loss.' Karp broke into a smile, showing gold molars. 'See, I learned how to say all that shit.'

Arkady stood. Their eyes were on a level, though Karp outweighed him. He said, 'I was stupid not to recognize you. You're twice as stupid to tell me who you are.'

Karp looked hurt. 'I thought you'd be pleased to see how I'd reformed and become a model worker. I hoped we could be friends, but I see you haven't changed at all.' Forgiving, he leaned closer to offer advice. 'We had a guy in camp who reminded me of you. He was political. He was an Army officer who wouldn't take his tanks into Czechoslovakia against the counter-revolutionaries – something like that. I was his section leader and he couldn't follow orders; he thought he was still in charge. You know, they'd take us out on a railroad spur and we'd drop trees and load them. A timber collective. Healthy reconstructive labour at thirty degrees below. The dangerous part is when you've got the trees on the flatbed; you don't want them rolling off. It's funny that the one guy with the education, this officer, is the one who had the accident, and he didn't even get his accident straight. What he said was he was held down on the track and somebody busted his bones with an axe handle. I mean upper arms, lower arms, hands, fingers – the works. Imagine. You've seen stiffs, the body has a lot of bones. But I was there and I didn't see anything like that. It's what happens when you make a mistake and a whole flatbed of logs rolls on you. He went crazy. He finally died of a ruptured spleen. I bet he wanted to at that point, or spend the rest of his life like a broken egg. The only reason I mention him is just because he reminded me of you, and you remind me of him, and because a ship way out at sea is such a dangerous place. That's what I wanted to tell you. You should be careful,' Karp said on the way out. 'Learn how to swim.'

Arkady's shakes came back twice as bad. Did he ever get so scared when he was an investigator? Maybe it was fitting that he'd come all the way from Moscow to sail with Karp Korobetz. Why hadn't he recognized him? The name wasn't that common. On the other hand, would Karp's own mother recognize him now?

The trawlmaster was the one who had thrown him into the fish hold; that was what his shakes were telling him. Three men had carried him and probably one had gone ahead and one had followed; that was Karp and his deck team, the well-organized winners of the socialist competition.

Sweat poured off Arkady, giving him a sheen of fear. Karp was crazy; no mere case of 'sluggish schizophrenia' here. Not dumb, though; so why would he draw attention to himself while Arkady had some temporary authority?

What had Karp said and what had he omitted? He hadn't mentioned the fish hold; why would he? But he hadn't mentioned Dutch Harbor, either. Everyone else was worried about the port call, but not Karp; he wanted to know about Hess. Most of all he wanted to spread some terror, which he'd done.

Again the sauna door opened. Arkady saw a dark foot and immediately reached behind for his knife. As cool air from the open door lifted the mist, however, he saw that the foot was a shoe, a blue Reebok. 'Slava?'

The third mate was irritably sweeping steam aside. 'Renko, I've been looking everywhere for you. I found it! I found the note!'

Arkady still couldn't get Karp out of his head. 'What? What are you talking about?'

'While you've been sleeping and taking saunas, I found the note from Zina Patiashvili. She wrote one.' Slava's face poked through a wreath of mist. 'A suicide note. It's perfect. We're going into port.'

Part Two

EARTH

Chapter Seventeen

Dutch Harbor was surrounded by a green ring of cliffs covered by thick sub-arctic grasses. There were no trees, nothing bigger than a bush, but as the wind moved over the grass the effect was magical, as if the hills were a wave.

The island was actually called Unalaska, and on one side of the bay there was an Aleut village by that name, a beachside line of cottages that led to a white, wooden Russian Orthodox church. The town of Dutch Harbor, however, was out of Arkady's sight, past a tank farm and beyond the breakwater that protected a loading dock with slag heaps of rusting trawl doors and rotting snow, and gas pumps and rows of the half-ton cages called crab pots. Beyond lay a pier of catcherboats and one large ship that had become a dockbound cannery with a fence of pilings around its hull. Behind all this, the hills of Unalaska rose rapidly to volcanic peaks edged in black stone and snow.

It was odd, Arkady thought, how the eye became starved for colour. The clouds were broken, so that sun-spots moved around the bay. Off the lower cliffs, puffins dropped like rocks to the water. Eagles lifted from the higher cliffs and soared to inspect the *Polar Star*; they were enormous birds, bear-brown with imperious white heads and amber eyes. It was like being at the top of the world.

The Americans had already gone ashore in the pilot boat. Soo-san was going home in a gift fishing jacket decorated with souvenir pins. On her way off the ship she'd distributed farewell kisses with the generosity of someone leaving jail. On the pilot boat as it came out had been a new head rep carrying a suitcase with $100,000, the *Polar Star*'s port-call foreign currency. The entire crew had waited while the bills were counted and then counted again in the captain's cabin.

Now, after four months' fishing, Arkady's co-workers were lined along the starboard rail and moving down the steps of the gangway to a lifeboat that would bear them and their allotted American dollars to the port they had dreamed of all this time. Not that they showed it. A Soviet seaman dressed for special occasions did not necessarily shave. He did shine his shoes, slick his hair back and wear his sports jacket even if the sleeves were too short. He also wore his most unimpressed face, not only for Volovoi's sake but for his own, so that his anticipation showed as a wary narrowing of the eyes.

With exceptions. Under the brim of a squat peasant's cap, Obidin's gaze was fixed on the church across the water. Kolya Mer had stuffed his coat with cardboard pots; he eyed the hills like Darwin approaching the Galapagoan shore. Women wore their nicest cotton dresses under the usual layers of sweaters and rabbit-fur coats. They had their grim tourist faces too, until they looked at each other and broke into nervous giggles, then waved up at Natasha, who stood on the boat deck with Arkady.

Natasha's cheeks were almost as red as her lipstick and she wore not one but two haircombs, as if she would need extra ammunition in Dutch Harbor. 'It's my first time in the United States,' she told Arkady. 'It doesn't seem so different from the Soviet Union. You've been before. Where?'

'New York.'

'That's different.'

Arkady paused. 'Yes.'

'Well, so you came to see me off?'

Natasha looked ready to fly from sheer excitement over the water to the waiting shops. In fact Arkady had come to see whether Karp was going ashore. So far the trawlmaster hadn't. 'To thank you and see you off,' he said.

'It will be just for a few hours.'

'Even so.'

Her voice and eyes dropped. 'It was a stimulating experience for me to work with you, Arkady Kirilovich. You don't mind that I call you Arkady Kirilovich?'

'Whatever you like.'

'You're not the fool I thought you were.'

'Thank you.'

'We came to a successful conclusion,' Natasha said.

'Yes, the captain has declared the inquiry officially over. There may not even be an investigation at Vladi-vostok.'

'It was good of Third Mate Bukovsky to find that note.'

'Better than good, unbelievable,' Arkady said, considering he had looked under Zina's mattress well before Slava found her note there.

'Natasha!' As her friends moved along the rail they waved frantically at her to claim her place in line.

Natasha was ready to run, to sail, to fly, but there was a line on her brow because she had witnessed Arkady's earlier search of the bed.

'At the dance, she didn't seem so down in the mouth.'

'No,' Arkady had to agree. Dancing and flirting were not the usual symptoms of depression.

Natasha's last question was the hardest for her. 'You really think she killed herself? She could have done something that rash?'

Arkady gave his answer thought because he knew Natasha had lived months for this one day's excursion, yet would stay loyally on board with him if he gave her any reason to. 'I think it's rash to write a suicide note. I'd refuse to, myself.' He pointed to the lifeboat. 'Hurry, you're going to miss your ride.'

'What can I get you?' Natasha's brow was clear again.

'A complete set of Shakespeare, a video camera, a car.'

'I can't get those.' She was already on the steps leading down to the deck.

'A piece of fruit will do.'

Natasha elbowed her way to her friends just as they were going down the gangway. They were like children, Arkady thought, the kind of Moscow children you see stamping their feet outside school on dark December mornings, bundled up to their hard little faces until the warm door is opened and their eyes light up. He wished he was going with them.

The lifeboat looked like a surfaced submarine; it could seal up forty passengers fleeing a sinking ship and was coloured that crayon hue called 'international orange'. For this holiday jaunt, the hatches were open so that the helmsman and passengers could stand in the fresh air. Natasha waved again before assuming a pose of resolute Soviet sobriety. They cast off, and the entire party appeared in their drab clothes on their orange boat to be headed for either a funeral or a picnic.

The *Merry Jane* was approaching to take more people ashore, and a whole new line had formed along the rail. Among those waiting was Pavel from Karp's deck team. Looking at Arkady, he drew a finger across his throat.

Land did smell, Arkady thought. Unalaska smelled like a garden and he wanted to walk on dry land and leave the scow on which he'd lived for ten months, if only for an hour.

So far, he hadn't told anyone about the attack. What would he say? He hadn't seen Karp or the other men. It would be his word against six politically reliable and socially responsible seamen first class. The only provable fact was that he had been inhaling fumes and inducing hallucinations. And attempting to set fire to the fish hold.

Smoke smudged the air above where Dutch Harbor must be. How large was the town? Cleaner wisps hung from the sides of the mountains. That's where they were, mountains that rose directly from the ocean floor. He imagined soaring over them and descending into a green valley, close enough to see those precious bog orchids of Kolya Mer's, close enough to pick up earth in his hand.

The lifeboat was now traversing the water in front of the Aleut houses; a pretty picture, the orange boat putputting by the white church. He imagined Zina on it.

'It's ironic,' Hess said as he joined Arkady.

The fleet electrical engineer was resplendent in a shiny black parka, jeans and Siberian felt boots. Arkady hadn't seen him since yesterday morning. Of course Hess was small; maybe even small enough to move invisibly around the ship through funnels and ventilator shafts.

'What is?' Arkady asked.

'That the only member of the crew who ever could have defected, the only man whose loyalty has really been tested, is the only one not allowed off the ship.'

'In irony we lead the world.'

Hess smiled. His stiff hair leaned in the breeze but he stood with the wide, solid stance of a sailor as he gazed around.

'A handsome harbour. During the war, the Americans had fifty thousand men here. If we'd had Dutch Harbor there'd still be that many, instead of a few natives and fishing nets. Well, the Americans can be choosy. The Pacific Ocean is an American lake. Alaska, San Francisco, Pearl Harbor, Midway, the Marshalls, Fijis, Samoa, the Marianas. They own it.'

'You're going ashore?'

'To stretch my legs. It might be interesting.'

Perhaps not to a fleet electrical engineer, Arkady thought, but to an officer of Naval Intelligence, yes, a stroll around the major port of the Aleutians might be informative.

Hess said, 'Let me congratulate you on resolving the case of that poor girl.'

'Your congratulations should go entirely to Slava Bukovsky; he found her note. I searched the same place and never saw it.'

Arkady had examined the note once Slava had stopped flourishing his discovery. It had been written on half a lined page that appeared to have been torn from Zina's spiral notebook. The handwriting was hers; the prints were hers and Slava's.

'But it was suicide?'

'A suicide note definitely is evidence of suicide. Of course, being fatally hit on the back of the head and being stabbed after death is evidence of something else.'

Hess seemed to be studying the trawler as it swung alongside the *Polar Star*. Was he a line officer? Arkady wondered. Considering the slow promotions that Germans got, he might be no more than a captain second rank. If he stayed near Leningrad, though, close to Naval headquarters, maybe taught at one of the officers' academies, he could have the title of Professor. Hess looked professorial.

'The captain was relieved to hear that you agreed with Bukovsky's conclusions. You were sick in bed or he would have asked you himself. You seem better now.'

The shakes had chased Arkady back to his cabin, it was true, and he *was* better now, well enough to light a Belomor and start poisoning himself again. He tossed the match away. 'And you, Comrade Hess,' he asked, 'were you relieved?'

Hess allowed himself another smile. 'It sounded too convenient for you to have anything to do with it. But you could have corrected Bukovsky and gone to the captain.'

'And stopped this?' Arkady watched as a Portuguese crewman helped Madame Malzeva off the gangway onto the trawler deck. She stepped down daintily, shawl over her shoulders, as if onto a gondola. 'This is the reason for their whole voyage. I'm not going to ruin their two days here. Is Volovoi ashore?'

'No, the captain is. You know the regulations: either the captain or the commissar has to be on the ship at all times. Marchuk went in on the pilot boat to make sure the merchants of Dutch Harbor are ready for our invasion. I hear they are not only ready but eager.' He looked at Arkady. 'Murder, then? When we're back at sea, will you start asking questions again? Officially the inquiry is over. You won't have the support of the captain, you won't even have the assistance of Bukovsky. You'll be entirely alone, one factory worker in the bottom of the ship. It sounds dangerous. Even if you knew who was responsible for the girl's death, it might be better to forget.'

'I could.' Arkady thought about it. 'But if you were

the killer and you knew that I knew, would you let me live until we returned to Vladivostok?'

Hess considered the idea. 'You'd have a long voyage home.'

Or short, Arkady thought.

'Come with me,' Hess said.

He motioned and Arkady followed into the aft house. He assumed they were going to some quiet spot to speak, but Hess led him directly out to the boat deck on the port side of the ship. A Jacob's ladder hung from the rail to another lifeboat already in the water. A lone helmsman waved up. Not for a fleet electrical engineer the crowded deck of a trawler.

'Ashore,' Hess said. 'Come with me to Dutch Harbor. Everyone else is enjoying a port call, thanks to you. You should have some reward.'

'I don't have a seaman's first-class visa to go in, as you know.'

'On my authority,' Hess said lightly, but also as if he meant what he said.

Even thinking about going ashore had the effect of a glass of vodka. Perspective changed, bringing houses, church and mountains closer. The wind freshened on his cheek and water lapped more audibly against the hull. As Hess pulled on black calfskin gloves, Arkady looked down at his own bare hands, stained canvas jacket, rough pants and rubber boots. Hess caught the self-scrutiny. 'You've shaved,' he reassured Arkady. 'A man who's shaved is ready to go anywhere.'

'What about the captain?'

'Captain Marchuk knows that initiative is the new order of the day. Also, trust in the loyalty of the masses.'

Arkady took a deep breath. 'Volovoi?'

'He's on the bridge watching the other direction. By the time he sees you going ashore you'll be there. You're like a lion who finds his cage door open. You hesitate.'

Arkady held the rail as if for balance. 'It's not that simple.'

'There is one little thing,' Hess said, and brought from his parka a sheet of paper that he spread on the bulk-head. The page bore a two-sentence acknowledgement that defection from a Soviet ship was a state crime for which an offender's family would suffer in his absence. 'Everyone signs it. You have a family? A wife?'

'Divorced.'

'She'll have to do.' When Arkady signed, Hess said, 'One other thing. No knives, not in port.'

Arkady took it from his jacket pocket. Up until yesterday that knife had lived in the closet. Now he and his knife felt inseparable.

'I'll keep it for you,' Hess promised. 'I'm afraid no foreign currency has been allotted for this unanticipated port call of ours. You don't have American dollars?'

'No, nor francs nor yen. There hasn't been the need.'

Hess neatly folded the paper and slipped it back inside his parka. Like a host who enjoys impromptu parties most, he said, 'Then you must be my guest. Come, Comrade Renko, I will show you the famous Dutch Harbor.'

They stood in the open hatches and breathed the sharp fumes of the water that was silky with oil. Arkady hadn't even been so near the surface of the water in ten months, let alone on land. As the lifeboat drew across the harbour he saw how the Aleut houses edged between mountain and bay, and how proudly they all seemed to march behind their white church with its onion dome. There were lights in the windows and human forms in the shadows, and the very existence of shadows seemed miraculous after a year's staring into fog. And the smell was overwhelming: the briny tang of the beach's grey sand and, powerful as gravity, the sweet breath of green grass and mosses. There was even a graveyard with Orthodox crosses, as if people could be buried without sinking directly to the ocean floor.

The lifeboat was built with a miniature bridge, but the helmsman, a blond-haired boy in a heavy sweater, used the outside wheel. Behind him, from a short pole, a Soviet ensign fluttered like a red hankie.

'Built for the war and then allowed to fall apart,' Hess said and pointed to a house on the crest of a cliff. Half the house had fallen in, exposing stairs and rails like the inner workings of a seashell. Looking around, Arkady saw half a dozen more Army-grey structures on other hills. 'That was the war when we were allies,' Hess added for the sake of the young helmsman.

'As you say, chief,' the helmsman said.

Protected by encircling land, the inner bay was calm. A mirrored, inverted ring of undulating green surrounded the lifeboat.

'That was before you were born,' Arkady said to the boy. He recognized him now, a radio technician named Nicolai. He looked like a recruiting poster – cornsilk hair, cornflower-blue eyes, and the big shoulders and indolent smile of an athlete.

'That was my grandfather's war,' he said.

Immediately Arkady felt ancient, but he pressed the conversation. 'Where did he serve?'

'Murmansk. He went to America and back ten times,' Nicolai said. 'Two boats were sunk under him.'

'But it's hard work, too, what you do.'

Nicolai shrugged. 'Mental work.'

By now Arkady recognized the voice of Zina's lieutenant. He could see Nicolai confidently navigating among the waitresses at the Golden Horn, the stars on his shoulder boards glittering, his cap askew. It occurred to Arkady, not for the first time, that he hadn't been attacked until he'd gone searching for Hess's assistant.

'Such a handsome harbour.' Hess's eyes wandered from the tank farm to the mile-long concrete dock to the radio tower on the hill, as if he were reviewing the charms of an uncharted tropical isle.

Perhaps no one had seen him climb down to the boat, Arkady thought. How simple it would be to dispose of him. It was a common enough practice for ships to dump their weighted garbage as they entered port. There was an extra anchor and chain inside every lifeboat.

But the lifeboat continued to slide over the iridescent surface, past the wet, primary colours of catcherboats that Arkady had never seen before, near enough to watch men hosing decks and hoisting nets to repair, and to hear shouts from docks previously hidden behind the slate-blue hull of the cannery ship.

As the hills closed in and the harbour narrowed to an inlet, Arkady glimpsed pinpoints of Arctic flowers and seams of snow hidden in the grass. The air carried the throaty taste of woodsmoke. As they cleared the cannery ship, the inlet trailed into a stream and he saw docks of smaller boats, including purse seiners no bigger than rowboats, a couple of single-engine sea-planes and the unmistakable orange of the first lifeboat from the *Polar Star*. Slava Bukovsky was on guard, watching with surprise that turned to dismay as the second lifeboat approached. Beyond Slava were dogs nosing around refuse heaps, eagles roosting on roofs and, most miraculous of all, men walking on dry land.

Chapter Eighteen

Forgotten were Siberian orchids. Kolya stood at the end of the aisle like a traveller faced by three signposts. To his left was a stack of stereo receivers with digital tuning and chrome, five-band graphic equalizers and black hi-tech speakers. To his right was a tier of twin-deck, Dolby-equipped cassette players that could not only play but could propagate tapes like rabbits. Straight ahead was a veritable tower of suitcase-sized receivers with cassette decks in a variety of pink, turquoise and ivory high-impact plastics for recording Western music right off the air. Kolya dared not look behind because there were racks of pocket cassette players, key chains that beeped when you clapped, cassette-fed toy bears that talked, calculator watches that recorded your mileage and took your pulse, the dizzying and proliferating armoury of a civilization based on the silicon chip.

Kolya dealt with this alien situation with time-honoured Soviet technique, stepping back and with snake eyes examining each article as if it were a tub of rancid butter, an excellent attitude in the Soviet Union, where the shelf for items 'broken when bought' was sometimes fuller than the display case; no experienced Soviet shopper left a store with his purchase until he'd taken it out of its box, turned it on and made sure it did *something*. Soviet shoppers also searched for the date of completion on the manufacturer's tag and hoped for a day in the middle of the month, rather than at the end, when the factory management was trying to meet its quota of TVs, VCRs, or cars with or without all the necessary parts, or at the beginning of the month, when the workers were in a drunken stupor from having met the quota. Here there was no shelf overflowing with defective goods, nor any dates on the manufacturers' tags, so having finally reached their destination, Kolya and a hundred other Soviet men and women now stood numbed before the foreign radios, calculators and other electronic exotica they had dreamed of.

'Arkady!' Kolya was overjoyed to see him. 'You've travelled before. Where are the clerks?'

It was true there didn't appear to be any. A Soviet store is amply staffed because a shopper must buy in three stages: securing a chit from one clerk, paying a second, exchanging the receipt with a third – all of whom are far too interested in personal conversations or the telephone to take kindly the interruption of some stranger who has come off the street. Besides, Soviet clerks hide any quality stuff – fresh fish, new translations, Hungarian bras – under the counter or in the back of the store, and they're people with pride, who are in no hurry to sell inferior goods. The entire business is distasteful to them.

'Try her,' Arkady suggested.

A grandmotherly woman smiled from a counter. She wore a mohair sweater as white as an Arctic fox, and her hair was an astonishing silver-blue. Spread out on the counter before her were sliced oranges, apples and crackers smeared with pâté. A card on an electric urn said in Russian, 'Coffee'. There was also a cash register, and she was taking money from some sophisticated seamen who simply carried their stereos to her. At her back a large sign announced, again in Russian, 'Dutch Harbor Welcomes the Polar Star!'

Kolya seemed relieved until another thought struck him. 'Arkady, what are you doing here? You don't have the right visa.'

'I have special dispensation.'

Arkady was still trying to get his land legs. There was roll and pitch even on a factory ship and after ten months his body didn't trust level, motionless ground. The fluorescent lights and shiny colours of the store displays seemed to swim around him.

'I thought you were a factory worker, and you become an investigator,' Kolya said. 'I thought you couldn't go ashore, and suddenly you're here.'

'I'm confused myself,' Arkady admitted.

Although Kolya had more questions, his eyes had lit on a rack of blank, low-bias cassette tapes which held a magnetic attraction for him. Arkady had caught a few other astonished glances in his direction, but everyone was too busy in this brief paradise to ask questions. One figure did stop; from the end of an aisle, the informer Slezko gawked in alarm, a gold tooth brightening his grey face. In his hands was a box of electric rollers; evidence that somewhere there was a Mrs Slezkova.

'Ugggh.' A machinist recoiled from his first bite of a cracker. 'What kind of meat is in this pâté?'

'Peanuts,' Izrail told him. 'It's peanut butter.'

'Oh.' The machinist took another nibble. 'Not bad.'

'Renko, you're a regular Lazarus,' Izrail said. 'You keep popping up. This business with Zina, it's not over, is it? I see your look of determination and my heart sinks.'

'Arkady, you came!' Natasha seized his arm as if he had appeared at a ball. 'This proves it. You are a trustworthy citizen or they wouldn't have let you. What did Volovoi say?'

'I can't wait to hear,' Arkady said. 'What did you buy so far?'

She blushed. The only purchase in her net bag was two oranges. 'Clothes are upstairs,' she said. 'Jeans, jogging gear, running shoes.'

'Bathrobes and slippers,' Madame Malzeva butted in.

Gury had strapped on a heavy safari watch with a compass built into the strap. He turned in different directions as he moved to the counter, like a man dancing alone. 'Apple?' the woman with blue hair offered him a slice.

'Yamaha.' Gury tried his English. 'Software, programmes, blank disks.'

Without money, Arkady felt like a voyeur. As the two women swept towards the stairs, he retreated in the opposite direction. Passing by the food aisles he saw Lidia Taratuta cramming her bag with instant coffee. Two mechanics shared a box of ice-cream popsicles; they leaned against a freezer, popsicles in hand, like a pair of drunks. How could they resist? Soviet advertising consisted of the directive 'Buy . . .!' The package might bear a star, a flag or a factory's profile. In contrast, American packaging was promiscuously splashed with colour pictures of untouchably beautiful women and winsome children enjoying 'New and Improved' products. Lidia had moved on to detergents and was starting to fill a shopping cart.

Even Arkady stopped at the produce section. Yes, the lettuce was browning and wrapped in Cellophane, the bananas were liverspotted with age, and the grapes were many of them split and weeping, but they were the first uncanned, unsyruped fruit he had seen in four months, so he paused long enough to pay his respects. Then the only member of the *Polar Star*'s crew able to resist the blandishments of capitalism went out into the road.

The northern afternoon had settled into a slowly dimming light that revealed as gently as possible the wide plaza of mud that was the centre of Dutch Harbor. On one side was the store, on the other the hotel. Both were prefabricated shells of ribbed metal walls and sliding windows, and were so long they suggested that some lower floors had sunk into the mud and disappeared. A score of smaller prefabricated houses took shelter on the lower ridge of a hill. There were shipping containers and dumpsters for storage and trash, and stray, unravelling heaps of suction hose used for offloading fish. Mostly there was mud. The roads were frozen waves of mud;

panel trucks and vans rocked like boats as they moved across the plaza, and each vehicle wore a skirt of mud. Every man-made structure was earthtoned, ochre or tan, a calculated surrender to mud. Even the snow was stained with it, yet Arkady could have lain down and wallowed in it, in the unyielding, toothy grip of cold mud.

A dozen Soviets stood outside the store, either because they were putting off the climactic act of shopping or because sheer excitement made them take a break and step out for a cigarette. They stood in a circle, as if it were safer to look at the town over another man's shoulder.

'It's not so different from home, you know,' said one. 'This could be Siberia.'

'We use pre-formed concrete,' said another.

'The point is, it's just like Volovoi said. I didn't believe him.'

'This is a typical American town?' asked a third.

'That's what the first mate said.'

'It's not what I expected.'

'We use concrete.'

'That's not the point.'

Looking around, Arkady saw three roads leading from the square: one along the bay to the tank farm, a second to the Aleut side of the bay and a third headed inland. Earlier, from the ship, he had noticed other anchorages and an airport on the island.

The conversation continued. 'All those foods, all those radios. You think it's normal? I saw a documentary. The reason their stores have so much food is that people don't have any money to buy it.'

'Come on.'

'True. Posner said it on television. He likes Americans, but he said it.'

Arkady took out a Belomor, though a papirosa seemed out of place. He noticed that the store also housed a bank on the first floor and some offices on the second. In the early dusk their lights had a stove-grate warmth. Across the road, the hotel had smaller, blearier windows, except for the blazing plate-glass front to a liquor store which the crew had been warned to avoid.

'There's a place like that at home. A seamen's hostel, ten kopeks a night. I wonder how much that is?'

'I wonder how many men to a room?'

The second floor of the hotel overhung the first, making a protected walkway that must have served during the rainy season or when snow piled high during the winter. On the other hand, the population of Dutch Harbor would halve in November when the fishing season ended.

'The point is, all your life you hear about a place and it becomes fantastic. Like a friend of mine went to Egypt. He read up on pharaohs and temples and pyramids. He came back with diseases you wouldn't believe.'

'Sshh, here comes one now.'

A woman about thirty was headed for the store. Her hair had been teased into a yellow froth and her face was made up into a pout. In spite of the cold, she only wore a short rabbitskin jacket, jeans and cowboy boots.

The circle of Soviet cosmopolitans admired the view of the bay. An African warrior with a spear could have walked by them without their attention wavering from the water. Not until she was past did they glance after her.

'Not bad.'

'Not so different.'

'That's my point. Not better.' This one kicked at the mud appreciatively, inhaled deeply and gave the dour hotel, hills and bay an authoritative sweep of his eyes.

'I like it.'

One by one they killed their cigarettes, tacitly arranged themselves into the prescribed groups of four and, working up their courage with an interchange of shrugs and nods, began moving back into the store. 'I wonder,' one asked on the way, 'can you buy those boots here?'

Arkady was thinking of the end of *Crime and Punishment*, of Raskolnikov redeemed on the bank overlooking the sea. Maybe he had been seduced in part by Dostoevsky's picture of the intelligent interrogator into becoming an investigator himself; yet here, at this midpoint in life, by some twist he wasn't the police but the criminal, a kind of unconvicted convict standing by the Pacific, just like Raskolnikov, but on the other side of the ocean. How long before Volovoi had him dragged back to the ship? Would he cling to the ground like a crab when they did so? He knew he didn't want to go. It was so restful, to stand still in the shadow of a hill and to know that the hill, fixed, unlike a wave, was not going to slide underfoot. The grass trembling in the breeze would still be on that same slope tomorrow. Clouds would collect at the same peaks and light like flames at sunset. The mud itself would freeze and melt according to the season, but it would still be there.

'I saw you and couldn't believe it.' Susan had come out of the hotel and crossed the road. Her jacket, the one she had worn from the boat, was askew, her hair was rumpled and her eyes were wild, as if she'd been crying. 'Then I said to myself, of course he's here. I mean, I had almost believed that someone on the slime line might just possibly have been, long ago, a detective. And spoke English. After all, that's the sort of man who would have gotten into so much trouble that he wouldn't have a visa to come ashore. It was just possible. Then I look out the lobby door and who do I see? You. Standing here like you own the island.'

At first he thought she was drunk. Women drink, even Americans. He saw Hess and Marchuk emerge from the hotel, followed by George Morgan. All three were in shirtsleeves, though the captain of the *Eagle* still wore his cap.

'What is today's story?' Susan asked. 'What is the operative fairytale?'

'Zina killed herself,' Arkady said.

'And as your reward you come ashore? Does that make sense to you?'

'No,' Arkady confessed.

'Let's try it a different way.' She aimed her finger at

him as if it were a sharp stick extended at a snake. 'You killed her and as your reward you come ashore. Now *that* makes sense.'

Morgan grabbed the sleeve of Susan's jacket and pulled her away from Arkady. 'Will you think about what you're saying?'

'You two bastards.' She swung her arm free. 'You probably cooked it up together.'

'All I'm asking,' Morgan told her, 'is that you think about what you're saying.'

She attempted to return to Arkady by going around Morgan, but he held his arms out.

'What a pair you make,' she said.

'Calm down.' Morgan tried a soothing voice. 'Don't say anything that we're all going to regret. Because it can get very messy, Susan, you know that.'

'What a perfect pair of bastards.' She turned away in disgust and stared at the sky – a trick, Arkady knew, to hold in tears.

When Morgan began, 'Susan—', she silenced him by holding up her hand, and without another word started back to the hotel.

Morgan turned a bent smile towards Arkady. 'Sorry, I don't know what that was about.'

Susan pushed between Marchuk and Hess as she went into the hotel. They joined Morgan and Arkady in the road. The Soviet captain already had the glitter of a man who has had a drink or two. It was cold enough now for breath to show. There was an air of male embarrassment about Susan's behaviour.

'Of course,' Morgan said, 'she has just learned that her replacement had to go back to Seattle. She's going to have to stay on the *Polar Star*.'

'That could do it,' Arkady said.

Chapter Nineteen

Arkady and the two other Soviets had beers at a table that was redwood caramelized in plastic. As a body bounced against the shoulder-high partition that separated them from the bar, Marchuk observed, 'When Americans get drunk they get loud. A Russian gets more serious. He drinks until he falls with dignity, like a tree.' He pondered his beer for a moment. 'You're not going to run on us?'

'No,' Arkady said.

'Understand, it's one thing to take a man off the slime line and let him loose on the ship. It's another to let him off the ship. What do you think happens to a master whose seaman defects? A master who allows a man with your visa to go ashore?' He leaned forward, as if pinning Arkady's eyes. 'You tell me.'

'They probably still need a watchman in Norilsk.'

'I'll tell you. I'll come after you and kill you myself. Of course, you have my wholehearted support. But I thought you should know.'

'Cheers.' Arkady liked an honest man.

'Congratulations.' George Morgan pulled up a chair and touched his bottle to Arkady's. 'I understand you solved your mystery. Suicide?'

'She left a note.'

'Lucky.' Morgan was the unruffled man in control again. Not a black-bearded tiger like Marchuk or gnome like Hess, but a professional's smooth face pierced by two blue eyes.

'We were just saying what an unusual place Dutch Harbor is,' Hess said.

'We're closer to the North Pole than to the rest of the States,' Morgan said. 'It's strange.'

Different, Arkady thought. A Soviet bar was quiet, a gathering place for sedated men; this bar was explosive with sound. Along the counter was a crowd of big men in plaid shirts and caps, with long hair and beards and a physical ease that seemed to naturally lead to backslapping and drinking from the bottle. The crowd and noise was doubled by a long mirror above a gemstone row of bottles. In a corner, Aleuts played pool. There were women at the tables, girls with drawn faces and extravagantly blonde hair, but they were mostly ignored, except for a circle of them where Ridley held court. Morgan's engineer also distinguished himself from the crowd by wearing a velvet shirt and a gold chain; he looked like a Renaissance prince mingling with peasants.

He came over to Arkady. 'The ladies want to know if you have a two-headed prick.'

'What is normal here?' Arkady asked.

'Nothing is normal here. Look at it, all these sea-going American entrepreneurs completely dependent on you Communists. It's true. The banks had the fishermen's balls in the drawer because they'd all borrowed during the king-crab boom. That's why even Gulf boats like ours are up here. When the crabs disappeared, everyone was losing boats, gear, cars, homes. We'd be pumping gas if we weren't fishing. Then the Russians come along in '78 and buy anything we catch. Thank God for international cooperation. We'd be on our asses if it were up to the United States. You want strange? That's it.'

'How much do you make?'

'Ten, twelve thousand a month.'

Arkady figured he himself made about one hundred dollars at a realistic black market exchange.

'That's strange,' he had to admit.

In their corner, under a hanging fluorescent light, the Aleuts played pool with sombre concentration. They wore caps, parkas and dark glasses, all but Mike, the deckhand off the *Eagle*. He whooped as the cue ball rolled toward a pocket, nudged another ball in and stopped short of a scratch. Three Aleut girls in pastel quilted coats sat along one wall, their heads together, talking. A white girl sat alone by the other wall, her jaw working on gum, her eyes following Mike's shots, ignoring the others.

'The Aleuts own the whole island,' Ridley said to Arkady. 'The Navy threw them off during the war, then Carter gave them the whole place back, so they don't need to fish. Mike, he just loves the sea.'

'And you?' Arkady asked. 'You love it too?'

Ridley not only brushed his hair into a ponytail and tied braids by his ears, but seemed to have supercharged his eyes and sharp smile. 'Fucking hate it. It's an

MARTIN CRUZ SMITH

unnatural act to float steel on water. Salt water is your
enemy. It tears iron apart. Life is short enough.'

'Your shipmate Coletti was in the police?'

'A patrolman, not a bilingual investigator like you.
Unless you count Italian.'

The Scotch came and Morgan poured.

Ridley said, 'What I miss at sea is civilization, because
civilization is women, and that's where the *Polar Star*
has us beat. Take Christ and Freud and Karl Marx, put
them in a boat for six months and they'd be the same
as us, just as foul-mouthed and primitive.'

'Your engineer is a philosopher,' Hess told Morgan.
'In fact, in the fifties we used to have cannery ships off
Kamchatka that had about seven hundred women and a
dozen men. They canned crabs. The process demanded
that no metal be in contact with the crab, so we used a
special lining produced in America. However, as a moral
point, your government ordered no more lining for those
Communist cans. Our crab industry collapsed.'

Arkady remembered the stories. There had been riots
on board the ships, women raping the men. Not a lot
of civilization.

'To joint ventures.' Morgan raised his glass.

Pool wasn't played in the Soviet Union, but Arkady
remembered the GIs in Germany and their obsession
with the game. Mike seemed to be winning, and gathering good-luck kisses from his gum-chewing girlfriend.
If the tsar hadn't sold Alaska, would the Aleuts be pushing pawns on a chessboard?

Ridley followed Arkady's eyes. 'Aleuts used to hunt

sea otters for Russia. They used to go after sea lions, walrus, whales. Today they're busy renting docks to Exxon. A bunch of Native American capitalists now. Not like us.'

'You and me?'

'Sure. The truth is fishermen have more in common with each other than with anyone on land. For example, people on land love sea lions. When I see a sea lion I see a thief. When you go by the Shelikoff Islands they're lying in wait for you – gangs of them, forty, fifty at a time. They're not afraid; they come right up on the net. Hell, they weigh six hundred, seven hundred pounds each. They're like goddamned bears.'

'Sea lions,' Hess explained to Marchuk, who rolled his eyes in understanding.

'They do two things,' Ridley said. 'They don't just grab a single fish from the net and jump. No, they take a bite out of the belly of each fish. If it's salmon in the net, they're stealing $50 a bite. Second, when he's tired of that, the son of a bitch grabs one last fish and dives in the water. Then he does something real cute. He comes to the surface with the fish in his mouth and waves it at you. Like saying, 'Fuck you, sucker.' That's what Magnums were made for. I don't think anything less than a Magnum will even slow a big male. What do you use?'

Hess carefully translated what Marchuk said. 'Officially they are protected.'

'Yeah, that's what I said too. We have a whole armoury

for them in the *Eagle*. They should be protected.' Ridley nodded.

Ridley had an ambidextrous quality, it seemed to Arkady, an ability to play both the charmer and the thug, all the while looking like a poet. The engineer had fixed on him as well. 'From your expression,' he said, 'you think it's murder.'

'Who?' Arkady asked.

'Not who. What,' Ridley said. 'Sea lions.'

Marchuk raised his glass. 'The main thing is that whether we're Soviets or Americans, we're all fishermen and are doing what we like to do. To happy men.'

' "Happiness is the absence of pain." ' Ridley drained his glass and set it down. 'Now I'm happy. Tell me,' he asked Arkady, 'working down on the slime line all wet and cold and covered in fish guts, are you happy?'

'We use a different adage on the slime line,' Arkady said. ' "Happiness is the maximum agreement of reality and desire." '

'Good answer. I'll drink to that,' Morgan said. 'That's Tolstoy?'

'Stalin,' Arkady said. 'Soviet philosophy is full of surprises.'

'From you, yes,' Susan said. How long she'd been standing by the table Arkady didn't know. Her hair was combed back wet and her cheeks were damp and pale, making her mouth redder and her brown eyes darker, the contrast lending her a new intensity.

*

Ridley had gone off with Coletti in search of a card game. Marchuk had returned to the ship to give Volovoi his turn ashore. Once the first mate learned that Arkady was on shore he would fly like a winged hangman. Still, two hours on land was better than none. Even in a bar, every minute on shore was like breathing air again.

Though the noise level continued to rise, Arkady noticed it less and less. Susan sat with her legs tucked underneath her. Her face was in shadow within a ring of golden hair. Her usual veneer of animosity had split, revealing a darker, more interesting plane.

'I detest Volovoi, but I can believe in him easier than I can believe in you.'

'Here I am.'

'Dedicated to truth, justice and the Soviet way?'

'Dedicated to getting off the ship.'

'That's the joke. We're both going back and I'm not even Russian.'

'Then quit.'

'I can't.'

'Who's forcing you to stay?' Arkady asked.

She lit a cigarette, added Scotch to her ice, didn't answer.

'So we'll suffer together,' Arkady said.

George Morgan and Hess shared their bottle. 'Imagine,' Hess suggested, 'if we did everything as a joint venture.'

'If we really cooperated?' Morgan asked.

'Did away with suspicion and stopped trying to pull each other down. What natural partners we would be.'

MARTIN CRUZ SMITH

'We take the Japanese, you take the Chinese?'

'Split the Germans while we can.'

'How would you describe Hell?' she asked Arkady.

He thought about it. 'A Party Congress. A four-hour speech by the Secretary General. No, an eternal speech. The delegates spread out like flatfish listening to a speech that goes on and on and on.'

'An imaginary evening with Volovoi. Watching him lift weights. Either he's naked or I'm naked. Whichever, it's horrible.'

'He calls you "Soo-san".'

'So do you. What's a name you say better?'

'Irina.'

'Describe her.'

'Light brown hair, very dark brown eyes. Tall. Full of life and spirit.'

'She's not on the *Polar Star*.'

'No.'

'She's home?'

Arkady changed the subject. 'They like you on the *Polar Star*.'

'I like Russians, but I don't like having my cabin bugged. If I mention there's no butter, suddenly I'm served a plate of butter. Bernie has a political discussion with a deckhand and the man is taken off the ship. At first you try not to say anything offensive, but after a while to keep your sanity you start talking about Volovoi and his slugs. The *Polar Star* is hell to me. You?'

'Only limbo.'

'It can all be joint venture,' said Hess. 'The shortest

sea route between Europe and the Pacific is through the Arctic and we could provide the icebreakers the same way the *Polar Star* leads the *Eagle* through the ice sheet.'

'And depend on you?' Morgan asked. 'I don't think things have changed *that* much.'

'You liked Zina,' Arkady said. 'You gave her your swimsuit, you let her borrow your sunglasses. In return, she gave you . . . what?'

Susan took a long time to answer; it was like holding a conversation in the dark with a black cat. 'Amusement,' she said finally.

'You told her about California, she told you about Vladivostok, an even trade?'

'She was a combination of innocence and guile. A Russian Norma Jean.'

'I don't understand.'

'Norma Jean bleached her hair and became Marilyn Monroe. Zina Patiashvili bleached her hair and remained Zina Patiashvili. Same ambition, different result.'

'You were friends.'

She refilled his glass so full that the Scotch swelled like oil above the rim, then did the same for herself. 'This is a Norwegian drinking game,' she said. 'The first one to spill has to drink. Lose twice and you sit in a chair while the other person hits you on the head and tries to knock you over.'

'We'll do it without the hitting. So, you and Zina were friends,' Arkady repeated.

'The *Polar Star* is like a deprivation tank. You know how rare it is to meet someone who actually seems to be alive and unpredictable? The problem is that you Soviets have a peculiar idea of friends. We're all peace-loving peoples of goodwill, but God forbid an American and a Soviet should get too close. Then the Soviet is next heard of on a ship off New Zealand.'

'Zina wasn't shipped off.'

'No, so we knew she was informing on us, at least to some degree. And I was willing to accept it because she was so alive, so naïve, so much fun, so much smarter than any of the men knew.'

'Which of your men did she sleep with?'

'How do you know she slept with someone?'

'She always did; it was the way she operated. If there were four American men on board she slept with at least one of them.'

'Lantz.'

Arkady remembered Lantz, the thin, languid observer from the sauna. 'After that, you warned her off? It wouldn't have been Volovoi.' Arkady took a sip. 'Good Scotch.'

Overfilled, the surface of the drink trembled but didn't break. Neon light lay on it like a moon.

'Who do you sleep with on the *Polar Star*?' she asked.

'No one.'

'Then the *Polar Star* is a deprivation tank for you too. I drink to you.'

For the first time, Morgan raised his head in her direction, then returned to a description by Hess of the latest invasion of Moscow. 'The Japanese are everywhere, at least in the best hotels. The best restaurant in Moscow is Japanese, but you can't get in because it's full of them.'

Arkady said, 'Zina told you about herself and Captain Marchuk, didn't she? Is that why you didn't tell me you saw them at the stern rail during the dance, so that you wouldn't embarrass him?'

'It was dark.'

'He didn't think she was suicidal. You talked to her, did you think she was depressed?'

'Are you depressed?' Susan asked. 'Are you suicidal?'

Arkady was thrown off the track again. He was out of practice at interrogation, too slow, too swayed by the counterflow of her questions.

'No, I would describe myself as a carefree reveller in life. I was more carefree when I was a Party member, of course.'

'I bet.'

'It's harder to get in trouble if you have a card.'

'Really. Like how?'

'Take smuggling. Without a Party card, tragedy. With a Party card, comedy.'

'How is that?'

'A drama. Say the second mate gets caught. He goes before the other officers and sobs, "I don't know what came over me, comrades. I have never done anything like it before. Please give me a chance to redeem myself." '

'So?' Susan had been lured into the light.

Hess and Morgan had fallen silent, listening.

'A vote is taken,' Arkady said, 'and a decision is

reached to place a severe reprimand on his Party record. Two months pass and another meeting is held.'

'Yes?' Susan said.

'The captain says, "We were all disappointed in the conduct of our second mate and there were times I felt I would never sail with him again, but now I see a sincere effort to redeem himself." '

'The political officer says . . .' Susan prompted him.

'The political officer says, "He has drunk again from the clear wellsprings of Communist thought. I suggest that, taking into consideration his spiritual rebirth, the severe reprimand be removed from his Party record." What could be more comic?'

Susan said, 'You're a funny man, Renko.'

'He's an angry man,' said Hess.

'That's how it ends if you're a Party member,' Arkady said, 'but if you're not a Party member, if you're just a worker and are caught smuggling videotapes or gems, the outcome is not comical or humane. Then it's five years in a labour camp.'

'Tell me more about Irina,' Susan said. 'She sounds interesting; where is she?'

'I don't know.'

'Somewhere . . .' She spread her arms to indicate the vaguest of directions. 'Out there?'

'Some people are like that,' Arkady said. 'You know, there's a North Pole and a South Pole. There's another place called the Pole of Inaccessibility. Once it was thought that all the ice in the Arctic Sea turned around one point, a mythical pole surrounded by wheeling floes impossible to cross. I think that's where she is.' Without a pause he asked, 'Was Zina depressed the night of the dance?'

'I didn't say I talked to her.'

'If you'd warned her off the Americans on the *Polar Star*, then wouldn't you warn her off the Americans on the *Eagle*?'

'She said she'd found true love. You can't stop that.'

'What exactly were her words?'

'That no one could stop her.'

'If you're talking about Mike,' Morgan spoke up, 'they only met at a couple of dances. Otherwise all they did was wave at each other. Anyway, all my men were back on my boat, so what does it matter?'

'Unless she was murdered,' Susan said.

Morgan reacted with the thin smile of a man whose patience for the simple-minded was wearing thin, and he seemed to find everyone but Hess in that category, Arkady thought.

'I'm out of cigarettes,' Susan said. 'There's a machine in the lobby. Are you allowed to come?' she asked Arkady.

He looked towards Hess, who slowly nodded. Morgan shook his head at Susan, but she ignored him.

'We'll just be a second,' she said.

The machine offered a dozen brands, like flavours. Susan, though, didn't have the correct change.

'I know you don't have any.'

'No,' Arkady said.

'I have cigarettes in my room. Come on.'

Susan's room was on the second floor at the far end

267

of the hall, a gamut of sounds. Each room had a different argument or played a different tape. She touched the walls twice for balance's sake and Arkady wondered how drunk she was.

She unlocked the door to a room not much larger than her cabin on the *Polar Star*, but offered twin beds, shower, telephone and, instead of a built-in Soviet radio with two stations, a television on a desk. The bureau held a disarray of Scotch, plastic ice bucket, gooseneck lamp. The beds were by the window and though it was thin and dirty, not even double-paned, Arkady felt bathed in utter luxury.

Outside, the sun was gone and Dutch Harbor drifted in the dark. From a hotel guestroom Arkady watched his shipmates emerge from the store and gather on the road, reluctant to walk to the dock even though their arms were weighed down with plastic and string bags stuffed with their purchases. They were used to standing in line for hours to buy one pineapple or one pair of stockings. This was nothing, this was heaven. Polaroid cameras flashed, capturing a closed rank of friends, blue-white in an American port. Natasha and Dynka. Lidia and Olimpiada. On a hill above the tank farm a fire burned like a beacon. Ridley said there were fires all the time, kids torching the wooden structures left from the war. Fog had thickened around the hill, turning the flames to a soft furze of light.

Arkady found the light switch and turned it on. 'What did you mean when you said that Morgan and I had "cooked up" something together?'

'Captain Morgan is not too careful about the company he keeps.' Susan turned the switch off. 'I guess I'm not either.'

'Someone tried to kill me two days ago.'

'On the *Polar Star*?'

'Where else?'

'No more questions.' Her hand was on his mouth. 'You seem to be for real,' she said, 'but I know you have to be a fake because everything is fake. Remember the poem?'

Her eyes seemed so dark that he wondered how much he'd had to drink. He could smell the dampness in her hair.

'Yes.' He knew which one she meant.

'Say it.'

' "Tell me how men kiss you." '

Susan leaned into him and rose at the same time, bringing her face up to his. Strange. A man considers himself nearly dead, cold, inert; then the right flame appears and he flies into it like a moth.

Her lips opened to his. 'If you were real,' she said.

'As real as you.'

He lifted her and carried her to the bed. Through the window he saw that the plaza outside was as bright with camera flashes as a celebration of silent fire-crackers, a last wave of picture-taking before the happy visitors, his shipmates, decamped for the dock. Out on the road, a camera's bright flash illuminated Natasha as she posed coquettishly, jacket open to a glass necklace, her head tossed in profile to display crystal earrings. Arkady felt oddly like a traitor seeing her from a hotel window.

He stood poised above the bed, at one of those points that make the difference in the rest of a lifetime. On the road a blue flash illuminated Gury and Natasha, and incidentally froze Mike, the Aleut, as he was leaving the hotel.

'What's the matter?' Susan asked.

Another flash bathed a happy Madame Malzeva with a bolt of satin, and also caught Volovoi rushing in the hotel door.

'I have to go,' Arkady said.

'Why?' Susan asked.

'Volovoi's here. He's looking for me.'

'You're going with him?'

'No.'

'You're going to run?' She sat up.

'No. I couldn't on this island even if I wanted to. You depend on us too much. Who else would the fishermen here sell their fish to? Who else comes all this way to buy stereos and shoes? If any Soviet tried to run here, you'd throw him back as fast as you could catch him.'

'Then where are you going?'

'I don't know. Not back. Not yet.'

Chapter Twenty

As he climbed the hill, Arkady felt the thick grasses softly yielding, then springing up behind his step. Behind him, the hotel lay bathed in electric light, its bright windows banked in mid-air above the walkway, which was a shaft of still, white light. A figure on the walkway seemed to move in slow motion. Volovoi looking right, then left.

The last few Soviets were joining the crowd on the road, and some of them were already moving towards the docks, like the vanguard of a herd. Some of the men lingered while Lantz visited the liquor store. Returning, he distributed pints of vodka, which they stuffed in their pants. Natasha and Lidia lingered too, as if to give the evening a last embrace. America? With so many Soviets in the street it could have been a Russian village, with Russian dogs barking in the yards, Russian grass blanketing the hills. Arkady imagined Kolya off in the dark digging up tender orchids, and Obidin entering the doorway of the church.

He had crossed the road away from the hotel and worked his way through the dumpsters beside the store. The building had windows only in front, so he slipped into the shadows in back, then manoeuvred between the pre-fab housing on the ridge, long metal homes with aluminium windows bathed in shifting colours of television sets. A couple of dogs, black-and-white animals with pale eyes, challenged him, but no owner appeared. The yards had pitfalls, auto parts and suction hoses covered by snow; but he slipped only once before reaching the hill. Mike was well ahead, keeping the beam of the flashlight on a path. So far he hadn't looked back.

Land was so seductive, dark but firm underfoot. Sometimes Arkady stepped on cushions of waterleaf or moss. Dried lupin brushed his hands. He couldn't so much see as sense the volcanic mountains rising like walls in the mist. Ahead, a fire lit one peak. Out in the harbour the lights of the ships at anchor were more distinct; the lamps of the *Polar Star* floated on a tilted sheet of black.

What if he did run? There were no trees to hide behind, few houses to beg at. There was an airport on the other side of the island. What could he do, jump on to a wheel as a plane took off?

Hummocks made climbing easy. Snow was cupped into the northern slope; there was just enough light to turn the drifts blue. After ten months at sea, it was like mounting heaven. A cold wind, a harbinger of the winter to come, stirred earthy vapours of berry bushes, parsley and moss. Mike seemed to be enjoying himself, too, following his flashlight at a leisurely pace.

Where the path joined a dirt road, the fog grew more intense. At points, the ground dropped away on either side, and Arkady could make out the difference between firm footing and air mainly by the sound of the sea breeze as it rushed up the face of the cliff. He knew which way to walk because the fire, though obscured, was closer and brighter, like a beacon.

Then, in a matter of steps, the fog dissipated and fell away. It was as if he had climbed to the surface of a second ocean and second set of mountains. The fog lay heavy, still and foamy white under a night sky as brilliantly clear as deep space. The mountain peaks floated like smaller islands, hideaways of sheer black rock and starlit ice.

The road ended at the fire. Around its glow Arkady saw signs of an abandoned military battery: earthworks turned to a grassy knoll, gunplates now rings of rust, a mare's nest of barbed wire. In the muffled tussling of the flames were boards, bed springs, oil cans and tyres. On the far side, Mike pulled open a heavy door built into the hill. For the first time, Arkady noticed that he carried a rifle.

The stars were so near. The Little Bear was still chained to Polaris. Orion's arm reached over the horizon as if tossing stars. In his ten months on the Bering Sea, Arkady had never seen a night so clear, yet they'd always been there, just above the fog.

He walked around the fire to the door. It was iron set in a concrete frame, an entrance to a wartime bunker. The concrete was chipped and stained with rust, but it had resisted both years and vandals. A new padlock hanging open on the hasp showed that someone had taken ownership and the door swung easily on the oiled hinges.

'Mike!' he yelled.

A kerosene lamp burned on the floor, and in its light Arkady saw that someone had done his best to turn the bunker into a fisherman's loft. A trawl net billowed artistically down from the ceiling. On the walls were shelves of starfish, abalone shells and jawbones of baby sharks. There was a cot and fruit-box bookcases stuffed with paperbacks and magazines, and barrels of salvaged webbing, twisted tow shackles and split corks.

When he saw the rifle on the cot, Arkady relaxed. 'Mike?'

On a stand and filling the entire middle of the bunker was the largest kayak Arkady had ever seen. It was at least six metres long, low and narrow, with two round hatches, and although it was only half finished an intrinsic sleekness and grace were evident. Arkady remembered the voice on Zina's tape describing a native boat, a *baidarka*, that the speaker would paddle around the *Polar Star*. The more he examined the boat the more impressed he was. The keel was wood, jointed with bone. The ribs were bent wood, lashed with sinew. He didn't see a nail in the whole construction. Only the sheath of the craft was a compromise with the modern age: a covering of fibreglass fabric sewn up to the rear hatch coaming by nylon thread held in place with a hemostat. On a workbench was an assortment of whittling knives and files, sail needles and twine, paint brushes, gas mask, electric hair dryer and half-gallon cans of epoxy resin. Epoxy was volatile material; pails of sand bracketed the bench and there was a toxic bite to the air from a sample that had been painted on the skin.

'Come on out,' Arkady called. 'I just want to talk.'

The way the bow of the craft split and curled backwards, Arkady could easily imagine the *baidarka* bending, riding lightly on the waves. He could also see why Zina was attracted to Mike. A 'merman' she had called him, a romantic who dreamed of sailing with her to all the points of the Pacific. How different from himself, who just wanted to stay on land.

The hairdryer meant there had to be power. Arkady found an extension cord on the floor and followed it to a blanket hanging on the end wall, pulled it aside and discovered a second, smaller room to the bunker. There was a gasoline generator, not running, with an exhaust pipe to a duct. A gasoline can lay on its side and a flashlight spilled its own light.

Just inside the doorway, Mike sprawled as if hugging the rough floor. The Aleut's left eye was open and had the sheen of dark wet rock. Arkady couldn't feel any breath or pulse. On the other hand, he didn't see any blood. Mike had walked into the bunker only steps ahead of him, had lit the kerosene lamp and then gone to the generator. Young men had heart attacks. He turned the Aleut over, unbuttoned his shirt and hit his chest while Mike watched with one eye.

'Come on,' Arkady urged.

Mike wore a religious medal on a chain of metal beads; it clinked at the back of his neck each time Arkady hit his chest. He was too warm to be dead, too young and strong, with a boat half built. 'Mikhail! Come on!'

Arkady opened Mike's mouth, blew in and inhaled

the taste of beer. He beat the chest again as if anyone inside could be roused. The medal clicked as Mike stared with a fading eye.

Or a stroke, Arkady thought, and put his fingers inside to clear the tongue. He touched something that felt improbably hard, and when he pulled his hand out, his fingertips were smeared red. He opened Mike's mouth as wide as he could, looked in with the flashlight and found a point emerging from the tongue like a silver thorn. Gently, he turned the boy's head to the side and brushed the thick black hair at the base of the skull away from two steel ovals that looked like an old-fashioned lorgnette tangled in the hair. American males had affectations: earrings, heavy finger rings, leather cuffs on long braids. But these two bright ovals were imbedded in the head, the handles of a pair of scissors that had been neatly driven like an ice pick, with hardly a drop of blood, halfway through the cranium. They were what Mike's medal had been hitting. One hand doesn't clap; one medal doesn't click. The body sagged gratefully as Arkady let it down.

Volovoi stepped into the bunker. After him came Karp.

'He's dead,' Arkady said.

The first mate and trawlmaster seemed more interested in the bunker than the body.

'Another suicide?' Volovoi asked as he looked around.

'You could say so.' Arkady stood. 'It's Mike from the *Eagle*. I followed him, and he was in here no more than a minute before me. No one came out. Whoever killed him could still be here.'

'I'm sure,' Volovoi said.

Arkady flashed the beam around the second room of the bunker. Except for the generator all it contained was bare walls scribbled with graffiti. There was a pool of water in one corner, and above it a shaft russet-striped with stains that led up through the bomb-proof ceiling to a closed hatch. The hatch was out of reach, though there were two broken flanges that had once supported steps.

'There must have been a rope here or a ladder,' Arkady said. 'Whoever got out probably pulled it up with him and then closed the hatch.'

'We were following you.' Karp took the rifle off the bed and admired it. 'We didn't seen anyone leave.'

'Why were you following an American?' Volovoi asked.

'Let's look outside,' Arkady said.

Karp blocked his way. 'Why were you following him?' Volovoi asked again.

'To ask him about Zin—'

'The inquiry is over,' Volovoi said. 'That's not a permissible reason to follow anyone. Or to leave the ship against orders, to disappear from your compatriots, to sneak alone at night out of a foreign port. But I'm not surprised, I'm not surprised by anything you do. Hit him.'

Karp jabbed the barrel like a spear into Arkady's back between the shoulder blades, then took a measured swing, like a farmer with a scythe, and drove the side of the barrel into the back of his knees. Arkady dropped on to the floor, gasping.

Volovoi sat on the cot and lit a cigarette. He plucked a well-thumbed magazine from the bookcase, opened the centrefold and tossed it aside, a flush of disgust spreading over his pink face.

'This proves my point. You've killed before, according to your file. Now you want to defect, to go over to the other side, to dishonour your shipmates and your ship the first chance you had. You picked the weakest of the Americans, this native, and when he wouldn't help, you killed him.'

'No.'

Volovoi glanced at Karp and the trawlmaster swung the rifle down on to Arkady's ribs. His jacket absorbed some of the force, but Karp was a powerful man and an enthusiastic assistant.

'The suicide note that Zina Patiashvili wrote', Volovoi said, 'was found in the dead girl's bed. I myself asked Natasha Chaikovskaya why you didn't search there. She told me you had, yet you didn't report a note.'

'Because it wasn't there.'

In spite of the bunker's dank cold, the first mate was sweating. Well, there was the climb, and Arkady had noticed in the past how interrogation was hard work for everyone involved. In the glare of the lamp, Volovoi's crewcut was a crown of radiant spikes. Of course Karp, who was doing all the heavy labour, perspired like Vulcan at his forge.

'You followed me together?' Arkady asked.

'I'm asking the questions. He still doesn't understand,' Volovoi complained to Karp.

Karp kicked Arkady in the stomach. So far it was all routine police work, Arkady thought, a good sign, still just intimidation, nothing irreversible. Then the trawl-master pinned Arkady's neck to the floor with the rifle stock and landed a more serious kick, one that endeavoured to enter the stomach and come out at the spine.

'Stop,' Volovoi said.

'Why?' asked Karp. His boot was cocked for a third go.

'Wait.' Volovoi smiled indulgently; a leader could not explain everything to an associate.

Arkady rose to one elbow. It was important not to be totally inert.

'I expected something like this,' Volovoi said. 'Restructuring may be necessary in Moscow, but we're far from Moscow. Here we know that when you move rocks you stir up snakes. We're going to make an example.'

'Of what?' Arkady asked, trying to hold up his end of the conversation.

'An example of how dangerous it can be to encourage elements like you.'

Arkady dragged himself against the workbench. He didn't sit up; he didn't want to appear too comfortable. 'I don't feel encouraged,' he said. 'You were thinking of a trial?'

Karp said, 'Not a trial. You haven't seen him in front of a judge, the way he twists words.'

'I didn't kill this boy,' Arkady said. 'If you didn't, then whoever did this is walking down the hill right now.'

He ducked because he saw the rifle stock coming, so instead of crushing his face it swept the cans off the workbench, and he became more worried, because while he could tolerate an officially authorized beating kept within certain rough bounds, this was getting out of control.

'Comrade Korobetz!' Volovoi warned Karp. 'That's enough.'

'He's just going to lie,' Karp said.

Volovoi said to Arkady, 'Korobetz is not an intellectual, but he is an outstanding worker and he accepts the direction of the Party, something you never did.'

Except for a white seam across the middle of his narrow forehead where the skin had been removed, Karp's face was red.

'Your direction?' Arkady hunched closer to a whittling knife that had fallen with the cans.

'We caught him running, we caught him killing someone,' Karp insisted. 'He doesn't have to be alive.'

'That's not your decision,' Volovoi said. 'There are hard questions to be asked and answered. Such as who, knowing how dangerous and unstable a personality Renko is, persuaded the captain to set him loose in a foreign port? What was Renko planning with this ring of Americans? New Thinking is necessary to increase the productivity of labour, but in terms of political discipline our country has become slack. A year ago he would never have been allowed ashore. That's why an example is so important.'

'I haven't done anything,' Arkady said.

Volovoi had thought about it. 'There's your provocative investigation, your attempt to sway the trusting captain and crew of the *Polar Star*, your defection as soon as your feet hit foreign soil. Who knows what else you've been involved in? We'll tear the entire ship apart, rip out every bulkhead and tank. Marchuk will get the message. All the captains will get the message.'

'But Renko's not a smuggler,' Karp said.

'Who knows? Besides, we'll always find something. When I'm done the *Polar Star* will be in small pieces.'

'You call that restructuring?' Karp asked.

Volovoi lost patience. 'Korobetz, I'm not going to debate politics with a convict.'

'I'll show you a debate,' Karp said.

He picked up the knife on the floor before Arkady could grab it, turned to the cot and stuck the blade up to the hilt in Volovoi's throat.

'That's how convicts debate,' Karp said, and cradled the back of Volovoi's head and pressed it forward against the knife.

While Volovoi struggled a jet of blood sprayed the wall. His face swelled. His eyes inflated with disbelief.

'What? No more speeches?' Karp asked. 'Restructuring answers the demands of . . . what? I can't hear you. Speak up. Answers the demands of the working class! You ought to know that.'

A man lifts weights, keeps himself in shape, but it's

not the same as real labour, and it was obvious that Volovoi's muscles were putty compared to Karp's. The first mate thrashed, but the trawlmaster kept the knife tight in the throat as lightly as a hand on a lever. This was how they did it in the camp, when the *urkas* discovered an informer. Always the throat.

'Demands for more work? Really?' Karp said.

As Volovoi's face became darker, his eyes turned whiter, as if all the lectures inside him had been choked off and the very pressure of them was building up. His tongue unrolled down to his chin.

'You thought I was going to kiss your cock and ass for ever?' Karp asked.

As Volovoi's face went black he rocked the cot against the wall, and his hands shot out. His eyes still looked full of wonder, as if he had to be watching someone else, this couldn't be happening to him.

No, Arkady thought, Volovoi's not surprised any longer. He's dead.

'He should have just shut up,' Karp spoke to Arkady and jerked the knife first one way and then the other before pulling it out.

Arkady wanted to fly through the door, but the best he could do was push himself to his feet with a can of epoxy to swing in defence. 'You got carried away.'

'Yeah,' Karp admitted. 'But I think they're going to say you got carried away.'

Volovoi still sat upright, as if he could rejoin the conversation. From neck to chest he seemed to have burst under the weight of blood.

Arkady asked, 'Have you ever spent any time in a psychiatric ward?'

'Have you? See?' Karp smiled. 'Anyway, I've been cured. I'm a new man. Let me ask you a question.'

'Go ahead.'

'You like Siberia?'

'What?'

'I'm interested in your opinion. Do you like Siberia?'

'Sure.'

'What kind of fucking answer is that? I *love* Siberia. The cold, the taiga, the hunting, everything, but most of all the people. Real people, like the natives. People in Moscow look hard, but they're like turtles. Get them east, out of their shells, you can just step on them. Siberia's the best thing that ever happened to me. Like home.'

'Good.'

'Just the hunting.' Karp wiped his blade on Volovoi's sleeve. 'Some guys go out in helicopters and blast away with Kalashnikovs. I like the Dragunov, a sniper rifle with a scope. Sometimes I don't even bother shooting. Like, last winter a tiger wandered into Vladivostok killing dogs. A wild tiger in the centre of the city. The militia, naturally, shot it. You know, I wouldn't have killed it; I would have taken it back out of town and let it go. That's the difference between you and me: I wouldn't have killed the tiger.' He propped Volovoi against the wall. 'How long do you think he can stay like that? I was thinking of making a matched set. You know, symmetry.'

Symmetry was always an interesting fetish, Arkady thought. There was a padlock hanging on the bunker door, he remembered; if he could get outside he could lock Karp in.

'But it wouldn't look right,' Arkady said. 'You can't want to leave three murders here. It's a matter of arithmetic. I can't be a victim too.'

'This wasn't my first plan,' Karp confessed, 'but Volovoi was such a prick. All my life I've listened to pricks like him and you, Zina . . .'

'Zina?'

'Zina said words freed you or fucked you or turned you inside out. Every word, every single one, was a weapon or a chain or a pair of wings. You didn't know Zina. And *you* didn't know Zina,' he added, turning to Volovoi. The political officer, his head askew, seemed to be listening. 'An invalid doesn't want to debate with someone from the camps? I could tell you about the camps.' He turned to Arkady. 'Thanks to you.'

'I'm going to send you there again.'

'Well, if you can,' Karp said and spread his arms as if to say, now we've finally come to the point, a point past words and into his domain. He added, as his personal conclusion, 'You should have stayed on the boat.'

When Arkady threw the epoxy, Karp casually lifted a forearm and let the can bounce off. In two steps Arkady was across the room and pushing open the door, but Karp's hand reached out and dragged him back in. Arkady ducked under the knife and grabbed Karp's wrist in the 'come along' grip he had been taught by a militia instructor in Moscow, which brought an appreciative laugh from Karp. He dropped the knife but swung

Arkady into the bookcase. Paperbacks fluttered out like birds.

As Arkady started for the door again, Karp lifted him and threw him over the *baidarka* into the opposite wall, rattling shark jaws and iridescent shells on to the bunker floor. He swept the boat aside. For all his power, he crouched in the favourite *urka* stance, with two fingers extended toward the eyes, a style Arkady had seen before. He moved inside the stabbing hand and hit Karp flush on the mouth, which didn't stop the trawlmaster's forward motion, so Arkady hit him in the stomach, which was like probing concrete, then brought an elbow back to the chin and dropped Karp to one knee.

Roaring, Karp tackled Arkady and drove him into one wall and then another, until Arkady reached up and clung to the fishnet hanging from the ceiling. As Karp ripped him down, Arkady brought a fold of net with him, smothered the trawlmaster's head in it and kicked his legs out from under him. Going for the door a third time, Arkady tripped on the open ribs of the boat, and before he could rise Karp had him by the ankle. On the floor, he had no chance against the trawlmaster's weight, and Karp climbed up his body, ignoring blows until Arkady brought the barrel of shackles down on Karp's head.

Arkady twisted free. He was trying to open the door when a barrel shot by his ear and slammed it shut. Karp tore him off the handle and threw him on the cot next to Volovoi. As if to commiserate, the dead man sagged against Arkady's shoulder. From his jacket, Karp took his own knife, the double-edged one that fishermen were urged to carry at all times in case of emergency. On the cot, Arkady found the knife that Karp had dropped earlier.

Karp was faster, and his stroke should have sliced Arkady from the navel up, but the dead Volovoi finally lost equilibrium and slumped sideways in front of Arkady. The knife thudded into the first mate, and for a moment, leaning forward, his blade imbedded in the wrong target, Karp was vulnerable from heart to neck. Arkady hesitated. Then it was too late. Karp tipped the bed over, trapping him against the wall. Trying to rise, Arkady lost the knife.

Karp lifted him up from behind the cot and tossed him over Mike's body into the smaller room. The trawlmaster paused to liberate his knife from Volovoi before following. Arkady could barely budge the generator, but he did manage to heave the gasoline can. Expecting it, Karp ducked until the can had flown by before he stepped over Mike.

There was a chime-like ring of glass breaking. The sound must have come before Karp entered the room, but afterwards Arkady remembered the man's surprise backlit by a white glare, as if the sun had suddenly risen behind him. The explosion of the kerosene lamp and gas can was followed by a whoosh of spilled epoxy igniting. As gasoline spread, the scattered books caught fire, the tangled sheet of the cot, the corner of the bench. Karp jabbed at Arkady, but half-heartedly, in a disconcerted way. There was a second explosion as the full bucket of epoxy blew and a flame shot to the ceiling. Thick, brown, acrid fumes spread up the walls.

'Even better,' Karp said. He waved the knife one last time and ran back through the burning room; he looked like a demon retreating from hell. After opening the bunker door, he stopped to give Arkady a last backward glance, his eyes lit by the flames. The he darted out and the door shut.

The *baidarka* ignited, its ribs black in the boat's translucent skin, which sweated burning beads of epoxy. Already the ceiling was concealed by poisonous smoke that rolled forward like a storm cloud. Arkady stood over Mike. A remarkable scene, he thought. Storm, fire, the Aleut stretched out towards his burning boat, Volovoi on his upended funeral pyre, one sleeve covered in flame. He thought of a phrase he had once read in a French guidebook: 'Worth a visit.' Sometimes the mind did that in a panic, going off on its own last-minute trips. There were two choices: burn in one room or choke to death in the other.

His hand over his mouth, Arkady darted through the burning room and flung himself against the door. It gave, it wasn't padlocked, only blocked by Karp on the outside. The same as the fish hold. Simple ideas were the best. Flames marched towards Arkady's feet. He bent beneath the smoke, wheezing between coughs. It wouldn't take five minutes, ten at the most; then Karp could open the door wide and check his success.

Arkady shot the door's inside bolt. He had once known a pathologist who claimed that Renko's greatest talent lay not in escaping disastrous situations, only in complicating them. Holding his breath, he waded back through the fire and focused on a barrel that he rescued and carried into the second room. Inside the barrel was trash, Mike's collection of loose netting. With a fisherman's eye, he picked the longest strip of nylon mesh. Illuminated by the flames at the door, the water in the corner had become a golden pond, and he could just see the broken flanges, two rusting tips of iron, under the closed hatch. He set the barrel upside down in the water and stood on it. On his toes he could just swing the strip of mesh high enough to reach. The hatch was not airtight, and by now smoke was lapping into the room, creeping along the ceiling, following the draft to where Arkady balanced. As he hooked a flange, the barrel tipped over and rolled away. While he climbed the net, he heard bottles breaking amid the growing, surf-like sound of fire. He pushed open the hatch. Smoke rushed up, as if trying to drag him back, but by then he was outside and over the earthworks, rolling over mist-slickened grass and falling back towards the sea.

Part Three

ICE

Chapter Twenty-one

The first sign of the ice sheet was a few broken pieces of ice as slick and white as marble floating on black water, and though the *Polar Star* with its company of four catcherboats moved easily into a north wind, there was a general sense of heightened apprehension and isolation. Belowdecks was the new sound of ice scraping the waterline. On deck the crew leaned back to study the gear that surmounted the bridgehouse and gantries: the slowly turning bars, the interlocked rings, the star-shaped, whip and line antennas that provided radar, VHF, short-wave, radio and satellite direction. The sense of a distant reality was increasingly important as scattered ice turned to an endless maze of ice rafts, circular and smooth. More and more the trawlers fell in line behind the *Polar Star*, especially the *Eagle*, built for the warm waters of the Gulf of Mexico, not for the Bering Sea.

By evening the wind had increased, as if sliding faster over ice than over water, and brought a fine rain that froze on the windshield of the bridge. Through the night, crewmen hosed ice off the *Polar Star*'s decks with water from the boilers. The trawlers, even more vulnerable to the destabilizing weight of ice, did the same, and so they moved as a steaming parade through the dark.

The *Alaska Miss*, its screws dented by a floe, turned back at dawn. The others stayed because the fish were there. In the morning light the boats found that the ice had melded into one solid sheet. Ahead lay a white and featureless shell under a blue arch; in the *Polar Star*'s wake stretched a fairway of carbon-black water into which the trawlers, spaced a mile apart, dipped their nets. For some reason, groundfish, particularly sole, chose the ocean floor just inside the ice sheet to mass practically in tiers. Nets thirty and forty tons heavy rose from the water, fish and mesh and plastic chafing hair immediately covered in dazzling crystals of ice, so it appeared that the trawlers were literally hauling gems from the sea. In a way it was true. The Americans were getting rich and the Soviets were doubling their daily plan.

All the same, the *Polar Star*'s flag hung at half-mast. The voyage's entire quota had been dedicated to the memory of Fedor Volovoi. Messages of sympathy were sent to the dead man's family; messages of support were received from fleet headquarters in Vladivostok and the company offices in Seattle. The Party cell had nominated a gloomy Slava Bukovsky to carry out the duties of political officer. Volovoi would be riding home in the No. 2 food store in a plastic bag next to the one containing Zina Patiashvili, who had been transferred; all the space in the fish hold would be needed. It was whispered on board that the first mate's throat was more than simply charred. In his capacity as trade union representative charged with writing death forms, Slava denied the rumours, but with all his new duties, the third mate seemed to be more afflicted with depression than inspired by opportunity. Arkady himself ached after the beating from Karp, but no worse than if he had fallen down a very long staircase.

On the slime line a half-ton of yellowfin sole poured like a quickening flood down the chute every ten minutes to be gutted, cleaned and trimmed. The fish were so laced with ice that Obidin, Malzeva, Mer and the others were numb from hands to shoulders. Over the sound of the saws and the incessant murmuring of cheerful tunes from the radio came the thumping of ice along the hull. The ice-breaking bow of the *Polar Star* had been designed to ride up and crash through ice a metre thick. Still the hull protested. The whole bulkhead would shudder, and individual plates bowed in and out like drums.

As she steered fish through the saw, Natasha again and again raised a questioning look at Arkady, but he was listening to the progress of the ship, to the ice resisting and then exploding under the bow, a sound like the earth splitting.

Marchuk looked as if he had been climbing mountains. Fog, never far away, had returned as a mist that froze on the windshield of the bridge and the captain had gone out on the flying bridge. His greatcoat, boots, open-finger gloves and captain's cap were lined in every fold with ice, and his beard had the shimmer of melting rime. As he stood now behind his desk, water began to pool on the floor. By the evidence of his red ears it was plain that Marchuk had not traded his cap for the flapped woollen cap of lesser men. Anton Hess had not been out on deck; still, he was padded with two sweaters and the same sort of gloves as Marchuk. A Soviet ship is overheated – the glory of a Russian home is heat – but nothing stayed warm on the ice sheet. Under his forehead and wild hair, Hess's eyes were hollowed by exhaustion. Two strong men, yet each seemed uncertain, even frightened. For the first time in their lives they were sailing on ships without a watchdog of the Party – worse, with a dead watchdog in the freezer.

Standing on the carpet next to Arkady, but not with him, as far as he could suggest by expression, was Slava Bukovsky. It was the same group that had assembled in the captain's cabin before, with one obvious exception.

'I apologize for not meeting when we raised anchor,' Marchuk said. 'Matters were unclear. Also, my attention is taken with the radio whenever we approach ice. Americans are not used to ice, so I have to hold their hands. Now, Comrade Bukovsky, I have read your report, but the others might like to hear it.'

Slava took the opportunity to step forward, a step further away from Arkady. 'My report is based on the American report. I have it here.'

As soon as Slava opened his briefcase, his papers escaped on to the carpet. It occurred to Arkady that if Marchuk had a tail it would be twitching.

The third mate found the paper he wanted. He read, 'The competent authorities in Dutch Harbor—'

'Who are the competent authorities?' Hess interrupted.

'The local fire chief. He said it appeared to be an accidental fire,' Slava went on. 'The native called Mikhail Krukov had been warned many times about the danger of using volatile materials in the construction of his boats, and there was evidence of a kerosene lamp, of gasoline and of alcohol. The accident occurred in a concrete construction dating back to the war, a bunker without sufficient ventilation and without safeguards for the generator that Krukov used. Apparently the natives have taken over a number of abandoned military structures without permission. Krukov was well known locally as some sort of boatbuilder. The Americans assume that he was showing one to Volovoi, that the two men shared a bottle and that in the closed space there was somehow an accident that broke a kerosene lamp, igniting toxic material which, in turn, exploded. Fedor Volovoi, apparently, was immediately killed by flying glass. The native, it seemed, died of burns and inhalation.

'Mikhail Krukov?' Marchuk raised his eyebrows. 'A Russian name?'

'He was called Mike,' Slava said.

'They were drunk?' Hess asked. 'Is that what the competent authorities suggest?'

'Like our own, their natives are known to be abusers of alcohol,' Slava said.

Marchuk smiled like a man who had heard a joke on the way to the gallows. He turned the smile towards Arkady. 'Volovoi didn't drink and he hated boats. But that's the report; that's what I'm supposed to tell Vladivostok. Somehow I have the feeling that you have something you could add.'

The ship trembled as it hit a larger ice floe. Arkady waited until the grinding slid past. 'No,' he said.

'Nothing?' Marchuk asked. 'I think of you as such a reliable source of surprises.'

Arkady shrugged. As an afterthought he asked Slava, 'Who found the bodies?'

'Karp.'

'Karp Korobetz, a trawlmaster,' the captain explained to Hess. 'He was searching for Volovoi in the company of an engineer from the *Eagle*.'

'Ridley,' Slava said. 'He showed Karp the way to the bunker.'

'What time did they discover the bodies?' Arkady asked.

'About ten,' Slava said. 'They had to break the door in.'

'You hear that?' Marchuk underlined the words for Arkady. 'They had to *break in*. It was locked from the inside. That's the touch I like.'

'Karp and Ridley entered the bunker?' Arkady asked Slava. 'They looked around?'

'I suppose.'

Slava jumped as Marchuk slapped his cap against a boot and shook off water. The captain replaced the hat on his head and lit a cigarette. 'Go on,' he encouraged Slava.

'Volovoi was found in the main room of the bunker

and the American was found in a second room,' Slava said. 'There was a trapdoor of sorts in the second room, but no ladder was found.'

'There was no way up from the inside,' Marchuk said. 'It's like a mystery.'

'I didn't see much of Dutch Harbor,' Arkady said.

'Really?' Marchuk said.

'I didn't notice much in the way of medical facilities.' Arkady continued. 'Did a doctor examine the bodies?'

'Yes,' Slava said.

'In a laboratory?'

'No.' Slava became defensive. 'There was clearly a fire and explosion, and the bodies were almost too badly burned to be moved.'

'The Americans accept that?' Arkady asked.

Marchuk said, 'They would have to fly the bodies to the mainland, and we're not going to let them have Volovoi. His body will be examined in Vladivostok. Anyway, Captain Morgan has accepted the report.'

'Just out of curiosity,' Arkady said, 'who was next at the scene, after Korobetz and Ridley?'

'Morgan,' Slava read.

'You accept the report, too?' Arkady asked Marchuk.

'Of course. Two men die, one of theirs and one of ours, and nearly every sign indicates that they got drunk and burned themselves to death. That's the kind of stink the Americans and we can mutually put behind us. Co-operation is the byword of a joint venture.'

The captain swung his attention to Slava. 'Volovoi was a real shit. I hope you can fill his shoes.' He leaned forward, turning again to Arkady. 'But how do you think this will look for me, returning to Vladivostok with two of my crew in bags? Do you know what a circus it will be? What will my next command be? A garbage scow in Magadan? They still float logs along Kamchatka. Maybe they'll save a log for me.'

'You went ashore on my authority,' Hess said to Arkady. 'Supposedly you were still gathering information about the dead girl, Zina Patiashvili.'

'Thank you,' Arkady said. 'It was invigorating to be on land again.'

'But now we have three dead instead of one,' Hess pressed on, 'and since one was the vigilant defender of the Party, the Party will have its questions when we return home.'

'Somehow,' Marchuk stared at Arkady, 'somehow I connect it all to you. You come on board; there's one dead. You go ashore; there are two more dead. Compared with you, Jonah was a ray of sunshine.'

'You see, this is the question: where were *you*?' Hess asked. 'Volovoi left the hotel searching for you. No one could find either of you, and the next time we see the commissar he's up on top of a hill and burned to death with an Indian—'

'An Aleut,' Slava said. 'It's in my report.'

'A native, whatever, to whom Volovoi had hardly ever spoken before. What was Volovoi doing drinking, which he never did, with a boatbuilder on top of a hill? Why would he be there when he was looking for you?' Hess asked Arkady.

'Do you want me to try to find out?'

Hess smiled at the answer from sheer professional appreciation, as if he had seen a goalie stop a difficult kick, then boot the ball into the opposite net.

'No, no,' Marchuk said. 'No more help from you. I can just see their faces in Vladivostok if we tried to explain why we assigned you to investigate the death of Volovoi. Comrade Bukovsky is in charge.'

'Again? Congratulations,' Arkady said to Slava.

'I have already questioned Seaman Renko,' Slava said. 'He claims that after leaving Susan, being drunk and feeling ill, he went out behind the hotel and passed out. Then he remembers nothing until he found himself in the water, having fallen off the dock.'

Marchuk said, 'Izrail, the factory manager, tells me that you were drunk in a fish hold the other day and almost froze yourself. No wonder you lost your Party card.'

'The hidden drunks are the worst,' Arkady agreed. 'But Captain, you just said you accepted the American report that there was an accidental fire. Then what is Comrade Bukovsky investigating?'

'I'm assembling our own findings,' Slava said. 'I'm not necessarily asking questions.'

'The best kind of investigation.' Arkady nodded. 'A straight line with no dangerous curves. Incidentally,' he said to Hess, 'could I have my knife back? You took it before we went ashore.'

'I'd have to look for it.'

'Please do. It's the property of the state.'

MARTIN CRUZ SMITH

Marchuk crushed his cigarette into an ashtray and glanced at the porthole, heavy-lidded with ice. 'Well, your days as an investigator are over once again. The death of Zina Patiashvili is a closed matter until we reach home. Gentlemen, the fish await.' He rose, pulled the peak of his cap forward, picked up the twisted butt and used it to light another cigarette. Everyone had been smoking Marlboros since Dutch Harbor. 'I like you, Renko, but I have to say this: if our Comrade Volovoi didn't die in the fire – if, for example, his throat was cut – I would suspect you first. We can't figure out how you could kill two men or escape the fire. I like the way you fell in the water. That would dampen the smell of the smoke and wash the grass off your boots.' He pushed up the collar of his coat. 'My Americans await. It's like leading little girls across a frozen pond.'

Chapter Twenty-two

From the stern rail Susan focused binoculars on the wake of the *Polar Star*. Her jacket was buttoned to her chin and, like a girl on skis, she wore mittens and a woollen cap.

'See anything?' Arkady asked.

'I was watching the *Eagle*. A Gulf boat shouldn't be here.'

'I've been looking for you.'

'Funny,' she said, 'I've been avoiding you.'

Out of habit, Arkady checked over his shoulder to see whether Karp was near. 'That's hard on a ship.'

'Apparently.'

'Can I look?' he asked.

She handed him the glasses. Arkady focused first on the water reaching up the *Polar Star*'s ramp, the waves almost a tropical blue as they flowed in and out of the rusty gullet. Water so cold seemed molten. Sea water started to crystallize at 29°F, and because it carried so much brine it formed first not as a solid but as a transparent sheen, undulating on black swells, going grey as it congealed.

The trawlers had to stay close to mother. Through the glasses he could see the *Merry Jane* slip by the *Eagle* as the first ship brought in a bag that lay fat and wet on its deck. The *Eagle* was just setting its net, and as it rose on a swell he had a clear view of two deckhands in yellow slickers. Americans didn't use safety gates. Water surged freely up and down the ramp, and the men expertly timed their every move, jumping on to gantry rungs when larger waves broke over the gunwales. The binoculars were 10×50 so Arkady could see it was the former policeman, Coletti, who was working the hydraulic levers on the gantry. The second fisherman threw loose crabs over the side, and only as the man turned did Arkady recognize the peaked brows and grin of Ridley.

'Just a two-man crew?' Arkady asked. 'They didn't replace Mike?'

'They're capitalists. One less share to give up.'

Setting a net was a delicate operation in the best of circumstances, which was a calm sea with room to manoeuvre. The *Aurora* had already tangled its trawl wires on a propeller and left, at a limp, for Dutch Harbor. In the wheelhouse, Morgan, in a baseball cap and parka, alternately worked the *Eagle*'s throttle and tended the controls of the winch behind him.

'Why didn't you stay at the hotel with me?' Susan asked.

'I told you that Volovoi was coming to take me back to the ship.'

'Maybe he should have. They'd be more people alive now.'

Arkady, always slow on the uptake, finally put the glasses down and noticed that Susan's cheeks weren't burning merely from the cold. What had he looked like when he suddenly left her? A coward, a seducer? More likely a buffoon.

'I'm sorry I left,' he said.

'Too late,' Susan said. 'You weren't just running from Volovoi. I watched you from the window when you crossed the road. You were following Mike.' The steam of her breath seemed like visible contempt. 'You followed Mike, Volovoi followed you. Now they're both dead and you're taking an Arctic cruise.'

Arkady had come to apologize, but there always seemed to be a barrier between the two of them he couldn't cross. Anyway, what could he say? Mike was dead when he had caught up? That a model trawlmaster had sliced the first mate's throat, though he had witnesses where he supposedly was and Arkady did not? Or, what were you looking for in the water?

'Can you tell me what happened?'

'No,' he admitted.

'Let me tell you what I think. I think you really were an investigator of some sort at some time. You're pretending to try to find out about Zina, but you've been offered a chance to get off the boat if you can blame an American. It would have been Mike, but now that he's dead you have to find another one. What I don't understand', she said, 'is me. Back at Dutch Harbor I actually believed you. Then I saw you running across the road after Mike.'

Arkady found himself getting warm. 'Did you tell anyone I was following him?'

In spite of her anger she looked back at the *Eagle*. Arkady looked through the glasses again. The boat went hull down, then disappeared behind a swell, and when it rose both Ridley and Coletti had climbed the gantry to stay out of water that would have been up to their knees. In the wheelhouse Morgan had already picked up his own binoculars and was watching Arkady in return.

'He'll stay close to us, won't he?'

'Or get iced in,' Susan said.

'Is he a dedicated man?'

A swell like a smooth rock streaked with foam grew between the two men, gathered momentum as it rolled to the *Polar Star* and then plunged up the factory ship ramp. Morgan held his binoculars steady on his target.

'He's a professional,' she said.

'Did you make him jealous?' Arkady asked. 'Was that why you asked me to your room?'

Susan's hand rose to slap him, then stopped. Why? Arkady wondered. Did she think a slap would be too banal, too bourgeois? Nonsense. On a Saturday night the Moscow metro resounded with slaps.

The ship's speakers squawked. It was 1500, time for light musical selections from Fleet Radio, beginning with a rumba suggesting Cuban beaches and waving palms. Socialist maracas struck up a Latin rhythm.

Arkady said, 'This music reminds me, before Dutch Harbor you were leaving us for a vacation. Soo-san, why did you come back to this Soviet ship you hate so much? The fish? The excitement of filling the quota?'

'No, but it might be worth it to see you rotting on the slime line again.'

The radio room was the first portside cabin behind the bridge. Nicolai, the young man who had piloted the lifeboat that had taken Hess and Arkady into Dutch Harbor, was idly working the crossword puzzle in *Soviet Sport* when Arkady entered. Nicolai's desk was occupied by stacked radios, amplifiers and a row of binders, one with the red stripe of classified codes, but there was room left for a hot plate and pot. Cosy. The rumba trotted in and out of the speaker. Not bad duty. Junior lieutenants with training in electronics were often assigned to fishing fleets to take an ostensibly civilian tour of foreign ports. Even in his warm-up suit and slippers he had the air of a freshly minted officer whose future was lined with gold braid. Nicolai raised his eyes lazily towards Arkady.

'Whatever it is, old-timer, I'm busy.'

Arkady checked to make sure no one was in the passage, then closed the door, kicked over the radioman's chair and planted a foot in his chest.

'You screwed Zina Patiashvili. You took her into an intelligence station in this ship. If your chief finds out, you'll go to a military labour camp, and by the time you get out you'll be lucky if you still have teeth and hair.'

On his back, Nicolai still held his pencil, his eyes two perfect pools of blue. 'That's a lie.'

'Then let's tell Hess.'

Arkady looked down at a young man who was experiencing all the terrors of free fall, for whom a comfortable and promising world had suddenly become an abyss.

'How do you know?' Nicolai asked.

'That's better.' Arkady removed his foot and helped him up. 'You can pick up the chair. Sit.'

Nicolai promptly did as he was ordered, always a good sign. Arkady turned up the speaker a notch as the rumba faded and was replaced by a Bulgarian folk song.

While the lieutenant sat at attention, Arkady considered the different ways to handle this interrogation: as a former lover of Zina himself, as a blackmailer, as someone still carrying out a ship's inquiry. But he wanted an approach that would throw an aggressive Naval Intelligence officer into a pit of despair, as if the young man were already in the hands of the military's most despised enemy. He deliberately chose the unlikely words with which the KGB always began its more informal chats.

'Relax. If you're honest, you have nothing to worry about.'

Nicolai shank in his chair. 'It was one time, that's all. She recognized me from Vladivostok. I thought she was a waitress; how did I know she was going to be on board? Maybe I should have told someone, but she begged me not to because she would have been sent back home on an off-loader. I had mercy on her, and then one thing led to another.'

'It led her to your cot.'

'I didn't plan it that way. There's no privacy on a ship. That was the only time.'

'No.'

'It was!'

'Vladivostok,' Arkady prompted him. 'The Golden Horn.'

'You were watching her then?'

'Tell me about it.'

Nicolai's story wasn't much different from Marchuk's. He'd gone to the Golden Horn with friends from the base and they'd all noticed Zina, but she seemed to be most attracted to him. When she got off work, the two went to her place, listened to music, danced, made love, and then he left and never saw her again until the *Polar Star*. 'I thought the investigation about Zina was over,' he said. 'I heard you were back in the factory.'

'She was a good waitress?'

'The worst.'

'What did you talk about?'

Arkady could feel the radioman's mind freeze like a rabbit wondering which way to run next. Not only was he implicated in the betrayal of his service on the ship, but the interrogation had dangerously expanded into the past, implicating him again, if only through coincidence. The worst construction was that Zina had infiltrated the Pacific Fleet not once but twice, both times through him. Not necessarily as a foreign agent, to be sure; the KGB was always and obsessively trying to worm into the military, and Naval Intelligence was always and paranoically testing the vigilance of its own officers to see if it could breach its own security.

Like other men in similar dilemmas, Nicolai decided to plead guilty to a smaller crime as evidence of his honesty. 'I have the best receivers in the world in Vladivostok. I can get American Armed Forces Radio, Manila, Nome. Sometimes I have to monitor them anyway, so I tape – just music and just for myself, never for profit. I offered one to Zina as a friend and said we ought to go someplace where we could play it. OK, it was a come on, but we never talked about anything but music. She wanted me to duplicate the tapes and sell the copies through her. Zina was Georgian through and through. I told her no. We went to her place and listened to the tapes, but that was all.'

'Not quite all. You got what you wanted; you slept with her.'

Arkady asked what Zina's apartment was like, and again Nicolai's description resembled Marchuk's. A private flat in a relatively new building, maybe a co-op. Television, VCR, stereo. Japanese prints and samurai swords on the wall. Doors and bar upholstered in red plastic. A rifle collection in a locked case. Though there were no photographs, clearly a man lived there too, and Nicolai had assumed that Zina's friend was powerful and wealthy, either a black-market millionaire or someone high up in the Party.

'You're a Party member?' Arkady asked.

'Young Communist.'

'Tell me about the radios here.'

The radioman was happy to leave the subject of Zina Patiashvili and expound on more technical matters. The *Polar Star*'s radio cabin had a VHF radio with a range of about fifty kilometres for communicating with the catcherboats, and two larger, single-sideband radios for longer range. One single-sideband was usually tuned to the fleet radio. The second single-sideband was for the radio conferences with other Soviet ships spread across the Bering Sea, or for contact with the fleet headquarters in Vladivostok and the company office in Seattle. In between, the radio monitored an emergency channel that all ships kept open.

The cabin also had a shortwave for Radio Moscow or the BBC. 'I'll show you something else.' Nicolai brought from under the desk a receiver no larger than an historical novel. 'A CB radio. Very short range, but this is how the catcherboats talk to each other when they don't want us to listen in. All the more reason for us to have it.' He turned it on to the voice of Thorwald, the captain of the *Merry Jane*, droning in a Norwegian accent, '. . . fucking Russians pounded the fucking George Bank to death and pounding the fucking African coast until there's no fucking fish there. At least we'll get some fucking money—'

Arkady turned the CB off. 'Tell me more about Zina.'

'She wasn't a real blonde. She was pretty wild, though.'

'Not sex. What you talked about.'

'Tapes. I told you.' Nicolai had the confused expression of a student who was trying to cooperate but didn't know what his new teacher wanted.

'The weather?' Arkady prompted.

'For her, anywhere but Georgia was too cold.'

'Georgia?'

'She said Georgian men would screw anything that bent over.'

'Work?'

'She expressed an un-Soviet philosophy about labour.'

'Fun?'

'Dancing.'

'Men?'

'Money.' Nicolai laughed. 'I don't know why I say that, because she didn't ask me for money. But she had a way of looking at you one moment as if you were the most handsome, desirable man on earth, which is a very erotic sensation, and then a minute later dismissing you with her eyes as if you couldn't possibly meet her expectations. It's crazy, but somehow I had the feeling that, with Zina, emotions and money never met. I'd say, "Why are you looking at me so coldly?" and she'd say, "I'm imagining you're not a little sailor boy, that you're an Afghantsi, a soldier sent off to fight against Allah and his madmen, and you've just come home in a zinc-lined coffin and it makes me sad." Cruel things like that – and right in the middle of love, too.'

'What about the guns in the apartment? Did she talk about them?'

'No. I had the feeling I'd be some sort of softie in her eyes if I asked. She did say that the guy, whoever he was, slept with a gun under his pillow. I thought, Well, that's typically Siberian.'

'Did she ask you questions?'

'Just about my family, my home, did I write often like a good son and send proper packages of coffee and tea.'

'Doesn't the Navy have its own system so that parcels don't arrive ripped apart months after they're sent?'

'The Navy takes care of its own.'

'And she asked you to send a parcel for her?'

There was something increasingly calf-like about the radioman in the widening of his eyes. 'Yes.'

'Tea?'

'Yes.'

'Already wrapped for you to take?'

'Yes. But at the last minute she changed her mind and I left without it. That was another time when she gave me one of those looks as if I couldn't measure up.'

'When you met on the *Polar Star*, did she tell you how she came to be on board?'

'She just said she'd got bored back at the restaurant, bored with Vladivostok, bored with Siberia. When I asked how she got a seaman's union card she laughed in my face and said she'd bought it, what else? The rules about that are well known, but they didn't seem to apply to Zina.'

'She was different?'

Nicolai struggled with words, then admitted failure. 'You had to know her.'

Arkady changed the subject. 'Our single-sideband radios, what's their range?'

'It varies with the atmospherics. The captain can tell you; one day we can get Mexico and the next day nothing. But the ship's crew often calls home all the way to Moscow through a radio-telephone link. It's a morale builder.'

Arkady asked, 'Can other ships listen to those conversations?'

'If they happen to be monitoring the right channel they can hear the incoming part of the conversation, but not what we say.'

'Good. Place a call for me to Odessa militia headquarters.'

'No problem.' Nicolai was eager to please. 'Of course all calls have to be cleared with the captain.'

'You don't want to clear this call; you don't even want to log it. Let's review,' Arkady said, because the radio technician was a young man who needed careful instruction. 'As a naval officer, simply for admitting Patiashvili into your station on the *Polar Star* you can be charged with betraying your sacred trust. Since this was an ongoing relationship the question of conspiracy to commit the state crime of treason comes up. Even if you were merely innocently attempting to seduce a citizen, you can still be charge with activities detrimental to the high standing of Soviet womanhood, failure to report illegal firearms, theft of state property – the tapes – and dissemination of anti-Soviet propaganda – the music. In any case, your life as a naval officer is at an end.'

Listening, Nicolai looked like a man swallowing a fish whole. 'No problem. It may take an hour or so to get through to Odessa, but I'll do it.'

'Incidentally, since you are a music lover, where were you during the ship's dance?'

'My other duties.' Nicolai lowered his eyes to indicate, belowdecks, the intelligence station Arkady had yet to find. 'It's funny you mention music. The tapes that Zina had in the apartment in Vladivostok? Some were rock, but most were *magnatizdat*. You know, thieves' songs.'

' "Cut my throat, but please don't cut the strings of my guitar"?'

'Exactly! You did know her.'

'I do now.'

On the way out, Arkady had to admit to himself that he'd been harder on the radioman that he'd really needed to be. It was the dig, 'old-timer', that had been Nicolai's mistake. He found himself running his hand over his face. Did he look old? He didn't feel old.

Chapter Twenty-three

Under Gury's bunk was a new nylon bag stuffed with plastic booty: Sony Walkmen, Swatch watches, Aiwa speakers, WaterPiks, Marlboros and a Mickey Mouse telephone. Taped on the wardrobe were Polaroid snapshots of Obidin, his beard cleaned and combed, standing before the wooden church in Unalaska like a man modestly posing on a cloud beside his Lord. Inside, the wardrobe was redolent with the exhalation of rows of jars of homemade brew flavoured by fresh and canned fruit from the Dutch Harbor store. Anyone reaching for his jacket was assaulted by the sugary fumes of peaches, cherries and exotic mandarin oranges. The most botanical corner of the cabin, however, was Kolya's shelves of specimens gathered on the island and brought back in cardboard pots: furry moss clinging to a rock bedded on moist page from *Pravda;* a miniature bush with minute purple berries; the sickle-shaped, papery leaves of a dwarf iris; a paintbrush that still claimed one fire-red petal.

Kolya was giving Natasha the tour; with the porthole laced by frost, his corner of the cabin resembled a greenhouse. It was the first time he'd ever impressed her. 'Any scientific voyage returned like this,' he explained. 'Cook and Darwin, their small ships were filled with botanical specimens in the holds, bulbs in the chain lockers, bread-fruit trees on deck. Because life is everywhere. The underside of the ice sheet around us is covered with algae. That's what brings the tiny creatures which, in turn, attract the fish. Naturally, predators follow: seals, whales, polar bears. We're surrounded by life.'

Arkady's mind was on botany of a different sort. He sat at the narrow table, enjoying one of Gury's cigarettes and thinking of wild hemp, thousands of square hectares of luxuriant, wild Manchurian hemp heavy with narcotic pollen, flowers and leaves growing like free rubles across the rugged Asian landscape. Every autumn what Siberians called 'grass fever' broke out as people flocked like Party volunteers – better than Party volunteers – to the countryside for the harvest. Often no travel was necessary because the weed grew everywhere – along the road, in the potato field, in the tomato patch. Called *anasha*, it was trucked in bags west towards Moscow, where it could be smoked loose like cigarettes or tamped into pipes.

Then there was *plan*. Hashish. *Plan* came in kilo bricks from Afghanistan and Pakistan, then travelled by different routes, some on Army lorries, some on ferries over the Black and Caspian Seas across Georgia, then north to Moscow.

'Polar bears wander for hundreds of kilometres out on the ice sheet,' Kolya was telling Natasha. 'No one knows how they find their way. They hunt two ways, by waiting at the holes where seals come up to breathe and by swimming under the ice and watching for a seal shadow above.'

Or poppies, Arkady thought. How many Georgian collectives overfulfilled their quota for magic flower? How much was swept from the threshing floor, how much dried, how much baled, how much processed into morphine, then seemingly blown by the wind to Moscow?

From an investigator's point of view, Moscow appeared to be an innocent Eve, surrounded by dangerous gardens, constantly seduced by oily Georgian, Afghani and Siberian snakes. The 'tea' that Zina had asked Nicolai to send was undoubtedly a block of hemp, *anasha*. She'd changed her mind, probably because it was such small change, but it meant that there was at least part of a network in place.

'You found all these flowers just around the road and the store?' Natasha asked.

'Well, you have to know where to look,' Kolya said.

'The seed of beauty is everywhere.' Natasha wore her hair back to show off the crystal earrings she'd bought in Dutch Harbor. 'Wouldn't you agree, Arkady?'

'It's undeniable.'

'You see how much more constructively Comrade Mer spent his time on shore, instead of getting disgustingly drunk and falling in the water.'

'Kolya, I bow to your scientific zeal.' Arkady noticed that his cabinmate's spiral notebook, with its grey, crocodile-textured binding, was the kind sold in the ship's store. The same as Zina's. 'May I?' He flipped through the pages. On each Kolya had noted a different plant by common name, Latin name, when and where picked.

'Were you alone when you fell in?' Natasha asked.

'It's less embarrassing that way.'

'Susan wasn't with you?'

'No one.'

'You could have been hurt.' Kolya was upset. 'A little tipsy, in the water, at night.'

'I was wondering,' Natasha said to Arkady, 'What you plan to do when we return to Vladivostok. When he was alive, Comrade Volovoi suggested that you might have difficulties with the Guard. Positive statements from your co-workers, from Party members, might be helpful. Then you might want to go elsewhere. There are some very nice hydro-electric projects starting on the Yenisei. Arctic bonuses, a month's vacation anywhere. With your abilities, you'd learn how to run a crane in no time.'

'Thanks, I'll consider that.'

'How many former investigators from Moscow can say they built a dam?' she asked.

'Not many.'

'We could keep a cow. I mean, *you* could keep a cow if you wanted. Anyone who wanted to keep a cow could keep a cow. In a private plot. Or a pig. Or even chickens, though you have to have some place warm for fowl in the wintertime.'

'Cow? Chickens?' Arkady shook his head. What was this about?

'The Yenisei is interesting,' Koyla said.

'It's *very* interesting,' Natasha emphasized. 'Beautiful taiga of pines and larches. Deer and grouse.'

'Edible snails,' Kolya said.

'But you'd have a cow if you wanted. Room for a motorcycle too. Picnics on the river bank. A whole town full of young people, children. You—'

'Did Zina know anything about ships?' Arkady interrupted. 'Did she understand terminology, what different parts of a ship are called?'

Natasha couldn't believe her ears. 'Zina? Again?'

'What would she mean by "fish hold"?'

'She's dead. That's all over.'

'The hold, or anything near to it?' Arkady asked.

'Zina knew nothing about ships, nothing about her work, nothing except her own self-interest, and she's dead,' Natasha said. 'Why this fascination? When she was alive you cared nothing about her. It was one thing when the captain ordered you to carry out an investigation. Now your interest is morbid, negative and disgusting.'

Arkady pulled on his boots. 'You could be right,' he said.

'I'm sorry, Arkasha, I shouldn't have said any of that. Please.'

'Don't apologize for being honest.' Arkady reached for his jacket.

'I hate the sea,' Natasha said bitterly. 'I should have gone to Moscow. I could have gotten work in a mill and looked for a husband there.'

'The mills are sweatshops,' Arkady said, 'and you'd have lived in a dorm with a curtain between your bed and the next. It's too cramped; you'd hate it there. A big flower deserves a lot of space.'

'True.' She liked that.

Below decks in the bow it sounded as if the *Polar Star* weren't breaking ice so much as ploughing through an unseen landscape, overturning houses and trees, unearthing boulders. Arkady wouldn't have been too surprised to see beds or branches puncture the rusty skin of steel. What did the rats think? They had left land generations before. Did this din evoke memories and odd dreams in rodent sleep?

Zina had said "fish hold", but what she must have meant was the chain locker next to the hold. The lowest and most forward point of the ship, the locker was an angular, catch-all space usually stuffed with hawsers and chains, a dark corner that might be visited twice on a voyage by a scrupulous bosun. Only a recessed peephole in the watertight hatch suggested that this door might be different from any other. Before he could knock, the hatch opened with a pop of air, like a bottle. As soon as he stepped in and the hatch closed behind him, he felt his eardrums compress.

A red overhead bulb lit Anton Hess, sitting in a swivel chair. In the light, his towering hair looked all askew. He had turned from three monitors that were tapped into the bridge's echo-sounder; on the screens, three green seas flowed over three orange sea floors; he looked like a magician hovering over vats of fluorescent colour.

Stacked on one side were two loran monitors with luminous crosshairs that marked latitude and longitude on glowing charts that matched the paper plotters Arkady had seen on the *Eagle* and that far outstripped anything on Marchuk's bridge. On the other side was a blank oscilloscope and what looked like a sound engineer's acoustical mixer, complete with headset. Above this was a screen showing in grey half-tones the passage between the locker and the fish hold, where Arkady had been standing a moment before. There was a small mainframe computer and racks of other equipment he couldn't make out clearly in the red haze, though all the gear, plus chair and cot, were crammed into an area not much larger than a closet. For a submariner, it must be just like home.

'I'm surprised it took you this long to find me,' Hess said.

'Me, too.'

'Sit.' Hess indicated the cot. 'Welcome to this little station. I'm afraid there's no smoking allowed because the air circulation is non-existent, but it's like the paratroops: you pack your own parachute. I designed it, so I have no one else to blame.'

One reason the space was so snug, Arkady realized, was the heavy soundproofing on every surface; there was even a false deck over insulation that muffled the grinding of ice and steel plate. As his eyes adjusted, he saw another reason: built into the deck where the bulkheads met was a white hemisphere a full metre across. The dome seemed to be the lid of something much larger built into the bottom of the ship itself.

'Amazing,' Arkady said.

'No, it's pathetic. It's a desperate resort to redress the unfirmness of geography and the burden of history. Every major Soviet port faces a choke point or is ice-bound six months of the year. Leaving Vladivostok, our fleet has to pass through either the Kuril or the Korea Straits. In a war we probably wouldn't get a single ship out. Thank God for submarines.'

On the three screens Arkady watched an orange tracery mounting like a wave, the signals of groundfish rising to feed. Why fish enjoy foul weather no one knew. Hess held out something glittering to Arkady, a flask; brandy at body temperature.

'Underwater we're equal?'

'Ignoring the fact that they carry twice as many warheads. And that they can keep 60 per cent of their missile boats on patrol while we can barely manage 15 per cent. Also that their boats are quieter, faster and dive deeper. But this is where irony comes in, Renko. I know you appreciate irony as much as I do. The only place where our submarines can safely hide is under the Arctic ice, and the only way the Americans can come after us from the Pacific is across the Bering Sea and through the Bering Strait. For once *we* choke *them*.'

Host and guest drank to geography. As Arkady sat back the cot squeaked and he thought of Zina on the same blanket. There hadn't been any lectures then. 'So you have a quota of fish too, in a sense,' he said.

'Not to catch, just to hear. You know that the *Polar Star* was in dry dock.'

'I did wonder what work was done. No one has noticed any improvements that have to do with fishing.'

'Extra ears.' Hess nodded towards the white dome set into the deck. 'It's called a towed array sonar. This is a passive system, a cable with hydrophones that plays out from an electric winch in that pod. On submarines we mount the pod over the stern. On the *Polar Star* we've mounted it near the bow to avoid getting it tangled in an American net.'

'And you pull in the cable before a net is brought on,' Arkady said. That was why Nicolai had time to dally with Zina, because a bag of fish was coming in.

'It's not a very effective system for deep water, but this is a shallow sea. Submarines, even theirs, hate shallow water. They race for the strait and the faster they go the louder they are and we hear them. Every boat sounds different.' Hess swivelled towards a rack with a computer, monitor and a file of floppy disks. 'Here we have the signatures of five hundred submarines, their and ours. By matching, we sort out their routes and missions. Of course, we would do the same on one of our submarines or hydrographic boats, but they hide their subs from those. The *Polar Star* is only a factory ship in the middle of the Bering Sea.'

Arkady remembered the map in the cabin of the fleet electrician engineer. 'One of fifty Soviet factory ships along their coast?'

'Exactly. This is the prototype.'

'It seems rather sophisticated.'

'No,' Hess said. 'Let me tell you what is sophisticated in terms of electronic intelligence gathering. The Americans place nuclear-powered monitors off the Siberian coast. Those containers hold six tonnes of reconnaissance equipment and a supply of plutonium so they can transmit indefinitely right under our noses. Their submarines go into Murmansk harbour and place hydrophones right on our submarines. They like coming out with trophies. Of course, if they could get hold of our cable it would be displayed in Washington in one of those news events they do so well, as if they had never seen a can on a string before.'

'That's what your cable is, a can on a string?'

'Microphones on a three-hundred-metre string, essentially.' Hess granted himself half a smile. 'The software is interesting; it was originally programmed in California to track whales.'

'Do you ever mistake a boat for a whale?'

'No.' Hess's fingers reached out and touched the round screen of the oscilloscope as if it were a crystal ball. There was a handcrafted quality to it, as there often was to the high technology produced by the Ministry for Electrical Apparatus. 'Whales and dolphins sound like beacons in deep space. You can hear some whales for close to a thousand kilometres, deep bass notes with the long waves of low frequencies. Then there are the other sounds of fish, of seals pursuing the fish, of walrus digging up the floor with their tusks. It's all like the sound of an orchestra constantly warming up. Then you hear a certain hiss that shouldn't be there.'

'You're a musician?' Arkady asked.

'When I was a boy I thought the cello would be my career. Such innocence!'

Arkady looked at the monitors, at the repeated image of orange fish rising in an electric-green sea. The white dome had clamps; it was removable; if the winch had to be serviced, what else would Hess do, send down a diver?

'Why do you think I had you taken off the slime line?' Hess continued. 'I heard something wrong: that this dead girl, Zina Patiashvili, went to the stern every time the *Eagle* delivered a net. To wave at a native boy? Let's not be silly. The only possible answer is that she was signalling Captain Morgan whether we had played the cable out or not.'

'Is it visible?'

'Not during tests, but she must have seen something besides Morgan's net.'

'They say Morgan is a good fisherman.'

'George Morgan has fished the Gulf of Thailand, off Guantanamo and Grenada. He should know how to fish. That's why I supported an investigation. Better to dig up the truth, to shake a traitor out of the tree sooner rather than later. But, Renko, I must tell you that too many bodies have been hitting the ground. First the girl, then Volovoi and the American. And you snake in and out, in and out of all this.'

'I can find out about Zina.'

'And our roasted first mate? No, we'll leave it to

Vladivostok, there are too many questions now. Including, how are you involved?'

'Someone's trying to kill me.'

'That's not good enough. Zina–Susan–Morgan, that's the chain I want. Fit into that and you justify my interest. The rest is none of my concern.'

'You don't care what happened to Zina?'

'By itself, of course not.'

'Would you be interested in evidence of smuggling?'

Hess laughed in horror. 'My God, no. It's an invitation to the KGB to stick its nose into the affairs of intelligence. Renko, try to lift your eyes above petty crime. Give me something real.'

'Like what?' Arkady wondered.

'Susan. I watched you in Dutch Harbor. Renko, you must be irresistibly charming in a wounded sort of way. She's attracted. Get closer. Serve your country and yourself. Find something on her and Morgan and I'll order an off-loader just for you.'

'Incriminating notes, secret codes?'

'We'll re-wire her cabin or we can put a transmitter on you.'

'We can do it any number of different ways.'

'Whatever you're comfortable with.'

'Well, no, I don't think so,' Arkady said after consideration. 'Actually I came for something else.'

'What did you come for?'

Arkady stood for a better view of the corners of the locker. 'I just wanted to see if Zina's body was stowed here.'

MARTIN CRUZ SMITH

'And?'

The light was dim, but the space was close.

'No,' Arkady decided.

The two men looked at each other, Hess with the saddened expression of a man who has sung confidences and aspirations to a deaf ear.

'Petty crime is my passion,' Arkady apologized.

The hatch popped open.

'Wait,' Hess said as Arkady started to go. The little man searched in a drawer and came out with a shiny object. This time, it was Arkady's knife. He handed it over. 'Property of the state, right? Good luck.'

Arkady glanced back on the way out. Under the black-and-white screen, Anton Hess was an exhausted man. The other, coloured screens seemed inappropriately gay, tuned into some happier wavelength. Behind their glow the dome nesting in the insulated floor resembled the tip of a vulnerable egg that the fleet electrical engineer was shepherding around the world.

Chapter Twenty-four

Rain beat the *Polar Star* with sharp, horizontal drops that beaded into soft, spongy ice. The crew worked under lamps, hosing the ship off with live steam from the boilers so that the trawl deck smoked as if it were on fire. Ropes stretched across the deck and men clung to the lines, slipping as the deck rolled. Wearing their hard hats under fur-lined hoods the team looked like a Siberian construction crew, all but Karp, who was still in a sweater as if the weather meant nothing to him.

'Relax,' Karp grandly offered a hand as Arkady approached. A radio hung from a strap on his belt. 'Enjoy the refreshing Bering weather.'

'You haven't been after me.' Arkady counted the deck team to be sure they were all in sight. On either side of the deck, pollack overflowed the bunkers. Surrounded by steaming mist, glazed by the freezing rain, the fish sparkled like silvery armour in the lamps.

'It's not as if you had some other place to go.' Karp pulled a block down by its rope to hammer ice from the sheave with the butt of his knife. The gantry operator was out of his cabin. With the ice sheet, no catcherboats were alongside. The entire deck was obscured by steam. 'I could probably throw you overboard right now and nobody would notice.'

'What if I hit the ice and didn't sink?' Arkady said. 'You have to think things through. You're too impulsive.'

Karp laughed. 'You have brass balls, I'll give you that.'

'What was it Volovoi said that made you stick him?' Arkady asked. 'Was it that Volovoi swore he'd take the ship apart when we got back to Vladivostok? Knifing him didn't help. The KGB is going to be all over us when we return.'

'Ridley will say I was with him all night,' Karp picked out the last ice with his blade. 'Say anything about Volovoi, it will come right back to you.'

'Forget about Volovoi.' Arkady shook out a papirosa, a cigarette that could stand up to rain, sleet or driving snow. 'Zina is still who interests me.'

Waist-high in a roar of clouds, Pavel worked his way along the rail with a hose of steaming water. Karp waved him off. 'What about Zina?' he asked Arkady.

'Whatever she was doing she wasn't doing alone, that was never the way she operated. I look around this ship and the only one she would have operated with is you. You told Slava you hardly knew her.'

'She was a fellow worker, that's all.'

'Just another worker, like you?'

'No, I'm a model worker.' Karp enjoyed the distinction. He spread his arms. 'You don't know about workers because you're not one, not at heart. You think the slime line's bad?' Karp tapped his knife on Arkady's chest to make a point. 'Ever work in a slaughterhouse?'

'Yes.'

'A reindeer slaughterhouse?'

'Yes.'

'Slipping around in guts with an oilskin on your shoulder?'

'Yes.'

'Along the Aldan?' The Aldan was a river in Eastern Siberia.

'Yes.'

Karp paused. 'The director of the collective's a Koryak named Sinaneft, went around on a pony?'

'No, he was a Buryat named Korin and he drove a Moskvitch with skis on the front wheels.'

'You really worked there.' Karp was amused. 'Korin had two sons.'

'Daughters.'

'One with tattoos, though. Funny, isn't it? All the time I was in the camps, all the time in Siberia, I said if there was any justice in the world you and I would meet again. And all the time, fate was on my side.'

Overhead, the crane operator carried a mug into his cabin. Across the deck, the American called Bernie made his way aft. Enveloped in a parka, holding on to the line, he looked like a mountaineer. From Karp's radio came Thorwald's throaty voice to say that the *Merry Jane* was approaching with a bag. The trawlmaster sheathed his knife and at once work tempo changed. Hoses were shut off, cables were dragged to the ramp.

'You're not dumb, but you never think more than one step ahead,' Arkady said. 'You should have stayed in Siberia or smuggled videotapes or jeans – small stuff, nothing big.'

'Now let me tell you about you,' Karp said. He brushed ice from Arkady's jacket. 'You're like a dog that's kicked out of the house. You live off scraps in the woods for a while and you think you can run with wolves. But really, in the back of your mind, what you want to do is bring down one wolf so they'll let you back in the house.' He picked a crystal from Arkady's hair and whispered, 'You'll never make it back to Vladivostok.'

People became winter animals, wearing their jackets while they ate. In the middle of the long table was a pot of cabbage soup that smelled like laundry and was consumed with raw garlic offered on separate plates, along with dark bread, goulash and tea that steamed enough to make the cafeteria as foggy as a sauna. Izrail slipped on to the bench next to Arkady. As usual, the factory manager bore fish scales on his beard, as if he'd waded to the crew's mess. 'You cannot ignore your socialist duty,' he whispered to Arkady. 'You must take your place on the work line with your comrades or you will be reported.'

Natasha sat across from Arkady. She still wore her factory-line toque, the high, white cap designed to keep her hair out of the fish.

'Listen to Izrail Izrailevich,' she told Arkady. 'I thought you must be sick. I went to your cabin and you weren't there.'

'Olimpiada has a way with cabbage.' Arkady offered

to ladle soup for Natasha; she shook her head. 'Where is Olimpiada? I haven't seen her.'

Izrail said, 'You will be reported to the captain, to your union, to the Party.'

'Reporting me to Volovoi would be interesting. Natasha, you're not having any goulash?'

'No.'

'At least bread?'

'Thank you, tea is sufficient.' She poured herself a dainty cup.

'This is serious, Renko.' Izrail helped himself to soup and bread. 'You can't go around the ship as if you had special orders from Moscow.' He bit into a clove and reflected. 'Unless you do.'

'You're dieting?' Arkady asked Natasha.

'Resisting.'

'Why?'

'I have my reasons.' With her hair pulled back inside her cap she was showing more cheekbone, and her dark eyes seemed larger and softer.

Obidin sat beside her and heaped his plate with goulash, which he examined for meat. 'I understand there is a feeling we should never take fish again where we found Zina,' he said. 'Out of respect for the dead.'

'Ridiculous.' Natasha's eyes grew hard at the thought of Zina. 'We're not all religious fanatics. This is the modern age. Have you ever heard of such a thing?' she demanded of Izrail.

'Have you ever heard of Kureyka?' Izrail asked in turn. A smile hid in his beard. 'It's where Stalin was exiled by the Tsar. Then when Stalin ruled, he sent an army of prisoners to Kureyka to nail his old cabin back together and build around it a hangar filled with lights that shone twenty-four hours a day on the cabin and on a marble statue of himself. A giant statue. One night years after he died, they secretly dragged the statue out and dropped it into the river. All the boats detoured so they wouldn't sail overhead.'

'How do you know about this?' Arkady asked.

'How do you think a Jew becomes Siberian?' The manager asked in turn. 'My father helped erect the hangar.' He bit into the bread. 'I won't report you right away,' he told Arkady. 'I'll give you a day or two.'

On his way to the radio shack, Arkady heard a voice that sounded like the one on Zina's tape. The voice and guitar, resonantly romantic, emanated from the infirmary door. It didn't sound like Doctor Vainu.

'In a distant blustering sea
A pirate brigantine is making sail.'

It was an old camper's song, though a camper had to be fairly drunk and probably incapable of walking around a tree to enjoy such weepy lyrics.

'The Jolly Roger flaps in the breeze,
Captain Flint is singing along.

And, our glasses ringing, we too
Begin our little song.'

When Arkady entered the infirmary the song stopped.

'Shit, shit, I thought it was locked,' Doctor Vainu said, rushing to block Arkady's way. At the far end of the hall Arkady saw the broad, borscht-red backside of Olimpiada Bovina running into an examining room. The doctor was in a leisure suit and slippers and looked only slightly rumpled, slippers on the wrong feet. Arkady would have thought that Bovina and Vainu made a pair like a steamroller and a squirrel.

'You can't just come in,' Vainu protested.

'I'm in.' Looking for the singer, Arkady led the doctor down the hall to the operating room, where a sheet covered the operating table. Arkady noticed that the box with Zina's effects was still on the counter.

'This is a medical office.' Vainu checked his zipper.

Beside the table was a steel tray with a beaker and, from the taste of varnish in the air, glasses of grain alcohol. Also, a half-eaten chocolate with a cream centre. Arkady laid his hand on the sheet. Still warm, like the hood of a car.

'You can't just break in,' Vainu said with evaporating conviction. He slumped against a counter and lit a cigarette to calm himself. On the counter beside the box was a new Japanese cassette player with its own miniature stereo speakers. Arkady pressed the player's 'Rewind' button, then 'Play.' '... Roger flaps in the breeze.' Then 'Stop'. 'Sorry,' he said.

The voice wasn't like the other singer anyway.

Col. Pavlov-Zalygin's sonorous voice travelled the telephone path and airwaves all the way from Odessa. His rich, unhurried baritone reminded Arkady that while the ice sheet might be moving south in the Bering Sea, in Georgia they were still pressing grapes, and on the Black Sea ferry boats were still filled with the last tourists of the year.

The colonel was happy to aid a colleague far at sea, though it meant digging through old files. 'Patiashvili? I knew the case, but lately the bosses are sticklers about the law. Lawyers are getting into everything, accusing us of violence, appealing perfectly good sentences. Believe me, you're better off at sea. I should study the case and call you back.'

Arkady remembered that if they happened to be monitoring the Soviet channel, other ships could hear the incoming half of the conversation. The less calls the better, even assuming he had a chance for another one. Nicolai studied the dials on the single sideband; the needles swayed with the colonel's voice. 'It's the weather,' he told Arkady. 'Reception is deteriorating.'

'There's no time,' Arkady spoke into the receiver.

'Criminals are having their letters printed in the newspapers,' Pavlov-Zalygin said. 'In the *Literary Gazette*!'

'She's dead,' Arkady said.

'Well,' the colonel said, 'let me think.'

There was a four-second gap in each transmission that only added confusion. Instead of a microphone, the radio had a telephone receiver with a daisy pattern on the mouthpiece as an old-fashioned nicety. It struck

Arkady that all the modern technology on the *Polar Star* was at the bottom of the ship with Hess.

'The trouble was we had no real case against her,' Pavlov-Zalygin said reluctantly, 'nothing we could take to court. We searched her apartment, we held her in custody, but we never had enough to charge her. Aside from that, the investigation was a great success.'

'Investigation of what?'

'This was in the newspapers, in *Pravda*,' the colonel said with pride. 'An international operation. Five tonnes of Georgian hashish shipped from Odessa on a Soviet freighter to Montreal. Very high-quality goods, all in bricks, inside containers marked "raw wool". Customs discovered the narcotics here. Usually we make the arrests and destroy the illegal shipment, but this time we decided to collaborate with the Canadians and to make arrests at both ends.'

'A joint venture.'

'Just so. The operation was a great success, you must . . . it.'

'Yes. How was Zina Patiashvili involved?'

'The ringleader was a boyfriend of hers. She had worked six months in the galley of the freighter; in fact, it was the only freighter she ever really worked on. She was seen on the dock when the ship was first loaded, but . . .'

As the static increased it pushed the needle in the radio's wattage meter.

'. . . to the prosecutor. Nevertheless, we ran her out of town.'

'The others involved are still in camps?'

'Camps of strict regimen, absolutely. I know there's been an amnesty, but it's not like the Krushchev amnesty when we let everybody go. No, when. . . .'

'We're losing him,' Nicolai said.

'You said that she worked on that freighter for six months, but her paybook shows that she worked in the Black Sea Fleet for three years,' Arkady said.

'Not as a galley worker exactly. She . . . with . . . recommendations and the usual titles. . . .'

'What did she do?' Arkady asked again.

'Swam.' Suddenly the colonel's voice was booming and clear. 'She swam for the Black Sea Fleet at meets everywhere. Before that she swam for her vocational school. Some said she could have tried for the Olympics if she'd had any discipline.'

'A small girl, dark hair bleached blond?' Arkady couldn't believe they were talking about the same woman.

'That's her, except her hair was just dark. Attractive in a cheap . . . foreign . . . Hello? . . . Re. . . .'

The colonel's voice faded like a boat sighted in a storm, moving from one fog bank of static to a thicker one.

'He's gone.' Nicolai watched the needle bounce out of control.

Arkady signed off and sat back while the lieutenant watched him anxiously. With good reason. It was one thing for a virile young radioman to slip an honest citizen into a secret intelligence post to seduce her; it was quite another to reveal the post to a major criminal.

'I'm sorry.' Nicolai couldn't stand the suspense any longer. 'I wanted to get you up here to the radio shack earlier when the transmission was better, but there was a lot of fuss about the trawl we lost, with calls to Seattle and the fleet. It was the last net from the *Merry Jane*.'

'Thorwald?'

'The Norwegians, yes. He blames us, but we blame him because he tried to transfer more than the maximum load. He lost his trawl and gear. There's no way of grappling for it in this ice apparently – and he has to return to Dutch Harbor.'

'We're down to the *Eagle*?'

'The company has already dispatched three catcher-boats to join us. They're not going to leave a factory ship like us depending on only one trawler.'

'Did Zina tell you that she swam?'

Nicolai cleared his throat. 'She just said she could.'

'Back in the Golden Horn, the restaurant, was there anyone else you recognized, someone on the ship?'

'No. Look, I have to ask about your report. What are you going to say about me? You seem to know everything.'

'If I knew everything I wouldn't be asking questions.'

'Yes, yes, but are you naming me in your report?' Nicolai hunched closer; he was the kind of boy, Arkady thought, who would try to read his marks upside down on his teacher's desk. 'I have no right to ask, but I beg you to consider what will happen to me if there are adverse comments in your report. It's not for myself. My mother works in a cannery. I always send one bolt of Navy cloth home, and she sews skirts and pants that she can sell to friends, that's how she gets by. She lives for me, and something bad like this would kill her.'

'Are you suggesting that I'd be responsible if your betrayal of your duty caused your mother's death?'

'Of course not, nothing like that.'

Vladivostok would listen to Zina's tapes no matter what happened to Arkady. On the basis of her trip to the chain locker alone the lieutenant faced the brig. 'Before we reach home port you'd better talk to Hess,' he said. He wanted to get out of the radio shack quickly. 'We'll see what happens.'

'I remember one other thing, on the subject of money,' Nicolai said. 'Zina never asked for any. What she wanted me to bring was a playing card, a queen of hearts. Not a payment, a . . .'

'A souvenir?'

'I went to the recreation officer and asked for a pack. Can you believe we have only one pack for the entire ship? And it didn't have a queen of hearts. The way he was smiling, he knew.'

'Who was the recreation officer?' Arkady asked, though since the position was the lowest function an officer could have only one name was likely.

'Slava Bukovsky.'

Who else?

Chapter Twenty-five

Arkady found Slava sitting in shadow on an upper bunk, wearing the headphones of a Walkman and playing the mouthpiece of a saxophone, his bare feet swinging with the beat. Arkady sat quietly at the cabin's table as if he'd arrived midway at a concert. Only the hooded light over the desk was on, but he could see the appointments that graced an officer's cabin: the desk itself, bookshelves, a waist-high refrigerator and a clock inside a waterproof case, as if Slava's were the cabin most likely to be flooded. He reminded himself not to be too disparaging; Slava had concealed successfully until now any involvement with Zina. The bookshelf held an entertainment officer's usual books on popular games and recommended songs, as well as forbidding tomes on Lenin's thought and on diesel propulsion; the second mate, Slava's cabinmate, was studying for his first mate's ticket.

As Slava's cheeks swelled, his eyes closed, his body swayed and soulful bleats emerged from the mouthpiece. There was a calendar on a pennant, a photo of a group of boys around a motorcycle, with Slava in the sidecar, and a typed list of the year's May Day slogans; No. 14, 'Toilers in the agro-industrial complex! Your patriotic duty is to fully provide the country with food in a short time!' was underlined.

The third mate pulled off his headphones. He squeezed a last mournful note from the mouthpiece, let it drop and finally looked at Arkady.

' "Back in the USSR.",' he said. 'Beatles.'

'I recognized it.'

'I can play any instrument. Name an instrument.'

'Zither.'

'A regular instrument.'

'Lute, lyre, steel drum, sitar, Pan's pipes, Formosan chong chai?'

'You know what I mean.'

'Accordion?'

'I can play that. Synthesizer, drums, guitar.' Slava looked at Arkady suspiciously. 'What do you want?'

'Remember that box of personal effects you took from Zina's cabin? Did you have a chance to go through her spiral notebook?'

'No, I didn't have time because I had to interview a hundred people that same day.'

'The box is still in the infirmary. I just came from going over the notebook for fingerprints more completely than I did the first time. There are Zina's and yours. I compared them with the prints on the suicide note you found.'

'So I did look in her dumb book. Too bad, you should have asked me in front of someone. Anyway, what are you doing running around the ship, not even bothering to show up in the factory?'

'We don't have that many fish to clean. The team isn't going to miss me.'

'Why isn't the captain stopping you?'

Arkady had thought about it. 'It's a little like the *Inspector General*. Remember that story about how a fool comes to town and is thought to be an official of the tsar? Also, murder changes everything. Nobody knows quite what to do, especially with Volovoi out of the way. As long as I don't argue with orders, I can ignore them for a while. As long as people don't know how much I know; that's what scares them.'

'So it's just a matter of calling your bluff?'

'Pretty much.'

Slava sat up. 'I could march right up to the bridge and tell the captain that a certain seaman second-class has been shirking work in order to pester the crew with questions he was ordered not to ask?'

'You can march better with your shoes on.'

'Done.'

Slava tucked the mouthpiece into his shirt pocket and hopped lightly from the bunk down to the deck. Arkady reached across the desk for an ashtray while the third mate pulled on his boots. 'You're going to wait here?' he asked Arkady.

'Right here.'

Slava threw on his running jacket. 'Anything else I should tell him?'

'Tell him about you and Zina.'

The door slammed and Slava was gone.

Arkady took a cigarette from his pants and found a book of matches in the desk's mug of pencils. He studied the design on the face of the book: the world 'Prodintorg'

341

emblazoned on a ribbon. As he remembered, Prodintorg was in charge of foreign trade in animal goods: fish,
crab, caviar, racehorses, cattle and animals for zoos, a
wholesale approach to the wonders of nature. He had
barely lit up when Slava returned shutting the door with
his back. 'What about Zina?'

'Zina and you.'

'You're guessing again.'

'No.'

A lifetime of bowing to authority shaped people. Slava
sat on the lower bunk and put his face in his hands.
'Oh, God. When my father hears about this.'

'He may not, but you do have to tell me.'

Slava raised his head, blinked and took the sharp
breaths of a man hyperventilating. 'He'll kill me.'

Arkady prompted him. 'I think you tried to tell
me once or twice and I wasn't smart enough to hear
you. What I couldn't solve, for example, was how Zina
was assigned to this ship. To have that much influence
in Fleet headquarters is highly unusual.'

'Oh, he tried to please, in his way.'

'Your father?' Arkady held up the matchbook.

'Deputy minister.' Slava was silent for a moment. 'Zina
insisted she had to be on this ship to be near me. What
a joke! As soon as we left port, everything was over, as
if we'd never known each other.'

'He made the call that put you on the *Polar Star*, and
then at your request ordered to have Zina assigned too?'

'He never orders; he just calls the head of the port
and asks if there's any good reason someone can't be

placed somewhere or something can't be done. All he says is that the Ministry is interested, and everybody understands. Anything: the right school, the right teacher, a Ministry car to bring me home. You know the first sign of restructuring was when he couldn't get me into the Baltic Fleet, only the Pacific. That's why Marchuk detests me.' Slava stared into the dark as if there were a ghost there at a desk with a battery of phones. 'You never had a father like that.'

'I did, but I disappointed him early and completely,' Arkady reassured him. 'We all make mistakes. You couldn't know that I'd already looked under the bed where you found the suicide note. Or, I should say, where you put the note, which came from her notebook that you took away from her cabin. I was slow not to figure that out right away. Was there anything else in the notebook that I didn't see?'

A nervous giggle overcame Slava. 'More suicide notes, two or three on a page. I threw the rest away. How many times could she kill herself?'

'So there you were, leading the ship's band and watching a woman you'd helped get on board dancing with American fishermen and ignoring you.'

'No one knew.'

'You knew.'

'I hated it. During the break I had a smoke in the galley just so I wouldn't see her. Zina came in and out and didn't give me a second glance. Because she couldn't use me any more I didn't exist.'

'That wasn't in your report.'

'Nobody saw us. Once I tried to talk to her, one day in the wardroom, and she said she'd tell the captain if I ever bothered her again. That's when I saw what was going on between the two of them, the leading captain and Zina. What if he knew about me? I wasn't dumb enough to say I might have been the last one to see her alive.'

'Were you?'

'Slava unscrewed the mouthpiece band and examined the reed. 'Cracked. It's hard enough to find a sax to buy, and when you do own one it's impossible to find reeds. They control you either way.' Gingerly he slipped the reed back on, like a man putting a ruby into a ring. 'I don't know. She took a plastic bag from a soup pot. The bag was all taped up. She put it under her jacket and went out. I've tried to figure it out over and over. I thought those people on deck saw her after I did, but they didn't say anything about a jacket or a bag. I'm not a good detective.'

'How big was the bag? What colour?'

'One of the big ones. Black.'

'See, you remembered that. How is your report on Volovoi going?'

'I was just working on it when you came in.'

'In the dark?'

'Does it matter? What can I say that anyone will believe? They have a way of checking the lungs, don't they, to tell whether he really died in a fire?' Slava laughed bitterly. 'Marchuk says if I do a good job he'll second my move to a Party school, which is another way of his saying I'll never make a captain.'

'Maybe you shouldn't. What about the Ministry?'

'Working under my father?' The question answered Arkady's.

'Music?'

After a silence Slava said, 'Before we moved to Moscow we lived in Leningrad. You know Leningrad?'

It hadn't struck Arkady so forcibly before how lonely Slava was. This soft young man sitting in the shadow was meant for a carpeted office with a view of the Neva, not of the North Pacific.

'Yes.'

'The basketball courts near the Nevsky? No? Well, when I was five I was at the courts and there were some black Americans playing basketball. I'd never seen anything like them; they could have been from another planet. Everything they did was different – the way they shot, which was so easy, and the way they laughed, so loud that I put my hands over my ears. Actually they weren't even a team. They were musicians who had been scheduled to play at the House of Culture but the performance had been cancelled because they played jazz. So they were playing basketball instead, but I could imagine how they made music, like black angels.'

'What kind of music did you make?'

'Rock. We had a high-school band. We wrote our own songs, but we were censored by the House of Creativity.'

'You must have been popular,' Arkady said.

'It was pretty anti-Establishment. I've always been a liberal. The idiots on this ship don't understand that.'

'Is that how you met Zina, at a dance? Or at the restaurant?'

'No. Do you know Vladivostok?'

'About as well as I know Leningrad.'

'I hate Vladivostok. There's a beach by the stadium where everybody swims in the summertime. You know the scene, a pier covered with towels, air mattresses, chessboards, gobs of suntan lotion and all the anatomy you'd just as soon not see.'

'That's not for you?'

'Thank you, no. I borrowed a sailboat, a six-metre, and sailed the bay. Because of the naval channel you have to stay fairly near the beach. Of course, most of the people don't go in the water any deeper than their waist, or any further than the buoy lines, certainly not past the lifeguards in the rowboats. Just the sound drives you crazy, the yakking and splashing and lifeguards' whistles. Sailing was like escaping all of them. There was one swimmer, though, who swam so far out and so easily that I couldn't help noticing her. She must have swum underwater some distance just to get past the lifeguards. I was so distracted that I spilled the wind out of the sail and luffed. There was a rope trailing off the side and she grabbed it and pulled herself on board, just as if we'd planned it. Then she stretched out on deck for a rest and pulled her cap off. Her hair was dark then, almost black. You know how water beads in the sun, so she looked like she was covered in little diamonds. She laughed as if it was the most natural thing in the world for her to leap out of the water on to the boat of someone she'd never met. We sailed all afternoon. She said she wanted me to take her to a disco, but that she'd have to meet me there; she didn't want me to pick her up. Then she dove in the water and was gone.

'After the disco, we went hiking in the hills. She never let me pick her up or leave her off at her apartment. I assumed she was living in such poor conditions that she was embarrassed. I knew by her accent that she was Georgian, but I didn't hold that against her. I was able to tell her anything and she seemed to understand. With hindsight I realize she never talked about herself at all, except to say that she had a seaman's ticket and wanted to come on the *Polar Star* with me. She played me for a fool, which is exactly what I was. She played everyone for a fool.'

'Who do you think killed her?'

'Anyone, but I was afraid a murder investigation would sooner or later point to me, which makes me a coward as well as a fool. Am I wrong?'

'No.' Arkady couldn't disagree. 'The water in the bay, was it cold?'

'Out where she was? Freezing.' Sitting on the upper bunk, Slava seemed suspended in the dark.

Arkady said, 'You told me before this is your second voyage.'

'Yes.'

'Both voyages with Captain Marchuk?'

'Yes.'

'Is there anyone else on the *Polar Star* that you sailed with before?'

'No.' Slava thought. 'No officers, I mean. Otherwise, only Pavel and Karp. Am I in trouble?'

'I'm afraid you are.'

'I've never been in real trouble before, I never had the nerve. It's new, a whole different range of possibilities. What are you going to do now?'

'Go to bed.'

'It's early.'

'Well, when you're in trouble even getting to bed can be exciting.'

On deck, Arkady could feel the ship ride away from the wind, which meant that Marchuk had delivered the *Merry Jane* to the edge of the ice sheet and turned north, into the sheet again. Rain made the ice around the *Polar Star* shimmer like the blue of an electrical field. Arkady hid in shadow until his eyes adjusted.

Slava hadn't known anything about the Golden Horn or about the apartment Zina had taken Nicolai and Marchuk to, so from the start she had treated Slava differently. No raucous seamen's restaurant, no apartment cum illegal arsenal to scare off the delicate third mate. She may have never seen Slava before that day she climbed on to his sailboat, but the trawlmaster had.

At any moment Karp could swing from a guy wire or pop out of a hatch. 'Relax,' he had said. Why hadn't Karp killed him yet? Arkady wondered. Not because of his intelligence or luck. Officers occupied the *Polar Star*'s wheelhouse, their realm of ignorance, and the rest of the factory ship's ill-lit passages and slippery decks were the trawlmaster's dominion. Arkady could vanish whenever Karp wanted. Each day since Dutch Harbor had been a day of grace. He was alive, he realized, only because a third death was more than Vladivostok would be willing to accept. The *Polar Star* would immediately be ordered home. When a ship returned under a cloud it was surrounded by Border Guard troops and the crew kept on board while the vessel was stripped down and searched. Yet Karp had to get rid of him. For the moment the trawlmaster's dilemma was the difference between Arkady wearing his head or not. Karp was still thinking, taking his time since what could Arkady tell Marchuk that wouldn't point more at himself than at anyone else? Karp had witnesses for where he was when the first mate died. Still, despite that 'Relax,' Arkady crossed the deck from pool of light to pool of light like a man connecting dots.

The crew was already packed away in their beds, and in Arkady's cabin only Obidin was awake.

'Some persons say there's an off-loader coming to get you, Arkady. Some say you're Cheka.' Cheka was the old, honoured name of the KGB. 'Some say you don't know yourself.' The smell of homebrew rose from Obidin's beard like the scent of pollen from a thistle.

Arkady pulled off his boots and climbed into his bunk. 'And what do you think?'

'They're fools, of course. The mystery of human action cannot be defined in political terms.'

'You don't like politics,' Arkady yawned.

'The black soul of a politician cannot be plumbed. Soon the Kremlin will join the other devil.'

'Which devil?' Americans, Chinese, Jews?

'The Pope.'

'Shut up,' Gury's voice said. 'We're trying to sleep.'

Thank God, Arkady thought.

'Arkady,' Kolya said a minute later. 'You awake?'

'What?'

'Have you noticed Natasha lately? She's looking nice.'

Chapter Twenty-six

In his sleep Arkady watched Zina Patiashvili swim from the Vladivostok beach, which was exactly as Slava had described except that the sunbathers were all seals, basking and craning their heads and long-lashed oriental eyes up to the sky. She was in the same bathing suit she'd paraded in on deck that sunny day. The same dark glasses, and her hair was blond, not even with telltale roots. It was a dazzling day. Long buoys were strung like candy sticks around a kiddy section. Timber had floated from the loading yards near by, and boys rode stray logs like war canoes.

Further into the bay Zina swam, even past the sailboats on the surface of the water so that she could turn on her back and look at the city's overlapping green trees and office blocks and the Roman arches of the stadium. Dynamo Stadium. Every town had its Dynamos, Spartaks or Torpedos. Why not names like Torpor or Inertia?

She dove to quieter, cooler water where light penetrated the water at an angle, as if through the blinds of a room, down to a level both translucent and black, pulling herself with sweeping strokes to the soft, silent floor of the bay. A fish darted in front of her face. Schools of fish flowed by on either side, herring as bright as a shower of coins, blue streams of sablefish, the floating shadow of a ray moving from two beams of light that approached with the sound of an onrushing train. Steel trawl doors ploughed the sea floor on either side, sending up plumes of roiled mud. The lights attached to the headrope were blinding, but she could see the bottom exploding with the groundrope's advance, both geysers of silt and wave after wave of groundfish rising to try to escape the trawl, which roared as it engulfed them. A wall of water first pushed her away from and then sucked her into the maelstrom, into the deep bass chord of straining mesh and clouds of silt and glittering scales.

Awake, Arkady sat up in the dark as wet with sweat as if he'd climbed from the sea. He'd told Natasha it was simply seeing what was before your eyes; no genius was needed. How do you smuggle on open water? What went back and forth twenty times a day? And where would the trawlmaster hide what he'd received? Another obvious answer came back: where on the *Polar Star* had he been attacked?

This time Arkady took a flashlight. Rats scurried from beams, slipping between planks, red pinpoints staring down as he went down the ladder in the forward hold. Cooling pipes swarmed with the adept clambering of rats. At least his descent was shorter with a light.

He stepped gently down on to the bottom of the hold, remembering how on his first trip he had picked up a loose plank and started beating on the walls in an attempt to drive out a lieutenant of Naval Intelligence, when all the while he had probably been standing on the lid of a treasure chest. The beam of the flashlight found the plank, the same paint cans and blanket, the same cat skeleton as before. But earlier the cat skeleton had been in the centre of the floor; this time it was curled up in a corner. There were heels and scuff marks on the floor planks. He touched them. Not scuff marks: wet.

The hatch at floor level opened and Pavel, the deck-hand on Karp's team, stepped halfway in. Wearing a helmet and jacket soaked with rain, he tried to squint over his hand through the glare of Arkady's flashlight. 'Still here?' he asked. Then he saw who it was, slammed the hatch and locked it shut.

Arkady climbed the ladder to the next level. Its hatch was locked. He continued up to the top level, the one he'd entered the hold through, his heart pounding like an extra prisoner willing his hands up the rungs. Kicking the hatch open, he ran to the stairs and down. When he reached the bottom level outside the hold Pavel was gone, but wet bootprints on the metal deck pointed like arrows in the direction he'd taken. There was the damp traffic of other boots on the same path.

Arkady ran, trying to catch up. The path led aft, passed the No. 2 fish hold and then took the midship stairs to emerge by the forward crane of the trawl deck. There was no sign of Pavel or anyone else. Rain swept the boards of the deck, wiping them clean, and Arkady

pocketed the flashlight and took out his knife. The main
winch lamp was off, the gantry lamps were caked with
ice. Across the deck the entrance to the stern ramp was
black.

At this point he didn't need arrows. What was surprising was that it was the first time he'd ever been on the
ramp. The gantry lights touched the rough hide of its
walls and the overlapping folds of ice at the top of the
slip. With each step down, though, the light faded and
the angle of the ramp became more precipitous. Far
forward, the prow of the *Polar Star* hit heavier ice and
shuddered. Deep within the stern, in the soundbox of
the ramp, the shudder swelled into a moan. A following
wave rushed up the ramp and subsided with a sigh,
the way the audiomechanics of a seashell amplified the
exaggerated sound, the way the inner ear gauged the
pounding of the heart.

If Arkady slid there was nothing between him and
the water but the safety gate. He held on as best he
could to the side of the ramp as he felt its deck start to
fall away. Overhead, at the well, was a second dim
intrusion of light. He could see that the chain of the
safety gate was taut on its hook on the wall of the ramp;
the gate had been swung up and out of the way. Too
late to grasp the hook, he began to slide. Just a bit to
begin with, the first millimetre that informs a falling
man of his situation, then with momentum that grew as
the curve of the ramp became steeper. Spread-eagled,
face forward, his fingers digging into ice, he saw the
white tracery of a wave rising towards him while his

knife rattled ahead of him, free. At the lip the ramp opened to the black of the fairway and the sky, the sound of the screws and, to the sides, wings of ice. As the water rushed up, his hand found a rope along the side of the ramp and he twisted his wrist around it. When he came to a stop he saw below him another man standing in boots at a steep angle like a mountain climber in the waves washing the bottom of the ramp. The lifeline was tied to his waist.

Karp wore a dark sweater and a wool cap pulled down to his heavy brow, and he held what looked like a cushion. 'Too late,' he told Arkady. He threw the cushion backhanded into the water. From the way it hit and plunged, the package was weighted. 'A fortune,' he said. 'Everything we'd bought. But you're right; they'll tear this ship apart when we get back to Vladivostok.'

Karp leaned back with both hands free and lit a cigarette, a man relieved and at ease. The wake had a luminescence that dissipated in the dark. Arkady pulled himself to his feet.

'You look scared, Renko.'

'I am.'

'Here.' Karp shifted, gave the cigarette to Arkady and lit another for himself. His eyes shone as they searched the ramp above. 'You came alone?'

'Yes.'

'We'll find out.'

Arkady's attention was fixed on the rain and a light swaying in the distance like a lamp in a breeze. It was the *Eagle*, maybe two hundred metres back. 'What you tossed in, what if the net picks it up?'

'The *Eagle* isn't towing now, they're busy enough hosing off ice. Pretty top-heavy in a boat like that. How did you know I'd be here?'

Arkady decided not to mention Pavel. 'I wanted to see where Zina had gone into the water.'

'Here?'

'She left her jacket and a bag either here or on the landing while she went to the dance. What did she look like in the net?' Arkady asked.

Karp gave his cigarette a long pull. 'Ever see anyone drown?' he asked.

'Yes.'

'Then you know.' Karp turned to study the *Eagle*'s light as it faded in a sweeping gust of rain. He seemed unhurried, as if waiting for a friend. 'The sea is dangerous, but I should be grateful to you for getting me out of Moscow. I was making with pimping and shakedowns, what? Twenty or thirty rubles a day? To the rest of the world, rubles aren't even money.'

'You're not in the rest of the world. In the Soviet Union a fisherman makes a lot of rubles.'

'For what? Meat's rationed, sugar's rationed. Restructuring is a joke. The only difference now is that vodka is rationed too. Who's a criminal? Who's a smuggler? Delegations go to Washington and come back with clothes, toilets, chandeliers. The Secretary General collected fast cars, his daughter collected diamonds. The same in the republics. This Party leader has marble palaces; that one had suitcases so full of gold you can't lift them from the floor. Another has a fleet of trucks that carry nothing but poppies, and the trucks are protected by the motor patrol. Renko, you're the only one I don't understand. You're like a doctor in a whorehouse.'

'Well, I'm a romantic. So you wanted something else, but why drugs?'

Karp's shoulders wore frozen beads of rain; their outline made Arkady think of the mist in a cloud chamber that betrayed the dewy track of ions.

'It's the one way a worker can make real money as long as he has the nerve,' Karp said. 'That's why governments hate drugs, because they can't control them. They control vodka and tobacco, but they don't control drugs. Look at America. Even blacks are making money.'

'You think it will happen in the Soviet Union, too?'

'It's happening already. You can buy ammo off a Red Army base, run it right over the border and sell it to the Afghans fighting us. The *dushmany* have warehouses with cocaine piled to the roof. It's better than gold. It's the new currency. That's why everyone's afraid of the veterans – not just because they're drug-users, but because they know what's really going on.'

'You're not part of any vast Afghani network, though,' Arkady said. 'You'd be dealing in Siberian goods, *anasha*. What's the rate of exchange as the nets go back and forth?'

Karp's smile flashed gold in the dark. 'A couple of bricks from us for a spoonful from them. It seems unfair, but you know what a gram of cocaine brings at an oil rig in Siberia? Five hundred rubles. You figured out the nets; that's clever of you.'

'What I don't understand is how you got *anasha* past the Border Guards and on to the *Polar Star.*'

The trawlmaster's voice became both flattered and confiding, as if it were a shame that the two of them couldn't pull up chairs and split a bottle. At the same time, Arkady was aware that the trawlmaster was only playing a role, enjoying the situation over which he had complete control.

'You'll appreciate this,' Karp said. 'What can a trawlmaster ask for in the way of supplies? Net, needles, shackles, ropes. The yard always gives you the worst, you can depend on that. What's the cheapest rope?'

'Hemp.' Manchurian hemp was grown legally for rope and packing; *anasha* was merely the potent, pollinating version of the same bush. 'You packed *anasha* in the rope, hemp in hemp.' Arkady was forced to admire it.

'And we end up trading shit for gold. Two kilos are a million rubles.'

'But now you'll have to sign up for another six months to bring back a second load.'

'It's a setback.' Karp looked thoughtfully up the ramp. 'Not like the one you're going to have, but still a setback. You say you came here in the rain in the middle of the night just to see where Zina went in? I don't believe it.'

'Do you believe in dreams?'

'No.'

'Neither do I.'

'You know why I killed that son of a bitch in Moscow?' Karp asked suddenly.

'In the train yard with the prostitute?'

'The one you nailed me on, right.'

'So it wasn't an accident, you meant to do it?'

'Long gone, fifteen years ago, you can't charge me a second time.'

'So why did you kill him?'

'You know who the whore was? It was my mother.'

'She didn't say. She had a different name.'

'Yeah, well, that son of a bitch knew it, and he said he was going to tell everyone. It wasn't like I was crazy.'

'You should have said so then.'

'It would have made her sentence worse.'

Arkady remembered a coarsely painted woman with hair dyed Chinese red. At that time prostitution did not officially exist, but she was sentenced for conspiracy to rob.

'What happened to her?'

'She died in corrective labour. In her camp they made padded jackets for Siberia, so maybe you or I wore one. They had a quota like anyone else. She died happy, though. There were a lot of women there with babies, a kindergarten with its own barbed wire, and they let her clean up there. She wrote and said she'd gotten better being around kids. Except she died of pneumonia, which she probably picked up from some runny-nosed brat. It's funny what can kill you.' He shook a knife from his sleeve.

Arkady turned at the sound of steps. Against the faint

glow from the trawl deck he could make out someone in a hard hat descending the ramp, holding on to the rope that led to Karp.

'It's Pavel.' Karp said. 'He took his time getting here. So you really did come alone.'

Arkady started back up the rope, pulling himself hand over hand. Karp was faster. Though the lifeline was tied around his own waist the trawlmaster didn't seem to need it and he strode easily up the icy slope.

Ahead, the figure from the trawl deck stopped. Arkady would have to go wide to get by, and he knew that as soon as he left the rope he would slide down the ramp to the water. His boots slipped. How did Karp move up the ramp so quickly, like a devil flying up steps?

'This was worth waiting for,' Karp said. He shook the rope so that Arkady slipped again, and then he had him by his jacket.

'Arkady?' Natasha called. 'Is that you?'

'Yes.'

The shape looming on the ramp above wasn't Pavel. Now that they were closer he saw that what had looked like a man's helmet was a scarf over her hair.

'Who are you with?' she demanded.

'Korobetz,' Arkady said. 'You know Korobetz.'

Arkady could almost hear the calculations in the trawlmaster's mind. Would it be possible to kill him *and* Natasha before she reached the trawl deck and called out?

'We're old friends,' Karp still held on to Arkady. 'We go back a long way. Give us a hand.'

'Get on deck,' Arkady told her. 'I'll follow.'

'You two?' Natasha asked suspiciously. 'Friends?'

'Go,' Arkady ordered. He stayed where he was so that Karp couldn't get past.

'What's the matter, Arkady?' She stood her ground.

'Wait,' Karp told her.

'Wait there,' Pavel added as he came down the ramp above Natasha. An axe dangled from his free hand.

Arkady kicked Karp's leg. The trawlmaster landed on his stomach and slid down the ramp the length of his lifeline. Arkady hoped he would go into the water, but Karp stopped just above the churning spine of the wake. At once he was back on his feet and scaling the ramp, but by then Arkady had reached the hook where the chain holding up the safety gate was fastened. He released the chain. With a rush of air, the gate swung down and with a metallic clap slammed shut in Karp's face, trapping him on the lower end of the ramp.

Arkady got ahead of Natasha. Behind him, he heard Karp shaking the gate as if its steel mesh could come apart in his hands. Then the gate was still. 'Renko,' the trawlmaster's voice came up the ramp.

Pavel hesitated as Arkady approached. His eyes were round hollows, more afraid of Karp than of Arkady. 'You're fucking up everything. He said you would.'

Karp's laugh filled the ramp. 'Where are you going to run?'

'Piss off.' Natasha said the magic words and Pavel backed away.

Chapter Twenty-seven

'We make a good team,' Natasha said.

She was still exhilarated by their escape from the ramp, her eyes bright, a long strand of hair hanging loose. Arkady led her into the cafeteria, which they found turned into a dance floor.

There had been no announcement over the loud-speakers. Third Mate Slava Bukovsky, the officer in charge of entertainment, had for purposes of morale spontaneously gathered his band and sent word below decks that music would be offered to the crew. As no nets were being taken and the night was foul, the entire ship's company had been holing up, bored and stifling, in their cabins. Now they holed up happily and commu-nally in the cafeteria. This time there were no Americans, not even reps, and for some reason no rock. The ball of mirrors spun, its reflections scattering like snow over dancers who moved in dreamy slowness. On stage, Slava squeezed from his saxophone a sweet, dirgelike blues.

Arkady and Natasha crowded on to a back bench with Dynka and Madame Malzeva. 'I wish my Mahmet were here now.' The Uzbek girl clasped her hands together.

'I've heard musicians in the Black Sea Fleet.' Malzeva wrapped a babushka around her shoulders for dignity's sake, but unbent enough to add, 'Actually, he's not so bad.'

Natasha whispered in Arkady's ear. 'We should go to the captain and tell him what happened.'

'What would we say? All you saw was me and Karp. A trawlmaster has any number of reasons to be on the ramp. I don't.'

'There was Pavel with an axe.'

'They've been chopping ice all day. Maybe he's a Hero Worker.'

'You were attacked.'

'I dropped the gate on Karp, not the other way round, and all you heard him say was that we were friends. The man's a saint.'

The next song was 'Dark Eyes', a syrupy tale of gypsy love. The girl on the synthesizer plunked out a sound something like a guitar's while Slava produced lush, brassy melody. It was shameless and irresistible. The floor was a slowly surging tide of dancers.

'You and Karp are like a mouse and a snake,' Natasha said. 'You can't share the same hole.'

'Not for much longer.'

'Why were you on the ramp?'

'Would you like to dance?' Arkady asked.

A metamorphosis came over Natasha. Light glowed not only in her eyes but from her face. Like a woman who has arrived in sable, she slowly removed her fishing jacket and scarf, gave them to Dynka and then pulled the comb from her hair so that it cascaded softly down.

'Ready?' Arkady asked.

'Absolutely.' Her voice had softened, too.

They made an unlikely pair, he had to admit: the Party's model member and a troublemaker from the slime line. As he led Natasha between tables to the floor she met astonished glances with a gaze at once imperious and serene.

Soviet dancers don't expect much room to dance in; there's always an attendant amount of bumping, like ballbearings in a bottle. It's a good-humoured aspect of the dance, especially one in the middle of the ice sheet with an Arctic wind frosting the portholes. For all her size and strength, Natasha seemed to float in Arkady's arms, her hot cheek tentatively touching his.

'I apologize for my boots,' she said.

Arkady said, 'No, I apologize for *my* boots.'

'You like romantic songs?'

'I am helpless before romantic songs.'

'So am I.' She sighed. 'I know you like poetry.'

'How do you know that?'

'I found your book.'

'You did?'

'When you were sick. It was under your mattress. You're not the only one who knows where to look.'

'Is that so?'

He pulled back for a moment. There was a frightening lack of embarrassment in her eyes.

'It wasn't even a book of poetry,' Arkady said. 'Just some essays and letters from Mandelstam.' He didn't add it was a gift from Susan.

'Well, the essays were too intellectual,' Natasha admitted, 'but I liked the letters to his wife.'

'To Nadezhda?'

'Yes, but he had so many other names for her. Nadik, Nadya, Nadka, Nadenka, Nadyusha, Nanusha, Nadyushok, Nanochka, Nadenysh, Niakushka. Ten special names in all. That's a poet.' She laid her cheek a little more firmly on his.

Slava and his sax leaned into 'Dark Eyes', extracting amber from sap. Dancers revolved slowly under the revolving ball. There was a cavelike quality to the low ceiling and flickering lights that eased the Russian soul.

'I have always admired your work on the factory line,' Natasha confided.

'I've always admired yours.'

'The way you handle the fish,' she said. 'Especially the difficult ones like hake.'

'You cut the spines off so . . . well.' He wasn't good at this, Arkady thought.

She cleared her throat. 'That trouble you had in Moscow? I think it's possible the Party made a mistake.'

A mistake? For Natasha that was like saying black might be white, or an admission that there might be grey.

'Oddly enough,' he said, 'this time it didn't.'

'Anyone can be rehabilitated.'

'Generally after they're dead. Don't worry; there's life outside the Party. It's unbelievable how much life there is.'

Natasha fell contemplative. Her train of thought

seemed much like the Baikal–Amur Mainline, with whole sections unfinished and tunnels going off in mysterious directions. Poetry, fish, the Party. He wondered what she would come up with next.

'I know there's someone else,' Natasha said. 'Another woman.'

'Yes.'

Was that a sniff he heard? He hoped not.

'There had to be,' she finally said. 'There's only one thing I ask.'

'What's that?'

'That it's not Susan.'

'No, it's not Soo-san.'

'And it wasn't Zina?'

'No.'

'Someone not on board?'

'Not on board and far away.'

'Very far away?'

'Oh, very,' he assured her.

'That's good enough.' She rested her head on his shoulder.

Well, Arkady thought, Ridley was right. This was civilized, maybe the acme of civilization, these fishermen and fisherwomen waltzing in boots on the Bering Sea. Dr Vainu clung to Olimpiada like a man rolling a boulder. Keeping a straight-armed, semi-Islamic distance, Dynka danced with one of the engineers. Some men were on the floor with men, some women with women, just to keep in practice. A few had taken the time to pull on fresh jerseys, but most of them had come as they were, in the spirit of a rare, impromptu event. Arkady also enjoyed the dance because now he had some idea of Zina's last hours on earth. There was a nice aptness to ending up with Natasha here, as if Zina herself might come dancing by.

'He's here.' Natasha stiffened.

Karp was moving slowly along the benches at the rear of the cafeteria, perfectly at ease, simply sorting out figures in the dark. Arkady steered Natasha towards the stage. 'Kolya would like to dance with you,' he said.

'He would?'

'If you see him, you should give him a chance. He's a bright man, a scientist, a botanist who needs to come down to earth.'

'I'd rather help you,' Natasha said.

'Then half a minute after I'm gone turn out the stage lights for just a few seconds.'

'This is still about Zina, isn't it?' Natasha's voice sank. 'Why are you so involved?'

Arkady was startled into an answer. 'I hate suicide.'

There was something newly liberated about Slava, as if the saxophone were a divining rod that had located his soul. While the third mate wailed, Arkady and Natasha reached the galley door.

'She didn't kill herself?' Natasha asked.

'No.'

'Karp killed her?'

'Now that's the strange part. I don't think he did.'

*

The galley was a narrow gamut of steel sinks, stacked trays as dented as war shields, towers of white soup bowls, industrial ranges under hanging pans of wash-tub size. The realm of Olimpiada Bovina. Cabbage bathed in boiling water, either being prepared for breakfast or being reduced to glue. A paddle stood upright in a mixing bowl of hardening batter. Arkady was aware he was following the same path Zina had taken the previous dance seven nights before. According to Slava she had removed a plastic bag from a pot. What was in the bag? Why plastic? Then the next witnesses placed her on deck.

Arkady opened the door to the corridor just enough to see Pavel anxiously sucking on a cigarette and watching for anyone leaving the dance. A moment later, 'Dark Eyes' ended amid shouts of 'Lights!' and 'Off my foot, you bloody bastard!' At once Pavel stuck his head inside the cafeteria while Arkady slipped out of the galley and down the corridor.

Who else but Kolya Mer would be at the rail taking in all the pleasures of rain turning to a wet, stinging snow that angled under a lowering fog? He grabbed Arkady as he ran past.

'I wanted to tell you about the flowers.'

'Flowers?'

'Where I picked them.' Bare fingers peeked out of Kolya's cut gloves.

'The irises?'

'I told Natasha I got them along the road outside the

store in Dutch Harbor. Irises actually grow higher up. I saw you check my notebook, so you know I found them on the hill. I saw you going up after the American.' Kolya took a deep breath for courage. 'Volovoi asked.'

'Volovoi ran into you on the hill?'

'He was looking for you. He even said he was going to take my samples away unless I told him. I didn't, though.'

'I didn't think you did. Was he alone?'

Say no, Arkady thought. Say that First Mate Volovoi was with Karp Korobetz and we'll go together to Marchuk right now.

'I couldn't tell in the fog,' Kolya said.

Karp would be coming on deck any second, Arkady thought, unless he was already on his way below decks to block him from the forward part of the ship.

Kolya was staring straight up. 'Like tonight. The snow will stop and then it will really get thick. I miss the sextant.'

'It's not very useful without stars,' Arkady said. 'Go inside. Get warm. Dance.'

Only because he was away from the dance, Arkady heard the change in pitch. The reverberation of the screws was deeper, which meant the *Polar Star* was slowing down. But the stream of glittering flakes created the illusion that the factory ship was rushing forward like a sleigh. Underfoot, he felt the tremor of the engines and the cracking of ice under the plate of the prow. Overhead, snow swayed on the booms and gantries, coating the antennas, directional rings and radar bars so that they shone in a lamplight intensified by the plane of fog directly above. If the senses were anything to go by, the *Polar Star* was flying between two seas, one above and one below.

The sound of boots scurried across the deck behind him. Ahead, someone else descended the stairs from the bow. Arkady slipped through the fishing net that surrounded the volleyball court. Snow on the mesh had turned it into a gauzy tent of ice that trembled in the wind. The deck lamp was a blur. Through this screen he watched the two figures converge and talk. He should have picked up a knife in the kitchen. The volleyball apparatus had been taken down. He couldn't defend himself with a pole; there wasn't even a ball.

First one figure and then the other entered the court after Arkady. He expected them to spread out but they stayed together as they crept forward. The bottom of the net was tied to cleats, tied and frozen; no exit there. Maybe he could climb the net like a monkey? Not likely. The deck was icy. If he knocked one down, perhaps both would fall.

'Renko? Is it you?'

The other silhouette lit a match. In a darting flame Arkady could see two faces with gnomish brows and anxious smiles with gold teeth. Skiba and Slezko, Volovoi's two slugs.

'What do you want?' Arkady asked.

'We're on your side,' Slezko said.

'They're going to get you tonight,' Skiba said. 'They don't want you to see morning.'

Arkady asked. 'Who is "they"?'

'You know,' Slezko said in time-honoured Soviet fashion. Why say more?

'We still know how to do our jobs,' said Skiba. 'There just hasn't been anyone to report to.'

The match went out. In the wind, the net billowed like sails of ice.

'There's no discipline, no vigilance, no line of communication any more,' Slezko said. 'To speak frankly, we're at a loss.'

Skiba said, 'You must have done something that set them off because they're searching the entire ship for you. They'll cut your throat in your cabin if they have to. Or on deck.'

'Why are you telling me?' Arkady asked.

'Reporting, not telling,' Slezko said. 'We're just doing our duty.'

'Reporting to *me*?'

Skiba said. 'We've thought about this a lot. We have to report to someone, and you're the only one with the experience to take his place.'

'Whose place?'

'Volovoi's, who else?' Slezko said.

Skiba said, 'We think that you might come from the appropriate organ anyway, the way you act lately.'

'What organ would that be?'

Slezko said, 'You know.'

I know, Arkady thought. The KGB. It was insane.

Skiba and Slezko were happy to inform on him as an enemy of the people while Volovoi was alive. Once he was dead, however, they were like guard dogs thrown into confusion. Allegiance wasn't what they craved so much as a new fist on the leash. Well, a farmer sowed corn, a shoemaker made shoes, informers needed a new Volovoi. They had simply changed Arkady from victim to master.

'Thank you,' Arkady said. 'I'll keep your advice in mind.'

'I don't understand why you don't just hold them in custody,' Skiba said. 'They're only workers.'

Slezko said, 'You won't be safe until you do.'

'My advice', Arkady said, 'is to watch out for your own necks.'

In the dark Skiba mournfully agreed. 'In times like these nothing is safe.'

On the bridge, the oncoming snow was lit by bow and wheelhouse lamps so that the eye could follow flakes individually, one or two out of the millions flowing out of the dark and over and around a windshield that had been hosed down with steam and wore its own frozen sheen. Wipers rhythmically brushed snow aside, but ice was already encroaching again from the corners.

Inside, the overhead lamp was dim. The radar and echo-sounder scopes cast green haloes. The gyro-compass floated in ball of light. Marchuk was at the wheel;

Hess stood at the windshield. Neither man seemed surprised to see Arkady on the bridge.

'Comrade Jonah,' the captain said softly.

There was no helmsman and no one was in the navigation room. The engine telegraph was set between
'Dead Slow' and 'Dead Stop'.

'Why are we slowing?' Arkady asked.

The captain had a pained smile. As he tapped out a
cigarette he looked like a man contemplating life from
the last step of a guillotine. Hess, caught in the moving
shadow of a wiper, looked like he was only one step
behind.

'I should have left you where you were,' Marchuk told
Arkady. 'You'd disappeared on the slime line, in the belly
of the whale. We must have been insane to pluck you
out.'

'Are we stopping?' Arkady asked.

'We have a slight problem,' Hess conceded. 'There are
problems beside you.'

The light from outside was pale and cold, but the
fleet electrical engineer appeared to Arkady to be
especially white, as if all the sun lamps on earth had
been wasted on him.

'Your cable?' Arkady suggested.

'I told you,' Hess reminded Marchuk. 'He found my
station today.'

'Well, your station is a pearl in an oyster, so a man
of Renko's abilities was bound to find it. One more
reason why I should have left him where he was.' The
captain let a reflective plume of smoke escape. To Arkady

he said, 'I told him the bottom we were going over was too grabby and too shallow, but he put the cable out anyway.'

'A hydrophone cable is designed not to snag,' Hess said. 'It's deployed from submarines all the time.'

'And now something's tangled in the cable,' Marchuk said. 'Maybe part of a crab pot, maybe a walrus head. Tusks dragging on the ocean floor. We can't reel the cable in and the tension on it is too great for us to go any faster.'

'Whatever it is will come loose eventually,' said Hess.

'In the meantime,' Marchuk said, 'we must proceed ahead delicately even while we're making way through ice and a Force 7 wind. The captains in the Navy must be magicians.' When he inhaled, his eyes reflected the ember. 'Excuse me, I forgot: in the Navy they are deployed from submarines, not from factory ships in the ice.'

The *Polar Star* trembled and heaved a little in the swell hidden below the sheet. Arkady was no engineer, but he knew that in order to break ice a ship, no matter how big, needed a certain amount of momentum. Too slow at too low a gear and the diesels would sooner or later burn out. 'How good a captain is Morgan?' he asked.

Marchuk said, 'We'll find out. A boat like the *Eagle* should be in view of a coconut palm and looking for shrimp, nowhere near ice. Now the waves are picking up in the fairway, and his bow and deck aren't high enough. He shouldn't head into the wind, but he has to stay behind us or get iced in. He's already iced up and getting top-heavy.'

Something occurred to Arkady. The quiet. A bridge always had one radio tuned to the distress frequency. Marchuk followed Arkady's eyes to the single-sideband. The captain left the wheel to turn up the sound, like pins dropping, of heavy static.

'Morgan hasn't sent an emergency call yet,' said Hess.

'He hasn't sent any call,' Marchuk said.

Arkady asked, 'Why don't you raise him?' Off Sakhalin, boats always talked each other through heavy weather.

'He doesn't respond,' Marchuk said. 'One of his antennas might be down.'

Hess said, 'Morgan can tell by our speed that something is wrong, and he probably knows that the cable is played out. A piece of the cable is what he's after. We're the ones in trouble, not him. This weather is perfect for him.'

On the radar screens the fairway carved by the *Polar Star* was a narrow line of green dots, sea returning the radar's signal. In the middle of the lane, about five hundred metres back, was the blip that was the *Eagle*; the rest of the screen was a blank. Arkady punched in a 50-k scale. Still there was nothing but the *Eagle*. Boats were supposed to be coming from Seattle, but the weather would be delaying them.

'Morgan has a radar, too,' Hess said. 'And a directional echo-sounder. If something is caught on the cable he will detect it. This is probably the opportunity he's been waiting for.'

Marchuk said, 'If he's lost a radio mast, then he's lost his radar, too.'

'The autopilot turned the wheel a notch, minding its job.

'Captain,' Hess said, 'I can understand your sympathy for another fisherman. Would that Morgan was, but he's not. George Morgan is their Anton Hess. When I see him I recognize myself. He will be silent and he will stay close to see if we make a mistake, such as picking up speed. Whatever is caught on the cable could lift it to the surface right beside the *Eagle*.'

'What if the cable breaks?' Arkady asked.

'It won't break if we stay at this speed,' said Hess.

'What if it does?' Marchuk asked.

'It won't,' Hess said.

What was Hess's musical instrument? The cello. Hess reminded Arkady of a cellist trying to play as his strings popped one by one.

Hess repeated, 'It won't, but even if it did break, the cable has negative buoyancy; it would sink. The only problem would be returning to Vladivostok and the Pacific Fleet after losing a hydrophone cable. Our voyage has been disastrous enough, Captain. We don't need any more disgraces.'

'Why doesn't Morgan answer our calls?' Marchuk demanded.

'I've told you why. Except for the radio, the *Eagle* is proceeding normally. Everything else is in your imagination.' Hess lost patience. 'I'm going below; perhaps I can wind in the cable a little.' He paused in front of Arkady. 'Explain to the captain that Zina Patiashvili didn't go to the stern rail every time the *Eagle* was close to throw kisses. It turns out that she got plenty of them from my own radioman. If Zina were here now, I'd kill her myself.'

The fleet electrical engineer left by the flying bridge. Before the door slammed shut, snow spun in the dark, then died.

'It *is* humorous,' Marchuk said. 'After all that time in dry dock putting in the cable and it's the only thing that breaks down.'

The captain leaned against the counter. He laid his hand affectionately on a compass repeater, opened its hood, closed it.

'I keep thinking things will change, Renko, that life can be honest and direct, that there's good and dignity in anyone who's willing to work hard. Not that people are perfect, not that I'm perfect. But good. Am I an idiot? Tell me, when we get to Vladivostok will you tell them about me and Zina?'

'No. But they'll take pictures of the officers and crew to the restaurant where she worked and the people there will recognize you.'

'So I'm dead either way.'

No, *I'm* dead either way, Arkady thought. Karp and his deck team will hunt until they find me. Marchuk was caught in the more significant drama of a trailing cable. How could he explain why Karp wanted to attack him if there was no evidence left of smuggling? At best he'd sound like a madman; more likely, he'd hang himself for Volovoi and the Aleut.

'You know how this ship was delivered?' Marchuk asked. 'You know the condition in which any ship is delivered from the boatyard?'

'Like new?'

'Better than new. The *Polar Star* was built in a Polish yard. When it was handed over it was handed over complete, with everything: tableware, linens, curtains, lights, everything so you could go to sea right away. But they never got to sea right away. The KGB comes on board. People from the Ministry come on board. They take the new tableware and replace it with old, take the linens and curtains and replace bright lights with bulbs you could go blind by. Exactly as if they were robbing a house. Rip out the good plumbing and replace it with lead. Even mattresses and doorknobs. Replace good with shit. Then they give it to Soviet fishermen and say, "Comrades, go to sea!" This was a pretty ship, a good ship.'

Marchuk bowled his head, dropped the butt of his cigarette on the deck and stepped on it. 'So, Renko, now you know why the ship is moving so slowly. Was there anything else?'

'No.'

The captain stared at the bright, blinded windshield. 'Too bad about us and the *Eagle*,' he said. 'The joint venture is good thing. The other way leads back to the cave, doesn't it?'

Chapter Twenty-eight

Arkady went through the bridgehouse corridor without knowing where he was heading. He couldn't simply go to his cabin and wait. The dance wouldn't be safe. This was the sort of prison situation that an *urku* like Karp excelled at. The lights would go out and when they came on again he'd be gone, headed down the ramp in a weighted sack. Or he'd be found in an empty bunker, paint can by his side, an obvious victim of sniffing fumes. Moral lessons would be drawn.

'We never finished our game,' Susan said.

Arkady took a step back to her open door. He'd passed it without noticing because her cabin was dark.

'Don't be afraid,' she said. She turned on the overhead lights long enough for him to see disconnected wires hanging from the radio and the base of the desk lamp. She sat on the lower bunk, her hair damp and dishevelled as if she had just stepped out of a shower. Her feet were bare and she was dressed in jeans and a loose denim shirt. Her brown eyes seemed to have gone black. In her hand was a glass filled to the brim. The cabin smelled of Scotch. She turned the light off with the bunk switch. 'Close the door,' she said.

'I thought you never closed the door when Soviet men came to call.'

'There's always a first time. Soviet ships never have unscheduled dances, but I hear you're having one right now. That's where all my boys have gone, so it's a night of firsts.'

Arkady closed the door and groped to sit where he'd seen a chair by the bunk. She turned on her bunk lamp, a 20-watt bulb not much brighter than a waning candle.

'For example, I said to myself that I would fuck the first man who walked by my door. Then, Renko, you walked by and I changed my mind. The *Eagle*'s in trouble, isn't it?'

'I have it on good authority that the snow will stop.'

'They lost radio contact an hour ago.'

'We still have them on radar. They're not far behind us.'

'So?'

'So their radio antenna is probably iced up. You know that happens up here.'

Susan put a glass in his hand and poured from a bottle so that the Scotch swelled over the brim. 'Remember,' she said. 'First one to spill gets hit.'

Arkady frowned. 'The Norwegian game again?'

'Yes. They don't call them roundheads for nothing.'

'Is there an American version?'

'You get shot,' Susan said.

'Ah, a short version. I have a different idea. Why not the first one to spill tells the truth?'

'That's the Soviet version?'

'I wish I could say so.'

'No,' Susan said, 'you can have anything but the truth.'

'In that case,' Arkady said and sipped, 'I'll cheat.'

Susan matched him with a swallow. She was well ahead of him, though she didn't seem drunk. The bunk light provided more corona than illumination. Her eyes were shadowed but not softened.

'You haven't been writing any suicide notes, have you?' she asked.

Arkady set his drink on the floor so he could get out a cigarette.

'Light one for me,' she said.

'It's an art in itself, suicide notes.' Arkady lit two Belomors off a match and put one in her hand. Her fingers were smooth, not rough and scarred from cleaning cold fish.

'You speak as an expert?'

'A student. Suicide notes are a branch of literature too often ignored. There's the pensive suicide note, the bitter note, the guilt-ridden note, rarely the comic note because there's always some sense of formality. Usually the writer signs his or her name, or else signs off in some fashion: "I love you," "It's better this way," "Consider me a good Communist."'

'Zina didn't.'

'And the note is generally left where it will be found at the same time as the body. Or found when someone is discovered missing.'

'Zina didn't do that, either.'

'And always, because this is the writer's last testament, she doesn't mind using a whole piece of paper. Not a scrap, not half a page from a notebook – not for the last letter of her life. Which reminds me, how is your writing going?' Arkady looked at Susan's typewriter and books.

'I'm blocked. I thought a ship would be the perfect place to write, but . . .' She stared at the bulkhead as if peering at some faraway, fading memory. 'Too many people, too little space. No, that's not fair. Soviet writers write in communal apartments all the time, don't they? I have this cabin to myself. But it's like finally having a chance to listen to your very own seashell and there's no sound at all.'

'On the *Polar Star* I think it would be hard to hear a seashell.'

'True. You know, you're strange, Renko, you're very strange. Remember that poem, the one—'

' "Tell me how men kiss you/Tell me how you kiss"?'

'That's the one. Remember the last line?' she asked, and recited,

> 'Oh I see, his game is that he knows
> Intimately, ardently.
> There's nothing from me he wants,
> So I have nothing to refuse.'

That's you. Of all the men on this ship, you're the only one who wants nothing at all.'

'That's not true,' Arkady said. He wanted to stay alive, he thought. He wanted to get through the night.

'What do you want?' she asked.

'I want to know what happened to Zina.'

'What do you want from me?'

'You were the last person to see Zina before she disappeared. I'd like to know what she said.'

'See what I mean?' She laughed softly, more at herself. 'OK. What she said? Honestly?'

'Try it.'

Susan took a more judicious sip. 'I don't know. This game gets dangerous.'

'I'll tell you what I think she told you,' Arkady said. 'I think she said she knew what the *Polar Star* was towing when we're not taking nets, and that she could give you information about the station where the cable was controlled.'

She shrugged. 'What cable? What on earth are you talking about?'

'That's why Morgan is where he is and that's why you're here.'

'You sound like Volovoi.'

'It's not an easy game,' Arkady said. The Scotch was good; it made even a papirosa taste as sweet as candy.

'Maybe you're a spy,' Susan said.

'No, I don't have the world view. I'm more comfortable in a smaller, more human scale. And I'd say you're a bit of an amateur, not a professional. But you got on the ship, and if Morgan says you stay on it, you stay.'

'Well, I do have a world view. I don't think Zina would have been so desperate to leave an American boat.'

'She—'

He stopped and turned his ear. There wasn't so much the sound of boots in the corridor as of boots suddenly standing outside the door. Along the corridor were six cabins, with stairs at each end up to the bridge and down to the main deck. Other boots ran down the stairs and came to a halt.

The door opened in the next cabin, then shut. A door opened across the hall. There was a knock at Susan's door. 'Soo-san?' Karp called.

She watched Arkady kill his cigarette. Was there panic in his eyes? He wondered. There was fascination in hers.

The second knock was harder. 'Are you alone?' Karp asked through the door.

'Go away,' she said, her eyes still fixed on Arkady.

The doorknob strained, resisting pressure. At least it was a metal door, Arkady thought. In Soviet housing projects the doors and frames were so easy to kick in that any locks were decorative. Susan stood, gathered a tape and cassette player from the upper bunk and turned on James Taylor very low.

'Soo-san?' Karp called again.

She answered, 'Go away now or I'll tell the captain.'

'Open up,' Karp ordered. He hit the door with probably no more than his shoulder, and the latch, nearly persuaded, almost popped.

'Wait,' she said and turned off the bunk light.

While Arkady moved himself and his chair from the line of sight, Susan took her drink across the cabin and edged open the door. The mirror over her sink was ajar, and in it Arkady found he had positioned himself directly facing Karp's reflection. A head taller than Susan, the trawlmaster gazed over her into the cabin. In the hall's dim light the rest of the deck team huddled like a pack behind a lead wolf. The room was black – black enough, Arkady hoped, so that they wouldn't see him.

'I thought I heard voices,' Karp hit a note of concern. 'We wanted to be sure there was nothing wrong.'

Susan said, 'There'll be something wrong if I go to the captain and tell him his crewmen are breaking into my cabin.'

'I apologize.' Karp seemed to be looking right at Arkady while he talked to her. 'It was for your own good. A mistake. Please excuse us.'

'You're excused.'

'Pleasant.' Karp kept his foot in the door and listened to the faint music, a man singing to a guitar. Finally he looked down at Susan and his smile of appreciation turned to an expression of concern. 'Soo-san, I am just a seaman, but I have to warn you.'

'What about?'

'It's bad to drink alone.'

When Susan shut the door Arkady stayed still. The boots outside marched away, too much in unison. He listened to her cross the cabin and turn the volume of her player up higher, though the words were oddly soft and meaningless. He heard her set her glass down; it sounded empty. After six months in a small space, she knew her way around it even in the dark. She crossed the cabin again and he felt her fingers touch where sweat had broken out on his temple. 'Are they after you?' she asked.

He put his hand lightly on her mouth. Someone, he

was sure, still stood outside. She took his wrist and slipped his hand inside her shirt.

Her breast was small. He took his hand out to unbutton the rest of her shirt. As she pulled his head close, he felt the rest of her body soften and let go. He kissed her face and lifted her towards him. If it was possible to step back to that moment in Dutch Harbor when he suddenly left, they were there now.

She seemed weightless. The rest of the world became soundless, as if the tape was playing in another room and the listener in the corridor were on another ship in another sea. Shirt and pants collected silently at her feet. Was this what women felt like? The damp hair at the nape of the neck? Teeth biting and lips yielding at the same time? How long had it been?

His jacket and clothes fell, sloughed off like an old skin. Perhaps this was what being alive was like. The heart hammering within the chest, a second heart answering outside, being doubly alive. His body was like another man who had been entombed and, now let free, was in control. He himself was swept along. She clung to him, climbed him, wrapped herself around him. They tottered dizzily against the bulkhead and then he was in her.

At what point does antagonism twist, turn and become desire? Is heat so interchangeable, or only masked? Why do suspicions already bear their answers? How did he know she would taste like this?

'I knew I was in trouble,' she whispered, 'when I heard

about Volovoi and Mike and my first thought was, How is Arkady?'

She curled against him as if dying even while, inside, she held him tighter. He held her and helped her move. Standing, they were like two people walking a tightrope in the dark, so high up that they preferred the dark.

'Susan—'

'Another first,' she said into his ear. 'My name.'

They slowly sank to their knees and then to her back on the deck. He felt her wide brown eyes watching. Cat's eyes, night eyes. Her legs spread like wings.

As he had borne her standing, she carried him now, both on top and deeper within, to the unseen torch in the dark, as if the cold metal of the deck were warm water.

'I like the name,' he whispered. 'Susan. Soo-san. Was it Susannah and the elders?'

'A virgin, I think. You know the Bible?'

'I know good story with elements of voyeurism, conspiracy' – he stopped to light his cigarette from hers – 'seduction and revenge.'

They lay on her bunk against her pillow and another one made of her blankets. Despite the cool, he wasn't cold. Her cassette player now stood on the floor, aimed at the door. Every time the tape ended, she turned it over and started it again.

'You're a strange detective,' she said. 'You like names?'

'There's Ridley. A riddler, someone full of riddles. Morgan? Wasn't there a pirate named Morgan?'

'Karp?'

'A fish, a big fish.'

'And Renko? What does that mean?'

'Son of. Fedorenko would be son of Fedor. I'm just son of . . . something.'

'Too vague.' She ran a finger around the line of his lips. 'A stranger detective by the minute. But then I make a strange virgin. The two of us are a perfect pair.'

At least for one night, Arkady thought. The door existed as a thin line of light in the dark. If Karp was still waiting outside, his team was probably up on deck. They could try to look in through the porthole, but all they'd see was a drawn curtain.

Arkady picked up the glass. 'We didn't finish the game.'

'Being honest? Look at me, isn't this honest enough? I'll be more honest. My door was open just on the chance you'd go by. I didn't know what I'd say. You make me mad.' In a softer voice she said, 'You *made* me mad. Then I admitted to myself that this ritual of animosity between us was because you were the last person I wanted to be attracted to.'

'Maybe we make a perfect pair of moths.'

But it was more than that, he knew. He'd been coming back to life and when he held her he found himself at last fully alive, as if her heat had melted some final frozen lock inside him. Though they were trapped in a small steel cabin in the middle of the ice, he was alive, even if just for a night. Or was that a moth's rationale?

'He recruited me in Athens,' Susan said.

'Morgan?'

'George, yes. I was doing a graduate course in Greek, which was the passion of my life – or at least at the time I thought it was. He was the captain of a yacht that belonged to some rich Saudi. He'd send telegrams to George to meet him here or there. The Saudi never showed up, but George had to move the boat from Cyprus to Tripoli and then back to Greece. He recruited me when I finally realized there was no Saudi.

'Slavic Studies were my next great passion. George said I had a talent for languages. He doesn't himself, though his Arabic is passable. He paid my way through school in Germany. I'd see him at Christmas and for a week in the summer. When I got out of school, though, he said he'd gone private. No more government hassle, he said.

'He had a small shipping company in Rhodes that specialized in beating embargoes. We re-labelled canned goods from South Africa, oranges from Israel, software from Taiwan. We always had buyers from Angola, Cuba, the USSR. George said that Communists trust you as long as you're making a profit, and that they'll trust you even more if you give them a kickback.

'It made sense. He didn't have to clear anything any more. No oversight committee, no paperwork, just lunch in Geneva every two weeks with someone from Langley.

George had to visit the bank anyway, so it was convenient.

'George is smart. He was the first one to notice the fishing venture and the possibilities for the Soviets here, because he was sure you were doing the same thing he was. He folded the company in a week and moved to Seattle. There were plenty of boats available. I think he deliberately got a bad one so he wouldn't make too much of a splash. He certainly could've gotten a better crew.

'So I've known George for years and been recruited for three. I was in Germany for one, worked on Rhodes for one, have been on Soviet ships for one. In all those years, he and I have actually been together for a total of six months. Two days together in the last ten months. It's too hard to stay in love with someone that way. I end up waiting for someone like you. Is that honest enough?'

Were ships like women or were women like ships? Something to cling to in a dream?

Outside in the hall, Arkady heard American voices, weary from the hour and the dance, staggering back to their separate quarters. He didn't have a watch.

He ran his hand softly down from the middle of her forehead as if he were tracing her profile. At one time he had thought of her looks as thin and triangular, but now it seemed the right frame for such a mobile mouth and wide-apart eyes, the only face for such childishly cut hair. As his fingers grazed down across her stomach she turned towards him, a warm, enfolding barque with a golden sail.

'Zina mentioned seeing something in the water,' Arkady said.

'She also mentioned a Navy officer she saw on board, the radioman.' Susan lay with her head resting on Arkady's chest. They shared a Winston, one of hers.

'You thought she was a provocateur?'

'At first. She did tell Volovoi about smoking grass with Lantz, just enough to keep him titillated.'

'Just enough to give her the run of the ship,' Arkady said. He passed the cigarette back to her and rested his hand where the corner of her jaw met her neck.

'Zina was too wild to be fake. Too bright,' Susan said. 'Men never realized that.'

'She manipulated them?'

'Volovoi, Marchuk, Slava. I don't know how many others. Maybe everyone but you.'

'Did she talk about Vladivostok, about her life there?'

'Just about waiting tables and fending off sailors.'

'So why did she come on the *Polar Star*?' Arkady asked. 'It was only more of the same.'

'I wondered, too. That was her secret.'

'Did she talk about a man in Vladivostok?'

'Marchuk and the radioman.'

'Guns?' he asked.

'No.'

'Drugs?'

'No.'

'So what do you think Zina was doing every time she joined you at the stern rail?'

Susan laughed. 'You never get tired of that question, do you?'

'No.' He felt the pulse in her neck begin to race. 'I never get tired of good questions. Was it fish? Why was she interested in fish just from the *Eagle*?'

'Men, not fish,' Susan said. 'Mike was on the *Eagle*.'

Arkady pictured Zina standing at the stern rail, waving to the American catcherboat. Did it matter who waved back? 'Morgan was on the *Eagle*,' he said.

'All Morgan needed from Zina was confirmation that there was something like the cable. She couldn't give him any real details. He had no other use for her.'

'What did she want from him?' Arkady asked.

'Too much.'

'Is that what you told her the night of the dance? Was that what you said to her just before she disappeared?'

'I tried to explain that in George's terms she wasn't a valuable asset.'

'Why not?' When Susan didn't answer, he asked, 'What did you mean when you said she wouldn't have wanted to leave an American boat?'

'She wanted to defect.'

He rested his hand on her shoulder. This was the most quiet, he thought, like a pillow on the moon.

'Do you want to get off the *Polar Star*?' she asked.

'Yes.'

He heard her hold her breath before she said, 'I can help.'

He held a cigarette in one hand and a match in the other, but he didn't light it. He concentrated on the soft tremor of her breast against his cheek. 'How?'

'You need protection. I can ask Marchuk to make you a translator. You're wasted on the slime line. That way we can spend more time together.'

'But how can you help me get off the *Polar Star*?'

'We can work on it.'

'What would I have to do?'

'Nothing. Who is Hess?'

Now he struck the match, a yellow flare in the hand, and let the first sulphurous haze burn off. 'Should we stop smoking?'

'No.'

He inhaled. Raw tobacco fumes, Soviet again. 'He's our Morgan, another fisherman.'

'You saw the cable, didn't you?'

'A cover over it. There wasn't much to see.'

'But you were there.'

Before he blew the flame out he reached down to the floor for the glass. It was half-full, the last of the Scotch. 'Should we stop drinking?'

'No. Go back and take another look.'

'Hess won't let me in again.' He killed the flame and drank half of what was left.

'Get in. You seem to be able to go wherever you want to on this ship.'

He passed the glass. 'Until Karp catches me.'

'Until then, yes.' She swallowed what was left and turned her head away. 'Then we can get you off or out.'

He rose on an elbow as if he could see her. Her hair was still damp to the touch. He turned her chin towards him. 'Off or out? What does that mean?'

'Just what I said.'

The bottle was empty and the Winstons had all gone up into a floating blanket of smoke. As if he and Susan had gone up in smoke.

'I want you in, not out,' she said.

The bunk lamp was more glow than light, but he could see her eyes looking up, and himself in her eyes. Inside of her and out.

'Did Hess mention length?' Susan asked. 'Number of hydrophones? Range? He has computers and software. It would be good if you could bring me a disk, even better if you can get a hydrophone.'

Arkady lit a Belomor. 'Don't you find it boring?' he asked. 'Doesn't spying ever seem like an endless game of cards?'

'George checked your bonafides while we were in Dutch Harbor. He has a secure line there. He wanted to know if you were for real.' She took the cigarette. 'The FBI says you can't be trusted.'

'The KGB says so too. At least they agree on something.'

'Don't you have a good reason for wanting to get out?' Her eyes were wide, trying to see into him by the sparks of the papirosi, the bonfire of Russian conspirators.

'At Dutch Harbor you suggested that Morgan and I might have murdered Zina together. You're attracted to murderers?' Arkady asked.

'No.'

'Then why did you say it? That's the man you want me to trust?'

'It wasn't George's fault.'

'Whose, then?' When she didn't answer, he said, 'You and Zina were on the stern deck. The dance was still going on. The ship was bobbing in the dark, the *Eagle* tied up alongside. At the rail you told her she was asking for too much. What did she say to you?'

'She said I couldn't stop her.'

'Someone stopped her. Did she show you a plastic bag?'

'A bag?'

'With a towel and clothes inside. She borrowed a bathing cap from one of her cabinmates. She never returned it.'

'No. Besides, you're different, Arkady. You're a known quantity, and if you can bring something from Hess to me, we really can help you. There's nothing for you at home, is there? Why would you want to go back?'

'Can you really help me? Can you really make us

disappear from here and find ourselves walking on a street, sitting in a café, lying in bed on the other side of the world?'

'You have to hope.'

'If you want to help, tell me what Zina was doing at the rail all those other times. Before she knew anything about Morgan or a radioman or a cable, why was she at the rail?'

She turned the lamp switch off. 'Funny, the whole night has been like holding hands over a flame.'

'Tell me.'

Susan fell silent in the dark for a minute, and then said, 'I didn't know. Not for sure. At first I thought she was simply being friendly, or sent by Volovoi. Sometimes you become aware of a pattern around you, but you can't tell quite what it is. After we became friends, I stopped noticing, because I liked having her there. It wasn't until you came around that I started asking questions again, and not until Dutch Harbor that I knew for sure, when I was told that I had to come back to the *Polar Star* and help keep things quiet. We had to keep the team together and cope with problems as they came up. Adjust and resolve. That's the problem with working in the private sector. There's no back-up and nobody pulls you out. Instead, you compromise and the hands you hire for dirty work are that much dirtier. George is a control freak who's lost control. He'll clean it up. He's indestructible, not like us. He caught on before I did what Zina was doing at the rail and if he says he'll deal with his side, he will. He didn't kill her, I can promise you that.'

'Why did you ever think I killed her?'

'Because you were so unlikely. An investigator from the factory? And because that night she said she was coming back.'

'Coming back?' Arkady thought of the girl swimming out into Vladivostok bay, borrowing a shower cap, taping up a bag. Again and again, it made no sense. There were two Zinas: the Zina who mooned over Mike and listened to the Rolling Stones, and the Zina with her secret tapes. If Zina had been defecting to the *Eagle* she would have taken the tapes and left one false suicide note, not pages of practice notes. And she knew better than to stage a suicide when any American boat was close. 'From where?'

When Susan spoke again she sounded exhausted. 'George said he needed more than fishermen, and that's what he got. He just needs some time to get the crew under control. He didn't know about Zina. He couldn't do anything about Mike and Volovoi; he was only surprised he didn't find you there too.'

Arkady thought of Karp. 'Tell Marchuk.'

'I can't say any of this again. I'll deny every word and you know it.'

'Yes,' Arkady had to admit.

'It was just a game,' she said. 'A "What If" game.'

'Like, "What if morning doesn't come"?' he asked.

Her hand sought his. 'Now you answer a question: if

397

you could run right now, disappear from the *Polar Star* and go to America, would you do it?'

Arkady listened to his answer, interested if it was simply a game. 'No.'

On the narrow space of her bunk their sleeping bodies folded together as the *Polar Star* slowly rose on the angle of its plated bow and fell, crushing the ice ahead. The sound was subdued, not much more than a wind cooling the skin, or distant thunder moving farther away.

Arkady pulled the curtain from a porthole of luminous grey. Not the glitter of snow, but denser and softer. Dawn, a new day in the Bering Sea. 'We've stopped,' he said.

The grating of steel on ice was gone, though through his feet he felt the engines running. He flicked the bunk lamp on and off; there didn't seem to be an electrical problem. The *Polar Star* seemed poised in a vacuum, not silent itself but still and surrounded by silence.

'What about the *Eagle*?' Susan asked.

'If we're not going anywhere, they're not going anywhere.' He picked his pants and shirt off the deck.

'It's follow the leader, and finally you people are the leader?' Susan asked.

'That's right.'

'So much for joint ventures. The *Eagle* isn't built for ice, and Marchuk knows it.'

Arkady buttoned his shirt. 'Go to the radio shack,' he said. 'Try to raise Dutch Harbor or try the emergency channel.'

'And where are you going?'

Arkady pulled on his socks. 'Into hiding. The *Polar Star* is a big ship.'

'How long can you do that?'

'I'll think of it as a form of socialist competition.'

He stepped into his boots and took his jacket from a chair. In the gun-slit haze of the porthole she was motionless, all but her eyes, which followed Arkady to the door.

'You're not hiding,' she decided. 'Where are you going?'

He lifted and dropped his hand from the knob. 'I think I know where Zina died.'

'This whole night was just about Zina?'

'No.' Arkady turned to face her.

'Why do you look so happy?'

He was almost ashamed. 'Because I'm alive. We're both alive. I guess we're not moths.'

'OK.' As she leaned forward the light covered her like dust. 'I'll tell you what I told Zina. I said, "Don't go." '

But he was gone.

Chapter Twenty-nine

The *Polar Star* lay at the bottom of a white well. Fog bounded the factory ship on every side, and the sunlight reflected by the ice sheet and trapped by arms of fog produced an illumination that was both indistinct and overwhelming.

The ship itself glowed; ice had formed on every surface. The deck was a milky skating rink. The net around the volleyball court glittered like a house that had been built crystal upon crystal; the antennas overhead hung heavy as glass. Ice lay on the portholes in opaque, extra lenses, and glazed the wood stacked on the superstructure. The ship looked as if it had surfaced like a fish from the Arctic Sea.

'It's the cable that could not snag which is, of course, thoroughly fouled on the sea floor,' Marchuk said. He had taken Arkady to a corner of the bridge away from the helmsman. The captain hadn't slept during the night. His beard was overgrown, and when he removed his dark glasses his eyes looked scoured. 'We have to sit at dead stop while Hess is below, winding and unwinding the cable, trying to pull out his dick.'

'What about the *Eagle*?' Arkady asked the question Susan had asked him.

Wipers were doing an effective job of smearing ice in arcs across the windshield. On the other hand, the ship was going nowhere, and there was nothing to see except blinding fog. At a squint, Arkady estimated visibility at a hundred metres.

'Be thankful you're on the right boat, Renko.'

'There's been no call?'

'Their radio is dead,' Marchuk said.

'Three different kinds of radio and backups, and they're all dead?'

'Maybe their mast is down. We know they iced up and that there was a lot of rolling. It's possible.'

'Send someone back.'

Marchuk felt his pockets for a pack, then leaned against the windshield counter and coughed, which was almost the same as having a cigarette. He cleared his throat. 'You know what I'm going to do when we get back? Take a rest cure. No drinking, no smoking. Go someplace near Sochi where they clean you out, steam you in sulphur and pack you in hot mud. I want to stay in that mud for at least six months until I stink like a Chinese egg; that's how you know you're cured. I'll come out pink as a babe. Then they can shoot me.' He glanced at the helmsman and then through the door to the navigation room, where the second mate was soberly working charts. The *Polar Star* was locked in ice but the ship had not stopped moving because, slowly and inexorably, the ice sheet itself moved. 'When you get this far north, curious things happen to equipment. There are illusions not just to our eyes. A radio signal goes up and bounces right back. The magnetism is so strong that radio-direction signals are absorbed. You don't have to go to outer space to find a black hole – it's right here.'

'Send someone back,' Arkady said again.

'I'm not allowed as long as the cable is not properly reeled in. If it's caught on something buoyant it could be right under the ice; perhaps it could even be seen.'

'Who is the captain of this ship, you or Hess?'

'Renko.' Marchuk flushed, started to bring his hands out of his pockets and stuffed them back in. 'Who is a second-class seaman who should be grateful he isn't chained to his bunk?'

Arkady stepped over to the radio. Though the *Eagle* was still two kilometres behind the *Polar Star*, the green dot on the scope was a blur.

'They're not sinking,' Marchuk said. 'They've just iced up, and ice doesn't give you an echo the way clean metal does. Hess says they're in good shape; their radios are in working order and they have a fix on his cable. You heard him say that we're the ones in trouble, not them.'

'And if they disappear from the screen completely, Hess will tell you the *Eagle* has turned into a submarine. Susan will be on the bridge in a second. How are you going to handle her and the rest of the Americans on board?'

'I'll give them a complete and frank analysis in the wardroom,' Marchuk said drily. 'The main thing is to keep them away from the stern until the cable is hauled in.'

Both factory ship and trawler were frozen into the sheet, bows to the southeast, aimed at the boats coming up from Seattle, though neither of the incoming craft showed on the screen no matter what range Arkady punched into the radar scan. He reset the scope at five kilometres to take the *Eagle*'s bearing at three hundred degrees.

Marchuk whispered, 'If after another hour Comrade Hess has still not pulled in his cable, I will personally cut it and break out of the ice. That will take time because water this cold is dense and the cable will sink slowly. Then I can go back and rescue the *Eagle*. I promise you, I am not going to let other fishermen die. I'm like you; I want them out on open water.'

'No,' Arkady said, 'I like them right where they are.'

Marchuk turned his back to the thump of the wipers. Below him the bow lifted its deck, rust and green paint wearing its ghostly sheen of ice. Beyond the gunwale there was only white: no water, no sky, no distinction of horizon.

'I can't permit anyone to leave the ship,' Marchuk said. 'First, I am not allowed. Second, it would be useless. You've walked on frozen lakes?'

'Yes.'

'This is not the same. This is not Lake Baikal. Ice from salt water is only half as strong as from fresh water, more like quicksand than cement. Take a look! In fog like this you can't see where you're going. In a hundred steps you'd lose your way. If a crazy man did go out on the ice, he should say goodbye to everyone first. No, not allowed.'

'Have you ever walked on the ice here?' Arkady asked.

Marchuk, the silhouette, bowed to memory. 'Yes.'

'What was it like?'

'It was' – the captain spread his hands – 'beautiful.'

From an emergency locker Arkady took a pair of lifevests and a flare gun. The vests were made of orange cotton over plastic foam briquettes, with pockets for missing emergency whistles, and straps that tied at the waist over his sweater. The gun was an ancient Nagant revolver, the cylinder and barrel replaced by the squat tube of a flare.

The trawl deck seemed clear. Crossing it, he noticed, too late, someone watching from the high vantage point of the crane cabin. Pavel was a shadow within the glass of the cabin, except where his face peered through a triangular crack. He didn't react, though. Not until Arkady was inside the aft house did he realize that with his hood up and the added bulk of the vests under his jacket he had, at least at a distance, disguised himself.

'Arkady, is that you?' Gury loitered in the corridor by the kitchen passing a hot *pilmeni* from hand to hand. Pasta flour covered the shoulders of his leather jacket like heavy dandruff.

Arkady was startled, but realized that it was the sheer normalcy of Gury and the cabbage vapours of the mess that had surprised him. With no fishing to occupy them, people could stay below, play dominoes or chess, watch films, catch naps. The *Polar Star* might be stopped for some unexplained reason, but reasons were rarely explained. They could feel the engines idling below; in the meantime, life went on.

'You've got to see this. The usual turd-shaped, meat-stuffed ravioli, but . . .' Gury bit, choked down half the *pilmeni* and displayed the remaining half.

'So?' Arkady asked.

Gury grinned and held the *pilmeni* even closer to Arkady's eyes, as if displaying a diamond ring. 'No meat. I don't mean the usual "no meat", with gristle or bone. I mean not within lightyears' distance of any mammalian life form. I mean fishmeal and gravy, Arkady.'

'I need your watch.'

Gury was nonplussed. 'You want to know what time it is?'

'No.' Arkady unbuckled the new safari watch on Gury's wrist. 'I just want to borrow your watch.'

' "Borrow"? You know, of all the words in the Russian language, including "fuck" and "kill", "borrow" is probably the lowest. "Lease", "rent", "timeshare" – those are words we must learn.'

'I'm stealing your watch.' The compass built into the band was even notched to indicate degrees.

'You're an honest man.'

'You're going to report Olimpiada for adulterating our food?'

It took Gury a moment to get back on track. 'No, no. I was thinking when we get back to Vladivostok of maybe opening an enterprise, a restaurant. Olimpiada's a genius. With a partner like her I could make a fortune.'

'Good luck.' Arkady strapped on the watch.

'Thank you.' Gury pulled a face. 'What do you mean, "Good luck"?' He became more concerned as Arkady moved towards the trawl deck. 'Where are you going dressed like that? Will I get my watch back?'

Arkady took the walkway to the stern deck, consciously assuming the deliberate gait of a heavier man. He didn't glance back at the boat deck in case one of Karp's team was watching. The red ensign at the stern rail hung still with ice. Few footsteps had marred the shiny patina of the deck. At the well over the stern ramp stood a pair of long-suffering crewmen with the red armbands of public-order volunteers: Skiba and Slezko in sunglasses and rabbit-fur hats. When Arkady neared, they recognized him. As they started to block his way he waved them aside. It was a gesture he had seen enough in Moscow, a brusque gesture more with the hand than the arm, but sufficient to prompt the trained response, to chase pedestrians away from speeding motorcades, send dogs racing around a perimeter, dismiss orderlies or disperse prisoners.

Slezko said, 'The captain ordered—'

'No one is allowed—' said Skiba.

Arkady took Skiba's sunglasses.

'Wait,' Slezko said. He handed Arkady his Marlboros.

'Comrades.' Arkady saluted them. 'Consider me a bad Communist.'

He went down the well. At the landing, the platform

where the trawlmasters usually watched nets rise from the sea, the rope was frozen to the rail and he had to kick it free. He climbed over the rail and wrapped the rope around his sleeve. Going down the rope was not much different from sliding down an icicle. He landed on his heels, which at once went out from under him; letting go, he slid the rest of the way down the ramp and on to the ice.

High overhead, Skiba and Slezko crowded to the stern rail like a pair of stoats peeking over a cliff. On his feet again, Arkady took a bearing from the compass built into the band of Gury's watch. The ice was solid as stone. He started to walk.

He should have worn double underclothes, socks and felt boots. At least he had good gloves, a wool cap inside his hood and the two life preservers, which provided a surprising amount of insulation. The more he walked, the warmer he got.

And the less he cared. The glasses didn't so much shade the brilliant fog as define it so that he could appreciate the veils of white vapour shifting around him. He'd once had a similar sensation looking through the window of a plane flying through clouds. The ice was solid, white the way the sea ice is when the brine freezes out. Bright as a mirror, though he couldn't see his image, only an aerated haze frozen within the ice. When he looked back, the ship was fading into the fog. And out of context, Arkady thought. The *Polar Star* was no longer a ship in water so much as a grey wedge dropped from the sky.

Two kilometres at a brisk pace. Twenty minutes, maybe half an hour. How many people got to walk upon the sea?

Arkady wondered whether Zina had looked up from the waves at the looming grey flank of the ship. It was much easier for him; the water was flat, frozen, so much alabaster pavement. When he glanced back again, the *Polar Star* had disappeared.

He was still on a bearing of three hundred degrees, though the compass needle swung from side to side. This close to the magnetic pole the vertical pull was so strong that the needle's tip seemed to be jerked left and right by strings. There was nothing else to get a fix on – no feature on the horizon, no horizon at all, no seam between ice and fog. Every direction was the same, including up and down. Total whiteout.

First, Arkady wanted to check the wardrobes in the cabins, then storage lockers and engine room. Zina had been stowed somewhere.

Marchuk was right about illusions. Arkady saw an old-fashioned black vinyl 78 record spinning by itself and without a sound in the middle of the ice. It was as if his mind had decided to fill in the white void with the first object it could grab from his memory. He checked the compass. Perhaps he had been going in a circle. That happened in fog. Some scientists said travellers wandered because one leg was stronger than the other; others even cited the Coriolis effect of the rotation of the earth, assuming that men had no more control over their direction than wind or water.

The record spun faster as he approached, then wobbled out of control; with his last steps, it trembled and dissolved into a rough circle of tar-black water edged by broken ice soaked red with blood.

Polar bears sometimes crashed through a seal's breathing hole just as the seal was coming up for air. The bears hunted two hundred or three hundred kilometres out on the sea ice. The sound of an ice breaker usually chased them away, but the *Polar Star* was at dead stop. Arkady hadn't heard the attack, so it couldn't have just happened. On the other hand, no blood or tracks led away from the hole. The bear had taken its kill straight down into the water and hadn't come back up yet. Or had headed underwater for another hole. The ice looked as if it had exploded. From the amount of blood ringing the hole, perhaps the seal had exploded, too. Only a piece or two of ice bobbed in the water, evidence of currents still moving under the sheet.

Now, that would be an unexpected conclusion to an investigation, Arkady thought: being eaten by a bear. A first? Not in Russia. How surprised that seal must have been. He knew the feeling. He took another reading from the compass and set off again.

Ahead he heard the sharp sound of a crack. At first he thought it might be the bear erupting through the ice, then it occurred to him that perhaps the ice sheet was splitting. On open water, pulled by tides and currents, the sheet shifted, broke and realigned. He didn't feel in any particular danger. Water carried sound faster and farther than dry air. Fog didn't muffle sound; it amplified it. If there was a fissure, it was probably far in the distance.

He wished the needle of the compass would stop jumping. How many minutes had he been walking? Twenty by the watch. How was Japanese quality control? There was no sign of the *Eagle*, but looking back he could see, on the outer ring of visibility, something following him, a figure so gauzy it seemed an apparition.

A grey streak of ice started to sag under his feet. He moved laterally to whiter ice and picked up the bearing again. Ice tended to break on a southwest–northeast axis, the wrong way for his path. It kept him alert. The object behind him moved at a steady lope, like a bear, but it was upright and black.

By now Arkady knew he was lost. Either he had gone off at an angle, or else he had underestimated the distance to the *Eagle*. As the fog stirred it flowed from left to right. For the first time he noticed the sideways movement of what he'd thought was a stationary bank, which might have been leading him astray the entire time. The cloud also flowed forward, enveloping him. Behind him, within a hundred metres now, his pursuer had developed legs, arms, head and beard. Marchuk. Skiba and Slezko must have run directly from the stern to the captain, and it was perfectly characteristic of a Siberian like Marchuk to follow by himself. In a matter of steps Arkady was into the fog. Marchuk faded away.

The captain hadn't called out. What Arkady wanted now was to reach the *Eagle* before Marchuk caught up and ordered him back to the *Polar Star*. They could go on board the trawler together, as long as Arkady got to look around. It would be safer with Marchuk along, Arkady had to admit. Ridley and Coletti were working with Karp. Probably not Morgan, though a captain couldn't be entirely innocent of what happened on his own boat.

Although he was walking blindly in the fog, in his mind's eye Arkady saw his footprints leading straighter than an arrow across the ice to the *Eagle*. It had a rightness, a sense of the magnetic. Unless, of course, he'd already missed the trawler and was heading for the Arctic Circle.

The cracking sound came again, more distinctly this time. Not ice splitting: ice being hammered, impact followed by an echo like splintering glass. Arkady found himself turning his head in a searching motion as if he could trace the source of the noise. Sound could mislead in fog by seeming too close, and Arkady resisted the temptation to run because it would be easy to veer in the wrong direction. By now the fog itself rushed over him like surf trying to bear him away. Imagine, he thought, how much courage it took to swim even a few metres in water almost this cold. He had seen men fall off a trawler and almost instantly go into shock before they were rescued.

The hammering was suddenly loud. The *Eagle* emerged no more than ten metres away, thrust up and tilted by ice. Fog whipping over the boat made it appear as if it were speeding through heavy seas.

Breaking the way, the *Polar Star* had iced up from

411

clean snow. On the fairway, the *Eagle* had iced up from salt spray, which froze in a grey ice that had accreted grotesquely like stalactites, then glazed as the temperature dropped. Ice seemed to cascade down the wheelhouse stairs and flood from the scuppers. Icicles hanging off the gunwales were rooted to the ice sheet. Coletti was outside the wheelhouse using a blowtorch to melt ice into sockets around the windows; the flame of the torch lit his sallow face. The light inside the bridge was as dim as a candle, but Arkady could see a figure sitting in the captain's chair. Ridley was hammering ice off the rungs of the radio mast. At the top of the mast the dipoles had disappeared and the whip antennas were bent at ninety degrees. Ice hung from them like torn rigging; the best Morgan would hear from them was static. The fog shifted, obscuring the *Eagle* again. They hadn't seen him at all. He began circling towards the stern.

How far ahead of Marchuk was he? Ten steps? Twenty? Sound would draw the captain, too. Arkady almost stepped on to the stern ramp before he saw it. A net was reeled on to the gantry overhead, strips of black and orange plastic turned into a dull shroud of ice. Fog was driven so hard over the boat that it left a ghostly wake, a dark tunnel at the end of which Marchuk was already visible. No matter, the captain wouldn't send him back now. It was all working out.

As the trailing figure separated more clearly from fog, Arkady saw that its beard was actually a sweater drawn up over the man's mouth. Karp pulled the sweater down as he neared. Better prepared than Arkady, he had dark glasses and Siberian felt boots. In one hand he held an axe.

For a moment Arkady considered his options. A dash right to the North Pole? The long run left to Hawaii?

The *Eagle*'s ramp was low but slick and Arkady pulled himself up on his stomach. On deck, fish and crabs were dusted in ice. Icicles fringed the shelter deck. Riding the fog high on the radio mast, Ridley had reached the radar bar, which was frozen solid in a white cowl. The fisherman's long hair and beard were frosted from his breath. With the care of a jeweller, he started to tap the bar free. Arkady estimated the distance from ramp to wheelhouse at fifteen metres, but the most exposed were the first five metres to the shelter deck that ran along the side.

Karp was closing in. Carrying the axe like a spare wing, he seemed to glide across the ice.

Chapter Thirty

Arkady ran the few steps to the shadow of the shelter deck. He could no longer see the bridge, but the bridge could no longer see him. Behind, Karp came up the ramp with the sure foot of a deckhand.

Arkady slipped into the wheelhouse through a wet room that opened into the galley of the *Eagle*. He removed his glasses to see in the dim light that filtered through two portholes crusted with ice; it was like visiting the murk of an underwater ship. A banquette curved around a table with anti-skid mats. Pots leaned on the sea rails of the stove top. Forward were two cabin doors, stairs up to the bridge and down to the engine room.

The port-side cabin had two bunks, though only the lower one looked used. Immediately, Arkady saw that there was no Soviet-style wardrobe where a body could have been stowed. On the bulkhead was an empty rifle rack. Arkady felt under the mattress for a handgun, a knife, anything. Under the soiled pillow was a magazine with nudes. Under the bunk was a drawer with dirty clothes, more magazines of nudes and of firearms and of survival tactics; a sock with a roll of $100 bills; a well-carved whetstone; a carton of cigarettes; an empty box of shotgun shells.

'Coletti's,' Karp said as he came in. He looked like a

woodsman who had set off into the *taiga* for a vigorous morning of felling trees. No jacket or lifevest, just an extra sweater, heavy gloves, boots, cap and dark glasses resting against his brow. Not even out of breath.

'You make it so easy,' Karp said. 'Getting rid of you on the ship was a little difficult. Out here you just disappear, and no one will know I was ever gone.'

The axe was probably from the wide selection of firefighting equipment on the boat deck of the *Polar Star*, and Arkady suspected that Karp had brought it for a practical reason – to break through the ice and dispose of a body. As usual, the trawlmaster's plan had the virtue of simplicity. From outside came sounds of the ongoing war on ice, more the hammer blows of a foundry than a boat. The Americans still didn't know anyone else was on board.

'Why did you come?' Karp asked.

'I was looking for signs of Zina.'

There was a flare gun in Arkady's jacket pocket; that would be a dazzling sight in a small cabin. As he moved his hand, Karp flicked it aside with the axe.

'Another investigation?'

'No, just me. No one else knows. No one besides me even cares.' His wrist where the axe hit it was numb. This, he thought, is what it would be like to be cornered by a wolf.

Karp said, 'Whenever someone is dead, you usually accuse me.'

'You were surprised when she came up in the net. You could have tried to pour her with the fish into a bunker and dumped her later. Instead you cut her out. You didn't know. Last night on the ramp you still didn't know.'

Casually, the axe nudged Arkady's hand from the pocket again. It wasn't fair to die feeling quite so helpless, yet panic was shutting the brain down.

'You're stalling,' Karp said.

Arkady had been too scared to stall. 'Don't you want to know who killed her?' he asked. *Now* he was stalling.

'Why should I?'

'You brought her,' Arkady said. 'I must have been smarter back in Moscow. For a long time I couldn't even understand how Zina got herself assigned to the *Polar Star*. It was Slava, of course. But who pointed him out to Zina when he was sailing on the bay? Who'd shipped with Slava before?'

'A whole crew.'

'But only three coming on the *Polar Star*: Marchuk, Pavel and you. You saw him from the dock.'

'Daddy's boy on his toy boat. His father was the only way he'd get on a real ship.'

'With Slava she acted the innocent. That's why she never took him to your apartment.'

Karp peeled off his sunglasses. 'You knew that was me?'

'Someone with money, rifles, the nerve to run drugs.' Arkady spoke quickly; it was wonderful what adrenalin could do for the ability to add two and two. 'The only man on the *Polar Star* who fits that description is you. Since she was making money at the Golden Horn, she would have come only for something better than rubles. You kept away from each other on board, but not as much as you claimed. You said you never saw her except in the mess, but every time the *Eagle* brought in a net you saw her on the stern deck. Before she knew any men from any boat, she was at the rail waiting for the *Eagle*. She was yours.'

'That's right,' Karp said proudly. 'You're not so dumb.'

Arkady imagined the Americans overhead, surrounded by the abrasive static of the radio, the anvil-hammering on ice. He and Karp were conversing as quietly as conspirators; no one knew they were on board.

'Volovoi's fear,' Arkady said. 'The theme of his life was smuggling. He had to inspect every package, even one thrown from one Soviet boat to another. The watch-word is what?'

'Vigilance.' Karp smiled in spite of himself. He lifted the axe, shouldered it. 'Keep your hands where I can see them.'

'The one thing he couldn't stop was the net going back and forth. How did you know when a package was coming?'

'Simple,' Karp said. 'Ridley waved if they were delivering something besides fish and Coletti waved if they weren't. I looked to see where Zina stood at the rail, starboard side or port. Then I told the men on the ramp the net looked heavy or it didn't.'

'If it was, they found a waterproof package on the headrope of the bag?'

'You'd be good at this. Pavel would cut it off, slip it in

his lifevest. Then we signalled Ridley if we were sending a package back. Renko, what's the point? You're not getting away alive.'

'When you don't worry about that, you can learn a lot.'

'Yeah.' Karp saw merit in the concept.

'And I'm interested in Zina,' Arkady added.

'Men were always interested in Zina. She was like a queen.' Karp's gaze wandered up towards the percussive chorus of hammers on deck, then dropped back. Arkady had never felt eyes so attentive.

'Could you have caught up with me on the ice?' Arkady asked.

'If I wanted to.'

'You could have killed me a minute ago, ten minutes ago.'

'Whenever.'

'Then you want to know what happened to Zina, too.'

'I just want to know what you meant on the ramp last night about Zina being thrown into the water.'

'Simple curiosity?'

Karp had the metallic stillness of a statue. After a long pause he said, 'Go on, Comrade Investigator. Zina was at the dance . . .'

'Zina went and flirted with Mike, but she didn't say goodbye to him when he transferred back to the *Eagle* because she had gone to the stern deck forty-five minutes before. She was seen there by Marchuk, Lidia, Susan. Thirty minutes before Mike transferred, Zina wasn't seen on the *Polar Star* again. By the time he transferred, she was dead.' From his jacket, Arkady slowly took out a piece of paper that he unfolded for Karp. It was a copy of the physical examination. 'She was killed by a blow to the back of the head. She was stabbed so she wouldn't float. She was stowed somewhere on this boat, bent and crammed in some small space that left these regular marks on her side. That's what I came to find – that space. A wardrobe, a closet, a hold, a bin.'

'A piece of paper.' Karp shoved it back.

'That space is here or it isn't. I have to look in the other cabin,' Arkady said but he didn't dare move.

Karp rolled the axe handle thoughtfully. The single-edged head turned reflectively, like a coin. He pushed the door open. 'We'll look together.'

Passing through the galley Arkady heard hammers taking full swings, as if the Americans were trying to carve their way home. He felt the axe cocked at his back and sweat rolling down his spine.

Karp prodded him into the starboard cabin. A real blanket covered his bunk. A railed shelf displayed books on philosophy, electronics and diesel mechanics. On the bulkhead hung a holster and a picture of a man sticking out his tongue. The man in the picture was Einstein.

'Ridley,' Arkady said in answer to himself.

'She disappeared from the *Polar Star* . . . then what?' Karp demanded.

'Remember, you pointed out Slava to her when he was sailing.' Arkady spoke faster. Ridley's bunk drawer held clean clothes neatly folded; leather wristbands and silver ear studs; photos of himself skiing with two women, touching wineglasses with a third; books of Hindu prayer; playing cards; an electronic game of chess; a lapel pin of Minnie Mouse. Arkady turned the cards face up, flipped through them and spread them on the bed.

'I wanted her on the ship, and Bukovsky had the connection. So?'

'She liked to visit men on their boats, and it must have seemed easy for a swimmer as strong as she was to take a few strokes to the *Eagle* when it was tied up to the *Polar Star*. She simply stepped off the stern ramp of the ship, Comrade Malzeva's shower cap on her head, her shoes and a change of clothes in a black plastic bag tied to one wrist. From the rail she was probably invisible.'

'Why would she do that?'

'That was her method. She moved from man to man and boat to boat.'

'No, that doesn't answer my question,' Karp said. 'She wouldn't have taken the chance just to visit. So, Comrade Investigator, why would she do it?'

'I asked myself the same question.'

'And?'

'I don't know.'

Karp used the axe like a long hand to push Arkady to the wall. 'See, where you went wrong, Renko, is saying that Zina would ever leave me.'

'She slept with other men.'

'To use them; that didn't mean anything. But the Americans were partners; that's different.'

420

'She was here.'

'Now that I look around, I don't see any space like
you said she was put in. Not a sign of her.' Karp glanced
at the open drawer. 'If you were hoping to find a gun,
forget it. On this boat everyone carries their guns all the
time.'

'We have to look around more,' Arkady said. He
remembered fighting the trawlmaster in the bunker; the
last place he wanted to dodge an axe was in the confines
of a trawler cabin.

Karp's attention fell on the playing cards spread across
the bunk. Still holding the axe high, he scanned the
cards back and forth. 'Don't move,' he warned. He set
the axe down to pick up the cards and painstakingly
thumb through them. When he was done, he squeezed
them back into a pack which he replaced in the drawer.
His small eyes receded into a stricken white face of love.
For a moment Arkady thought Karp would actually drop
to the floor. Instead, he picked up his axe and said, 'We'll
start in the engine room.'

As they opened the door to the galley another furious
assault on ice began overhead. The trawlmaster only
glanced upward as if at the sound of heavy rain.

The *Eagle*'s two diesel engines throbbed on their steel
beds, a six-cylinder main and a four-cylinder auxiliary.
This was Ridley's domain, the warm innerboat beneath
the deck where it took manoeuvring to walk safely
around layshafts and pulleys, generators and hydraulic

421

pumps, wheel valves and convoluted piping. Low pipes, belt guards and every other dangerous possibility were painted red. The path between the engines was cross-hatched plating.

While Karp prowled Arkady went into the forward space, a repair room with tools, hanging belts, a table with a threader and vice, a rack with saws and drills. There was also what appeared to be the door of a refrigeration unit, though since the *Eagle* delivered its catch to the *Polar Star*, why would it need refrigeration? When he opened the door he had to laugh. Stacked to waist level were mahogany-brown, resinous one-kilo bricks of Manchurian hemp, *anasha*. Well, it was the way the major companies worked. Because the ruble wasn't hard currency, international business was always done by barter. Soviet gas, Soviet oil, why not Soviet *anasha*?

In the narrow bow end of the refrigerator were crammed a table and chair, headphones and oscilloscope, amplifier and equalizer, mainframe, dual console and a file of floppy disks. It was much the same as Hess's station except that the hardware was shinier and more compact, with names like EDO and Raytheon. Sure enough, below the table was a fibreglass dome. He picked a disk from the file; the label read, 'Bering Menu. File. SSBN-Los Angeles. USS *Sawtooth*, USS *Patrick Henry*, USS *Manwaring*, USS *Ojai*, USS *Roger Owen*.' He flipped through the other disks; their labels read 'SSBN-*Ohio*', 'SSGN', 'SSN'. On the table was a clipboard with a paper divided into columns that listed 'Date', 'Boat', 'Position',

'Transmission Time', 'Duration'. The last transmission had been of the *Roger Owen* yesterday. Arkady opened the desk drawer. Inside was an assortment of manuals and schematics. He flipped through the pages. 'Acoustic simulator . . .' 'Polyethylene-covered tow cable with acoustic section and vibration isolation module . . .' 'Winch drum traverses axially . . .' There was a book titled in red letters: 'You Cannot Take This Book From This Office.' The subtitle was 'Reserve, Decommissioned, Dismantled Status – 1/1/83.' Under submarines he found that the USS *Roger Owen* had been dismantled a year ago, and that the USS *Manwaring* and the USS *Ojai* had been removed from service.

The outline of a wonderful joke was taking shape. The electronics were similar to Hess's with one difference: at the end of Morgan's cable wasn't a hydrophone for listening; instead, there was a waterproof acoustic transmitter trailing sounds like a lure. The disks were recordings, and all the submarines on them had been decommissioned or dismantled. Morgan and Hess were circling the Bering Sea, one spy sending false signals for another spy to collect in triumph. Hess must think that American subs were swarming like schools of fish. Arkady replaced the book, but he pocketed the disks. From the engine room Karp paid no attention, as if nothing Arkady did at this point could matter.

Together they returned to the wet room's intermediate damp and pegs of slickers and boots, then went back outside. Under the cover of the shelter deck lay rolls of mesh laced with ice, net bags of buoys, a welder's table with vice, storage lockers and oil drums of shovels and grappling hooks. The hammering overhead was quiet, but there was no stopping Karp now. The *Eagle* had fish holds it had never used since it began transferring nets to factory ships. With his axe, the trawlmaster chipped away the ice covering the holds. As it split it flew up in prism-like flashes. He had to use a grappling hook to lift the hatch. After all his effort, the hold was empty.

Arkady hastily concentrated on the storage lockers under the shelter deck. From the first one he emptied loose rope and blocks; from the second, rubbery legs of coveralls, gloves, torn slickers, tarp. At some previous point the box must have held wire rope, because the bottom had a mixed residue of lubricant and rust. A coffin. He could clearly see the marks where Zina's knees and forearms had rested. On one side was a row of six nuts, about five centimetres apart, that had bruised her side.

'Come and look,' Arkady whispered.

Karp leaned in and came up with a tuft of hair, blond with dark roots. As Arkady reached for it, he felt something brush his neck.

'What are you doing here?' Ridley pressed the gun's cold muzzle more firmly against Arkady's head as Coletti came through the wet-room door with a double-barrelled shotgun.

'This is an unofficial visit?' Morgan stood halfway down the wheelhouse ladder.

Ridley and Coletti looked inflated by the parkas under their slickers. Their left hands were huge with heavy

424

gloves, their right hands bare to fit in trigger guards. Their mouths were raw and frosted by their breath, proper faces for a boat draped in white. In contrast, with his down vest and cap Morgan looked as if he'd stepped out of a different climate. Except for his eyes; they had facets in them as crystalline as ice. Slung over one shoulder was a stubby automatic weapon, a military piece, its ammunition clip longer than its barrel.

'Looking for vodka?' Morgan asked. 'You won't find it there.'

'The *Polar Star* sent us,' Arkady said. 'Captain Marchuk would probably appreciate a call that we made it.'

Morgan pointed to the mast. For all Ridley's labour, the radar bar was still locked in place, the antennas still sheathed in ice. 'Our radios are down. Besides, you two don't look like an official rescue party.'

'Here we are, freezing our asses off to de-ice this tub and we hear this banging on the deck and come around to find you two going through gear like a pair of bag ladies. You understand "bag ladies"?' Ridley twisted the barrel into the back of Arkady's head.

'I think so.'

'I have the feeling,' Morgan said, 'that no one on the *Polar Star* knows you're gone. And if they do, there's no way they can know you and the trawlmaster made it here. What were you looking for?'

'Zina,' Arkady said.

'Again?' the captain asked.

'This time we found her, or the only evidence that's left of her here.'

'Like what?'

'Some hair. I took a sample from the muck at the bottom of the box, and I think I can match that with the marks on her pants. I'd prefer to have the whole storage box, of course.'

'Of course,' Morgan said. 'Well, we'll have the box clean before you get back to the *Polar Star* and as for the hair, you could have gotten that anywhere.'

What Arkady could see of Ridley's weapon was the cylinder of a large revolver, a cowboy gun. The approach to the back of the skull was the same style used on Mike and Zina, but whoever killed them was a knife artist. There was no help from Karp; the trawlmaster stood immobilized, his eyes desperately chasing a foreign conversation, the grappling hook hanging limply from his hand.

'Consider the situation,' Ridley said to Morgan. 'We have a lot to lose and you have a lot to lose.'

'You mean the *anasha*?' Arkady asked.

Ridley paused, then told Coletti, 'They've been below.'

'This is where I draw the line,' Morgan told Ridley. 'I'm not going to let you kill someone in front of me.'

'Captain, my captain,' Ridley said, 'we're trapped in the fucking ice. Renko goes back and reports what he's seen, the next thing you know we've got fifty more Soviets traipsing over for an interested look. This is a case of national security, right?'

'You just want to protect your drugs,' Morgan said.

'I could get personal, too,' Ridley answered. 'At Dutch Harbor, Renko was balling your woman. He took her right away from you. He's probably been balling her on the big ship ever since.'

Morgan looked at Arkady. The moment of denial came and went.

'How about that?' Ridley said. 'Bingo! Cap, you going to let him go back now?'

'That's the difference between you and me,' Morgan said. 'I'm a professional and you're a greedy little bastard.'

'We have a right to our stake, too.'

Arkady asked, 'Why didn't you unload the *anasha* at Dutch Harbor?'

'Mike was crazy about Zina,' Ridley said. 'He was ready to start talking. Then when he was dead, with all those Aleuts watching we just wanted to get out of port. We'll offload on the mainland later.' Ridley turned to Morgan. 'Right, Captain? We all have different interests, some rational and some purely patriotic. The question is,' Ridley said and switched to Russian to ask Karp, 'what team you're on? Are you Renko's partner or are you *our* partner?'

'You speak Russian,' Arkady said.

'Better than Esperanto,' Ridley said.

'I followed Renko to get rid of him,' Karp said.

'Do it,' Ridley said.

'Let Renko go, alone,' Morgan ordered.

Ridley sighed and said to Coletti, 'Who needs this shit from Captain Bligh?'

Arkady was amazed at Morgan's reaction time. Coletti turned, aimed and fired, and only punched in a window by the stairs Morgan jumped from. But while Morgan was in mid-air, Coletti fired the second barrel. The vest exploded. The captain landed on the deck covered in feathers and blood.

'Like a fucking duck.' Coletti broke the shotgun and reloaded a single shell.

Morgan squirmed against the winch, trying to rise and reach his own weapon, which lay under him. One shoulder and ear were red pulp. His jaw was pocked red.

'Your turn,' Ridley told Karp. 'You wanted Renko? Take him.'

'Who killed Zina?' Karp asked.

Coletti stood over Morgan, the shotgun at the captain's head, but he paused at the sound of Karp's voice.

'Renko told us she drowned,' Ridley said.

'We know Zina was here,' Arkady said. 'At the dance you pretended to be drunk. You came back early to the *Eagle* and you waited for her to swim over.'

'No,' Ridley said. 'I was sick. I told you before.'

'She followed you,' Arkady said. 'We found marks, her hair; there's no doubt she was here.'

'OK, I came back and suddenly she was on board.' Although Ridley was behind him, Arkady could feel the gun waver. 'Look, Karp, the entire enterprise depended on everyone acting normal and staying in place: Americans here, Soviets there, a joint venture.'

'Zina was very attractive,' Arkady said.

'Who killed her?' Karp repeated.

Coletti's shotgun started to rise from Morgan.

'No one,' Ridley said. 'Zina sprung this crazy plan. She had this bag and she wanted to take back one of our survival suits, so she could wear it the next time she went overboard. Insane. She'd jump when we were far away, then we would pick her up miles away from the *Polar Star*. She said as long as they weren't missing any survival gear they'd give her up for dead.'

'I'm sure you have excellent survival suits.' Arkady admired Zina's plan. That's what she came for, of course. 'It could have worked.'

'Karp, I blame myself,' Ridley said. 'I told her she was your girl and she'd have to go back to the *Polar Star* the way she came. I guess she didn't make it.'

'You're missing a card,' Karp said.

Ridley paused. 'Missing a card?'

'The queen of hearts,' Karp said. 'She collected them from lovers.'

Coletti was exasperated. 'What the fuck is Karp talking about?'

'I don't know, but I think we've got another bad partner,' Ridley said. 'Cover the ape.' He took the gun from Arkady's head. 'Have to save shots.' From inside his slicker he took an ice pick. As Arkady tried to turn, Ridley drove the pick into his chest.

The force of the blow dropped Arkady to the deck. He sat against the storage box and groped inside his jacket.

Ridley turned to Karp. 'She seduced me. Who was going to resist Zina after four months at sea? But blackmailing me to help her defect?' He raised the gun. 'You people live in a different world. A fucking different world.'

Arkady fired the flare gun. He'd aimed at Ridley's back, but the flare caromed off the engineer's cap, leaving it ablaze like a matchhead.

Ridley whipped off the burning cap. As he swung around to Arkady, a black spider flew over the engineer's shoulder and stretched across his face. It was the three-legged grappling hook that the trawlmaster had been holding. While one prong sank through a cheek, another probed his ear. Karp wrapped the line around Ridley's neck, shutting off the air to his scream. Coletti looked for an angle of fire, but Karp and the engineer were too close together. Karp wrapped the line around Ridley like a man binding barrel staves. Ridley fired his cowboy gun wide twice, and the third time the hammer came down on an empty breech. His eyes twisted back as he dropped the gun.

'Jesus Christ,' Coletti said.

Arkady freed the pick. The tip was red, but the rest of the shaft had been buried in the two lifevests he wore.

'You only have one shell left.' Morgan nodded at Coletti's shotgun. The captain had finally rolled off his own weapon. He pointed it at his deckhand.

Ridley struggled as Karp yanked him backwards along the gunwale, snapping icicles like chimes. Sometimes a boat brought up a halibut, a fish that was as big as a man and could thrash like a man and had to be killed as quickly as possible with a spike through the brain. With his arms tied tight, Ridley looked a little like a landed fish, though Karp was taking his time finishing him.

Arkady got to his feet. 'Where are her jacket and bag?'

'We dumped them at sea long ago,' Coletti said. 'No one will ever find them. I mean, what were the odds she was going to come up in a fucking net?'

'Ridley killed Zina. And Mike, too?' Arkady asked.

'Not me. I was in the bar, I have witnesses,' Coletti said. 'What does it matter?'

'I just like to be absolutely certain.'

Karp threw the loose end of the line four metres high over the stern gantry, caught the line on the way down and started hauling Ridley up hand over hand. The engineer was good-sized, but the rope slipped friction-free over the icy transom. He'd stopped kicking.

'How are you?' Arkady asked Morgan.

'Nothing broken. I have morphine and penicillin.' Morgan spat beads on to the deck. 'Steel shot. Not as bad as lead.'

'Really?' Arkady recalled that Susan had called Morgan invulnerable; perhaps not impenetrable, he thought, but fairly invulnerable. 'Even a superhuman can't run a boat with one arm.'

'The captain and I can work something out.' Coletti's face showed the strain of a man making fresh calculations. 'I can tell you this, I've got a better chance than you. How far do you think Karp will let you get?'

Karp secured the rope around the hydraulic levers on the gantry post so that Ridley swayed clear of the deck. His head seemed to be unscrewing from his shoulders, east to west.

'This is an American boat in American waters,'

Morgan said. 'You don't have proof of anything, not really.'

As Karp took a step from the gantry, Coletti raised the shotgun. 'I still have one shell,' he told Arkady. 'Get that psycho out of here.'

Karp eyed Coletti speculatively, gauging the distance across the deck and his chances against the spreading pattern of a shotgun, but the fire in him was gone.

Arkady joined Karp. 'Now you know.'

'Renko,' Morgan called.

'Morgan?' he called in return.

'Go back,' Morgan said. 'I'll get the radios up and tell Marchuk everything is under control.'

Respectfully Arkady gazed around the frozen ship, the shattered window, Ridley's smouldering cap on the deck, his body dangling from the crosspiece of the gantry.

'Good,' Arkady said. 'Then you can tell Captain Marchuk he has *two* fishermen coming back.'

Chapter Thirty-one

Arkady fished out Slezko's cigarettes, which he shared with Karp. The walk had some aspects of a stroll.

'You know the song *Ginger Moll*?' Karp asked.

'Yes.'

' "Why've you gone and plucked your eyebrows, bitch? And why've you put your blue beret on, you whore?" ' Karp's voice rose to a husky tenor as he sang. 'That was Zina and me. She treated me like dirt. "You know for a fact that I'm crazy about you, I'd be glad to spend all my time thieving for you, but lately you've been stepping out a bit too much." '

'I heard you on her tape.'

'She liked my songs. That's how we met. I had a table of friends at the Golden Horn. We were singing and having a good time, and I could see her watching and listening from across the restaurant. I said to myself, "That's for me!" She moved in a week later. She slept around, but men meant nothing to her, so how could I be jealous? She operated outside the rules. If Zina had a weakness it was all her ideas about the West, as if it was paradise. That was her only flaw.'

'I found a jacket with a hem full of jewels.'

'She liked jewels,' Karp granted. 'But I watched her take over the *Polar Star*. I couldn't get her on board with any amount of money. Then we found Slava, and she took care of Marchuk. When we left port she worked her way through the ship. If she'd wanted you, she'd have had you.'

'In a way she did.' Arkady thought of the tapes.

By the compass, they were on a line to the *Polar Star*. A curiosity of the fog was that they seemed to be making no progress at all. With every step they were surrounded by the same periphery of fog, as if they were continually stepping into the same place.

The ache in Arkady's chest seeped through the rest of his body. Hail to tobacco, the poor man's sedative. Morgan might radio Marchuk that two men were returning, but who could prove one hadn't lost his way, met a bear, walked on to soft ice and slipped from the glittering face of the earth?

'You met Ridley when he spent those two weeks on the ship?' Arkady asked.

'The second week he said to me, "Religion is the opium of the masses." He said it in Russian. Then he said, "Cocaine is the business of the masses." I knew right then. When I got back to Vladivostok, I told Zina about this fantastic connection, and that it was too bad she couldn't get on board. But she found a way. What is fate? Birds fly from a nest in Africa to a branch in Moscow. Every winter the same nest, every summer the same tree. Is it magnetic? Can they tell by the angle of the sun? Every eel in the world is born in the Sargasso Sea, then each one heads to his predestined stream, sometimes swimming for years. When Zina was born in Georgia, what led her to Siberia, then to the sea?'

'The same things that led you to me,' Arkady said.

'What's that?'

'Murder, money, greed.'

'More than that,' Karp insisted. 'Someplace to breathe. Right now this is the freest you or I will ever be. Morgan isn't going to do anything about Ridley; he was ready to kill him too. I sank what I was smuggling. So far I haven't done anything wrong at all.'

'What about Volovoi? When Vladivostok takes a look at his slit throat, there'll be questions asked.'

'Fuck! I can't go straight even if I wanted to.'

'It's tough.'

Karp coaxed a drag from his butt. 'Rules,' he said. 'It's like the blue line you see on the wall at school. Blue line on a shitty plaster wall. In every room, every hall, every school. It starts at shoulder level, and as you get bigger the line sinks to the belt, but it's always there. I mean, it seems to stretch right across the country. In reform camp, same line. Militia office, same line. You know where it stops? I think it stops at about Irkutsk.'

'Norilsk for me.'

'East of there, no more line. Maybe they ran out of paint, maybe you can't paint Siberia. You know, what I feel worst is about Ridley sleeping with Zina. She always took a playing card, a queen of hearts, like a trophy. Did you see the cards on Ridley's bunk? I looked through the whole deck. No queen of hearts. That's how I knew she was on the *Eagle*.'

Arkady pulled up his jacket sleeve and gave Karp a card with a stylized queen in a robe of hearts. 'I palmed it before I spread the deck,' Arkady said.

'You prick!'

'It took you for ever to notice.'

'Brass bastard.' Karp stopped to stare at the card in disbelief. 'You're the one man I thought was honest.'

'No,' Arkady said. 'Not when I'm trapped by a man with an axe. Anyway, it worked; we did learn who killed her.'

'Fucking devious all the same.' Karp threw the card away.

They started walking again. 'Remember the director at the slaughterhouse?' Karp asked. 'His girls raised a reindeer like a pet, and one day it wandered into the wrong pen and they went running through the slaughterhouse looking for it. It was funny. Who can tell one dead reindeer from another? One of the girls left after that. She was the one I liked.'

Ahead, sooner than Arkady had expected and clearer with every step, was the breathing hole. On an otherwise featureless surface it was a black pool within a ring of red ice, a startling break in the mist.

Automatically Karp began to slow down and look around. 'We should have gotten drunk together sometime, just the two of us.' He snapped his butt into the water.

Arkady tossed his in, too. Pollution of the Bering Sea, he thought, one more crime. 'Morgan radioed the *Polar Star* to expect the two of us,' he reminded Karp.

'If he ever got his radio going. Anyway, it's dangerous out here. A call doesn't mean anything.'

The hole was more circular than Arkady remembered. It was only two metres across, but it gave definition to the fog. A Pole of Inaccessibility reached. Some of the ice was soaked through with blood, some pinkly tinged. The black water lapped against it with rhythmic slaps. There was a pulse in there, Arkady suspected, that a man watching long enough might detect.

'Life is shit,' Karp said. With a sideways kick, he knocked Arkady's feet from under him, straddled his back and started to twist his head. Arkady rolled and swung his elbow against Karp's jaw, turning the trawl-master over.

'It feels like I've been trying to kill you for ever,' Karp said.

'Then quit.'

'I can't now,' Karp said. 'Anyway, I've seen guys get stuck before. I think you're hurt worse than you know.' He hit Arkady in the chest, directly on the wound, and it felt as if a lung had collapsed. Arkady couldn't move. Karp punched him again, and all the air seemed to leave his body.

The trawlmaster rolled him over, sat on him and pressed Arkady's shoulders back over the edge of the ice. 'Sorry,' he said and pushed Arkady's head under. Air bubbles exploded from his mouth. He saw silvery air in his lashes and hair. The water was incredibly cold, like molten ice, stingingly salty but clear, not black, magnifying Karp as he leaned forward, pushing Arkady down.

He actually did look sorrowful, like a man performing an unpleasant but necessary christening. Arkady's hand came out of the water, took his sweater and pulled him down.

As Karp reared back, Arkady came out of the water, gasping, holding in his other hand the ice pick Ridley had used on him, and pressed its stained tip against Karp's neck, twisting the jaw back from the bulging vein. Karp's eyes rolled as he tried to watch the shaft. Why not stab him? Arkady thought. Put his whole weight behind the steel, prick the vein and press straight through to the backbone. Eye to eye, what better time?

Karp rolled to the side. He was uninjured except for a scratch, yet all his strength seemed to have left him, as if the gravity of a lifetime had suddenly come down on his chest. 'Enough,' he said.

'You're still going to freeze. It won't take long,' Karp said. He sat by the water, legs crossed, relaxing with a cigarette like a Siberian at ease. 'Your jacket's soaked. You're going to be walking in a block of ice.'

'Then come on,' Arkady said. It was already hard to choose between the dull pain of the wound and the shakes of the cold.

'I was just thinking,' Karp didn't stir. 'What do you think life would have been like for Zina if she'd made it? That's the sort of thing you can spend the rest of your life dreaming about. Ever know anyone who went over?'

'Yes, but I don't know how she's doing.'

'At least you can wonder.' Karp blew a trail of smoke the same colour as the fog; he looked surrounded by a puffy world of smoke. 'I've been thinking. Pavel's already shitting like a rabbit. You're right, once we get to Vladivostok they're not going to let up until somebody talks – Pavel or one of the others. It doesn't matter whether you get back or not; I'm finished.'

'Admit to the smuggling,' Arkady said. 'Testify and they'll only give you fifteen years for Volovoi, and you might get out after ten.'

'With my record?'

'You've been a leading trawlmaster.'

'Like you've been a worker on the leading slime line? The winners of socialist competition, you and me. No, it will be aggravated murder. I don't want to lose my teeth in a camp. I don't want to be buried in a camp. Ever see those little plots right outside the wire? A few daisies for those miserable souls who never left. That's not for me.'

Ice had formed on Arkady's hair and brows. His jacket was glazed with ice, and when he moved his sleeves cracked like glass. 'Alaska is a little out of reach. Let's go; we'll argue on the way to the ship. It will keep us warm.'

'Here.' Karp got to his feet and pulled off his sweater. 'You need something dry.'

'What about you?'

Karp pulled off Arkady's jacket and helped him on

with the sweater. The trawlmaster wore another one underneath.

'Thanks,' Arkady said. Along with the lifevests, the sweater might provide enough insulation. 'If we walk fast enough, we may both make it.'

Karp brushed ice from Arkady's hair. 'Someone who's been in Siberia as long as you have should know you lose most of your heat from your head. Your ears are going to be frostbit in another minute. It's a trade.' He placed his cap on Arkady's head, pulling it tight over his ears.

'What do you get?' Arkady asked.

'The cigarettes.' Karp fished them out of the jacket before handing it back. 'I worry about you sometimes. There's got to be a dry one here.'

He broke off an unsoaked half and lit it from the fag he was about to toss. Though Arkady felt as if his blood were congealing in ice, Karp didn't seem cold. 'Joy.' He exhaled. 'That was one of the signs at the camp. "Rejoice in Work!" and "Work Makes You Free!" We made cameras, in fact – "New Generation". Look for them.'

'Are you coming?'

'Our last day in Vladivostok, Zina and I went on a picnic outside town, on the cliffs overlooking the water. There's that lighthouse there at the cape, looks like a grey castle going to sea, with a red-and-white candle stuck on top. Renko, it's fantastic. Waves crash at the foot of the cliffs. Seals stick their heads out of the water. On top of the cliffs, pines are bent by the wind. I wish I'd had a camera then.'

Holding the cigarette in his lips, Karp peeled off his other sweater. He still seemed clothed because of the *urka* tattoos that covered his torso and arms to his neck and wrists.

'You're not coming?' Arkady asked.

'Or you can go into the woods. It's not the taiga; it's not what people expect. It's a mixed forest – fir and maple on the hills, slow rivers with water lilies. You want to sleep in the woods, so you can hear a tiger. You'll never see one, and anyway, they're protected. But to hear a tiger at night, that's something you never forget.'

Karp stepped naked from his pants and boots. He pinched the butt of his cigarette in his mouth. He was smoking an ember. As his skin pinkened from the cold, his tattooed decorations stood out.

'Don't do this,' Arkady said.

'The main thing is, nobody can say I ever hurt Zina. Not once. If you love someone, you don't hurt them and you don't run away. She wouldn't have stayed away.'

The tattoos were freshened by the air. Oriental dragons climbed Karp's arm, green claws splayed from his feet, ink-blue women wrapped around the columns of his thighs, and with each steamy breath, the vulture picked at his heart. More vivid were the whitening scars, dead stripes on his chest, where the accusations had been burned away. Across his narrow brow spread a livid band. The rest of his skin was reddening, the muscles trembling and jumping in reaction to the cold, animating each tattoo. Arkady remembered what agony it had been for him, even when dressed, in the fish hold. Each second

441

it visibly took more effort and concentration for Karp to get out a word, even to think.

'Come back with me,' Arkady said.

'To what? For what? You win.' By now Karp shook so hard that he could barely stay upright, but he took a final, burning drag before dropping a butt that was no more than a spark into the water. He spread his arms triumphantly. ' "I smile at the enemy with my wolfish grin, baring my teeth's rotten stumps. We're not wolves any more." ' He grinned at Arkady, took a deep breath and dived in.

Arkady could see Karp swimming straight down in powerful strokes as glutinous air bubbles trailed behind. The tattoos looked appropriate, more like scales than skin in the twilight water beneath the ice. About four metres down, he seemed temporarily stalled, until he released a chestful of air and descended to the next, darker layer of water. There a current caught him and he began to drift.

The soles of Karp's feet were not tattooed. After the rest of him disappeared, Arkady saw his feet still swimming, two pale fish in black water.

Chapter Thirty-two

Arkady looked down at the patrol boat's broad radar rig, grey turtleshell guns, torpedo tubes. All night, it seemed, sailors of the Soviet Pacific Fleet had clambered on and off the *Polar Star* removing sealed boxes of equipment. Now, before dawn, the time had come for Anton Hess to make his exit, and like an actor between costume changes the fleet electrical engineer still wore a fishing jacket over pants with a military crease.

'It's good of you to come to see me off. I always believed that you would prove yourself useful with the right goad, the right prize. And here we are.'

'In the dark,' Arkady said.

'In the clear.' Hess gathered Arkady from the rail. 'You don't know how toothsome a bone a failure of Naval Intelligence can be to the KGB. This will not go unappreciated.' He ended his sigh with a laugh. 'Did you see Morgan's face when we freed the *Eagle* from the ice? Of course his boat was a wreck. Worse, he knew what you had brought back to us.'

As soon as it was independently free of the ice sheet the *Eagle* had limped towards the Alaska mainland, while the *Polar Star* cancelled the rest of its fishing. The ship dropped Susan Hightower and the other reps and Lantz off on a pilot boat outside Dutch Harbor.

443

'The only thing I didn't understand was Susan, when she went,' Hess said. 'Why was she so amused?'

'We shared a joke. I told her how valuable her help had been.' After all, she had told him what to steal, even if he had used her advice on a different boat.

Nicolai was waiting inside the transport cage with a marine. The soldier, a moon-face between black fatigues and a beret, carried an assault rifle. The young radioman did not appear happy; on the other hand, he was not in irons. For a moment Hess seemed reluctant to leave, like any man reflecting at the end of a long and successful trip.

'Renko, you understand that your name can't come up in connection with the disks. We don't want to taint them. I wish I could share the credit.'

'Credit for sounds of submarines that were dismantled years ago? You were listening to submarines that don't exist,' Arkady said.

'That doesn't matter. Morgan was compromised. And this time we have the trophy.'

'Disks of nothing.'

'Very well, ghosts and phantoms hissing in the dark. Careers have been made on less.' Hess boarded the cage and hooked the chain across the gate. 'Let me tell you something, Renko. It's round after round and it never stops. I'll be back.'

'That's another reason Susan was smiling,' Arkady said. 'She won't be.'

Hess's good humour could not be defeated. 'Nevertheless.' He put out his hand and shook Arkady's. 'We shouldn't argue. You served well. You rose early to say goodbye.'

'Not really.'

'Nevertheless,' Hess insisted.

'Good luck.' Arkady shook Nicolai's hand.

With the patrol boat gone, the *Polar Star* picked up speed again. Coastal trawlers increased by the hour on the night horizon. A kilometre away, they made a dazzling string of fishing lamps, each boat its own constellation, a different scene from the leave-taking at Dutch Harbor; there it had been a wet afternoon, with the kind of damp that was a second skin and the Americans huddled inside the bridge for the ride to the dock – all but Susan, who stood on deck, not waving, but never taking her eyes off the ship she was leaving.

A curious life, he thought, when he always cared most for whatever he was losing. He'd felt her gaze across the widening water as strongly as when they'd been in bed. Some flaw in him led to futile connections.

'Comrade Jonah.' Marchuk joined Arkady.

'Captain.' Arkady stirred from his reverie. 'I always like night fishing.'

'It'll be day in a minute.' Marchuk leaned on the rail. The captain tried a casual attitude, though for the first time on the voyage he wore dress blues, four gold stripes on the cuffs, gold braid on his cap, bright smudges in the dim light of the deck. 'Your cut is better?'

'It proved to be within Vainu's level of competence,'

Arkady said, though he wasn't taking any deep breaths. 'Too bad about your quota.'

'We revised the quota.' Marchuk shrugged. 'That's the beauty of a quota. But it was good fishing. We should have just fished.'

With the start of dawn, the trawler lamps began to fade into traceries of ordinary gantries and booms against a background of retreating shadow. Chains rang across the surface of the water as the fleet dipped its nets. In the twilight, claques of gulls shifted from boat to boat. On the *Polar Star* more crew came up on deck all the time. Arkady could see them by their cigarettes up on the boat deck and along the rail.

'You weren't the Jonah,' Marchuk added. 'You know, on the radio they're starting to refer to you as *Investigator* Renko, whatever that suggests.'

Below, a line of angular shadows flew by, their bills tucked, skimming the trough behind the bow wave, pelicans at work.

'It could mean anything,' Arkady said.

'True.'

The trawlers shimmered in a grey haze, not fog but the normal exhalation of the sea. This was the in-between moment when the mind had to complete each ship, connect a bow here or a stack there, paint them, people them, give them life. Arkady looked up at the boat deck, where Natasha had turned her face towards the breaking sun, her eyes shining, her black hair momentarily edged with gold. By her Kolya checked his watch, and Dynka rose on tiptoes as she looked east.

Along the rail Arkady saw Izrail in a sweater so clean of fish scales he looked like a burly lamb; Lidia, her face wet with tears; Gury unfolding his dark glasses.

Arkady hadn't risen to see Hess off; what he'd waited all night for was only now emerging.

Gulls burst over the *Polar Star* as if blown by light that rolled like a wind over the factory ship. Clouds lit. The windows of the trawlers flashed and at last, out of the dark rose the low, green shore of home.

447

HAVANA BAY

Martin Cruz Smith, former journalist and magazine editor, is now a full-time writer. He is the author of nine previous novels, including *Gorky Park*, *Polar Star* and *Red Square* – the Arkady Renko trilogy which has sold millions of copies worldwide. *Havana Bay* is his long-awaited new Arkady Renko novel which Macmillan publish in hardback on 22 October 1999. What follows overleaf is the first chapter . . .

Chapter One

A police boat directed a light toward tar-covered pilings and water, turning a black scene white. Havana was invisible across the bay, except for a single line of lamps along the seawall. Stars rode high, anchor lights rode low, otherwise the harbor was a still pool in the night.

Soda cans, crab pots, fishing floats, mattresses, Styrofoam bearded with algae shifted as an investigation team of the Policía Nacional de la Revolución took flash shots. Arkady waited in a cashmere overcoat with a Captain Arcos, a barrel-chested little man who looked ironed into military fatigues, and his Sergeant Luna, large, black and angular. Detective Osorio was a small brown woman in PNR blue; she gave Arkady a studied glare.

A Cuban named Rufo was the interpreter from the Russian embassy. 'It's very simple,' he translated the captain's words. 'You see the body, identify the body and then go home.'

'Sounds simple.' Arkady tried to be agreeable, although Arcos walked off as if any contact with Russians was contamination.

Osorio combined the sharp features of an ingenue with the grave expression of a hangman. She spoke and Rufo explained, 'The detective says this is the Cuban method, not the Russian method or the German method. The Cuban method. You will see.'

Arkady had seen little so far. He had just arrived at the airport in the dark when he was whisked away by Rufo. They were headed by taxi to the city when Rufo received a call on a cellular phone that diverted them to the bay. Already Arkady had a sense that he was unwelcome and unpopular.

Rufo wore a loose Hawaiian shirt and a faint resemblance to the older, softer Muhammad Ali. 'The detective says she hopes you don't mind learning the Cuban method.'

'I'm looking forward to it.' Arkady was nothing if not a good guest. 'Could you ask her when the body was discovered?'

'Two hours ago by the boat.'

'The embassy sent me a message yesterday that Pribluda was in trouble. Why did they say that before you found a body?'

'She says ask the embassy. She was certainly not expecting an investigator.'

Professional honor seemed to be at stake and Arkady felt badly outclassed on that score. Like Columbus on deck, Captain Arcos scanned the dark impatiently, Luna his hulking shadow. Osorio had sawhorses erected and stretched a tape that read NO PASEO. When a motorcycle policeman in a white helmet and spurs on his boots arrived, she chased him with a shout that could have scored steel. Somehow men in T-shirts appeared along the tape as soon as it was unrolled – what was it about violent death that was better than dreams? Arkady wondered. Most of the onlookers were black; Havana was far more African than Arkady had expected, although the logos on their shirts were American.

Someone along the tape carried a radio that sang, '*La fiesta no es para los feos. Qué feo es, señor. Super feo, amigo mío. No puedes pasar aquí, amigo. La fiesta no es para los feos.*'

'What does that mean?' Arkady asked Rufo.

'The song? It says, "This party is not for ugly people. Sorry, my friend, you can't come." '

Yet here I am, Arkady thought.

A vapor trail far overhead showed silver, and ships at anchor started to appear where only lights had hung moments before. Across the bay the seawall and mansions of Havana rose from the water, docks spread and, along the inner bay, loading cranes got to their feet.

'The captain is sensitive,' Rufo said, 'but whoever was right or wrong about the message, you're here, the body's here.'

'So it couldn't have worked out better?'

'In a manner of speaking.'

Osorio ordered the boat to back off so that its wash wouldn't stir the body. A combination of the boat's light and the freshening sky made her face glow.

Rufo said, 'Cubans don't like Russians. It's not you, it's just not a good place for a Russian.'

'Where is a good place?'

Rufo shrugged.

This side of the harbor, now that Arkady could see

453

it, was like a village. A hillside of banana palms overhung abandoned houses that fronted what was more a cement curb than a seawall that stretched from a coal dock to a ferry landing. A wooden walkway balanced on a black piling captured whatever floated in. The day was going to be warm. He could tell by the smell.

'*Vaya a cambiar su cara, amigo. Feo, feo, feo como horror, señor.*'

In Moscow, in January, the sun would have crept like a dim lamp behind rice paper. Here it was a rushing torch that turned air and bay into mirrors, first of nickel and then to vibrant, undulating pink. Many things were suddenly apparent. A picturesque ferry that moved toward the landing. Little fishing boats moored almost within reach. Arkady noticed that more than palms grew in the village behind him; the sun found coconuts, hibiscus, red and yellow trees. Water around the pilings began to show the peacock sheen of petroleum.

Detective Osorio's order for the video camera to roll was a signal for onlookers to press against the tape. The ferry landing filled with commuters, every face turned toward the pilings where, in the quickening light floated a body as black and bloated as the inner tube it rested in. Shirt and shorts were split by the body's expansion. Hands and feet trailed in the water; a swim fin dangled casually on one foot. The head was eyeless and inflated like a black balloon.

'A *neumático*,' Rufo told Arkady. 'A *neumático* is a fisherman who fishes from an inner tube. Actually from a fishing net spread over the tube. Like a hammock. It's very ingenious, very Cuban.'

'The inner tube is his boat?'

'Better than a boat. A boat needs gasoline.'

Arkady pondered that proposition.

'Much better.'

A diver in a wet suit slid off the police boat while an officer in waders dropped over the seawall. They clambered as much as waded across crab pots and mattress springs, mindful of hidden nails and septic water, and cornered the inner tube so that it wouldn't float away. A net was thrown down from the seawall to stretch under the inner tube and lift it and the body up together. So far, Arkady wouldn't have done anything differently. Sometimes events were just a matter of luck.

The diver stepped into a hole and went under. Gasping, he came up out of the water, grabbed onto first the inner tube and then a foot hanging from it. The foot came off. The inner tube pressed against the spear of a mattress spring, popped and started to deflate. As the foot turned to jelly, Detective Osorio shouted for the officer to toss it to shore: a classic confrontation between authority and vulgar death, Arkady thought. All along the tape, onlookers clapped and laughed.

Rufo said, 'See, usually, our level of competence is fairly high, but Russians have this effect. The captain will never forgive you.'

The camera went on taping the debacle while another detective jumped into the water. Arkady hoped the lens captured the way the rising sun poured into the windows of the ferry. The inner tube was sinking. An arm disengaged. Shouts flew back and forth between Osorio and the police boat. The more desperately the men in the water tried to save the situation the worse it became. Captain Arcos contributed orders to lift the body. As the diver steadied the head, the pressure of his hands liquefied its face and made it slide like a grape skin off the skull, which itself separated cleanly from the neck; it was like trying to lift a man who was perversely disrobing part by part, unembarrassed by the stench of advanced decomposition. A pelican sailed overhead, red as a flamingo.

'I think identification is going to be a little more complicated than the captain imagined,' Arkady said.

The diver caught the jaw as it dropped off from the skull and juggled each, while the detectives pushed the other black, swollen limbs pell-mell into the shriveling inner tube.

'*Feo, tan feo. No puedes pasar aquí, amigo. Porque la fiesta no es para los feos.*'

The rhythm was . . . what was the word? Arkady wondered. Unrelenting.

Across the bay a golden dome seemed to burst into flame, and the houses of the Malecón started to express their unlikely colors of lemon, rose, royal purple, aquamarine.

It really was a lovely city, he thought.

*

Light from the high windows of the autopsy theater of the Instituto de Medicina Legal fell on three stainless-steel tables. On the right-hand table lay the *neumático*'s torso and loose parts arranged like an ancient statue dredged in pieces from the sea. Along the walls were enamel cabinets, scales, X-ray panel, sink, specimen shelves, freezer, refrigerator, pails. Above, at the observation level, Rufo and Arkady had a semicircle of seats to themselves. Arkady hadn't noticed before how scarred Rufo's brows were.

'Captain Luna would rather you watched from here. The examiner is Dr Blas.'

Rufo waited expectantly until Arkady realized he was supposed to react.

'*The* Dr Blas?'

'The very one.'

Blas had a dapper Spanish beard and wore rubber gloves, goggles, green scrubs. Only when he appeared satisfied that he had a reasonably complete body did he measure it and search it meticulously for marks and tattoos, a painstaking task when skin tended to slide wherever touched. An autopsy could take two hours, as much as four. At the left-hand table Detective Osorio and a pair of technicians sorted through the deflated inner tube and fishnet; the body had been left tangled in them for fear of disturbing it any more. Captain Arcos stood to one side, Luna a step behind. It occurred to Arkady that Luna's head was as round and blunt as a black fist with red-rimmed eyes. Already Osorio had found a wet roll of American dollar bills and a ring of keys kept in a leaky plastic bag. Fingerprints wouldn't have survived the bag, and she immediately dispatched the keys with an officer. There was something appealingly energetic and fastidious about Osorio. She hung wet shirt, shorts and underwear on hangers on a rack.

While Blas worked he commented to a microphone clipped to the lapel of his coat.

'Maybe two weeks in the water,' Rufo translated. He added, 'It's been hot and raining, very humid. Even for here.'

'You've seen autopsies before?' Arkady asked.

'No, but I've always been curious. And, of course, I'd heard of Dr Blas.'

Performing an autopsy on a body in an advanced stage of putrefaction was a delicate as dissecting a soft-boiled egg. Sex was obvious but not age, not race, not size when the chest and stomach cavities were distended, not weight when the body sagged with water inside, not fingerprints when hands that had trailed in the water for a week ended in digits nibbled to the bone. Then there was the gaseous pressure of chemical change. When Blas punctured the abdomen a flatulent spray shot loudly up, and when he made the Y incision across the chest and then to groin, a wave of black water and liquefied matter overflowed the table. Using a pail, a technician deftly caught the viscera as they floated out. An expand-ing pong of rot – as if a shovel had been plunged into swamp gas – took possession of the room, invading everyone's nose and mouth. Arkady was glad he had left his precious coat in the car. After the first trauma of the stench – five minutes, no more – the olfactory nerves were traumatized and numb, but he was already digging deep into his cigarettes.

Rufo said, 'That smells disgusting.'

'Russian tobacco.' Arkady filled his lungs with smoke. 'Want one?'

'No, thanks. I boxed in Russia when I was on the national team. I hated Moscow. The food, the bread and, most of all, the cigarettes.'

'You don't like Russians, either?'

'I love Russians. Some of my best friends are Russian.' Rufo leaned for a better view as Blas spread the chest for the camera. 'The doctor is very good. At the rate they're going you'll have time to make your plane. You won't even have to spend the night.'

'Won't the embassy make a fuss about this?'

'The Russians here? No.'

Blas slapped the pulpy mass of the heart in a separate tray.

'You don't think they're too indelicate, I hope,' Rufo said.

'Oh, no.' To be fair, as Arkady remembered, Pribluda used to root through bodies with the enthusiasm of a boar after nuts. 'Imagine the poor bastard's surprise,' Pribluda would have said. 'Floating around, looking up at the stars, and then bang, he's dead.'

Arkady lit one cigarette from another and drew the smoke in sharply enough to make his eyes tear. It occurred to him that he was at a point now where he knew more people dead than alive, the wrong side of a certain line.

'I picked up a lot of languages touring with the team,' Rufo said. 'After boxing, I used to guide groups of singers, musicians, dancers, intellectuals for the embassy. I miss those days.'

Detective Osorio methodically laid out supplies that the dead man had taken to sea: thermos, wicker box, and plastic bags of candles, rolls of tape, twine, hooks and extra line.

Usually, an examiner cut at the hairline and peeled the forehead over the face to reach the skull. Since in this case both the forehead and the face had already slipped off and bade adieu in the bay, Blas proceeded directly with a rotary saw to uncover the brain, which proved rotten with worms that reminded Arkady of the macaroni served by Aeroflot. As the nausea rose he had Rufo lead him to a tiny, chain-flush lavatory, where he threw up, so perhaps he wasn't so inured after all, he thought. Maybe he had just reached his limit. Rufo was gone, and walking back to the autopsy theater on his own, Arkady went by a room perfumed by carboys of formaldehyde and decorated with anatomical charts. On a table two feet with yellow toenails stuck out from a sheet. Between the legs lay an oversized syringe connected by a tube to a tub of embalming fluid on the floor, a technique used in the smallest, most primitive Russian villages when electric pumps failed. The needle of the syringe was particularly long and narrow to fit into an artery, which was thinner than a vein. Between the feet were rubber gloves and another syringe in an unopened plastic bag. Arkady slipped the bag into his jacket pocket.

When Arkady returned to his seat, Rufo was waiting with a recuperative Cuban cigarette. By that time, the brain had been weighed and set aside while Dr Blas fit head and jaw together.

Although Rufo's lighter was the plastic disposable sort, he said it had been refilled twenty times. 'The Cuban record is over a hundred.'

Arkady bit the cigarette, inhaled. 'What kind is this?'

' "Popular." Black tobacco. You like it?'

'It's perfect.' Arkady let out a plume of smoke as blue as the exhaust of a car in distress.

Rufo's hand kneaded Arkady's shoulder. 'Relax. You're down to bones, my friend.'

The officer who had taken the keys from Osorio returned. At the other table, after Blas had measured the skull vertically and across the brow, he spread a handkerchief and diligently scrubbed the teeth with a toothbrush. Arkady handed Rufo a dental chart he had brought from Moscow (an investigator's precaution), and the driver trotted the envelope down to Blas, who systematically matched the skull's brightened grin to the chart's numbered circles. When he was done he conferred with Captain Arcos, who grunted with satisfaction and summoned Arkady down to the theater floor.

Rufo interpreted. 'The Russian citizen Sergei Sergeevich Pribluda arrived in Havana eleven months ago as an attaché to the Russian embassy. We knew, of course, that he was a colonel in the KGB. Excuse me, the new Federal Security Service, the SVR.'

'Same thing,' Arkady said.

The captain – and in his wake, Rufo – went on. 'A week ago the embassy informed us that Pribluda was missing. We did not expect them to invite a senior investigator from the Moscow prosecutor's office. Perhaps a family member, nothing more.'

Arkady had talked to Pribluda's son, who had refused to come to Havana. He managed a pizzeria, a major responsibility.

Rufo went on. 'Fortunately, the captain says, the identification performed today before your eyes is simple and conclusive. The captain says that a key found in the effects was taken to the apartment of the missing man where it unlocked the door. From an examination of the body recovered from the bay, Dr Blas estimates that it is a Caucasoid male approximately fifty to sixty years of age, one hundred sixty-five centimeters in height, ninety kilos in weight, in every regard the same as the missing man. Moreover, the dental chart of the Russian citizen Pribluda you yourself brought shows one lower molar filled. That molar in the recovered jaw is a steel tooth which, in the opinion of Dr Blas, according to the captain, is typical Russian dental work. Do you agree?'

'From what I saw, yes.'

'Dr Blas says he finds no wounds or broken bones, no signs of violence or foul play. Your friend died of natural causes, perhaps a stroke or aneurysm or heart attack, it would be almost impossible to determine which for a body in this condition. The doctor hopes he did not suffer long.'

'That's kind of him.' Although the doctor appeared more smug than sympathetic.

'The captain, for his part, asks if you accept the observations of this autopsy?'

'I'd like to think about it.'

'Well, you accept the conclusion that the body recovered is that of the Russian citizen Pribluda?'

Arkady turned to the examining table. What had been a bloated cadaver was now split and gutted. Of course, there had been no face or eyes to identify anyway, and finger bones never did yield prints, but someone had lived in that ruined body.

'I think an inner tube in the bay is a strange place to find a Russian citizen.'

'The captain says they all think that.'

'Then there will be an investigation?'

Rufo said, 'It depends.'

'On what?'

'On many factors.'

'Such as?'

'The captain says your friend was a spy. What he was doing when he died was not innocent. The captain can predict your embassy will ask us to do nothing. We are the ones who could make an international incident of this, but frankly it is not worth the effort. We will investigate in our own time, in our own way, although in this Special Period the Cuban people cannot afford to waste resources on people who have revealed themselves to be our enemy. Now do you understand what I mean?' Rufo paused while Arcos took a second to compose himself. 'The captain says an investigation depends on many factors. The position of our friends at the Russian embassy must be taken into account before premature steps are taken. The only issue we have here is an identification of a foreign national who has died on Cuban territory. Do you accept it is the Russian citizen Sergei Pribluda?'

'It could be,' Arkady said.

Dr Blas sighed, Luna took a deep breath and Detective Osorio weighed the keys in her palm. Arkady couldn't help feeling like a difficult actor. 'It probably is, but I can't say conclusively that this body is Pribluda. There's no face, no prints and I doubt very much that you will be able to type the blood. All you have is a dental chart and one steel tooth. He could be another Russian. Or one of thousands of Cubans who went to Russia. Or a Cuban who had a tooth pulled by a Cuban dentist who trained in Russia. Probably you're right, but that's not enough. You opened Pribluda's door with a key. Did you look inside?'

Dr Blas asked in precisely snipped Russian, 'Did you bring any other identification from Moscow?'

'Just this. Pribluda sent it a month ago.' Arkady dug out of his passport case a snapshot of three men standing on a beach and squinting at the camera. One man was so black he could have been carved from jet. He held up a glistening rainbow of a fish for the admiration of two whites, a shorter man with a compensating tower of steel-wool hair and, partially obscured by the others, Pribluda. Behind them was water, a tip of beach, palms.

Blas studied the photograph and read the scribble on the back. 'Havana Yacht Club.'

'There is such a yacht club?' Arkady asked.

'There *was* such a club before the Revolution,' Blas said. 'I think your friend was making a joke.'

Rufo said, 'Cubans love grandiose titles. A "drinking society" can be friends in a bar.'

'The others don't look Russian to me. You can make copies of the picture and circulate them.'

The picture went around to Arcos, who put it back into Arkady's hands as if it were toxic. Rufo said, 'The captain says your friend was a spy, that spies come to bad ends, as they deserve. This is typically Russian, pretending to help and then stabbing Cuba in the back. The Russian embassy sends out its spy and, when he's missing, asks us to find him. When we find him, you refuse to identify him. Instead of cooperating, you demand an investigation, as if you were still the master and Cuba was the puppet. Since that is no longer the case, you can take your picture back to Moscow. The whole world knows of the Russian betrayal of the Cuban people and, well, he says some more in that vein.'

Arkady gathered as much. The captain looked ready to spit.

Rufo gave Arkady a push. 'I think it's time to go.'

Detective Osorio, who had been quietly following the conversation, suddenly revealed fluent Russian. 'Was there a letter with the picture?'

'Only a postcard saying hello,' Arkady said. 'I threw it away.'

'*Idiota*,' Osorio said, which nobody bothered to translate.

'It's lucky you're going home, you don't have many friends here,' Rufo said. 'The embassy said to put you in an apartment until the plane.'

They drove by three-story stone town houses transformed by the revolution into a far more colorful backdrop of ruin and decay, marble colonnades refaced with whatever color was available – green, ultramarine, chartreuse. Not just ordinary green, either, but a vibrant spectrum: sea, lime, palm and verdigris. Houses were as blue as powdered turquoise, pools of water, peeling sky, the upper levels enlivened by balconies of ornate ironwork embellished by canary cages, florid roosters, hanging bicycles. Even dowdy Russian cars wore a wide variety of paint, and if their clothes were drab most of the people had the slow grace and color of big cats. They paused at tables offering guava paste, pastries, tubers and fruits. One girl shaving ices was streaked red and green with syrup, another girl sold sweetmeats from a cheesecloth tent. A locksmith rode a bicycle that powered a key grinder; he wore goggles for the sparks and shavings flying around him as he pedaled in place. The music of a radio hanging in the crook of a pushcart's umbrella floated in the air.

'Is this the way to the airport?' Arkady asked.

'The flight is tomorrow. Usually there's only one Aeroflot flight a week during the winter, so they don't want you to miss it.' Rufo rolled the window down. 'Phew, I smell worse than fish.'

'Autopsies stay with you.' Arkady had left his overcoat outside the operating theater and separated the coat now from the paper bag holding Pribluda's effects. 'If Dr Blas and Detective Osorio speak Russian, why were you along?'

'There was a time when it was forbidden to speak English. Now Russian is taboo. Anyway, the embassy wanted someone along when you were with the police, but someone not Russian. You know, I never knew anyone so unpopular so fast as you.'

'That's a sort of distinction.'

'But now you're here you should enjoy yourself. Would you like to see the city, go to a café, to the Havana Libre? It used to be the Hilton. They have a rooftop restaurant with a fantastic view. And they serve lobster. Only state restaurants are allowed to serve lobster, which are assets of the state.'

'No, thanks.' The idea of cracking open a lobster after an autopsy didn't sit quite right.

'Or a *paladar*, a private restaurant. They're small, they're only allowed twelve chairs but the food is much superior. No?'

Perhaps Rufo didn't get a chance to dine out often, but Arkady didn't think he could even watch someone eat.

'No. The captain and sergeant were in green uniforms, the detective in gray and blue. Why was that?'

'She's police and they're from the Ministry of the Interior. We just call it Minint. Police are under Minint.'

Arkady nodded; in Russia the militia was under the same ministry. 'But Arcos and Luna don't usually go out on homicides?'

'I don't think so.'

'Why was the captain going on about the Russian embassy?'

'He has a point. In the old days Russians acted like lords. Even now, for Cuban police to ask questions at the embassy takes a diplomatic note. Sometimes the embassy cooperates and sometimes it doesn't.'

Most of the traffic was Russian Ladas and Moskviches spraying exhaust and then, waddling as ponderously as dinosaurs, American cars from before the Revolution. Rufo and Arkady got out at a two-story house decorated like a blue Egyptian tomb with scarabs, ankhs and lotuses carved in stucco. A car on blocks sat in residence on the porch.

''57 Chevrolet.' Rufo looked inside at the car's gutted interior, straightened and ran his hand over the flecked paint. From the back. 'Tail fins.' To the front bumper. 'And tits.'

From the car key in the bag of effects Arkady knew that Pribluda had a Lada. No breasts on a Russian car.

As they went in and climbed the stairs the door to the ground-floor apartment cracked open enough for a woman in a house-dress to follow their progress.

'A concierge?' Arkady asked.

'A snoop. Don't worry, at night she watches television and doesn't hear a thing.'

'I'm going back tonight.'

'That's right.' Rufo unlocked the upstairs door. 'This is a protocol apartment the embassy uses for visiting dignitaries. Well, lesser dignitaries. I don't think we've had anyone here for a year.'

'Is someone from the embassy coming to talk about Pribluda?'

'The only one who wants to talk about Pribluda is you. You like cigars?'

'I've never smoked a cigar.'

'We'll talk about it later. I'll be back at midnight to take you to the plane. If you think the flight to Havana was long, wait till you go back to Moscow.'

The apartment was furnished with a set of cream-and-gold dining chairs, a sideboard with a coffee service, a nubby sofa, red phone, a bookshelf with titles like *La Amistad Russo-Cubana* and *Fidel y Arte* supported by erotic bookends in mahogany. In a disconnected refrigerator a loaf of Bimbo Bread was spotted with mold. The air conditioner was dead and showed the carbon smudges of an electrical fire. Arkady thought he probably showed some carbon smudges of his own.

He stripped from his clothes and showered in a stall of tiles that poured water from every valve and washed the odor of the autopsy off his skin and from his hair. He dried himself on the scrap of towel provided and stretched out on the bed under his overcoat in the dark of the bedroom and listened to the voices and music that filtered from outside through the closed shutters of the window. He dreamed of floating among the playing fish of Havana Bay. He dreamed of flying back to Moscow and not landing, just circling in the night.

Russian planes did that, sometimes, if they were so old that their instruments failed. Although there could be other factors. If a pilot made a second landing approach he could be charged for the extra fuel expended, so he made only one, good or not. Or they were overloaded or underfueled.

He was both.

Circling sounded good.

ROSE

For Em

Acknowledgements

I would like to thank Christopher Maclehose and Anne O'Brien for setting me on the road to Wigan, Nikki Sheriff for the map room, Kristin Jakob for the right garden, Jean Sellars for the proper attire, George Thompson for the poetry and Ian Winstanley for the world underneath the surface.

Most of all, I owe Joe Fox, who for five books over fifteen years lit the way.

Chapter One

The most beautiful women in the world were African.

Somali women wrapped in robes suffused with purple, vermilion, pink. Around their necks beads of amber that, rubbed together, emitted electricity and the scent of lemons and honey.

Women of the Horn who peered through veils of gold, strands in the shape of tinkling teardrops. They stood veiled in black from head to toe, their longing compressed into kohl-edged eyes. In the Mountains of the Moon, Dinka women, dark and smooth as the darkest smoothest wood, tall and statuesque within beaded corsets that would be cut open only on their wedding nights.

And the women of the Gold Coast in golden chains, bells, bracelets, dancing in skirts of golden thread in rooms scented by cinnamon, cardamom, musk.

Jonathan Blair awoke tangled in damp sheets and shivering to the rain, gas fumes and soot that pressed against his lodging's single window. He wished he could slip back into his dream, but it was gone like smoke. The Africa in his bloodstream, though, that was for ever.

He suspected he had typhoid. His bedclothes were

dank from sweat. The week before, he had been yellow from his eyeballs to his toes. He pissed brown water, a sign he had malaria. Which last night had demanded quinine and gin – at least he had demanded it.

Outside, morning bells rang in another foul day, resounding like blood vessels exploding in his brain. He was freezing and on the room's miniature grate a pitiful mouthful of coals was fading under ash. He swung his feet to the floor, took one step and collapsed.

He came to an hour later. He could tell by another outburst of bells, so there was some point to God after all – as a celestial regulator with a gong.

From the floor Blair had a low but excellent view of his sitting room: threadbare carpet of tea stains, bed with wrestled sheets, single chair and table with oil lamp, wallpaper patched with newspaper, window of weepy grey light that showed dead ashes on the grate. He was tempted to try to crawl to the chair and die in a sitting position, but he remembered that he had an appointment to keep. Shaking like an old dog, he struck out on all fours towards the fireplace. Chills squeezed his ribs and twisted his bones. The floor pitched like the deck of a ship, and he passed out again.

And came to with a match in one hand and a newspaper and kindling in the other. He seemed to do as well unconscious as conscious; he was pleased with that. The paper was folded to the Court Circular for 23 March 1872. 'HRH The Princess Royal will attend a Patrons' meeting at the Royal Geographical Society with Sir Rodney Murchison, President of the RGS, and the

ROSE

Right Reverend Bishop Hannay. In attendance will be . . .' That was yesterday, which meant he had missed the festivities, had he been, well, invited, and possessed the cab fare. He struck the match and used all his strength to hold the sulphurous flame under the paper and sticks, and to push them under the grate. He rolled on his side to the scuttle. Please God, he thought, let there be coal. There was. He laid a handful on the fire. A kettle hung over the grate. Please God, he thought, let there be water. He tapped the kettle and heard its contents slosh from side to side. He fed the fire more paper and more coal, and when the coal had caught he lay as close as he could to the fire's warming breath.

He didn't like English tea. He would have preferred sweet Moroccan minted tea served in a glass. Or thick Turkish coffee. Or a tin cup of American boiled coffee. In London, however, he thought this was probably about as pleasant as life could get.

Once he'd had his tea, Blair chanced getting dressed. Fashioning his scarf into a sort of tie gave him problems, since he couldn't raise his arms without triggering the shakes. Because he hadn't dared put a razor near his throat for days he had the beginnings of a beard. He did still have decent clothes and a pocket watch to tell him that if he was going to walk from Holborn Road to Savile Row – he certainly didn't have money to ride – he had to leave at once. Ordinarily the route was an hour's stroll. Today it lay before him like a passage through mountains, deserts, swamps. He leaned against the window and stared down at the hunched backs of cabs

3

and vying streams of umbrellas on the pavements. The glass reflected a face that was raw and high-coloured by a life spent out of doors. Not a friendly or comfortable face even to its owner.

Going down the stairs he swayed like a sailor. As long as he didn't break a leg he'd be fine, he told himself. Anyway, this was an appointment he couldn't afford to miss, not if he wanted to get out of England. He'd crawl on his elbows to do that.

London assaulted him with the steaming smell of horse droppings, the shouts of a rag-and-bone man contending with a line of hackney cabs, the argument punctuated with explosive discharges of phlegm. The boulevards of Paris were washed once a day. In San Francisco dirt at least rolled down to the bay. In London filth accreted undisturbed but for the daily piss from the heavens, creating a stench that made the nose weep.

Well, that was what England itself was like, a snuffling nose set by the blue eye of the North Sea, Blair thought. This other Eden, this sceptred isle, this chamberpot beneath the sky. And every subject proud of his umbrella.

At this end of Holborn Road the local tribes were Jews, Irish and Romanians, all dressed in bowlers and drab rags. Every street had its pawnshop, mission hall, tripe house, oyster stall, brace of beerhouses. If the surrounding stench was a miasma, the inhabitants on the street took no more notice than fish took of salt water. Horse-drawn buses with open upper decks lurched through layers of drizzle and fog. Men in sandwich boards carried the offers of chiropractors, dentists, psychics. Women in sodden boas offered glimpses of rouge and venereal disease. Corner vendors sold French rolls, penny rolls, hot potatoes and newspaper headlines announcing 'Heartsick Strangler Kills Babe, Mum!' How the editors sorted out which of the daily multitude of urban atrocities to sell, Blair couldn't imagine.

Halfway, by Charing Cross, billboards advertised the staples of middle-class life: liver pills and elderberry, Nestlé's milk and Cockburn's sherry. Here the population was transformed to a masculine society in black suits and top hats: clerks with one hand clutching their collars, tradesmen with cotton gloves and ribboned boxes, barristers in waistcoats festooned with silver fobs, all jostling with umbrellas. Blair had no umbrella himself, only a broad-brimmed hat that diverted rain on to the shoulders of his mackintosh. On his feet he had a pair of leaky wellingtons, the soles lined with pages torn from a mission hymnal: 'A Closer Walk with Thee' in the left boot. He stopped every five minutes to rest against a lamp-post.

By the time he reached St James's, the chills had returned as spasms that made his teeth chatter. Although he was late, he turned into a public house with a blackboard that declared 'Cheapest Gin'. He laid his last coin on the bar and found himself given ample room by the regulars, a lunchtime gallery of shop assistants and apprentices with the drawn faces of mourners in training.

The bartender delivered a glass of gin and said,

5

'There's pickled eggs or oysters comes with that, if you want.'

'No, thanks. I'm off solids.'

Every eye seemed to watch him down the glass. It wasn't simply that their faces were white. Compared with other complexions, British skin had the sallow shine that reflected a sun long lost in a pall of smoke. A boy with brighter eyes edged along the counter. He wore a green band on his hat, a purple tie squashed as flat as a cabbage leaf, and yellow gloves with rings on the outside.

'*Illustrated London News*,' he said, and extended a hand.

A reporter. Blair didn't wait for his change. He pushed himself away from the bar and plunged through the door.

The boy had the grin of someone who had found a pearl in his oyster. 'That was Blair,' he announced. 'Blair of the Gold Coast. Nigger Blair.'

His destination was in the sort of Savile Row townhouse that merchant banks and clubs were fond of: an entrance between banded columns, three floors of windows over-hung with marble crenellation that expressed confidence, propriety, discretion. A brass plaque on a column read 'The Royal Geographical Society'.

'Mr Blair.' Jessup, the steward, was always solicitous for reasons Blair never understood. He helped Blair off with his hat and coat, led him to the rear of the cloakroom and fetched him tea and milk. 'How are you feeling, sir?' he asked.

'A little chilled, just the smallest bit.' Blair was trembling so hard from the short dash from the pub that he could barely keep the tea in the cup.

'Gunpowder tea will set you straight, sir. It's good to see you again, sir.'

'A pleasure to see you, Jessup. The Bishop is still here?'

'His Grace is still here. One of the men just took him some cheese and port. You catch your breath. I read the reports of your work with great interest, sir. I hope there will be more accounts to come.'

'I hope so, too.'

'Do you think you can stand, sir?'

'I believe I can.' The shakes were subsiding. He got semi-briskly to his feet and Jessup brushed his jacket.

'Gin will rot your insides, sir.'

'Thank you, Jessup.' He started to move while he was still faintly refreshed.

'You'll find the Bishop in the map room, sir. Please be careful. He's in a mood.'

The map room was testimony of the Society's contribution to exploration and knowledge. It had started as the African Association. A great map delineated expeditions the Society had sponsored: Mungo Park up the Niger, Burton and Speke to Lake Victoria, Speke and Grant to the White Nile, Livingstone to the Congo, Baker to Uganda in search of Speke. The walls were two levels of book and map shelves, the upper gallery supported by cast-iron columns and a spiral stairway. Watery light showed through the glass roof. In the middle of the room a mounted globe showed the British possessions as an earth-girdling corporation in Imperial pink.

By the globe stood Bishop Hannay, a tall man of middle age in a black woollen suit and the inverted V of an ecclesiastical collar. Because most English dressed in black they seemed a nation in perpetual grief, but the sombre cloth and white collar only emphasized the Bishop's inappropriate vigour and the bluntness of his gaze. He had ruddy skin with red lips, and dark hair gone grey and wild at the temples and brows as if singed.

He said, 'Sit down, Blair. You look like Hell.'

Two high-backed chairs were at a map table set with cheese and port. Blair accepted the invitation to collapse.

'It's good to see you again, too, Your Grace. Sorry about being late.'

'You stink of gin. Have some port.'

Hannay poured him a glass, taking none for himself.

'You're in bad odour altogether, Blair. Embezzlement of charitable funds, wilful disobedience of orders, abetting slavery, for God's sake! You embarrassed the Society and the Foreign Office. And you were my recommendation.'

'I only took funds that were owed me. If I could meet with the Board of Governors—'

'If you did, they'd slap your face and turn you out of the door.'

8

'Well, I'd hate to provoke them to violence.' Blair refilled the glass and looked up. 'You'll listen to me?'

'I'm not as easily shocked as the others. I expect moral turpitude.' The Bishop sat back. 'But, no, I won't listen because it would be a waste of time. They resent you for reasons that have nothing to do with the accusations.'

'Such as?'

'You're American. I know you were born here, but you're American now. You have no idea how abrasive your style and voice can be. And you're poor.'

Blair said, 'That's why I took the money. There I was in Kumasi on survey. I'm not like Speke, I don't need an army, just five men, assay equipment, medicine, food, gifts for the chiefs. I had to pay the men in advance, and I'd already spent all my own funds. Those people depend on me. Twenty pounds. It's little enough money anyway and half the men die. Where was all the money promised by the Foreign Office and the Society? Spent by the colonial administration in Accra. The only thing I could get my hands on was the Bible Fund. I used it. It was food or books.'

'Bibles, Blair. The food of souls. Even if it was for Methodists.' The Bishop whispered so low that Blair couldn't tell whether he was inviting a laugh.

'You know what the office in Accra spent my money on? They splurged on ceremonies and honours for a murderous cretin – your nephew.'

'It was an official visit. Of course they put on a show. If you weren't so poor it wouldn't have been a problem.

9

That's why Africa is a field for gentlemen. Whereas you are—'

'A mining engineer.'

'Let's say more than just a mining engineer. A geologist, a cartographer, but definitely not a gentleman. Gentlemen have sufficient private means so that unexpected situations don't become painful embarrassments. Don't worry, I made good on the Bible Fund for you.'

'With the money I spent in Kumasi, the Society still owes me a hundred pounds.'

'After the way you disgraced them? I don't think so.'

The Bishop stood. He was as tall as a Dinka. Blair knew for sure because Hannay was the only member of the Board of Governors ever to go to Africa, the real Africa south of the Sahara. Blair had taken him into the Sudan, where they encountered first the flies, then the cattle, and finally the camp of nomadic Dinkas. The women ran from the visitors' white faces. Africans usually did: the story was that whites ate blacks. The Dinka men stood in a bold line, naked except for a ghostly dusting of ash and armbands of ivory. Out of curiosity the Bishop stripped off his suit and matched himself limb for limb with the largest warrior. From the shoulders down in every physical particular the two giants were identical.

Hannay rose. He gave the globe a light spin. 'This slavery business. Explain that.'

Blair said, 'Your nephew, Rowland, came inland slaughtering animals.'

'He was gathering scientific specimens.'

10

'Specimens with holes. When someone shoots fifty hippos and twenty elephants in half a day, he's a butcher, not a scientist.'

'He's an amateur scientist. What has that to do with slavery?'

'Your nephew revealed he had a commission from the Foreign Office to investigate native affairs, and he declared that he was shocked to find slavery in a British colony.'

'British *protectorate*.' Hannay put up his hand.

'He had troops and a letter from you retaining me as his guide. He announced he would free the Ashanti's slaves and put the king in irons. It was a statement designed to provoke an Ashanti reaction and bring in British troops.'

'What's wrong with that? The Ashanti grew fat off slavery.'

'So did England. England and the Dutch and the Portuguese set up the slave trade with the Ashanti.'

'But now England has shut the slave trade down. The only way to do it completely is to crush the Ashanti and make British rule secure throughout the Gold Coast. But you, Jonathan Blair, my employee, took the side of black slavers. Just when did you find it in your competence to frustrate the policies of the Foreign Office or to question the moral vision of Lord Rowland?'

Blair knew Hannay used Rowland's title to emphasize his own far inferior status. He swallowed the impulse to make an angry, democratic exit.

'All I did was advise the king to retreat and live to

11

fight another day. We can slaughter him and his family a few years from now.'

'The Ashanti fights well. It won't be a slaughter.'

'The Ashanti goes into battle with a musket and boxes of verse from the Koran stitched to his shirt. The British infantryman goes into battle with a Martini-Henry rifle. It will be a glorious slaughter.'

'Meanwhile the evil of slavery goes on.'

'England doesn't want their slaves, it wants their gold.'

'Of course it does. That's what you were supposed to find and didn't.'

'I'll go back for you.' He had meant to introduce the offer slowly, not to blurt it out as desperately as this.

The Bishop smiled. 'Send you back to the Gold Coast? So you could abet your slaver friends again?'

'No, to finish the survey I've already started. Who knows the land as well as I do?'

'It's out of the question.'

Blair was familiar enough with Hannay to understand that the Bishop answered personal appeal with contempt. Well, there were many routes to Africa. He tried a different one. 'I understand there'll be an expedition to the Horn next year. There's gold there. You'll need someone like me.'

'Someone *like* you, not necessarily you. The Society would prefer anyone to you.'

'You're the major sponsor, they'll do what you say.'

'At the moment that does not work to your benefit.' Hannay managed to look amused without a smile. 'I see through you, Blair. You hate London, you detest England, every hour here is odious to you. You want to get back to your jungle and your coffee-coloured women. You are transparent.'

Blair felt a warm flush on his cheeks that had nothing to do with either malaria or port. Hannay had diagnosed him in a brutally accurate way. And perhaps dismissed him, too. The Bishop crossed to the bookshelves. Burton's *First Footsteps in East Africa* was there. Also Livingstone's *Missionary Travels*. Both had been bestsellers on a scale usually reserved for Dickens's maudlin myths of London. Hannay ran his fingers lightly across Society reports: 'Trade Routes of the Arab Dhow', 'Superstitions and Rituals of the Hottentot', 'Mineral Resources of the Horn of Africa', 'Certain Practices among the Peoples of the Horn'. The latter two had been Blair's own minor contributions. As if he were alone, Hannay moved in a leisurely fashion to the shelf devoted to South Africa, to Zulus and Boers.

No protest or exit line came to Blair's mind. Perhaps he had been expelled and the expulsion had been so swift that he had missed the kick. In the silence he calculated how much he owed for his miserable lodging. Besides the clothes on his back he owned nothing that didn't fit into a pack. His only valuable possession was his surveying equipment: chronometer, brass sextant, telescope.

'What are your prospects?' Bishop Hannay asked, as if Blair had been wondering aloud.

'There are other mining companies in London. The East India Company or an Egyptian interest. I'll find something.'

'Any employer will ask for a recommendation, and you'll be publicly infamous before the week is out.'

'Or go to New York or California. There's still plenty of gold there.'

'Not without a steamship ticket. Your hat is soaked. You didn't have enough for a cab here.'

'For a bishop you are a mean son of a bitch.'

'I'm Church of England,' Hannay said. 'That gives me a great deal of latitude. That's why I tolerate you.'

'I've engineered Hannay mines in America, Mexico, Brazil. You're the one who sent me to Africa.'

'Asked, not sent, and you were off like a shot.'

'I'm not asking for money, not even what the Society owes me. Just a ticket to New York, nothing more.'

'That's all?'

'The world is full of mines.'

'And like the white rabbit, you'll pop down a hole and never be seen again.' To emphasize his point, Hannay dropped his own frame into the chair opposite Blair.

'Right.'

'Well, I would miss you, Blair. You may be many things, but a rabbit is hardly one of them. I do feel responsibility for you. You've done some good work in difficult places, that's absolutely true. Your company, when you control your language, isn't disagreeable. It's pathetic to see you reduced to this condition. Tomorrow you'll be boiling your boots and dining on them. Or dining on the citizens of London. No, you're not a rabbit.'

'Then get me out of this place.'

The Bishop put his hands together in a way that on

anyone else would have looked like prayer; on him it was simply concentration. 'You'd ship to New York out of Liverpool?'

Blair nodded, for the first time with a little hope.

'Then there might be something for you on the way,' Hannay continued.

'What's "on the way"?'

'Wigan.'

Blair laughed, surprised that he had the strength. He said, 'Thanks, I'd rather starve.'

'Wigan is mining country. The world is full of mines, you said so yourself.'

'I meant gold mines, not coal.'

'But you started in coal mines.'

'So I know the difference.'

'A hundred pounds,' Hannay said. 'And expenses.'

'You owe me the hundred. Expenses in Wigan? You mean all the meat pie I can eat?'

'And a place on next year's expedition. They'll be mustering in Zanzibar and attempting to cross the continent from the east coast of Africa to the west, aiming for the mouth of the Congo. I can't guarantee the position – I'm only a sponsor – but I will speak for your character.'

Blair refilled his glass and tried to keep the decanter steady. This was all he could have hoped for, weighed against Wigan.

'Just to look at a coal mine? There are a hundred better men for that already in Wigan.'

'No. What I want you to do is for the Church.'

'Lectures? Lantern slides of Africa? Missionaries I have admired, that kind of thing?'

'That would strain credulity too much. No, something better suited to your nature, your curiosity, your peculiar background. Something private. I have a young curate in Wigan. A "low church" kind of curate, the evangelical kind. Practically Methodist, almost Wesleyan. A zealot for preaching to fallen women and convicted men. The problem is not that he's a fool but that I can't find him. Like the white rabbit, he has gone down a hole and disappeared.'

'You mean he went down a mine?' Blair asked.

'No, no, just that he's vanished. It's been two months since he was seen in Wigan. The police have asked questions, but our constables are local lads trained mainly for subduing drunks and finding poachers.'

'Bring in a detective from the outside.'

'Miners despise detectives as strikebreakers, which they usually are. You, on the other hand, blend in. You did it in Africa as well as a white man could.'

'You could get someone from London.'

'Someone from London would be lost. They wouldn't understand five words a Lancashireman said. Your mother was from Wigan, wasn't she? I seem to remember the two of us sitting at a campfire in the middle of the Sudan and your confiding that information.'

'We'd talked about everything else.'

'It was completely natural. My home is Wigan. It's a mutual bond between us. You lived in Wigan before your mother took you to America.'

16

'What's your point?'

'That when someone in Wigan speaks to you, you will comprehend what he's saying.'

Gin and port was not a bad combination. The chills faded. The mind focused.

'There's more to it,' Blair said. 'You're not going to all this trouble simply for a wayward curate. Especially a fool.'

Bishop Hannay sat forward, pleased. 'Of course there's more. The curate is engaged to my daughter. If he was outside a pub and skulled by an Irishman, I want to know. If he was saving a prostitute and seduced in turn, I want to know. Quietly, through an agent of mine, so my daughter and I and the rest of the nation won't be reading about it in the newspapers.'

'Anything could have happened. He could have fallen down a shaft, into a canal, under a coal wagon. Maybe he dipped into *his* Bible Fund and ran off with gypsies.'

'Anything. But I want to know.' From under his chair the Bishop drew a cardboard envelope tied with a red ribbon. He untied it and showed Blair the contents. 'John.'

'His name is John?'

'His Christian name. Also, fifty pounds in advance for any costs that you incur.'

'What if he walks into church tomorrow?'

'You keep it all. Get a decent meal in you and some more medicine. I've had you booked into a hotel in Wigan. The bills will go to me.'

'You mean, the bills will go to Hannay Coal?'

'Same thing.'

A hundred pounds was still owed to him, Blair thought, but fifty pounds was generous. The Bishop was a host who offered a spoon of honey for a spoon of bile. Blair was sweating so hard he was sticking to the back of the chair.

'You think I'll do this?'

'I think you're desperate, and I know you want to return to Africa. This is an easy task. A personal favour. It's also a form of minor redemption.'

'How is that?'

'You think I'm the hard man, Blair? Anyone but you would have inquired about my daughter, what condition she was in when she realized that her fiancé had gone to ground. Was she distressed? Hysterical? Under a doctor's care? You ask not a single word.'

The Bishop waited. Blair watched rain tap on the window, collect in beads, coalesce, and then sluice to the bottom of the pane.

'Very well, how is your daughter?'

Hannay smiled, getting the performance he was paying for. 'She's bearing up, thank you. She'll be relieved to know you've consented to help.'

'What's her name?'

'It's all in there.' The Bishop closed the envelope, tied it and placed it on Blair's lap. 'Leveret will be in contact with you at the hotel. He's my estate manager. Good luck.'

This time there was no doubt Blair was being dismissed. He stood, steadying himself with the chair, holding on to the envelope and its precious money. 'Thank you.'

'You overwhelm me,' Hannay said.

On his way out, Blair had negotiated the globe and was at the door when the Bishop called after him.

'Blair, since you will be working for me and near my home I want to remind you that some parts of the public do think of you as a sort of explorer. You have a reputation for getting close to the natives, first in East Africa, then in the Gold Coast. Picking up the language is one thing; dressing like them and acting like them is something else. People like to call you "Nigger Blair". Discourage that.'

Chapter Two

Blair rode in a railway car as hushed and polished as a hearse, with oil lamps that were as low as candles. He thought all he was missing were lilies on his chest. It didn't help that mourners seemed to have climbed in with him, because the rest of his compartment was occupied by two men and a woman returning from a Temperance rally. They wore militant black with red sashes that said 'Tea – The Drink That Cheers and Does Not Inebriate'. Since he still hadn't shaved, he hoped that he made a travelling companion too unsavoury to speak to, but they eyed him like vultures presented with a dying lion.

Though Blair had invested in quinine and brandy, fever came in tides that lifted him from crest to crest of sweat and left him exhausted between waves. Not that he could complain. Malaria was the minimum, the price of admission in Africa. There were far more extravagant tropical souvenirs for the unlucky – sleeping sickness, marsh fever, yellow jack, unnamed exotic diseases that caused haemorrhaging, paralysis or swelled the tongue like a pig's bladder until the air passage was choked. In comparison, malaria was minor discomfort, a sneeze, a bagatelle.

He rested his forehead against the cold window.

Outside passed the bucolic scene of a farmer ploughing behind a shire horse, man and beast plunging into a sea of mud. The English monsoon. Mud rose in brown waves, carrying the farmer away. When he closed his eyes, a conductor shook him and asked if he was ill. My eyes are as yellow as your brass buttons; does that look well to you? Blair thought.

'I'm fine.'

'If you're sick, I'll have to put you off,' the conductor warned.

There was a moment of embarrassment among the teetotallers after the conductor left. Then the one across from Blair licked his lips and confided, 'I was once as you are, brother. My name is Smallbone.'

Smallbone's nose was a rosy knob. His black suit shone, the sign of wool revived with polish. Blue lines tattooed his forehead. The blue was permanent, Blair knew: dust in the scars every miner collected from coal roofs.

'But my husband was saved,' said the woman at his side. She pressed her mouth into a line. 'Weak and worthless though we may be.'

There was no access to another compartment unless he crawled along the outside of the train. He considered it.

'Would you mind if we prayed for you?' Mrs Smallbone asked.

'Not if you do it quietly,' Blair said.

Smallbone whispered to his wife, 'Maybe he's a Papist.'

'Or a thug,' said the other man. He had a full beard with a black, curly nap that crept nearly to his eyes. An almost Persian beard, Blair thought, one of which Zoroaster would have been proud.

'I would have said a cashiered officer until you opened your mouth, which pronounces you American. I can see that you are usually clean-shaven, which is the habit of artistic types, Italians or French.'

The miner's wife told Blair, 'Mr Earnshaw is a Member of Parliament.'

'That must account for his manners.'

'You make enemies quickly,' Earnshaw said.

'It's a talent. Good night.' Blair closed his eyes.

Gold was what drew the British. The Ashanti had so much that they seemed the Incas of Africa. Their rivers were flecked with gold, their hills veined with it. What better investment than a man with a tripod and sextant, auger and pan, and bottles of quicksilver? Let heroes discover the source of the Nile and the Mountains of the Moon, slaughter lions and apes, baptize lakes and peoples. All Blair searched for was pyrites and quartz, the telltale glitter of aurora.

In a feverish dream he was back on the golden sea-sands of Axim. This time Rowland was with him. He knew the Bishop's nephew was insane, but he hoped the ocean would soothe his blue eyes. The sea breeze tugged at Rowland's golden beard. Surf rolled in with the steady pace of wheels. 'Excellent,' Rowland murmured. 'Excellent.' At Axim, women panned the sands with wooden plates painted black to let the sun find the gold. Naked, they waded into the water to rinse the sand away, and rose and fell in the waves, holding the pans high. 'Wonderful ducks,' Rowland said and raised his rifle. A pan flew and the woman who had been holding it sank into a reddening wave. While he reloaded, the other women waded for shore. Rowland shot again, methodically, casually. As a woman fell, gold dust dashed across the sand. He rolled her with his foot so that she was dusted with sparkling flecks. Blair gathered the remaining women to lead them to safety, and Rowland reloaded and turned the rifle on him. He felt the barrel press against the back of his neck.

Sheer terror brought Blair half awake. It was sweat on his neck, not a rifle. It was only a dream. Rowland had never done anything like that – at least not at Axim.

We live equally in two worlds, an African had told Blair. Awake, we plod on with our eyes downcast from the sun, ignoring or not seeing what lies around us. Asleep, eyes open behind their lids, we pass through a vibrant world in which men become lions, women become snakes, in which the vague fears of the daytime become, through heightened senses, revealed and visible.

Awake, we are trapped in the present like a lizard in an hour-glass that crawls for ever over the falling sand. Asleep, we fly from the past into the future. Time is no longer a narrow, drudging path but an entire forest seen at once. Blair's problem, the African said, was that he lived only in the waking world. That was why he needed maps, because he saw so little.

Blair claimed he rarely dreamed, and this sent the African into paroxysms of laughter. Only a man without memory couldn't dream. What about Blair's parents? Even if they were far away, he could visit them in dreams. Blair said he had no memory of his parents. His father was anonymous, his mother was buried at sea. He was about four then. How could he have any memories?

The African offered to cure him so he would have memories and dreams.

Blair said, No!

He opened his eyes. On his lap was a Temperance pamphlet. 'Drink drowns all feelings of Sorrow and Shame! Drink turns the Labourer into the Sluggard, the Loving Father into the Prodigal! Does this sound Familiar to You?'

It certainly did. He would never get back to the Gold Coast. With open eyes, with the clarity of fever, he saw that Hannay's promise was like a bauble dangled above a child's hand. Missionaries were the rage, and none of them would accept a man with Blair's reputation as a member of his team, no matter what the Bishop said, and Hannay knew it. So all that was really being offered was the hundred and fifty pounds, one hundred of which was already owed him. Which left whatever he could steal from expenses.

Wigan? A single minute spent there was money wasted. Blair thought he might even forget the hundred pounds that was owed. He could stay on the train to Liverpool and catch the first steamer to West Africa. The problem was that as soon as he set foot in the Gold Coast, the consulate would have him put back on board the ship. If he went into the bush to find his daughter, soldiers would follow. They had before. In which case she was better off without him.

He saw her dancing on a mat, winding and unwinding herself within her mother's golden cloth back in his house in Kumasi. The girl glowed from the threads. An entire language was spoken by the hands during a dance and her hands said: No, go away. Stop, stay there. Come here. Closer, closer. Dance with me.

He had no talent as a dancer, whereas the Ashanti seemed to have extra joints in their bodies just for dancing. She would cover her mouth because he was so clumsy. He watched her dance and wondered, Where am I in her? She had distilled everything that was decent in him and he wondered what she had done with all the rest. Perhaps there was some other child, black on the inside. It wasn't the gold that made her shine, the glow came from herself. If she was at all a mirror of him, why was the mirror brighter?

'The prostitute, at least, plays a traditional role in society. She is a fallen woman, perhaps weak, perhaps depraved, usually ignorant and poor, pawning her greatest prize for

25

a few coins. A pathetic creature but understandable. The pit girls of Wigan, however, are a far greater threat for two reasons.' Earnshaw paused.

His eyes closed, trying to sleep, Blair listened to the sleepers passing underneath to the endless formula, *wiganwiganwiganwigan*, over a trestle bridge, *africafricafrica*, then again, *wiganwiganwigan*.

'For two reasons,' Earnshaw went on. 'First, because she has traduced her very sexuality. She has denied it and perverted it. A prostitute is, at least, a woman. But what is a pit girl? I have seen pictures of them for sale throughout England. Freaks wearing mannish pants, looking at the camera with mannish stares. The reaction of any decent woman is repulsion and disgust. Indeed, the instinctive reaction even of fallen women is the same.

'The second reason is that pit girls do the work that should be done by men. There is no other instance in industrial England of women shouldering labour meant for the stronger, more responsible sex. By doing so, the pit girl steals food not only from men but from the families of those men. Wives and children are the victims, a suffering to which mine owners turn a blind eye because they can pay less to a pit girl than they would to a man.'

'The union is with you,' the miner said. 'The lasses are a danger to labour and a threat to the institution of family life.'

Earnshaw said, 'Parliament has twice before tried to chase them from the pits and failed, which has only made the women more brazen. This time we cannot fail. Christ has made this my crusade.'

Blair looked through slitted lids. Earnshaw's brows looked electrified, as if Jehovah had anointed him with a lightning bolt. Besides his wiry beard, subsidiary tufts exploded from his nostrils and ears. Blair thought of suggesting butter to train the beard, the way Somali women groomed their hair, but Earnshaw didn't look receptive to new ideas.

As afternoon faded, the conductor came through the car to turn up the lamps. Earnshaw and the Smallbones perused their Bibles. Blair's pulse was too rapid for him to sleep, so he opened his knapsack and extracted the envelope Bishop Hannay had given him. He had removed the money before without bothering with the rest of the contents, which consisted of two onionskin pages and a photograph of a rugby team. The pages were written in the meticulous hand of a bookkeeper. Blair glanced at the signature at the end. O. L. Leveret, Hannay's man. He returned to the beginning.

I write these words as a friend and confidant of Revd John Edward Maypole, whose disappearance and continued absence has deprived the Wigan Parish Church and the town of Wigan of a vigorous and earnest spirit.

As Curate of our Parish Church, Mr Maypole

assisted Revd Chubb in every regular parish duty, such as services, instruction in the Catechism, Bible School, calls on the sick and poor. On his own, Mr Maypole gathered the funds and founded the Wigan Home for Single Women Who Have Fallen for the First Time. It was during his work for the Home that he met a soulmate in Bishop Hannay's daughter, Charlotte. They were engaged to be married this July. She has been inconsolable. Otherwise it is the working class that has most keenly suffered the absence of Mr Maypole. He was a constant visitor to the poorest households, and although much of his social work was among women, he was a man's man who could take the rugby field with the brawniest miner, play fair and hold his own.

I apologize if what follows sounds like the contents of a police blotter. It is merely an attempt to reconstruct John Maypole's activities on 18 January, the last day he was seen. He performed the Morning Service for Revd Chubb, who was ill, and from then until noon visited convalescents. Dinner for Mr Maypole was bread and tea taken at the home of Mary Jaxon, widow. In the afternoon, he gave Bible class at the parish school, delivered food to the town workhouse and visited the Home for Women, where he oversaw instruction in nursing and domestic service. By this hour the work day was done. Mr Maypole spoke to returning miners, inviting them to a social at the parish rectory the following Saturday. The last person he is known to have invited was Rose Molyneux, a pit girl at the Hannay Pit. He was not seen afterwards, Since he often took tea alone with a book and had no obligations for the evening, Mr Maypole may well have concluded what was for him a normal day. Likewise, the following day, because his duties and interests were so wide and various, his absence was not commented on until evening, when Revd Chubb asked me to visit John's rooms. I reported that his housekeeper told me that his bed had not been slept in. Inquiries through the police have, since then, proved fruitless.

It is the desire and expectation of the Parish Church, of the Hannay family and of John's friends that any questions into his whereabouts be conducted in a manner that ensures that no scandal or public sensation attaches to the modest, Christian life he led.

O. L. Leveret, Estate Manager, Hannay Hall.

The photograph was stiffened with pasteboard. Twenty rugby players in makeshift uniforms of sweaters and shorts posed in two rows, one sitting and one standing, before a painted backdrop of a garden. Instead of shoes, they wore clogs with leather uppers and wooden soles. The men were slope-shouldered, powerful, some with legs as bowed as a bulldog's. The middle man in front marked the occasion by holding a rugby ball on which was written in white ink, 'Wigan 14–Warrington 0'. The group was balanced by the placement of the only two tall men at opposite ends of the back row. One was dark, with thick hair and a fierce glare directed at the lens. The other was fair, with eyes as placid as a veal calf's. By this figure was the notation in Leveret's hand, 'Revd John Maypole'. Etched on the reverse was 'Hotham's Photographic Studio, Millgate, Wigan. Portraits, Novelties, Stereoscopics'.

Even taking into consideration the dramatized language of letters, Leveret's words were a eulogy. A confused eulogy since he didn't know what tense to use in writing about the missing curate, past or present, dead or alive. It also struck Blair that for such a public figure as Maypole there was little indication of much hue and cry when he disappeared.

He studied the photograph again. About the other men there was a worn quality. In the youngest this was a gauntness around their eyes, in the oldest a trademark smudging on the foreheads and hands that wasn't ordinary dirt. By comparison, John Edward Maypole's hair was brushed back from a smooth brow. A chinless quality marred his profile, but it made him look more sincere.

Blair put the letter and picture away. He liked the name. Maypole. A good English name with both rustic and erotic connections, a hint of maids honouring pagan gods as they braided garlands around an ancient symbol of fertility. He doubted such a picture had ever come to the curate's mind, no more than thought could penetrate solid marble, he decided. The same could probably be said for the 'inconsolable soulmate', Miss Charlotte Hannay. Blair imagined different possible Miss Hannays. A virtuous Miss Hannay with a corset and a bun, dressed in mourning just in case? A pretty and brainless Miss

Hannay who would ride a pony cart to visit the poor? A practical Miss Hannay ready with bandages and remedies, a local Florence Nightingale?

The dark sky turned darker, not with clouds but with a more pungent ingredient. From the window, Blair saw what could have been the towering effluent plume of a volcano, except that there was no erupting volcanic cone, no mountain of any size, in fact, between the Pennines to the east and the sea to the west, nothing but swale and hill above the long tilt of underground carboniferous deposits. The smoke rose not from a single point but as a dark veil across the northern horizon, as if all the land thereafter was on fire. Only closer could a traveller tell that the horizon was an unbroken line of chimneys.

Chimneys congregated around cotton mills, glass works, iron foundries, chemical works, dye works, brick works. But the most monumental chimneys were at the coal pits, as if the earth itself had been turned into one great factory. When Blake wrote of 'dark Satanic mills', he meant chimneys.

The hour was almost dusk, but this darkness was premature. Even Earnshaw stared through the window with some awe. When enough chimneys had passed one by one, the sky turned the ashen grey of an eclipse. On either side private tracks connected pits to the canal ahead. Between the pall and the lines of steel lay Wigan, at first sight looking more like smouldering ruins than a town.

Coal was worked into the town itself, creating coal tips that were black hills of slag. On some, coal gas escaped as little flames that darted from peak to peak like blue imps. The train slowed beside a pit as a cageload of miners reached the surface. Coated in coal dust, the men were almost invisible except for the safety lamps in their hands. The train slid past a tower topped by a headgear that, even in the subdued light, Blair saw was painted red. On the other side, figures crossed in single file across the slag, taking a shortcut home. Blair caught them in profile. They wore pants and coal dust too, but they were women.

The track bridged the canal, over barges heaped with coal, then travelled by a gas works and a rank of cotton mills, their high windows bright and the chimneys that drove their spinning machines spewing as much smoke as castles sacked and set ablaze. The locomotive slowed with its own blasts of steam. Tracks split off to goods sheds and yards. In the middle, like an island, was a platform with iron columns and hanging lamps. The train approached at a creep, gave a last convulsive shake and stopped.

The Smallbones were up at once and in the corridor, ready to engage the forces of darkness. Earnshaw pulled a bag off the rack overhead. 'Getting off?' he asked Blair.

'No, I think I'll ride to the end of the line.'

'Really? I would have thought that Wigan was your sort of place.'

'You'd be wrong.'

'I hope so.'

Earnshaw joined the Smallbones outside on the platform, where they were greeted by a priest in a cassock, making a happy circle of wraiths. At something Earnshaw said, the priest lifted an owlish gaze towards the train. Blair sat back and the group's attention was diverted by the arrival of a tall man in a bowler.

Blair was two hundred pounds ahead – well, one hundred pounds ahead. Passage from Liverpool to the Gold Coast was ten pounds, and he knew he'd have to use a different name and disembark north of Accra, but doctors always ordered ocean voyages, didn't they, so he'd recuperate on the way. With luck, he could be gone tomorrow.

He replaced his hat over his eyes and was attempting to get comfortable when a hand prodded his shoulder. He tipped the hat back and looked up. The conductor and the tall man from the platform stood over him.

'Mr Blair?'

'Yes. Leveret?' Blair guessed.

Silence seemed to be Leveret's form of assent. A young man and a creature of contradiction, Blair thought. Leveret's bowler was brushed but his jacket was crushed. His striped silk waistcoat looked uneasy. His earnest, deep-set eyes pondered Blair's lack of movement.

'It's Wigan.'

'So it is,' Blair agreed.

'You don't look well.'

'You're an astute observer, Leveret. Not quite well enough to rise.'

'You were thinking of staying on, from what I hear.'

33

'The idea occurred to me.'

'Bishop Hannay advanced you funds to perform a task. If you don't, I'll have to ask for those funds.'

'I'll rest in Liverpool and return,' Blair said. The hell I will, he thought, I'll be on deck and at sea.

The conductor said, 'Then you'll have to buy another ticket in the station.'

'I'll buy it from you.'

'That may be the way you do things in America,' Leveret said. 'Here you buy tickets in the station.'

When Blair pushed himself to his feet, he found his legs frail and his balance untrustworthy. He fell in one long step to the platform, stood and gathered his dignity. The last disembarking travellers – shop girls with hat boxes – leaned away as he reeled by at a leper's pace into the station. A stove sat between two empty benches. No one was at the ticket window, so he leaned against the window sill and hit its bell. At the same time it rang, he felt a shudder; he turned and saw the train pulling away from the platform.

Leveret came in the station door with Blair's pack under his arm. 'I understand it's been a long time since you were in Wigan,' he said.

Leveret had the long face and shamble of an underfed horse and he was tall enough to have to duck under shop signs. He led Blair up the station steps to a street of shops of greasy red brick. Despite the gloom of gas lamps, the pavement was crowded with shoppers and outdoor displays of waterproof coats, wellington boots, silk scarves, satin ribbons, Pilkington glass, paraffin oil. Stalls offered sides of Australian beef, glutinous tripe, herring and cod arrayed in tiers, iced baskets of oysters. The smells of tea and coffee insinuated like exotic perfumes. Everything lay under a faintly glittering veil of soot. The thought occurred to Blair that if Hell had a flourishing main street it would look like this.

They slowed by a shopfront with the newspaper placard: 'London Slasher'. 'The local newspaper,' Leveret said, as if they were passing a brothel.

The Minorca Hotel was in the same building. Leveret ushered Blair up to a second-floor suite furnished in velvet and dark panelling.

'Even a rubber tree,' Blair said. 'I do feel at home.'

'I reserved the suite in case people would be visiting you in the course of your inquiry. This way you have an office.'

'An office? Leveret, I have the feeling that you know more about what I'm supposed to do than I do.'

'I care more about this investigation than you do. I'm a friend of the family.'

'That's nice, but I'd appreciate it if you stopped calling this an "investigation". I'm not the police. I'll ask a few questions that you have probably already asked, and then I'll be on my way.'

'But you'll try? You took the money for it.'

Blair felt his legs start to buckle. 'I'll do something.'

'I thought you'd want to get started right away. I'll take you around now to the Reverend Chubb. You saw him at the station.'

'And more fun than a barrel of monkeys, from what I saw.' Blair aimed himself into a chair and sat. 'Leveret, you found me on the train and you have dragged me here. Now you can go.'

'The Reverend Chubb—'

'Does Chubb knows where Maypole is?'

'No.'

'Then what's the point in talking to him?'

'It's a matter of courtesy.'

'I haven't got time.'

'You ought to know that we've warned the ship's captains in Liverpool that if you show up there with any funds, they've been stolen.'

'Well, so much for courtesy.' Blair gave Leveret a broad wink. 'The English are so grand to work with, such a smug little nation.' Talking was exhausting. He let his head loll back and shut his eyes. He heard scribbling.

'I'm putting down addresses,' Leveret said. 'I wasn't trying to offend you about the captains, but I do want to keep you here.'

'And a great pleasure it is.' Blair sensed welcome oblivion on the rise. He heard Leveret open the door. 'Wait.' Blair stirred from his torpor for a moment. 'How old is he?'

Leveret took a moment.

'Twenty-three.'

'Tall?'

'Six feet. You have the photograph.'

'An excellent photograph. Weight, about?'

'Fourteen stone.'

Almost two hundred pounds, to an American. 'Fair hair,' Blair remembered. 'Eyes?'

'Blue.'

'Just in case I bump into him on the stairs. Thanks.'

His eyelids dropped like leaden gates. He was asleep before Leveret was out of the door.

When he awoke, it took Blair a moment to comprehend where he was. The fever had ebbed, but in the dark the unfamiliar furniture seemed suspiciously animated, especially chairs and tables so draped in tassels and cloths that they were virtually dressed. Standing, he felt lightheaded. He thought he heard horses but when he made his way to the window and looked down on the street he saw only people, which puzzled him until he realized that half of them wore clogs. Clogs were leather shoes with wooden soles protected by iron rails that could last a working man ten years. The perfect sound for Wigan: people shod like horses.

It was eight o'clock by his watch. The thing to do, it seemed to him, was to talk to the smallest number of locals in the shortest amount of time and get out of town. In Africa he had marched with eyes sealed shut with infection, with feet covered in sores; he could overcome a little chill to get out of Wigan.

He read Leveret's note on the table. The Reverend

Chubb's address was the parish rectory, John Maypole's seemed near by, the widow Mary Jaxon's was in Shaw's Court, Rose Molyneux's was in Candle Court. There was no address for Miss Charlotte Hannay.

The widow Jaxon sounded like the best choice, more likely to be home, readier to gossip. As he picked up the paper he caught sight through the open bedroom door of a man in a mirror. Someone in a slouch hat, bad beard and eyes staring back like two dim candles.

Blair was not quite as ready for an excursion as he'd imagined. He had no sooner climbed into a cab before he passed out. Between black spells he was vaguely aware of shopping streets giving way to foundries, the sharp fumes of dye works, a bridge and then row upon row of brick houses. He revived as the carriage pulled up.

The driver said, 'This is Candle Court.'

Blair said, 'I wanted Shaw's Court.'

'You told me Candle Court.'

If Blair had made a mistake, he didn't have the strength to correct it. He got out and told the driver to wait.

'Not here. I'll be on the other side of the bridge.' The driver turned his cab around briskly in retreat.

The street was a paved trench between terraced houses built for miners by mine owners, two storeys back to back, under a single roofline of Welsh slate so that it was impossible to tell one house from another except by their doors. It was a maze of shadow and brick. The gas jets of street lights were far apart, and most illumination came from the paraffin lamps of beerhouses and pubs, or open windows where sausages, oysters or hams were for sale. Everyone else seemed to be at the evening meal; he heard a sea sound of voices within.

According to Leveret the Molyneux girl lived at number 21. When he knocked on the door it swung open.

'Rose Molyneux? Miss Molyneux?'

As he stepped into a parlour the door closed behind him. Enough of the street's faint light entered for him to see chairs, table and a cabinet filling the tight space. He had anticipated worse. Miners' houses usually had families of ten or more, plus lodgers stepping over and on top of each other. This was as quiet as a sanctuary. Relatively prosperous, too. The cabinet displayed ornamental pots: a ceramic Duke of Wellington, with his hook nose, was the only one Blair could identify.

The next room was lit by a rear window. Heat and the aroma of milk and sugar emanated from a kitchen range. A large pan of hot water sat on top. Blair opened the oven and raised the lid of the pot inside. Rice pudding. Two plates for it lay on a table. Wash tubs crowded in the corner and, curiously, a full-length mirror. A hook rug softened the boards of the floor. On the wall opposite the range a flight of stairs rose to a quiet bedroom floor.

Feet shuffled outside. Blair looked through the window at a miniature yard with a wash boiler, slop stone for washing and a pig rubbing against the slats of its pen. The pig raised its eyes yearningly. Someone was expected home.

Blair knew that to wait outside would be self-defeating because any loitering stranger was, until proven otherwise, a debt collector to be avoided. He went into the parlour to sit, but neighbours were passing by the front window and he couldn't lower the curtain without drawing attention: a lowered curtain was a public notice of death among miners. Odd he remembered that, he thought.

He retreated to the kitchen and sank into a chair set in the shadow of the stairs. The fever was between swings, leaving him limp. He told himself that when he heard the front door open he could return to the parlour. As he tipped back into shadow the wall pushed his hat forward over his face. He closed his eyes – just for a second, he told himself. The sweetness of the pudding scented the dark.

He opened his eyes as she stepped into the bath. She had lit a lamp but turned the wick low. She was black with silvery glints of mica, and her hair was twisted up and pinned. She washed with a sponge and cloth, watching in a full-length mirror not in admiration but because fine coal dust had insinuated itself so completely into the pores of her skin. As she washed she progressed from ebony to blue, and from blue to olive, like a watercolour fading.

ROSE

She stepped into a second tub and directed a pitcher's stream of water over her face and shoulders. Turning within the confines of the tub her movements were a private, narrow dance. Steam hung as an aureole around her face, water ran in braids down her back and between her breasts. Minute by minute she transformed from black to grey to shell-like pink, though her eyes revealed a cool disregard for the flesh, as if another woman were bathing.

When she was done she stepped out of the tub on to the rug. For the first time Blair noticed a towel and clothes laid over a chair. She dried herself, raised her arms and let a chemise slip over her and stepped into a skirt of linen that was thin but of good quality, what a maid might steal from a house. Finally she released her hair, which was dark copper, thick and vigorous.

As Blair let his chair settle forward she stared into the dark like a fox startled in its den. If she cried for help, he knew that the house would quickly fill with miners happy to mete out punishment to any stranger who violated the privacy of their hovels.

'Rose Molyneux?'

'Aye.'

'Bishop Hannay asked me to look into the matter of John Maypole. Your door was open. I came in and fell asleep. I apologize.'

'When did you wake up? If you was a gentleman you'd have spoke up right away.'

'I'm not a gentleman.'

'That's clear.'

She looked towards the front door but made no move

41

to it, and though the shift clung damply to her, she left her dress on the chair. Her eyes were dark and direct. 'I know nowt about the priest,' she said.

'On January 18th, Maypole was seen talking to you, and then he wasn't seen again. Where was that?'

'Scholes Bridge. I told the constables. He asked me to a social, a dance with songs and lemonade.'

'You were friends?'

'No. He asked all the girls. He was always at us for one thing or another.'

'What kind of things?'

'Church things. He was always trying to save us.'

'From what?'

'Our weaknesses.' She watched his eyes. 'I fell into a coal car, that's why I had t'wash.'

'Did you go to the social?'

'There was no social.'

'Because Maypole was missing?'

She gave a laugh. 'Because there was an explosion down the pit. Seventy-six men died that day. Nobody here gave a damn about a priest.'

Blair felt as if the bottom had dropped out of his chair. Seventy-six men had died the same day Maypole vanished from sight and Leveret hadn't mentioned it?

From next door came a cannonade of clogs down a stairway. Bricks between houses were a membrane so thin that the stampede sounded as if it had descended the steps above Blair's head. A bead of water like a ball of light ran down the girl's cheek, coursed down her neck and disappeared. Otherwise she was still.

'No more questions?' she asked.

'No.' He was still trying to assimilate the news of the explosion.

'You're really not a gentleman, are you?'

'Not a bit.'

'Then how do you know the Bishop?'

'You don't have to be a gentleman to know the Bishop.' He got to his feet to go.

Rose said, 'What's your name? You know mine, I don't know yours.'

'Blair.'

'You're a bastard, Mr Blair.'

'That's been said. I'll see myself out.'

He was so dizzy the floor seemed to be on a slant. He guided himself with seatbacks through the parlour to the front. Rose Molyneux followed as far as the kitchen door, more to make sure he went than to say goodbye. She was framed by the sash and the kitchen light, white muslin and red hair. From the house on the other side came a volley of cabinets slamming and domestic denunciations joined by the wails of a baby.

'It's a small world, Wigan?' Blair asked.

Rose said, 'It's a black hole.'

Chapter Three

In the morning Blair found himself feeling strangely better. Malaria did that, came and went like a house guest. He celebrated with a bath and shave and was eating a breakfast of cold toast and dry steak when Leveret arrived.

'There's some terrible coffee on the table,' Blair offered.

'I've eaten.'

Blair went back to his meal. He'd had nothing but soup or gin for a week and he intended to finish the remains on his plate.

Leveret removed his hat respectfully. 'Bishop Hannay is up from London. He has asked you to dinner tonight. I'll gather you here at seven.'

'Sorry. I don't have anything to wear.'

'The Bishop said you would say that and I should tell you not to worry. Since you are American, people will assume you don't know how to dress for dinner.'

'Very well, you can go back to His Grace and tell him that his insult has been delivered. See you at seven.' Blair returned to his steak, which had the texture of incinerated rope. He became aware that his visitor hadn't moved. 'You're just going to stand there? You look like a doorstop.'

Leveret edged towards a chair. 'I thought I'd accompany you this morning.'

'Accompany me?'

'I was John Maypole's best friend. No one can tell you as much about him as I can.'

'You assisted the police?'

'There hasn't been a real investigation. We thought he was away and then ... well, he still may be away. The Bishop doesn't want the police involved.'

'You're the Hannay estate manager, haven't you got things to do, cows to tend, tenants to evict?'

'I don't evi—'

'What's your first name, Leveret?'

'Oliver.'

'Oliver. Ollie. I know Russians in California. They'd call you Olyosha.'

'Leveret will do.'

'How old are you?'

Leveret paused, like a man stepping into high grass. 'Twenty-five.'

'The Hannay estate must be quite a responsibility. Do you evict aged tenants personally or do you have a bailiff for that?'

'I try not to evict anyone.'

'But you do it. You get my point? No one is going to talk confidentially to me if I have you at my side.'

Leveret looked pained. Besides making his point, Blair had meant to offend him; if brushing him aside with a paw left him scratched that was fine, but Leveret seemed to take the exchange as his own fault, which irritated

Blair more. The man had an inward expression, as if the failing of the world was due to himself.

'I was in Africa, too. In the Cape Colony,' Leveret said.

'So?'

'When I heard you might be coming here, I was thrilled.'

Blair visited the newspaper office next to the hotel and Leveret followed.

Eight pages of the *Wigan Observer* were posted on the wall, announcing auctions of farm stocks and saw mills, vivid church pantomimes, complete railway timetables. Advertisements, too, of course. 'Glenfield's Starch Is the Only Kind Used in Her Majesty's Laundry.' The *Illustrated London News* was also offered; its front page was devoted to the Lambeth Slasher.

'You notice there are no washday encomiums from the Slasher,' Blair pointed out. 'Now there would be an endorsement.'

Punch, the *Coal Question* and the *Miners' Advocate* were offered to men, *Self-Help*, *Hints on Household Taste*, the *Englishwoman's Review* to ladies. There were local histories like *Lancashire Catholics: Obstinate Souls* and for the popular reader a selection of sensational novels about Wild West cowboys and Horse Marines. Glass cases displayed stationery, fountain pens, stamp boxes, steel nibs, Indian ink. A wooden rail divided the shop from an editor in an eye shade scribbling at a desk. On the walls around him were framed photographs of derailed locomotives, gutted houses and mass funerals.

Blair called Leveret's attention to the railway timetable in the newspaper. 'Have you noticed this? Timetables are the most reassuring information of modern life. Yet according to the *Observer*, same page, we read that five local people were run over in separate railroad accidents on Saturday night. Are these regularly scheduled executions?'

'On Saturday night workers drink and to find their way home they follow the tracks.'

'Look at this, steamship notices that include free transport to Australia for female domestics. In what other nation would a ticket to a desert on the far side of the world be a lure?'

'You're not an admirer of England.' The idea pained Leveret so that he almost stuttered.

'Leveret, go away. Count the Bishop's sheep, set mantraps. whatever you usually do, but leave me alone.'

'Can I get you something?' the editor said. His speech was lengthened by the Lancashire 'o' and shortened by a 'g': 'soomthin'.'

Blair pushed through the gate of the bar to study the photographs more closely. It was always educational to see what gas and steam could do to metal and brick. In one picture a building façade was sheared away like the front of a doll's house, exposing a table and chairs set for tea. In another a locomotive had propelled itself like a rocket on to the roof of a brewery. Two pictures were labelled 'Unfortunate Victims of the Hannay Pit

Explosion'. The first was of the coal-mine yard. Standing figures were blurred while the bodies laid on the ground were in deathly focus. The other was of a long line of hearses drawn by horses with black plumes.

The editor said, 'Miners believe in a proper send-off. The *Illustrated London News* covered that one. Still the biggest disaster of the year so far. Intense interest. You must have read about it.'

'No,' Blair said.

'Everyone read about it.'

'Do you have copies of that edition?'

The man pulled out a drawer of newspapers hung on rods. 'Most of the inquest nearly verbatim. Otherwise you have to wait for the official report of the Mines Inspector. You seem familiar.'

Blair flipped through the newspapers. He had no interest in the explosion at the Hannay Pit, but the editions that covered the accident, rescue attempts and inquiries into the disaster also covered the weeks after John Maypole disappeared.

In the 10 March issue, for example: 'There will be a meeting of the patrons of the Home for Women Who Have Fallen for the First Time despite the absence of Revd Maypole. It is thought that Revd Maypole has been called away by urgent family affairs.'

In the 7 February issue: 'Revd Chubb led prayers for the souls of parishioners who tragically lost their lives in the Hannay Pit Explosion. They are now with Christ. He also asked the congregation to pray for the safety of the curate, Revd Maypole, who has not been heard from for two weeks.'

And on 23 February: 'All Saints' Parish Church 21–St Helen's 6. Marked by William Jaxon's two tries, the victory was dedicated to Revd John Maypole.'

The rest of the editorial columns were taken up with the disaster. An engraved illustration showed rescuers assembled around the base of a pit tower that was decorated at the top with a Lancashire rose.

'Could I buy these?'

'Oh, yes. We did special editions.'

'I'll pay for the gentleman,' Leveret said.

'And a notebook, red ink, black ink and your best local map,' Blair said.

'An Ordnance Survey map?'

'Perfect.'

The editor wrapped the purchases without taking his eyes off Blair. 'The Hannay Pit explosion was a major story. It's things like that put Wigan on the map.'

On the way out, Blair noticed among the books for sale one titled *Nigger Blair*, with a cover illustration of him shooting a gorilla. He had never worn a moustache and never seen a gorilla. They got his slouch hat right, though.

New country was best seen from a high point. Blair scrambled through a trapdoor to the open top of the Parish Church tower, startling doves off the finials.

Leveret struggled to pull his long frame through, picking up feathers and dust on his bowler as he did. It was midday, but the sky was as oily as dusk. When Blair opened and spread his map, granules of dirt immediately, visibly appeared on the paper.

Blair loved maps. He loved latitude, longitude, altitude. He loved the sense that with a sextant and a decent watch he could shoot the sun and determine his position anywhere on earth, and with a protractor and paper chart his position so that another man using his map could trace his steps to the exact same place, not a second or an inch off. He loved topography, the twist and folds of the earth, the shelves that became mountains, the mountains that were islands. He loved the inconstancy of the planet – shores that washed away, volcanoes that erupted from flat plains, rivers that looped first this way, then that. A map was, admittedly, no more than a moment in that flux, but as a visualization of time it was a work of art.

'What are you doing?' Leveret asked.

From a chamois purse Blair unwrapped a telescope; it was a German refractor with a Ramsden eyepiece, and easily his single most precious possession. He turned in a slow 360 degrees, sighting off the sun and checking a compass. 'Getting my bearings. There's no north indicated on the map, but I think I've got it now.' He drew an arrow on the map, an act that brought him a small, reflexive satisfaction.

Leveret stood, grabbing his bowler to keep it from

being snatched by the wind. 'I've never been up here before,' he said. 'Look at the clouds, like ships from the sea.'

'Poetic. Look down, Leveret. Ask yourself why this seems to be an especially senseless jumble of streets. Look at the map and you see the old village of Wigan that was the church, market place and medieval alleys, even if the green is overlaid now by cobblestones and the alleys are turned into foundry yards. The oldest shops have the narrowest fronts because everyone wanted to be on the only road.'

Leveret compared eyesight and map, as Blair knew he would. People could no more resist maps of where they lived than they could portraits of themselves.

'But you're looking at other places,' Leveret noticed.

'Triangulation is the mapmaker's method. If you know the position and height of any two places and you see a third, you can work out its position and height. That's what maps are, invisible triangles.'

Blair located Scholes Bridge, which he had crossed the night before. In the dark and with his fever, he hadn't appreciated how completely the bridge divided the town. West of the bridge was prosperous, substantial Wigan, an orbit of business offices, hotels and stores topped by the terracotta coronets of chimneypots. East of the bridge was a newer, densely packed community of miners' terraced houses with brick walls and blue slate tiles. North\ from the church, avoiding the bridge completely, a boulevard of well-to-do townhouses with a blaze of gardens ran to a thickly wooded area. A note on the map read, 'To Hannay Hall'. South lay the battlefield smoke of coal pits.

What was obscured to the eye but apparent on the map was that Wigan was vivisected and stitched back together by railways: the London & Northwest, the Wigan and Southport, Liverpool and Bury and Lancashire Union lines extended with sweeping geometric curves in every direction, connecting to the private tracks that ran to the mines. Haze veiled the southern horizon, but on the map Blair counted a full fifty active coal pits, incredible for any town.

He turned his glasses to the miners' terraces across the bridge. Perhaps they had been erected on straight lines, but since they were built over older, worked-out mines where underground props rotted and tunnels gave way, the walls and roofs above had shifted in turn until the houses presented a rolling, sagging, slowly collapsing landscape that was as much a product of nature as man-made.

Leveret said, 'I heard the story about the Bible Fund. And the, the—'

'Debauchery?'

'Fast living. However, it seems to me from a careful reading of the facts that you've been a champion of the African.'

'Don't believe what you read. People have many reasons for what they do.'

'But it's important to let people know, otherwise you'll be misjudged. It sets an example.'

'Like Hannay? Now there is one hell of a bishop.'

'Bishop Hannay is . . . different. Not every bishop will support costly expeditions to the far corners of the world.'

'It's a luxury he can afford.'

'It's a luxury you need,' Leveret pointed out gently. 'Anyway, no matter how private your reasons for doing good in Africa, don't let people paint you quite so black.'

'Leveret, let me worry about my reputation. Why didn't you mention the explosion at the Hannay Pit in the information about John Maypole?'

Leveret took a moment to adjust to the change in subject.

'Bishop Hannay felt that information didn't apply. Except that everyone was so occupied with the explosion that we didn't take proper notice at first that John was gone.'

'You read Dickens?' Blair asked.

'I love Dickens.'

'Miraculous coincidence doesn't bother you?'

'You don't like Dickens?'

'I don't like coincidence. I don't like it that Maypole disappeared on the same day as a mine explosion. Particularly when the Bishop chose me, a mining engineer, to find him.'

'It's simply that we didn't pay sufficient attention to John's disappearance because of the explosion. The Bishop selected you, I believe, because he wanted someone from the outside whom he could trust. Your mining background is appropriate for Wigan, after all.'

Blair was still unconvinced. 'Was Maypole ever down in the mine?'

'It's not allowed.'

'He could only preach to the miners when they were up?'

'That's right.'

'But he did preach to them?'

'Yes, as soon as they came to the surface. And to pit girls. John was a true evangelist. He was of selfless, absolutely stainless character.'

'He sounds like someone I would cross streets of deep mud to avoid.'

With red ink Blair initialled the addresses of John Maypole, the widow Mary Jaxon and Rose Molyneux.

His mind stayed on Rose. Why hadn't she called for help? Why hadn't she even dressed? Her clothes were on the chair. Instead she had stayed in her damp chemise. When she had looked towards the door, was she as afraid of being discovered as he was?

John Maypole's room was near Scholes Bridge in an alley of brick walls leaning together so acutely that their roof lines almost touched. Between them a slice of grey air dropped on to Leveret and Blair. Maypole was obviously the sort of evangelist who chose to mingle with his congregation day and night, a man who was willing not only to descend to the depths but to sleep there.

Leveret opened a room furnished with bed, table and

chairs, cast-iron range, chest of drawers, wash basin, chamberpot set on linoleum of a dark, indecipherable pattern. Blair lit an oil lamp hanging on the wall. Its wan illumination reached to the glory of the room, an oil painting of Christ in a carpenter's shop. Jesus appeared delicate and unaccustomed to hard work, and in Blair's opinion His expression was overly abstracted for a man handling a saw. Shavings curled around His feet. Through His window was a glimpse of olive trees, thorn bushes and the blue Sea of Galilee.

Leveret said, 'We left the room as it was, in case he returned.'

A pewter crucifix hung in the centre of another wall. On a shelf leaned a Bible, well-thumbed theological books and a single slim volume of Wordsworth. Blair opened the chest of drawers and felt through the black woollen cassocks and suits of a poor curate.

'John wasn't interested in material goods,' Leveret said. 'He owned only two suits.'

'And they're both here.' Blair returned to the shelf, flipped through the Bible and books and stood them upright. They stayed. They hadn't leaned long enough for the bindings to warp. 'Is anything missing?'

With a deep breath, Leveret said, 'A journal. John recorded his thoughts. It's the one item that's gone. It was the first thing I looked for.'

'Why?'

'In case it might tell where he was going or what he was thinking.'

'Have you ever read it?'

'No, it was private.'

Blair walked around the room and to the window, which was dirty enough to serve as a shade. 'Did he ever have visitors?'

'John chaired meetings here for the Explosion Fund and the Society for the Improvement of the Working Classes, not to mention the Home for Women.'

'Practically a radical.' Blair sniffed. 'He didn't smoke?'

'No, and he didn't allow smoking here.'

'Leveret, you described yourself in your letter as not only Maypole's friend but his confidant. Which suggests that he confided in you. What?'

'Personal matters.'

'Do you think this is a good time to hold out, after he's been gone for two months?'

'If I thought that the sentiments John shared with me in the intimacy of friendship had anything to do with his disappearance, naturally I would divulge them to you.'

'How intimate were you? Damon and Pythias, Jesus and John, Punch and Judy?'

'You're trying to provoke me.'

'I'm trying to provoke the truth. The sort of saint you describe doesn't exist. I'm not writing his tombstone, I'm trying to find the son of a bitch.'

'I wish you wouldn't use that language.'

'Leveret, you're a specimen, you really are.'

Even in the dusk of the room, Blair saw the estate manager's face heat to red. He lifted the painting and felt the back of the canvas. He paced off the linoleum: ten by twenty feet, ending in walls of whitewashed brick.

He touched the plaster ceiling: seven feet high in one corner, six in another. He went to the centre of the room and knelt.

'Now what are you doing?' Leveret asked.

'The way Bushmen teach their children to track is to give them turtles as pets. The father releases the turtle and the child has to find it by following scratches the turtle claws make on bare rock.'

'You're looking for scratches?'

'I was looking for blood, actually, but scratches would do.'

'What do you see?'

'Not a damn thing. I'm not a Bushman.'

Leveret pulled out his watch. 'I'll leave you now. I have to invite the Reverend Chubb for tonight.'

'Why will he be there?'

Leveret answered reluctantly. 'Reverend Chubb has expressed some concerns about your fitness.'

'My fitness?'

'Not your intelligence,' Leveret said quickly. 'Your moral fitness.'

'Thank you. This promises to be a delightful dinner party. Will there be other guests concerned about my moral fitness?'

Leveret backed towards the door. 'A few.'

'Well, I'll try to stay sober.'

'The Bishop has faith in you.'

'The Bishop?' Blair could hardly keep from laughing.

*

The night before, darkness had softened the terraced houses on the eastern side of Scholes Bridge; now daylight and soot outlined every brick and slate. The mystery cast by gas lamps was replaced by a meanness of block after block of back-to-back construction that showed in leaning walls and the reek of privies. The daytime sound was different because women and children were in the streets and the din of their clogs on stone rang through the singsong of vendors and tinkers. Miners wore clogs, mill workers wore clogs, everyone in Scholes wore clogs. What had Rose Molyneux called Wigan? A black hole? It was a loud hole.

John Maypole had met her at the bridge. It was a logical place to follow the martyr's steps.

It wasn't quite the Via Dolorosa. The corner beerhouse was a parlour with long tables, barrels of beer and cider, and the commercial hospitality of pickled eggs. Blair introduced himself to the owner as Maypole's cousin and suggested that the family would reward good information about the priest, last seen two months ago at the bridge.

The owner reminded Blair that in March dark came early. And, as the man put it, 'Your Maypole might be a curate, he could be the Pope with a bell on, but unless a man comes in with his mates for a drink he's pretty much invisible this end of Wigan.'

A butcher's shop looked out on the next block. The butcher was Catholic, but he recognized Maypole from rugby. He said the curate had been walking at a stiff pace with the Molyneux girl, lecturing her or being lectured by her.

'She's a Catholic girl, she stood right up to him. It caught my eye how Maypole was pulling off his choker – you know, his ecclesiastical collar.' He paused significantly. 'In a furtive manner.'

'Ah.' Blair brushed a fly away.

The fly returned to a swarm browsing on what looked like torn flannel: tripe. Pigs' feet and black pudding lay under a glass as scummy as a pond. The butcher leaned across to whisper, 'Priests are human. The flesh is weak. It never hurt a man to wet his willy.'

Blair looked around. He wouldn't have been too surprised to see a willy or two hanging from hooks. 'They looked friendly, then? I thought you said that one seemed to be lecturing the other.'

'That's Rose, complete with thorns, as the saying goes.'

The butcher was the last person who recalled anyone resembling Maypole. These things happened in Africa, Blair thought. Missionaries vanished all the time. Why not in darkest Wigan?

Blair spent the afternoon asking about his missing cousin John Maypole at the Angel, Harp, George, Crown and Sceptre, Black Swan, White Swan, Balcarres Arms, Fleece, Weavers' Arms, Wheelwrights' Arms, Windmill, and the Rope and Anchor. Along the way he bought not new but old clothes from a 'shoddy shop'. 'Shoddy' were clothes so old they were ready to be torn up and used as fertilizer; in fact, they were more valuable as fertilizer than as clothes. Perfect miner's clothes.

By six he was in a pub called the Young Prince. Outside, the establishment looked to be falling down. Corner bricks had dropped like rotted teeth; slate tiles had skated off the roof. Yet the interior boasted a mahogany bar, a glowing hearth and the Young Prince himself, mounted on a pedestal beside the door. The Prince was apparently a fighting dog of some renown, a bull terrier white when alive, now stuffed and turning grey with immortality.

Miners were just arriving. A few had been home, washed and returned in clean caps and white silk scarves. The majority, however, had stopped on their way from the pit to rinse their throats first. Where their caps tipped back was a peek of white skin and hairlines tattooed from coal scars; the older men smoked long clay pipes and wore scars on their foreheads as blue as the veins in Stilton cheese. Blair ordered a hot gin for his fever, which was returning in a spiteful manner, as if it had left him alone too long, and listened to arguments about racing doves, the decline of rugby, whether a ferret or a dog could kill more rats. This was edifying company, he thought. He had once spent a day listening to an Ethiopian describe different ways to skin and cook a snake, which was a discourse by Socrates compared with this.

This was not a job for him, he thought. He was serious

with Leveret: Maypole was too opposite. How could he retrace the steps of a man who was practically a martyr? The curate was an Englishman who saw the world as a battle between Heaven and Hell, whereas he saw it as geology. Maypole thought of England as a shining lamp unto all nations, which to him was like claiming that the world was flat.

Blair became aware that he had been joined at his table by a familiar face, Mr Smallbone from the train, except that he had traded his suit for a miner's moleskin jacket and a leather pouch like the kind used by book-makers at race courses hung from his shoulder. His prominent nose, set off by blank smudges on his cheeks, was in crimson bloom.

'I'm not drinking,' Smallbone said.

'I can see that.'

'I came in with the lads, I didn't spend a penny, I was only being sociable. It's a very friendly situation, the Young Prince.'

'That's what you tell Mrs Smallbone?'

'Mrs Smallbone is another story.' Smallbone sighed as if his wife was a volume to herself, then brightened. 'You're come to the right place, especially tonight. Oh, if you'd gone to the Harp.'

'I was at the Harp.'

'Irish. Is it me or is it dry in here?'

Blair caught the barman's attention and held up two fingers.

'The fights at the Harp. Every night it's one Irishman biting off the nose of another Irishman. They're good

61

men. Oh, there's no one better for digging a hole than an Irishman. But for the day-in, day-out getting of coal there's nothing like a Lancashireman.' Smallbone sighed as the gins arrived and took his before it hit the table. 'Your Welshman, your Yorkshireman, but above all, your Lancashireman.'

'Underground?'

'So to speak. Your health.'

They drank, Blair half his glass at a go, Smallbone with a careful, parsimonious sip – a man for the long haul.

'You must have known the men who died in the fire.'

'Knew them all. Worked with them thirty years, fathers and sons. Absent friends.' Smallbone doled himself another sip. 'Well, not all. There are always miners from outside Wigan. Day workers. You never even know their last names. If they're Welsh you call them "Taffy", if they're Irish they're "Paddy", and if they're missing two fingers you call them "Two Pints". As long as they can get coal, that's all that matters.'

A group of women entered. Respectable women were relegated to an area called the snug; their bustles would upset glasses if they even tried to make their way to the bar. These four, however, pushed through. Boldness was not the only difference: from the waist up they dressed in woollen head shawls and flannel shirts, but their sack skirts were rolled up to the waist like cummerbunds and sewn to stay permanently out of the way of their corduroy trousers. Their hands were blue on one side, pink on the other, their faces raw and damp from washing.

The bartender didn't seem surprised. 'Beers?'

'Ales,' said a big girl with ginger hair. She told the other girls, 'He'd forget his balls if they weren't in a bag.' Her eyes roamed the pub until she noticed Blair. 'You're a photographer?'

'No.'

'I do photographs. My friend Rose and I pose in work clothes or Sunday dresses. We're very popular.'

'Rose who?'

'My friend Rose. No artistic poses, if you know what I mean.'

'I know what you mean,' Blair said.

'Call me Flo.' Ale in hand, she approached his table. Her features were plain but she had painted her lips and cheeks with enough rouge to look like a tinted photo. 'You're American.'

'You have a good ear, Flo.'

The compliment brought pink to her face. Her hair seemed to spring electrically from her shawl. She put Blair in mind of Queen Boadicea, the mad queen of the Britons who almost drove Caesar's troops back into the sea.

She said, 'I like Americans. They don't stand on ceremony.'

'I don't stand on any ceremony at all,' Blair promised her.

'Not like someone from London.' There was a dramatic

quality to Flo; London was clearly her equivalent of a nest of lice. 'Members of Parliament who wanted to put honest girls out of work.' Her gaze swooped down on Smallbone. 'And the little arse-kissers who help them.'

Smallbone listened unprovoked, a pat of butter that wouldn't melt in a furnace. She turned her attention back to Blair. 'Could you see me in a factory? Flouncing around in a skirt, seeing to a bobbin here and a spool there? Going pale and deaf and tied to a machine? Not me. And not you, because you never see any photographers in a factory. People only want to buy pictures of women at a mine.'

A voice behind them said, 'He's no photographer.'

Blair looked up at a young miner wearing a jacket with a velvet collar and a silk scarf with brown spots. He recognized Bill Jaxon from the picture of the rugby team.

Jaxon said, 'Last night he visited Rose.'

The rest of the pub was silent, a tableau. It struck Blair that Jaxon's entrance was expected. Relished. Even the Young Prince's glass eyes seemed to show a fresh gleam.

Jaxon said mildly, 'You didn't knock, did you? She said she was lucky to be dressed.'

'I apologized.'

Flo said, 'Bill, he's drunk. Besides, he's got no clogs. He'd be no sport at all.'

Jaxon said, 'Hush up, Flo.'

What clogs had to do with sport, Blair didn't know.

Jaxon delivered his attention back to Blair. 'You're from the Bishop, Rose says.'

'From Reverend Maypole's family, I heard,' Smallbone said.

'Both.'

'A distant relation?' Jaxon asked.

'Very distant.' When Blair twisted in his chair to look up at Jaxon he had a sensation of envelopment, like a mouse in a large hand. It wasn't comfortable. Bill Jaxon had fair features and straight dark hair, exceedingly combed, a pearly scarf tucked under a ploughshare of a jaw, the sort that could make an actor's career. Blair said, 'I was asking Rose about Reverend Maypole. Weren't you on the same rugby team?'

'We were.'

'Maybe you can help.'

At a signal Blair hadn't caught, Smallbone jumped from the chair and Jaxon sat. The man was the centre of attention, a sun in the benighted universe of this pub, Blair thought. He remembered how in the photograph Maypole had been looking at Jaxon instead of at the camera. Jaxon's eyes said he took questions as seriously as charades.

'Ask away.'

'Did you see Reverend Maypole that last day?'

'No.'

'Do you have any idea what happened to him?'

'No.'

'Did he seem unhappy?'

'No.'

That seemed to cover it, Blair thought. For form's sake, he added, 'What did you talk about with John Maypole?'

'Sports.'

'Did you ever talk about religious matters?'

'The Reverend said Jesus would have been a champion rugby player.'

'Really?' This was a revelation, a contribution of muscular theology: Christ in a scrum, breaking tackles, dashing upfield between centurions.

'The Reverend said Jesus was a working man. He was a carpenter and fit, so who can say He wasn't a great athlete as well? John said that Christian competition was a joy to God. He said he'd rather be on the field with our team than in church with all the dons at Oxford.'

'Makes sense to me.'

'All the disciples, the Reverend said, were working men, fishermen and the like. John said that impure thoughts undermined the athlete as much as any archbishop, and that it was the special duty of the strong to be patient with the weak.'

'I'm glad to hear that.' Blair didn't feel at his own physical peak. 'Exactly what positions did the disciples play?'

'What do you mean?'

'What positions on the team? Peter and Paul? Wingmen, you think? And John the Baptist? Lots of brawn, I would guess. Right wing?'

The pub became quiet. Jaxon liked sending up a visitor, he didn't like being sent up himself.

'You shouldn't make fun.'

'No, you're right.' Blair caught a glow in Jaxon's eyes. It was a bit like stirring coals. 'So my lost cousin John was a theologian and a saint?'

'That's one way of putting it.'

'Two ways, actually.' Blair decided to get out while he could navigate. He picked up his knapsack. 'You've been so helpful I can't say.'

'Are you going back to America now?' Flo asked.

'Maybe. Leaving Wigan, at any rate.'

'Too quiet?' Jaxon asked.

'I hope so.'

Blair wove to the door. Outside, an early twilight was turning to the dark of a cave. The street was a tunnel of gas lamps and beerhouse doors. Too late he remembered the fear expressed by his driver the night before. The man had plainly exaggerated, but there wasn't a cab in sight.

Mill girls in wool shawls and cotton dresses and carrying food cans rushed by, and the sound of their clogs was deafening. He felt the gin circulating sluggishly in his brain. When he had walked a couple of blocks, however, he realized what Bill Jaxon had said – or not said. When Blair had asked if he had seen Maypole that last day, Jaxon's answer shouldn't have been 'No'; it should have been, 'What day was that?'

Though it was a small point and Blair knew he should

hurry to meet Leveret, he turned around and made his way back to the Young Prince. When he arrived, he wondered whether he had walked into the wrong pub because the room that had been full was empty. From his pedestal the Young Prince presided stiffly over abandoned chairs, fireplace and counter.

Blair knew that no crowd had passed him. Through the rear door of the pub he heard shouts. He opened it and edged carefully past a hole used as a pissoir to a junction of back alleys. Here, where there were no gas lamps, there was light from lanterns held on poles and clamour from at least two hundred people, including patrons and employees of the Young Prince, other miners, women in skirts, pit girls in trousers, families with babes, all of them festive as if at a fair.

It was a scene from Bosch's *Garden of Earthly Delights*. Or an ancient Olympic contest, Blair thought. Or a nightmare. He stayed in the dark unseen, though he could see Bill Jaxon standing naked in the middle of the crowd. He had a miner's overly defined body, the pinched waist and stark muscles that were the result of hard labour in extreme heat. His skin, pale as polished marble, contrasted with his dark hair, which now looked ruffled and wild. A second man had also stripped. He was shorter, older, with a barrel chest and bow legs. His head was shaved and his shoulders bore a backlit nimbus of curls. Behind him waved a green satin banner embroidered with an Irish harp.

Jaxon bent and laced on his clogs tight. Lancashire work clogs were leather uppers on ash soles, irons shaped like horseshoes on the soles for wear. Jaxon's were tipped with brass studs. He draped his scarf lightly around his neck and paraded like a thoroughbred in a paddock.

Jaxon's opponent advanced with the intent rolling gait of a bulldog. His shins were crosshatched with scars. His clogs were tipped with brass, too.

It wasn't human, Blair thought. More like cockfighting between rooster men wearing razors. In California they would have boxed with bare knuckles, which was effete by comparison. The mining-camp behaviour was familiar: backbreaking work relieved by blood sport. The wagering was also familiar; now Smallbone's money pouch made sense.

The bartender from the Young Prince said, 'The rules are: no high kicking, punching or biting. No wrestling to the ground. When a man goes down or breaks off or calls "Quit", the match is over.'

The other man was Irish. He told Jaxon, 'You'll look grand with a tin dick.'

'Fuck the rules,' Jaxon told the bartender. The smile released on his face was reckless, nearly gleeful.

The two opponents stepped back for a moment. A brass-tipped clog made a massive club, especially when swung with the full force of a miner's leg, and particularly against unprotected flesh. A miner could batter down a wooden door with his clogs.

In the lull Blair took in the feverish brightness of the bartenders' aprons, the whiteness of the two men in the swaying lights of the lanterns. It was a saturnalia, he thought, nothing English about it. It was clear from their faces that Jaxon was the favourite of Flo and the other pit girls and the object now of their anxiety.

The two men placed their hands on each other's shoulders and touched their foreheads together. Even while the bartender tied them loosely together at the neck with Jaxon's scarf they started pushing and angling for position. At close quarters a shorter, more experienced man had the advantage. The Irishman's threat was a veteran's trick, Blair thought. Let Jaxon try to protect his manhood and he'd be fighting on one leg. More likely he would go down with a shattered leg than a ruptured testicle.

The bartender held another scarf high. Waiting for it to drop, the two fighters leaned forward, heads touching. Flo and her friends put their hands together in prayer.

The bartender snapped the scarf down.

Ballet, Blair thought, as danced in Wigan. The first kicks were so swift that he couldn't follow them. Both men were bleeding from the knees down. With each hit a violent red blush spread on their skin. The Irishman tried to cave in Bill Jaxon's knee from the side. As Jaxon slipped the Irishman slashed his clog up, slicing Jaxon from knee to groin.

Jaxon leaned away and hammered his forehead down on the other man, whose shaved head split like a porcelain bowl of blood. Jaxon sidestepped a blind, retaliatory butt and swung his own leg from the outside, scooping the smaller man into the air. The scarf shot up into the air. As the Irishman hit the ground Jaxon swung his foot with his full weight. Clog and ribs met with a crack. A moan rose from the men below the banner of the harp.

The Irishman rolled and coughed black phlegm on to the dirt. As he hopped to his feet he struck back, stripping skin from Jaxon's flank. Jaxon's next blow caught the Irishman in the stomach and lifted him into the air again. The Irishman bounced from the ground to his knees and swayed. A bright effusion of blood flowed from his mouth. In that moment the fight was already over, except that it wasn't.

Jaxon announced, 'The man who bothered Rose, he's put me in a mood,' and his kick swung forward like the blur of a wing.

Chapter Four

The Cannel Room was the strangest formal dining room Blair had ever seen.

Bishop Hannay sat at the head of the table. Around it were his sister-in-law, Lady Rowland; the Reverend Chubb; a union man named Fellowes; Lady Rowland's daughter, Lydia; Earnshaw, the Member of Parliament from the train; Leveret; Blair; and at the foot of the table an empty chair.

The Cannel Room's ceiling, walls and wainscoting were panelled in polished black stone. Table and Queen Anne chairs were hand-turned work of the same material. Chandelier and candelabra seemed carved of ebony. Yet the walls showed no marble veins. The weight of the chairs was wrong. The temperature was wrong; marble always felt cooler than the air around it, but when Blair laid his hand on the table it was almost warm. Properly so, since cannel was jet, a form of clean, exceedingly fine coal. He had seen sculptures in black cannel. The Cannel Room was the only room made entirely of coal and it was famous. Its effect was heightened by contrasts: the luminous shimmer of silver and crystal on the black table, the deep purple of Lady Rowland's gown, the camellia white of Miss Rowland's dress.

The men – except for Blair of course – were all dressed for dinner in black, Hannay and Chubb in cassocks. The butler was assisted by four footmen in black satin livery. The floor was carpeted in black felt to silence the sound of their feet. The effect was as if they were dining in an elegant hall far below the surface of the earth. Blair ran his hand over the table and looked at his palm. Clean: not a speck of carbon dust, not an atom, not a mote.

'Mr Blair, exactly what is it that you do?' Lady Rowland asked.

Blair felt Leveret watching anxiously. He also felt contending waves of gin on one side of his brain and fever on the other. He wished the room were a little less hallucinatory. The only reassuring note of reality was a pail of sand by each footman in case of fire.

'The Hannay interests own different kinds of mines in different parts of the world. North America, South America, England. I work as a mining engineer.'

'Yes, I know that.' Lady Rowland had the theatrical quality of a flower that was slightly past its prime, still beautiful but pouty. She asserted the ancient right of aristocratic *décolletage*, and had a manner of playing with the string of pearls that lay upon it. 'I meant, what were you doing in Africa? We read about explorers and missionaries. It seems to me so important that the first white man that Africans encounter be the right sort. They frame their impression from the first contact, don't they?'

'Well said,' agreed Hannay, a host who liked to see

the conversational ball in play. Lady Rowland was young Lord Rowland's mother, the same Rowland whom Blair had described to Hannay as a 'murderous cretin'. Maybe this was family courtesy, he thought.

Blair refilled his wine glass, prompting a footman to come to life and bring out another bottle. Leveret lowered his eyes from the sight. The estate manager had tried to be a social palliative and was obviously dazzled by the sheer radiance of Lydia Rowland, but small talk was not in his nature, no matter how well he dressed for the occasion. It was like asking a walking stick to be an umbrella.

'Well, explorers are good at finding lakes, and missionaries are good at singing psalms, but neither of them are good at finding gold,' Blair said. 'That's what I was in West Africa for, to map where gold was most likely to be found. It's there; that's why they call it the Gold Coast. As for being the first white man, the Ashanti have already met Arab slavers, Portuguese slavers and English slavers, so I'm probably not going to lower their respect for the white race too much.'

Lydia Rowland was seventeen or so, Blair guessed. She was as fresh and milk-white as her dress. Her hair swept back in golden wings tied with velvet bows, and everything she said was with a breathless sense of discovery. 'I understand that you're the only man in England who can say what Ashanti women are like. Flirtatious?'

'Don't be grotesque, dear,' Lady Rowland said.

'It's a rash matter to send men who have no moral base,' the Reverend Chubb said. 'Missionaries don't just

74

sing psalms, Mr Blair. They also conduct the saving of souls and the introduction of civilization. That never requires fraternization.'

Blair said, 'You can always stay ignorant of people you're supposed to save. Anyway, the missionary is there to introduce English business, not civilization.'

Earnshaw said, 'Surely the second white man into such places is the scientist. Your Grace, the Royal Society sponsors botanical expeditions around the world, does it not?'

'The rhododendrons at Kew Gardens were spectacular this year,' Lady Rowland said.

'Yes,' Blair said, 'but the botanist who brings rhododendrons from Tibet also smuggles out tea plants, and the botanist who brings orchids out of Brazil also smuggles out rubber trees, and that's why there are tea and rubber tree plantations in India. That's also why botanists are knighted, not because they find flowers.'

'That's a very jaundiced view of the world, isn't it?' Earnshaw looked over his beard. If on the train from London he had regarded Blair with suspicion, he now had the certain air of a man who had identified a snake by species and size.

'It may be a different point of view, but it's rather exciting,' Lydia Rowland said.

'It's not exciting to support slavery. Isn't that what you were doing in the Gold Coast?' Earnshaw asked.

'I think the stories we've heard about Mr Blair are just that – stories,' Leveret said.

'But there are so many stories,' Earnshaw said. 'How

did you ever pick up that interesting sobriquet "Nigger Blair"? From your close association with Africans?'

Blair said, 'Funny you should ask. In the Gold Coast if you called a free African a "nigger", he could sue you. There "nigger" means slave, nothing else. He'd sue you for libel in a Gold Coast civil court and he'd win. The word was fixed on me by the newspapers in London, that's all. I can't sue here.'

'They have lawyers there?' Lydia Rowland asked.

'African lawyers, the first crop of civilization,' Blair said.

'So you're not offended when someone says, "Nigger Blair"?' Earnshaw asked.

'No, no more than I would be if another man called a springbok a spaniel because he doesn't know the difference. I can't be offended if someone is uninformed.' Blair was so pleased with himself for producing such a moderate response that he accepted another glass of wine. 'Whether he's a Member of Parliament or not.'

Teeth showed in Earnshaw's beard. It was a smile. He said, 'The interior of the Gold Coast is not civilized, it is the kingdom of the Ashanti. Just where did you stand in the Ashanti War?'

Blair said, 'There was no war.'

'Pardon?'

'There was no war,' Blair repeated.

'We read about it in *The Times*,' Earnshaw said.

'They marched out to have a war. They had dysentery instead. No war.'

'The disease?' Lydia Rowland asked, to be certain.

'An epidemic. Wiped out whole villages, and also hit the armies, British and Ashanti. They were both too sick to fight. And many people died.'

Earnshaw said, 'I read that you helped the Ashanti escape.'

'Members of the king's family were sick, some dying. Women and children. I led them out.'

'So you were practically a member of the Ashanti retinue. Why else would they trust you with their women?'

'Don't worry, Earnshaw, there'll be another Ashanti war and this time you'll get to kill the king and his family, too. Or maybe we can introduce syphilis.'

'He really is fully as awful as my son promised,' Lady Rowland told the Bishop.

'Then you're not disappointed,' Hannay said.

Turtle soup was followed by poached trout. Aspic made Blair queasy. He had more wine and wondered whether anyone was ever going to take the empty chair at the end of the table.

'I read something fascinating,' Lydia Rowland said. 'That the African explorer Samuel Baker bought his wife at a Turkish slave auction. She's Hungarian – I mean, she's white. Can you imagine?'

Bishop Hannay had more wine himself. 'Is this what all the young ladies of your set are imagining, Lydia?'

'I meant that it's terrible. She speaks four or five languages, goes to Africa with him and shoots lions.'

'Well, as you said, she's Hungarian.'

'And he's famous and successful. He was received at court by the Queen.'

'But his wife was not, dear, and that's the point,' Lady Rowland said.

'Whom we receive at court and whom we send to Africa can be two different sorts,' Hannay said. 'We could send a thoroughbred horse, for example, but it would be a total waste. Most of Central Africa is fly country. The insects carry some sort of malady that kills horses, even the best, within weeks. What you want is any four-legged animal that has been "salted" – bitten by the flies and survived. The same with men. The Royal Society selects its explorers from gallant officers. Then they get into the jungle and rot with fever or blow their brains out. But you could cut Blair's leg off and he would walk on the other. Cut off both and he would walk on the stumps. That's his gift: he absorbs punishment.'

Lady Rowland said, 'May I change the subject from Africa? Mr Earnshaw, what is it that brings you to Wigan?'

Earnshaw laid his knife and fork down. 'It's kind of you to ask. I am a member of a parliamentary committee looking into the employment of women called "pit girls" in the coal mines. They're women who work on the surface, sorting and moving coal as it comes up. We are, in fact, the third parliamentary committee that has tried to remove these women from the mines, but they are obstinate. That's why I've been talking to the Reverend Chubb and Mr Fellowes.'

Fellowes had spent the evening trying to choose between different knives and forks. He spoke for the first time; his voice was geared to union halls. 'It's an economic issue, Your Ladyship. It should be men doing that work and getting decent wages, with the women staying at home. Or if they do want to work, work in the cotton mills like decent girls.'

'It's a moral issue,' the Reverend Chubb said. 'The sad truth is that Wigan is the most degraded city in England. The cause is not the men, who are the coarser sex. The reason is the women of Wigan, who are so unlike their softer gender anywhere, except perhaps for Africa or along the Amazon. Earnshaw tells me he has seen picture cards sold in London, sordid cards for low tastes, of French "models" and Wigan pit girls. Their notoriety only makes them more brazen.'

'Why Wigan?' Lady Rowland asked. 'Surely women work at pits in Wales and other parts of the country?'

'Not in trousers,' Chubb said.

Revulsion was shared by Lady Rowland and her daughter; for a moment they were mirrors of each other.

'Not dresses?' the girl asked.

'A mockery of a dress rolled up and pinned above the trousers,' Fellowes said.

Earnshaw said, 'They claim for reasons of safety, but the fact is that factory girls in full skirts work surrounded by intense heat and spinning gears. So we have to ask ourselves, why do pit girls *choose* to unsex themselves? It seems a deliberate provocation.'

'An insult to every decent woman,' Fellowes said.

'And damage to marriage itself,' Earnshaw said. 'The commission has gathered information from medical experts, including Dr Acton, the author of *The Functions and Disorders of the Reproductive Organs*. With your permission?' Earnshaw waited for a nod from Lady Rowland. 'Dr Acton, who is *the* authority, says that a young man unfortunately often forms his ideas of the feminine sensibility from the lowest and most vulgar women, hence has the mistaken impression that the sexual feelings of the female are as strong as his, an error that only leads to heartbreak when he forms a union with a decent woman.'

Lydia Rowland lowered her eyes, held her breath and blushed delicately; the effect was like a faint stain on fine porcelain. Blair marvelled at her; a person didn't need language if she could manage the colour of her cheeks so well.

'I want to be fair,' Earnshaw added, 'but there does seem to be a scientific correlation between dress and behaviour, because statistically pit girls have the highest rate of illegitimate births in the country.'

'We see them carousing naked in and out of the beerhouses every night,' Chubb said.

'Pit girls?' Blair asked.

'Yes,' Chubb said.

'Totally undressed?'

'Their arms bare,' Chubb said.

'Ah,' said Blair.

The main course was saddle of mutton, beetroot, mustard. The empty chair was still unclaimed.

'Actually, what I saw, besides bare arms, was a fight between miners. A kicking fight,' Blair said.

'It's called "purring",' Hannay said. 'Lord knows why. A traditional local sport. The miners love it. Barbaric, isn't it?'

'It vents the tension,' Fellowes said.

Hannay said, 'They vent their tension on their wives, too. Taking clogs off a drunken miner is like unloading a cocked gun.'

'How horrible,' Lydia Rowland said.

'There's a pit girl or two knows how to use her clogs, too,' Fellowes said.

'That's a domestic scene to contemplate, isn't it?' Hannay said.

Blair asked, 'What did John Maypole think of pit girls?'

There was quiet the length of the table.

'Maypole?' Earnshaw asked.

The Reverend Chubb explained that the curate of the parish church was missing. 'We continue to trust that John's fate will become known to us. In the meantime, the Bishop has imported Mr Blair to make unofficial inquiries.'

'Looking for John?' Lydia Rowland asked her mother.

'Like setting a black sheep after a white,' Earnshaw said.

'Does Charlotte know about this?' Lady Rowland asked her brother.

Chubb set his fork down. It rattled with the fury transmitted by his body. 'The truth is that John Maypole was naïve about the character of pit girls. The fact that more illegitimate children are born here than even in Ireland marks Wigan as a moral cesspool. They are women totally beyond the bounds of decency or social control. It is my duty, for example, to disburse church funds to unwed mothers who apply, making sure not to give money so lavishly as to encourage animal conduct. It would be a lesson to pit girls for me to withhold money from them, but since they refuse to request assistance the lesson is utterly lost.'

There was a silence after Chubb's explosion.

'Do you think they'll find a lake in Africa for Princess Beatrice?' Lydia Rowland asked Blair finally.

'For Princess Beatrice?'

'Yes. They've found lakes and falls to name for the rest of the royal family. The Queen and Albert, of course. Alexandra, the Prince of Wales, Alice, Alfred, Helena, Louise, Arthur, even poor Leopold, I think they all have something discovered and named after them. All but Beatrice, the baby. She must be feeling left out. Do you think there's anything left worth finding and naming for her? It just makes it more personal if you can find your own lake on the map.'

Lady Rowland gave her daughter's hand a touch of maternal concern. 'Dear, it doesn't matter what Mr Blair thinks.'

Meat was followed by fowl. Fellowes chased a round plover egg around his plate with a knife and spoon. In the shifting light of the candles Blair detected a Paisley pattern on the opposite wall like a watermark in black stone. Not Paisley, he realized, but ferns fossilized within the cannel. He moved the candelabra and other small, graceful, intricately delicate fronds came into focus. They were seen best in the corner of the eye. On a second wall what he had first taken to be irregular striation was in fact ghostly fossil fish. Moving diagonally across another wall were the imprints of a great amphibian.

He said, 'If it's all right, I'd like to visit the mine where you had the explosion.'

'If you want,' Hannay said. 'It seems a waste of time since Maypole was never below. The last thing we'd allow is preachers down the shaft, the men's work is difficult and dangerous enough. But when you want to, Leveret will arrange it.'

'Tomorrow?'

Hannay took a moment. 'Why not? You can tour the surface too, and see the notorious pit girls in action.'

Earnshaw rose to the bait. 'I'm surprised, My Lord, that you tolerate those women for a moment, considering the reputation they give Wigan. It seems to me that the question is not whether a handful of brazen women wear skirts or not, it's whether Wigan joins the modern world.'

Hannay asked, 'What do you know about the modern world?'

'As a Member of Parliament, I know the spirit of the age.'

'Such as?'

'The upwelling political reform, the social conscience of modern theatre and books, the call for elevated subjects in the arts.'

'Ruskin?'

'John Ruskin is a perfect example, yes,' Earnshaw agreed. 'Ruskin is the greatest art critic of our time, and also a friend of the working man.'

'Tell him, Leveret,' Hannay said.

Earnshaw was wary. 'What?'

'We invited Ruskin.' Leveret told the tale as deferentially as he could. 'We invited him to give a lecture on the arts to the workers. But when he arrived he looked out of the window at Wigan and he wouldn't leave the train. He refused. No entreaty made him budge. He stayed on the train until it left.'

Hannay said, 'It's public knowledge that Ruskin couldn't consummate his marriage, either. He does seem to be easily shocked.'

Lady Rowland's blush burned through her pallor. 'We will leave the table if you speak like that.'

Hannay ignored her. 'Earnshaw, I appreciate that unlike other visitors from London, you had the courage to leave the train. Before you lecture us about Wigan's place in the modern world, though, let me suggest that the question is not one of politics or art, but one of industrial power. The best measure of that is steam engines *per capita*. Between mines and mills and factories, there are more steam engines per person in Wigan than in London, Pittsburgh, Essen or anywhere else. It happens to fit nicely that the palm oil we import from Africa lubricates those engines. The world runs on coal, and Wigan leads it. As long as we have coal we will continue to do so.'

'What about religion?' Chubb asked.

'That's the next world,' Hannay said. 'Perhaps there'll be coal there, too.'

'Does this mean you insist on employing pit girls?' Earnshaw asked.

Hannay shrugged. 'Not at all, as long as someone sorts the coal.'

'How long will the coal in Wigan last?' Lydia Rowland asked. The thought had never occurred to her before.

'A thousand years,' Leveret assured her.

'Really? The price of coal shot up last year because of a supposed shortage. We heard in London that English coalfields were running out,' Earnshaw said.

Hannay said blandly, 'Well, the good news is that we aren't.'

Dessert was pineapple cream and a meringue that rose to a snowy peak in the middle of the table.

'The importance of family,' Lady Rowland said.

Fellowes said, 'Social reform.'

'Moral life,' said Chubb.

'Blair, what do you think has been the Queen's greatest gift to England?' Hannay asked.

Before he could answer, a new voice said, 'Chloroform.'

A new arrival had slipped in through a service door.

She was not much more than twenty but wore a matron's soberly purple dress and long gloves and apparently had just arrived at the house because her hair of brooding Celtic red was dragged under a dark bonnet that shadowed a face of sharp features and small, severe eyes. Blair was put in mind of a fierce sparrow.

The men, all but Hannay, stood. He said, 'Charlotte, how flattering of you to join us.'

'Father.' She took the chair that had been empty opposite Hannay and waved off a footman bearing wine.

The men sat.

'Chloroform?' Blair asked.

'That the Queen had chloroform for labour and made it acceptable not to give birth in agony will go down in history as her greatest gift.' Charlotte Hannay redirected her gaze. 'Cousin Lydia, you look like a freshly picked peach.'

'Thank you,' Lydia said uncertainly.

Hannay introduced the table and said, 'Charlotte doesn't often join us for dinner, although we always hope. Remove your hat and stay.'

Charlotte said, 'I just wanted to see your white African.'

'American,' Blair said.

'But your reputation is from Africa,' she said. 'Slaves and native women, isn't that what you're known for? What was it like to be in a position of such power? Did it make you feel like a god?'

'No.'

'Perhaps you have a charm that only works on black women.'

'Perhaps.'

'Mr Blair is actually very charming,' Lydia Rowland said.

Charlotte said, 'Really? I look forward to seeing that.'

'Many of us do,' Earnshaw said drily.

'And you've been hired by my father to inquire after John Maypole. What a bizarre proposition,' Charlotte said.

'Tell him to go away, Charlotte,' Lady Rowland said.

Hannay said, 'I'm sure Charlotte wants to know what happened to Maypole. After all, he was her fiancé.'

'Is, until I know otherwise,' Charlotte said.

'I know we will receive a letter from the Reverend Maypole that will explain everything. You have to carry on,' Lydia Rowland said.

'I do. I just don't carry on like you.'

Lydia Rowland blinked as if she'd been slapped, and for the first time Blair felt sympathy for the girl. She might be a fool, but in contrast to Charlotte Hannay a fool was positively attractive. He instantly saw Charlotte's future: she had a mouth on which no smile would ever perch, eyes that would never soften, a body that would never be unbound from mourning. She might have arrived late but she was a proper mistress for the Cannel Room.

From his end of the table, Hannay said, 'Charlotte, it seems to me that your devotion to Maypole grows in proportion to his absence.'

'Or in proportion to your inconvenience,' she suggested.

'Maybe Blair will put an end to both,' Hannay said.

Charlotte regarded Blair with, if possible, increased hostility. 'You'll do anything to get back to Africa?'

'Yes.'

She told her father, 'Congratulations, you certainly have found your man. And, Blair, are you being adequately recompensed?'

'I hope so.'

Charlotte said, 'You had better hope. My father is like Saturn, except that he doesn't eat all his children. He lets them fight it out, and then he eats the survivor.'

Lydia Rowland put her hand over her mouth.

Hannay stood. 'Well, it's been a very successful party.'

The men moved to a library fully as large as the Royal Society's. Two storeys of stacks and chart drawers with an iron balcony surrounded birds of paradise in bell jars, tables of fossils and meteorites, a rose-marble fireplace, ebony desk and deep leather furniture. Blair noticed the steady gas glow of wall lamps. Apparently only the Cannel Room was lit with candles.

'The women are happy in the study.' Hannay poured port left to right. 'The family has been building Hannay Hall for eight hundred years, so that now it's a perfect monster. You exit from a Gothic gallery and enter a Georgian ballroom. Step out of a Restoration library and run into the plumbing of a modern water closet. The scullery dates back to the Black Prince. Pity the wretches who work there.'

'My aunt works there,' Fellowes said.

'Excellent.' Hannay proposed a toast. 'Your aunt.'

'Very kind, Milord,' Fellowes said.

They drank. Blair asked, 'Do you mean there's another library?'

'Yes. This was a chapel,' Hannay said.

'Roman Catholic,' Chubb whispered.

Hannay pointed to a small oil portrait of a long-haired man wearing an ear-ring and a flamboyant Elizabethan collar. 'The Hannays were resolute Catholics, hiding and running priests from here to the Highlands. The tenth earl, whom you see there, was an abject coward who converted to save his neck and estate, for which his descendants eternally thank him. The chapel was allowed to go to rack and ruin. The lead was stripped, roof and windows fell in. Being in a back courtyard no one much noticed. I decided to make something of it.'

Earnshaw and Chubb were reduced to reverence by a framed manuscript of gilded Latin designed into Celtic knots. Leveret and Blair lingered over the fossils: a fiddlehead fern curled like the scroll of a cello, the cross-section of a fossilized tree as iridescent as a peacock's tail.

Hannay opened drawers with maps in Greek, Persian and Arabic drawn on tree bark, papyrus, vellum, and pilot charts written in Dutch and Portuguese. On them Africa evolved and grew from Egyptian delta, to Carthaginian empire, to indeterminate land mass guarded by boiling waters, to the saints' names of a newly navigated but still ominous continent, to a modern, well-plotted coastline and beckoning interior.

'Africa does seem to be your special interest,' Earnshaw said.

'Not entirely. This is the prize of the library.' Hannay opened a velvet slipcase and as painstakingly as if he were lifting air brought out a book with a badly worn leather cover faded to a powdery mauve. He raised the front just enough for Blair and Earnshaw to read, handwritten on the frontispiece, 'Roman de la Rose'. 'Every fine medieval lady had her copy of *The Romance of the Rose*,' Hannay said. 'This was written, fittingly enough, in 1323 for Céline, Dame de Hannay.'

'What is it about?' Fellowes asked.

'Chivalry, spirituality, carnality, mystery.'

'Sounds interesting.'

'Would you like to take it home with you, share it with the wife?' Hannay handed it to him.

'No, no!' Fellowes backed away, horrified.

'Very well.' Hannay took it back.

'She doesn't speak French,' Fellowes told Blair.

The library doors flew open. The book emitted a faint bouquet of roses as the room was invaded by Charlotte, still in her bonnet, driving her aunt and cousin before her like a demon.

Charlotte announced, 'I want to know what new arrangements you're making behind my back. Your Blair has probably the most loathsome reputation on the face of the earth, and you've hired him to foul the name of a better man under the pretence of an investigation. I would no more answer questions from Blair than I would willingly sit in stinking offal.'

'But you *will* answer them,' Hannay said.

'Father, when you rot in Hell. Since you're a bishop of the Church, that's not very likely, is it?'

She gave the company in the library a contemptuous rake of her small, hard-set eyes and marched away. If this were Joan of Arc, Blair thought, he'd light the first torch. Gladly.

Chapter Five

Blair rose at the sound of clogs ringing on the cobble-stones like gongs. In the light of the street lamp he could make out miners and women heading for the pits on the west side of town, and mill girls in dresses and shawls streaming in the opposite direction.

He had dressed in the secondhand clothes he had bought the day before and had his coffee by the time Leveret arrived. They climbed into the state manager's modest one-horse gig and took the road south towards the Hannay Pit. In dark fields on either side Blair could make out miners in the dark by the glow of their pipes and the mist of their breath. The fields smelled of manure, the air of ash. Ahead, from a high chimney, issued a silvery column of smoke that at its very peak was coloured by dawn.

'Last night was a rare appearance by Charlotte,' Leveret said. 'For weeks you can't find her, and then she bursts on to the scene. I'm sorry that she was rude.'

'The nastiest little monster I ever met. You know her well?'

'I grew up with her. Not actually *with* her, but on the estate. My father was manager before me. Then I was John's best friend when he came here and he and

Charlotte became allied. It's just that she feels strongly about things.'

'Are there any brothers or sisters?'

'Deceased. Charlotte's oldest brother had a hunting accident. Tragic.'

'So in the house it's just the Bishop and her and a hundred and forty staff?'

'No. The Rowlands live at Hannay Hall with the Bishop, but Charlotte lives in a separate cottage. A nice house, actually. Very old. She lives her own life.'

'I bet she does.'

'She used to be different.'

'She *is* different,' Blair said.

Leveret laughed timidly and changed the subject. 'I'm surprised you want to take the time to go down the mine. You were in such a rush to look for John.'

'I still am.'

There was no gate or clear demarcation between farmland and the Hannay Pit. Miners on either side converged, and Blair found himself entering a yard lit by gas lamps and surrounded by sheds where sound and light seemed to have been stored and at that moment unleashed: the heavy breath and hoofbeats of horses pulling wagons across stones, the amber glow and rhythm of farriers shaping iron, the sparks and whine of picks being sharpened. Donkey engines chuffed out of railway sheds. Tram wagons, chained, not coupled, crashed together. Barely audible overhead, like a bow drawn across a cello, came a vibration from the cables running from the winding gears in the tower that stood above the shaft.

Metal tubs full of coal rolled off the cage on to a scale, connected to an 'endless chain' and moved mechanically on rails up to the shed to be sorted and graded. Blair hopped off the gig and kept pace with the parade of tubs. Each full tub weighed, according to the scale, at least two hundred pounds. The shed had a cover, no sides, more to protect coal from water than workers from weather. All the workers in it were pit girls. Those at the top unlinked arriving tubs, rolled them to a tippler, locked a tub in and slowly released a brake lever so that as the tippler rocked, the tub disgorged a black stream of coal on to a conveyor belt where, by the light of a lamp, other women cleaned the coal of dirt and stones.

The pit girls wore flannel shirts, corduroy trousers and vestigial skirts greasy with coal. Their hair was hidden in shawls from the dust. Their hands were black and their faces blurred from clouds of pulverized carbon that erupted as coal from the belt flowed down a slanted screen, or fell through to finer screens.

Cleaned and graded coal poured down a chute to the shed's railway siding, where two girls manhandled the chute mouth over wagons. Blair recognized Flo from the Young Prince and Rose Molyneux.

Flo had a voice that sawed through the din. 'It's him.'

Blair shouted to Rose, 'I want to talk to you.'

Rose turned towards him and put one hand on her

hip. Her eyes were two prisms of concentration, accentuated by the black dust that covered her face. It was the sort of unhurried gaze a man might receive from a cat at ease on a chair she claimed for her own. She took in Blair, engine drivers, haulers and miners, as if they were all of equal unimportance.

'You look debonair,' she said.

He glanced down at his shabby jacket and trousers. 'For the occasion.'

Somehow she managed to imbue her own dirty apparel with stylish impudence. 'Going down pit? You'll be black as a pipe cleaner when you come back.'

'We have to talk.'

'Was it such a fascinating conversation the first time?'

'It was interesting.'

She held his gaze. In that moment he saw that she knew she had the power to catch his eye when she wanted.

'Bill won't like that,' Flo said.

'Bill Jaxon?' Blair asked.

Rose laughed at Blair's reaction. 'Did that make your pecker drop?'

'Blair!' Leveret shouted from a shed across the yard.

Because the lamp shed was where the miners were issued their safety lamps it burned on the inside like a chandelier. On the lower shelves were lamp oil, rolls of wick cord and caulking in cans that read 'Good Enough for the Royal Navy!' Hanging on the back wall, six canary cages sounded a chorus. Yellow heads peeked through the grilles.

'Maybe you should wait here,' Blair told Leveret. In the light he could see that under a borrowed leather jacket the estate manager wore a silk waistcoat and white shirt, not to mention a nicely brushed bowler.

'No, I've always wondered about the mining experience. I've never been more than ten feet deep in an old mine before.'

'You could tie yourself into a sack of coal and jump up and down,' Blair suggested.

The safety lamps were eight inches tall, with brass caps and bases and, in between, a cylinder of brass gauze to cool the heat of the flame below the ignition point of explosive gas. The lamp man lit and locked lamps for Leveret and Blair. Within the safety gauze, the flames were murky embers. Scratched into each lamp base was a different number that the lamp man wrote into a ledger that he turned for Blair and Leveret. 'That's how we know who went down pit and who come up. Just in case. I should warn you, gentlemen, the Hannay Pit's a mile down, the deepest pit in Lancashire. If closets make you uncomfortable, best to think twice.'

They went back into the dark to join men waiting under the tower at the pit head. The miners wore dirty wool jackets and moleskin trousers; moleskin had no nap to rub the wrong way underground. Cloth caps and clogs, of course. Tommy tins of food hung on straps over their shoulders. The men lounged against one another with an ease particular to soldiers, athletes, miners. In spite of himself, Blair felt at home among them, just as Leveret showed signs of middle-class unease. Air whistled down the shaft – it was the ventilation intake for eight miles of workings underground – and the wind set the flames in the safety lamps trembling. Blair could just see the white warning fence around a ventilation upshaft fifty yards away; at the bottom was a furnace that drove foul air from the pit and drew in good – at least, that was the theory.

The wind subsided at the same time as the improbable sound of a freight train approached from beneath the ground. Blair watched the winding wheel slow, the vertical line of cable shake as the load lessened, a hook emerge, followed by a cage – an iron square with two wooden sides and ends open except for two loose chains. Immediately the chains were unhooked and tubs of glossy coal were rolled from the cage to the scale. Just as quickly, the miners pushed into the cage, taking the place of the tubs, putting their feet around the rails, and Blair and Leveret joined them.

Everyone crowded in; miners were paid by coal they produced, not the time they spent waiting for a ride. They didn't force Blair or Leveret to the open ends, and that was courtesy enough, Blair thought. In the glow of the lamps, fainter than candles, he saw coal dust on Leveret's collar and knew the same inescapable smudges were on him.

'Last chance. You'll look like a pipe cleaner when we

come back,' Blair said. He liked Rose's expression. Another woman would have said 'chimney sweep'. Leveret was tall, so 'pipe cleaner' fitted him.

Leveret's bravado was lost in the deafening clatter of a bell. One ring: going down.

The cage started slowly, down through the round, brick-lined upper mouth of the shaft, past round garlands of Yorkshire iron, good as steel, into a cross-hatched well of stone and timber and then simply down. Down into an unlit abyss. Down at twenty, thirty, forty miles per hour. Down faster than any men anywhere else on earth could travel. So fast that breath flew from the lungs and pressed against the ears. So fast that nothing could be seen at the open end of the cage except a blur that could whip away an inattentive hand or leg. Down seemingly for ever.

Past the lamplight of an older landing. It could have been a firefly. Blair caught Leveret crossing himself and shook his head; the less movement the better. At its fastest, the cage dropped so smoothly that the men almost floated. In a shaft it was always the moment of greatest danger and greatest bliss. Blair thought that with their massed lamps they might resemble a meteor to a spectator, to a dazzled worm.

Brunel, the great railway engineer, claimed that the drivers of trains should be illiterate because only the unlettered man *paid attention*. Miners paid attention, Blair thought. The faces in the cage were more concentrated than the School of Plato for the way they listened to the unravelling of round steel cable, the slightest yawing of the cage, the growing pressure on the wooden soles of their clogs.

They were slowing. At two minutes by Blair's watch at an estimated average speed of thirty miles per hour, a mile down, the cage settled into a subterranean well of lights and stopped. At once the miners poured out, followed by Blair and Leveret, the latter in a state of confusion.

For good reason. There was the converging traffic of underground roads, out of which emerged ponies in heavy harness and boys in caps and jackets, both beasts and tenders even more stunted by dim lamps hanging from the timbers. Behind each pony followed a row of loaded tubs on rails.

There was the smell emanating from a long row of low pony stalls. Underground stables were always placed by the downshaft and built on planks, but they never totally dried out; instead, the pungent aroma of horse manure and urine seemed both ancient and distilled.

There was the gale-force wind that whistled down the shaft, fresh air now tainted by the stable it passed through.

There was the heat, the opposite of a dank cave. A stifling heat ripe with sweat, muck, carbon dust. A reminder that the earth was a living organism with a burning core.

All these were sensory evidence that a visitor took notice of, sorted through, made order of. It took a minute for a visitor to comprehend that the pit eye was a hundred yards across. What the visitor had simply to ignore was the subtler, stronger report of his senses that a mile of earth stood over him, or that he was that far from escape. Blair checked his compass anyway.

Just as there was a manager's office on the surface there was an underlooker's office below, a square and simple room of brick. The underlooker was named Battie, a happy Vulcan in shirtsleeves, bowler and braces.

Battie was expecting them; he had cleared his desk, spread a map and weighted the corners with lamps. On the north end of the map were the cage and furnace shafts. The south was a gridiron of large and small tunnels that ran to an irregular border.

Battie registered with a noncommittal glance the different fashions of his visitors' dress. 'Mr Leveret, Mr Blair, will you please turn your pockets inside out?'

Blair pulled out his watch, compass, handkerchief, penknife and loose change; Leveret produced a more substantial pile of watch, purse, wallet, locket, comb, visiting cards, briar pipe, tobacco, matches. Battie locked the pipe, tobacco and matches in his desk.

'No smoking, Mr Leveret. I wouldn't want you to even think about it.'

The map was dated the day of the explosion and bore circles with numbers ranging from one to three digits. Lamp numbers, Blair realized. There were seventy-six victims in the fire and that was the total he counted. It wasn't difficult because so many were clustered in a central tunnel, while others were evenly spaced along the coal face. One number, however, was right outside the underlooker's office.

'What happened here?' he asked.

'The cage was up. The shaft itself goes further down, you know. A boy had just come with his pony and tubs. When the smoke reached here, the pony backed over the edge. The boy tried to save it. That's how they went – pony, tubs and then the boy.' Battie paused. He lifted the lamps and let the map roll up, and put it in a leather satchel along with a ledger. He replaced his bowler with a red bandanna tied around his forehead. In a second, he had regained his poise, as if he were about to stroll through a park. 'Well, gentlemen, I have to make my rounds. If you still want to, we have a long way to go.'

'You can wait here or go up in the cage,' Blair offered Leveret again.

'I'm with you,' Leveret said.

'"Onward, Christian Soldiers"?' Blair asked.

'I won't hold you back,' Leveret promised.

Swinging his satchel, Battie led the way around the shaft and darted into the right-hand tunnel. 'Tunnels we call "roads",' he said over his shoulder. 'When they're as wide as this, it's a "main road".'

There was nothing high about it, however, and as soon as they entered, Leveret was in trouble. The only light was the safety lamps, three flames so obscured by wire gauze that they barely lit the rails on the floor or the timbers on the ceiling, and when Leveret tried to avoid one he stumbled into the other, and he didn't know when to step and when to duck.

Battie slowed but didn't stop. 'When you want to turn around, Mr Leveret, look for a sign saying, "Out". If you don't find one, just follow the air in your face. If the wind's at your back, you're going further in. Mr Blair, you've done this before.'

Blair hadn't even realized he'd slipped into the miner's stride: a half crouch with the head up, steps unconsciously measuring the sleepers of the track.

'When do we reach the coal?' Leveret asked.

'We're in it now. You're in the middle of the Hannay Seam, one of the richest coal seams in England,' Battie said. 'That's what's holding up the roof.'

Black walls. Black roof, too, Blair thought, because coal cushioned timbers better than stone. The irises of his eyes had dilated so that dark became shadow, and shadow took on form. Ahead of Battie a shaggy outline and lamp came from the opposite direction.

'Pony,' Battie said and stepped into a refuge hole that not even Blair had seen. Blair followed and they pulled in a startled Leveret the moment before a pony passed, a Shetland with sooty locks tended by a boy with a lamp and trailed by four full tubs. Leveret looked a little shorter.

'Lost your hat?' Blair asked.

'Actually, yes.' Mournfully Leveret watched the tubs roll by.

Blair asked Battie, 'You can tell when someone's been in mines before no matter how they're dressed?'

'With their first step. And whether they're drunk or not. If they are, I send them up. You're only as safe as the stupidest man in the mine.'

To join the conversation, Leveret asked, 'Why do the men wear clogs? I understand that most people in Wigan do, but I'd think that down in a mine they would be clumsy.'

Battie said, 'Rockfalls, sir. When the roof comes down on you it doesn't crush a clog's wooden sole the way it does a shoe. Then they're easier to squirm and get your foot out of, too.'

Leveret fell silent.

Walking underground was called travelling. They travelled twenty minutes, encountering only ponies and tub trains. The road became lower and narrower and began to slant down, and the sound of the trains was muffled by the constricted breath of the wind and the press of weight on wooden timbers. Battie halted regularly to hold his lamp where stones packed into dry walls or timbers propped up the roof.

He explained to Leveret, 'When we cut the coal, we let out firedamp. A funny word, isn't it, gentlemen?'

'It is a funny word,' Leveret agreed.

'As if it would put out fire.' Battie poked into a niche.

'And it does?'

'From the German *Dampf*. Meaning vapour. Explosive gas.'

'Oh,' said Leveret.

'Methane. It likes to hide in cracks and along the roof. The point of a safety lamp is that the gauze dissipates enough of the heat so that you won't set the gas off. Still, the best way to find it is with a flame.' Battie lifted the lamp by a rough column of rock and studied the light wavering behind the screen of the gauze. 'See how it's a little longer, a little bluer? That's methane that's burning.'

'Should we evacuate?' Leveret asked.

The flame lit Battie's grin as he pulled off his waistcoat and fanned the rock. He went back in the tunnel and returned a minute later with a folded frame of canvas and wood that he opened into a standing panel that redirected the flow of air at the rock.

'Mr Leveret, if we closed a pit every time we found a whiff of firedamp, England would freeze.' He took the ledger from his pack and noted the time, location and amount of gas. 'We watch the firedamp, we chase the firedamp, and we don't let it blow us to kingdom come.'

From here the road got worse, which didn't slow Battie in the least. 'This is a "sit",' he said at a place where the ceiling buckled, and made a note in his book. 'This is a "creep",' he said where the floor rose, lifting the track. 'There's pressure up and down. We have limestone above and gritstone below. We haven't lost the coal yet, though.'

The further they walked the more Blair understood that Battie didn't need the map. The man knew the Hannay Seam the way a riverman knew a river. Probably his father and grandfather had worked the same coal. A man like Battie knew where the black banks twisted left, right, up and down, or plunged from sight at a geologic fault. He knew the Hannay Seam's density, cohesion, water content, lustre, lighting point and ash. He could follow it in the dark.

Leveret was falling behind. Blair was about to ask Battie to relent when the underlooker stopped on his own and set his lamp by a coal pillar. He spread his map across the floor and pointed to two lamp numbers. 'This is where we found these two lads. They were the nearest casualties to the cage except for the boy and pony.'

A trail of numbers led to the west coal face, still twice as far as they had gone so far. The victims on the main road had fallen in groups, some huddled in refuge holes.

Leveret arrived, gasping and covered in coal dust as if he'd been dragged behind a pony.

'I'm . . . fine,' he said and sank to his knees.

Blair and Battie returned to the map.

'Were they burned?' Blair asked.

'No. No one was burned until we get to the end of the main road, close to the face. The lads here were stretched out like they'd gone to sleep.'

'But facing the air? Running when they'd dropped?'

'Right.' Battie seemed darkly satisfied. 'Mr Leveret, your friend here knows something about coal.'

'They were crushed?' Leveret asked.

'No,' Battie said. 'When firedamp explodes it turns to afterdamp. Carbon monoxide. The strongest man in the world could be running through here at top speed, but two breaths of that and he'll drop to the floor. Unless you drag him out, he'll die. In fact, I've seen rescue attempts where one, two, three men will drop trying to pull one man out.'

The floor jumped, followed by a roar that rolled

through from one end of the tunnel to the other. Pebbles rained in the dark.

Leveret was on his feet. 'Fire!'

'Just blasting, Mr Leveret. There's a difference. When there's an explosion you can feel it in Wigan. I'll let you know.' Battie rolled up the map and added, 'There won't be any more demonstrations like that, I hope, Mr Leveret. Around the men, I mean.'

Battie's lamp led the way again, pausing only as he mentioned that three miners had died here, four there, all trying to outrun afterdamp. It wasn't an unsafe mine, as mines went, Blair thought. It was dirty and close and uncomfortable, of course, but tunnels were kept clear, tracks well maintained, and Battie seemed to be a punctilious supervisor. It was just that all mines were an inversion of the natural order, and coal mines in particular were stupid and deadly.

The tunnel started to plunge. It would go deeper as the whole underground strata tilted south, Blair thought. The seam had likely first been worked as an easy outcropping north of Wigan. Roman troops had probably dried their sandals by fires of Hannay coal. With each step down, he was more aware of heat. The mine's breath parched the throat even as the skin turned to a slough of black sweat.

The tunnel opened into a crypt-sized chamber where a boy walked a pony on a ring of track, making a ghostly carousel. When the pony stopped, a man silvery with coal dust, naked except for improvised kneepads and clogs, emerged from a low tunnel and hooked full tubs to the animal's harness. Giving Battie the briefest of nods, he disappeared like an apparition back into the tunnel, pushing an empty tub ahead of him. Pony and boy vanished in the opposite direction.

'Hot.' Leveret found his voice.

'Tea, sir?' Battie offered a tin flask from his pack.

Leveret shook his head and dropped to the track in exhaustion. The first time in a mine was always the worst, no matter how fit you were, Blair thought. Even with malaria, he was simply doing what he had done all his life.

Leveret said, 'Sorry to be so clumsy.'

'No bother, sir,' Battie said. 'Miners get too comfortable. They know a single spark is dangerous, but they will come skating down the rails here on the irons of their clogs, sparks flying like fireworks. Or sneak away from work into a side tunnel and sleep like a fieldmouse.'

'Sounds quite cosy,' Leveret said.

Battie said, 'Sometimes. There was a pony here the day of the fire. Dropped and blocked that tunnel. We found ten men on the other side.'

'Afterdamp?' Blair asked.

'Yes. You know, I read a London paper that said the greatest modern fear is being buried alive. There were advertisements for coffins with speaking tubes and semaphores. Why would they worry about being buried alive in London?' Battie turned to Leveret. 'Better?'

'I'm ready to move.'

'Good.'

They ducked into the tunnel that the miner had

vanished into. There were rails and just enough room for a crouching man to manoeuvre a tub through a gallery of wooden props. Through the tunnel came a concussive sound, as if a wave of surf had curled and crashed.

Leveret asked, 'What's that?'

'The roof falling in,' Battie said.

'Good Lord,' Leveret said, and Blair heard him trying to backtrack.

Battie said, 'No, that was normal, Mr Leveret. That's the system.'

'System?'

'You'll see. A cave-in is a sharper noise, a mix of timbers and stone, usually,' Battie said. 'You'll see what I mean.'

On either side now their lamps lit not so much tunnels as a honeycomb of pillars of coal a little like the columns of a black mosque. At the edge of conscious hearing Blair became aware of a new sound: crystalline, percussive, distorted and amplified by the vagaries of rock. Battie led the way for ten more minutes, and suddenly he and Blair crawled out into a narrow tunnel, the length of which was populated by shadowy figures wearing only trousers and clogs, some only clogs, covered by a film of dust and glitter, swinging short, double-pointed picks. The men had the pinched waists of whippets and the banded, muscular shoulders of horses, but shining in the upcast light of their lamps what they most resembled was machinery, automatons tirelessly hacking at the pillars of coal that supported the black roof above them.

Coal split with a sound nearly like chimes. Where the coal seam dipped, men worked on knees wrapped in rags. Other men loaded tubs or pushed them, leaning into them with their backs. A fog of condensation and coal dust rose from them.

Blair looked at his compass. 'You're working backwards.'

'Correct,' Battie said.

The miners were attacking the inner wall of the west face, working back towards the pit eye and not along the outer wall, as Blair had expected. The outer wall didn't exist, it was a low space that receded into impenetrable murk.

Battie opened his map. 'I think you'll appreciate this, Mr Blair. This is the Lancashire system. We drive the main tunnels, the roads, through the coal to the border of the vein. We cut smaller tunnels to connect the roads and circulate the air, and then we start working backwards, as you say, to get the rest of the coal, just leaving enough stone pillars and props to hold up the roof until we're clear. The props collapse and the roof does fall – that's the sound we heard – but by then we're gone.'

'This is where victims were burned?' Blair asked.

'Along this coal face, but about fifteen yards in.' Battie faced the worked-out void behind the miners. 'That's where we were two months ago. That's two thousand tons of coal. Anyway, no one is allowed in old workings. Those are pit rules.'

The line of miners swung their picks at a relentless pace. Blair had seen the same phenomenon around the world: deep-shaft miners worked as if sheer physical effort could mesmerize the mind. In this case, perhaps there was also a sense that they were cutting their way back to the shaft. A bull's-eye lantern might have cut the murk, but the dim glow of a safety lamp was hardly better than an ember and barely lit the man holding it. Beyond the perimeter of the coal face it was impossible to say how far the worked-out area extended behind the miners, or whether the roof was six feet or six inches high. Blair picked up a stone and threw it sidearm. The stone was swallowed by the dark, its sound lost in the din of the picks.

'How far in is the roof up?' he asked.

'Ten yards some places, a hundred yards in others. It could stay up a month, a year. It could come down while we're here,' Battie said.

Leveret caught up with them, gasping, the worse for wear in the last, low stretch of tunnel. Blood smeared his forehead, and sweat and coal dust made black soup around his eyes. 'What could come down?' he asked.

'Nothing. Leveret, I couldn't be prouder if you had found Livingstone.' Blair gave him a handkerchief. 'A few minutes and then we'll head back.'

For every man with a pick, another shovelled the coal and loaded it in tubs. Every twenty yards the track split into short parallel lines so that tubs could pass. Into a coal pillar a man cranked a drill that was a barrel of cogs steadied by an iron brace that reached from floor to roof. He was a head taller than any other man along the

110

coal face, and though the drill must have weighed forty pounds, he handled it easily. Black powder poured from the bore hole. The rod turned so smoothly the man could have been drilling into cheese.

Because of the poor light and the fact that they were so black with dust, Blair didn't notice at first that the man wore bandages on both his legs. At the sight of Blair he stopped work. 'Still looking for Reverend Maypole?' Bill Jaxon asked.

'You never know,' said Blair.

He was amazed that Jaxon was capable of walking after last night's fight behind the Young Prince, but he reminded himself that miners took pride in the amount of pain they could ignore. With his long hair tied back, Jaxon looked like a statue by Michelangelo, but carved from coal, not marble.

'Still got your clogs on?' Blair asked.

'Want to try them?' Jaxon answered.

At Jaxon's side appeared a gnomish figure that Blair recognized as an ebony version of Smallbone, his drinking partner from the Prince. Smallbone cradled a long tin box. Jaxon unscrewed the top leg of the brace and extracted the bore rod from the hole. From the box Smallbone took a long straw that he slid in the hole and puffed into with his eyes closed. A jet of dust flew out. Blair enjoyed seeing a specialist at work. Next, Smallbone brought out a ten-inch waxed paper tube from the box.

'What . . .?' Leveret asked.

'Gunpowder. He makes the shots himself,' Jaxon said.

MARTIN CRUZ SMITH

Battie said, 'Smallbone is a fireman. On the surface a fireman puts out fires. Down here a fireman fires the shots.'

The bore hole had a downward slant. With a wooden rod Smallbone pushed the paper tube in as far as it would go, carefully punctured its end with a copper needle and fed in a fuse, a 'slow match' of rough cotton cord soaked with saltpetre. He led the cord out and tamped the hole with clay so that one foot of fuse hung free. Very homemade, Blair thought. In the meantime, Battie had moved his lamp along the roof in search of firedamp. 'It looks clear,' he said.

'Shot!' Jaxon yelled.

The shout was passed along. All the miners in sight gathered their tools and moved to the main-road tunnel out of the line of fire. Battie led Leveret and Blair. Jaxon followed with his drill while Smallbone stayed at the hole alone.

Battie advised Leveret, 'Look the opposite way, sir, and open your mouth.'

Blair watched Smallbone pass the lamp slowly along the roof and down the wall to satisfy himself there was no gas, a sign of intelligence better than any written examination. He knelt by the dangling fuse and blew against the flame of his lamp until it flared in response and tilted towards its protective gauze. He blew harder and the flame grew brighter and pushed until a tongue of fire penetrated the wire screen and reached out to the cord. On his third breath the fuse end reciprocated with an orange bud of light.

The fireman returned with quick, short steps and had joined the group for five seconds when the tunnel behind him erupted with a clap like thunder and swirling billows of black dust. The blast was more powerful than Blair had expected. The miners rocked like men on a deck, while the report divided into echoes that subdivided into other tunnels. One by one the men shook their heads and opened their red-rimmed eyes wide.

'Doubling up on the charge, Mr Smallbone?' Battie said. 'Do that again and you can find employment in another pit.'

It was the first hint of hypocrisy Blair had seen in the underlooker and Battie seemed uneasy at his own protest. Everyone – owners and underlookers – knew that miners were paid only by the tubs they filled, not by the time they spent picking at deep, hard coal. That was why firemen blasted in spite of firedamp. Smallbone's shot had dropped a wide shelf of coal to the floor and fractured the wall besides. The miners dug reviving snuff from their tins and returned to work. Jaxon shouldered his drill and brace and moved down the tunnel to start the next hole. As he moved, an avenue of admiration formed around him.

Smallbone, with no chagrin, lingered by the fallen shelf and expanded to Leveret. 'Yer German dynamite, well, it's a fart in t'wind.'

'I thought it was powerful,' Leveret said. 'I've read about it in scientific journals.'

'On German coal,' Smallbone said. 'This is English coal.'

Nothing like a pit as a leveller, Blair thought. Where else could you find an estate manager discussing explosives with a naked miner? He noticed that Battie was contemplating the worked-out void again, where airborne dust still shivered from the blast.

'About twenty more yards along the face, that's where I think the explosion was. How far in, Mr Blair, I don't know. I've thought about it a thousand times.'

'You think it was touched off by a shot?'

'No. Only Smallbone was firing shots at this end of the face. He and Jaxon, the man with the drill, would be dead, too. They lived to save a half-a-dozen men, thank God. There was a spark. Someone did something incredibly stupid. Some fool forced open his lamp to light his pipe. Or pulled the top off just for more light to swing a pick by. There *was* gas. A real "blower". And there was a complication. The blast unsettled some waste – stones and small coal – that we'd bricked in. Gas loves waste. After we aired the blower out, gas leaked from the waste until we bricked it up again. Had to if we wanted to bring in lamps to search.'

'How big a section did you rebrick?'

'Maybe two foot high, three wide.'

'Show me.'

Battie stared into the void. 'We had the Mines Inspector here and we had the inquiry. It's all done with, Mr Blair. So what are you after? Clearly you know your way around a mine but it's very unclear to me why you're in *this* mine. What are you looking for?'

'There's a man missing.'

'Not here. After the fire there were seventy-six lamps and seventy-six bodies accounted for. I made sure of that.'

'Each and every one identified? There was enough left of them to tell?'

'They were identified officially by the coroner – every one, Mr Blair.'

'All from Wigan? I saw some Irish in town.'

'There were some day workers from outside.'

'And nobody's been in there since?'

'It's against the rules. Anyway, nobody would go with you.'

'I hate coal mines,' Blair muttered. He held his lamp out to opaque eddies of suspended dust. 'Could you check the map one more time?'

While Battie was distracted with his satchel and sorting through it for the map, Blair stepped into the dark.

The way was surprisingly open for the first steps, and blackness swam around him. But within a few feet the roof lowered steeply and pressed him first into a crouch and then down to all fours, crawling on the floor and pushing the meagre light ahead, he and the lamp invisible from behind. Battie's blinded, furious shouts and curses chased after him ineffectually.

Dust rolled like waves before the lamp. Above the

lamp was a faint nimbus, like a ring around a moon. It was the scope of Blair's sight and knowledge. He held his compass to the light, aiming west.

Once he stopped at the sound of an abandoned timber giving way with a slow tick, like a clock. The roof was settling, but easing down. That was why miners preferred wooden props to iron, for the warning.

Twice he had to correct around stone pillars. At one point he had to squeeze on his stomach through a rockfall, but the other side was clear up to where a whole section of subterranean roof had collapsed and the air was foul enough for the flame of his lamp to start sputtering. He backed away and followed the line of the collapse south. Overhead, the roof was moist and glittered like stars. It was like navigating, he thought, in a world where everything was solid.

He struggled around gritstone slabs that had crept up from the floor. What he wanted to avoid was falling in a pocket and having his lamp go out.

His foot was caught. When he tried to pull free, he heard Battie's voice close behind him. 'You're a miner, Mr Blair.'

'I have been.'

He lay still and let Battie pull himself level. The underlooker had a lamp, though all Blair could see in its light was Battie's eyes.

'The Bishop's man, they say. Wants a tour. Not so unusual. The board of directors comes by. They turn around before we're a hundred yards into a tunnel. A big thank you. Other appointments, wrong clothes. Not you.'

'So I've broken the rules,' Blair said.

'You'll never be allowed back down this pit.'

'So I might as well see.'

Battie was silent for a moment, then hitched himself forward on his elbows. 'Bugger all,' he muttered. 'Follow me.'

For a barrel-chested man, Battie was an eel at sliding over and around rockfalls, rising boulders, holes. Blair scrambled to keep the irons of the soles of Battie's clogs in sight until the underlooker's progress slowed and became uncertain.

'Should be here. It changes all the time, though. I can't—'

Battie stopped. Blair pulled closer and set his lamp next to Battie's. The doubled glow showed a yard-high gap between roof and rubble that was filled by a wall of bricks of the maroon variety used for Wigan houses. About forty bricks in all. The mortaring looked sloppy – hasty might be a better word.

Battie asked, 'Have you ever had to rebrick after an explosion, Mr Blair? You don't know what's lurking on the other side. Could be firedamp, could be afterdamp, could be both. You do it in turns. Hold your breath, lay a brick, back out and let the next man lay his. Jaxon and Smallbone. Each with a rope around his waist.'

'This was where the explosion was?'

'Next to it as far as we could tell.' Battie craned to

look at the roof. 'It will all fall in sometime. Not soon enough for me.'

Like a watermark, the impressed words 'Hannay Brickworks' appeared on a brick, then on a second and a third. Blair caught a rotting odour of firedamp, like marsh gas. As the lamps grew brighter he saw that the mortar between the top bricks was cracked, perhaps from Smallbone's shot or from one days earlier. Battie's face shone, his eyes widening.

In the lamps the flames lengthened to blue columns. The wicks themselves went out, but enough gas had already infiltrated to ignite and float in the gauze like plasma. Illuminated, Blair thought three thoughts. To blow the lamps out would press the fire through the safety gauze and set off the surrounding gas. To wait was useless because as the safety gauze heated the wire itself began to glow like an orange web of fuses. Third, he had worked very hard to kill himself.

As it didn't happen immediately, he remembered that methane was lighter than air. He started scooping out the rubble at the base of the brick wall and pulled out loose rocks and dust to a depth of a foot. He took a lamp by the base and, balancing the flame within, set it down in the hole as straight up and down as he could. Hairs burned off the back of his hands as he did so. Battie understood. Just as carefully, he did the same with the second lamp, so that they stood side by side in the little excavation, two brilliant spears of blue cupped by bristling red wires.

The spears burned steadily for a minute, then pulsed

and shortened reluctantly, from the bottom to the top. Wires dulled from gold to grey. The first flame seemed to swallow itself in a gulp of tarry smoke. The other vanished a second later, leaving Blair and Battie in utter darkness.

'No gentleman would have thought of that,' Battie said.

Blair became aware of Leveret desperately shouting his name; he had forgotten about the estate manager. Miners were calling also. Stiffly, like two men swimming in black shallows, he and Battie followed the sound.

Chapter Six

Hannay Hall was barely visible through greening branches. Between tree roots lay pools of violets. As always, after Blair had been down a pit, the colour of flowers seemed as intense as polished gems. Most miners were the same in this regard, and he sometimes thought it was a mercy for them to come and go in the dark, not to be tantalized by senses whetted by deprivation.

He followed a gravel path along a wall of yew trees and around a lily pond to the conservatory, an oriental pavilion of iron and glass. Entering, in one step he left cool England for a steamy world of palms, mangoes and breadfruit trees. Pink hibiscus unfurled. Spotted orchids hung from plaques of moss. A path edged with aromatic jasmine and orange bloom led to Bishop Hannay, who sat by a garden table on which lay newspapers and a cup of Turkish coffee. In his linen shirt Hannay resembled a viceroy enjoying colonial ease. Around him was subdued activity: gardeners tapping pots to listen for the hollow note of a dry fern, sub-gardeners spraying with water syringes the size of rifles. Above him a forest of date palms lifted glossy fronds as large as fans.

'All you need is a fruit bat,' Blair said.

Hannay gave Blair a long study. 'Leveret says you two were down in the mine. He came back looking like a casualty. I gave you permission to visit the pit, not to lead a chase through it. What on earth were you doing?'

'What you hired me for.'

'I asked you to look for John Maypole.'

'That's what I was doing.'

'In the mine?'

'It never occurred to you?' Blair asked. 'You have a curate who happens to disappear on the same day as seventy-six other men die in your mine and you think there's no connection? Then you happen to hire a mining engineer to look for the missing man? It seems to me you might as well have pointed where to go, so I went.'

At a discreet distance a boy sprayed a rainbow over banana palms. Each bead of water sparkled within a luminous arc of hues.

'And you found Maypole?' Hannay asked.

'No.'

'So he was never down there?'

'I can't say that. Your man Battie is a competent underlooker, but he can't identify everyone who comes down a cage at the start of a shift. Six days a week their faces are black.'

'Those men grew up together. They'd know each other in the dark.'

'But you also have day workers from outside Wigan, men whose real names no one even knows. Day workers arrive from Wales, Ireland, everywhere. They come into Wigan, rent a bed and look for work. Didn't Maypole like to preach at the mine surface?'

'He was fanatical,' Hannay said. 'Worse than a Methodist.'

'Well, he may have taken his preaching underground. When I came back from the mine I read the newspaper accounts again. Twelve of the dead were day workers. Another ten were badly burned. Maybe one of them is Maypole but you won't find out without exhuming the bodies.'

'Blair, all anyone in Wigan expects from life is a proper burial. Miners scrimp so that when they die they'll be drawn in a decent hearse with black plumes and matched black horses. And you suggest that a bishop uproot the recently departed?'

'If Maypole is in one of those graves, the sooner we dig him up the better.'

'There's a pleasant prospect. The last Wigan riot was less than twenty years ago. The miners looted the town and the police locked themselves in the gaol until the militia arrived. And that was over a small matter of wages, not the desecration of graves, thank you.'

'Or—'

'Or what?'

'Or Maypole took off and is happily spending your Bible Fund in New York or New South Wales, in which case I'll never find him. At least you know one thing: he's not in your mine now. That was the point, I suspect. You didn't want to reopen the inquiry into the explosion, but you didn't want your curate discovered dead in a Hannay mine. And the way you set me up by telling poor Leveret to omit obvious information like a disaster that took seventy-six lives on the same day, it all seems like my idea.'

Hannay listened without a change of expression. No, he didn't look like a viceroy, and certainly not like a bishop, Blair thought. Something far more powerful, a Hannay in his dominion. At a barely audible thump, Hannay looked down at his newspaper, where a drop of water had hit and spread; he looked up at panes clouded by condensation.

'Humidity. Maybe we should have a fruit bat.'

'Or a tapir rooting around the pots,' Blair suggested.

'Yes. What fun we could have here if you stayed. Don't you think you should linger in Wigan and search out your family background?'

'No, thanks.'

'As I remember from our campfire conversations, your father was anonymous and your mother died when you were young. Blair is not a Wigan name.'

'It wasn't hers. An American took care of me, so I took his name. I have no idea what hers was.'

'Which makes you a regular curiosity. You have no idea of who or what you are. A blank slate. Sometimes I think that's why you have such an obsession with maps, so that at least you know where you are. Well, that's fun for you, but what about poor Charlotte? She'll want more proof than your speculation.'

'I've done what a mining engineer can do. I want to be paid and I want to go back to Africa. That was our bargain.'

'Our agreement, Blair, was that you would conduct a

diligent search, above ground as well as below. I think you're doing extremely well. If you could just find something more definite.'

'Do you want to dig up the graves?'

'Good Lord, no. We're not ghouls or resurrectionists. Carry on. Quietly. Console Charlotte. Speak to Chubb. I'll let you know when you're done.'

On his way back, Blair saw the same luminous carpet of violets. This time he noticed that the trunks of the beech trees themselves were black from coal soot. On the bark were moths as dark as miners.

Blair went from Hannay Hall to Wigan and John Maypole's room in the alley near Scholes Bridge.

He knew Portuguese traders in Sierra Leone – the worst men in the world – who had plaster saints on bureau altars. These men sold liquor, rifles, still the occasional slave, yet they felt a commonality with saints who, before their enlightenment, had themselves often lived lives of deep venality. After all, saints included murderers, prostitutes, slaves and slave owners. A statuette was a reminder that no one was either perfect or beyond redemption.

A portrait of Christ, however, was a different matter. Who was going to measure up to that? Yet Maypole had risen from his bed every day under the ceaseless scrutiny of the character in this painting. The olives and thorns seen through the window and the wood shavings around His feet were rendered with better than photographic precision. The Saviour Himself looked less like a Jewish carpenter than a blue-eyed, underfed London clerk, but his gaze filled the room with limpid, impossible expectations.

Blair went through the contents of the room in the same order he had with Leveret. The closet with two suits. The range, chest of drawers, wash basin. Bible and books. The simple possessions of a dedicated curate. This time, however, he had murderous resolve. There was nothing like a visit to the Bishop to give him more faith in his own cynicism.

He had accepted Maypole's reputation as pure white, but no man was so good. Everyone had secrets. Saint Francis must have eaten a sparrow or two. Saint Jerome in his hermit's cave probably whiled away the hours with some private vice.

He riffled through *Re-Reading the Bible, Early Italian Poets, Sesame and Lilies, The Utilitarian Christian, The Athletic Christ, Taking the Gospel to Africa*, which sounded like good reading for the high-minded, though wasted on him. Ransacked and examined the backs and undersides of the drawers. Emptied the dry sink of bowl, knife and fork, tin and wooden spoons. Opened the ovens and groped inside. Upended the bed. Peeled back the edge of the linoleum. Turned over the painting and probed the frame with a penknife. Which left nothing but the brick walls.

Not that he was different, Blair admitted. If anyone examined his history, what would they find? He didn't have a history, only a geographic location. His memory wasn't a blank, but his English and American memory was a bare room compared with the richness of his African experience. English coal miners trudged through their tunnels; the black gold miners of Brazil sang in time to the hammering of their drills.

The African climate had a mesmerizing effect on him. The dry season and the wet season had rhythms – one of insects, the other of rain – that held him in thrall. His status as a white among the Ashanti kept emotional attachment at the right pitch, first testing and then acceptance, but never true inclusion, always a distance.

The apparent simplicity of his work – mapping rivers and examining rocks – masked its real intent from the Ashanti. Perhaps this was the lie that impelled him to help them, the knowledge that missionaries weren't the threat. The real threat was his surveys, which would lead to gold sluices, navigable streams and railway grades, and would change the Ashanti more than any Bible.

England, land of bricks. There were whitened Tudor bricks, red Elizabethan bricks, orange Georgian bricks, blue railway bricks and the blackened cottage bricks of Wigan. Maypole had scrubbed his walls, revealing their mottled colours and uneven surface. Blair could trace fault lines stepping from brick to brick, but testing each brick by hand might take all day and night.

He remembered the gardeners in the greenhouse tapping the pots. With Maypole's wooden spoon he started rapping the bricks, row by row, wall by wall. Well-mortared bricks responded with a solid sound, while the looser bricks were almost silent. Though more than a few were dislodgeable, they hid nothing.

Blair worked his way to the last wall until he had to remove the painting and lay it on the bed to continue. Below the nail, a brick in the centre sounded dead. Blair dropped the spoon and, fingers on the corners of the brick, drew it out.

Behind was an open space, a poor man's vault.

There were no coins or notes, no jewels or heirlooms, nothing but a leather notebook with a clasp. He opened the clasp and looked at the frontispiece, which read, in a modest and precise hand, 'This is the property of Revd John Thos. Maypole, D.D. If found, please return to the Parish Church, Wigan, Lancs.'

Blair leafed through the pages. They ran from the previous June to January and each week showed the same virtuous parade. On Mondays: Morning Service, call on parish sick and needy, Evening Service; Tuesdays: Morning Service, Young Men's Bible Study, Evening Service, Temperance League; Wednesdays: Morning Service, afternoon prayer at Home for Women; Thursdays: Morning Service, Bible Study at Ragged School, Evening Mass, Society for Improvement of the Working Class; Fridays: Morning Service, sick calls, workshop prayer, Evening Service; Saturdays: Morning Service, christenings and burials, miners' prayer, rugby, Workers' Evening Social; Sundays: Communion Service, Bible Study, Pensioners' Tea, 'dinner with C'.

Hardly a week of fleshly pleasures, Blair thought.

'Dinner with C' – which Blair took to mean dining with Charlotte Hannay – was the capper.

In the margin of every page were cryptic notations of a different tale: TSM–ld, Bd–2d, Ba–2d. Because Blair had himself come close to starving, the figures were easy to decipher. Tea with sugar and milk one penny, bread two pence, bacon two pence. In the midst of all his good deeds and while engaged to one of the wealthiest women in England, the Reverend John Maypole had been living on drippings and crust.

Maypole had also used the poor man's trick of writing both horizontally and vertically, economically filling every page with a dense, interwoven pattern of words and rendering the act of reading like unravelling a sleeve. Patiently Blair plucked out stern remonstrations like 'Unworthy Thoughts, Vanity, Denial'. The kind of cold shower a curate was expected to turn on himself.

In the first week of December, however, this had changed.

Wed. C. ill and bedridden so instead of "Home" to prayer meeting at the pit, brief wds. on the 'Working Jesus'. My suspicions confirmed.

Thurs. Mass. Ragged Sch., Soc. for Imp. Evening Service. At the meeting Oliver asked if I was well. (*That would be Leveret, Blair thought.*) I lied. Difficult to sustain concentration. In total confusion and shame.

Sun. After Morning Service confronted her. She is

totally wo guilt. Accuses me of hypocrisy! Carried
on, but can't confess, certainly not to Chubb. Spent
the day in Hell.

What happened at the workplace meeting, and which
women he had confronted, Maypole didn't say. On 23
December, however, the journal was clear enough.

Sat. Mass. She has a point. One cannot go among
people as a Roman or a Pharisee.

Sun. Chubb ill and so allowed me to give the
sermon, which was, I believe, the best I've delivered.
On Job 30: 28–30 – 'I went mourning without the
sun . . . My skin is black upon me, and my bones are
burned w heat.' How like the miners' workplace! She
was right.

Christmas! Infant Saviour, snowy day, starry night.
First an innocent pantomime for the miners' children
and then midnight service. Even Chubb cannot dwell
on death at this great event. I feel reborn, at least in
contemplation. A generative turmoil of the soul.

Sat. Mass. Rugby vs Haydock, played in mud and
snow. Bill magnificent as usual. Afterward, I was
accosted by a so-called 'sportsman' called Silcock,
whom I had seen before at the fringe of matches.
That I was a clergyman who enjoyed the sweat of
honest games seemed to insinuate to him that I was
also interested in more sordid entertainments, and he
offered to introduce me to vices worthy of my

interest. I offered to introduce him to the police and he left, shaking his fist and threatening to take my head off 'at the dog collar'.

Mon. Mass. Parish calls. The New Year and Chubb warns again about the 'Sink of Pollution' that I am sinking into. That 'Sink' is despairing mankind!

Thurs. Mass. Ragged Sch. I have been practising in the hole. Alone, only for an hour at a time but agony such as I have never known, and can barely lead the evening service.

Fri Chubb now in a fury over 'insubordination', i.e. my going down to London and speaking to a Parliamentary Comm., where a cabal of reformers and the miners' union are trying to 'save' women from employment at the pits, in consequence of which they would be forced into the mills or prostitution. I knew Earnshaw at Oxford, now an energetic MP. Unfortunately his interest was not matched by his sympathy.

Sun: Chubb felled by another attack of croup and left it to me to read the sermon. Trusting to let the Bible choose, the first passage I saw was Isaiah 45:3, and so I spoke on a divinely inspired message: 'I will give thee the treasures of darkness and hidden riches of secret places, that thou mayest know that I, the Lord, which call thee by thy name, am the God of Israel.'

Whatever the psalm was, the entries for the following days were code and in such an agitated tangle of lines as to be illegible, more the scribblings of a conspirator than a diarist. When Blair turned the page, he was back where he had started, the last week Maypole was seen in Wigan, starting on 15 January.

Mon. The Song of Solomon has never been more apt:

'I am black but comely,
O ye daughters of Jerusalem,
as the tents of Kedar, as the curtains of Solomon.
Look not upon me because I am black,
because the sun hath gazed upon me.'

The Queen of Sheba came to test Solomon, and he answered all her questions and she gave him gold, spices and precious stones. She was African and Solomon had, of course, black concubines.

Tue. 'There is nothing better for a man than that he should eat and drink, and that he should make his soul enjoy good in his labour,' says Solomon. What of the hellfire that Revd Chubb blows in the face of any miner who slakes his thirst with beer?

At one time I was like Chubb. I admired scholarship and single-minded preparation for the world to come. Wigan has taught me differently. Now I would say that foremost are the warmth of family, friendship and the light at the end of the tunnel. All else is vanity!

We have two worlds here. A daylit world of houses

with servants and carriages, shopping for kid gloves and fashionable hats, annuities, and rides across the countryside. And another world led by a tribe that labours underground or in pit yards so obscured by steam and soot that every hour seems like dusk. In circumstances of mortal danger and with the sweat of great physical effort, the second world wins wealth and ease for the first. Yet for the inhabitants of the first world, the second world is literally invisible except for the daily parade of black and exhausted men and women returning through Wigan to the alleys of Scholes. (*Here the writing again became almost impossible to read.*) How to enter that second world? This is the key.

The puffed-up barrister may have his house and parlour. But the miner, in the words of the Psalm, 'was made in secret and curiously wrought in the lowest parts of the earth'. The lady begs the praise of her maid. Instead, the pit girl lifts her eyes to the Lord and sings, 'I will praise thee; for I am fearfully and wonderfully made!' It is a wonderful, secret, most favourite psalm.

Wed. Call on Mary Jaxon, widow. Home for Women. The duties of a curate suddenly seem small and safe. I feel as though I am setting off from a world of comfortable verities and travelling to another, realer land. Tomorrow is the great adventure!

The remaining pages were blank. Inside the back cover Blair found a photograph the size of a playing card. The picture was of a young woman, a flannel shawl angled gypsy-fashion to reveal only half her theatrically smudged face. She wore a man's rough work shirt and trousers. A skirt was rolled and sewn at her waist, and both hands rested on a shovel. Behind her was a crudely painted landscape of hills, shepherds and sheep. Printed on the other side was, 'Hotham's Photographic Studio, Millgate, Wigan'.

The photographer's magnesium flash caught the bold-ness of the subject's eye. In fact, the misshapen clothes accentuated the litheness of her body, the heavy shawl only framed the bright curve of her brow, and although she was half hidden and there was no identification of the subject either by the photographer or Maypole, Blair recognized no Queen of Sheba but Rose Molyneux returning the camera's gaze.

Chapter Seven

Rose and her friend Flo were leaving the house; though they hadn't cleaned the coal dust from their faces, they had exchanged their shawls for velveteen hats. Even as Flo hulked in the door to block Blair's way, her eyes shifted impatiently over his shoulder to the brassy salute of a sweet vendor's bugle on the street outside.

Rose said, 'It's the African explorer.'

'Ah thought he was a photographer last night,' Flo said.

Blair asked, 'May I go with you? Buy you a round?'

The women traded looks, and then as coolly as a queen making plans, Rose said, 'Flo, you go on. I'll talk t'Mr Blair here for a minute and then I'll find you.'

'Tha sure?'

'Go on.' Rose gave her a push.

'Don't be long.' Flo balanced to polish a clog against the back of a trouser leg; she had switched to fancy ones with brass nails. A gay bouquet of silk geraniums festooned her hat. Blair made way for her and as she hauled herself out into the street he thought of a brightly dressed hippo hitting the water.

Rose let Blair in and quickly closed the door. The front room was dark, and the coals in the grate were dim bars of orange.

'Are you afraid of Bill Jaxon seeing you with me?' he asked.

She said, 'You're the one who should be afraid, not me.'

The rhythm of her words was Lancashire but it was obvious that she could leave out dialect when she wanted to, otherwise she would be speaking in ancient 'ah's and 'tha's. So she had some education. Most workers' homes had only a Bible. She had books on the parlour shelves that actually looked read. The coals produced a soft ringing. In spite of them, he shivered.

'You look pot,' Rose said.

Blair said, 'It's been a full day.'

She hung her hat on the rack. Released, her hair was a full Celtic mane. Coal dust gave her face a faint sheen and, like extravagant make-up, made her eyes look even larger. Without a word she turned and went into the kitchen, the same kitchen he had found her in two nights before.

'Should I follow you?' he called.

'Parlour's for company,' she called back.

He hesitated at the kitchen threshold. A kettle was on the stove; in miners' homes there was always a kettle of steeping tea on a hot stove. Rose lit an oil lamp and turned the flame low.

'And what am I?' he asked.

'That's a good question. Peeping Tom? Police? Reverend Maypole's American cousin? The man at the newspaper says he recognized you for an African explorer.' She poured tea and gin into a cup and set it on the table. 'So, Mr Blair, what are you?'

Rose kept the light so low that the air was smoked glass, and a scent of carbon lingered on her. Her eyes stayed on him as if to read his mind; likely she could predict the thoughts of most of the denizens of her small world. Probably she was the most seductive creature in it, and that was disconcerting, too, because it gave her confidence.

Blair supplemented the cup with quinine powder. 'Medicine. I'm not contagious. It's just a reminder to us all not to sleep in tropical swamps.'

'George Battie says you're a miner. Or maybe from the Mines Inspector's Office.'

Blair drained the cup; the fever made him feel as if he had a slight charge of electricity. The last thing he was going to do was let Rose ask the questions. 'You told me that the Reverend Maypole talked to all the pit girls.'

Rose shrugged; her shirt was flannel, as stiff with soot as a snail shell. 'Reverend Maypole was very evangelical,' she said. 'A regular threat t'break into preaching any time. He was always about the pit yard. Men didn't want to come up for fear of an earful about the sanctity of labour. They'd stay down. Not just Hannay Pit, but at all the mines.'

'I meant pit girls, not men.'

'He preached t'pit girls, mill girls, barmaids, shop girls. Fanatical. But you knew your cousin, right? I mean, you rushed here from Africa out of concern.'

'I'm from the California branch of the family.'

'People say you were born in Wigan. You must be

going round t'all your childhood haunts, knocking up relatives.'

'Not yet.'

'What was your mother's name?'

'I think we're getting off the point here.'

'You had a point?'

'When I started. Rose, you're a bit like a cross-current, aren't you? There's no straight sailing with you.'

'Why should there be?'

Blair realized it wasn't going to be quite as simple as he had thought.

Rose said, 'Now you're back, does Wigan seem smaller than you remembered? Or has it become a Garden of Eden?'

'I don't remember. Rose, Wigan is like Pittsburgh plunged into eternal darkness, does that satisfy you? It is not the Garden of Eden, it is either a city sinking into a volcanic pit or the rising outskirts of Hell. Does *that* satisfy you?'

'You're blunt.'

'You asked.'

'Actually, Liverpool is the outskirts of Hell,' she said.

Blair shook his head. 'Rose. Rose Molyneux.' He could see her in Hell, laughing, wearing a garland. 'Let me get back to Maypole.'

'You have preachers in California?'

'Oh, yes. Bible thumpers pour over the sierras. Every fanatic in America ends up in California. You said that Maypole wanted to preach at the mine.'

'Maypole would preach at rugby games, at pigeon races, at pantomimes. You like rugby?'

'From what I understand, it's like watching men run around in the mud chasing a pig, except there's no pig. Is that all Maypole wanted, just to preach to you?'

'He preached t'all the girls. I was just one more dirty face t'him.'

'No, Rose. He had a special interest in you.' He laid the photograph on the table. 'This was in John Maypole's room.'

Rose was so visibly surprised that he wondered whether she would tilt to outrage or confession. Instead, she laughed. 'That stupid picture? Have you ever tried t'pose with a shovel? That card is for sale everywhere in England.'

'Men are strange,' Blair admitted. 'Some men like pictures of undressed women, some men like pictures of women in trousers. The Reverend had only one picture, though, and it's of you.'

'I can't stop someone from having a picture of me. Flo saw a book about you. It called you "Nigger Blair". Why do they call you "Nigger Blair"?'

'The penny-dreadful writer is a low form of life. I can't stop them and there's no controlling them.'

'All the same, they don't come into your house and ask all about your personal life like they're the police when they're not. What are you? I'm still not clear on that. Why should I talk to you?'

'I'm just doing a job for the Bishop.'

'That won't do.'

Blair found himself at a loss. So far he'd learned nothing and this girl, this *pit girl*, was in control.

'I'm not police, not Maypole's cousin, not a Mines Inspector. I'm a mining engineer and I've been to Africa, that's all.'

'Not good enough.' Rose stood. 'Bill and Flo are waiting for me.'

'What do you want to hear?'

'Considering your first visit, you know more about me than I do about you.'

Blair remembered opening his eyes to the sight of her bathing. He conceded the point. 'Such as?' he asked.

'Any reason t'talk.'

'A reason? Maypole may be dead—'

When Rose stood and started toward the parlour, Blair grabbed for her arm. She was too quick and he only caught her fingertips, which were rough and black from sorting coal, though her hand was slender. He let go. 'I have to get back to Africa.'

'Why?'

'I have a daughter there.'

Rose smiled, triumphant. 'That's better,' she said. 'Is the mother white? Or is that why they call you "Nigger Blair"?'

'On the Gold Coast, it's women who pan for gold. They use pans painted black and swirl water around. Usually in riverbeds, the same as anywhere in the world except that they don't have quicksilver to draw the gold. Still, they get an amazing amount. My job was to map the rivers, determine how navigable they were and find out where the gold was washing down from. The trouble is that the Ashanti don't trust the English because they aren't fools. Is this boring you?'

Rose topped his tea with gin and sipped some from her cup, her lips turned red from the hot drink. 'Not yet,' she said.

'The Ashanti capital is Kumasi. Orange-earth country, ferrous soil. Outcroppings of rose quartz. Very pleasant. Huts and guava trees and banana. The king's palace is the one big building. I stayed with Arabs because they're traders. Gold, palm oil, slaves.'

'Slaves for America?' Rose asked.

'Slaves for Africa. That's how anything is harvested, how anything is carried. By slaves. This Arab traded gold and slaves. He had a fifteen-year-old girl who had been captured in the north. She had unusually fine features. They thought she'd bring a good price in Kumasi. Obviously she wasn't being sold to carry bananas. But she cried. She cried all the time. Usually Africans accept their fate. They beat her, but not too much because that would damage the goods. She went on crying, and finally the Arab told me he was giving up and was going to sell her back to the raiders, who could make her their entertainment on the way south. That didn't sound very nice, so I bought her. You're sure this isn't boring you? Maybe you've heard this kind of story before.'

'Not in Wigan,' Rose said.

'I set her free. But how was she going to get home? How was she going to live? Unless I took care of her she'd have to sell herself back into slavery. I hired her as a cook – tried to teach her how to cook, how to clean. There was nothing she could do and I was afraid to leave her on her own in Kumasi, so I married her.'

'Did she ever stop crying?'

'At about that point, yes. I don't know how legal the marriage was. A mixture of Islam, Methodist, Fetish.'

'Was the Arab there? The trader?'

'Oh, yes. Best man. Anyway, she took being a wife very seriously and insisted on my taking it seriously: otherwise she said she'd be ashamed. Other people would know, and that would make her no better than a slave. So she got pregnant.'

'Was it yours?'

'Oh, without a doubt. A brown girl with green eyes? The Wesleyans said I had stained the white man's reputation. They closed down their mission. Maybe if they'd had women they'd still be in Kumasi.'

'You chased the Wesleyans out?'

'In a way.'

'You're better than the Devil.'

How much of this did Rose understand? Blair wondered. Did she know where the Gold Coast was, let alone what an Ashanti looked like? Or seen a nugget of gold in her life? He had started talking about Kumasi only because she was about to go and he didn't know what else to say. Now that he'd started on this disastrous course, on his disastrous life, it was hard to stop.

'I was never an explorer in the Gold Coast. There are Ashanti roads, caravans, toll collectors, unless you insist on cutting your way through the bush. There are lions, but the real dangers are worms, mosquitoes and flies. I was three years with the Ashanti. They were curious and suspicious because they couldn't quite figure out why a man wanted to look at rocks. The Ashanti think you find gold where there are giant baboons or smoke or a particular fern. I was looking for quartz reefs and diorite. Making maps and delivering them to the coast and the mail boat so they could be brought to Liverpool and then to here. But there was a war last year. Also dysentery. In Africa every disease hits like the plague. My wife died. The girl survived.'

'Did you love her, your wife?'

Blair couldn't tell if Rose was serious or not. He did see despite the low light that while each feature of her face was individually perhaps too bold, as a composition they had balance and her eyes were as bright as two candles.

'No,' he said. 'But she become a fact through perseverance.'

'So why did you leave?'

'I had to go to the coast because I had run out of medicine and money. However, the funds that were supposed to be waiting for me at the District Commissioner's office had been diverted to help celebrate the arrival of a distinguished visitor from London who had helped incite the war. I especially needed the money because I had squandered the Bible Fund on my porters, the men who carry my gear. They walked as far as I did, and carrying ninety extra pounds. Anyway, I was found out, which made me worse than a criminal on the Gold Coast.'

'A black sheep?'

'Exactly. So I am here to rescue my fortunes, to please my patron, to carry out this small mission and be reinstated.'

'Where is the little girl?'

'With the Arab.'

'You could have stayed.'

Blair contemplated his cup; at this point, it was less tea than gin. 'When a white man slides in Africa, he slides fast.'

Rose said, 'You were finding gold. You must've been rich. What happened t'that?'

'That went to paying for the girl. The Arab does nothing for free, but he's a relatively honest business-man.' He raised his eyes to hers. 'Now tell me about John Maypole.'

'Th'Reverend didn't know when t'quit. He was at us when we walked t'work and at us when we walked back. T'share our burden, so he said. But he grew into an irritation. Then after work he was at the door.'

'Your door especially,' Blair said.

'I told him I was pairing with Bill Jaxon and it was best for him t'stay away. Bill didn't understand at first, but they got on. Maypole was a boy. That was why he was so moral, he didn't know any better.'

'You saw a lot of him?'

'No. I'm Catholic. I don't attend his church or his do-good clubs.'

'But he sought you out. The last time anyone saw him, the day before the fire, he met you at Scholes Bridge. How far did you walk with him?'

'I was walking home and he followed me.'

'You were talking, too. What about?'

'I might have teased him. He was easy to tease.'

'As he was talking to you, he pulled off his priest's collar. Do you remember why?'

'I don't remember him doing that at all. Ask me about the blast, I remember *that*. The earth jumping. The smoke. Maybe it blew Mr Maypole out of my head.'

'But the last time you saw him, you just went home?'

'I was seeing Bill.'

'Have you ever seen Bill fight? Pretty bloody.'

'Isn't he fooking glorious?'

'Fooking glorious?'

'He is,' Rose said.

He thought of her watching Bill fight, the sound of wooden soles on naked flesh, the gore smeared on skin. How did Bill and Rose celebrate afterwards? An interesting choice of words, 'fooking glorious'. And they talk about savages in Africa, he thought.

'Did Bill Jaxon ever threaten Maypole?'

'No. The Reverend only wanted t'save my soul, he didn't have any interest in the rest of me.'

'That's what you keep telling me.' Blair turned the picture on the table for her to see better. 'But that's not a picture of the soul.'

Rose studied it more closely. 'I extra washed and then

144

I get t'studio and they wipe that muck on my face. I look like an Irish potato farmer.'

'You look ferocious with that shovel. Dangerous.'

'Well, I never touched a hair on Reverend Maypole. I don't know why he had a picture of me.'

'I like the picture. I even like the shovel. It's far more interesting than a parasol.'

'Gentlemen don't cross the street to meet a girl twirling a shovel.'

'I've crossed jungles to meet women with plates in their lips.'

'Kiss any?'

'No.'

'See!'

As coal collapsed it sent a shower of sparks up the chimney. Rose stared at the grate. She was small for moving steel tubs, Blair thought. Her face was as delicate at rest as it was wild when animated. What sort of life did a creature like her look forward to? Gin, babies, beatings from a man like Bill? This was her all-too-brief flowering, and she seemed determined to make the most of it.

'I should be getting on t'Bill and Flo,' she said. 'I don't think he likes you.'

'Bill didn't mind Maypole.'

'Bill likes t'rule the roost. Maypole let him.'

'Well, they played together.'

'You'd have thought the rules of rugby were laid down by Christ t'hear Maypole preach.'

'What did he preach to girls?'

'Chastity and higher love. Every mother had t'be the Virgin Mary. Every girl who sported was Mary Magdalene. I don't think he ever had a real woman.'

'Now, I'm not a gentleman—'

'We all know that.'

'—but I have the feeling that for a man like Maypole, there was nothing more attractive than a woman in need of saving.'

'Maybe.'

'Did he ever call you "Rose of Sharon"?'

'Where did you hear that?' The question was so casual that it stood out like a half-driven nail, a small slip.

'Did he?'

'No.'

'You said he never had a real woman. You don't count his fiancée, Miss Hannay?'

'No.'

'You've met her?'

'I don't meet the Hannays any more than I've been to the moon. But I've seen the moon, I have an opinion about it. Have you met her?'

'Yes.'

'And what do you think?'

'She's thin on charm.'

'Thin on everything, but she has money, clothes, carriages. Going t'see her again?'

'Tomorrow.'

'Sounds like you can't resist her.'

'Compared with you, she's a thorn, an icicle and sour wine.'

Rose watched him silently from across the table. He would have liked to see her face clean. He'd seen her bathe, but what he remembered was her body within a glowing sheath of water. He hoped the image didn't shine from his eyes.

Rose said, 'You have t'go.' She added, 'You're not so sick as you say.'

Later, at his hotel, Blair asked himself if he was crazy. He had hidden the reason for his return to Africa from everyone with a right to know: Bishop Hannay, the Royal Society, even the innocuous Leveret, and now he had blurted everything to a girl who would spread this most irresistible of stories to all the pubs in Wigan, whence it would quickly work its destructive way to Hannay Hall. What a combination he had given her – slavery and racial mixing! The tragedy of the young black wife. The poignancy of a white father and his half-caste issue, set against the barbarism of an African jungle and the rapaciousness of Arabian traders. England itself would go to war to save that child if she were white. What was he thinking? To impress a coquette like Rose Molyneux by telling the truth?

Look at the lies she had told in return. The only treasure John Maypole possessed was a picture of her, and she said he only wanted to save her soul?

147

Consider the house. How was it that while all the other homes on Candle Court were stuffed with families and day lodgers like herrings in a net, Rose and her friend Flo had an entire, well-furnished house to themselves? How did honest girls pay for that?

Her secrecy. She'd made him quit the house alone and said she would wait till he was out of sight to leave herself.

Was it her revenge for his first visit, catching her in her bath? Was it his fever? Though he didn't feel that ill. Sometimes a brain that was warm made inspired choices. The reason he hadn't told her about finding Maypole's journal was that the book was the only advantage he had over her.

He had to laugh, though. If she could do this to him, what had she done to Maypole?

Chapter Eight

'An ounce of quinine?'

'Two ounces,' Blair said.

'You're sure?'

'Quinine is what keeps the British Empire going.'

'Very true, sir.' The chemist added a second weight on one side of the beam scale and tapped more white powder on to the other. 'I could break this into any number of doses wrapped in rice paper for easier swallowing.'

'I drink it with gin. It swallows very easily.'

'I dare say it does.' The chemist poured the quinine into an envelope. He frowned. 'Might I ask if you are doubling up, though?'

'A bit.'

'Have you considered Warburg's Drops? A combination of quinine, opium and sloes. Plums to you, sir. Very smooth going down.'

'A little too sedative.'

'If it is a pick-me-up you're after, then might I suggest arsenic? Clears the head wonderfully. Some of our veterans have had excellent results.'

'I've tried it,' Blair said. Arsenic could be used for almost anything: malaria, melancholy, impotence. 'Sure, I'll take some of that, too.'

'The Bishop is paying, you said?'

'Yes.'

The chemist cleaned the scale on his apron and from the drug run, the long set of drawers behind the dispensary counter, brought out a jar of actinic green to mark it by colour as poison. The shop itself was tinged an underwater hue by cobalt blue bottles arrayed in the window. Dried botanicals scented the air and a coolness emanated from two creamware urns with perforated lids for leeches. The chemist poured out a pyramid of chalky powder. Blair dipped in his finger, licked it and let the bitter taste sting his tongue.

'You appreciate the importance of temperate dosage, sir?'

'Yes.' I'm eating arsenic in front of you, Blair thought. How temperate can a man get?

'A little coca extract for vigour?'

'I might be back for that. Quinine and arsenic for now.'

The chemist filled a second envelope and was giving them both to Blair when the scales swayed and glass stoppers jiggled. Starting at the top shelves and moving to the bottom, brass measures and stone mortars, poison rounds and perfume jars began to tremble as a heavy resonance shook the plate-glass front of the shop. Outside, a mover's steam-powered van lumbered by, a two-storey locomotive with boiler, black stack and rubber wheels that made the cobblestones of the street groan. Behind his counter, the chemist moved quickly from side to side to reach up and keep first one leech urn and then the other from falling.

Blair opened the envelopes, poured lines of arsenic and quinine across his palm and tossed them into his mouth. As the van passed he saw Leveret's carriage outside the hotel. He pocketed the envelopes and left.

'You seem revitalized today,' Leveret said.

'Yes.' And motivated, Blair thought. He had to show progress before any rumours were spread by Rose Molyneux. If she started to entertain friends with lurid reports of his half-African daughter, the news would not take long to reach Wigan's monitors of virtue, and then not even Bishop Hannay could ignore the scandal of miscegenation. What had he told Blair about the name 'Nigger Blair'? 'Discourage it.' The Bishop would drop him without paying another penny.

'Today's Wednesday?' Blair climbed up into the carriage seat.

'Right,' Leveret said.

'Maypole was last seen on a Wednesday. Wednesday afternoons, he always went to the Home for Women. You wanted me to pay a courtesy call on the Reverend Chubb, we'll do that. Then let's talk to the police. There's a Chief Constable Moon we should see.'

'We should at least inform Charlotte that we're going to the Home.'

'We'll surprise her.'

As they drove, Blair became aware that besides being uncomfortable about etiquette, Leveret sat a little stiffly.

'You're all right?'

'Yesterday's tour of the pit took a toll, I'm afraid. My grandfather was a miner. He always had stories, but now I know what he was talking about. Explosions, falling rocks.' He lifted his hat to show off bandages. 'Low roofs.'

'Nice. Gives you panache.'

Beyond the entrance to Hannay Hall was a smaller gate and a meandering path. As they progressed, Blair realized they had entered a private park. Trees – plane, chestnut and beech – became regularly planted, footpaths were edged in purple crocus and the carriage joined a swept avenue at the end of which sat a small fortress. A mock fortress, he saw as they approached. Three storeys of brick with limestone parapets, decorative towers and loopholes filled with stained glass, the whole surrounded not by a moat but by various colours of primroses. Two young women wearing plain, grey dresses with no bustles sat in a garden arbour. A third girl, also in grey, emerged from the door with a swaddled baby.

Leveret said, 'This is the Home for Women. It was a Hannay guest cottage.'

'A cottage?'

'The Prince of Wales stayed here once. Hannays have always done things in the grand style. Wait here.'

Leveret went inside. Through a window opened to the warm air Blair saw young women in grey uniforms around a blackboard scribbled with rows of arithmetic. He was aware of being an interloper of the wrong gender, and he wondered how, even armoured by a clerical collar, Maypole had felt. Through the next open window he saw a class huddled around prosthetic limbs wrapped in bandages. Some of the students had the robust frame and red cheeks of pit girls, others were sallow from life in the mills. They sat stiffly and unnaturally in their uniforms, like girls posing in paper wings for a Christmas pageant.

Leveret returned and followed Blair's gaze. 'Charlotte wants them to have professions. Nursing is one. She insists that they read, too.'

'Poets?'

'Economics and hygiene, mainly.'

'That sounds like Charlotte.'

Leveret spoke hesitantly, as if about to commit an act he knew he would regret. 'She's in the rose garden.'

They went around a side of the Home where a lawn sloped down between rounded masses of rhododendron to the terminus of a boxwood hedge. From the other side rose two sharp, familiar voices.

Earnshaw was saying, 'It is simply my conviction, Miss Hannay, that charity can be overdone and that the best intentions often lead to the worst results. Your father tells me that you have argued for paying pit girls and mill girls *not* to work during the last stage of pregnancy.

What is that if not an invitation to immorality and sloth? Don't you think women, as much as men, should suffer the consequences of their acts?'

'Men don't get pregnant.'

'Then consider the inevitable outcome of educating women above their husbands and above their class.'

'So that they might be dissatisfied by life with a drunken, ignorant lout?'

'Or by life with a perfectly acceptable and sober man.'

'Acceptable to whom? You? *You* marry him. You speak of these women as if they were cows waiting for a bull with four good legs.'

Blair came around the hedge to a garden of pea-gravel paths and rosebushes so bare and severely pruned that they looked like iron rods. Charlotte Hannay and Earnshaw stood at the central, circular bed. Was this the woman 'black and beautiful' who had invaded the mind of John Maypole, the figure who led the curate to suspect that a pit girl in corduroy had more life than a lady? Blair doubted it. Charlotte was an example of how silk could subdue a small woman, her bosom compacted by stays, her legs swimming somewhere within a bustle of purple silk, pruning shears poised in a hideous purple glove. Blair removed his hat. Did her eyebrows arch at the sight of him or were they pinned high on her forehead because her hair was combed so tautly under a sun hat as black as crêpe? He saw a coppery flame at the nape of her neck, but she could have been a novitiate for all he could tell of her hair's colour. At her side was Earnshaw's beard shining in the sunlight. Behind them at a respectful distance was a nurseryman in a smock and straw hat holding a sack of dripping liquid manure.

Leveret said, 'If we could beg your indulgence, Blair has a question or two.'

Earnshaw suggested to Charlotte, 'I can return later. Or would you rather I stayed?'

'Stay, but I can manage visitors by myself,' Charlotte said.

'She could probably geld visitors by herself,' Blair muttered to Leveret.

'What was that?' Earnshaw demanded.

Blair made a vague gesture towards the building. 'I was just saying that this must be a golden opportunity for all these women.'

'If you were a reformer or a pedagogue, Miss Hannay might conceive some interest in your opinion. Since you are a confessed associate of traders in flesh, your opinion could not be less welcome.'

'Wrong,' Charlotte Hannay said. 'Since Mr Blair is such a depraved individual, his opinion is all the more valuable. Blair, speaking from your wide experience, what will more likely keep young women in a condition of financial need and sexual peril, the ability to think as an independent person or, as Mr Earnshaw insists, training for domestic service so that a penniless, ignorant maid can bring a brandy to her master in his bed?'

She was remarkable, Blair had to admit. Like a sparrow chasing men around a garden. 'I've never had a maid,' he said.

'Surely in Africa you had female servants. You must have taken advantage of them.'

Had rumours from Rose already reached her? Blair wondered.

'Sorry, no.'

'But you have a reputation as a man who will try anything at least once, from ostrich eggs to snake meat. Supposedly no man in England knows more about African women than you. Mr Earnshaw, who knows nothing about either African women or English women, says it is unnatural to educate a woman above her station.'

'To make her unfit and unhappy in her station,' Earnshaw explained. 'It's unfair to her and unhealthy for England.'

'Like God, he proposes to create women fit for only one station. Like a politician, he presumes to speak for England when, in fact, he speaks only for those allowed to vote – men.'

Earnshaw said, 'If I might ask, what has this to do with Blair?'

'Blair,' Charlotte asked, 'is there another tribe anywhere that degrades women as thoroughly as the English?'

Earnshaw protested, 'Miss Hannay, think of any Muslim country. Polygamy, women dressed like tents.'

'While in England,' Charlotte said, 'a man is allowed by law to beat his wife, force himself physically on her and dispose of her property as his own. You've been in

Africa, Blair. May the most vicious Muslim legally do that?'

'No.'

Charlotte asked, 'What better witness than a man who has infamously used women of every race? Testimony from the Devil!' She moved on to the next bare stems and asked the nurseryman, 'Joseph, what do we have here?'

'Tea roses, ma'am. Pink Carrière. Dooble-white Vibert. Red General Jacqueminot. Wi' mulch an' gravy.' He indicated the sack he held. 'Cow droppings soaked wi' ground hoof an' horn. It'll be beautiful, ma'am.'

White, red, yellow, pink; it was amazing what future blooms were expected. Yet it was clear to Blair that Charlotte at a young age was already everything she would be, a prickly armature of thorns.

Over her shoulder she asked, 'Oliver, why are you bandaged like a veteran of the Crimea?'

'I went down the pit with Blair yesterday.'

'Be glad you weren't a girl.'

'Miss Hannay, why *do* you dislike me so much?' Blair asked. 'I haven't had a chance to earn so much contempt.'

'Mr Blair, if you saw a slug on a flower petal how long would you let it stay?'

'I've done nothing—'

'You're here. I told you not to come and yet you did. You either have no manners or no ears.'

'Your father—'

'My father threatens to close the Home for Fallen Women at the first sign of scandal, but he is willing to hire you, a man who would embezzle a Bible Fund. The story is well known, along with tales of foul habits and black harems. My father did not choose you for this task because you possess any investigative skills; he chose you because you are the most loathsome individual on not one but two continents. He chose you because the choice of you is in itself an insult to John Maypole and me.'

'Oh.' Blair felt wound in the web of an industrious little spider. 'So where do you think John Maypole is?'

Charlotte dropped the shears into a pocket of her skirt and turned to Earnshaw. 'I might as well get this over with, otherwise we'll have him following us for ever like a tradesman with a cigar.' She faced Blair. 'Where the Reverend John Maypole is at present I have no idea. Until it is proved otherwise, I assume he is well and that he will make the reasons for his absence known when he cares to. In the meantime I will carry out the work we began together in the full anticipation of his return.'

'The last day he was seen was a Wednesday. Meetings for the Home were on Wednesdays. Did you see him there?'

'No. I happened to be ill that day.'

'Miss Hannay has a frail constitution,' Leveret said.

She didn't appear frail to Blair. Small of frame, but not frail. 'When was the last time you saw him?' he asked.

'Sunday Services.'

'Sounds romantic. And not a word since?'

'No.'

'Did he ever talk to you about his visits to the coal mines? To the Hannay Mine?'

'No.'

'The pit girls there?'

'No.'

'Or indicate any frustration that he couldn't extend his ministry down into the mine itself?'

'No.'

'He liked to preach, didn't he? At the drop of a hat?'

'He felt he had a calling,' Charlotte said.

'And wanted to be part of the working class, at least long enough to preach. Did he ever mention a miner named Bill Jaxon?'

'No.'

'Did he have any history of melancholia?'

'No.'

'Did he like to roam the countryside? Swim in the canal? Take lonely walks on slag heaps or high cliffs?'

'No. His only pastime was rugby, and he did that to reach the men.'

'But you didn't spend much time with him outside meetings, did you? You had a spiritual relationship.'

'I hope so.'

'So he could have a tattoo of the Royal Navy and you wouldn't know.'

'No, no more than you would know whether any of the women you debauched had a brain or a soul,' Charlotte answered passionately, toe to toe. Put a pair of clogs on her and she would be a dangerous creature,

Blair thought. Earnshaw and Leveret faded from his conscious view.

'Was Maypole intelligent, would you say?'

'Intelligent and sensitive.'

'So he knew he would break your heart if he disappeared and didn't even drop a line?'

'He knew I would understand whatever he did.'

'Lucky man. That's the kind of woman *I've* always needed.'

'Stop it,' Earnshaw said from somewhere, but Blair felt an accelerating rhythm of mutual loathing and knew Charlotte Hannay felt it also, like a crescendo heard by two.

'Did he mention wealthy relatives who might be old and sick?' he asked.

'No.'

'Pending lawsuits?'

'No.'

'Spiritual crises?'

'Not John.'

'Anything pending but your wedding?'

'No.'

'Mail is delivered twice a day. I understand that lovers write to each other every post. Did you keep his letters?'

'If I did, I'd rather put them in the hands of a leper than deliver them to you.'

'No sense he felt he might have been missing out on simple pleasures?'

'Simple as in animal? No, that particular depth is your level, Mr Blair.'

'I meant simple as in human.'

'I don't know what you mean.'

'Human weakness. This is the Home for Fallen Women, Miss Hannay, so there must be some humans here. Maybe Maypole met one.'

Charlotte stooped to snip a long stem with her shears. With more force and speed than he expected, she stood and whipped the stem across Blair's face, which immediately burned.

'You will leave now,' Charlotte said. 'I will have dogs here next time and I will have them set on you if you ever dare return.'

'I personally will set on you if you return,' Earnshaw said.

Blair felt blood wet his cheek. He plopped his hat back on.

'Well, regretfully, I must be going. Thank you for all your help. My best to your father.' As he walked away he paused by the nurseryman. 'Knew a man in the Gold Coast raised roses. Retired sergeant major. Roses big as a platter. Used guano. Guano's the key.'

Leveret retreated in reverse, leaving excuses. 'I had no idea, no idea. So sorry.'

As they went around the hedge, Blair used a handkerchief to mop his face and motioned Leveret to stop and be silent. They heard a furious Charlotte Hannay on the other side.

'And you, Mr Earnshaw, do you have any idea how obnoxious it is to offer your protection before it's asked?'

'I was merely supporting you.'

'When I'm so weak that I need support I will let you know.'

Smiling through the blood, Blair walked up the lawn.

'Now you've set *them* to arguing,' Leveret said.

'It doesn't matter how much people like that argue, they're moralists. They were made for each other.'

At the river, Blair washed his face. The clouds were high and edged sideways by the sun, and although the cuts on his face burned, he felt strangely braced.

Leveret was distressed. 'You can't speak to people like Charlotte like that. That was a terrible scene. The language was unforgivable, Blair. You goaded her.'

Blair picked out a thorn. In his reflection on the water's surface he saw three gouges, otherwise only scratches, and felt a hot sense of satisfaction.

'I goaded her? That's like accusing somebody of goading an asp.'

'You were cruel. What were you getting at with insinuations about John being human?'

Blair dried himself on his jacket and put a dab of arsenic in his palm. 'What we are, Leveret, is a sum of our sins. That's what makes us human instead of saints. A perfectly flat surface has no character. Allow some cracks, some flaws and shortcomings, and then you have contrast. It's that contrast with impossible perfection that makes our character.'

'You have character?' Leveret asked.

'Tons.' Blair put his head back and threw the powder into his mouth. 'It turns out that Maypole might have, too, in a demented, religious sort of way.'

'Questions like that can ruin a man's reputation.'

'I'm not interested in his reputation. I'm more of a geologist, I look for feet of clay. So I find it interesting that a penniless curate managed to connect to a girl with so much money.'

'Everything in Wigan is connected to the Hannays. Half the people work for the Hannays. Besides the Hannay mines, the Hannay Iron Works manufacture boilers, iron plate and locomotives. There are the Hannay Cotton Mills and Hannay Brick Works. They build their own chimneys to burn their own coal to spin their own yarn on a quarter of a million spindles. I haven't travelled the world like you, but I would venture to say that the Hannays are one of the most efficient industrial complexes anywhere.'

'And making a fortune.'

'And providing employment. Well-paid employment compared to average wages. But there's more to the Hannays than commerce. The family supports the Church, which means paying for clergy and organs and pews. The Ragged Schools for poor children. Evening Schools for men. Dispensary for the Sick. The Explosion Fund, the Widows and Orphans Fund, the Clothing Society were all started by Bishop Hannay himself. Without the Hannays there would be less work in Wigan and very little charity. Everyone is connected to the Hannays, including you. Or did you forget?'

'The Bishop doesn't let me forget.'

'Charlotte has probably gone to him already and told him about our disastrous visit. He'll have to discharge you now.'

'I won't spend any more delightful days with the sanctimonious Miss Hannay? Bring my money and I'll be gone.'

'You don't understand her situation.'

'I understand that she is a rich young woman whose hobbyhorse is a charity for poor girls she dresses up in Quaker grey. She probably knows as much about real life in Wigan as she does about the moon. It doesn't matter because she'll be the richest spoiled brat in England when her father dies.'

'Not quite.'

The way Leveret said it made Blair pause.

'You just described the Hannay empire.'

'Yes, but Bishop Hannay is also Lord Hannay. When he dies, the estate will pass with the title. A woman cannot inherit the title. Everything – land and properties – will go to the nearest male heir, her cousin, Lord Rowland, who will become the next Lord Hannay. Charlotte will be well settled, of course.'

'You mean rich.'

'Yes, but whoever she marries, John Maypole or anyone else, would have full disposition of whatever she inherits.'

Blair watched bees buzz by with golden satchels of pollen. Which explained Earnshaw, he thought, though he hovered by Charlotte Hannay more like a beetle than a bee.

The visit of the Municipal Committee for Health and Sanitation to Albert Court, a U of two-storey red-brick housing, was a form of war. All the residents stood in the middle of the courtyard as disinfectors dressed in white smocks and caps rolled in caissons bearing bright pumps and canisters of polished brass. At every third or fourth house, a disinfector manned the pump while his partner unreeled the hose, dashed into the front door and sprayed a poisonous mist of strychnine and ammonia. The stench was choking, but the Reverend Chubb, in command, a red committee sash over his cassock, issued directions like a general oblivious to the smoke of battle. The residents were women and children; Blair noticed that a number cradled bird cages. Among the committee matrons in official sashes he recognized Mrs Smallbone, her skirt of black bombazine adding a menacing bounce to every stride. She dug into a boy's head with a comb and signalled to two other committee members, who bore down on the boy with water and carbolic soap. Chubb acknowledged the arrival of Leveret and Blair in the courtyard with no more than a flicker of his concentration.

Blair remembered having his own head clipped and washed, hands clamping his neck to hold him still as if he were a dog. It was the smell of the soap that did it.

'Medicine doesn't taste good,' Chubb said.

'It wouldn't be medicine if it did, would it?' Blair asked. 'Shouldn't there be a medical officer in charge?'

'He's ill. Fumigation can't wait. If these people insist on crowding five in a bed with lice-ridden bedclothes, not even bothering to use the sanitary facilities the landlord provides, creating a miasma from which spread cholera, typhus and smallpox, then community measures are called for. A sink of pestilence affects us all. Think of the mince rats.'

'Mince rats?' Blair didn't want to think about them.

'Some of the houses will have to be sealed and left with sulphur candles.'

'Where do the people from those houses go?'

Chubb marched ahead. 'The children should all be in school, where they can be properly inspected.'

Certainly some of the residents had crusted bare feet and ragged clothes, just as some houses had split doors and broken panes. Most, however, looked merely angry, rousted from homes that showed lace curtains in the windows and thresholds that must have been zealously scrubbed with stone to be clean at all. Chubb seemed to send in the fumigators on an arbitrary basis.

'How does he know which houses to attack?' Blair asked Leveret.

Leveret whispered, 'Simple. He wouldn't dare break into a miner's house. The miners would break into the town hall. In defence of the people here, there are only two privies for two hundred occupants.'

Chubb returned. 'Sufficient, if there is social discipline. Look at their clothes. Rags, probably infested. If it were up to me, we'd burn them.'

'Too bad you can't have an *auto da fé*,' Blair said.

'That's a Papist practice. There has always been an obstinate core of them here. The Hannay family, as the Bishop told you, was once, long ago, Roman. And of course we have Irish among the miners – Irish and pigs.'

'They go together?'

'Filth and immorality go hand in hand. Squalor breeds disease. No doubt, Mr Blair, in your travels to the sinkholes of the world you have noticed that smell itself is pestilential. I know that in time these people will come to appreciate the effort we make on their behalf.'

'Maypole used to do this?'

'He was on the Committee for a time.'

The cart rolled forward, leaving in the air an acrid taste that coated the lips.

'Reverend, you're a born missionary. You mean Maypole quit.'

'He was disobedient. He was young. Rather than stamp out pollution, he sheltered it.'

'You mean, the Home for Women?'

'Home for Women Who Have Fallen for the First Time,' Chubb corrected him. 'As if in Wigan there is such a thing as women who have fallen *only* for the first time. It is a dangerous thing for even the most hardened man to save a fallen woman. A young curate's interest in such a pursuit has to be suspect. Philanthropy has masked weakness more than once. It is not the woman who is saved but the saviour who goes under.'

'Are you thinking of any particular woman?'

'I don't know any women that *particular*. I washed my hands of Maypole and his "Magdalenes".'

Blair walked to stay abreast of Chubb and the disinfection carts. 'Otherwise he was satisfactory? He conducted services, did sick calls, that sort of thing?'

'Yes.'

'He seemed to have little money.'

'Men do not join the Church to make money. It is not a trade.'

'He was broke.'

'He didn't yet have a living, a post as a vicar and the remuneration that comes with it. He was of good family, I was given to understand, but his parents died when he was young, leaving him little. What did it matter? He was about to marry far above his station.'

'Did he give you any indication that he was considering some sort of adventure, that he might leave?'

'Leave? When he was engaged to the Bishop's daughter?'

'He seemed happy?'

'Why shouldn't he be? As soon as they married it was preordained that he would rise to the highest ranks of the Church.'

'What about his preaching at the mines? Do you know anything about that?'

'I warned him that open-air sort of thing was for Wesleyans. Unfortunately Maypole had low-church leanings. Like his playing at rugby. What I needed was a man to serve Communion, visit the sick, take food to the deserving poor. That is enough work for two.'

'What do you think happened to him?'

'I don't know.'

'Did you ask the police?'

'We don't want to overly bother the police. It's not a scandal unless we make it one. If Chief Constable Moon hears anything, he'll tell us.'

'Tell me, do you still want to find Maypole?'

'I don't know that I care. Saint Maypole, here and gone. I serve at the Bishop's pleasure, of course. We all do. But tell him when you see him that I've waited long enough. I need another curate.'

The cart rolled ahead, sunlight smeared over brass, and Chubb hurried to keep pace.

Chief Constable Moon had an indentation in the middle of his forehead. 'Brick.' He pulled a sleeve back from a white scar that ran the length of a meaty forearm. 'Shovel.' He lifted a trouser leg. His shin was cross-hatched with scar tissue and punched in as if shot. 'Clogs. Enough to say that today when there's a set-to with miners we wear stiff leather leggings. And what happened to you?' He peered at the scratches on Blair's face.

'A rose.'

'Oh, well, we can't report that, sir.'

'No.'

Moon's uniform was blue, embroidered in silver at

the collar and cuffs, and he had mobile features that suggested he enjoyed authority dispensed with nudges and winks. Blair himself enjoyed the luckless state of mind of a man with nothing to lose. Arsenic coursed through his veins like a secondary fever. Leveret had left to plead Blair's case to the Bishop. By now Charlotte Hannay must have gone to her father and demanded his dismissal. Moans issued from holding cells of white-washed stone and straw bedding across the corridor, but the Constable's office offered the comfort of a tile firegrate, a desk of mahogany, deep chairs of Russian leather, gas lamps that illuminated maps of the worlds of Lancashire and Wigan. There was the prosperity of a new business to Moon's office.

'Nice, isn't it? The old station and town hall were damaged by the miners when we had some troubles a few years back. The Hannays, of course, were major contributors to the improvements.' Moon allowed him-self a pause. 'We want to set the Bishop's mind at ease. It's just a little late in the day. What with the Hannay explosion, the rescue, identifying bodies, accident inquiry, funerals, no one mentioned Maypole to us until long after. Well, I think they wanted to be quiet about it, don't you? Young curate engaged to the Bishop's daugh-ter. Best solved privately. Never been a formal complaint, not in the log.'

'But you did ask about Maypole?'

'Using discretion. At railways, in case Maypole bought a ticket. Walked the ditches and canals. Sad business, but you never know. Of course it's coal country. Old shafts everywhere. If a man walks in the dark and doesn't know where to stop, then he might never be found.'

'Maypole had trouble with a man named Silcock. Is that name familiar to you?'

'An expert with a cosh. Preys on hotel guests, gentlemen who've had too much to drink. Has a fair, square-rigged look. That's his guise.'

'Like Maypole?'

'Now that you mention it, in a general fashion. Anyway, we were on top of that. We ran him out of Wigan the same day we saw him bother the Reverend.'

'You arrested him?'

'No, but we put the pressure on. Had to warn him twice, but he disappeared.'

'Have you located Silcock since then?'

'No.'

'Don't you think you should have?'

'Someone else's problem.' Moon shuffled his jaw back and forth. 'Mr Leveret couldn't be with you?'

'He went to Hannay Hall to report on the day's progress. Chief Constable, do you recall seeing Maypole the day before the explosion?'

'You have so many questions you could be a regular detective. No.'

'When was the last time you talked to him?'

'The week before. He was always bringing an excuse for a drunken miner. I understood. Forgiveness is a young curate's job, after all.'

Moon made it sound like the drooling stage of a baby; Blair felt a dislike for the man.

'Do you remember which miner it was that week?'

'It was Bill Jaxon.'

'Jaxon and Maypole played on the same rugby team, didn't they?'

'Ah, Bill's a famous boy. He gets in scrapes. Miners do. That's why they're so good at rugby, what does a split nose mean to them? They say if you want a good rugby team in Lancashire, just shout down a shaft.'

'What had Bill done to attract the attention of the law?'

'He broke another man's head for squeezing the wrong girl. I couldn't blame Bill myself. You see, we get travellers who don't know Wigan ways, who get confused.'

'By what?'

'Pit girls.'

'How so?'

Moon had his front teeth, but not the side ones, which made his smile wet and gummy. 'Well, they do what they want, don't they? Drink like men, work like men, live like men. And draw a certain sort of gentleman who travels up here by train to see an Amazon in trousers. That sort of gentleman thinks he can take liberties, and then finds himself squaring up to someone like Bill.'

'Who was the Amazon in Bill's case?'

'A girl named Molyneux.'

'Rose?'

'The same. A pit girl, attractive in a sluttish way. A fairly new arrival in Wigan.' Moon appeared taken aback. 'However do you know her?'

'She was on the list you supplied Leveret of the last people to see Maypole.'

'That's right. I never liked it that the Reverend Maypole wasted time with her. I warned him about over-socializing with miners, letting them drag him down to their level.'

'What level is that?'

'They're good folk but they're primitive. A fact, sir.' Moon shifted his attention to Blair's cheek. 'Know what miners use to clean wounds? Coal dust. So they end up tattooed like savages. You don't want to look like them.'

From the police station Blair walked so that Leveret would have time to bring word of his dismissal to the hotel.

The night clerk poked into message boxes. 'Sorry, sir, nothing for you.'

'There has to be.' Blair couldn't believe that the Bishop would not at least warn him after Leveret's report or Charlotte Hannay's complaint. 'Look again.'

The clerk ducked under the desk. 'There *is* something, sir.' He brought out a heavy, unshapely package wrapped in brown paper and string. Written on the paper in a thick pencil was, 'For Mr Blair. From a friend.'

'Do you know who brought this?'

'No, it was here when I came on. A gift, I suppose. Seems to be in two pieces.'

The clerk waited expectantly for Blair to open the package. Instead he carried it up to his room, set the parcel on the sitting-room table, lit the lamps and allowed himself a quinine and gin. He told himself he had done his best, at least as much as the police had done for the saintly John Maypole. Tomorrow he would be in Liverpool booking passage, even steerage, to escape. In a year his three nights in Wigan would seem a passing dream.

Reinforced with another gin, Blair loosened the string of the package and unwrapped the contents, which proved to be a pair of shoes. Not shoes. Clogs with stout leather uppers attached by brass nails to solid ash soles edged on the underside by horseshoe irons. Shamrocks were stitched into the leather and extra brass heads studded the toes. They were the clogs that Bill Jaxon had won from the Irishman.

Out of curiosity, Blair sat down and pulled off his boots. He slipped on the clogs, closed the clasps and stood. Because wood didn't bend, his feet rocked within, lifting at the heels. The sound of the clogs on the floor when he stepped was like rolling balls. But they fitted.

Chapter Nine

When Blair arrived at the Hannay yard, miners on the day shift were already below, but Battie, the underlooker, had come up in the cage to supervise the lowering of a pony, a mare with a milk-white mane and tail. The pony was in blinkers and trailed a harness with two extra-long cinches. While Battie attached a chain and hook to the bottom of the cage, a stableman with hay lured the little horse close to the platform.

The underlooker noticed Blair. 'Are you planning to take another tour of the pit? We won't be crawling on our hands and knees again, will we?'

'No.' Blair dropped his pack from his shoulder to the ground.

Battie finished hooking the chain and stepped back. He wore a dusting of carbon powder. He shielded his eyes from the sun to peer at Blair's face. 'You've been crawling through brambles?'

'I met a human bramble.'

'Mr Leveret with you? I don't see a carriage.'

'I walked out on my own.'

'Carrying your pack all the way? You're not still asking about the Reverend Maypole?'

'Still,' Blair said, although he had left a note at the hotel desk saying where he was headed and hoped to see

Leveret roll into the pit yard at any moment with word that the Bishop had fired him. 'Did Maypole come here often?'

'Yes. He was a preacher of opportunity, very good at drawing parallels from the Bible – workers in a vineyard and men in a pit, that sort of thing. I feel bad now.'

'Why?'

'I'm afraid I told him that a pit yard was not a church. You can't preach around rolling wagons and tubs. He was welcome to visit as a friend of the Hannays, but not as a minister. That was a week before the explosion. I should have kept my mouth shut.'

The cage rose, trailing its extra hook below while workmen laid planks across the shaft. The stableman was wiry as a boy, with a beaked nose and a fierce moustache. He walked the pony on to the planks, forced her to her knees, and then to her side. He folded her front legs into the forward cinch and strapped them tight, then did the same with a second cinch around the rear legs so that only her four hoofs were free. He yanked the cinches to test their tension before he connected a ring in the harness to the hook hanging from the cage. At his shout, the cage rose and lifted the pony to a sitting position and then over the hole. The workmen pulled the planks aside, opening the shaft.

'Pretty little horse,' Blair said.

Battie nodded. 'And expensive. I like Welsh ponies, but they're in short supply. This one is all the way from Iceland.'

'White as the proverbial snow.'

'Well, the poor girl won't be white for long.'

The pony hung, trussed, between cage and shaft. Though the stableman tucked hay under her nose and held her reins, she rolled her eyes. A shadow of horse, cage and tower stretched across the yard.

'It's her first time. She'll quiet,' the stableman called. 'We don't want her bucking when we send her down pit.'

'Some of the ponies die their first month down,' Battie told Blair. 'Maybe lack of light or air or proper mucking. A mystery. You forgot something?'

Blair stepped on to the platform. 'No, it was just something you said the other day. You showed me where you found the victims of the explosion, the ones who suffocated and the ones who were blown up. You said you'd "thought about it a thousand times".'

'Anyone would, a fire like that.'

'It was the word "thought". As if there was something you were trying to figure out, going over it in your mind. You didn't say "remembered", you said "thought".'

'I don't see the difference,' Battie said.

'There may not be.'

'That's why you came out here?'

'One reason. Was there something you were thinking about?' Blair asked.

The pony didn't calm. Instead, she began to thrash until the cage above her swung against the guide wires like a jointed pendulum. Loose hay spilled, straws of gold sucked by the downdraft into the shaft. Once a pony went down a pit it wouldn't come up again except once a year for a week, until it was finally lame and hauled up for the knacker's cart. In spite of her reins and all the stableman's pulling, she twisted her head to bite the cinch. The cage ticked the tower's wooden props.

'I think about everything that goes on below. That's what an underlooker does,' Battie said.

'I'm not talking about accusations, but maybe something that didn't make sense.'

'Mr Blair, perhaps you haven't noticed, but a dark tunnel deep in the earth is not where you find sensible men.'

The cinch broke. As the pony kicked more freely, she gyrated, which caused her to kick more violently. The stableman ducked her hoofs and tried to pull her back over the platform by her reins so that if she broke or reared out of the bottom cinch she wouldn't pour herself into the open shaft.

'Pull her clear,' Battie shouted.

But the weight of the pony started to drag the stableman towards the shaft. The irons of his clogs slipped across the platform. Battie grabbed him by the waist. Blair removed his jacket, threw it over the pony's head and then held on to Battie.

The three men clung to the reins as the pony thrashed and tried to shake the jacket off. Slowly the kicking stopped. The pony spun but ever more idly, sedated by blindness. Battie took the reins while the stableman fetched a hood, which he expertly slipped over the pony's head even as he snatched Blair's jacket off. Blair took it and staggered against a prop. Activity in the pit yard had ceased around the spectacle. Blair's heart kicked. He was as covered in the pony's lather as if he had rolled in foam.

The stableman was furious. 'Tha' shouldna' done that. Think Ah don't know me job?'

'Sorry,' Blair said.

'You made him look a fool,' Battie said. 'He'd prefer to die.'

More stablemen arrived to pull the pony to the platform and truss her with a new cinch. Across the yard, men again began to weigh tubs, drivers to back their engines into wagons, blacksmiths to beat iron. Battie shouted to the winding house. A tremor ran the length of the cable as it rose, but the pony in her hood was pacified. As the cable reversed and unreeled, she dropped from sight down into the hole, followed by the cage, which stopped momentarily at platform level for Battie to get on.

The underlooker hit the cage bell and said, 'The numbers agree, Mr Blair. Seventy-six lamps, seventy-six men. That's what matters.'

Blair was still trying to get his breath. 'It's hardly a mystery.'

'What?' Battie called back.

'Why the ponies die. Fear.'

An unhappy smile stole on to Battie's face. Then he disappeared under the top of the cage as it descended, gathering speed but moving smoothly, anchored by the pony hanging underneath.

Blair went over to the sorting shed. A locomotive was

shifting a train of loaded wagons away from the siding. Connected only by chains, the wagons slapped together as they transmitted the stop-and-go of the engine. Pit girls walked alongside, collecting larger pieces of coal that fell.

Over the shed itself a cloud of coal dust glittered in the sun. Blair didn't see Rose Molyneux at the siding tippler or among the women picking rocks and dirt from the belt or tending the coal as it cascaded through the grates. The first time he had seen them at work had been in the dark. In daylight their uniforms – work shirts and trousers, head covering of flannel shawls and rolled-up skirts – were neither male nor female but fashion for hermaphroditic drudges. He did recognize the large form of Rose's friend Flo as she disengaged from other women at the bottom of the chute and came his way.

'It's t'gentleman caller,' she said and nodded towards the tower. 'Ah saw thi ride t'carousel.'

Blair swung the pack off his shoulder. 'I have something for Rose. Is she here?'

'She is, but she got hurt. Not bad. She'll be back later, Ah can't say when.' Flo put out a black hand. 'Give it t'me, Ah'll pass it on.'

'I want to give this to Rose myself. I have to talk to her.'

'Well, Ah can't say when she'll be back.'

'When do you quit work? I'll talk to her then.'

'Five. But it wouldn't do for her t'talk then, not when t'men are up.'

'Then I'll meet her in town.'

'No. T'best place is Canary Wood. It's t'trees closest t'pit. She'll meet thi there after work.'

'I'll look for her in Wigan if she's not there.'

'Rose will be there.'

Flo seemed pleased with the negotiation. Also, suddenly afraid to trade more words. 'I mun t'work,' she said.

'If you mun you mun.'

'Aye.'

She edged towards the coal chute. She was too large to slip away on light feet, though, and no shawl or black smudges could hide the satisfaction in her backward glance.

Blair had walked halfway back to Wigan when he came to a halt. Most of the road was by fields black with fresh-turned earth. His plan was to find the widow, Mrs Jaxon; according to Maypole's journal, he called on her the day he disappeared. Other people saw him later, but maybe he had said something to the woman.

Yet Blair found that he had stopped walking, as if the power to do so had left his legs. Rather than the dark fields, he saw the pony thrashing on the chain. Fear welled up like the dark of the shaft, but it wasn't fear of falling. Something worse the way the mare whipped its head back and forth as it struggled to escape. The sweat of its terror covered him still.

He found himself on the ground on his knees. It wasn't malaria. The horse was gone, replaced by a memory of a paddle steamer pushing between black seas and a grey sky. The hoarse sound of the waves vied with the uneven churning of side wheels as the ship made way, wallowed, made way. The captain held the Bible flat to read in a wind that was strong enough to lift beards. Six sailors shouldered a plank on which lay a body wrapped in a muslin sheet. They lifted the plank and the body shot out like a wingless angel through the air. The little boy pulled himself up on the railing to watch.

Above the water the descent stopped. The plank had snagged the sheet and it had unwound in a fluttering white arc down to the knot that secured the body within the first turn of the cloth. As the ship plodded forward, the body sank into a wave, reappeared and swung into the side of the ship, sank into a wave, reappeared again. Because she was weighted with lead he heard her hit the ship.

A sailor cut through the sheet. Released, it immediately trailed behind and, dropping, whipped as if escaping grip after grip. The body, covered by a foamy wave, was quickly out of sight, although he thought he saw the sheet on the water for a minute more. Blair, a gold miner whom the boy and his mother had met on deck, patted him on the head and said, 'These things happen.' It was young Blair's experience as he grew that things like that happened all the time.

Now he bent over and sobbed. The goddamn pony, he said to himself. The sheet unwinding from the plank, his jacket whipping back and forth. The cage slamming against the guide wires, her hitting the side of the ship. He couldn't remember the last time he had cried, except that now memory was born kicking painfully from the inside out. The fucking pony.

'Are you all right?'

Blair raised his head. A blurry Leveret looked down from a carriage that Blair hadn't heard come.

'Sure.'

'You seem upset.'

'Leveret, you are one sharp observer.' Blair rolled on to his back; he wouldn't have been surprised if his eyes flowed out. His ribs were racked as if they weren't used to this form of exercise. He'd been walking along, remembered that burial at sea and suddenly turned into a fountain.

'Can I help you up?'

'If you want to help, tell me that I've been dismissed, that the Hannay family no longer needs my services.'

'No, the Bishop says he is very satisfied with your work. He wants you to continue just the way you are.'

Blair sat up. 'What about Charlotte Hannay? He wants me to stay away from her?'

'The opposite. The Bishop wants you to talk to her again.'

'You told him what happened?'

'He says you should turn the other cheek.' When Blair laughed through his wet face, Leveret added, 'However, the Bishop says that if you don't possess sufficient sympathy to do that, you should feel free to defend yourself from attack.'

'The Bishop said that? He knows that his daughter despises the sight of me?'

'I told him what happened. Charlotte and Earnshaw had already reported to him in detail. The unpleasantness of the episode in the garden has been thoroughly described.'

The episode in the garden! What an English way to describe anything from murder to a fart, Blair thought. He pulled himself to his feet. 'Hannay is mad,' he said.

'The Bishop says that the Reverend Maypole's disappearance is too urgent and important a matter for any personal considerations to interfere. He seems to be more convinced than ever that you are the right man for the job. He said there may be a bonus for you.'

Disgustedly Blair threw his pack on to the carriage and climbed up to the seat next to Leveret. 'I don't want a bonus and I have no idea how to do "the job". Your Chief Constable Moon thinks Maypole will never be found. He's probably right.'

Leveret sniffed. 'Have you been riding? Were you thrown by a horse?'

Blair thought the question over. 'Close.'

He changed clothes at the hotel. He felt strangely invigorated and cleansed. Colours were rawer, fresher, more vibrant to his eyes. He bought a magnifying glass at a stationer's for reading Maypole's journal. He even had an appetite and talked Leveret into visiting a Scholes eating house for rabbit pie and pickled eel.

184

The air inside was a cloud of pipe smoke so sharp it made the nose wince. Crutches and a cripple's cart parked by tables where old men in caps and stained scarves played games of dominoes between arguments, mixed with younger workers taking the day off. They ate their pies with clasp knives, an etiquette that made Leveret stiff and fastidious. Blair was used to Arabs and Africans eating with their hands. He also had a weakness for this sort of tableau, the timeless scene of luckless men gambling, the same here as in Accra or Sacramento. With the games came two rhythmic choruses, the pop of men drawing on their clay pipes, the slap of ivory tiles.

The beer was dark and sent an almost visible ripple through Leveret. He still wore stamps of plaster and appeared slightly crimped, as if he had been posted. He whispered, 'I haven't been to one of these places since I used to sneak in with Charlotte.'

'She used to come here?'

'When we were children. We both loved eel pie.'

'Charlotte Hannay? I can't see that.'

'You don't know Charlotte.'

'A grim little mollusc.'

'No. She . . . at least she used to be the opposite.'

'A fish?'

'Adventuresome, full of life.'

'Now she's full of opinions. Isn't she a bit young to be so much smarter than everyone else?'

'She's educated.'

'What does that mean?'

'The classics, science, French, Latin, a little Greek—'

'I get the idea. Does she know anything about the miners and pit girls?'

'It's a Hannay tradition to slip into town. When he was young, the Bishop himself was always in the working part of Wigan. Boys used to leap over old shafts. It was a dare, you know? Some wouldn't jump at all. Hannay was the champion.'

'Well, they were his shafts, weren't they? Maybe that should be a requirement for ownership, jumping over an open shaft. Did Maypole come here?'

'For a time. He wanted to eat like the miners and suffer with them. But he told me that he discovered that miners actually eat quite well. Roast beef, mutton, ham, and of course great quantities of beer. John couldn't afford it and he went back to living like a curate.'

'Most people went to his church?'

'No. I don't know if you noticed, but in the newspaper office there was a book called *Lancashire Catholics: Obstinate Souls*. That's because Lancashire has remained the most Catholic county in spite of the Reformation. We're also the most Methodist. We're the most at whatever we are. In the Middle Ages Wigan was a refuge for runaway slaves. In the Civil War we were Royalist. Not like Southerners.'

'Southerners?'

'London people. Southerners are convenient people, they do whatever is convenient for them. Mining is not a convenient sort of occupation.'

'Did Maypole ever wear clogs?'

'For rugby, yes, because the other men did.'

'I didn't see them in his room. Do you ever wear clogs?'

'Good Lord, no.'

'Did you as a kid?'

'My father would never let me. Remember, he was the estate manager before me. Being the son of a miner, it was a great step up for him, starting as a clerk, rising to assistant manager, then manager. He said, "No more bow legs for this family." My grandfather had legs like hoops from hauling coal as a boy when his bones were soft. In one generation the Leverets sprouted up.'

'Like evolution?'

Leveret thought. 'Improvement, my father said. My mother's father was a lock-keeper and I would spend all day at the canal – a canal's a fascinating place for a boy, between fishing, horses and boats – until my father put an end to the visits. He was a great friend of Chief Constable Moon, and Moon always believed in the improvement of workers in general and miners in particular. Although Moon says improvement starts at the end of a stout club. An intimidating man. A chief constable is an important figure in a town like Wigan.'

'Moon is a goon in a uniform.'

'Rather catchy.' Leveret suppressed a smile.

Blair nodded towards a corner table. 'See the man cutting sausage? Face black with coal. Coal in his hair, his nails, every crevice of his skin. Moleskin waistcoat falling off his back. Speaking a language unintelligible to any other Englishman. Wearing clogs. Bring him back an hour from now, washed, shaved, in London clothes, sounding like a London man, in shoes, and you wouldn't believe he was the same man. He couldn't convince you. But is that improvement?'

'The clothes make the man?'

'And soap,' said Blair.

'Do you know what people believe here? People believe that English woollens are the best insulation for tropical heat. They do. They think it's the advantage that English explorers have. You have to be English to understand.'

'No doubt. That's why I don't understand why the Bishop is more convinced than ever that I'm the right man for the job. If I'm not finding Maypole, what am I doing right?'

Leveret strained for a positive answer. 'I don't know,' he confessed. 'Although I think your approaches are imaginative, I can't say that I feel we are any closer to finding John or discovering what happened to him. After the argument you had with Charlotte I was certain that the Bishop would let you go. Instead he was quite clear that it was her duty to cooperate. In fact, he wanted me to tell you that while Charlotte might resist at first, you mustn't be discouraged.'

'Maybe I can catch his daughter where there are no weapons. Or roses.'

'Charlotte can seem difficult because she has so many causes and takes them so seriously.'

'Like Maypole. Tell me, what kind of relationship did she have with him?'

'They shared the same ideals: to better Wigan through education, sobriety, sanitation.'

'If that doesn't win a girl's heart, what will? What I meant was, did they ever hold hands, kiss, dance?'

'No, nothing the least coarse or physical.'

Sometimes Blair wondered whether he and Leveret spoke the same language. 'Were Maypole and Charlotte happy? I'm not talking about the higher contentment of doing good, I mean the lower contentment of another warm body.'

'They didn't think that way. They were allies, fellow soldiers fighting for the same social goal.'

Blair tried a different tack. 'Tell me, did you ever see any disagreement between them? We're talking about a woman with a, let's say, flammable temperament.'

Leveret hesitated. 'Charlotte could be impatient with John, but that was because she wanted to help so many people.'

'Maybe also because she's the daughter of a bishop and he was a lowly curate?'

'No, she has never had anything but contempt for class distinctions. That's why she doesn't live in Hannay Hall. She refuses to have a servant.'

'Exactly, she just orders everyone around. How did John Maypole get on with Hannay? What did the Bishop think of his daughter marrying someone who wasn't an aristocrat?'

'A bishop and a curate don't ordinarily have much to do with each other. Also, John is a reformer, which the

Bishop does not necessarily approve of. The marriage *was* going to be an enormous step down socially for Charlotte. However, since she couldn't inherit the title or land, the question of whom she married wasn't all that important.'

'Tell me, how is it that Hannay is both a bishop and a lord?'

'Well, there were three brothers. Being the second, the Bishop went into the Church and Rowland's father, the youngest brother, made a career in the Army. When the older brother died without issue – sons, I mean – the Bishop succeeded to the title.'

'And after the Bishop?'

'Charlotte's brother would have been next in line, but he died in a riding accident two years ago. Rowland's father died in India a dozen years ago, so it would appear that Rowland will be the next Lord Hannay.'

'Charlotte's out of the picture?'

'As a woman, yes. The Bishop never mentioned any of this to you?'

'Why would he?'

'After his son's death he was distraught. That was when he went off to Africa with you. It might be why he thinks of you so fondly.'

'"Fondly"?' Blair had to laugh at that.

'Charlotte changed too. She was riding with her brother when he fell. It was after the accident that she began to turn into someone more serious – which was what appealed to John, of course, when he came to Wigan.'

'Of course.'

Blair actually felt a twinge of sympathy until Leveret added, 'You're not unlike her brother in a way. I can't think why she despises you so.'

'Kismet. Did Maypole pick Charlotte or did she pick him? You don't have to explain mating rituals, just tell me who asked who.'

'Considering their different social stations, it would have been impossible for John to ask her. But he worshipped Charlotte.'

'So you can't imagine Maypole in love with someone he might have met in a place like this? A flesh-and-blood dirty working girl from Wigan?'

'That's a peculiar question to ask.'

'What's the weekly rent for a Hannay company house at, say, Candle Court?'

'Three pounds.'

'The weekly wage for pit girls?'

'Ten pence a day. Before deductions. After, just under five shillings a week.'

'Who said England was against slavery? Which leaves a couple of pit girls nearly three pounds short of making the rent, let alone paying for food and clothes. You're sure Maypole never helped a girl in that kind of situation?'

'There was no one but Charlotte. Blair, there must be other lines of inquiry.'

'Other lines? To really question people would take a police campaign, which would be public and which the Hannays refuse to do, so I follow the feeble lines that I have.'

'Which are?'

'Envy. Reverend Chubb dislikes his overly fortunate curate so much that he brains him with a candlestick and hides him in a crypt.'

'No.'

'I don't think so, either. Money. Mr Earnshaw, Member of Parliament, listens to Maypole's passionate appeal for pit girls, but what really catches his attention is that his friend is engaged to a wealthy woman. Earnshaw secretly takes the train to Wigan, slits Maypole's throat, goes back to London and then returns to Wigan as the white knight of temperance to court the grieving Miss Hannay.'

'No.'

'Probably not. Then there's you, honest Oliver Leveret, who always loved Charlotte Hannay and must have been shocked when she perversely chose your best friend to share her bed and bank account. You, who are supposed to help me and have done nothing but describe a saint who never existed. That Maypole I never could find. But John Maypole wasn't a saint. He disobeyed Chubb. He lusted after pit girls. Most likely he considered Charlotte Hannay an expendable witch. You suspected something was happening. One week before he disappeared you asked him about it, and when he said everything was fine, you knew it was a lie. You are my last line, Leveret.'

Leveret reddened as if he'd been slapped. 'John did tell me not to be concerned. How did you know I asked?'

'What made you ask?'

192

'He was so agitated.'

'Exactly what did he say?'

'That he was experiencing a spiritual crisis. That miners were closer than priests to the ideal of Heaven. That minute to minute he swung from ecstasy to despair. But he did assure me that he was fine.'

'That sounds fine to you?'

'I knew John was human. So am I. If I loved Charlotte, I never aspired to her. No one was happier for John when their engagement was announced.'

'Let's get back to ecstasy and despair. Was the ecstasy a working girl? Was the despair Charlotte Hannay?'

'There was only Charlotte.'

'Both? Quite a woman.'

'Blair, do you actually suspect me?'

'No, but I think it's time you started helping. Can you do that?'

Leveret's colour rose to the roots of his hair. 'How?'

'Get me the inquest for the Hannay explosion.'

'That would be the Coroner's Report. We discussed this before. There is a copy at our offices here in town, but to be kept there at all times, as I told you.'

'Bring it to my hotel.'

'Why?'

'It makes me feel I'm doing something. I don't understand England. I do understand mines.'

'Anything else?'

'I need your carriage.'

'That's all?'

Blair remembered King Solomon. 'You haven't had

any black women passing through Wigan, have you? African women?'

'No.'

'Just a thought.'

As Blair drove towards the Hannay tower, miners and pit girls trudged home in the opposite direction beside the road. Riding in Leveret's carriage literally put him in a class above. He saw neither Flo nor Bill Jaxon. No one raised their eyes. They might have been sheep or cattle in the gloaming.

He missed an equatorial sun and a sharp division between day and night, but he admitted that English light had eccentric charms. Thunderheads towering so high that a train of coal wagons looked like a fold on the landscape. Sparrows that tumbled from high to low, from light to dark, around hedgerows and chimney towers. There was a stillness that no locomotive could shake, a stirring that no veil of soot could hide.

Everything was contradiction. Bishop Hannay, who didn't care for Maypole, wanted him found. Charlotte Hannay, Maypole's fiancée, wouldn't help. The more Blair infuriated her, the happier the Bishop seemed to be. Leveret was correct when he said that Blair didn't understand. Day by day, he understood less.

Close to the Hannay yard was a rise of leafless, dun-coloured willows and oaks swaying in the wind over a lower canopy of brambles and gorse. Blackthorns showed white buds; otherwise this last remnant of Wigan forest was as drab as a feather duster. There was no access by road and no sign of Rose Molyneux. Blair tied the horse and found a footpath that wandered between bushes. As thorns reached out he pushed them away with his leather pack.

The wood was nesting for moles, foxes, stoats; there was little wild woodland left around the mines and Blair could almost feel the concentrated animal activity around him. Within minutes he reached what he judged to be the centre of the little wood, a small clearing around a silver birch, and saw a finch sitting on a branch pour forth a stream of musical notes. He was dumbfounded, as if while touring an urban ruin he had stumbled into an ancient, miniature chapel, and the finch itself was pulling the bell ropes.

'It's a canary,' Rose said.

She slipped out from the shadow of a willow, though with the fading light, her shawl and so much coal dust on her face she was a shadow of herself. A food tin hung in her hand.

Blair asked, 'How is that?'

'They escape from the pit, or sometimes they're let go and this is the first wood they fly to. They mix with the birds here.'

'That's hard to believe.'

'Not for me.'

Her hair hung loose in red-brown coils, her corduroy coat was velvet with coal dust and she wore a satin ribbon around her neck to balance her ensemble. One hand was bandaged and he remembered Flo had said she'd had an accident.

'You're hurt?'

'We weren't serving tea t'day, we were sorting coal. Sometimes there's a sharp stone on the belt. What did you have t'tell me?'

The birch lit up. Startled, the bird flew away, followed by a clap of thunder. In that moment of illumination Blair realized that he had never seen Rose Molyneux before in a good light. She was always half covered with dust or weakly lit by a candle or lamp. The lightning showed a forehead as high as Charlotte Hannay's but over brighter eyes, and as fine a nose but with a more relaxed and fuller mouth, red against her black cheek. She seemed taller than Charlotte, but beyond that she was more physically present, a civet compared with a domestic cat.

'I want you to return something for me,' Blair said. From his pack he took the pair of clogs that had been delivered to his hotel. 'These were left for me by Bill Jaxon. I saw him win them off an Irishman he kicked half to death. I know Jaxon is your beau. I think he has the idea that I have designs on you and these clogs are a warning that if I don't leave you alone he will kick *me* half to death. Tell Jaxon that I got the message and that I don't need any clogs.'

'They're handsome ones. Shamrocks.' She looked at the stitching and the brass-studded toes.

'Well, they didn't bring the Irishman any luck.' He held the clogs out but Rose still didn't take them.

'Bill scares you?'

'Bill certainly does scare me. He's violent and he's not half as dumb as he looks.'

'Oooh, he'll like that description.'

'You don't have to repeat it to him.'

'Maybe it's clogs that bother you? Are you getting grand now? You'd prefer pistols or swords?'

'I'd prefer having no trouble at all. The only reason I talked to you in the first place was to ask about John Maypole.'

'You came twice,' Rose said.

'The second time was because of the photograph Maypole had of you.'

'And you said you wouldn't bother me again.'

'I'm trying not to bother you, believe me.'

A few raindrops began to fall through the trees. Rose was oblivious, picking up spirit like an actress on a stage. 'If I was Miss Hannay it would be different. If I was a lady, you wouldn't come throwing clogs in my face. You wouldn't be badgering me with questions like a poor-house inspector.'

'Rose, your friend Flo arranged for us to meet here. I'm not throwing clogs, I'm trying to give them to you. And as for Miss Hannay, you're twice the lady she is.'

'Just say you're a coward. Don't give me sweet words.'

Blair lost patience. 'Will you take the damn clogs?'

'See? Is that how you speak t'a lady?'

Nothing with Rose went as he hoped. As the rain began to beat down, hair stuck to her sooty brow, yet he was the one who felt bedraggled. 'Please?' he asked.

She placed her hands behind her back. 'I don't know. A famous explorer like you, you can answer t'Bill yourself. You have all the world to hide in if Wigan isn't safe enough.'

'What do you want, Rose?'

'Two things. First, a ride t'town. You can set me down when we're close. Then you must promise never t'come t'my house or bother me at work again. I don't need another Maypole.'

Comparison with Maypole was an unexpected sting.

'Rose, take the clogs and I will never bother you again.'

'I'll take them on that account only.'

While Blair led her out, the storm arrived with a heave of tree boughs. He asked himself why he was leading the way when Rose knew the path through the wood better than he did, but she seemed to expect it, like the princess of a tiny kingdom.

Chapter Ten

'Ah went down pit when Ah were six. They lifted us oop an' down in baskets. Ah worked a brace o' canvas an' frame t'let air in. Otherwise folk below coodn't breathe, they'd die.

'When Ah was eight Ah was big enough t'draw coal. That means drag it. Ah had a chain went around m'neck an' between m'legs t'sledge, same as me mum an' all m'sisters. Ah was a strong lass an' Ah'd draw forty, fifty pound o'coal. No ponies in that pit. So tight tha could barely squeeze through.

'Was it hot? Up face, where they took t'coal, everyone was stripped. Like Adam an' Eve. Tha were crawling through water an' muck. Things happened t'girls. That's wha there was t'big Reform an' Parliament put all t'girls on top o'pit. Not because of our work but because of our morality. That's how Ah become a pit girl.

'Ah didn't mind t'work. Sortin' coal. Tipping tubs into wagons. Cold in t'winter. Tha danced just t'stay warm. There's worse than freezin'. M'first girl, when she coom t'work on the brew she was caught b'tween wagons an' was crooshed. She was ten. T'owners an' t'managers coom by t'give us five shillin's for her. That's t'death rate. Five shillin's fur oldest girl, three shillin's fur each girl after.'

'What did you do?' Blair asked.

'Tha genuflect an' say, yes sir, no sir, three bags full, sir.'

When the kettle rattled, Mary Jaxon moved it to a cold burner and put in a tea ball to steep. The centre of any miner's home was a cast-iron range. Its fender was polished to a shine. The smell of bread emanated from the oven. The design of the house was the same as Rose Molyneux's, but in Mary Jaxon's kitchen there were a dozen children packed on the stairs to stare at the visitor.

Around the table were Blair and a circle of neighbours, men with the black necks and red-rimmed eyes of miners, no one Blair knew except the little stableman who had cursed him at the Hannay Pit. Behind them stood their wives; it was understood that men home from work had the first rights to chairs. Though the women had covered worn dresses with their best shawls, from the way they folded their sinewy arms and narrowed their eyes Blair detected a higher general level of suspicion. Like Mary Jaxon, they had gone from the pit brow to a terraced house, bearing children one a year on wages that dried up in the summer when coal prices dropped or stopped completely during strikes. Mary Jaxon made a curious hostess, like a mother of a wolf pack, a combination of ferocity and hospitality. Blair had returned the carriage to Leveret and come alone on foot to draw as little attention as possible, but Mary Jaxon had at once stepped out of the back of her house and summoned neighbours from the entire alley. She said

Scholes was the sort of community where interesting visitors were shared.

'Tha like tay?' Mary asked.

'I'd enjoy some, thanks,' Blair said.

'Art tha really from America?' a girl asked from a middle step.

'Yes.'

A boy from the bottom of the stairs asked, 'Art th'a Red Indian?'

'No.'

They watched him fixedly, undiscouraged, as if he might turn into one.

Blair asked Mrs Jaxon, 'The last time the Reverend Maypole came by, what did you talk about?'

'About t'boons God's given t'workin' man. Patience, sufferin' an' all t'wee angels we supply. For a woman t'boons are dooble.'

The miners shifted uneasily in their chairs but nods from the wives said that Mary Jaxon spoke for them.

'Anything else?' Blair asked.

'Reverend Maypole wanted us all t'kneel an' pray fur t'health of t'Prince of Wales, who'd got a sniffle. There's that Queen with her huge German family, an' that we don't hang them Ah think is mercy enough.'

A titter went up the steps.

'An' he was a great one fur Christian sports,' one of the men offered.

'Which are?' Blair asked.

A small boy on the stairs said, 'Cricket.'

'Rugby,' a larger boy said and hit the first.

Mary Jaxon said, 'Remember, t'following afternoon, seventy-six men was laid like burnt matches around pit head at t'Hannay Mine. No one noticed a priest comin' or goin'. Not unless he could raise t'dead. Tha understand everythin' Ah'm sayin'?'

'Yes.' Blair also understood that he would be getting no information. Maybe it was the explosion, he thought. Every family had lost a son, father, husband, brother – at the least a close friend. Perhaps that was why they were in the kitchen, because front parlours were used for laying out the dead. Possibly Mrs Jaxon and her neighbours were upset about his questions. In any case, he was ready to leave even though everyone else in the kitchen continued to stare at him with dumb anticipation.

'Tell us about Africa,' Mary Jaxon said.

'Africa?'

'Aye.' Her eyes shot to the stairway. 'T'babs know nothin' of t'world. They plan t'be ignorant aw their lives. They think they can't be bothered t'read or write 'cause they're goin' down pit.'

'A lecture for "the babs"?' Blair asked.

'If tha don't mind.'

Entertainment from the outside was rare in Wigan, Blair knew. This was a world where a hurdy-gurdy drew a crowd. Still, it also struck him that other travellers on their return from Africa delivered their talks in the Map Room of the Royal Society. Gentlemen travellers, of course. Celebrated explorers. In formal clothes with official guests, champagne, toasts and a silver medal from the Society. Blair never imagined they would give him one, but the disparity was telling. The Society had his maps and reports, even a monograph or two, and here he was at his début in Wigan, in a kitchen suffused by the close smells of stew and wet wool, accompanied by the occasional knock of a child's clog against a stair.

Blair stood. 'I have to go. Thanks for the tea.'

'Tha art *the* Blair from Africa?' one of the miners asked.

'Maybe not. Good night.'

'I knew it. A fake,' the miner's wife said.

On his way through the dark parlour to the front door he walked into a table. Stopped short, he looked at an oval mirror beside the hat rack and saw a gaunt man in the bent hurry of a thief, although he hadn't taken anything but their decent opinion of him. Of course the decent opinion had nothing to do with him. It was a gift because they had little else to give. What did it matter? It had nothing to do with him at all.

'Something does occur to me,' Blair said as he returned to the kitchen. The adults were still trading expressions of outrage over his departure. Half the children had trooped down the stairs; at the sound of his voice, they climbed back up. Blair took his seat as if he hadn't left. 'If you do go to Africa or anywhere in the world, you will need to write legibly and read with understanding, a perfect case in point being the late governor of Sierra Leone, Sir Charles Macarthy, who led a thousand Fanti troops against the Ashanti of the Gold Coast. Although the brave Macarthy was warned by scouts how badly he was outnumbered by Ashanti warriors, he spurned retreat and so the two armies clashed at the Battle of Assamacow.'

His audience, even the stableman, resumed their earlier seats and positions. Mary Jaxon poured more tea.

'The Fanti were stalwart soldiers drilled in the British manner, but the Ashanti were from a kingdom that had not only conquered other African tribes, but withstood the Danish, Dutch and Portuguese. The fate of West Africa stood in the balance. Although Macarthy was a courageous general, the enemy host swarmed on all sides. The fight was close, first with riflery, then with spears and swords. Then the worst possible thing that could happen to Macarthy did happen: he ran out of ammunition.'

Blair paused to sip from his cup. From the stairs a diagonal of eyes watched every move.

'Fortunately, he had an excellent runner. Macarthy wrote a message to his ordnance-keeper demanding the ammunition and the runner ran off with it, dashing through a momentary breach in the Ashanti lines. Macarthy and his Fanti allies held on grimly, harbouring every shot. You can imagine their relief when, following the bank of the river, the runner returned leading two pack mules laden with crates. And then imagine their disappointment and disbelief when they opened the boxes and found not ammunition but macaroni. The ordnance-keeper had not read Macarthy's request correctly. Hunched under enemy bullets, Macarthy wrote a second note. Again the runner slipped into shifting mists of smoke. Again Macarthy and his loyal, dwindling troops held out, this time with no ammunition of their own at all, defending themselves only with steel. And again the runner broke through the siege and returned with yet two more mules and crates. They broke open the crates.'

Blair sipped again, very slowly, and set down his cup.

'More macaroni. The ordnance-keeper simply could not make out anything Macarthy wrote. The rest of the story gets pretty nasty. The Ashanti completely overran them. The Fanti were slaughtered almost to a man. Macarthy fought as long as he could, propped himself against a tree and shot himself rather than be captured. It was probably wise. The Ashanti cut off his head and boiled his brains. They roasted the rest of him, and his skull they took back to the capital of Ashantiland to worship along with a pile of skulls of other enemies they admired, because Macarthy was a valiant fighter although he was an unusually bad penman.'

A silence followed. Around the table faces were warm and flushed.

'B'gum, that was a gripper,' one of the men said and sat back.

'T'ole story was macaroni,' a woman said.

''S true?' the man asked.

'Pretty much, for an African story. In fact, it's one of the truest I know,' Blair said.

'Gor,' said a boy.

'Watch tha mouth,' a mother said.

A miner hunched forward. 'Is there gold mines in th'Gold Coast?'

'Yes, and deposits of granite, gneiss and quartz that suggest there is a good deal more gold undiscovered. A person who learned some geology would have a great advantage.'

'We're aw geologists here when it comes t'coal.'

'That's true,' Blair said.

'Did tha shoot a gorilla?' the smallest boy asked.

'No, I've never seen a gorilla.'

'Elephant?'

'Not shot one.'

'Real explorers do,' the boy maintained.

'I've noticed. But real explorers travel with as many as a hundred porters. Porters may carry shaving soap and fine wine, but it's the explorer's job to get fresh meat for the expedition. Besides, he has the rifles. Since I only had a few men with me, I shot only antelope, which are like deer.'

The stableman finally spoke. 'So a man could make a fortune in gold down there.'

'Absolutely. More likely, though, he'll die of malaria, Guinea worm or yellow jack. I wouldn't send any man there who had a family or a chance of happiness nearer home.'

'Tha went.'

'With blinkers on, if you know what I mean.'

'Ah do.' The stableman's face split into a grin.

Blair told them how to prepare dried rats and bats,

drink palm wine, weather the winds of the dry season and the tornadoes of the rains, wake to the screams of monkeys and go to sleep to the mad laugh of hyenas. How to address the Ashanti King, which was through an intermediary, while the King sat on a golden stool under a golden parasol and pretended to hear nothing. How to back away from the King, staying low. How the King moved slowly and majestically, like Queen Victoria, but bigger and browner and in flashier clothes.

The questions around the kitchen had none of the archness of a salon. Their interest was so pure and intense that it lit faces – both parents' and children's – as if a window to the sun had been thrown open. If his answers weren't the lecture he'd ever imagined giving, but more like the sort of shapeless baggage of impressions that a traveller opened for assembled relatives, the experience was still curiously enjoyable.

When he left Mary Jaxon's door an hour later, he found that he had forgotten about the rain, a cold, steady deluge that ran off the rooflines in ropes. Shops had closed their shutters. Beerhouses and pubs were muffled by the downpour. The streets were almost cleared of wagons and there were certainly no cabs. He pulled his hat brim low and set off towards his hotel.

Lamps lit only the corners of long, dark blocks. Lakes appeared where streets had sunk over old mine shafts. He found himself making a detour through side streets and back alleys to find his way to the centre of town. The further he went, though, the narrower the alleys got and the more ash pits and fewer people he saw. He seemed to be trapped within a maze of backyard fences, pigeon lofts and pig sties. The locals obviously knew a better route but, by the time he'd decided to ask, there was no one else around.

Blair had spent half his life trying to find his way. He never minded asking where he was. Africans loved giving directions; African etiquette could turn simple instructions into an inescapable hour of sociability. He was trying to find his way now and there wasn't even an African in sight.

As he came out of the alley he found himself at a field of high grass and thistles that rose to a horizon edged with the sulphuric glow of mill ovens fading in and out of the rain like chain lightning. He climbed the ridge and discovered that it ended abruptly at a black dune stretching into the dark in either direction. The dune was coal slag, the mountain of rock and dirt and carbon dust left after the lifetime of a mine, after it had been driven, worked out and abandoned. The slag had dropped down with its own weight into the collapsed workings of the mine like the caldera of an ancient volcano. Like a volcano there were lingering, opalescent signs of life, votive candle glimmers as coal dust heated and ignited spontaneously within the slag, producing relatively harmless blue flames that worked their way through dirt to dart here and there – a second in each place – as evanescent, almost animated imps of fire. Rain couldn't quench them; in fact, low pressure brought them out.

There was light enough for Blair to see an abandoned brick kiln with the stub of a chimney teetering on the edge of the grass and, in the deepest point of the slag pit, an inky pool with the rest of the chimney standing diagonally up from the middle. How deep the water was depended on how tall the chimney was. There was even enough light for him to use his compass.

'Lost?'

It was Bill Jaxon's voice. He was the only person Blair would have expected to see. He finished reading the compass and discovered that he'd changed direction and was headed north. If he skirted the slag to the west he could reconnect with streets that would take him directly back to Scholes Bridge.

'I said, are you lost?' Bill emerged from the shadow of the alley and walked up the ridge to where Blair stood.

'Not any more, thanks.'

Jaxon topped Blair by half a head. With his cap and longish hair, bunched-up woollen jacket and white scarf trying to fly in the wind as it swept up the face of the slag, he looked even larger. Or was it the clogs? Blair reminded himself to add an inch for them.

'I asked you to not bother Rose Molyneux, but you keep at her. Now you're at my mother. Why are you doing this?'

'I'm asking about the Reverend Maypole, the same as I asked you. That's all.'

'You think Rose or my mother did something to Reverend Maypole?'

'No, I'm just asking what Maypole said, what he seemed like, the same as I ask everyone else.'

'But I told you not to.'

That was true. Blair had faith that he could talk himself out of a pinch. The main thing was never to make an adversary – Ashanti, Fanti, Mexican, whatever – lose face. It also helped to have no self-respect. All the same, he put the compass in his pocket to keep his hands free.

'Bill, the Bishop hired me to do this. If I don't, someone else will.'

'No, they won't. This has nothing to do with finding Maypole.'

'For me it's just Maypole.'

'But you've put me in a position. People hear about you socializing with Rose and it puts me in a position.'

'I understand. Bill, the last thing I want is to put you in a position. You're the champion here, ruler of the nether world. I'm not even a challenger.'

'You're not a fighter.'

'Or a lover. I'm a mining engineer, and there are some mines calling to me from the other side of the world right now, but I can't go until I've found out what happened to Maypole.'

Rivulets of water ran down his neck and under his collar. Under his cap, Bill's face was blank as marble. He looked down at Blair's feet.

'What are you wearing?'

'Not clogs. I'm not going to fight.'

'Afraid?'

'Yes.'

Bill seemed to think the problem through. 'I wish I had a choice.'

'You do.'

'But you got the clogs?'

'I got your gift. No, thanks. I gave the clogs to Rose to give back to you.'

'So you did see Rose again.'

An unanswerable question. Blair had the sense – the sense of falling from the top of a tall ladder – that words, no matter how glib, would never replace wings.

'To give back—'

He didn't see the kick. His left leg felt paralysed from the hip down. Bill bounced back quickly, lightly for a big man, and using his other foot like a scythe, scooped up both Blair's legs. Blair landed on his side and rolled away from a kick that raked his back.

'I told you to stay away from Rose, didn't I?' Bill said.

Blair got to his knees, his left leg numb. Bill feinted from side to side, and Blair ducked as a clog swung at his face and crawled backwards from the kick that followed that. There was something ignominious about the situation, he thought. He had survived attacks with spears and guns in the most exotic parts of the world, and here he was on the verge of being kicked to death in an English coal town.

A clog caught him above the ear and he saw beads of blood fly to the side. Jaxon skipped playfully from right to left, manoeuvring Blair so that he slipped over the edge of the grass with one knee in the slag. Wind stung his eyes with carbon dust.

'Bill, if you kill me, they'll come right after you.'

'Not if you disappear.'

'You want me to leave Wigan, Bill? Give me a couple more days and I'll be gone.'

For a moment, Bill Jaxon seemed genuinely uncertain. His gaze travelled down the slag to the water at the bottom. 'They won't find you,' he said.

Bill pretended to pull his foot back. Blair dodged and the move sent him sliding over the lip of grass and down the slag, which was warm, almost hot. When he half swam, half clambered up, Jaxon stomped on his hand.

'You should have brought clogs,' Bill said.

Blair grabbed Jaxon's ankle. Instead of merely stepping back, Bill tried to kick free, and Blair changed his grip to the cuff of the other ankle. The harder Bill kicked, the more off-balance he became, until he toppled next to Blair on to the slag and the two slid down together through waves of black dust. Flames touched them briefly, harmlessly. They rolled down to the bottom of the slope, by the edge of the water.

The slag pit was like a cup, boggy at the base, worse footing for clogs than shoes. The chimney rose like a sunken cannon aimed at the sky. When they stood, Blair didn't let Jaxon get room to kick. He hit Bill in the face, moved forward and hit him again until Bill backed into the water and went under, immediately out of his depth. It was a tall chimney, Blair thought.

Jaxon struggled in the water and gasped, 'I can't swim!'

Blair gave him a hand, and as he was pulling him up, hit him and watched him sink a second time.

Bill surfaced. 'For God's sake.'

Blair let him bob for a while before waving him out. He offered Bill help, and as Jaxon swung up the bank he hit him harder than before.

A minute passed before Bill floated to the surface again, face down. Blair fished him out by his hair and dragged him up on the sandbank. He wasn't breathing. Blair turned him over and pumped his back until Bill's mouth discharged an eruption of rank water. Satisfied that he was alive enough, Blair removed Bill's clogs and threw them in the pool.

Blair crawled up the sand, wearing a second skin of black dust, losing half his progress in sliding for every inch he rose. On either side, flames popped out of the slag like flowers, and as quickly disappeared. His left leg was not functioning well; neither was the hand Bill had stomped on. At the end he was feebly clawing his way towards the same ridge of grass he had fallen from. He saw waiting for him, obscured by rain and dark, the roofline of terraced houses and chimneypots and what appeared to be a looming, headless figure.

'Is 'e dead?' it asked Blair.

Blair gained the ridge and swayed to his feet. 'No.'

There was momentary stupefaction in the dark. A latch swung open and the focused light of a bull's-eye lantern blinded him, though he glimpsed the pit girl Flo, her head and shoulders covered with a shawl that sparkled in the rain.

'Then tha best run,' she said.

Blair kept his weight on his good leg; he could just picture himself hopping on one foot through the alleys. 'I don't think I'm running anywhere.'

'Ah'll help.'

Flo offered her back to lean on; it was like holding on to an energetic locomotive that carried as much as led him, the beam of her lantern aimed ahead. It made sense to him that she chose the alley instead of staying anywhere near the sand, but she continued to guide him between backyards rather than cut to the streets even when they had the chance. Through fence boards he saw the white flash of a pigeon loft. At this point, he didn't need a compass to know she was not taking him towards his hotel.

'Where are we going?'

Flo didn't answer. Like an engine, she pressed forward on a track of mud, slats and perpendicular turns until she pushed open a gate Blair never would have noticed. A pig squealed and scurried around its corner sty. Brick steps led between wash tubs to a back door that Flo rushed him through.

Inside, she let him sink into a chair. The room was dark except for a fire grate and she played the lantern on him. 'You're black an' bloody, too. But you're safe now.'

Blair's leg was numb and vaguely throbbing. He put fingertips to the side of his head and felt matted hair and a spongy flap of scalp. A little safety sounded good. While Flo lit the lamp he leaned back and let his eyes close. He listened to her stoke the grate. The smell of warm sugar and sweet milk penetrated his headache. He sat forward and looked. The grate was in an oven. A pot simmered on the range. By the stairs stood a full-length mirror that was familiar. From her knees, Flo turned to footsteps descending the stairs.

Rose Molyneux came down into the kitchen in a plain muslin blouse and skirt that made her hair, unbrushed and damp from a bath, appear like coppery knots. Her eyes were dark, charged with anger.

'What's he doing here?'

'Ah followed Bill, like tha said. They had a brawl an' Ah didn't know where else t'take him, Ah didn't. He's hurt.'

It was a wonder to witness, Blair thought. Rose dominated the room in a way that made the bigger girl quail. 'You were stupid t'bring him. Mr Blair looks black as a miner, is all. He only needs water and soap t'change back.'

'Believe me, this is the last place I want to be,' Blair said.

Rose said, 'You're the last person I want t'see, so we're even.'

'Rose, all you had to do was give the clogs to Bill, as I asked you to, and tell him that you're his and his alone, and that I didn't want to fight. Then Bill wouldn't have tried to kill me and I wouldn't be here now.'

'I'm not a maid t'do your errands.' She pointed with the poker to a corner of the kitchen. 'There are the clogs. Take them yourself.'

Flo said, 'He's not walkin' anywhere. Take a look at 'is head.'

Rose took the lantern from Flo and ran her hand through Blair's hair, roughly to begin with and then with more care. He felt her stiffen at the sight of something. 'Maybe water and gin,' she said.

Flo fed the fire to heat water. Rose fed Blair the gin. One item of trade you could always get in Africa was good Holland gin, so there were constants in life.

'Why don't you get a doctor?' he asked.

'You need a surgeon. At this hour he's so drunk I wouldn't trust him t'sew up a cat.'

Blair felt light-headed. The scene of the two women and the bright oven grate seemed to float around him. The lid of the pot began to rattle.

'Water's ready.' Flo pulled a zinc tub across the floor to the oven.

Rose tied on an apron and waited, hands on hips. 'Well?'

'I can bathe myself.'

'You've more than dirt t'worry about. Anyway, I've seen naked men before. And you've seen me.'

Which was true, although Blair was sure that she was far more attractive undressed than he was. He pulled off his boots and socks and stood shakily, supporting himself with the table to unbutton his shirt. Looking down, he saw how coal dust had collected down the centre of his chest. He opened his trousers and long johns and stepped out of them, feeling not so much bare as embarrassed. In the Gold Coast he had always been aware how pale and scrawny he appeared. In Wigan, too, as it turned out.

Moving made him dizzy. Flo gave him an arm to help him kneel on the ribbed bottom of the tub. Rose opened the oven grate. With a cloth she took an iron pan from the coals and from the pan she removed a needle glowing orange that she dropped into a bowl of water. He heard the hiss.

'You really make ten pence a day? Serfdom has not come to an end.'

'That's none of your business,' Rose said.

'And pay three pounds a week in rent? How do you manage that? Maybe you're tipping more than coal.'

'Drink this.' Flo gave him a second cup of gin.

Scissors appeared in Rose's hand.

'You're giving me a haircut?' This seemed the final indecency.

'Just t'see what I'm doing.'

He listened to the click of the blades and was aware of matted hair falling to the floor, but he didn't seem to have any sensation on that side of his head. Nothing was making sense. He should be in a proper surgery, Blair thought. Wasn't that one of the glories of civilization, trained medical men? He noticed that the gas lamps of the kitchen were suddenly turned to their brightest.

'You're not going t'cry like a bab, are you?' Rose asked.

He was wrong, he did have sensation on that side of his head. When she tipped the bowl of cold water over it he had to lock a scream inside his teeth. Flo gave him a twisted rag to bite on, and handed Rose a needle and red thread.

Rose said, 'Think about Africa.'

Blair thought about Bill Jaxon. If Jaxon had wanted to kill him before, how much more implacable an enemy would he be once he heard where Flo had taken Blair? The more he thought about it, he realized he couldn't even go to the police. Chief Constable Moon would ask first what the fight was about, and second where he had gone afterwards. It would sound like a sordid Wigan romance. As the needle tugged he gripped the edges of the tub.

Flo mixed hot and cold water in a pitcher. Rose cut the thread, put the needle down and again emptied the pitcher over Blair. Water felt like an electric shock. Then she began washing his hair, which was no worse than massaging a wound. He spat the rag from his mouth because he couldn't breathe from the water running into his nose. He didn't shake so much as quiver with every muscle in his body.

Flo refilled the cup of gin and said, 'Ah best find 'im clothes.'

'Then hurry,' Rose said.

As Flo left, Blair reached for the cup and finished it in two swallows, trying to rush sedation. He felt isolated in a shroud of pain, trying to keep his balance, awash in water that was black and red.

Rose rinsed his hair, poured a pitcher of hot water over his shoulders and started to rub him with soap and a sponge. He rocked from the effort of her scrubbing. Steam rose around them.

'Flo says you beat Bill. You don't look it.'

'I don't feel it.'

'You could have left 'im for dead, she says.'

'Is that why you're taking care of me, because I didn't? Is he in love with you?'

'Quiet and sit up.'

Although her hands weren't broad, they were strong, and when she washed his neck he let his head loll back drunkenly. In the mirror by the stairs he saw himself, the tub and her. Her hair was loose and wild; all she needed in it, he thought, was a briar rose to be a muse of summer. Add a lute and a silvery streak and she could be a model. Between the steam and washing him, she was almost as wet as he was, damp muslin clinging to her arms. Her hair brushed his cheek. It was the sort of deep brown that became red with the looking. No fizzy orange but threads of sable, copper, sienna, gold.

She poured more water over him to sponge his chest. It was the heat of the water combined with the gin in his veins, but he felt himself start to harden. The tub water wasn't so soapy that she couldn't see. He was astounded and ashamed. The rest of him was bruised and dead, yet this single part was unmistakably alive, rising like Lazarus, a traitor from the water. He shifted on his side to make the physiological fact less evident. Rose washed around the bruise on his hip, a circular motion repeated by her breasts against his back. From their friction he became aware that they had stiffened, too.

He felt his blood pound, but Rose didn't break

contact, as if they were both mesmerized and complicit in the steady rhythmic motion of the sponge in her hand and the heat of the stove.

'Understand, you can't come here again,' she said. Her voice was thick.

'Too bad.' He had meant to say it sarcastically but it didn't come out that way.

'Bill won't rest until he has you down.'

'It's you and Bill, then?'

'In Bill's mind.'

'Which is enough?'

'Enough for everyone else.'

'For you?'

He felt her breath on his neck as her hand came to a stop. He was amazed that through the pain and gin he could be so aware of her touch, of her heartbeat through the slight tremor of her breast, the very air of her.

'You don't want the answer,' Rose said.

'I do.'

'Not really. You're Nigger Blair. You make your mess and move on. Maybe you sneer at the Hannays, but you sneer at everyone. At least Bill left his mark on you, I'll give him credit for that.'

'I don't sneer at you.'

He didn't. Rose had seemed a liar and coquette before. Now she was a different person. She had become real. Being real, she didn't have another ready word. Neither did he. They were trapped like two people who had encountered each other in the dark, neither wishing to back away. He felt her soft exhalation and the brush of her hair on the side of his cheek. The sponge in her hand rested motionlessly on his thigh. He didn't know who would have moved first if Flo hadn't returned.

'Success,' she announced as she marched down the stairs, oversized trousers hanging from one hand and a cap and shapeless jacket in the other. 'Everythin' but a silk scarf.'

Immediately Blair felt himself subside into uncomplicated pain. Rose sat back silently and wiped her brow while Flo bustled around the kitchen. Blair didn't understand what had transpired but he did know that the moment was gone and that without its tension he was progressively more drunk.

Rose got to her feet and gave the sponge to Flo. 'Dry him, dress him, take him back t'his hotel.' She untied her apron and went up the stairs that Flo had just come down.

'Sure.' Flo was surprised by Rose's retreat but still full of momentum. She said to Blair, 'Your shoes are full o' muck, but you can wear clogs.'

'Great.' It was his last coherent word.

Chapter Eleven

In the middle of the night Blair woke and lit the lamp in his hotel room. The flame burned away some of his stupor, though the oversweet taste of gin coated his tongue.

The visit to Mary Jaxon and her neighbours, and memories of being bodily transported by Flo, had the quality of dreams rather than actuality. The fight in the slag pit, especially, seemed more hallucination than fact, except that his hands were raw with scrapes and one leg was bruised black.

When he approached the mirror he saw that the hair above one ear had been cropped. He lifted the hair and turned to see out of the corner of his eye a semi-circle neatly stitched, the edge faintly coloured blue from coal dust that couldn't be removed. Not Bill Jaxon's mark. Her mark.

While his head throbbed, Blair opened Maypole's journal, attempting for a second time to make sense of the entries the curate had written the week before he disappeared. The weave of vertical and horizontal lines was a maze of Indian ink and they were in transposed letters. If the lines had simply been in Latin they would have been safe from him. Codes were different. Miners knew codes; old Blair had kept a notebook of claims before they were registered, hidden in a variety of ciphers: keyword, picket fence, Porta's and pigpen.

'Jbn uif spt fpg tib spo . . .'

Blair had it. The Augustus code, a one-letter shift in blocks of three – baby's play. Maypole was an Oxford man? He should have been ashamed of himself.

I am the rose of Sharon, and the lily of the valleys.

My beloved spake and said unto me, 'Rise up, my love, my fair one, and come away.

'Let me see thy countenance, let me hear thy voice; for sweet is thy voice, and thy countenance is comely. Take us the foxes, the little foxes, that spoil the vines: for our vines have tender grapes.'

These are words I wish I could say to her.

As there were no vineyards around Wigan, Blair assumed that Maypole had slipped into the Bible, and while he could easily identify Charlotte as, say, the murderous Judith, who cut off the head of an Assyrian and hung it on a bed, he didn't see her as a vixen.

She tells me how people visit the pit yard to gawk at the women as if they were another race. Can coal dust and trousers make people so blind? Don't her intelligence and spirit shine through that disguise? She charges that my cassock is a stranger costume than any trousers she might wear, and though I rebuff her accusation, in private I begin to agree.

Blair remembered the last time Maypole was seen, running after Rose Molyneux and pulling off his ecclesiastical collar.

'Thy lips are like a thread of scarlet . . . Thy two breasts are like two young roes . . . which feed among the lilies.
'How much better is thy love than wine! and the smell of thine ointments than all spices!'

Why was Maypole coding what was in the Bible? Blair wondered. Unless it had some particular power for him. The Song of Solomon really shouldn't be placed in the hands of young curates, he decided. The Good Book ran like a railway engine on a track of sanctified slaughter, and then, out of nowhere, came Solomon's verses of love. He pictured conductors shouting, 'Don't look out of the windows at the naked man and woman! We'll be pulling into Isaiah and the degradation of Zion in five more minutes!'

The lines switched to plain text.

'It is the voice of my beloved that knocketh, saying, Open to me . . . my love, my dove . . . for my head is filled with dew, and my locks with the drops of the night.
'My beloved put in his hand by the hole of the door . . . I rose up to open to my beloved; and my hands dripped with myrrh, and my fingers with sweet smelling myrrh upon the handles of the lock.'

The next entry shifted to a different cipher, too much for Blair's headache. One thing was clear, though. If this was the fiancé of Charlotte Hannay, he was a man in trouble.

Chapter Twelve

Blair lifted a leech from a jar and set it in a row of its companions feeding on his bruised and swollen hip. Not that he expected leeches to draw anything but subcutaneous bleeding. He lay on his side to keep deeper blood from pooling, wearing only a loose shirt and socks, his skin red from the overstoked fire of his hotel sitting room. Since his veins swam in aspirin, arsenic and brandy, he expected the worms to soon swoon and drop.

Leveret had delivered a bound copy of the Coroner's report, and Blair had sent him off for a list of pit girls who had attended the Home for Women. Where else could Rose have learned how to stitch a wound? What better place to meet John Maypole?

The report weighed an imperial pound.

Being the Inquest of the Coroner's Jury into the Circumstances and Causes of the Explosion at the Hannay Pit, Wigan, Lancashire, held at the Royal Inn, 21 January 1872.

The site didn't surprise him. Inquests were held in a local public room, which usually meant any inn with space enough to seat the jury, witnesses, bereaved families and interested parties.

The first page was a fold-out map of the Hannay Mine, the scale fifty yards to an inch, marked with arrows to show how fresh air arrived from the downshaft, branched from the tunnel called the main road, and circulated through cross tunnels to the far periphery of the coal face. Ventilation returned through the back-road tunnel until it was sucked up a diagonal channel called a 'dumb drift' to join the upshaft far enough above the furnace so that the tainted, gassy air wouldn't explode.

The map was also marked from '1' to '76' to indicate where men had died. There was a capricious quality to mine explosions because blast and smoke underground could multiply like a dozen locomotives racing through tunnels, suddenly swerving from a likely victim to chase down a less fortunate man half a mile away. Also, in the insidious alchemy of a blast, the methane that fuelled a fire was always followed by afterdamp – carbon monoxide – and no man was safe until he had reached the surface ahead of the spreading gas.

Death certificates followed. Blair's eye skipped around because there were so many.

1. Henry Turton, eight years, pony tender. Attempting to aid his pony, Duke, he became tangled in the reins and was carried to the bottom of the shaft . . .

23, 24 and 25. Albert Pimblett, sixty-two; his son, Robert Pimblett, forty-one; and grandson Albert, eighteen, found side by side and apparently unmarked in the main road. It is surmised that as one succumbed to gas, the others stayed to help, and so all perished. They were identified by their wives . . .

45. In the main road, an Irishman called Paddy, no other name known. Age unknown. He was identified by a Fenian tattoo . . .

48. William Bibby, fourteen. Identified by his brother Abel, who had not gone to work that day because of a headache . . .

53. Bernard Twiss, sixteen. Burned. Recovered at the coal face by his father, Harvey, who failed at first to recognize him. Identified later by a red cloth he used to hold up his trousers . . .

66. Arnold Carey, thirty-four. Found burned and disfigured at the coal face. Identified by his wife, who recognized his clogs . . .

73. Thomas Greenall, fifty-four. At the coalface. Burned and mutilated, recognized by the fact that he had previously lost a finger . . .

74 and 75. George Swift, twenty-one, and John Swift, twenty. Burned and mutilated. Identified by George's belt buckle and John's watch . . .

76. A day worker known as Taffy. Age unknown. Identified by a black tooth . . .

A missing finger, a watch, a tattoo. It was enough to make a man take a personal inventory.

The thirteen members of the jury were listed: three bankers, two retired Army officers, a builder, one insurance agent and six shop owners, all of a social caste that

turned to the Hannays the way flowers heeded the sun.
A jury of one's peers.

George Battie was the first witness.

Coroner: As underlooker, you are one of the employees
most responsible for the day-to-day safety of the
Hannay Pit and the men who work in it, is that not
true?

Battie: It is, sir.

Coroner: Last week seventy-six men died in that mine.
Every home in Wigan lost a husband, a father, a
brother. Their widows are gathered here today, asking
how it is possible that such a mass calamity could have
been allowed to occur. We will hear testimony and
opinion from survivors and rescuers, experts who were
called immediately to the scene of the disaster, as well
as experts who visited the pit later, agents for the mine
owner and miners' union, and finally from Her Majesty's
Mines Inspector. However, you may be the most important witness of all, since you were the individual charged
with the safety of those victims.

Blair could see Battie strapped into a Sunday suit,
facing the questions like a pony staring down a shaft.

Coroner: What did you do on the morning of 18
January to ensure the safety of the men in the Hannay
Pit?

Battie: I am always first man down pit at four in the

229

morning to hear the report of the night underlooker whether there have been accidents or complaints since the previous day. There were none. I then checked the barometer and thermometer.

Aaron Hopton, Esq., Counsel for the Hannay Pit: Why is that?

Battie: If the barometric pressure falls, gas creeps out of the coal. When that is the case, I caution the men against setting off any shots that might ignite the gas. The barometric pressure did drop that morning and I issued such a caution as the men came down in the cage. I then visited workplaces to make sure that the caution was understood, paying particular attention to districts of the coalface I knew to be fraught with gas. As I did so, I also examined the ventilation to be sure that every part of the mine had access to good air, and that every workplace had two routes of escape.

Miles Liptrot, Esq., Counsel for the Hannay Pit: Did you examine where the explosion originated?

Battie: Yes, sir. That is, I believe I can estimate where the explosion took place, and I did inspect that area the morning of the fire.

Enoch Nuttal, Esq., Counsel for the Hannay Pit: Did you detect gas that morning?

Battie: Yes.

Isaac Meek, Esq., Counsel for the Hannay Pit: Determined by?

Battie: Passing my lamp across the coalface and observing a lengthening of the flame. I moved a brattice—

Hopton: Brattice?

Battie: A frame of wood and canvas for directing ventilation. And I told Albert Smallbone—

Liptrot: That would be the fireman at that location?

Battie: Yes, sir. I told him to watch the gas and not to fire any shots.

Nuttal: To set off any gunpowder for the easier getting of coal?

Battie: Yes, sir.

Meek: Describe, Mr Battie, where you were and what you did when you became aware of an explosion?

Battie: I was at my desk at the bottom of the shaft at two forty-five in the afternoon when the floor jumped and hot clouds of coal dust shot from the tunnels. The ponies were in a turmoil. One carried a boy to his death in the cistern beneath the cage shaft. The cage arrived almost at once, seconds too late for the poor boy.

Hopton: Go on.

Battie: I wrote a note for the pit manager, explaining the situation, and sent the cage back up. Then I took men with rescue supplies that are always at the ready – picks and shovels, litters and splints, brattices and timber, block and tackle, canaries in cages – and started with them into the main road because that is the main artery of fresh air. The first men and ponies we encountered were rushing out. I soon began to find brattices that had been blown out of position, disrupting the inward draft of good air and allowing afterdamp to spread. We repaired the canvas to improve ventilation and push the gas back. Only as the quality of air improved could we move forwards. It is one thing for fate to take a life; it is another matter altogether for the leader of a rescue party to endanger more lives through recklessness or haste.

Five hundred yards in, we found men who had succumbed to gas and fallen face forward unconscious to the floor, a sign they had fallen while running. We turned them on their backs so they could breathe and tended some twenty men in this fashion as proper ventilation took hold. All survived. Another fifty yards on, however, the canary in the cage I held dropped, and we now started to find men stretched out on the floor, unmarked by violence but beyond any ministration. We also started to meet cave-ins and were forced to dig through obstructions, propping up rock as we went, rigging block and tackle to move fallen props. There were pockets of good air as well as gas, and we were able to extricate another eighteen men alive, besides finding the bodies of thirty-five more.

Coroner: What about the canary? Canaries are sensitive to carbon monoxide, hence their use in mines. You said the canary in the cage you held dropped to the bottom of its cage. Were you progressing with a dead canary?

Battie: We had three cages. Only one was in the lead. When it dropped, it was handed back to revive while one of the other canaries was handed to the front. We were indeed slowed by thicker concentrations of gas, which required men as well as birds to take turns in the lead. Five of us were overcome and had to be carried out. However, we were reinforced by survivors who chose to participate in the rescue rather than to run for safety. Smallbone had been injured by a rockfall and was being assisted to my office by William Jaxon when the explosion took place. Both joined us and took such extreme risks I had to restrain them.

Hopton: They heard cries for help?

Battie: After an explosion, timbers make all manner of sounds. However, from a thousand yards on there were no more survivors.

Liptrot: And you advanced quickly?

Battie: It was three forty-five when Jaxon and Smallbone joined us, but our progress slowed despite their efforts. If you can't see the bird in the cage and the flame in your lamp sinks to a nub, you order everyone back until fresh air lifts the flame again because dead rescuers are no help at all.

Nuttal: You cite the zeal of Smallbone and Jaxon. Why do you think they pressed so hard?

Battie: The explosion was at their district of the coalface. When we emerged at the near end of the face, the bodies there were singed. With every step, the destruction was more severe. Midway, the victims were burned. Some were buried under coal tubs thrown off the track, others blown by the force of the explosion into old workings. The far end of the coal face was Smallbone's and Jaxon's station. Had they been there at the time of the explosion nothing would have been left of them.

Meek: Who was the last victim recovered?
Battie: A dayworker, a Welshman we called Taffy.

The black tooth, Blair remembered.

Coroner: At least we can trust that the death of these men was mercifully swift. The watch later identified as that of John Swift was found with its crystal shattered and its hands stopped at two forty-four, the very moment of the blast.

Progressing with a dead canary was an accurate description of Blair's own life. He shuffled stiffly across the carpet to feed the fire grate. Since they were along for the ride, he decided to name the leeches on his leg Famine, Death, Conquest and War after the Four Horsemen of the Apocalypse.

Blair was self-taught. What had there been to do in a Sierra winter but read through the old man's library of classics? Sober, old man Blair had no conversation beyond engineering or, drunk, the Revelation of Saint John the Divine. The women the boy saw were either Chinese or whores. To win attention he told them stories that he stole. His favourite was a version of *Robinson Crusoe* in which the castaway was a woman instead of a man, and Friday was a boy instead of a native. They lived so happily on the island that they let ships pass rather than wave them down.

Hopton: I appreciate that you and the other members of the rescue party were operating under strain and emotional upset. Did you, however, immediately examine the coalface for evidence that a worker had fired a shot contrary to your caution?

Battie: Not immediately.

Liptrot: Why not?

Battie: There was more gas.

Coroner: From what?

Battie: From old workings, sir. Waste stone and unusable small coal that we'd bricked to help support the roof. It's normal practice but, unfortunately, all sorts of gases accumulate in waste. The explosion had cracked the bricks. The whole tunnel lit up when our lamps felt the gas. The choice was to abandon the coalface with any bodies in it that we hadn't found or stop up the leak.

Nuttal: What was the condition of your lamps?

Battie: Red, sir. Too hot to hold.

Nuttal: Because of gas?

Battie: Yes.

Meek: What access did you have to this leak?

Battie: Poor. The gas was blowing from a bricked-up area deep in the coal seam under a low shelf, and the way was partially blocked by debris. While we tried to ventilate as best we could, I sent for bricks and the makings for cement that we store in side tunnels, and when they arrived I sent everyone out but Smallbone and Jaxon. We mixed mortar at the face and they took turns crawling with two bricks at a time in almost total darkness to repair the wall. They succeeded, and as a consequence I was able to bring lamps to that area of the coal face that I most wanted to examine.

Hopton: Why that part?

Battie: It was the area where I had detected gas that morning.

Hopton: Did you suspect that, contrary to the caution you issued, one of the victims had set off a shot?

Battie: No, sir.

Liptrot: Perhaps you feel it would be uncharitable to speculate?

Battie: I couldn't say, sir. Besides, sir, the only fireman in that district of the coalface was Smallbone.

Nuttal: And he was with you. So it was unlikely that Taffy or the Swift brothers or Greenall or any of the deceased set off a shot of gunpowder in the absence of Smallbone.

Battie: Yes, sir.

Meek: But if they did, they would be less expert.

Battie: Yes, sir.

Hopton: Isn't it true that Greenall had been reprimanded in the past for lighting a pipe in the mine?

Battie: Ten years back.

Liptrot: It's true, though?

Battie: Yes.

Nuttal: Any heavy drinkers among the men at the coal face?

Battie: I wouldn't say heavy.

Nuttal: Weren't John and George Swift reprimanded by police only last week for carousing on the street?

Battie: John was just married. They were celebrating.

Hopton: Does drink affect a miner's judgement?

Battie: Yes.

Hopton: Miners drink.

Battie: Some.

Nuttal: Do you drink?

Battie: I'll have an ale on the way home.

Nuttal: An ale or two?

Battie: The temperature down pit is one hundred degrees. You sweat off five pounds in a day. When you come up, you need something to drink.

Hopton: Are you suggesting that ale is purer than Wigan water?

Battie: You said it, sir, not I.

Meek: You are involved with the miners' union, are you not?

Battie: I am a miner and I am in the union.

Meek: More than that. An active leader. A defender, is that right?

Battie: I suppose so.

Meek: With no insinuation intended, would it be fair to say that the last thing a union leader would admit was that one of the unfortunate victims was himself to blame?

Battie: I don't know what happened down pit that day. I do know mining is dry and dangerous work, that's a fact of life. Nothing is ever going to change that.

Blair felt dry himself, and the ache from his head was crowding out his ability to focus. He drank a brandy, wished it was ale, set down the report, peeled off the leeches and napped.

He lunched on cold beef, cheese and wine, keeping in mind Battie's warning about the water. The leeches lunched on him. A different foursome now. Juliet, Ophelia, Portia and Lady Macbeth.

He hated coal mines. Gold was noble and inert. Coal, which had been living material, was still alive, exhaling gas as it changed into rock. Of course all the easy, shallow coal was long gone. As mines went deeper, coal was harder, air fouler, firedamp stronger. For what? No nugget of gold.

Coroner: Mr Wedge, you are the Manager of the Hannay Pit. Were you aware of a danger of explosive gas at the coal-face on the day of 18 January?
Wedge: I was so informed by George Battie, and I agreed with Battie's caution against firing shots. That's what an underlooker is for, to take such precautions and protect property.
Coroner: As Manager, where were you and what did you do when you became aware of the explosion?
Wedge: I was in the yard and knocked almost off my feet by the explosion. With my very first breath, I sent runners for medical assistance and help from the nearby pits. A bad fire requires the transport of injured and

dead for long distances underground at a time when your own miners are incapacitated. Next, I looked after the cage, which was, thank God, operative although a volume of smoke rose from the shaft. A messenger had come from Battie to say he had started rescue operations below. Although we had to wait for the cage to return to the surface again, we immediately sent volunteers down with lamps. It is a sad fact that in mine disasters rescuers are often among the victims. That is why we strictly count lamps, so that we know by simple arithmetic when *everyone* is out of the pit. The worst for a family is not knowing if someone is found.

Blair wasn't certain of his own age and had no idea of his birthday. Old Blair, however, taught him geometry, and when Blair was probably no more than nine he figured with a protractor – using the average time of an Atlantic crossing and taking into consideration trade winds and winter seas – the approximate latitude and longitude where he last saw his mother. Since then he had crossed the same position only once. He had stood at the rail and looked down at dark swells that moved under sheets of foam. The sense of cold and isolation was overwhelming.

Coroner: Your name is?
Jaxon: William Jaxon.
Liptrot: You are the miner who usually drills holes for the fireman at the coalface where the explosion took place?
Jaxon: Yes, sir.

Nuttal: Did you drill any holes that day?

Jaxon: No, sir. When Mr Battie issued a caution against shots, no one drilled any holes.

Hopton: But you were not at the coalface when the explosion erupted?

Jaxon: No, sir. I was helping Albert Smallbone to the cage because his pick hit a rock that shot out and hit his leg. We were in the road when it gave a shake like a rope. Smoke blew us along until we rolled into a refuge hole. We couldn't see, couldn't hear, because of coal dust and because we were concussed, like. We worked our way through side tunnels and that's when we met Battie and the others.

Meek: And decided to return to the coalface with them rather than seek your own safety?

Jaxon: You could put it that way.

Coroner: Your name is?

Smallbone: Albert Smallbone.

Liptrot: And you are the only fireman for that district of the coalface where the explosion took place?

Smallbone: Yes, sir.

Liptrot: Smallbone, were you given a caution about gas from Battie?

Smallbone: Yes, sir.

Nuttal: You must feel fortunate to be alive.

Smallbone: I would feel more fortunate if my friends were alive.

Meek: Was your leg badly injured when the rock hit it? When you chose to return with Jaxon and Battie?

Smallbone: I disregarded it, sir, in the heat of the moment.

In spite of aspirin, Blair's head still throbbed. Good stitching only went so far. He felt like Macarthy of the Gold Coast after his head was severed, boiled and stacked with the other honoured skulls.

Molony: My name is Ivan Molony. I am Manager of Mab's Pit, one mile distant from the Hannay Pit. On the afternoon of 18 January, I saw smoke rise from the Hannay Pit and knew that an underground explosion of some sort had taken place. I gathered a party of volunteers and rushed to the Hannay yard.

Nuttal: It is a tradition among Lancashire mines to lend assistance at the first sign of a fire?

Molony: Yes, it is a form of mutual aid.

Nuttal: And at the yard you proceeded down the shaft into the pit?

Molony: With other volunteers.

Hopton: You were the first expert to arrive at the coalface where the explosion is believed to have originated. Describe the scene as you found it.

Molony: A smooth wall at one end and a tangle of burned bodies and wagons at the other. Terrible carnage, like soldiers mown down by grapeshot. In the midst of it, Battie and two of his men had erected brattices for ventilation and were just setting the last brick in the wall to stop a secondary leak of gas.

Liptrot: You are aware from previous witnesses that

there was a caution in effect at the Hannay Mine before the explosion. In your expert opinion, what besides a shot of gunpowder might have set off such a disaster?

Molony: At Mab's Pit we search miners to prevent them from taking pipes and matches underground. We lock the lamps and keep the keys. It doesn't matter. They bring pipes anyway, and if a miner doesn't detect gas and unlocks his lamp to light up – which they do, in spite of every warning – he could certainly kill himself and all his mates.

Hopton: I would like to ask you, as an expert, how miners regard cautions against the discharge of gunpowder underground?

Molony: They're not happy about it.

Liptrot: Why not?

Molony: A shot of gunpowder will loose more coal face than a day's worth of swinging a pick. It's a matter of economics. Miners are paid by how much coal they send up, not how much time or labour they put into it.

Nuttal: Are there other ways in which a miner can undo the best efforts of a mine owner?

Molony: Any number. The first impulse of an improperly trained man, if he finds himself in a gas-saturated tunnel, is to run. If he runs fast enough, the flame will bend through the safety mesh of his lamp and ignite the very gas he is trying to escape.

Nuttal: Considering the force of the explosion at the Hannay Pit, was the tunnel necessarily saturated with gas?

Molony: No. A small initial explosion would do,

242

considering that miners recklessly stuff every coalface in Lancashire with canisters of gunpowder waiting to be used in charges. Once initiated, the canisters can set themselves off in a series of explosions the length of the tunnel.

Hopton: From your long experience, what do you feel was the more likely cause of the Hannay explosion, inadequate supervision on the part of the owners of the pit or a breach of safety regulations on the part of a miner?

Molony: As there was no deficiency in the regulations or their supervision, nothing is left but error on the part of a miner, is there?

According to the report, at this moment a disturbance broke out among the families attending. The uproar continued until a representative of the miners was given permission to speak. The name was familiar to Blair although he had met the man only once, clumsily chasing peas around a dinner plate at Hannay Hall.

Walter Fellowes: I am Agent of the Miners' Union and Mutual Insurance Fund. Acting in those capacities, I went down the Hannay Pit the day after the explosion, and while I agree with Mr Molony that it was a heartrending scene of hellish destruction, I am outraged by his attempt, familiar to us from past inquests of this nature, to lay the blame for a mining disaster on the very victims who suffered its fatal consequences. I would like to remind Mr Molony that it is not mine owners who are brought up lifeless and disfigured to the grief of their widows and children but the miners sent down by those owners. As to whether there is culpability on the part of the owners and compensation due the victims' families, this is a matter for the Civil Court and I would appreciate it if Mr Molony kept his opinion, expert or otherwise, to himself. I would also like to remind Mr Molony that a man who does not bring a certain amount of coal from a pit will soon be unemployed, so it is hardly the miners' greed that leads to the extensive use of gunpowder. I would like to ask Mr Molony a question.

Hopton: I object.

Meek: Fellowes has no standing with the Court.

Coroner: Nevertheless, would Mr Molony entertain a question from Mr Fellowes?

Molony: If Fellowes wants to. Go ahead.

Fellowes: Mr Molony, at all the numerous inquests you have graced with your opinions, have you ever found a wealthy pit owner, rather than a poor miner, responsible for an explosion?

Molony: No, for the simple reason that you do not find wealthy gentlemen swinging a pick or lighting a tube of gunpowder. I would, however, consider them very dangerous if they did.

The report said that, 'General laughter relieved the tension in the room', preparing the way for the most expert and indisputable witness in the realm.

Coroner: The inquest welcomes the comments of Benjamin Thicknesse, Her Majesty's Inspector of Mines.

Thicknesse: I have listened to the testimony delivered today. I have studied the ventilation map and cross-section details of the Hannay Pit. I have some thoughts and conclusions that duty and conscience urge me to share.

First, I offer the sympathy of the Queen and the Royal Family. A disaster on a scale of the Hannay explosion touches the entire nation. Her Majesty mourns with you.

Second, that the mining of deep coal is the most hazardous occupation short of war, has always been and likely always will be.

Third, that the prompt and intelligent actions of the underlooker George Battie and the rescuers he led were the salvation of numerous miners overcome by afterdamp. The swift bricking up of a second gas leak by Battie, Smallbone and Jaxon possibly staunched a second disaster.

Fourth, I cannot take issue with the opinions of any of the expert witnesses. They may all be right; they may all be wrong. A miner might have rashly opened his lamp to light his pipe, but we will never know. A spark, a flame, a gunpowder tin may have contributed singly or collectively to the force of the explosion. The answer is buried at the coal face. Was ventilation sufficient to clear the gas? After all, fresh air had to travel down a full mile from the surface, and then circulate through eight miles of tunnels and cross-tunnels. Based on safety standards as we currently know them, our calculations say that the ventilation was sufficient, yet a boy and his pony could have knocked one piece of canvas down and disrupted the whole carefully planned flow of air. It is a fact that the Lancashire coalfield is a 'fiery' coalfield – that is, particularly given to the accumulation of explosive gases. This fact is exacerbated by another one. The deeper the coal, the more fiery the coal. Yet the deeper the coal, the harder the coal, making gunpowder more necessary.

Finally, there is one more element: coal itself. Coal dust that lingers in a tunnel atmosphere and reddens the miner's eye and blackens his lung is, in proper ratio to oxygen, almost as explosive as gunpowder. This is, of course, a controversial point. No matter, one might ask how any man would chance work in subterranean chambers so fraught with known and unknown perils? How could any father kiss his children goodbye in the morning with the knowledge that by the afternoon they might be orphans?

This would, however, be an emotional and short-sighted response. It would bring British industry to a halt. Mills would lie empty, locomotives would stand and rust in their yards, ships would idle at their docks.

It is also an insult to science. British technology is improving every day. As knowledge increases, safety assuredly follows.

Finally, a single human error, one breach of orders, may well have been to blame for this catastrophe.

Tragically, the answer is buried. We will simply never know.

The record indicated that the jury deliberated for fifteen minutes, then returned with their verdict.

We the jury find that seventy-six men came to their deaths by an explosion of firedamp at the Hannay Pit on 18 January; by what means or by whom the gas was ignited there is insufficient evidence to show.

The jury is also unanimous in stating that the mine in which the calamity has happened has been properly conducted, and that there is no blame to be attached to the proprietors of the said company.

Not that the jury had been asked about the company's blame, but in a sentence they had effectively destroyed the chance of any victim's family bringing a claim against the Hannay Pit.

Blair raised a bitter toast of arsenic and brandy. What a surprise.

Appended to the report was a copy of the lampman's ledger for anyone who had signed for a lamp the day of the explosion. The list included survivors and rescuers as well as victims.

Battie, George	308
Paddy	081
Pimblett, Albert	024
Pimblett, Robert	220

The names went on at numbing length, but the point was, as Battie had said, that there were seventy-six lamps for seventy-six bodies.

Blair wore blankets like a Turkish pasha to make himself decent when dinner was brought by a girl with popped eyes who set out grilled chops and claret.

'Everybody's talkin' about what tha said.'

'What did I say?'

'About t'Africans an' t'macaroni. Ah laughed an' laughed.'

'It's not a bad story.'

'Art feelin' well or pot?'

'A little sore, thanks. Definitely pot.'

'It's terrible out, a night t'stay in.'

'I'm not stirring.'

'Oh, an' there's a letter, too.'

The girl produced it from her apron. Her hands lingered so long on the creamy envelope and raised monogram that she dropped it, but Blair caught it on its way to the floor. He tore the flap open and removed a single page that said, 'Come to Theatre Royal tomorrow at noon. Prepare yourself for a cultural occasion. H.'

A typically imperious summons from Hannay, with

no chance to beg off. A Wigan 'cultural occasion'? What was that?

When Blair looked up, he saw that the girl's eyes had popped even more, and he realized that in saving the letter his blanket had slipped from the leeches that formed a row of dark, fat commas along his flank.

'Sorry. They're not pretty. Of course at this point they're practically family.'

'Nawh.'

'Yes. They even have names. Hopton, Liptrot, Nuttal and Meek.' He covered up. She was on tiptoe, as if he might next reveal a tail or a horn on his head.

She folded her thin arms and shivered. 'Gives me goosepimples.'

'I hope so. It's girls who don't get goosepimples that come to a bad end.'

'True?'

'It's the last form of decency.'

Give me leeches rather than lawyers, though, Blair thought. Despite what Hannay's Counsel claimed, miners did not make certain mistakes. Experienced miners did not open safety lamps or run recklessly through gas. If in those last seconds they had noticed their lamp flames start to float, they would have hastily organized brattices to clear the gas. Or, failing that, made an orderly retreat through the fresh air that was still blowing through the main road.

Which raised other questions. Before the explosion, why did Jaxon and the injured Smallbone choose to make their way from the coal face through the fouler air of the back road?

Something even more curious had emerged. George Battie told the inquest that his first act after the explosion was to send messengers up in the cage. Wedge, the Manager, testified that after the messenger arrived on the surface the volunteers there had to wait for the cage to come up again. Why had the cage gone down? Who took it? Was it possible, Blair thought, that he had finally caught sight of John Maypole?

It was strangely pleasant to engage in an intellectual puzzle. His mind had raced ahead so fast that he had not noticed that the serving girl was still standing at the door.

'Something else?' he asked.

'Just everyone's talkin' abowt how tha beat Bill Jaxon. That's never happened before.'

'Is that so?'

'And how he's looking for tha.'

The inquest vanished from Blair's mind. 'Now *I've* got goosepimples. Anything else?'

'That was all.' She backed out.

Blair waited a minute, pushed the tray away, peeled off the leeches one by one and dressed.

Chapter Thirteen

Rain gave Blair an excuse to pull his collar up. Curtains were drawn and the pavements empty except for urchins chasing through the water that rushed out of the gutters. He pounded on her door to be heard over the downpour.

When Rose finally opened, he hobbled through and leaned against the jamb, resting his weight on one leg. The kitchen was lit only by an angle of lamplight from the parlour. Why did she always keep the house so dark? Her hair was wild, spilling from a comb. Skin olive from coal dust, in a skirt and blouse of patched muslin, sleeves too short for her wrists, the same as she had worn the night before. There was no sign of her friend Flo.

'I told you not t'come back,' she said.

'I didn't want to, but word is going around that I beat Bill Jaxon in a fight. I'd rather hear that Bill beat me, or that there was no fight at all.'

'I couldn't care either way.'

'Someone is spreading this story.'

'Not me. I haven't thought about you or Bill all day.'

From the open doorway, neither in nor out, he glanced around as if he might have missed Bill sitting on a kitchen chair in the dark. The house seemed as empty as ever, which again made no sense in the Calcutta conditions of Scholes.

'Tell Bill I'm not his rival. I have no interest in you.'

'Such pretty words. You're no more a poet than a gentleman.'

'I just want to leave Wigan as soon as possible. I don't want to get involved.'

'Involved in what?'

'Anything. I told Bill I was a coward.'

'Well, he should have listened.'

'Tell him—' Blair started when the sound of the rain on slate roofs accelerated to a drumming that drowned out his words and, without thinking, he moved away from the open door. Without conscious intent, he found his hand on her waist. By itself it drew her close. Rose could have hit him or driven her comb into his hand. Instead, she raised her mouth to his and gave him the taste of coal.

'Take off your hat,' she said.

He let it drop to the floor. She turned his head to the side to see the shaven patch, then turned it again to study his eyes. How he had gone from one point to another, Blair didn't understand. Some sign had passed that he hadn't caught, only acted on.

'That must hurt,' Rose said.

'It should.'

Through his hand he felt her heart, beating as hard as his. He couldn't hear the clock over the rain, but he saw the pendulum stirring by the grate. If he could have stepped back in time a mere minute and undone his touch, he would have. He couldn't. Besides, at a moment when her usual coquetry could have been expected and would have set him free, Rose seemed as astonished as he was. Or she was a better actor.

Upstairs, her room had an unlit lamp, the shadow of a chest of drawers, a bed with cotton sheets as worn as cambric. In his arms she was more slender than he had expected, and paler. He caught the flash of her back in a long mirror.

A year of deprivation made the slightest touch feverish, as in a reverie. Need was a form of insanity, he thought. He entered her with desperation, as a drowning man rises to the surface. She couldn't have been more than nineteen or twenty, but she waited for him with patience. He felt like a satyr upon her younger body, until, when he was firmly set, her face coloured and he felt her legs around his back.

What would the first drink of water in a year be like? What is water to the soul? What is astonishing about a primal act is the wholeness of two bodies, as he was astonished to find himself in a bed and made complete by a mere pit girl. He was aware of her sooty hands and face, and of his hands and face growing as dark, but mostly of her eyes, which watched him with a glow of triumph.

Sweat shone on her brow and welled around her eyes, making the lids darker, the whites brighter, avenues to a gaze that drew him in. Should an ignorant girl be shallow? There was a depth to Rose he was unprepared for, but now had fallen into. More than fallen: plunged.

Pain washed away. Or he had gone to a level where

pain could not follow, a level that was all Rose, where he felt himself gladly disappear then reappear, his whole body hard as a stone she clung to, then shudder and dissolve from stone to flesh.

'How old are you?' Rose asked.

'Thirty, thirty-two, somewhere there.'

'Somewhere? How can you not know?'

Blair shrugged.

She said, 'I hear people go t'America and start over. I didn't think they forgot that much.'

'I started early and I forgot a lot.'

'You know where you are now?'

'Oh, yes.'

She had lit the smallest blue flame on the lamp and sat against pillows packed against the pipes of the headboard. She exhibited – if that was the word – a complete lack of shame. Quantitatively – and he was an engineer, after all – she had a slim, almost wiry body with sharply pointed breasts and a twist of brown, not red, hair at the base of her stomach. Her eyes, in turn, looked across her body and met his gaze with an unblinking assertion that there was yet more he would have to recognize and contend with.

'I don't mean Wigan,' she said.

'I know.'

He sat against the foot of the bed, his bad leg trailing to the boards on the floor. Flo might be out another hour or all night, she told him.

'You have a house to yourself? How do you manage that?'

'That's my business.'

'You're not a simple girl.'

'You wanted a simple girl?'

'I wanted no girl at all. That's not what I came for. That's not what I thought I came for.'

'Then what happened?'

'I don't know.' He couldn't explain to himself what had guided his hand to her. 'All I know is that your madman Bill is out in the rain looking for me.'

'You're safe here.'

'That doesn't sound likely.'

'Do you want t'go?'

'No.'

'Good.'

In their voices was the excitement shared by two people who had cast off from shore in a small craft on to high seas in the dark with no plan at all. She wasn't his equal, he reminded himself. He had seen four continents; she had spent her life close by the mines. Yet from the platform of this bed they seemed to be equals. Now her claims of distinction – like the velvet ribbon she wore, even in trousers – didn't look ridiculous. Was he misleading himself, or was it intelligence aimed from her eyes?

'You've been living like a grandee. Can you bear t'spend the night here?'

'I've been living like the dead. Yes, I'd rather be here.'

'"Living like the dead"? I like that, I know what you

MARTIN CRUZ SMITH

mean. Working at the pit, sorting coal, I feel like a chambermaid in Hell.'

'Do you hate it?'

'No. Working in a mill, that I'd hate. The noise? I've friends who hardly hear any more. Air so full of cotton you can't breathe? Wearing skirts around all those spinning gears? You lose a leg, choke t'death or die of consumption. And for less money. I'm lucky.'

'You could be a domestic.'

'Be a maid? I know that's more respectable, but I'd rather have my self-respect.'

Talk died for a second because they didn't know each other, he thought. They had nothing in common, had gone through no period of wooing, only found themselves impelled towards each other, like planets falling into a mutual gravitational pull.

'How many maids have you seduced?'

'How many men have you seduced?'

She smiled, as if that erased the questions. 'Was it different, having a white girl again? Or is it true what they say, that all cats are grey in the dark?'

'I haven't had all that many women, but all were different.'

'How?'

'Touch, smell, taste, motion, heat.'

'God, you're a scientist. And what do I taste like?'

He ran his hand over her flank and across her belly, then licked his palm.

'Rose. A slightly burnt rose.'

She shifted to one elbow. Though her brow hid in the

256

tangle of her hair, the jet picked out in her irises scattered bits of brown and green. And though coal dust lay like a resident shadow across her face, her body had a red-head's extreme fairness, with veins so blue around the swell of her breasts that he could almost watch her pulse.

She ran her hand up his leg and held him there. 'I see you're alive again.'

Rose was no ordinary girl, Blair thought. He had brought a year's hunger to her bed and yet her passion matched his, as if a single night would have to feed the rest of her life, too. She had the abandon that willingly, consciously accepted damnation if she could find someone to be damned with.

As *she* was *someone*. Not dismissable, not a tourist's photographic curiosity, nor a silhouette standing on a slag heap. As real as any Hannay.

Was it love? He thought not. Their bodies beat together with a ferocity more like anger, like crazed, sweating cymbals. He felt his eyes starting, the muscles of his shoulders straining as her nails travelled the groove of his back.

White smeared black, the sheets spread infinitely from side to side. Above the bed was ordinary space. Within her a deeper place. Not Wigan. A different land altogether.

*

'You're starting t'heal.'

She straddled him and parted the hair from the cut on his head.

'That's my plan,' he said.

'It's a brilliant plan if you can stay away from Bill.'

'That's the major part of the plan – at least, it was.'

She hopped off Blair and was back a moment later with a shawl. She sat on his chest and turned his head to the side.

He asked, 'What are you doing?'

She spat on the wound and blew on coal dust from the shawl. 'What miners do,' she said.

Chapter Fourteen

A piano piece by Mendelssohn was followed by a brass band playing 'Onward, Christian Soldiers' while children costumed in huge paper collars and cotton beards as martyrs of the Reformation marched on to the stage of the Theatre Royal.

'The children are orphans of miners. The benefit is for them,' Leveret whispered to Blair. They stood in the rear of the theatre, under a bust of Shakespeare with pen in hand. The theatre bowed to all the Bard's plays, with murals of tragic figures and ardent lovers, on the proscenium the sight of Othello the Moor poling a gondola across the Grand Canal.

Blair had arrived late and kept his hat on the blued stitches on his head. He saw Hannay in a box seat; the Bishop seemed to be looking down from his height at a simple-minded but profoundly amusing comedy.

Leveret explained, 'Queen Elizabeth has the prettiest dress and all the red hair. You can tell Bloody Mary by the blood on her hands.'

'Reminds me of Charlotte.'

'Wyclif, the martyr, is tied to a stake, naturally. That's why most of the children are carrying torches.'

'That's the way I feel.'

'There will be two tableaux, one religious, one cultural.'

'Wonderful, but why did Hannay ask me here?'

Leveret was evasive. After some hesitation he said, 'I have the list you asked for.'

'Of "Women Who Have Fallen for the First Time"?'

'Yes.' Leveret handed him an envelope as covertly as if he were passing French postcards.

Two executioners in black hoods led the martyrs out. A string quartet played 'Drink to Me Only with Thine Eyes', J. B. Fellowes of the Miners' Union reported on the status of the Widows' Fund, and the quartet finished the first half of the programme with 'Annie Laurie'.

During the interval, Wigan gentry moved down the staircase to the lounge. This was the class whose coaches stood outside the drapers and milliners on Wallgate and Millgate, whose servants polished the brass and swept the pavements every morning, who invested in government funds at 5 per cent; in other words, people who wore shoes instead of clogs. When Blair thought of the effort involved in dressing for a charitable event such as this – the lacing of corsets, the mating of hooks and eyes on boned bodices, the hoisting of crinoline cages to squirming waists and laying of petticoats on top – every woman represented a battery of chambermaids with bloody fingers. The final effect was a flow of ladies in watered silk, foulard and grosgrain in hues of fuchsia and grenadine, accompanied by men who in their cravats and black suits seemed as static as burned trees. Some of the younger women affected the 'Alexandra limp', after the princess left lame by rheumatic fever. As Blair's own leg was stiff, he felt to some degree in style.

He was mystified about what was supposed to transpire in the theatre, although he was aware that around him there was a whisper of anticipation. In the centre was Lady Rowland, wearing the erotic glow of a woman accustomed to masculine attention. Her black hair, veined with silver, pillowed a hat with a green stone. Blair couldn't hear the banter, but he saw the way she skilfully led it with her fan, rewarding each sally with the appreciative smile of a mature and extravagantly attractive woman. On an outer ring of her solar system bobbed Chief Constable Moon, resplendent in a black frockcoat with black silk braids that hung from his shoulder to his cuff, carrying a dress helmet with a black ostrich plume. Blair didn't think word of his nocturnal visit to Rose Molyneux could have reached Moon already, but he kept a distance from the Chief Constable anyway.

A coterie of younger admirers surrounded Lydia Rowland, and if the mother glowed, the daughter, with less effort, glittered. A circlet of white roses framed her golden hair and blue eyes, with their gaze of crystalline innocence. Was it innocence or complete blankness? Blair asked himself.

He was so mesmerized that it took him a moment to notice Charlotte Hannay and Earnshaw in a corner. It had to be punishment for her to be in the same room as Lydia Rowland, for where her cousin shone, Charlotte was a pale figure in a dour, purplish gown, her hair a margin of angry red under a tangle of black lace. Here she was, the local heiress, and she could as well have been a governess or an émigrée from some cursed Middle European state. Earnshaw was at her side, his beard looking as brushed as his suit.

Charlotte's response to some riposte from Earnshaw was a basilisk stare that would have plunged a normal man into silence, but the Member of Parliament maintained a confident air of satisfaction. Which was why politicians were assassinated, Blair thought, because nothing else would faze them.

'So the benefit is for orphans?' he asked Leveret.

'A special subscription for their pageant.'

The band had come downstairs and lined up in front of bowls of punch and trays of meringues. The blue serge and brass buttons of their uniforms brought out the English pinkness of their cheeks. Behind the table hung oversized paintings on uplifting themes: *The Sermon on the Mount*, *The Quelling of the Waves*, *Judith Bearing the Head of Holofernes*. Blair became aware of Bishop Hannay and Lydia Rowland at his side.

'*The Sermon* is such a peaceful painting, Mr Blair, don't you agree?' Lydia asked. 'The crowd, blue skies and olive trees, and Jesus in the distance.'

'The wrong painting for Blair. He's not a man for fair weather,' Hannay said. 'He's one for storms and sharp knives. We don't want him too tame. I wish we had more than Temperance punch, Blair. From what I understand, you've earned it.'

'How is that?'

262

'Rumours have reached me that you are actually beating people to extract information.'

'That would be terrible, Your Grace, but he hasn't, I promise,' Leveret said.

'Why not? If Blair is finally getting interested, that's good.'

Blair looked at the black worn by other guests. 'I should have dressed differently.'

'No, you're blending in very well,' Hannay said. 'Leveret, don't you have a little surprise to see to?'

'Yes, Your Grace.' Leveret rushed off.

From different points across the gallery, Blair sensed the icy regard of Lady Rowland and an electric loathing from Charlotte Hannay. He felt the cut on the side of his head. He didn't feel that he was blending in.

Although Hannay drew Blair aside, the presence of a bishop created a kind of vortex. All heads turned to the Bishop, though few guests were secure enough in social status to approach. It did strike Blair as a public place to hold a private conversation.

Hannay said casually, 'Give me the benefit of your opinion. Who among the women here would you say was a shining light? Who is a diamond among dull stones?'

'Lydia Rowland, I suppose.'

'Lydia? Lydia is a stunning girl in an ordinary way. Next month the London season starts. My sister will take Lydia down to London to present her at Court, pay calls at the right houses and drive in the right carriages and dance at the right balls until she attracts a husband. No different from the customs of tribes we've met. No, I don't mean Lydia. What do I care about Lydia?'

'You mean Charlotte?'

'You can't see it? Of course, she is my daughter. She also used to be the brightest, most amusing child in the world. A dazzling princess. When she went down to London for her début she wouldn't have any of the Horse Guards or fops strutting in Court, and I didn't blame her. Now I hardly recognize her. It is as if she pours ashes over herself every morning to hide how bright she is. Look at her next to that sack of gas, Earnshaw. A professional politician. He defeated an old friend of mine, Lord Jeremy. Jeremy was a fool to run. He stood for office on the whimsical platform that his family had served the country since the Black Prince and that he employed ten thousand men and paid a hundred thousand pounds in wages, whereas Earnshaw was a nobody who employed a single clerk. Earnshaw won and now proposes that peers not be allowed to run for the Commons at all, that they be confined like relics to the House of Lords. Serves Jeremy right.'

'Why?'

'You don't run against professional politicians, you buy them.'

'Earnshaw is bought?' This was a different view of the champion of moral reform, Blair thought.

'It's been a great waste of money if he isn't.'

'Even for a bishop that sounds cynical.'

'As a young man I preached the Golden Rule, in

middle years I tried to persuade by reason. I don't have that sort of time any more.'

'What did you pay Earnshaw to do? He seems to be a suitor for Charlotte.'

'Earnshaw is not a suitor, he is a locomotive. He will huff and puff, and then, when he's scheduled to, will disappear down the track.' Hannay stopped to welcome an ancient matron cobwebbed in veils, inquire after her health, direct her to the meringues. He returned to Blair. 'Orphans always draw a crowd.'

'There were a lot of orphans on the stage today.'

'Orphans are the price of coal.'

'I read the Coroner's report. Seventy-six men died, and your lawyers succeeded in making sure that the mine was held blameless. You don't want the inquest reopened.'

'I believe everything is back to normal now.'

'Not for the dead, not for widows who weren't allowed a legal claim against you.'

'Blair, as I remember, the Coroner's jury indicated that one of the dead miners was responsible. We lost two weeks' production. I made no legal claim against the widows for my financial losses, which were substantial. Please don't feign compassion. You merely hope that I will be so frightened of reopening the inquest that I will declare you done and send you happily away. But I won't do that.'

'You don't mind if I ask more questions about that report?'

'On legal grounds? I have no anxieties.'

Blair saw Hannay's quick look through the crowd towards four men huddled by the stairs. They were all in their thirties, balding, edgy as whippets. Four dowdy wives in flowery dresses stood close by.

'Hopton, Liptrot, Nuttal and Meek?'

'Hopton, Liptrot, Nuttal and Meek, *Esquires*. Very good. Yes, I feel adequately represented in the courts.'

Blair caught enough of their return glances to tell that the lawyers would not be so comfortable with his questions as Hannay claimed to be. Inquests, like the dead, were best buried. He also sensed the approaching glare of Charlotte Hannay. 'Why did you ask me here? Why do I feel that the orphans aren't the show, that I am?'

'Well, you are. Half.'

Charlotte brought Leveret, who had returned. 'Mr Blair, I understand that you bullied Oliver into stealing the names of women who have sought help from the Home. Do you have any sense of privacy? What good purpose could a morally debased individual like you have for those names?'

'It's to find John,' Leveret said. 'It's for you.'

'On my behalf? Inform me, then. What villains has the famous Blair encountered in his investigation? Footpads, assassins, highwaymen?'

'Just miners,' Blair said.

Like a man dropping a pin, sure that it would be heard, Hannay asked, 'Any women?'

Lydia had returned, just in time to catch her breath. 'Uncle, that's an outrageous suggestion.'

'Is it?'

'Not with John,' Leveret protested.

Hannay said, 'I want to hear Blair's answer. As Charlotte's father and as John Maypole's bishop, I should want to know if he was involved with another woman. Blair?'

'Maypole was involved with a lot of women, especially women in trouble. Whether that meant something besides good works, I don't know.'

'You wanted names, so there was someone,' Hannay said.

'It's too soon to say.'

'One of those girls from Charlotte's Home? A pit girl, a mill girl?'

'What does it matter?'

'Mill girls are consumptive and ethereal, pit girls are robust. I see Maypole as being more attracted to the consumptive type.'

'I really don't know.'

'Well, one thing is clear,' Hannay announced. 'Blair is making progress. Charlotte, it's time to give up Maypole. Either his ghost or, worse, his sins will emerge soon. Blair has the bit now and I will whip him on until he finds your little curate or his bones. It's time to rearrange your life.'

A moment passed before the Hannays and Rowlands noticed that the rest of the lounge was watching, rapt. Not that the Hannays or the Rowlands ever seemed to care particularly; it had occurred to Blair before that the Bishop and his family set their own laws of conduct, and that for them other people existed no more than as faces daubed on a backdrop. In that distorted context, Hannay seemed to have especially staged this event.

The Bishop turned to all. 'Now for the surprise. In the first part of the programme, a pageant of children engagingly portrayed the martyrs who suffered gloriously for their mission: to spread the Bible and the Word of God throughout England. Today Britain has a mission to lift the many new peoples of the earth out of their ignorance and to take to them that same Word. Fortunately, we are blessed with new heroes, as you shall see when we reassemble upstairs.'

In the middle of the stage was a closed mahogany case as tall as a man. While the band played 'Rule, Britannia!', the orphans returned to the stage in blackface, black wigs and 'leopard skins' of spotted muslin. The boys held bamboo spears and cardboard shields; the girls carried coconuts. Their eyes and teeth shone.

'Africans,' Lydia Rowland told Blair.

'I can see that.'

A solemn girl in a tiara and an ermine robe of braided wool rolled over the boards on a canvas ship pushed by two 'Africans'.

'The Queen,' Lydia said.

'Right.'

'Rule, Britannia!' quavered to a finish, and Queen and ship trembled to a halt next to the case. When the applause diminished, Bishop Hannay joined her, thanked her and the other orphans, and let a second round of applause die.

'This is the dawn of a new age. We are exploring a new world, bringing it light in exchange for dark, freedom in exchange for shackles and, instead of primitive survival, a share in a trade that brings tea from Ceylon, rubber from Malaya, steel from Sheffield and cloth from Manchester on steamers from Liverpool that burn Wigan coal, never forgetting that our enterprise is blessed only when the Bible leads the way.

'As you know, my nephew, Lord Rowland, has manifested a passion for this dangerous task. Particularly on the Gold Coast of West Africa, he has laboured to free natives from the yoke of slavers, to bring those natives under the protection of the Crown, and to deliver them from superstitious ignorance by the lamp of the Church.

'Only this morning Lord Rowland arrived in Liverpool from Africa on an Atlantic mail ship. He was on his way at once to London to address the Royal Geographical Society about his explorations in the Gold Coast and the Congo and to report to the Anti-Slavery League about his efforts to stamp out that inhuman trade. Telegrams flew back and forth until we persuaded him to honour this benefit not with a formal speech, but with his presence. He will go immediately from this theatre to the station. I know that London is anxious to receive him, but Lord Rowland shares the family sentiment that Wigan comes first.

'During his travels in Africa Lord Rowland has incidentally gathered artefacts and curiosities that he deemed worthy of study at the Royal Society. He has consented to a first public exhibition of one such specimen here today for this benefit before it travels with him to London. Perhaps I do so with special pride, but I know I speak for us all in welcoming Lord Rowland.'

A slim man with golden hair appeared on stage to take Hannay's handshake. As the Bishop left him on stage alone, every row in the theatre stood to applaud. Lady Rowland proudly rose on tiptoe. As Lydia Rowland clapped, her fan spun on her wrist. The band roared back into 'Rule, Britannia!' with more fervour than before.

'Explorer! Emancipator! Missionary!' the girl Queen started to read her scroll. The rest of her words were overwhelmed by acclamation.

Rowland accepted the homage with an absolute still-ness that focused all the more on him. It was a natural theatricality that had worked in Africa as well, Blair remembered. He was a little changed from the more robust man who had first arrived in Accra. That was the effect of Africa, Blair thought. First the skeleton came home, then the flesh, then the shock of leaving equatorial weather for the cold piss of the English spring. He almost felt sorry for the man.

Rowland's hair fell in wings at his forehead and was matched by a wispy beard. The stage lights seemed to lean towards him, to illuminate a balance of even features. Staring towards the rear of the theatre, he had the beauty of someone philosophical, Hamlet before a

soliloquy. Like Hamlet, responding absently to adulation
as if it were irrelevant, which provoked it more. Hannay
made his way back to the front row. Rowland's attention
followed the Bishop; his eyes found his sister in the
crowd and focused on her for a moment, then on
Charlotte, whose arms were stiff by her side. His eyes
moved restlessly on until he located Blair in the row
behind. There was a glitter to the gaze, a shifting of light
within.

'Rule, Britannia!' ended with a flourish of horns,
followed by murmurs throughout the theatre. Rowland
stepped in front of the mahogany case and executed a
diffident nod that seemed to be interpreted as a hero's
modest bow. Still sharing the stage, the orphans were a
line of white smiles on dark faces. Of course if they really
were Africans, Blair thought, they would be running for
their lives.

'That is too kind, much too kind. The Bishop has
asked me to say a few words.' Rowland paused as if
reluctant to intrude. His voice filled the theatre effort-
lessly. Which was important for explorers; they made
their fame with books and lectures as much as exploration. Perhaps he was being petty, Blair told himself, just
because he himself hadn't been invited to lecture anywhere but Mary Jaxon's kitchen.

'The journey itself', Rowland said, 'was not remarkable. Passage from Liverpool on a mail ship of the
African Steam Ship Line bound for Madeira, the Azores,
the Gold Coast, Sierra Leone. Endless trip until we

271

transferred to a frigate of the Royal Navy on patrol to interdict slave ships. Thence to Accra, on the Gold Coast, to pursue slavers on land.'

Rowland brushed his hair from his eyes and took note of the 'native' orphans for the first time. 'On land. The worst feature of coastal Africa is the proliferation of mixed bloods. While Portuguese half-castes are super-ficially attractive, English blood mixes badly with the African and produces a muddied, mentally enfeebled race. It is one more reason for an Englishman to remember that he has a higher mission in Africa than the Portuguese or Arab trader of flesh.'

What about a mix of Celts, Vikings and Normans? Blair thought.

'Imagine, if you can,' Rowland said, 'a world of profuse and untamed nature, peopled with slaves and slavers, infested by every kind of predator that God in his curiosity could create, infected by a spiritual ignor-ance that can worship the baboon, the chameleon, the crocodile.' He touched the mahogany case. 'Animals were, in fact, another objective, with the aim to further science – British science, through the study of rare specimens. I repeat that this exhibit is purely scientific and pray that it does not offend.'

Rowland opened the doors of the case. Inside, bedded on white satin, were two black hands cut off at the wrist. Spiky black hair covered the back of one hand. The other was reversed to show a black, deeply creased, leathery palm with flat, triangulate fingers. The wrists wore bands of beaten gold.

'These are the hands of a great soko, or gorilla, that I shot near the Congo River. I had surprised him and his group while they were feeding. I felt deeply privileged to see them because, despite their great size, sightings are so rare. This is only the third specimen brought from Africa.'

Blair heard Charlotte Hannay whisper to Earnshaw, 'You approve?'

Earnshaw said, 'Absolutely. Not only on scientific grounds, but also for national prestige.'

Blair saw Charlotte's eyes darken with revulsion.

'What do you think, Blair?' Earnshaw turned and demanded.

'Maybe the rest is coming in another box.'

'Imagine a gentleman like him standing up to savages and apes.' Chief Constable Moon insinuated himself next to Blair. 'He seems to know you.'

'I think we know each other.'

'He must cut a figure in Africa.'

'Excellent posture, beautiful clothes.'

'Something else, surely.'

Charlotte looked to catch Blair's answer. Blair saw Rowland look down from the stage at the same moment. 'Totally insane.'

Blair's words were swallowed as the brass band picked up the self-satisfied strains of 'Home Sweet Home'. Rowland listened in the distracted manner of someone listening from a distance. Or about to escape.

Moon tugged on Blair's sleeve.

'What is it?' Blair had to shout to be heard.

Moon shouted back, 'I said, I've found Silcock.'

'Who?'

'Silcock, the man you were after. If you want. It's your investigation.'

Chapter Fifteen

They rode along the canal in the Chief Constable's carriage, all black lacquer and brass like an undertaker's coach. Blair kept his hat on despite the pricking on his temple where the stitches rasped against the hat band. Leveret had come along at Moon's insistence. The afternoon had narrowed to a tunnel of dark clouds. Mill chimneys were lit sideways like columns along the Nile.

Moon was still thrilled by the event they had left. 'Quite a sight, those hands. Educational, as Mr Earnshaw said. What do you think, Mr Leveret? Should we show those hands to every naughty boy in Wigan and scare some improvement?'

'Is that what you'd do?' Blair asked.

'Made all the women take a step back, didn't they? I'd say having a pair of hands like that to show would improve behaviour all the way around.'

'Ask Lord Rowland. Maybe he could get you another pair. The Royal Society could have one pair and you'd have the other. Use them at school or in the home.'

'You're being humorous? Is Mr Blair being humorous?' Moon asked Leveret, who squirmed on his seat like a tall man trying not to be noticed. 'One of the things I liked about your father was that he had no sense of humour at all.'

'He didn't,' Leveret agreed.

'I always knew where he stood, and I'd like to think I know where you stand.'

Leveret looked out of the carriage and nodded.

'I wasn't joking,' Blair told the Chief Constable. 'You're at least the scientist that Rowland is.'

Moon swung the weight of his attention from Leveret to Blair. 'But it must deeply impress the natives when Rowland stands up to a giant ape.'

'It does, I'm sure. He not only stands up to the ape, he tracks it, traps it and blows its head off.'

'Lord Rowland is a marksman, I hear. And specimens, as Mr Earnshaw was saying, are the beginning of zoology.'

'Taxidermy.'

'Well, whatever you call it, it's the start of science and civilization, isn't it?'

Blair let it go. He had thought Rowland was in Cape Town or Zanzibar, halfway round the world. It was a shock to see him in Wigan, hailed like the Second Coming. He also smarted from the idea that he had misread Earnshaw. If the man wasn't a suitor, why was he wasting Charlotte Hannay's time? He poured powder across his palm.

'Arsenic?' Moon said. 'I don't believe that in his expeditions Dr Livingstone uses that, does he?'

'He uses opium.' Blair tossed the dose down and felt a bitterness spread through his mouth and brain. 'Tell me about Silcock.'

'Sort of a thug, sort of a sport. If he didn't take your

money at cards, he'd catch you in the alley afterwards. I warned him off Wigan twice in January, the second time after the fire. Anyway, we have him in a corner now.'

'Has anyone asked him about Maypole?'

'No. Have you ever been in trouble with the law yourself, Mr Blair?'

'Why do you ask?'

'Because you have the look. Not quite a wolf in sheep's clothing. More like a wolf with a scarf around his neck. Someone might say, "Oh, he's wearing a collar." I would say, "No, he's planning to eat." When I hear you had a dust-up with Bill Jaxon and got the better of him, it inclines me to think my instinct was right.'

'Where did you hear that?'

'Everywhere. I hear he thinks you're after a favourite girl of his. You're not so stupid as that, are you?'

Blair felt a frying along the sutures that Rose had sewn. Could be arsenic, could be Moon.

'Not so stupid, surely, as that?' Moon repeated. 'The women are worse than the men. A fact. Are you aware that in the infirmaries of the British Army most of the beds are filled with victims of venereal disease passed on by prostitutes and loose women?'

'It's passed both ways, isn't it?'

'But innocently or professionally, that's the difference.'

'In peacetime I thought it was the soldier's profession to pass venereal disease.'

'You have your joke again, Mr Blair, but in the south of England loose women are isolated in special hospitals for their own good. Here in the north there is no control.'

'How would you identify them? Bare arms? Trousers?'

'It's a start.'

'You mean pit girls?'

'I mean that pit girls are females who have reverted to the wild state. It's not just a matter of dresses or trousers. Do you think Parliament would investigate these women if it was just a matter of trousers? Trousers are merely a symbol of civilization. Do I care whether they wear trousers or sea-shells or go about stark naked? Not a fig. But I care about the rules. I can tell you from sad experience that civilization is nothing but rules adopted for the general good. I don't know how it is in the South Seas, but once an Englishwoman has dressed in trousers she has divorced herself from decency or the considerations due her sex. Granted it's only a rule, but it's what separates us from the apes. The pit girl has her allure, there's no denying that. The Bishop himself, when he was a young man, before he was a man of the cloth, used to slip into town through the old Hannay tunnels to call on the girls. Was it Saint Valentine said, "Give me chastity, Lord, but not yet"?'

'Saint Augustine.'

'Well, that was Hannay. More than one girl had to leave Wigan with her ticket punched, if you get my meaning.' Moon leaned forward intimately. 'I ask you, how do Africans civilize their women?'

Blair sat back. 'I've never heard it put that way before. You're a regular anthropologist.'

'A policeman has to have an open mind.'

'They scarify them, put plugs in their noses, plates in their lips, weights on their legs, cut off part of their sexual organs.'

Moon pursed his lips. 'Does it work?'

'The women think it's normal.'

'There you are,' Moon said. 'Best rule of all.'

Canal traffic had to stop at locks to rise or fall to the next stretch of water, but it was clear to Blair as he scrambled down to the towpath that the last lock in Wigan was not functioning at all. Boats idled bow to stern in long lines on either side of the lock, and on the towpaths a crowd had gathered, boatmen joined by patrons from canalside beerhouses, boat children spread out on the banks above.

The boats themselves were marvels of design; fifty-foot narrow boats were capable of carrying twenty-five tons of coal or, for pottery factories, flint and bones. More, each boat was a home with a six-foot cabin into which a family of seven typically squeezed, the bows of their boats decorated with fanciful white castles or red Lancashire roses. Despite the imminence of rain there was an atmosphere of a crowd diverted by a street pantomime. Tow horses, Clydesdales, stood forgotten at their lines. Dogs raced back and forth on boat decks. Moon, Leveret and Blair had to push their way through.

A boat aimed upstream was in the south lock. Its crew – father, mother, two boys, three girls, agitated dog, goat with enormous teats, two moulting cats – were on deck and looking over the stern tiller at a man chin-deep in water. His clothes swam around him.

A lock was a simple affair of two basins – one for up traffic, the other for down – each with two pairs of gates. The dimensions, however, were exacting; the boat was seven feet across and the lock was eight feet across, leaving six inches of clearance on each side and about a foot at each end. The boat was tied forward until the bow fender nudged the gate, otherwise the man in the water couldn't have been seen at all.

Water level in the locks was controlled by paddles built into the lock gates; these had to be cranked up or down. But it was an old lock, pounded by boats every day; the up gate leaked in noisy sprays and the level was perceptibly rising. It wasn't a bad problem in normal circumstances; the water level would equalize with the down gate open. Now the motion of the water rocked the boat against the walls and thumped it against the downstream gate. Each time the man in the water had to go under and then climb back up to a tenuous handhold on the punched and splintered oak of the gate or the slime-covered bricks of the lock wall.

Moon said, 'Somehow Silcock seems to have caught his foot in a paddle in the down gate. The lock isn't big enough for Silcock and the boat, but we can't open the up gate without raising the water and drowning him. We can't open the down gate because the boats behind are packed so tight. He's trapped himself very smartly.'

'Why don't you crank the paddle off his foot?' Blair asked.

'That's the obvious solution,' Moon said. 'Every boat carries a crank – a "key" we call it, as Mr Leveret could tell you, one of his grandfathers being a lock-keeper – but the boatman managed to rip off the ratchet nut the key fits on. We could have a hundred keys, but none will work.'

Blair saw divers in the water outside the downstream gate. Moon said, 'The men are diving for the nut but this canal, with all the coal dust that's fell in it, is black as the river Styx. We're waiting for another; in the meantime, how does the old saw go: "For want of a nail a horse was lost, for want of a horse a battle was lost"?'

'How long has Silcock been in?'

'Since six this morning. I told you we'd warned him off twice before and he wouldn't admit to the men who he was until just before the ceremonies.'

'You could have told me as soon as you got there.'

'And miss Lord Rowland? I only trust you'll remember to tell His Lordship and the Bishop how helpful Chief Constable Moon was to you and brought you personally to carry out your private investigation. Mr Leveret, will you make sure of that?'

'Of course.'

'How did it happen?' Blair asked.

'You'll notice there's no bridge here. We tell them not to, but some fools will cross by walking on the gates, usually when they're staggering out of a beerhouse.

Silcock must have fallen in. He makes an example, doesn't he?'

'The Chief Constable likes examples,' Leveret said.

'It's what people remember,' Moon said.

Across the top of Silcock's skull wet hair splayed from a gash that was open to the bone.

'How'd he manage that?' Blair asked.

'The boat was tied up in the lock for the night. He must have hit it on the way down.'

'Didn't the boatmen see him?'

'No.'

'You're telling me that the boatman cranked the paddle on to a man's leg and didn't notice?'

'I'm telling you that the boatman was so drunk he wouldn't have noticed the parting of the Red Sea. He was drunk, his wife was drunk, their children were drunk. Probably the dog and cats were drunk too. Right, Mr Leveret?'

Leveret, however, had vanished. As the boat wallowed, a jet of water arced from the up gate the length of the basin. Blair realized that if Silcock's leg wasn't jammed in the paddle and draining the lock to some extent he would have drowned already. Of course if he wasn't trapped he wouldn't drown at all. One of those ancient conundrums. And Wigan did seem to be the sort of place where people slept on the tracks and slipped down old shafts, so why not swim in a canal lock?

Moon shouted down until he got Silcock's attention. 'Silcock, there's a man here with questions for you.'

Fish-eyed, Silcock gasped up from the water.

Blair tried to imagine him dry, with a bowler and a deck of cards. 'Can you move the people away?' he asked Moon.

'These people get little enough entertainment. No pageants, no lords or bishops, no great apes.'

True enough, this was the sort of audience that appreciated public dramas, be it a train wreck or a hanging. This was a tribe the Bible did not mention. Men in plug hats, the descendants of gypsies and Irish navvies, the dark captains of the waterways, and women in blowzy skirts white with ground bone or orange from iron ore. They had assembled before Blair's arrival and were intent on staying for the duration of the performance. Which wouldn't take much longer.

Blair told Moon, 'While I talk to him, you can send for a fire pump or a pump from a mine.'

'And try to lower the Leeds–Liverpool Canal? I think not.'

'Back up the boats and open the gate.'

'Rehitch twenty horses and twenty boats? Not at this point.'

'Amputate,' shouted a man in the crowd.

'Underwater?' another voice asked reasonably.

'Help me.' Silcock grabbed for a diver and almost pulled him under.

Moon said, 'Mr Blair, I'd say you have the stage. If you have any questions, there's no time like the present.'

Blair asked, 'Can you at least get me a rope?'

A boy on the deck eagerly volunteered a mooring line.

Blair made a noose and lowered it to Silcock, who slipped his head and arms through, gaining a quarter inch above the water, and fought off the tiller as it swung his way.

'Let the tiller be,' Blair called down. 'Don't think about it.'

Silcock focused on Blair. 'What should I be finking about?'

'Who did this to you?'

'I don't know. I only come back to Wigan last night and I fell in, I suppose, and split my head. I don't remember.'

'Were you drunk?'

'I hope so.'

'What pubs did you go to?'

'I don't know. I was drunk after the first one.'

This drew a laugh from the men on the far side of the lock, which lifted his spirits.

'After the last?'

'I slept for a while, I fink. Then I got up and fell in.'

'Can you think of any enemies?'

'I can fink of a lot,' Silcock claimed, playing to the crowd.

The boat wallowed sideways and chased him under. Being the objects of public attention, the family on board gathered close and watched with acute interest, father and mother both soberly sucking pipes now, the girls lined up with bows in their hair, the boys preening for friends on the bank.

'It's a wonderful example,' Moon said. 'A felon

brought down by the hazards of trespass on private property.'

When Silcock came up on the rope, he had lost the little ground he had gained. Blair gave up on subtlety. 'What about Maypole?'

Even *in extremis*, Silcock was baffled. 'What?'

'You saw a Reverend Maypole here in December. You approached him after a rugby match and caught the attention of Chief Constable Moon, who ran you out of town.'

Silcock squinted at the Chief Constable. 'I might've made conversation wiff the man, that's not a crime.'

Blair said, 'You offered to introduce him to a variety of vices. Which vices in particular?'

Silcock took cognizance again of his greater audience; it was an age, after all, of gallows orators.

'Entertainments, maybe. One man's meat, anover man's fish.'

'Girls or boys?'

'Buggery's a bit upper-class for me. Anyway, cards was what I had in mind.'

'Why would you approach a clergyman at all?'

'He played rugby. That's a queer taste for a churchman. If he liked that, maybe he'd like somefing else.'

'You threatened him if he told the police.'

'Never. I fink I said, "No harm done." Those were the words. But not a minute went by before the Chief Constable here had me by the neck. For doing nofing but passing the time wiff a priest. Is that fair?'

He went under. Blair dug in his heels and hauled.

285

When Silcock came up, the rope screwed his head into his shoulders and he had to twist his head to talk. 'This is a difficult fing, being saved.'

The diver outside the lock surfaced and rolled, exhausted, on to his back.

'Are you still game?' Blair asked.

'I'm drowning,' Silcock said.

'Are you game?'

'Yes. I'm game.' His eyes clung to Blair's as if they were hands.

'Did anyone in Wigan point out Maypole to you?'

'The people I associate wiff do not attend church. Not in my circles.'

'Your circles?'

'Travellers, sportsmen, men who like the fancy.'

'The "fancy". You mean fighting circles?'

'Pugilistic circles.'

'With gloves?'

'Bare knuckle. Gloves take away the featrical aspect.'

'The blood?'

'Where there's blood there's silver. When you stop a fight for cuts, you bet again. Makes for more action all around.'

'Rugby?'

'Not a real better's sport. More for miners. I like dogs, cocks, dogs an' rats, ferrets an' rats.'

'Purring? You know, the way miners fight with clogs?'

''S good.'

A diver hauled himself out, walked to Moon and

shook his head. Silcock watched as water lapped his nose, the shelves of his eyes.

'Get some other men in,' Blair told Moon.

Moon said, 'There's no point warning a man off if I treat him like a bab when he does come back.'

'Ask me somefing else,' Silcock said.

'Who's the best at purring you ever saw?'

'A poser. Overall, Macarfy in Wigan.'

'You never saw Jaxon?'

'Not in action. I've heard of Jaxon.'

'What did you hear?'

'He's best, according to some. At purring.'

'Who said so?'

'A man named Harvey said he worked wiff Jaxon.'

'Was Harvey his first name or last?'

'I don't know.'

'A miner you played with?'

Silcock went under and his hair lifted like underwater grass. Blair pulled him up, though he felt Silcock's arms almost wrench from their sockets.

Silcock said, 'I wouldn't play wiff a miner. Get me cards all black and bent?'

'Harvey was too clean to be a miner?' To Moon he added, 'Get some divers in the water.'

Moon did nothing but magisterially motion for no one else along the lock to move.

'Clean and unlucky.' Silcock lifted a smile. 'Never knew a man wiff a worse run of luck. I stuck to him like his best friend.'

'He was clean but he worked at the mine with Jaxon? How did you meet Harvey?'

'Cards. If I could do nofing but play cards wiff Harvey, I wouldn't be here.'

He went under again. Silvery bubbles erupted from his mouth. Blair wrapped the rope around his back and heaved, to no effect. The drowning man's eyes were wide above ballooning cheeks, purple from Blair's pulling.

Blair didn't see Leveret return, didn't notice the Hannay estate manager at all until he fitted a foundry wrench the size of a man's leg on to the shaft of broken nut and hauled on the handle as if he were pulling an oar. He adjusted the wrench jaws and hauled again. A deep sound issued from the bottom of the lock and the boats lined up outside the gate shifted from side to side. Moon looked at him and coloured while Leveret turned the wrench more furiously.

Other hands helped Blair pull Silcock out and pump the water from his lungs. Out of the lock, Silcock was a small, sopping figure, a rag still wrapped around the rope. Water had magnified him.

Leveret walked across the lock with the wrench. 'That's what my grandfather, the lock-keeper, would have done.'

Chapter Sixteen

When Blair got back to his hotel room, he went to the brandy on the stand by the bedroom window. Because the room was lit, he was faced with a reflection that looked like a man underwater.

In his all-but-last moments, when Silcock had claimed whatever dignity he could, bantering from his end of the rope like a sailor on the yardarm of a sinking ship, until only his nose was above water and then only his hands were trying to climb the rope, he had telegraphed his fear to Blair. Blair's hands trembled as if he were still getting the message.

The sluice gate had been so tight it had broken Silcock's ankle bone. He was no innocent victim, God knew; by Silcock's own account, he was a thief, a cheat and a drunk when he hit the water. Though Blair had talked to the family on board, all of them had been inside the cabin because the lock always filled so slowly, it was dark, and no one had heard a sound like a head bouncing off a gunwale.

Someone had laid open Silcock's head, dragged him down into the water of the lock, cranked the gate paddle on to his ankle like the bar of a rat trap and removed the crank. Or, as Moon maintained, Silcock fell head first from the gate, hit the gunwale on the way into the water and was swept into the draining paddle before it could close. As Silcock boasted even after his rescue, he couldn't start to list his enemies. He had never seen Bill Jaxon, and Blair knew from his own experience that Bill couldn't swim. Nothing had been gained by saving Silcock except that the wretch was alive, and that Blair's palms burned from the rope.

First the horse at the pit, now Silcock. Nothing was safe. One moment they were prancing along the green grass, and the next they were sucked under, as if water and mines were alive. He had a comic image of himself roped to everything in sight: Saint Blair, patron of the disappeared.

He carried his glass to the parlour and to the Coroner's report. There was no Harvey, first name or last, among the listed victims of the Hannay explosion, though he was sure he had seen the name before. He went through the list of survivors. No Harvey. Through the witness list. No Harvey. Which pointed out how peculiar it was for Silcock to say that anyone who worked with Bill Jaxon was clean enough to play cards. Men in a coal mine weren't clean. Even brake men and wagon men who worked on the surface were dusted black.

Did it matter? Silcock had nothing to do with Maypole aside from a single conversation after a rugby match and some suggestions that the curate had turned down.

He laid the Coroner's report aside to study Leveret's list from the Home for Women Who Have Fallen for the First Time. Rose Molyneux's skill at surgical stitching was not something picked up by the annual lacing of a

Christmas goose. Someone had trained her. Not at the Home, though; no Molyneux had ever registered there.

He was at a dead end. A day with nothing to show but a new enemy in Chief Constable Moon. That was his talent, as Earnshaw had said: making enemies. A bizarre day illuminated by the deliverance of Silcock and the even more miraculous emergence of Rowland. Who had been in the wilderness. Before whom all bowed. Who by now would be in London.

Gorillas had been discovered only thirty years earlier. The first gorilla hide had been shipped ten years ago. Now there were gorilla hands in Wigan. And the wreck of 'Nigger Blair'. Not washed up on the sands of Zanzibar, but on a bishop's leash.

Why should he care? No one else cared about Maypole. He wasn't a detective or a patron saint. It wasn't like him at all.

He returned to the bedroom for the brandy. Rather than face his reflection again, he turned the light down and saw a wall of wrecked, soiled, ruined clouds falling on the town. On the street, specimen bottles shone in the chemist's shop, stacks of tinware towered inside a hardware store, blank faces loomed in the milliner's window. In the alley by the milliner's, a piece of metal caught the street lamp. He thought it might be a coin on the ground until it shifted and he recognized the brass toe of a miner's clog.

Blair stepped back and watched for ten minutes, long enough for his eyes to see legs in the shadow of the alley. It didn't take a man that long to answer a call of nature.

He wasn't smoking, so he didn't want to be seen. He could be anyone, but if it was Bill Jaxon that was fine, because now Blair knew where Bill was. Jaxon wasn't about to batter down the doors of Wigan's most respectable hotel, as long as Blair stayed in the Minorca, a ship in port, he was safe.

He filled a glass of brandy and tried to concentrate on Maypole's journal. The sight of densely interwoven lines made him think of the priest bent over the page, like a giant doing needlepoint. He still hadn't decoded the ink-spotted entries for 13 and 14 January, and the only reason to think they might be worth the effort was that they were such knots. Untangled, they were still nonsense, but he reminded himself that Maypole was only a curate, not a devious miner. The lines looked like a Caesar code of transposed letters in blocks of four, which should have been no more than middling difficult, starting with the most frequently used letters, doubled letters, common combinations. The problem was that some combinations seemed so different as to be in another language. Ignoring the blocks and reading the lines again and again for the rhythm, he felt a familiar voice in his inner ear and then the first small words provided the vowel that evoked a name that turned a key that unlocked the rest.

But King Solomon loved many strange women, together with the daughter of the Pharaoh, women of the Moabites, Ammonites, Edomites, Zidonians, and Hittites.

So a childhood listening to religious fanatics hadn't been wasted. Brandy didn't hurt, either.

His wives turned away his heart after other gods, for Solomon went after Ashtoreth, the goddess of the Zidonians, and after Milcom the abomination of the Ammonites.

The abomination of the Ammonites? There was a title for a lawyer's card, Blair thought. Maybe Milcom could join Nuttal, Liptrot, Hopkins and Meek.

Love undid Solomon, the wisest of men. But is it love or clear vision? Solomon saw these women for how beautiful they were. As I feel my own eyes open I sense how dangerous clarity can be. If I have been blind, so has everyone else in Wigan. Perhaps blindness is safety, but now my eyes are unsealed, what can I do?

Blair wished his eyes were opened. At what point had Hannay switched from a quiet inquiry into Maypole's whereabouts to public humiliation of his daughter? Charlotte Hannay might be a nasty bundle, but the process made Blair feel small.

If, instead, it is my imagination and not my eyes, is that wrong? Was it a sin for Solomon to see the beauty in another skin, darker eyes, a fuller mouth? Some day, perhaps, C. and I will see the Holy Land.

Every night, though, I am visited by the dreams of
Solomon. It is not the Holy Land of Our Lord's
blessed agony, which I have imagined like a series of
lantern slides, each scene motionless and serene, an
awesome progression from Gethsemane to Golgotha,
which is a contemplation, in fact, on death. Instead,
every sense of mine is alive, and each dream has the
colour and tactile vibrancy of revelation.

To Blair, English middle-class character was a coin.
Heads: cool, asexual persona. Tails: the visions of the
sexually deprived. If Rose Molyneux batted her eyes at
Maypole, as a flirt casually bats her eyes at any male,
who knew what romance a curate could create in his
mind? Unless, of course, they read his journal.

In my dreams I am as dark, sweat as hard and laugh
as freely. And escape with her, slipping all the weight
of class and learning. If I had the courage to follow
her.

A curate refusing a bishop's daughter for a coal-yard
belle? Not likely, and yet . . .

Each morning, before light, I hear them pass. Her
and a thousand others, with the sound of their clogs
like a river of stones. As the Psalm says, they seem
'made in secret, and curiously wrought in the lowest
parts of the earth'. It is a Psalm written for Wigan. I
found the sound of their passing so odd when I first

arrived, and now it seems as natural as the dawn that
follows. Later, as I prepare for Low Mass, a counter
tide of sheep floods the streets before carriage traffic
starts. Christ was a carpenter, he knew the labour
and sweat of the men to whom he preached. All
morning I attend my rounds with half the heart I
should, ashamed that I have never shared the work
of Wigan miners. I have the man and only lack the
place in which to gain sufficient skill to pass as one
of them. Just for a day.

At night, of course, a different agony awaits, when
I would, as Solomon said, 'rise now, and go about
the city in the streets' and seek her whom I love. I
would if I dared.

Two hours later, brandy made a little puddle at the
bottom of the glass. The last entry was a weave of lines
in a more complex code. Credit was due. Maypole had
recapitulated the progress of ciphers, from most primitive to most maddening. The last entry suggested a
numerical system. Numerical ciphers were simple puzzles
– a matter of transposing letters according to a pattern
like 1–2–3, repeated over and over – 'Cat' became 'Dcw'
– but it was impossible to break without the key. When
the shortcut of birth dates didn't work, Blair understood
at once and with a groan from the heart that the key
would come from that wellspring of Maypole's inspira-
tion, the Bible. Number of Apostles, years of Methuselah,
cubits of the Holy Tabernacle, or something more
divinely, manically obscure like Nehemiah's census of

Jerusalem; the children of Elam, numbering 1254, or the children of Zatu, 845.

The second hand of his watch twitched under the crystal, the arrow of a compass seeking a new north.

Blair put the journal in a hiding place behind the mirror, left the lamp on, let himself into the hall, then went down the hotel restaurant stairs and out of the rear entrance through the steam of the kitchen. He didn't feel like a wolf, as Moon had described him. He felt like a goat walking in the track of another goat. Wasn't that his method of finding Maypole?

Flo said, 'Tha can't come here.'

'I want to see Rose.'

'Wait.' She blew out the kitchen lamp and left him to stand in the dark outside.

He waited on the back step, above the mud of the yard, surrounded by the smell of slops and ashpits. To the west, the clouds had ignited into an electrical storm too far off for audible thunder. He couldn't see individual strokes of lightning, only illumination in one valley of thunderheads and then another. Was it distance, he asked himself, or did the screen of smoke that rose from the overlapping lines of chimneypots cut Wigan off? The town seemed to exist as a world to itself – and, as always, to be slightly on fire.

Rose came to the kitchen door so quietly he didn't notice her at first. She wore a dress damp at the shoulders from her hair, and he saw the reason he hadn't heard her approach was that she had rushed from her bath in bare feet. A scent of Pear's soap surrounded her like an aura of sandalwood or myrrh.

'I took the alleys. I know the way now.'

'That's what Flo said.'

'Flo—'

'She's gone. Bill's still looking for you.'

'I'm still hiding from him.'

'Then run somewhere else.'

'I wanted to see you.'

'Bill will kick you t'death if he finds you here.'

'Bill is sure I'm not here. Did Maypole ever talk to you about different kinds of beauty?'

'You came t'ask me that?'

'Did he come seeking through the city, wandering through the streets to say he loved you?'

'Will you go?' Rose pushed him.

Blair leaned against her hands. 'No.'

A curious torpor spread through his body, and he could feel the same lassitude in her, so that she pushed without force and they leaned together. Her hand slid up to his temple and brushed the hair where she had stitched him together.

'I heard there was almost a drowning. They say you helped the man and ruined the Chief Constable's little show, which makes you more fool than hero. Now Moon or Bill will catch you and ruin my good work. You think it's worth it?' She bunched his hair in her fist so that the skin burned. 'Or d'you just want t'go back to Africa?'

'Both.'

'You're a greedy man.'

'That's true.'

Rose led him in. So much for Maypole, he thought. So much for Solomon, too.

Lovely was an inanimate word. Carnality was alive, and Rose had carnality from the thick, darkened curls of her hair to the fine coppery down where her neck sloped to her shoulder. It was the way the cheap dress shifted on her hips as she led him upstairs lit by the cat's eye of a kerosene lamp turned down to its slit. It was stupid animal poetry. Better than poetry because appreciation entered every sense. She was victory over the mind. The Greeks placed physical grace on a level with the arts. Rose would have done well in ancient Athens. Or in Somalia or Ashantiland.

Not that she was a beauty. Someone like Lydia Rowland outshone her easily, but outshone her as a diamond might outshine a fire. A diamond was mere reflection, a fire was alive.

Nor delicate. Her shoulders were wide, the calves of her legs muscled from work. Nor voluptuous. In fact, she was slight of body more than round.

What was it? The allure of the lower class? He didn't think so; he was too lower-class himself to find any erotic quality in rough hands or thin cotton.

But she was all of a piece. She was *there*. In the hall he felt heat on the floorboards where her feet had stepped.

She made herself a small throne of pillows while he rested against the headboard. The room had more variations of shadow than any real light, but to him she looked like a happy jinnee released from a bottle. His body stretched out, as pale and bruised as a body brought down from the cross.

'What would you do now if Bill came in?'

'Right now? I couldn't move, I know that.'

'Bill's big. He's not bright, though, not like you.'

'I'm so bright I'm here with his girl.'

She sprang forward on to his chest, her hair wild around her eyes. 'I'm no one's girl.'

'You're no one's girl.'

While she was on him, she turned his head and examined his temple where it was shaved and stitched.

'Where did you learn nursing?' he asked.

'Sewing cuts is a good thing t'know around a mine is all.'

She kissed him and sat back on the pillows, assembling herself with animal disregard for being naked. He became aware again of the fact that she seemed to have the house only for her own use. For all its age, it was built under a single slate roof that spanned the whole row of houses from corner to corner, looked out on a cobbled court-yard, and was surrounded by terraces of other, almost identical houses and courts.

'Where's Flo? She seemed to dematerialize.'

'That's an expensive word. You went t'school.'

'You did, too. There are a lot of books downstairs.'

'I'm not much of a reader. It's all rote in the schools

here. Remember the answer or they whip you with a rule. They beat me all the time. Name a country, I'll tell where it is. I know a hundred words of French, fifty of German. You'll teach me Ashanti.'

'You think I will?'

'I know it. And dance like them, too.'

He had to smile because he could see only her, out of all Englishwomen, in a golden cloth with golden bracelets on her arms.

'You're laughing,' she said.

'Not at you. I like the idea. Tell me, did you know the man who nearly drowned today? Silcock?'

'"As I was going to Saint Ives, I met a man with seven wives." But I never met a man called Silcock.' It was as firm a denial as he had heard from Rose, and he was relieved. 'Tell me about the big affair today. The Hannays and Rowlands and a pair of murderous hands off a great ape, I heard.'

'It wasn't the ape that was murderous. They should have had the hands of the Liverpool ship owners who made their fortunes off the slave trade and now send Rowland to Africa to shoot whatever moves and spread the word of God. The men looked like pallbearers, which is appropriate for the poor gorilla, I suppose. The women each wore a hundred yards of silk, and not one of them looked as good as you.'

'Well, I've nothing on.'

'A chain of gold would suit you fine.'

'That's the sweetest thing you've said so far.'

'If I ever get back to Africa, I'll send one to you.'

'That's sweeter yet.' She had the power to make her whole body look pleased. There were harems that could learn from Rose, Blair thought. 'You're not friends with our Chief Constable Moon.'

'Not quite.'

'I wouldn't let you touch me if you were. He's scary, isn't he, like a fright mask? They say he wears iron leggings for miners' clogs. I wonder if he takes them off when he goes to bed. He told you about pit girls?'

'A menace to the country.'

'Him and the Reverend Chubb. They think they're guarding the gates of Heaven and Hell. They want us crawling t'them for charity, so they can punish us by handing out one crumb instead of two. They say they want us on our knees t'pray, but they just want us on our knees. The union is with them is the sad part. As soon as they drive women off the coal chutes, the wages'll double. Then it'll be a blow for the working class, as long as the class is men. They ask me, "Don't you want a home and kids, Rose?" I say, "If I could have them without a great, slobbery man, yes!" Let them rave about my trousers. I'd shake my bare bum at them, too, if it made them madder.'

'You would, wouldn't you?'

'Then they'd lock me up as a lunatic, of course. Moon would personally swallow the key.'

'How did you know about me and Moon?'

'You've got your spies, I've got mine. Right now I spy a little lie.' She stretched her leg up his. 'You said you couldn't move.'

Lamplight was golden in her eyes. He thought of brass toes waiting in the dark.

She wasn't much more than a girl, but instead of fleshy weight and satiation, she offered abandon, the chance to leave gravity and exhaustion behind. As if he and she were crew and oars and, having made the trip once already, could now take longer strokes that dipped and left iridescent rings expanding in the air.

Why was this profound? Blair wondered. Better than philosophy or medicine. Why are we made to probe beneath the skin so far? Who was in control? Not him, but neither was she. What was frightening to him was how well they orchestrated, how tightly they *fit*, tumbling slowly until the master explorer did not know up from down, his hands on the bedpost, feet against the bar, their breathing grown hoarser and more rhythmic while a rope wrapped around his heart, stiffening with every turn.

There was one more twist. He asked himself, was he following Maypole or becoming Maypole?

'I'll think of you with native girls, won't I?' she said. 'I'll be with some hairy miner. You'll be surrounded by black Amazons.'

'When I am, I'll think of you.'

She wrapped herself in a sheet and hopped from the bed, promising to find something for them to eat.

Idly Blair rose on an elbow and turned the flame up a half turn. On the nightstand by the lamp, a mirror ball offered a smaller, foreshortened version of the room.

He leaned closer to the face in the ball. Africans had been trading with Arabs and Portuguese and Liverpool merchants for years, but there were people up the rivers of the interior who hadn't ever had contact with the outside. When he had shown them a looking-glass, they were first astonished and then wanted to protect the mirror at all costs because it was clearly a piece of them. Which impressed him, because he had always had trouble identifying himself.

He looked at the side of his head where the hair was shaved. Though the skin was black with a vitreous sheen, he could count eight stitches neatly sewn and could even see, despite dried blood, that Rose had used red thread. Which was how Harvey came to him.

Blair remembered the inquest for the Hannay explosion and the death certificate for Bernard Twiss, sixteen, 'recovered at the coal face by his father, Harvey, who failed at first to recognize him. Identified later by a red cloth he used to hold up his trousers.'

Harvey Twiss.

Chapter Seventeen

Blair returned to his hotel and slept until the pre-dawn clatter of miners passed below his window, followed by the muffled baas of sheep being herded into town, the tide and countertide that Maypole had written about in his journal. With this double alarm, he rose and dressed to ride to the pit.

At the Hannay Mine, the mist was a steady downpour in the dark that Wedge, the Manager, ignored. He had a ginger beard and brows that glistened like a hedgerow in the light of his lamp. Outfitted in mackintosh and wellington boots, he led and Blair splashed in his wake across the yard. Beside the tub rails and railway lines that ran to the sorting sheds, other railway lines stretched across the pit yard to the mile-long complex that was the Hannay foundry, brickyard, lumber platform. Hannay-built locomotives, six-wheeled and pony four-wheelers, their boilers cowled in water tanks, stirred blindly without lanterns across the yard, hauling in wooden-bodied wagons spewing sand or hauling out wagons spilling coal. As a train stopped with the rapid fire of buffers colliding, a man ran alongside the wagons, setting brakes with a shunting pole. Simultaneously, coal carts and wagons pulled by heavy horses steaming in the rain lurched over crossings. Miners emerged from the lamp shed with safety lamps dim as embers. Kerosene lanterns hung on poles. A circle of smoke and dust rose from around the yard, from the surface stables, workshops and sorting sheds where coal arrived still warm from the earth.

Blair couldn't see Rose, and he had no intention of visiting her, playing the lord while she tipped coal, though Wedge saw where his gaze had wandered. 'Women are the most extraordinary creatures. Work as hard as a man, paid half as much. But thieves! One of those frail little maids will tuck a forty-pound lump of coal in her knickers and skip all the way home. Some managers try to run their yards from a desk. You have to do the paperwork, but that's what clerks are for. My experience is that if you're not in the yard, the yard will walk away from you. Coal, cable, lamps, you name it. I keep my eye on everybody, and I make sure everybody knows it, including Mr Maypole.'

'He came here often?'

'Often enough.'

'Maybe more than enough.'

'Could be. I tried to impress on him that a pit yard was not a pulpit, that sermons had their time and place. There are, I admit, among the miners, lay ministers who might lead meetings down pit, strictly during their tea. Methodists, in the main. The Bishop says if getting on their knees helps miners get out coal, it's all right with him. I'm afraid, however, that the Reverend Maypole took it the wrong way. Being a young clergyman and all, he thought it gave the other side an unfair advantage. I finally had to ask him not to come till end of day. Very embarrassing. But in the yard, spontaneous preaching can be a hazard.'

'You were in the yard when the fire broke out?'

'Yes, and thank God I was. Every second counts in a situation like that. Fortunately I was in a position to organize immediate assistance to the men below.'

'Exactly where?'

Wedge slowed for a step. 'Here, in fact. I remember the blast as good as knocked me off my feet right here.'

It was too dark for Blair to estimate distances. 'Was there any confusion?'

The manager splashed on. 'Not a bit. As I told the inquest, a properly run pit is prepared for the unexpected. With my first breath I sent runners for help and medical assistance. Then I organized a corps of volunteers and, with the emergency supplies we had on hand, sent them down in the cage. They were on their way in less than five minutes.'

'You know a miner named Jaxon?'

'Jaxon was one of the heroes of the fire.'

'Did you see him before the explosion?'

'Waiting to go down pit with the others. He seemed to be out of sorts, quiet, wearing a muffler. Of course it was a wet day, which brings out the methane, which makes miners glum.'

Something stood out in Blair's mind, though he wasn't

sure what. 'There was a manager from another pit, a Molony, who said he saw the smoke from his pit.'

'No wonder.' Wedge waved his arms. 'Smoke like that is half coal dust. Like volcano ash. Here in the yard you couldn't see your hand in front of your face. Horses bolting everywhere. Trains still rolling, and you're trying to remember if you're standing on a track or not. It takes a while to stop a loaded train. Now that I think about it, it was a dark, nasty day, but Molony saw our smoke, no doubt about it.'

'A messenger arrived from George Battie, the underlooker, so you knew the cage was working. But you had to get rescuers organized and that meant have them each sign out a lamp.'

'From the lamp man, right. That's the purpose of the lamp system, to know who is down pit and who is up, especially during the mayhem of a fire.'

'But then the volunteers had to wait at the shaft for the cage to come up. Why was that?'

Wedge slowed and twisted his eyes back towards Blair. 'Pardon?'

'Where was the cage? Battie's messenger had come up. The cage should have been here, you shouldn't have had to wait. Why wasn't the cage still at the surface?'

'I don't see that it matters. It didn't hold us up for more than ten seconds.'

'When every second counted, as you said.'

'Not that much. It didn't matter at the inquest, and it matters less now. Ten seconds, maybe twelve, who knows, and the cage came up and the properly assembled and equipped rescue party went down.'

'No experienced miner, no experienced rescuer, would have tried to go down without your direction?'

'That's correct.'

'What about someone inexperienced, not a miner?'

'Mr Blair, perhaps you've not noticed, but I'm aware who's in my yard.'

'Where is Harvey Twiss?'

Wedge came to a halt. 'Not here, not any more.'

'Where can I find him?'

'Why do you want him?'

'Harvey Twiss was not on the list of rescuers, but according to the inquest report Harvey Twiss found his son. I assume you sent him down. I want to ask him about the explosion.'

'I didn't send him down.'

'The report says he went down.'

'I didn't send him.'

Blair was baffled. He didn't know what they were arguing about.

'Where is he?'

'Harvey Twiss is in the parish graveyard. The same day he buried his boy Bernard, Harvey laid his head on the railway track in time for the London train. Now they're both in the ground, side by side, father and son. But I didn't send him down.'

A rivulet of water ran off Blair's hat. Feeling immensely stupid, he started putting together the Pit Manager's hostility about Twiss and his touchiness about the cage. He squinted through the rain up to the tower, then followed the diagonal of winding cables down to the windowless brick structure of the engine house.

'Twiss was your winder?'

'The only bastard in the yard I couldn't see. The only man I couldn't keep my eyes on, and he abandoned his post.'

'When did you find out?'

'I caught him sneaking up with the boy in his arms. Both black as spades, but I was keeping a sharp look-out for him by then.'

'Then?'

'I discharged Twiss on the spot. No reason to be in the inquest report, nothing to do with the fire, but son or no son, he abandoned his post.'

Inside, the winding house was tall, built to accommodate a steam engine the size and design of a locomotive, although instead of driving and carrying wheels, the rods drove a single vertical eight-foot drum. As cable groaned off the drum and angled up through a door in the house peak, the slates of the roof resonated.

Winding houses appealed to Blair, their great stationary engines like something powering the rotation of the earth. The Hannay machinery was handsome work – a drum of heavy iron, twin pistons and rods of yellow brass, the boiler of riveted steel – all huge and intricate and dwarfing the winder, a man with a pinched face who sat in a mourner's dark hat, overcoat and gloves, a drop suspended from the tip of his nose. Levers at hand, his attention was so given to a white dial lit by two gas lamps that his only reaction to the entrance of Wedge and Blair was a tic of his eyes. Although he was in the centre of an industrial yard, he could have been a creature interred in a tomb. By the door a sign said, 'Admittance to the Engine House is Absolutely Restricted. Signed, The Manager.' Another sign said, 'Do Not Distract the Winder.'

'Don't mind us, Joseph,' Wedge said. He shook water from his beard. 'Joseph is watching the indicator.'

Indicators were familiar to Blair. It was a big word for a simple dial with a single hand. The face of the indicator was marked 'S' at three o'clock for Stop, 'T' at two o'clock for Top, 'B' at ten o'clock for Bottom and 'S' at nine o'clock for Stop. The hand of the indicator was perceptibly inching counter-clockwise to 'B', which meant that a cage of men or tubs was descending the shaft at a speed approaching forty miles an hour. When the hand reached 'B', Joseph would apply the brakes to slow the cage and stop at 'S'. There were no automatic brakes. If he didn't stop the reel, the cage would hurtle with undiminished speed into the bottom of the pit. The metal cage itself might be salvaged, but nothing inside it would survive. Or, going in the opposite direction, if he didn't apply the brakes at 'T', the cage would overwind, crash into the headgear and catapult its contents off the top of the tower.

'No one else comes in?' Blair asked.

'Not allowed,' Wedge said. 'The engine furnace is stoked from the outside.'

'No friends?'

'No.'

'No girls?'

'Never. Joseph is a Temperance man, not like Twiss. Free of vice and gossip and idle tales.'

As the indicator arrow hit 'B', Joseph switched to the brake lever until the dial came to rest at 'S'. The moan of the cable died. For a minute the cage would now stay at the bottom of the pit to be unloaded and loaded again.

Wedge said, 'Joseph, Blair here has a question for you. The day of the explosion, you were stoking outside. On his own volition, short minutes after we felt the force of the explosion, Twiss ran out of this building and sent you in to run the cage. I did not see him do so and I certainly did not send him down pit, isn't that true?'

When Joseph nodded solemnly, Wedge shot Blair a look of vindication.

'You have a clean job indoors now, don't you?' Wedge went on.

Joseph drew a handkerchief from his sleeve. Rain and the first grey, downcast light of day crept through the cable door. Blair wondered whether a little arsenic would be out of place. 'When Harvey Twiss grabbed you and made you winder, was that before the first party of volunteers went down or after?' he asked.

'After,' Joseph said.

'So it's all worked out for the best, hasn't it?' Wedge said.

Joseph blew his nose. Blair was ready to go, but as if his own internal flywheel had been started, Joseph added, 'Twiss was a victim of foul habits. Cards and drink. How Mrs Smallbone put up wi' him, ah'll never know.'

A bell by the dial rang twice, signalling that the cage was ready to be brought up.

'Why would Mrs Smallbone have to put up with Twiss at all?' Blair asked.

Joseph raised his eyes sadly, as if from a bier. 'Twiss roomed at Smallbone's. Making a penny is not a sin, but letting a sinner into a Temperance house never led t'good.' He pushed the cable lever and the drum began its counter-revolution, ponderously to begin with and then with growing speed.

Now that he had light, when he got back outside and was alone, Blair paced distances from the engine house to the shaft, to the overlooker's shed, then to the middle of the yard. Rain was falling too hard for him to see more than an outline of the sorting shed, and nothing of Rose at all.

He saw Charlotte as soon as he returned to his hotel. She was leaving the chemist's shop across the street, a small figure in a walking dress of an obscure colour that he couldn't distinguish as either purple or black. Her face wrapped in a bonnet and veil of the same inky hue, with matching umbrella and gloves, she could only be Charlotte Hannay or someone bereaved. What caught his attention was that she wasn't moving at her customary brisk pace. An unopened umbrella hung in her hand and she went only as far as the milliner's window before she stopped and stood in the rain as if unsure which direction to take. Or more likely, he decided, waiting for her carriage.

He avoided her the way he would walk around a spider, went up to his room, slapped off the rain, had a brandy for the circulation and spread out a map of the Hannay yard. What was clear to him now was that the yard had been a scene of blind confusion as smoke poured out from the explosion below. He was ever more impressed with the heroic efforts of George Battie in the tunnels underground, but Wedge was a poor witness as to what had happened above. The Manager claimed he had dispatched a rescue party in a cage within five minutes of the explosion. Adding the time it would have taken Wedge to get his bearings, find wagons with horses that hadn't bolted, collect volunteers and distribute safety lamps, Blair thought that fifteen minutes was a better estimate.

He opened Maypole's journal, flipping through pages until he found the entry he wanted. Because the lines ran across one another, he had misread the words for 17 January. Not 'How to enter that second world. This is the key,' but 'Twiss is the key.'

If the one place in the Hannay yard that Wedge's eye did not reach was the engine house, the possibility existed that, with the connivance of the winder Harvey Twiss,

Maypole could not only have hidden there, but, obscured by the smoke of the fire, crossed unseen the short distance from the house to the shaft and descended in the cage to that realer world he craved just as it was exploding, an act equally idiotic and badly timed. In his fervour it might not occur to a would-be saviour like Maypole that in a mine fire anyone who was not a miner was, at best, an obstacle.

The slightest chill pricked the hairs of Blair's arms and he allowed himself another brandy. From the window he was surprised to see Charlotte Hannay still outside the milliner's shop. She could exchange her bonnet for a hat, he thought – something in barbed wire, perhaps. The milliner herself bobbed out under an umbrella to pantomime an invitation of shelter. Charlotte appeared not only deaf to the offer but blind to traffic as she stepped off the kerb. She crossed Wallgate in front of a milk cart, startling the driver. In his room, Blair threw up his own hand reflexively. A churn tumbled off the cart and spilled a white skirt over cobblestones. Without taking the least notice, Charlotte continued at the same abstracted pace into an alley on the hotel side of the street.

Blair had never had an opportunity to observe Charlotte Hannay apart from their confrontations, when she had always had the busy focus of a wasp. Perhaps it was the rain, but from the perspective of his window there was such a wet and beaten quality to her that he almost felt sympathy and there was something dreamlike about the way she glided out of sight.

He went back to the inquest report and spread out the underground map of the pit. If Maypole did go down, what happened there? Thanks to Battie's cautious advance on the main road, no rescuers were overcome by afterdamp. All the bodies were identified, all the workings searched. Had Maypole, covered in soot, come back up in the cage holding one end of a stretcher? Had he then wandered off in shock? The curate had preached so often about Hell, how had he liked his first taste of it? But wandered to where? Blair found himself back at square one. The more he speculated, the more farfetched his theory appeared. On the other hand, no one had seen Maypole since. And it was all after the fact. Nothing Twiss or Maypole did or didn't do could have affected the explosion itself.

He returned to the window. Diluted by water, dashed by wheels, the spilled milk was still a visible lace among the stones. A little stone lady, he thought, was what Charlotte Hannay was. He didn't know why, but he picked up his hat and went out in search of her.

The alley was crowded with whelk and oyster stalls, sheep heads crowded together, tripe draped like rags. Blair pushed through to a row of fish barrows, salt cod stacked under canvas sequinned with scales. There was no sign of Charlotte; it didn't help that she was small and dark.

At the other end of the alley was an outdoor market of shoddy-clothes hawkers, mostly Irish, and tinsmiths, mostly gypsies. Stitched and restitched greatcoats and overshirts hung like wet sails. Where the market forked he chose the street that he realized led towards both Scholes Bridge and Maypole's room. In the mud he found the dull imprints of clogs and the single impression of a lady's shoe. Mixed in the mud were twists of sheep scat. He remembered the flock he had seen in the morning and the sheep Maypole had noted in his journal.

Beyond a court of small foundries was another track of clog-flattened mud and the imprint of a shoe so small it could have been a child's slipper. Brick walls bowed and, overhead, rooflines almost touched, admitting a narrow sheet of rain that disappeared into shadow. He stopped at Maypole's door, sure he would find her visiting, but the room was as bare as he had left it days before, the portrait of Christ the carpenter still hanging in the dark, the boards of the floor dry except for the threshold, where someone had opened the door to glance in only minutes before.

Back in the alley, the way became ever more foul from sheep. Blair come to the knacker's house and pen he had noticed on his first trip to Maypole's. For all the signs of sheep, the pen was empty. Fluffs of sodden wool clung to the chute that ran into the house. Because the house was a terminus without shutters or door, he saw Charlotte within. He checked the impulse to call her name because he could tell she was standing on the edge of the knacker's drop.

What knackers did was to drive sheep off a drop of

thirty feet or so to break their legs and make them that much easier to kill. Blair crept close enough to see that an enterprising Wiganer had used the shaft of an old mine. Work had just finished because a faint lantern revealed walls and floor that had been plastered and whitewashed, butcher blocks, meat hooks screwed into walls, and a blood trough that ran below the hooks and emptied into a pail. Blood and offal covered the floor and smeared the walls. What light reached up from the drop had a rose-coloured hue.

The toes of Charlotte's shoes were over the edge and she leaned forward, headfirst. A dive at that distance would do the job, Blair thought. Although he saw her mainly in silhouette, he imagined her white brow pointing down, her dress snapping out behind her.

'The Ashanti don't have sheep,' Blair said. 'Goats, yes. Monkeys, guinea fowl, lizards, too.'

She balanced, eyes forward, concentrating like a tightrope walker on her next step.

'And grasscutters, which are giant rodents, and forest snails, also giant. A knacker in Kumasi would have a real menagerie.'

When he moved in her direction, she teetered more towards the drop. He retreated a step and she straightened. Magnetic repulsion, he thought, the best example he'd ever seen.

'The snails take enormous cunning. Set out cornmeal and lie in wait by moonlight.'

'And elephants?' she asked softly. 'Do you shoot them, or do you wrestle them to the ground?'

'Snails are more in my line.'

'But not gorillas. You didn't like Rowland's gift, or is it that you don't like my cousin Rowland?'

Although her voice was small, it had its usual allotment of contempt. Under the circumstances, he took this as a good sign.

'I just wonder what Rowland did with the rest of the gorilla.'

'You don't like him,' Charlotte said.

'And Earnshaw, what happened to him?' Blair asked. 'He's not interested in the abattoirs of Wigan?'

'Mr Earnshaw has returned to London.'

On schedule, as Hannay had said? Blair wondered. When he tried to look at Charlotte, she turned her face away. Her dress was spotted and soiled at the hem and her shoes were ruined. At least the draught rising from the old shaft seemed to press her away from the edge. He was surprised that the red reek – the oily, airborne taint wherever blood or animal matter was processed – didn't knock her back. She was tougher than he had thought.

'Blair, what kind of a name is that?' she asked. 'You are supposed to have been born in Wigan. I looked at all the church records. There were no Blairs.'

'It wasn't my mother's name.'

'What was her name?'

'I don't know.'

'Your father's name?'

'No one knows.'

'Haven't you tried to discover who they were?'

'No.'

'You're not curious? You're more interested in John Maypole than you are in yourself?'

'As soon as I find Maypole, I can leave Wigan. That's what I'm interested in.'

'You're the most anonymous man I've ever met.'

'The fact that I'm not interested in Wigan does not make me anonymous.'

'But you are. Not American, African or English. Perhaps you're Irish. Celtic hermits used to sail away from Ireland, letting Providence set their course, praying to be cast ashore in distant lands so they could become anonymous. Do you feel Irish?'

'Sometimes cast ashore, but not Irish.'

'Then there were penitential pilgrims who wandered to the Holy Land to atone for the worst crimes, murder or incest. Do you have something to atone for?'

'Nothing that grand.'

'You haven't been in Wigan long enough, then.'

He tried to circle and inch closer, but she seemed to sense his every move, like a bird ready to take flight. A little dark bird with an umbrella in one wing.

'You don't like anonymity,' Blair said.

'I envy it.' Her voice dropped. 'I envy it. How close are you to finding John?'

'Maypole? I don't know. It would help if you told me something about him.'

'I can't help you. I'm sorry.'

'Anything. He didn't hint about any big plans or fears?'

'John was always full of great plans. He had a great heart.'

319

'*Had?*'

'See, there you go, picking my words apart.'

'Only trying to understand whether I'm looking for someone dead or alive. Who left on his own or under pressure. Why do I feel I'm the only one who wants to find him?'

'What do you mean?'

'The Bishop hired me to find Maypole, but now he seems to care more about your forgetting him.'

'Is that what you're asking me to do?'

'No. Just tell me, do *you* want me to go on looking?'

'It doesn't matter. Let's not pretend it does.'

'You were engaged to him. You loved him.'

'No. John wanted to help me. I let him, and that was weak of me.' She spread her arms wide.

'Maybe I can help you,' Blair said.

'Is that pity I hear?' she asked as if he had offered her a handful of worms.

'How can I help?' He resisted the urge to try to snatch her back from the drop.

'Can you fly?' Charlotte took a deep breath, turned and planted her toes on the ground and her heels over the edge. With her back to the drop and the poor light, the draught pressed her dress around her so it appeared she was falling. 'When my father was young, he used to leap over shafts.'

'I heard. You're as crazy as he is.'

'You're hardly one to talk. Is it true that you're fighting with miners?'

'No.'

'And seeing a pit girl?'

'No.'

She lost her balance for a moment. Her arms wavered. Dirt ticked off the wall of the drop and a stone echoed from below.

'I'll leave Wigan,' Blair said.

'What makes you think I'd care whether you left Wigan?'

'I thought that's what you wanted.'

'My father will find someone else just as terrible as you. Worse, if possible. Thank you for the offer, though. It makes your lies complete.' She raised her umbrella with both hands as a counterweight and stepped from the edge. Blair offered his hand. She ignored it. And walked through the dark and muck of the house as if she were crossing the rug of a parlour.

'You've done this before,' Blair said.

'As a girl, a hundred times.' At the door she looked back. 'Was the famous Blair afraid?'

'Yes.'

'Well, I don't think you're lying about that. That's something.'

Chapter Eighteen

It was a wet dusk when the miners returned from the pits. The warming smoke of chimneys created a new layer of clouds, like the smoke of battle after a city had been razed to the ground.

From the belfry of the parish church, Blair focused his telescope from street to street, lamp to lamp. Rain had dissipated to a drizzle that made stone shine and reflected sound. What looked like white smoke rose from a crumbling wall, moved laterally in the wind, turned on itself, scattered, regrouped and wheeled around and around the roofs. Doves.

More doves appeared as miners opened more dove-cotes. Dogs barked. A darker plume of smoke approached the London & Northwest station. Horse cabs rolled at a trot down Wallgate to the station. When Blair lifted the telescope he could follow the transit of coal trains across every quadrant of the horizon. It could have been the Russian steppes or the Great Wall of China for all it had to do with him, he thought. He was annoyed that Charlotte Hannay had tried to find his name in a church register. Why would she bother, unless the Hannays maintained a feudal interest and thought of everyone in Wigan as a serf and everyone who left it as an escapee?

He found the blue slate roof of Candle Court. The terrace was all Hannay houses. He had checked at the company office on his way to the hotel, and Molyneux had been the name on the rent book since the previous October. Every week, Rose and Flo paid in rent six times what they earned.

Doves returned to their yards. Night spread in grey and black bands of smoke and haze. In front of hardware stores, assistants cleared pavements of washtubs and hoes. Bone barrows made the rounds of stalls behind the Town Hall. Butchers locked their shutters.

Maypole had always intercepted pit girls at the Scholes Bridge, the main crossing between the miners' neighbourhood and the centre of Wigan. Blair borrowed the tactic with the use of a telescope. At six, he spied a row of black dresses with bustles making a snakelike parade that appeared and vanished at different points, to emerge finally on Wallgate and march to the door directly below him. A Church society that looked like a witches' coven, he thought.

The image of Charlotte on the edge of the drop continued to distract him. She had been so desperate that, in spite of himself, he had felt sympathy, until she stamped on it. Which was fine, he preferred his dislike pure.

At seven, Bill Jaxon passed under the lamp at Scholes Bridge. He was alone and, for all his size, moved quickly out of sight. Blair swept the streets and alleys with his glasses until he found him at the butchers' stalls. From the stalls he had an improved view of the front entrance and side exit of the hotel. Blair had left the lamps burning in his room so that Bill would have something to watch. The safe thing would have been to stay in his room. He decided that safer still was to plunge ahead, find Maypole and leave Wigan completely.

There was a flaw in this reasoning, he knew. It was a little like Charlotte Hannay standing at the drop.

Smallbone lived on a narrow street that had half subsided into ancient mines and left the remaining houses leaning as if arrested in the act of collapse. A shout answered Blair's knock and he let himself in.

Though the parlour was unlit, Blair was aware of the gaze of Mrs Smallbone multiplied in portraits and pictures of different Temperance assemblies; the smaller frames had rounded glass that magnified her severe, unrelenting eyes. Chairs were draped in crêpe. A table wore a black skirt, as if half of Mrs Smallbone were present. As he passed, he touched the keys of a harmonium. Ivory: the elephant's graveyard discovered in Wigan. The air itself was pungent with a gritty, oddly familiar scent.

Smallbone was at the table of a kitchen identical with those of Mary Jaxon and Rose Molyneux – a small room ruled by a massive range and warmed by the grate – except that his had been turned into a kind of bomb factory. A rack of strings soaked in great pots of saltpetre on the range. Rope lines of fuses hung from wall to wall to dry. On the floor was the source of the smell that

Blair had recognized: small open kegs of gunpowder. Grains of it covered the floor planks and table, and a shadowy haze of it hovered in the air. On the table were empty flutes of waxed paper, a scale and coin-shaped weights, and a coffee mill. There was stature to the scene and to Smallbone, as if he were sitting in no mere miner's kitchen but was a business magnate among glowing foundries and volcanic chimneys.

If Smallbone was startled by his visitor, he recovered well. 'What a pleasant surprise,' he said. 'I wish Mrs Smallbone was here. She's out for the evening. She's a woman for good works. I think tonight it's the improvement of ladies of loose morals, or stoning them t'death. She runs the north of England for the Queen, that's all I know for certain.'

'May I?' Blair slapped rain from his hat into the basin.

'How are you feeling?' Smallbone asked. He seemed to think Blair should be crippled.

'Good.'

'You seem to be. Well, I wish I could offer you something on such a nasty night. Mrs Smallbone left me bread and tea t'dip it in. Us being a Temperance house.'

Blair had brought brandy from the hotel. He set it on the table. 'Is this a mistake, then?'

Smallbone's nose quivered like a root for water, as if it could smell through glass. 'Not that I don't deserve a drink, mind, after a day's work and the long walk back in the rain.'

'I know that Dr Livingstone, the missionary, advised red wine for chills.'

325

'Well, there you are.'

Smallbone found two cups and, with the interest of a fellow chemist, watched Blair pour. The miner's face was washed to his collar, his hands clean to the cuffs, the lids of his eyes red from the occupational irritation of coal dust. With his first swallow, his eyes teared with relief. 'Mrs Smallbone is probably praying over some heathen right now. The Reverend Chubb is probably kneeling at her side. They're pulling the oars for both of us, bless them.'

'To Mrs Smallbone.'

They drank to her.

'You don't mind if I go on?' Smallbone asked. 'I make my own shots and I make extra to sell on the side.'

'I wouldn't want to bring business to a stop.'

'Thank you.' He produced a long clay pipe and topped the tobacco in the bowl with an ember from the grate.

'You've got enough powder here to blow up half of Wigan.'

Smallbone said proudly, 'All of Wigan.'

'All?'

'Because of the old mines underneath. Firedamp creeps up into closets and cabinets. We had neighbours who looked in the closet with a lamp and blew themselves up. But the rent is low.'

'They should pay you to live here.'

'I'll tell that t'Bishop Hannay next time I see him.'

'Those are Hannay mines underneath?'

'Hannay mines, Hannay workings. Going back

hundreds of years. When the Hannays were Catholic, they used t'run priests underground all the way from Hannay Hall t'Wigan. Catholics knew where t'go for Mass because there'd be a candle in the window. Shall I show you my secret?'

'Please.'

Smallbone scooped gunpowder from the open sack into the funnel of the coffee mill and starting cranking. 'Any idiot can buy gunpowder readymade. It's a government monopoly – fuses, too. Which sounds t'an idiot like a seal of approval, never stopping t'consider that where there's monopoly, quality goes out of the window. Then he makes a shot and it fizzles or kicks up late and blows off his head. See, an anti-monopolist, an expert, understands that it's air between the granules slows down a proper detonation. That's why loose gunpowder will burn but won't blow. So I grind it again because fine grains mean less air and your more dependable blast. Look.'

Smallbone pulled out the drawer of the mill and stirred the powder inside with his finger. 'Fine as ground glass. Of course you need a brass mill or you'll blow yourself up. And you have t'use the powder fresh, especially in rainy weather, or it soaks up water. I've been considering a touch of ammonium nitrate for added punch. What do you think, Mr Blair?'

'I wouldn't bother. You want to break up coal, you don't want it to disappear.'

'An excellent point.' Smallbone emptied the drawer

into his hand, poured a stream of powder from his fist
on to a scale, sipped from his cup. 'It makes my hand
steady.'

When the scales balanced, he poured the gunpowder
into a flute, twisted the ends tight and laid his finished
shot in the canister.

'Harvey Twiss lived here?' Blair asked.

'Yes. That was a sad case, Harvey and his boy,
Bernard.'

'The fire?'

'Harvey didn't get over finding Bernard. We laid the
boy out right there in the parlour. Closed coffin. Bernard
wasn't a member of the Burial Club, but Mrs Smallbone
throws herself into these things. It was all done in crêpe.
Mauve. Ham and tea. Poor Harvey was already in his
cups, half off his head at the funeral. We never should
have let him wander off.'

'To lay his head on the track?'

'So they say.'

'It was Christian of Mrs Smallbone to allow a sportsman to room here.'

'It was,' Smallbone agreed. 'Also, the extra pennies
didn't hurt. Saintliness is an expensive business. Between
letting the room, selling the shots and winning the bets
on Bill we're just able to afford Mrs Smallbone's attendance at Temperance rallies up and down the country. Of
course, they would be empty exercises without her.'

'Of course. Twiss was a good mate?'

'We weren't close. A sportsman, but a reliable winder.'

'Were you surprised to hear that Twiss left the

winding house to join the rescue? A winder never leaves the house because everyone else counts on him to run the cage. Twiss must have been through explosions before.'

'Maybe not with his boy down pit.'

'Maybe not.'

'In the confusion and all.'

'How's your leg?'

'Pardon?'

'The one you hurt in the explosion?'

'I wasn't hurt.'

'Before the fire.'

'Right, *before*. I'd forgot.' Smallbone relit his pipe. Tiny flashes lit his hands. 'Now that I think about it, tonight's issue was women of questionable morals. Mrs Smallbone wants t'lock them all into hospitals as a sanitary measure t'protect the men. The Reverend Chubb and the police say a loose woman is categorically identifiable by the exposure of her upper arms. The trouble is that all the pit girls in Wigan go about with bare arms.'

'That must keep Mrs Smallbone busy.'

'It does. I tell her she could spare herself the worry and the pit girls the aggravation if she would reclassify whores according t'more pertinent parts of the anatomy.'

Blair refreshed their cups while Smallbone filled another flute of paper. The charge looked like a church candle.

'Between Mrs Smallbone's good works and rugby matches, you must have seen a good amount of Reverend Maypole.'

'An earnest man, very sincere.'

'And a great admirer of miners. Did he ever ask you to show him how to wield a pick?'

'No.'

'Maybe go down an old pit?'

'No.'

'You're sure?'

'One quality I'm proud of is my memory.'

'Which leg was it?' Blair asked.

'Leg?'

'That you hurt before the Hannay explosion?'

'Left. It was my left leg.'

'I thought it was the right.'

'It could have been my right.' Smallbone attacked the crank again. 'It was a terrible blow. I leaned on Bill and we started for the pit eye.'

'Which way?'

'The back road.'

'The main road was closer to your work station and it had fresh, incoming air while the back road had foul. Why would you take the back?'

'A tub was off the rails at the main road. It was easier to try the back.'

'You were lucky. The men in the main road didn't survive.'

'See, that was a good reason t'stay on the back.'

'But you *did* turn to the main road. That's the way Battie was coming with the rescue party, and that's where you met him.'

'Bill heard them.'

'Bill was concussed, he said so at the inquest. When your ears are ringing you don't hear much. Lucky again. Were you waiting for George Battie?'

'For George Battie?'

'I'm just wondering what took you so long? A watch on one of the victims stopped at two forty-four, when it was broken by the explosion. It took Battie more than an hour to locate bodies and clear the gas to reach the point where he met you and Jaxon. It was three forty-five when you and Bill emerged from a cross tunnel midway on to the main road and met up with Battie. I'm just finding it difficult to understand what happened. You must have been clear of the blast and gas, but you only got midway when you met Battie? I wondered what took you so long unless Jaxon was carrying you.'

'Where d'you get all this information?'

'The inquest.'

'I had a bad leg, that's for sure.'

'Yet when you met Battie, you shrugged off the agony of this injured leg to join in the rescue. You "disregarded" the pain, you told the Coroner. Even so, can you explain what took you so long before you met Battie?'

Smallbone filled his fist with gunpowder. 'You know, Bill Jaxon and I are heroes. Everyone agreed. The rest of that inquest is full of shite. Thirteen men in shoes deciding about miners? Lords and lawyers who know as much of us as Mrs Smallbone knows of natives south of the Equator? And expert witnesses who wouldn't know coal from caramels? No one pays attention to a Coroner's report and you shouldn't, either.'

Gunpowder streamed in a black line from Smallbone's fist into a tube. His hand *was* steadier, Blair realized.

'All I want to know is why you and Bill left the coalface, why you took the back road, and what you waited for after the blast.'

Smallbone stacked weights on the scale for a double charge. 'What you should do, Mr Blair, is go back t'where you came from, either Africa or America. You have no idea what you're stirring up.'

'You mean Bill Jaxon and Rose? Tell Bill from me that Rose is a lovely girl, but there's nothing going on between us – just questions about Maypole, that's all.'

'It's not so simple. You can't come t'Wigan and decide in a day who is who or what is what.'

'Unfortunately I can't get out of Wigan until I find Maypole.'

'Then you could be here for ever.'

On his way out the parlour, Blair noticed one picture not in the spirit of the sombre portraits, a photograph of the Smallbones on a beach.

'Blackpool,' Smallbone said from the kitchen door. 'On holidays. All of Wigan goes.'

On a shelf by the photograph was an engraved silver shaving cup. Blair held it to the kitchen light and read, 'A. Smallbone. 3rd Place. Aquatics.'

'Handsome. From Blackpool, too?'

'Years and years ago,' Smallbone said.

'All the same, swimming in the open ocean? Winning

third place at Blackpool? Where did you learn to swim like that in Wigan?'

'Canals. In a straight line I can swim for ever.'

Afterwards, standing in the back alley, Blair resisted the impulse to go to Rose's house. He realized he knew the way too well.

Ashpits steamed in the rain. Although windows were shut he heard an oath, a hymn, children screaming up and down stairs. Wigan was a miniature landscape that kept adding new dimensions: clouds, echoes, subterranean chambers.

Smallbone as a swimmer was a new factor. The attack on Silcock was a two-man job. Not the hitting over the head, that was simple. But carrying him to the canal, and there one man to drag him into the water to the bottom of the lock while the other cranked the gate paddle shut on Silcock's leg. All next to a boat of witnesses who would swear they heard not a thing. That was sly, that was Smallbone's sort of work.

He went over the lies Smallbone had told, but he also heard his own dissembling to Charlotte and Smallbone, mostly about Rose. Why would he care what Charlotte thought? Why should he care at all for a pit girl? He could feel the pull, though, as if she were a luxuriant vine that grew at night and reached in his direction.

Chapter Nineteen

'Bishop's weather,' Hannay said.

Which meant that the night's rain had evaporated into a morning of high, blue skies and green hills bright as glass. Atop his ecclesiastical gaiters and frockcoat, the Bishop wore a broad straw hat for the expedition. In the same spirit, the Rowlands dressed like a pair of bouquets, Lydia in a dress and sun hat of tulip pink, the mother in a complicated outfit of peony red. In the breeze their silks, tulle and satin trim emitted scents of lavender, and their parasols shuddered like blown flowers. Blair kept pace in boots still damp from the day before. Behind him followed Leveret with a brace of yapping spaniels, and gamekeepers bearing wicker hampers.

'Poor Leveret, he does have his hands full.' Lydia covered her smile as Leveret prevented first one dog and then the other from racing up the path. 'Did you have dogs in Africa?' she asked Blair.

'No, too many things in Africa eat dogs.'

Hannay said, 'That's our Blair, always a cheery answer. Look around, Blair. Creation all fresh and new, literally humming with life. You were starting to look a little drawn, that's why I ordered this day up.'

They crested a hill where butterflies trafficked above drifts of small, early daisies. What was disturbing was that at some level Blair felt that the day had indeed been ordered by Hannay. A westerly wind not only polished the hills but pushed smoke east, so that they could not even see evidence of Wigan's chimneys behind them. The only thing that didn't fit was himself: he felt like a poacher who had wandered into a garden party.

He looked back at the oversized hampers. 'I'm surprised we didn't bring a piano.'

'We can next time, if you want,' Hannay said. 'It's all for you.'

'If you want to do me a favour, give me a berth back to the Gold Coast.'

'Forget Africa just for a second, can't you? Here we are on this glorious morning, surrounded by decorative lilies of the field, assured of a healthy outing and a good appetite.'

The spaniels yelped at the faint report of a shot.

'Think of Wordsworth,' Hannay said. '"Am I still a lover of the meadows and mountains and all that we behold from this green earth." Poetry, Blair, is the frame of life. England is a small landscape, but we have exquisite frames.'

The path led up the hill to higher hills of steeply sloping meadows divided by upright stones that enclosed flocks of ewes and lambs, the younger sheep marked with dyes of bright red and blue. A blush of pleasure showed on Lady Rowland's face, as if the climb had caused younger blood to fill her veins.

'We have a game,' she said.

'Daisies,' the Bishop said.

'"My thirst at every rill can slake, and gladly Nature's love partake of Thee, sweet Daisy,"' his sister-in-law said.

'Wordsworth,' Hannay told Blair. 'Too bad Charlotte isn't here. She always wins.'

The sheep started as one at a volley of shots, walked a few steps, then reassembled as an anxious still life. Blair looked for a hunting party, but the sound had drifted from a still higher ridge. The dogs whined for Leveret to let them free.

'You're making progress,' Hannay said.

'You think so?'

'The Reverend Chubb, Chief Constable Moon and Wedge, our Manager, have all complained to Leveret. If that's not progress, what is? Leveret, on the other hand, is your great supporter.'

'And Charlotte?'

'Oh, Charlotte thinks you are a plague. Aren't these butterflies wonderful? Called peacocks, as if we were in Babylon. Well, as close as we can come in England.'

'That Charlotte thinks I'm lower than the pox, is that progress, too?'

'It helps make up her mind. The sooner she helps you, the sooner you'll be gone and then you'll both be happy.'

The miniature peacocks led the way. If England didn't have the fantastical variety of life that Africa did, Blair admitted some relief on encountering insects that weren't intent on sucking, stabbing or boring into him. He looked at his compass and caught Lydia Rowland at his elbow.

'Have you been successful in your search for the Reverend Maypole?'

'No.'

'Do you have suspicions?'

The word was innocent on her lips. The butterflies circled her as if she were delicious.

'No.'

'But Blair has been working hard,' Hannay said. 'I understand he has been interviewing people from every level.'

'That is wonderful to hear,' Lydia said. 'I visited the poor once with the Reverend Maypole and his parishioners were good people with the most patience and the brightest children. We sometimes forget while we go on with our daily lives that we are being made comfortable by men who are hard at work beneath the very ground we walk on.' She faltered at the thought. 'There might be men chipping at coal underneath us at this very moment.'

'That's profound to contemplate,' Leveret said.

'We're a bit far from the pits,' Hannay said.

'Violets,' Lady Rowland said to change the mood.

Lydia brightened gratefully. '"A violet by a mossy stone half hidden from the eye! – Fair as a star, when only one is shining in the sky." Another flower?'

'Hemlock,' Charlotte said. She had come up the path so quietly that no one had noticed. Or she had dodged from shadow to shadow, Blair thought, because she was in a sort of anti-sundress of black silk with matching bonnet, boots and gloves, a cross of the sporting and the funereal. A glare lurked within the shadow of her veil like a flame in a safety lamp. Blair was struck by how young she was despite such grim attire.

At a knoll where the jagged stones of a wall were set into high grass like dragon's teeth, gamekeepers unrolled a Turkish carpet and set out from a hamper a blinding service of silver and mother-of-pearl. The hampers disgorged rabbit pies, Cumberland sausage, potted duck, savoury pies, porcelain jars of chutney, sauce and mustard, biscuits, cheeses and bottles of wine. The gamekeepers imitated footmen, carving pies and handing out plates, and then retired behind the wall. Hannay bowed his head and asked God's blessing on people who were, it struck Blair, already generously blessed. Nevertheless, he felt the site's undeniable appeal, the walls of stone adding a backdrop to the roll and toss of high grass in the wind. A lark lifted from a nest and rose vertically, trilling like a waterpipe. Air played with the ribbons on the brim of Lydia Rowland's hat as she bent her neck in prayer. When they began to eat and Lydia lifted her veil, kid gloves still on, she delicately cut her rabbit pie and raised each forkful to her bow-shaped mouth. In contrast to Charlotte, who refused to raise her veil to drink or eat.

'Do you ever eat?' Blair asked her.

'When I can stomach it.' She asked her father, 'Why do you persist in inflicting Blair on me?'

'To find my missing curate. You know that. To drag

the Reverend John Maypole from wherever he is hiding. Or until it no longer matters whether we find him or not.'

'What do you have against John?'

'What do I have against Maypole?' Hannay repeated the question and answered it idly. 'Not his idealism, because that is a natural stage of a man's life. Not his stupidity, because the greatest fool can sound wise if he simply sticks to the breviary and the Bible. But one thing I did not appreciate was his obsession with reform. Which leads to social agitation, which is not welcome in a Hannay mine.'

'Your uncle means unions,' Lady Rowland told Lydia.

'Blair is going to find him, though,' Lydia said. 'I feel quite sure this will all have a happy ending.'

In the distance, two shots sounded as quickly as a fusillade. The dogs liberated themselves with a sudden tug and escaped in the direction of the sound, their leashes dragging after them.

'Cousin Lydia, what is a happy ending to you?' Charlotte asked. 'Marriage, baby, house calls, balls? Have you considered that it might simply be the chance to have your own life?'

'I do.'

'Pit girls are freer than you. They make a pittance, but have you ever made a penny? Would you uncover your arms, pay your own rent, wear trousers?'

'Who would want to?' Lady Rowland asked.

'Perhaps she wouldn't, but would she dare? Or would freedom crush her life like an empty hatbox?'

'She has all the freedom in the world. Also expectations and obligations,' Lady Rowland said.

'To keep her dance card full but not tiresome, to be bright but not clever, to order dresses from Paris but store them for a year so she will be fashionable but not French.'

'And to marry well and be a benign influence on whoever that man is, yes.'

'Well, cousin,' Charlotte turned back to Lydia, 'you can start with Blair. You pretend to be interested. Scrub him and groom him and teach his tongue softer words until he pads by your side like a lapdog.'

Lydia's eyes welled with hurt. A nearer round of gunshots approached. She shook at the sound and her tears spilled.

Blair said to Charlotte, 'Your father's paying me or I wouldn't be within a thousand miles of this hill. If you're so free, why are you here?'

'Who said I was free?'

Blair escaped. He left the Hannays and Rowlands, climbed the stones, hiked along the wall and watched clouds arrive from the sea. They could be ships bearing him away, he thought. As a boy he had watched clouds, wondering about their routes, and here he was again, as if a day hadn't passed. They sailed overhead while their shadows slid across the hills from west to east. A kestrel hung on the breeze, watching for mice. If the little hawk could stay at this latitude, Blair thought, what points would it pass over? Newfoundland, the Aleutians, Lake Baikal, Minsk, Hamburg, Wigan.

He sank into the grass, closed his eyes and listened to the far-off trill of larks, the oboe calls of crows. Beneath him he could almost hear the trooping of ants, the tunnelling of moles and worms. He felt his eyelids and hands relax. Grass was better than a bed. He was only aware of falling asleep when he awoke to see a man with a shotgun silhouetted against the sun.

'"I wandered lonely as a cloud that floats on high o'er vales and hills, when all at once I saw a crowd, a host, of golden daffodils." And you.'

Blair rose to his elbows. Rowland had eyes as blue as the sky at his back.

'I see daisies, no daffodils.'

'No matter.' Rowland had hair of tarnished gold worn wild, old tweeds, high boots. He broke the breech, extracted smoking cartridges, and smoothly fed in new ones. *Dispassionately* – that was the word that came to Blair's mind – which carried both the denial and the residue of passion. Rowland reminded him of Maypole's painting of Christ the carpenter. Christ with a gun. The spaniels came running up, one with a bloody magpie in its mouth, the other with a lark.

'I wasn't really hunting. It's just that a gun lends punctuation to a walk.' Rowland patted the dogs and they nuzzled close, smearing his boots and trousers. 'You're somewhat far afield, aren't you? Dreaming of home?'

Blair had been dreaming of the hills outside Kumasi,

of palm fronds shifting before a rain and the muezzin's call to prayer.

'Yes.'

'I often come here, too. Out of sight of human habitation. Sometimes I think of Adam. The hunting he must have had in the Garden of Eden. All the animals freshly created. We can search the earth and never know its like.'

'I don't think there was any hunting in the Garden of Eden. Adam survived on fruit, anything but apples. No sex and no blood – I think those were the rules.'

'No hunting?'

'Not at first.' Blair got to his feet. 'Remember, it was only after the Flood that God let Noah hunt and put the fear of man in animals.'

'You're with the Bible Society now?'

'With the Bishop.'

'So I'm told.'

Rowland's attention was distracted by sweat on his brow. From a snuffbox he emptied white powder into his palm, twice as much arsenic as Blair had ever seen in one hand before, and ate it in a single swallow.

'Malaria?' Blair asked.

'What a good guess.'

'No guess at all.'

But there was more. Rowland proceeded to wipe the wet residue from his palm on to his cheeks. Blair had heard of women using arsenic to lighten their complexions, but not men.

'White faces frighten the natives,' he said.

'I think in your case that's gilding the lily.'

'You look like Hell too, Blair.'

'White man's graveyard.'

'West Africa?'

'Wigan.'

Rowland brushed the muzzle across Blair's chest. 'You could be right.' His eyes trailed along the wall. 'Are my mother and sister here, too?'

'And the Bishop and your cousin, Charlotte. I thought you were going to bask in glory in London for a while, educate the Royal Society, write a book, entertain the Queen. Why are you back?'

'Something I saw.'

'What?'

Rowland smiled and said simply, 'Something wrong.'

When the two men joined the picnic, Lady Rowland and Lydia were overwhelmed with surprise and delight, but Blair saw nothing so innocent on Hannay's face. Charlotte's greeting to her cousin was a cold kiss through her veil.

It was all strange to Blair. He knew nothing about families. All the same, after the first flurry of excitement and when the Hannays and Rowlands had settled back down on the carpet, it struck him how distant they were with one another. Of course Rowland was at least ten years older than his sister. From what Blair had heard about the English of their class, children were almost instantly shipped off to school, so they might hardly be friends. Charlotte took the farthest corner of the carpet, a still life in black. Lady Rowland was the most natural; she sat close enough to her son to stroke his hand, as if to reassure herself that he had returned in the flesh.

Hannay distributed champagne with the mock solemnity of a Mass. 'The father of the Prodigal Son said, "Quickly, bring out a robe – the best one – and put it on him; put a ring on his finger and sandals on his feet. And get the fatted calf and kill it, and let us eat and celebrate; for this son of mine was dead and is alive again; he was lost and is found!" Even better than a Prodigal Son is a nephew who returns bearing honour and fame.'

Rowland said, 'That is me, I assume, not Blair.'

'That is not amusing. Please,' Lady Rowland said. 'How was London? Tell us about your reception at the Society. How did they like the gift?'

'Those frightening hands,' Lydia said.

Hannay said, 'Since you decided to return, Rowland, the Reverend Chubb would like you to meet some working men. Not a bad idea.'

'Blair says you must have shipped the rest of the gorilla in another box. Is that true?' Charlotte asked.

'Blair would hardly understand what an explorer does,' Lady Rowland said. 'No disrespect to Blair, but he was your father's employee in Africa. He worked for money. Isn't that true, Blair?'

'Still am and still do,' Blair said.

'Such a wonderful familiarity with all of us,' Rowland said.

'Do you feel the slave trade will be coming to an end soon?' Lydia asked her brother.

'Only when Britain protects free men,' Rowland said.

'Britain shipped eight million slaves to the Indies and America,' Blair said. 'Walk around Liverpool and see the African heads carved over the doors. Britain is simply pulling out of the business.'

'If that doesn't show you the difference between idealism and the man who works for cash, what does?' Lady Rowland asked Charlotte.

'What happened to your head?' Rowland asked Blair.

Blair knew that, out of them all, Rowland would be the one to sniff out blood.

'Maybe he tripped in the dark,' Charlotte said.

'Which reminds me,' Rowland said. 'Is Maypole dead yet?'

Hannay said to Charlotte, 'Not dead, but almost buried. Until Maypole is, Blair will be hard at work.' He gave the gamekeepers a nod towards the hampers. 'My God, I've worked up another appetite.'

As soon as the hampers were open, the spaniels stole meat and raced around the perimeter of the party, dodging the efforts of the gamekeepers to catch them. Blair helped Leveret chase them up the hill, and when one of the leads tangled between rocks, free the leash and take the dog in hand.

'Leveret, what the hell is going on?'

The estate manager had been almost perky since the incident at the canal. His face fell at Blair's tone. 'What do you mean?'

'I was supposed to find Maypole. Now it's either find Maypole or look until Charlotte loses interest?'

'Breaks her engagement to Maypole. That's what the Bishop wants.' Leveret kept his head down and worked busily with the leash even though it was unsnagged. 'Then you can go on your way, I suppose.'

'Why wouldn't she? He's disappeared, missing for months. Sorry, Leveret, but I know there was no great romance there, not on her part. She has a walnut for a heart as far as I can see. Why shouldn't she get engaged to someone else?'

Leveret whispered in a rush, 'The Bishop wants her to marry Rowland.'

'Her cousin?'

'Nothing unusual about that.'

'Rowland?'

'The Bishop seized on this idea as soon as John disappeared. Charlotte is resisting. Rowland is a change from John.'

'From Christian martyr to mad dog.'

'Do you know the hundred and thirty-ninth Psalm? "I was made in secret and curiously wrought in the lowest parts of the earth." It seemed to John especially to evoke miners and pit girls. Lord Rowland does not share that sympathy.'

'The hundred and thirty-ninth?'

'It was John's favourite. He started every sermon with it.'

*

Leading the spaniel along the wall, seeing the black Hannays and the golden Rowlands together, they did seem complete to Blair. Like a completed puzzle, he thought, though exactly what the puzzle was, he still didn't know. Complete and beautiful, the Hannays in their sombre wool and ebony silk, the Rowland women in petal-like folds of crêpe de Chine on the little field of the Persian carpet, on the greater carpet of the hill.

Chapter Twenty

At his hotel was a note from George Battie asking him to visit him at home, but Blair went to his room, poured a brandy by the lamp and read the final cipher in Maypole's journal by the number of the curate's favourite psalm.

139139139 . . .

'*Ukn Bsxduhqkj* . . .' became:

The Apocrypha speaks of Darius, the King of
Persians, who was so great in his power that all lands
feared to touch him. Yet he would sit with Apame,
his concubine; she would sit at his right hand and
take the crown from his head and put it on her own,
and slap the King with her left hand. At this Darius
would gaze at her with mouth agape. If she smiled at
him, he laughed; if she lost her temper with him, he
flattered her, so that she would forgive *him*. I have
seen Rose do as much. Taunt and leave a man
pawing the earth like a tethered bull. And now the
Rose for whom I would give all does the same to me.

Blair could picture Rose Molyneux at the table of Darius the Great, giving the King a tap, a pout, a steamy glance. She would have left Darius spinning.

It was no shock to learn that Maypole didn't understand women. Someone in the Bible hadn't either. Blair knew he didn't, he hadn't met enough ordinary women to shape an informed opinion. There had been the crib girls, who were indentured, which meant practically slaves even if they were in California. Natives in Brazil, who *were* slaves. The Ashanti, on the other extreme, who all dressed and acted like the Queen of Sheba. It wasn't the normal range from which to make even a biblical judgement.

'*The Rose for whom I would give all.*' He checked the date on the entry. 14 January. Four days before Maypole disappeared. If Rose Molyneux had also disappeared, the vow would make more sense. Instead she had gone nowhere and denied any tragic romance with Maypole, no matter how obsessed he was with her.

> She says that the Hannays are crazy. Must be, for
> having ruled so long, since the Conqueror, eight
> hundred years in Wigan, by custom and by law for
> being bishops, sheriffs, magistrates, ready to send
> down or ship off any threat to their authority. It's
> not a way she says she'd live.

Bold stuff from a pit girl, Blair thought.

A sound like rocks rolling in a flood drew him to the window to see the miners fill the street, shoulder to shoulder, on their trudge home. Wagons and carriages made way. Shoppers and maids shrank into doorways to escape the touch of coal. Some of the miners had lit their pipes, embers bright in the dusk, little lamps for the road. A pebble rapped off Blair's window. He couldn't see who among the dirty caps and dark faces had thrown it.

That deserved a second brandy. The warmth of it grew as he deciphered Maypole's next words.

I have been toughening my hands with brine and secretly practising the walk and work of a miner in an old tunnel. Bill Jaxon, reluctantly, has been a help. His co-operation is essential, but it is based purely on his Rose's mood, not on my mission. I feel like the Pilgrim who sets out on the long journey through the Slough of Despond, into the Valley of Humiliation, to the Hill Difficulty. My muscles ache, even my bones are bent from training. I will only be going a mile down, yet I approach the day with as much excitement as if I were setting off for Africa, the price of my ticket the cost of a pick and lamp. Thus I put my trust in God.

Trust in God? Often a miner's last mistake, Blair thought.

And in my Rose.

Now, that was faith.

Chapter Twenty-One

The backyards of Scholes were black ditches with boilers, turnip plots, sties, ashpits.

George Battie was bent over a tub, shirt off, braces hanging to his knees, to wash his hands by the light of a paraffin lamp. His house was no larger than an ordinary miner's, but as a pit underlooker he was afforded a longer, flagstoned yard, with beds of bare rosebushes and what Blair presumed was a garden shed.

As he let himself in at the alley gate, Blair saw two small girls chasing back and forth on the stones, their frocks so long that they seemed to move without benefit of feet. Each time a rose thorn snagged them, the girls squealed and jumped with mock surprise. Battie was as huge as a statue beside them, his arms and torso grey from coal dust, face black and eyes rimmed red. Vulcan at home, Blair thought. At this time of year, the girls hardly ever saw their father in the daylight. In the dark he left for the mine and in the dark he returned.

'Mr Blair, good of you to come.' Battie applied a bristle brush to his palms. 'I'm sorry, you caught me "in between". When I was young and ambitious I used to have a proper wash every night. Almost died of pneumonia. Have you found the Reverend Maypole?'

'No.'

'You're still asking questions?'

'Yes.'

'Do you mind if I ask *you* a question? Why are you asking about Harvey Twiss? Wedge says you were at the pit.'

'Twiss was a winder who left his post.'

'Twiss had nothing to do with the cause of the fire.'

'He didn't sign for a lamp. According to the Coroner's inquest, the lamp system is foolproof. Every lamp is numbered. Each man was supposed to sign out a lamp before going down, even rescuers. Twiss proved the system didn't work.'

'Mr Blair, you know your way around mines, so you have to know a Coroner's inquest is a fine shower of piss. Girls!'

Battie dried his hands with rags and, still bare to the waist, motioned Blair to pick up the lamp and follow him to the garden shed. The girls trailed after. He opened the door and entered to a sound more like lapping water than clay pots. The girls held their breath until Battie reappeared with a white dove on each hand.

'Fantails. Some prefer acrobatic tumblers or racing homers, but I love the fancies. Each one thinks she's a queen, or a princess at the very least.'

The birds had delicate heads and extravagant tails of crisp snowy white. They preened and spread their feathers as if Battie were their mirror. He set them on the girl's shoulders, and immediately there was a flurry of wings from a hole in the roof of the shed and two more doves lit on Battie's hands.

'See, they fix on you. When you buy a new pair, you keep them in their nests, feed and water them until they mate, and then the family's yours. You cull the squabs for dove pie, but we like to keep as many as we can.'

'Pretty,' a girl said.

'Like miniature swans.' He turned to Blair. 'Harvey Twiss was my wife's brother. Did you think Wedge would make anyone like Harvey an engine winder without a push?'

'I didn't know you were connected.'

'In Wigan everyone's connected.' Battie turned his hands so that the doves climbed his fingers. 'Did you know that Albert Smallbone's father was a poacher?'

'No.'

'Him and Albert used to sneak out at night. I used to sneak out with them. Pheasant was easiest because they don't roost high up and if you've gentle hands you can pluck them one at a time. Ferrets for rabbits. Albert and I had a pair of spades, and our job was to dig up the ferret before he ate the rabbit. My father would have tattooed me if he knew, but it was the most fun I ever had, flitting like a goblin in the moonlight.' He smiled at the girls as they chased each other, birds hanging on and flapping. 'The lamp system, that's just to make the company sound safe and the families feel better. There are times when we've had to brick in bodies and come up with a number later by sorting out lamps. Were we right? Who knows? But the women think we do. Or pretend to. Were the men dead when we laid the final brick? God, I hope so. But sometimes it's them or all the men in the mine. You hear a blower of gas and it's the breath of Hell. The funny thing is, the last thing you'll probably ever see is a dead canary.' Battie's smile came and went. 'It's a short dash through the smoke from the winding house to the cage. Twiss went down, took a lamp off a body he found in the tunnel and joined the crowd coming from the yard. When they caught up with us at the coalface, I knew at the sight of him that Twiss had broken the regulations. There was nothing to be gained by putting all that in an inquest. He'd lost his boy, and a few days later he had his head crushed by the London train. Anyway, he didn't cause the explosion.'

'What did?'

'I don't know. It was where a shot was going to be. But the fireman, Smallbone, wasn't there. Neither was Jaxon or they would have been dead.'

'Where were they?'

'As I remember, Smallbone says he was injured by a falling rock and Jaxon was helping him out.'

'He can't remember if it was his right leg or his left.'

'Because he's probably lying. If he doesn't have a shot to fire, Albert's a great one for nesting in holes where his sleep isn't bothered by the sound of picks. We'll never know because anyone who could tell us whether Albert left the coalface is dead. And it's a difficult subject to bring up at an inquiry when Smallbone and Jaxon were celebrated heroes. Anyway, what set off the explosion had to be a shot, a lamp or a spark. But no one was there. That's what I go over again and again.'

The girls balanced doves on their heads like plumes, pointed at each other and laughed.

'Twiss was killed by the London train?' Blair asked.

'On the London and Northwest track. It was night. A coal train might have seen him in time, but passenger trains go twice as fast. The Constable said poor Twiss was so drunk he probably didn't feel a thing. I don't see what any of this has to do with finding the Reverend Maypole.'

'It's the cage. After the explosion you sent messengers to the top. The cage should have been up there to bring rescuers back, but they had to wait because someone else had already taken the cage down. It wasn't Twiss, he went down *after* them. So who took the cage?'

'It could have gone down empty.'

'It could have been the Prince of Wales. You said Twiss took a lamp from a body in the tunnel.'

'I asked him because I knew no lamp man would let a winder sign out a lamp. He took it off a dead man in the main road.'

'After the explosion, were all the lamps accounted for according to the numbers in the lamp man's ledger?'

'Every lamp for every man. This time the numbers matched. Why are you dragging in Maypole?'

'Because I think he got as far as the winding house and when the explosion happened he seized his opportunity. It was a short dash to the cage, as you said.'

'But the Reverend was not allowed in the Hannay yard, not during working hours. It's an easy thing for a miner to slip in, there are no guards and he's only one more dirty face, but a clergyman is something else.'

'That I haven't figured out,' Blair said.

'And where did Maypole go if he did take the cage? No one saw him in the pit and no one saw him come out.'

'I don't know.'

'Twiss stole a safety lamp. What lamp did the Reverend use if all the other lamps in the pit were accounted for?'

'I don't know.'

'Well, it's a fascinating theory, Mr Blair – up to a point.'

Considering the theory's shortcomings, Battie's reaction struck Blair as exquisitely polite.

'Maypole was training in an old tunnel to go into the mine. Where do you think those tunnels would be?'

'Anywhere. You could be standing on them. It's all a honeycomb underneath the houses and you can go for miles if you know how they connect.'

Which was the story with everything in Wigan, Blair thought. 'Twiss was drunk when he died. Who was he drinking with?'

'Bill Jaxon. Jaxon said Harvey went off by himself.'

'Ah. Very melancholy, no doubt?'

'And inclined to rest his cheek on a cold rail. You don't plan to drink with Bill, I hope.'

'I avoid Bill Jaxon when I can.'

'The first sensible thing you've said tonight.'

'I want to come out to the pit tomorrow. There *is* one place he could have gone.'

'Come early. I'd like to see, too.'

The girls circled Battie, crying, 'Daddy, Daddy, Daddy, Daddy, Daddy!'

'A second,' he promised them. He told Blair, 'I don't want to leave you with a false impression. The inquest isn't real, it's only an official version, a procedure for the owners to blame the miners and open up the pit. But on our side, if the pit was shut, if they said it wasn't safe for us, know what we'd do? Rather than starve? We'd fight to go back down again, so we're guilty too.'

The girls begged, 'Be an angel, Daddy, be an angel!'

Battie re-entered the shed. Dark smells of boiled beef and burned dripping drifted across the yards. From the direction of the street, calls to tea vied with the tin horn of a rag man. Battie reappeared with a line of doves perched on each black outstretched arm. As he let his arms drop an inch, the doves fluttered, giving the illusion that he was taking wing.

'You just caught her. She was going,' Flo said.

'Going where?' Blair asked, but the big girl ducked inside the kitchen door, leaving him on the step. How he had gone from Battie's yard to Rose's he wasn't sure. He seemed to have dream-walked and found himself at her back door. It opened again with Rose on the threshold, a shawl round her shoulders, the velvet ribbon at her neck, a hat on red hair that was half pinned and wild.

'The siren herself,' he said.

'Did Bill see you?' She looked over Blair's shoulder.

'I don't know. We'll find out. There'll be kisses for you and kicks for me.'

She brought her eyes down to him. '"Siren"? I don't remember singing for you.'

'Well, I was coming here anyway. I am Odysseus shipwrecked. Dante stuck in the ninth circle of Wigan, looking for a glass of gin. My feet led me.'

'I don't think it was your feet.'

'I get your meaning,' Blair admitted.

'My meaning is I don't need your condescension.'

The blue colour cast on her was more than an effect of the night. She had half washed after the day's work, leaving carbon dust like kohl around her eyes and a faint metallic shimmer on her brow. Rose Molyneux, the muse of industry, with a sooty sheen made visible by the pale skin underneath.

'If you want me, say so,' she said.

'If you put it that way, I do.'

'One minute. Then you're gone.'

'Then I'm gone.'

He had graduated to the rank of company because she took the gin into the parlour, perched on the edge of a chair and gave him the settee. She was unwilling to light a lamp that might show him to the street, so they sat in the dark except for the glow cast by the fireplace. Though there were no goblets of gold, she could have reigned at Darius' table, alternately giving the King kisses and taps. She made her own rules. Where Flo had gone to, or how two girls managed a house alone when every room in Scholes was stuffed with lodgers, he didn't ask. She flavoured the gin with tea, that was her nod to etiquette.

'You found the Reverend Maypole?'

'I'm getting to know Maypole, but I haven't found him.'

'How's that, getting t'know him?'

'From his journal.' This was the first Blair had told anyone. 'It's full of notes and thoughts. It's full of you. It's interesting, seeing you through two sets of eyes.'

'Different sets of eyes. You're nowt like him.'

'What was he like?'

She gave him the full pause and let him hang for a moment.

'Good.' In the shadow that hovered around her, the fire lit only her eyes.

'Rose, I don't even know what you really look like. I haven't seen your face clean except that first night, when I was too addled to notice. You're always in the dark or decorated with dust.'

'It's dark when I leave work, and if you have skin in Wigan you wear coal. Should I wash my face for you?'

'Sometime.' He sipped his gin and looked around the room. England was giving him the ability to see in the dark. Pasteboard photographs were stacked by a viewer on the sideboard. He leaned back to pick out the gilt title of *Every Gentlewoman's Guide to Poetry* on a shelf. In a carpetbag were balls of red and orange yarn.

Rose said, 'Flo makes her own hats and knits her own shawls.'

'I remember. But we were talking about you.'

'We were talking about the Reverend Maypole.'

'His obsession with you. The night before he disappeared, you were walking up Scholes Lane with him and he pulled off his collar. I'm still wondering what that was about.'

'I'm still saying it never happened.'

'Maypole wanted to go down the mine.'

'Is that so?'

'He was a pilgrim. He had the Hannay Pit confused with the Slough of Despond. He thought you were some kind of angel.'

'I won't be blamed for what men think.'

'But why would he think that?'

'Find him and ask him. That's what you're paid to do.'

'Actually, no. What I'm discovering is that Maypole doesn't matter, dead or alive, found or disappeared. Not to the Bishop. What matters to him is Charlotte. When she gives up her engagement to Maypole, the Reverend can rot and Hannay wouldn't care. He'll pay me, send me on my way and I'm done.'

'You sound pleased.'

'It's a relief if I don't have to find a body. Sometimes I think I've just been hired to drive her crazy.'

'Can you do that?'

'I seem to do it without even trying. She's cold, though. There certainly wasn't any passion between her and Maypole – not on her part.'

'Maybe she didn't want passion. Maybe she wanted a marriage where she was free.'

'Well, she won't have that with Rowland. I didn't believe it when I heard about an engagement to him. They're first cousins. I thought that was frowned on.'

'Not for them, not for nobility.'

'Well, it's what Hannay wants.'

'And Charlotte?'

'At least she'll be rid of me.'

'You'll be sad t'see the last of her?'

'Hardly. Anyway, she's as good as sold.'

'"Sold"? That sounds African.'

'It is. Here's to the upper classes.' He touched his glass to hers.

Rose watched him as she drank, then took off her hat and let it drop to the floor. Not exactly a commitment to stay. A gesture of her own royal interest, Blair thought, the same way Charlotte once dropped shears into a pocket of her skirt.

'"An angel"?' She allowed a smile to suggest itself.

'Well, we can't help what men think.'

'And himself a pilgrim? In the Slough of Despond?'

'The Slough of Despond, the Valley of Humiliation, the Hill Difficulty. What pilgrims need is some bouts of dysentery, malaria and yellow jack.'

'Said he like a devil. You're living up t'your reputation.'

'Or ill fame.'

'Rowland's the one with the great reputation, isn't he?' Rose asked.

'Oh, his reputation is glorious. Explorer, missionary, humanitarian. He took some troops and a guide and found a slave caravan in the Gold Coast. There were a dozen raiders with about a hundred captives from the north on their way to Kumasi. Men yoked together to stop them from escaping. Women and children, too. Rowland started picking off the raiders one by one. He's a hell of a shot.'

'Served them right.'

'When the raiders hid behind the captives, Rowland had his men shoot the captives, too, until the raiders tried to run and he finished them off. The rest of the captives were overjoyed about going home, but Rowland insisted they keep going to the coast so they could report to the Governor and ask for British protection. It's a glorious story, isn't it?'

'It is.' Rose refilled his glass.

'When the chief objected, Rowland shot him and named a new chief. So they went on to the coast. The guide released the women and sneaked them off at night. Rowland kept the men yoked, but every day a few escaped and he shot some to keep the rest in line. About twenty made it to the Governor on the coast to beg for English care, which is why Rowland's reputation has such shine. I was the guide, so I enjoy the darker, more African version of the tale.'

'And he's t'be the next Lord Hannay?'

'It seems that way.'

There was a masklike quality to Rose's face, only

betrayed by the glint and roundness of her eyes. 'Maybe you're just envious,' she said, 'because you don't have a name like Hannay.'

'Rowland and Hannay. He'll have two names. Why shouldn't I be envious?'

'Blair isn't a Wigan name.'

'Blair was the man who took me when my mother died.'

'You don't talk about him.'

'He was a gold miner who wore a beaver coat and a bowler hat, confused Shakespeare and the Bible when he was drunk, and was silent when sober. I don't know why he took me when we got to New York, though I'm sure the shipping company was happy to have me off their hands. I think I was like a stray dog to him, and as long as I didn't cry too much or cost too much, he'd keep me. At that time, people with nothing to lose were going to California. He went and I went with him.'

'And struck it rich?'

'Not quite. He was a good enough miner, but it was as if he lived under a dark star. He staked a creek claim when he should have filed for the hillside, and filed for the hillside when he should have dug on the flat. Scientific principles stood on their head to spite him. Quartz led to gravel banks, and when he sold the gravel banks a flood would wash the gravel off a motherlode. That was a good time to steer clear of him. But I wouldn't see him for months at a time, once for a year.'

'A year? How did you live?'

'There were Chinese in the camp and he paid them to feed me. For a long time I thought my name in Chinese was "Hih!" Then I found out it meant "Eat!"'

'He was mean t'leave you.'

'I didn't mind. The Chinese were a big family, and the big brothers were explosives experts for the railway. They were my idols. Then there were the crib girls across the road, which was a "Home For Women Who Fall Hourly". It was fairly entertaining, and Blair was okay as long as I returned his books to the shelf after I read them and made him coffee when he was drunk. He gave me and the dog equal attention.'

'Did you love him? Blair, I mean.'

'Sure. I loved the dog too and to be fair, I have to say the dog was more lovable than Blair or me. The old man took me to the School of Mines the last time I saw him and then he went back to California and blew his brains out with a Colt.'

'You're hard.'

He could be harder. He had never pressed her on the issue of her house rent, how she and Flo managed on the wages of pit girls. The money came from somewhere, and Bill Jaxon – with bets won on purring matches – was a likely source. Blair realized that he was willing to preserve the illusion of her independence and the unreal quality of the house because he was afraid that one wrong word would drive her away.

'So you're going to be Mrs Bill Jaxon.'

'Bill thinks so.'

'Bill's still hiding outside my hotel. He'd make a good newel post.'

'Do you envy Bill?'

'A bit.'

'What I mean is, he's real, isn't he? You're some creature from the papers. From the shipping news.'

'I am.'

'Sprung from nothing, you say.'

'Self-created out of my severely limited social exposure to Chinese, whores and miners.'

'No home.'

'Always moving, out of place, *sui generis*.'

'Is that Latin for lonely?'

'Miss Molyneux, you could have made a lawyer.'

She topped his glass. 'What do you call your daughter, the one in Africa?'

'Ah. Her mother and I went around on that. She wanted something English and I wanted something African. We compromised on something biblical.'

'And what was that?'

'Keziah. It means "Rainbow". From the Book of Job.'

'It's a beautiful name,' Rose said.

'A beautiful girl. We're pretty far from the Reverend Maypole.'

'I hope so.'

An unbidden image of George Battie and his two girls came to mind. Blair had assumed plainness in Battie's life and out of a black hole George had scooped up doves.

'You'll be leaving us soon,' Rose said. 'What do you miss most about the Gold Coast, the women or the gold?'

'Hard to say.'

'Why's that?'

Blair picked up the orange ball of yarn from the bag, pulled free a foot of wool shot through with brilliant aniline dye, and tied the yarn into a series of knots. 'They're hard to separate.'

'Knots?'

'Women and gold.'

He cut the knotted yarn with his pocket knife, slid the shawl off Rose's shoulders and tied the yarn around her upper arm. In the light of the fire, with her skin shadowed by coal dust, the bright yarn stood out.

'From top to bottom, a head band of royal purple and golden cloth, necklaces of gold filigree, breastplates of gold threads, armlets and bracelets of glass beads and gold, a skirt of pink, black and gold thread, and anklets of amber beads and golden wires. We'll simply have to use our imagination.'

He cut another length of yarn, knotted it and tied it to her other arm, then cut and knotted more and tied them around her wrists.

'Some of the gold is gold thread and some of it is cast. Some into chains, some into shapes of disks, bells, shells, seeds, cocoons.'

He untied and slipped off her clogs and tied yarn around her bare ankles. He helped her stand. 'Completely covered,' he said.

Her dress was cotton with a vestigial print and shell buttons, as many split as whole. He undid the buttons carefully, not to break them, and revealed a chemise of thin muslin. He slipped his fingers through the shoulder loops and slid the dress and chemise down.

With longer yarn he tied thicker knots. 'Think of a mass of golden necklaces with amulets and Dutch glass beads so heavy that with every move they sway. Strings of golden talismans and animals and in the middle, large as a lump of coal, a golden nugget.'

'My hair?' she asked.

'Your hair's already gold.'

She had a single petticoat of muslin, the meanest cloth of all. She stepped out of that and spread her arms. Someone could look in the window any time, Blair knew. If they squinted, they could see. He tied a final strand around her waist as a golden belt and stood back.

'Am I naked?' she asked.

'To someone else. Not to me.'

He carried her upstairs. He sensed that she wanted no man who couldn't do that much. Their faces and mouths pressed together, he tasted gin and salt and coal dust that made him take the steps two at a time. She held him and wrapped around him like a knot. Then they were in bed, his face hot against her belly. Wrapped in gold. She arched and stretched across the bed so that they travelled together and as one.

In Rose, hard work had created grace, the curved

muscularity of a wild animal, the lightness and, for her size, the strength. More lithe than thick, steel like a dancer through the legs, an arch to lift both their bodies. Then she turned and devoured him as he devoured her, demanding that nothing be held back. He was besotted with her, soaked, gilt in her black dust, her breasts washed pink from his mouth.

What were they now? English? African?

Lost, Blair thought. Something about making love muddled time and space, rearranged them like limbs. No past, no future, and the present so attenuated that he could breathe fifty times within a second. Bent over her, running his finger between her shoulderblades and down her spine, he could feel time shudder to a halt.

She turned. Her hair, a mop dark with sweat, swept back. The glint of coal dust on her face, her lips swollen, her brow white. Despite her darkness she was lit by a faint reflection of lamplight from his body, the way the moon was sometimes lit only by reflection from the earth, a ghostly illumination called an 'ashen glow'. In that faint light appeared – for a moment – a disturbing, secondary image of someone finer.

'You call this love?' Blair asked.

'I call it fair and equal,' Rose said. 'You're a mess, Mr Blair. You need someone like me.'

'And what would Bill Jaxon do?'

'Bill wouldn't know till we were gone. Then he could

kick in somebody else's head for spite.' The flame
guttered. She slipped from the bed, knelt by the night
stand and lit a new candle. She didn't move like a woman
who wore bustles. It was a paradox that hard work had
given her so much grace. Fresh wick light in her hair, she
jumped back on the bed. 'We could be gone before
anyone knew.'

'Gone? I thought you were happy here.'

'I was until you dressed me all in gold. What do I
need t'know for Africa?'

'Some pidgin English.'

'Not what we talk in Wigan?'

'Not really. Swahili for general travel. Twi is what the
Ashanti speak. If you can read a map, shoot the sun and
stay dry in the rainy season, you've pretty much got it
licked. Then it's largely a matter of knowing the difference between pyrite and gold and taking quinine in every
conceivable form.' He touched the stitches on his head.
'The surgery you've got. You'd do fine in Africa. You
could be an Amazon.'

'Then I don't need you? I could go without you.'

'Of course. Just follow the trade winds. That's what
trade is, just winds and currents.' He put his hand on
her heart and slid his palm down. 'Coal south from
Liverpool on the Canary current.' Diagonally up. 'Palm
oil west from Africa on the equatorial current.' Across.
'Gold east from the Americas on the Gulf Stream.'

'It's very simple when you put it that way.'

'That's about all I know,' Blair said.

'And you know other routes?'

'Yes.'

'Take me.' She placed her hand on his. 'Take me from Wigan, Mr Blair, and I'll love you t'the day I die.'

Chapter Twenty-Two

The furnace was as yellow as the vent of a volcano, its light so intense that Blair pulled down the brim of his hat to shield his eyes. The design was plain, a firegrate in an arch of bricks mortared three deep in the stone, an approach ramp lined in brick to separate the fire from a tunnel that ran to seams of Hannay coal. Although the furnace was a mile underground, its dimensions were outsized: two men abreast could have walked on to the grate, and the fire sucked air with a thirst that tugged at Battie and Blair.

Battie shouted, 'It always seems a contradiction to burn oxygen to build a draught, but that's what draws more air from the cage shaft and blows the foul air out. We have to draw fresh. If we introduced foul air full of gas directly into the fire the furnace would explode.'

'You drift it?'

'Right. We channel foul air in a shaft we call the dumb drift that joins well up the chimney, where the updraught's cool enough so gas won't ignite. Good air in, foul air out and that's our ventilation. Twenty-four hours we have to keep it going or the pit stops breathing and then any man down here would be dead.'

A golden plasma floated over a bed of brilliant coals that seemed to shift as if animated by the heat. The furnace fed on Hannay coal mined from the Hannay seam, a dragon that thrived by consuming itself. A coal bunker had been hacked out of stone at the end of the ramp, where two stokers in gauntlets and sacks with holes cut for their arms waited with a tub of coal. There were always two stokers in case one swooned, Battie had explained.

'Six tons of coal a day we burn in there,' Battie said. Once again, the underlooker had left his hat in his office and tied a handkerchief on his head.

Blair squinted, trying to look into the furnace and protect his eyes at the same time. 'The ashes?'

'Fall through the grate to be collected and dumped. It's been emptied twice since the accident.'

'Could we look anyway?'

'For what?'

'Buttons, bones. Clogs would be burned, but clog irons might be caught in the grate. Maybe nails.'

Battie looked at the stokers, just out of earshot. 'That would be wonderful news down pit, that the Bishop's man is sifting for bodies.'

'Tell them whatever you want.'

Battie motioned Blair to follow him down the ramp to the stokers, who had been watching with gaping curiosity.

'Men, this is Mr Blair, a special visitor to the mine. He's an American who likes to examine every cranny and stir every pot. Do we have a spoon?'

The 'spoon' was a long shovel. Battie took off Blair's hat and replaced it with a canvas hood with a viewplate of smoked mica. 'Mr Blair, you are a great pain in the fundament,' he muttered. He shoved on to Blair's hands a pair of padded canvas gloves that reached to the elbow. 'You're going to have to do this alone. I won't roast a man for a lunatic whim. Wait.' He picked up a wooden bucket and poured water over Blair's hood and gloves.

Dripping, Blair took the shovel and climbed back up the ramp. Despite the viewplate the coals burned white, too bright to look at directly. Like the sun. The heat was stunning, a physical blow.

When stokers threw coal they did it from a safe distance. Blair stabbed the fire directly at the grate. Superheated air forced itself down his throat. Coals rang like glass bells under the shovel's blade. Within his shirt, he felt the hairs of his chest stand and curl. But the beauty was overwhelming. Molten gold shimmering in its own consummation, fold lapping over radiant fold, sparking as he thrust the shovel, looking for what on the dragon's tongue? A gleaming thigh bone, a well-picked rib? Vapour exploded around him and he realized that someone had thrown water at him from behind. He dug away, trying to scratch down to the red of the grate. There was a tug at his arm, and at his side he found Battie in hood and gloves wrapped in steam. Battie pointed. What he was saying, Blair couldn't tell until the underlooker dragged him from the furnace and Blair realized that the shaft of his shovel was on fire and the iron of the blade was a dull, angry red.

The stokers met them halfway down the ramp, doused Blair's shovel and his hood with water. Only when he took off his gloves did he notice that they and his shirt front were scorched.

'Have you been to Hell before?' Battie asked. 'You seem used to the work.'

'I didn't find anything.'

'Nor will you, not without shutting down the fire. Is insanity a requirement for an explorer?'

Blair staggered down the ramp, dizzy from the flames, almost hilarious. 'Now I know what toast feels like.'

Battie followed. 'Absolutely mad. Mr Blair, I'll keep my eyes open. If I find anything more suspicious than the cinder of a cricket's dick, you'll be the first to know.'

A morning downpour greeted Blair at the surface and for once he didn't care because he felt as if he were still smouldering. The yard was an inky pond. Steam hung over engines and horses and the sorting shed, obscuring the screens and pit girls under the overhang. Smoke emanated from kiln, forge and engine chimneys. Devil's weather, he thought, and welcome.

He found his mackintosh under the carriage seat, pulled the coat around himself and staggered to the lamp man's shed. Battie had said that after the explosion all the lamps had been accounted for. Blair didn't doubt him, but there was a way to check. He didn't remember all the safety-lamp numbers listed in the Coroner's report but he recalled two: 091 signed for by Bill Jaxon and 125 by Smallbone. What if one or other lamp had never been signed out again? It was just an idea and he didn't know where it led, but he went through the lamp man's ledger until the pages were almost as wet as he was. Safety lamps 091 and 125 had been signed out every working day since the explosion. Blair decided he was about as good a detective as Maypole was a miner.

The window of the shed streaked with rain, and this reminded him of Maypole's journal, the lines reading down as well as across. What was it the poor son of bitch wrote the day before he disappeared? 'Tomorrow is the great adventure!'

Blair found Leveret at Hannay Hall, in the stables, a brick court with a tower and a portcullis, like a defendable castle. The estate manager was in the courtyard, kneeling on wet cobblestones in boots and great coat, intent on the task of grooming a giant Shire mare, combing mud from her feathers, the long hair around the hoof. The giant horse rested her muzzle on Leveret's back. Despite the rain, beast and man both looked content.

In a corner, a farrier hammered a red ribbon of iron on an anvil. As stalls were mucked out, horses clopped across open passageways; one side seemed given to workhorses, the other to hunters. It was a scene stately and bucolic, Blair thought, where gentry massed in hunting pink to ride to hounds. Maybe where generations of Hannays had deflowered maids. It was odd how he now looked at things through Rose's eyes.

He was feverish, whether from malaria or the furnace

he couldn't tell. Rose kept coming unbidden to his mind because he didn't know if she had been serious or playing when she suggested leaving with him. It wasn't only his feeling responsible for someone's rash decision. It made her real. Perhaps what made her more than a series of moments all in the present was – because of her suggestion – a sense of her future. If it took the setting of her bed and a smudge of coal transferred from her skin to his – well, that was the coarse nature of man. He had promised nothing. Perhaps it had all been a joke of hers. Or a mystery, like her house. It left him distracted. Stabbing at the furnace, he had thought of her. He tipped his head back and let rain cool his face. '"The deeper the shaft, the greater the heat" is a miner's rule.'

'Blair!' Leveret blushed. 'I'd never heard that.'

'You don't have enough stablemen to do the grooming?'

'Yes, but I enjoy it. To manage an estate, you can't just keep your eyes open, you have to put your hands on.' Leveret snapped mud off the comb with each pass; where he had combed, the hair was white and silky. 'I've worked in every part of the estate. Farming, stables, sheep, gardens, even the brewery. I was raised to be the estate manager. John used to say I was like Adam in the Garden of Eden, because Adam was put there to oversee Eden, not to own it. I feel fortunate that Bishop Hannay has so much faith in me. I've never aspired to be a Hannay, I wouldn't want to be a Hannay.'

'Maypole could have owned it – some of it.'

'Charlotte's income is all.'

'Quite a lot for a curate with two suits to his name.'
Even as Blair spoke, Rose returned to mind. What dowry
could a pit girl bring? Wages? A jar of coins, money she
had earned, which lowered its value in the eyes of the
world. Better an heirloom that came with family prospects, expectations a man could borrow against. 'When
we went down the mine you said something I should
have asked you about. You said you had been down a
mine before, an old one about ten feet deep.'

'An abandoned pit on the Wigan side of the grounds.'

'Did you ever mention it to Maypole?'

'That's why I went down. He asked if I knew of one,
so I took him.'

'When?'

'It was after the New Year. John was curious. There
are a number of tunnels here, actually, some used as
priest holes – hiding places – when the Hannays were
Catholic hundreds of years ago. This tunnel is inside the
grounds at the north gate, about fifty yards to your right
as you leave.' Leveret shifted and picked up the opposite
hoof. 'I feel I've served you badly. I've served John
poorly, too.'

'You have been conspicuous by your absence. Except
for the picnic yesterday and you were busy with dogs
then. You're always busy with four-legged animals.'

'Just hiding my embarrassment because I didn't tell
you everything when you first arrived on the train.'

'You didn't tell me about Charlotte. About the Bishop's
getting her to give up on Maypole and agree to Rowland.'

'I'm afraid so. This gives you such a wrong impression of the Hannays and of Charlotte. You've caught them at a bad point.'

'And I'm sure the sun shines in England most of the time. So it's me or Rowland in a way. Charlotte is stuck with me until she agrees to marry him? In the meantime I'm stuck with them?'

'That's one way to put it.'

'Fine, I'll drive Charlotte to it.'

'That's beneath you. You wouldn't do that.'

'Nothing is beneath me. I'm wet, I'm burned and I'm ready to leave. Like Earnshaw. Earnshaw was a set-up, wasn't he? The great reformer? He was brought by Hannay to keep Charlotte entertained. You told me Earnshaw wasn't courting, so you knew everything.'

'Charlotte is wealthy and attractive.'

'Charlotte has the allure of a young asp. Anyway, I don't like being another Earnshaw, and I don't like being part of the set-up for Rowland.'

'He's the future Lord Hannay.'

'He is a homicidal maniac. What a family!' Blair combed his hair with his fingers, it occurred to him that the horse was better groomed. 'You told me that Charlotte has her own cottage in the grounds. Where?'

'Why do you ask?'

'I want to talk to her, to reason with her.'

'It's the quarry cottage. Back on the lane, past the Home, you'll see the quarry, and then you can't miss the house. What if she won't talk to you?'

'Well, I still have my original option. I find Maypole

wherever he's rotting or hiding. Hannay didn't pay Maypole to disappear, did he?'

'John wouldn't, no more than you.'

'You never stop hoping, do you?'

The lane was two furrows in a blanket of last year's leaves. Beeches green with moss and black with soot held back a tangle of thorns dripping water. Half a mile on, one side opened to a meadow with a flock of sheep white against a backdrop of trees while the other side offered glimpses of houses on Wigan Lane, no longer distant but approaching the perimeter of Hannay Hall.

One last turn brought Blair over a hill and along a stone wall that protected the traveller from falling into an abyss where the entire other side of the hill had been carved out. He stopped to look from the height of the carriage he had borrowed from Leveret. The drop was at least a hundred feet, the gritstone wall overgrown with algae and desperately hanging shrubs, the bottom a dismal lake lost in shadow. The house that seemed to go with the quarry, though, made a contrast. Its bottom storey was built from dun-coloured quarry stones, but the upper façade was white Tudor, a chevron of black beams capped with a cheerfully coxcombed red-tile roof. Between cottage and quarry were a small stable, greenhouse and dovecote. Around the house itself was a border of rosebushes that were bare and daffodils just opening their hoods. Smoke trailed from a tall brick chimney. Everything about the house seemed inviting.

When Blair knocked at the door there was no answer. Since he had seen the smoke, he went back to the kitchen door. There was no response there, either. Through the window the kitchen was dark, a long table set for one, a pastry on a plate beside an exotic orange. In the hallway were candlelight and a young woman in a white dress that mirrored the flame. He saw her clearly only for a moment before she blew the candle out.

From her red hair he had thought at first that she was Rose, but her face was too round. In a way she resembled both Charlotte and Rose; yet Charlotte would have regarded him with cool outrage, Rose with the languid indifference of a cat. All he had seen staring out of this girl's eyes was panic.

He called through the door, again received silence in return, and he could almost feel the easing of floorboards as she retreated deeper into the hall. The quality of her dress, a watered silk, suggested a specimen of the upper class. Her fear, though, made him speculate that she might be one of Charlotte's charges from the Home for Women, a fallen pit or factory girl hiding in the cottage from a righteous father. Whichever, neither rapping nor calling could entice her to the door.

He gave up and drove away. Rain steamed off his horse. He remembered that he looked like a gypsy, a tinker, trouble of one sort or another. Not the kind of face that opened doors.

To a degree, not finding Charlotte at home was a relief. He didn't know what he had expected to say to her, whether to explain his relative innocence about the

Bishop's motives, or to give the devil in himself full rein
and whip her towards Rowland. If he had received
anything but aristocratic contempt from Charlotte,
detected a single heartbeat of human softness or warmth,
anything like Rose, it would be different. At the knacker's
drop he had offered to leave Wigan, and Charlotte had
thrown the offer back in his face, as if she were picking
up a rag on a stick.

His mood was accompanied by a darkening wind and
a scrabbling of branches overhead. He lit the carriage
lamps, though he trusted more to the horse's good sense
than to what he could see. Why he had even contemplated a second offer of truce to Charlotte he no longer
knew.

The grounds were coming to an end; by his compass,
the lane was bearing north, away from Wigan. A gust
picked leaves and swirled them around him like bats.
When he was beginning to think he had lost his way, the
road showed two brilliant, parallel lines of light and
from far ahead came the low beat of thunder.

In that blinding instant it struck Blair how extraordinary in their different ways Charlotte and Rose were,
and how nothing but the most ordinary prettiness shone
from the face of the girl in the house. Charlotte and Rose
were fashioned in opposite ways, but both were gold,
just as the third girl was dross.

The north gate was of wrought iron that had long
ago rusted open. Tall beeches had been replaced by

evergreens limping in the wind. Following Leveret's instructions, Blair paced off fifty steps and found himself waist-high in bracken. In the beam of his bull's-eye lamp, over a wave of ornate ferns, was a birch, always the first tree growing on coal slag.

At the tree he heard a ping of rain on metal. He tracked the tapping to a three-foot iron square that he swung back on a hinge, and the ping was blown away by a draught rising from below. He lowered the lamp slowly. Methane loved old pits, and he wanted to leave Wigan on foot, not through the air. Unlike a miner's lamp, a bull's-eye lantern was not designed for reading gas because the flame was enclosed in metal and aimed through a lens. All he could go by was the colour. The light stayed a safe yellow as it picked out a tunnel floor ten feet down. There were no rails, placing the mine back in a time when coal was dragged in sledges. Blair went to the carriage and returned with a rope that he secured to the birch. He rigged the lamp through his belt and went hand over hand down the rope into the shaft.

The floor was wet and slick, the timbers of the walls and roof bowing from age and rot. The open area of the pit eye was supported by free-standing pillars of corrupted stone; he thought a hard breath might bring them down. The tunnel was a miniature operation compared to the Hannay Pit, but the genesis of Hannay industry. There were hundreds of mines like this around Wigan, and thousands of even earlier ones, 'bell pits' that were nothing but holes hollowed out for coal until they collapsed.

Feeling one-eyed, he followed his lamp into the tunnel. He saw no footprints, but the fact that the shaft cover had opened at all suggested that the mine had been visited recently.

As the tunnel dipped, water striped the walls at the angle of descent. Toadstools fringed the ceiling. On damper walls glittered a remnant of coal carved out and hauled away long ago. His light caught a tail vanishing into a hole; there would be rats, mice, beetles; nature abhorred a vacuum. As the roof lowered, he fell into a miner's stooped walk. Big men had trouble learning the gait. 'My muscles ache,' Maypole had written.

The tunnel ended fifty yards on, where the coal strata had abruptly dipped and dropped out of reach, and dust had accumulated against a gritstone wall. A free-standing pillar of coal was left in the middle of the tunnel and Blair imagined the temptation it must have been to miners who were paid only by the coal they brought out. Still, it was important to come out alive.

He searched in sweeps of the light. Pearly, half-formed hands of stalactites reached down from the roof. A blank pool lay underneath. In the ebony powder at the pillar's base was the horseshoe print of a clog iron. Scuff marks on the stone floor could have been made by someone trying to get used to the stiff, rocking action of clogs. But more than walking had been practised. The walls were scarred with pick marks that ran straight as a chord and then scattered in clumsy imitation.

The tunnel had the chill of a crypt. Blair shivered and treated himself to a sip of brandy. When he put the flask away, he saw another curiosity, a brattice – canvas stretched on a wooden frame – leaning against the end wall. Brattices were used to direct ventilation between tunnels. This was a single, primitive tunnel with no need for brattices at all. Unless it was hiding something behind it.

As he approached the canvas a timber knocked off his hat. When Blair twisted to catch it, he was blown off his feet. He spun through the air and rolled end over end. The tunnel filled with powder smoke, he was choking on it even while he didn't know whether he was up or down. His eyes smarted, blinded. His head rang as if his eardrums had burst.

On hands and knees, he crawled around the floor, found the lamp, still lit, and burned his fingers before he got it upright because he could tell only by touch. He crawled in the other direction, feeling his way until he reached water falling through the shaft. He looked up into the rain with his eyes wide open until they were washed enough for him to see. His body felt slapped by a giant hand, though he found no blood or broken bones, only a round hole that ran through the oilskin of his raincoat, jacket and his shirt. He wet a handkerchief, tied it over his nose and mouth, and went unsteadily back into the tunnel.

In the atmosphere at the end of the tunnel, smoke and dust still swirled and eddied. The canvas had been knocked aside by a device with a fat, wooden stock and a short, flared barrel that sat like a cannon on a steel ring. It was called a spring gun. Below the trigger ran a chain with rings tied to strings. Blair brushed dirt away. The strings were attached to cords stretched across the tunnel floor. When a man tripped a cord, as he had, the gun swivelled in his direction and the trigger snapped shut. A spring gun wasn't for game, but for poachers. A mankiller, outlawed, but still used.

Blair aimed his lamp along the muzzle. In the coal pillar just behind where he had stood was a steel rod an inch in diameter, and driven so firmly into the coal that it couldn't be budged. But for his stumble, he would be bleeding to death. Born and died in Wigan. Funny when he thought about it. To leave, go around the world and come back home for this. With his penknife he cut off a piece of trip string. It was woven cotton, the sort for wicks and fuses.

Hearing returned as the sound of water insinuated itself, dripping with clocklike regularity from the roof to the smooth, pulsing surface of the pool below.

He had never before experienced the panic of being trapped underground. Standing in what should have been his grave, he felt fear blow down the back of his neck.

It was midnight when Blair got back to his room. He tore off his shirt. A red sear ran along his ribs.

He pulled off the rest of his damp clothes, poured himself a brandy and went to the window. The street was black and yellow, wet stones reflecting lamps. A constable in a helmet and cape shuffled up Wallgate as slowly as a sleepwalker. He stared into the void behind the shops. There was no reflection from brass toecaps to be seen, no knock of clogs to be heard.

Traps had an anonymous character. Anyone could have set the spring gun. Maypole's journal and the height of the pick marks on the tunnel walls indicated Jaxon. But the use of fuse string as trip wire and the slyness of the trap suggested Smallbone, that one-man factory of homemade explosives. As a former poacher, Smallbone would be familiar with spring guns.

This didn't exhaust the possibilities. George Battie had been a poacher and he didn't want the Coroner's inquest reopened. And who had directed Blair to the tunnel but Leveret? He had proof of nothing. He could have been assassinated by the Temperance League or the Wigan Brass Band.

He touched the welt, proof of only one thing. It was time to go.

Chapter Twenty-Three

At the ironmonger's, Blair bought the stout sort of luggage covered in American canvas called a Railway Companion, along with rope, bath towels, a four-inch length of one-inch-diameter rod, a pair of wrenches and a pound sack of gunpowder. He didn't buy one, but noticed miner's safety lamps at attention on a shelf. Then he drove out to Hannay Hall and detoured to the Home for Women.

This time he approached the mock castle of the Home from the garden side. Through the long windows at the stairs he saw grey uniforms rushing to class or catechism, a stir like doves in a stone loft. Damp weather had cleared the benches outside. No one, not even a gardener, was visible on the long slope of the lawn between the Home at the top and the hedge at the bottom.

On the near side of the hedge was one small, recognizable figure. In a black dress and leather gauntlets, Charlotte Hannay was again pruning her roses. Her wide-brimmed hat sagged in the mist and copper strands of hair stuck to her cheek. Between trees and garden was a space of twenty yards. Blair knew she saw him coming, though she didn't look in his direction. The raw welt on his ribs asked to be coddled, but he had the sense that no weakness should be revealed to Charlotte Hannay.

'Do they ever bloom?' he asked. 'You seem to get most of your pleasure from cutting them back.'

She gave him not a glance. The rose garden was a perfect setting for her precisely because there were no roses. A rose garden should have roses as pink as English faces, Blair thought. If there were, though, she would probably decapitate them. With her pruning shears' curved blades, Charlotte Hannay put him in mind of a figure from the French Revolution, one of those women who happily attended Madame Guillotine. Her dress glistened as if she had been in the garden all morning, although there were few clippings in the basket that straddled the path. Except for her pallor and habitual frown, she could have made a not unattractive young woman, he thought, though that was like saying a wasp made a pretty insect except for its sting.

'Didn't I warn you not to come here again?' Charlotte asked.

'You did.'

She snipped off a long cane with red barbs. Switch in one hand, shears in the other, she straightened up.

'You intend to whip me, neuter me, or both?' Blair asked.

'Whatever would serve as the best reminder.'

She tossed the cane towards the basket and bent over the next plant. She trimmed the top twigs, making a way to reach in and prune the middle stems. Though the gauntlets protected her to the elbow, the silk sleeves of her arms were torn.

Blair said, 'No need, anyway. I'm leaving Wigan.

You're not the only one, apparently, who'd like to see me go.'

Charlotte didn't bother to respond. As she trimmed dead wood, he noticed that her work slowed to a meditative pace. He expected her to charge him with prowling outside her cottage too, but she said not a word about it.

Blair said, 'I think in time I could have found Maypole. What I have discovered already is that I'm more interested in finding him than anyone else. It's clear this is not about a missing man. All your father wants is for you to give up a dead engagement and then I'm free to go back to Africa. Am I correct so far?'

'It doesn't actually matter.'

'You don't care if I find Maypole. You would have helped me if you did. I got interested in him and his fate, but that's not worth being killed for. It makes me feel stupid to admit it. Anyway, I apologize for being used against you. I had no idea this was about you. The main thing is, I want to go and you want me to go.'

Charlotte bent among the stems. With each snip, Blair pictured another red rose dropping. 'The main thing is,' she said, 'I won't marry Rowland.'

'Marry who you want. The problem is the longer I'm here, the more I find. He had another life besides you. I think you want me to go now rather than later. Just tell the Bishop you're no longer interested in Maypole. Then the Bishop blesses me and sends me on my way, and you and I are square.'

'You are a worm, Blair.'

'That's not the answer I was looking for.' He felt a rush of blood as if she had hit him. 'Very well, do you know a pit girl named Rose Molyneux?'

Wind pressed the brim of Charlotte's hat. Blair realized that she must be cold in her thin dress and shoes. But where was she colder, he wondered, inside or out?

'I don't recall the name.'

'Reverend Maypole was infatuated with her.'

'I doubt that.'

Blair glanced towards the Home. 'She has some skill at surgery. I thought she might have picked it up in one of your classes. Maypole might have met her here.'

'Describe her,' Charlotte said.

'Physically, I'd have to say she was ordinarily attractive. She has red hair and a great deal of spirit, and that sets her apart. I wouldn't say she was intellectual, but she's quickwitted and direct. A free spirit. You rescue these girls, you must have a fair opinion of them.'

'I rescue them because they are not free, because they are working girls who are abandoned by their suitors or abused by their fathers. Otherwise the babies go to the orphanage, and the mothers, who are usually not much more than children themselves, descend in three steps – from Reverend Chubb's care, to the workshop, to prostitution. We make them free.'

'Well, Maypole thought Rose was a free spirit without your care. He was taken with her.'

'And was this regard reciprocated?'

'No. I think Rose was flattered by Maypole's attentions, but that's all. I don't think she had anything to do with his disappearance. The affair was mainly in his head.'

'As if you knew John Maypole.'

'What I'm getting at—'

A cane snapped. Charlotte threw it lightly aside. 'Let me guess. That I will be embarrassed by revelations of the Reverend Maypole's romantic attachment to another woman – an earthy, working-class woman – unless you end your inquiry? Is that right?'

'More or less, since you put it that way.'

'Devoid of emotion as I allegedly am, I can work these things out.'

'Good. Do you remember what your father said about closing the Home if there was a public scandal? I think Maypole's infatuation would qualify as that. All your saintly work will be undone.'

Charlotte approached a bush with canes already pruned to the nub. While she removed her gauntlet to feel for shoots, a liqueur of water and compost swam into her shoes.

'Let us be clear. You would force me to marry Rowland so that you could collect money from my father and go back to Africa? If that's the case, I'll give you money and the ticket.'

'But you can't give me the work in West Africa your father can, and that's what I need.'

'You are lower than a worm. You are an extortionist.'

'It's not hard. I haven't seen one tear, one sign of human sympathy from you for that poor bastard Maypole. Not one word of help for me. Now you can find him on your own, if you care.'

'Perhaps you are simply too ignorant to understand the dimensions of the damage you could do. This is the only haven in the north of England where women pregnant out of wedlock are not treated as criminals or outcasts. We turn them from victims into employable, useful persons. Can you grasp that?'

'This is a doll's house where you dress poor girls in grey dresses. Your little world. You're the grey princess, the coal princess. What fun they have, I'm sure.'

'You'd wreck it all to get at me?'

'Unless you tell your father what he wants and I get what I need. As soon as I'm gone, you can change your mind. Or don't.'

Charlotte turned her back on Blair and moved to a plant already cut to a single Y of bare canes. She ran her hand lightly over the barbs in a slow, reflective search for shoots, until Blair realized she wasn't going to say anything more to him, that he had been dismissed.

Blair lowered himself by rope down into the mine and followed the same route as the night before, wrenches in his belt, taking care to sweep the floor with the light of his bull's-eye lantern for new trip wires. The spring gun sat at the end of the tunnel, the rod it had shot still lodged in the coal. The gun looked more like a stepson of a cannon than a rifle, and the sight of it made him wince.

He studied the pick marks on the wall as if he were an archaeologist in an ancient tomb. Miners used short-shafted picks because they worked in cramped conditions, and, all things being equal, the height of the work tended to indicate the size of the man. The marks were unusually high from the floor, Bill Jaxon's height, and expertly straight as a taut string, except where they went suddenly askew. At the same height but off-line and badly hit: too hard, too soft, or off the point. As the mishits went on, however, they improved. Jaxon and Maypole were both big men. Blair imagined the miner instructing the curate on the stroke and rhythm of the ancient craft of hewing coal. But why? If Maypole just wanted to slip underground to preach, he needed only to look like a miner, not to attempt the work. Winning coal with a pick was not something learned in a day or a week. Real miners would turn him out as a fraud and a danger.

A mystery never to be solved, Blair decided. The spring gun was all he'd come for. It was an ungainly forty pounds of hardwood stock and iron barrel on a base made from an iron wheel. Even after he had unbolted the gun from its base, the barrel made hard carrying under a roof that stooped to four feet in places. He laid the gun near the pit eye, went back for the base and was returning when an apparition of a spider the size of a man dropped through the shaft and hung in mid-air.

'Who is that?' The Reverend Chubb blinked at the dark and made vaguely swimming motions with his arms and legs. His hair, tie and wattles swayed as he hung. A hand from above held on to his belt.

'Is it Blair?' a voice asked.

'It is too black down here,' Chubb said.

'It's me.' Blair set the base down beside the gun.

'Good work, Chubb,' the voice said, and the Reverend rose again like an angel on a wire. Blair pulled himself up the rope to the surface, where Chubb stood dizzily reassembling his loose parts. Rowland kicked the shaft cover shut and leaned against the birch in a negligent way, like a poet who happened to be carrying a shotgun rather than a poem. His yellow hair was uncombed, his eyes bright as crystal set off by red lids.

'Very disagreeable and uncomfortable,' Chubb muttered to his chin.

'The work of a moment,' Rowland said, 'for which you have my gratitude, which is no small matter when you consider that I will be Lord Hannay and your living will be dependent on my good will. Otherwise you will eke out your final years like a cockle sucking on a pier.'

'I was pleased to oblige,' Chubb said.

'That is the wonderful thing about the Established Church,' Rowland told Blair. 'They do oblige. What are you doing here? We found a carriage standing in the lane and began beating the bushes for the driver.'

'Looking for the Reverend Chubb's missing curate. Chief Constable Moon suggested that he might have fallen down an old shaft.'

'There are a thousand abandoned shafts in Wigan.'

'I can only try.'

'Well, we'll prove the veracity of your claim. Moon is with us. Besides, there's something I want to tell you about. You'll join the party.'

They moved through stands of larch and oak. Besides Rowland, Blair, Chubb and Moon ranged gamekeepers on either side. Amid a fine rain fell heavier drops from branches. Wet leaves muffled the men's steps and soiled their trouser cuffs.

After being underground, Blair enjoyed the open air in spite of the company. Rowland bragged about his shotgun, a gift from the Royal Geographical Society. It was the custom product of a London gunmaker, with narrow double barrels and a breech engraved with lions and elands like the head of an elegant cane.

A woodpecker made an undulating flight across a clearing and alighted on the trunk of a larch fifty yards ahead. The bird crossed its black and white wings behind its back and had started to probe beneath the bark when Rowland fired and nailed its head to the tree. 'A tight pattern,' he said.

A finch panicked across the clearing. 'Too far,' Blair said.

Rowland shot and the bird split like a pillow, golden feathers wafting to the ground.

The advantage with arsenic, Blair thought, was that it did hone the eye and induce illusions of omnipotence; he wished he had brought some himself. Of course the peak was usually followed by a trough.

MARTIN CRUZ SMITH

The keepers ran forward to pluck the kills and stuff the fluffs and feathers into silk sacks.

Rowland reloaded as he walked. 'There is a use for everything and employment for every man. England's strength is specialization, Blair. One man collects iron, another tin, another rags, another bones. One man collects horse manure for fertilizer, another dog shit for dye works. Feathers make fish lures. Nothing wasted, everyone gainfully employed. I think it will be wonderful to be Lord Hannay.'

Moon loomed at Blair's shoulder. 'First you fish in the canals. Now, I understand you have been popping in and out of holes.'

'You told me Maypole might have fallen in a shaft.'

'I'm flattered you took my suggestion so much to heart. I have to warn you, though, that this side of Wigan is practically a Swiss cheese. There are tunnels, they say, that go all the way to Candle Court.'

'In Catholic days,' Chubb said, still smarting.

You don't put the local vicar down a hole like a ferret even if you are lord of the manor, Blair thought. Which would be precisely why Rowland did it, to establish his exception to all rules. It was the way the Hannays did everything.

Rowland said, 'I've been teasing Chubb about evolution. The problem with the Bible is that it claims we are all created in the image of God. It makes a great deal more sense that we share a mutual ancestor with the apes, and that the races of man show the same scientific evolution from Negroids and Asiatics to Hamites, your

Arabs, and Semites, your Jews, to the modern Anglo-Saxon.'

'I've seen too many Englishmen tip over canoes.'

'There are different English, just as there are ladies and pit girls. There's a reason those women do that sort of work. It's natural selection. I forget, Blair, what was your mother?'

'I forget, too.'

'Anyway, it gives me a sense of welcome and confidence to have representatives of the Church and the Law at my side. To know that they look forward to a time when I will be truly home. Of course the Bishop will be Lord Hannay for many years to come, I'm sure. We wish him the longest possible life.'

A starling passed with the flight of a stone skipping on water. Rowland fired and the bird turned a cartwheel. He asked Blair, 'Take you back to Africa?'

'It certainly does. Too bad you can't have some dead pachyderms lying around the grounds.'

'Shooting is the pinprick of reality, Blair. Otherwise everything is dull. A little bang, a little blood, and things come to life. Are you following this, Chubb? You might be able to use it for a sermon.'

'I don't understand why you want Blair along, My Lord.' Chubb was stumbling after them.

'Because Blair knows what I'm talking about and you don't. Moon, do you?'

Moon swept a branch aside for Rowland. 'I have some appreciation, My Lord.'

'Then we'll have some interesting times. But, Moon,

you should have seen Blair in the Gold Coast. There are
plenty of English on the coast, but in the interior there
was only Blair. And Arabs, but they don't count. Not
much of a marksman, but he knew his way. Spoke the
lingo like a pasha. See, there are two Blairs. The mythic
Blair in Africa and the lifesize Blair here. Have I done
your portrait, Blair? Is your nose too long or out of joint?
It's just that in Africa you had a certain style. It's sad to
see you so reduced. There you go, looking at your
compass again.'

'Thanks for the walk. I'm off,' Blair said.

Rowland said, 'Wait.'

From the mine, they had gone east through the first
stands of trees and south-east through a screen of willows
to the slag heap of another abandoned mine. Birches, as
if they preferred to slum, grew on the slag. Behind the
trees was a box hedge and a house.

Rowland climbed the pile. The wind was warmer, and
the sky, if anything, was lower and darker than before.
His face had a malarial shine. He pointed to a greening
copse of alders another fifty yards on and directed Moon
to lead Chubb and the keepers in that direction and
scare the game up. Again he asked Blair to wait.

'I didn't tell you about the reception at the Royal
Geographical Society. I wish you could have been there.
I think every member of the Society was. Some of the
Royal Family, too, to show their interest in items African
and geographic and anti-slavery. We began with a
champagne and an exhibit of the maps and intriguing
artifacts. The hands of the gorilla were a great success.

They wanted more parts, of course. At the end they hung a silver medal and ribbon around my neck and presented me with the gun. A brilliant affair. I could have stayed in London and been fêted for the next six months, but I felt I should be here. You haven't found Maypole.'

'No.'

'But you've found something. Charlotte can't hate you this much for nothing. What is it?'

'You want to marry her?'

'That's the whole point of your exercise. Have you learned anything that would help force the issue? The Bishop is not the only man who can send you to Africa.'

'You'd do that?'

'I would describe how you came to me full of contrition, begging for a second chance. Just tell me about Maypole.'

'Miss Hannay would want to keep the Home for Women going.'

'Who cares about her Home for Women? Keep her busy. Why not? I could shut it when I want. What is this information?'

Rose's name was on Blair's lips , but a hooting and cranking of noisemakers broke out among the trees. Moon and the gamekeepers could have been boys let out of school, he thought. A flock of redwings lifted, sleek black with chevrons of crimson. Rowland fired twice rapidly. The keepers kept up the din and as the birds turned in confusion, Rowland reloaded and shot again while the men stamped through underbrush.

Blair walked around the hedge to the driveway of the

house, noticing that the gravel was unraked and the flagstones leading from the driveway to the door were obscured by weeds. It was not a worker's house but a full three storeys of brick propriety isolated in a corner of the Hannay grounds; he would have said an estate manager's house or the residence of a pretentious Hannay company officer. Wrought-iron balconies too grand for their windows decorated the front. An oppressive pediment of stone, a cap from Athens, weighted the brick facade. Ugly, empty, perhaps, but not in disrepair.

Rowland fired and a window shattered.

Blair asked, 'Have you considered the possibility that someone's inside?'

'I don't think so. Do you know why I was in Africa?'

'I don't know why the English do anything.'

Rowland aimed his gift from the Royal Society, fired and a second pane split.

'I had no occupation, only expectations. I went to make a name for myself, and who was there to get in my way but you. I return home and here you are again. That's perverse.'

'I'm working for the Bishop, that's all.'

'He says you're helping us. I want you to prove it. What can this information about Maypole be?'

'Shall we go attack some barns?'

Rowland shot at two upper windows. One blew in, the other left a fang of glass.

'There's something I don't understand,' Blair said. 'You're the next Lord Hannay anyway. There must be any number of eligible women who'd like a title. Beautiful, talented, as avaricious as you. Why do you want to marry Charlotte?'

Rowland's eye wandered from Blair to take in the alders, the mist and the hills beyond, and a wistful expression appeared on his face. 'Because I have imagined it all my life. Because she comes with the property.'

He shivered. Blair caught an overripe mix of cologne and sweat and garlicky breath, the scent the body surrendered when arsenic burned to the bottom of the wick.

'No, I don't have any information. Nothing about Maypole and as for Charlotte Hannay, she hates me,' he said. 'I don't think that's news.'

As rain drummed, ringlets drooped on Rowland's marble brow. Blair didn't think about the house with broken windows. He imagined the dimmed lights of the map room of the Royal Society, the white rows of evening clothes, a medal around Rowland's neck. He said, 'Let me see your hand.'

Rowland put out his left hand. White streaks lined his nails, and the heel of his hand was a horny callus, trademarks of arsenic addiction. Did any member of the Royal Family notice them on the reception line? Blair wondered. Would they have noticed antlers sprouting from Rowland's head? When he scratched the palm, Rowland yanked it back in pain. Burning palms were another sign of arsenic collapse. 'You'll be dead in a year,' he said.

'So might we both of our diseases or our cures.'

'We have that in common.'

'If I felt better I'd shoot you now, but I don't have the strength to drag your body anywhere.'

'It comes in waves. You'll feel better soon.'

'I expect so.'

Blair left Rowland on the driveway and went around the screen of the hedge, controlling the urge to break into a run. By the time he was past the slag heaps, though, his stride lengthened and, gaining speed, he dodged through the willows on the far side.

Reference points were different in the rain, but Blair followed his compass. Water poured in when he opened the mine cover. He let himself down, found the spring gun and, like a man putting the shot with both arms, threw it up through the shaft on to the ground, then swung the base up and hauled himself out. Carrying gun and base, he waded through bracken to where the carriage was still tied, the horse snickering in the downpour. He opened the suitcase, the Railway Companion, and packed the gun and base in towels. Soaked and covered in mud, he whipped the horse on to the path as if Rowland might ride one more wave of energy and fly after him.

At the hotel, he assembled the gun on the threshold of his bedroom with three separate trip strings stretched into the sitting room and rigged between chairs. He approached the bedroom from different ways; each time he touched a string, the snout of the barrel swivelled in his direction and the flintlock slapped shut. He rammed home gunpowder, a linen wad and the rod and sat down in the dark to have some of his own arsenic and brandy. But with the image of Rowland before him, arsenic lost its appeal. Brandy wouldn't help either. The problem wasn't malaria, he decided, it was fear. Between Bill Jaxon, Smallbone and Rowland, he was afraid to leave his room, afraid to answer the door without artillery.

He heard clogs marching home in the street below. The storm ended and the night went from dark to black, as if Wigan had been inverted over an abyss. He felt the fear lapping like water. Nigger Blair in a chair too afraid to move.

Finally, he stepped carefully over the trip strings, uncocked the gun's hammer, pushed the spring gun under the bed, opened his knapsack and from a chamois cloth unwrapped a gleam, the brass tube of his telescope.

He went out of the rear door of the hotel and took the darkest crossing of the street to the parish church, where the whisper of an evening service was taking place at the front pews. The Reverend Chubb shuffled around the altar. While the congregation muttered a response, Blair slipped into the tower and climbed the stairs.

From the parapet at the top, the lack of a moon revealed how little illumination street lamps actually cast. Wigan was a black lake, the pavements incidentally visible by the spill of window light.

For once, rain had succeeded in cleaning the air. Stars shone with a clarity and generosity that made the tower seem to rise towards them. He brought out both the telescope and a tripod of adjustable legs with brass fittings that he screwed into the bottom of the telescope and set on the wall.

It depended where a viewer was. Orion stalked the Equator, where the Gold Coast lay. The stars of the southern hemisphere gathered in white archipelagos, leaving dark seas in between. Wigan's northern sky was more evenly ablaze, a bed of burning coal. Where a viewer was, however, depended on the planets – on the Pole Star and the Morning Star, but most of all on Jupiter. It was white to the naked eye. To the telescope, though, the planet revealed rose-coloured bands and three moons. Io, a pinpoint of red, hung to the left of Jupiter, and to the right were the grey pearls, Ganymede and Callisto.

As his eye continued to focus and adjust, Jupiter grew and intensified into a disc of roseate paper. Features sharpened: the Great Red Spot and ribboned currents light and dark. With nothing but addition, it was possible to determine the longitude of any visible place on Jupiter. Better, with Blair's dog-eared book of Jovian tables and Jupiter's moons, he could determine his longitude on Earth. This was the way navigators did it before the chronometer. It was the way, without an expensive watch, that Blair still did it.

In an hour, the moons shifted. Io swung wider. Blair had once seen them through a big Newtonian telescope which revealed colours that he had never forgotten, so that as Ganymede and Callisto overlapped they changed colour to bitter, frozen blue. From Jupiter's shadow rose the fourth and largest moon, Europa, smooth as a yellow stone.

'What are you doing?'

Blair glanced behind him. He had allowed his attention to depend too much on everyone in Wigan wearing clogs or boots; Charlotte Hannay had climbed the tower in shoes like slippers. She seemed dressed the same as she had been in the morning, perhaps a little more disarranged, although it was hard for him to tell in the dark.

He put his eye back to the telescope. 'Finding out where I am. What are *you* doing here?'

'Leveret told me the different places that you went.'

Which meant she had been looking for him, Blair thought, although she didn't seem ready to say for what.

'Why are you doing that? You can look at any map,' Charlotte said.

'It's interesting. It calms the nerves. Jupiter has four moons, and they've been observed for centuries. We know when each is supposed to rise according to Greenwich Mean Time. The difference in time is where you are. The longitude, at least. And it's a lovely fact: there's this clock up in the sky that we can all check.'

Moons rose fast. Europa was already half into the light shared by its sister moons. He made notes on paper.

'You're covered in dirt. Where have you been?' Charlotte asked.

'Poking around.'

'Exploring?'

'Yes, "walking up and down in the earth". That's what Satan says in the Bible, which proves Satan was an explorer. Or at least a miner.'

'You've read the Bible?'

'I've read the Bible. When you're snowbound in a cabin for the winter, you read the Bible more than most preachers. Although it's fair to say I think missionaries are stooges for millionaires who are trying to sell Manchester flannel to the world. Of course that's just one man's opinion.'

'So what else have you gleaned from the Bible, aside from the conceit that Satan was a miner?'

'God was a mapmaker.'

'Really?'

'Without a doubt. Nothing but maps. In the beginning a void, waters, heavens, earth, and then He lays out the Garden of Eden.'

'That is indeed the reading of a small mind.'

'No, of a fellow professional. Forget Adam and Eve. The important information is, "A river flows out of Eden to water the garden; and from there it divides and becomes four branches. The name of the first is Pishon; it is the one that flows around the whole land of Havilah, where there is gold; and the gold of that land is good."'

'You are obsessed with gold.'

'So was God, obviously. Take a look.'

Blair moved to the side, but Charlotte waited until he was at arm's length before she took his place at the eyepiece. She looked through the tube longer than he expected.

'I do see little white dots. I didn't even know you could see that much,' she said.

'In Africa it's even better because there are no lights at all. You can see the moons without a telescope. Straight up is best, of course. Lie down and you can feel the universe move.'

She stepped back into the dark. 'You were shooting with Rowland today?'

'I watched him blast some inoffensive birds.'

'You didn't tell him anything?'

'No. I don't think you're quite so terrible that I'd put you directly into Rowland's hands.'

'So where are we? By the moons, I mean.'

'Well, I haven't figured that out yet. You didn't know about this escapade Maypole had in mind, to go underground with the miners, pursue them and preach to them during their miserable half-hour break for tea?'

'John wanted to preach in the yard.'

'No, down the pit, a mile down at the coalface. What I don't understand is what put it in his mind. Being a preacher is one thing; a masquerade is something else. You see what I mean? It's not unusual for a curate to join miners in sports, but it would be unique for him to try to pass himself off as a miner. He wasn't that imaginative. Where did he get the idea?'

'What else don't you understand?'

'Why anyone would help him.'

He waited for her to mention the fright he had given the girl in her cottage. Since this was the second time that she hadn't brought it up, he assumed that the girl hadn't reported his visit.

'You can't wait to get back to Africa, can you?'

'No.'

'It seems to have great allure. I'm beginning to understand how much you miss it.'

What is this? Blair wondered. A little light in the dark? Sympathy? Something besides withering scorn? It struck him that Charlotte's voice wasn't as tight as usual, and there was more shine to her eyes in the dark than in the day.

'You obviously care about the Africans,' she said. 'We are supposed to send troops to help them but all we do is shoot them.'

'The English are good soldiers. They're fighting for beer and silver-plated spoons and Pear's soap . . . they don't know why they're fighting, they're just sent. But I know. I know the maps I draw bring more troops and railway engineers and hydraulic hoses to wash out the gold. I'm worse than a thousand troops or ten Rowlands.'

'At least you're doing something. You're out in the world, not playing with – what did you call it – a doll's house?'

'It's not a doll's house. I was impressed by the Home. You're helping those women.'

'Perhaps. I think I've educated a girl, and then she steps out of the door and goes right back to the man who ruined her. It doesn't matter whether he's a miner, a footman or a shop boy. I've learned that a girl will believe anything a man says. Anything.'

'Sometimes it's the other way around. I met a girl here who could convince a man she was the Queen of Sheba.'

'She convinced you?'

'Almost.'

'But that's a flirtation. I mean otherwise sensible women with babes in arms who listen to a man declaim that the moon is a round of bread that goes best with ale and a feather pillow.'

'That's not believing, that's wanting a man and a feather pillow.'

'So what other landmarks do you search for?' Charlotte looked up.

'I travel everywhere. A poor man's odyssey. I used to do this when I was a boy and made up stories. See Virgo chasing Leo, instead of the other way around? What did the ancient Greeks make of that? Then a swim across the Milky Way over to Orion and his faithful Canis Major.'

'You had a poor but loving family?'

'Yes, but it wasn't mine. A Chinese family fed me. Later I found out that the mother's greatest fear was that one of her daughters would fall in love with me, a barbarian.'

'Did one of them?'

'No, I was a barbarian through and through. I did fall for one of them, though.'

'You seem to have a weakness for exotic women.'

'I don't know that it's a weakness. You were never in love with Cousin Rowland?'

'No, but I understand him. A Rowland is a Hannay without money. Not poor as you understand it. Worse. You were poor among poor. I mean, to be poor when the society you move in is rich. The humiliation when the family money has gone into gowns so that your mother and sister might attend the proper balls. Without my father's assistance, the Rowlands would live in three rooms in Kew. Rowland doesn't see the stars, he sees only money.'

'Don't marry him.'

'My father will shut the Home if I don't. I'll never have sufficient funds to start another. I'm as trapped as Rowland.'

'It sounds as if you're more trapped than the girls in the Home. They may suffer the consequences, but they did have some fun. Did you have any fun with Maypole?'

'I don't think I gave John a moment's fun.'

'He still loved you.'

'I thought you said he was infatuated with a pit girl.'

'That's one more thing I haven't figured out. Are you cold?'

'No. What constellation is that triangle?'

He followed her hand across the stars. 'The Cameleopard.'

'What is a cameleopard?'

'A giraffe.'

'I thought so. I've seen pictures of cameleopards and

thought they looked like giraffes. So they *are* giraffes. I can go to my grave with that question off my mind.'

'Were you going to jump? At the knacker's drop?'

'No, I didn't have the nerve.'

'Not that time, you mean?'

'I'm not at all sure *what* I mean.'

They were silent. The sound of a cab horse below seemed miles away.

She said, 'I abused John. He would have accepted such a meagre marriage and let me go my own way. He was too good, too pure, a Christian snowman.'

'Not a complete snowman.' He thought of Rose.

'Better than me.'

'Earnshaw?'

'Hideous. I wish I had made him suffer.'

'If you couldn't make him suffer, no one could. I mean that as a compliment.'

'Thank you. For your sake, I should tell you that you'll never find John Maypole. Where he is exactly I don't know, but I do know that he's gone. I'm sorry you became involved. You're an interesting man. I've been unfair.'

She came to the edge of the parapet. An ashen light from the street crept up to her face. 'I'll leave you to your stars,' she said.

He felt the briefest touch on his hand and then she was gone, swiftly descending the ladder to the stairs of the belfry.

Blair found Jupiter again. The moon Io was still suspended to one side. On the other side, Ganymede and

Callisto merged into blue twins. Europa had risen clear of Jupiter like a stone cast by a giant arm.

But his mind still turned on Charlotte. When she had stood in the faint light from below she had been a completely different Charlotte, and a new thought had been born. He was too distracted to work out longitude by the Jovian moons. Now he had no idea where he was at all.

Chapter Twenty-Four

What swam into Blair's mind was Rose, when he caught her paler than pale reflection. And the girl in Charlotte's cottage. How she had hidden in the dark like a maid caught trying on her mistress's dress. In silhouette there was a shadowy resemblance to Rose, but whether it was a matter of height or a glint in her hair he couldn't say. He saw again the interrupted tea on the kitchen table, a place without a book, without even a lamp. What struck him was that, in spite of her fear, she hadn't said a word to Charlotte about a strange man at the window.

He packed the telescope and tripod into his pack, climbed down into the belfry and rushed down the tower steps. The service was over, the church a barrel of black except for watery votive candles in side chapels. When he went out of the door there was no sign of Charlotte at the front of the church or among the gravestones at the back. Most likely she had a carriage near his hotel.

The fastest way was the alley by the butchers' stalls. Blair was running after her when he tripped and his hat flew. A foot come out of the dark and kicked him in the stomach. He rolled and tried to breathe while other feet continued to stamp and kick. An oil rag was pushed and tied into his mouth, almost stuffing his tongue down his throat. Hands tied belts around his wrists and ankles and threw him on to a wooden plank, which began to roll. A cart, he thought. Crossing the street there was enough light for him to see that the cart's side walls were red. Though it had no horse, the cart gathered speed to the sound of a dozen clogs on cobblestones.

Bill Jaxon looked over a side of the cart and said, 'He can see.'

A sack was pulled over Blair's head. Within it a pungent cloud of gunpowder stung his eyes and stopped what little breath he had. The cartwheels crushed shells, slid on sheep muck, raced from alley to alley. The procession squeezed through a door and flew down an incline. He hoped they would only roll him around town to scare him and let him go. Maybe it was a good sign that Jaxon wasn't alone. Heavy doors opened and the cart lumbered into the echo of a tunnel. Blair couldn't think of any functioning mine in the middle of town. His hand felt a loose peg on the cart floor. It was smooth and split on one end and woolly at the other, and he understood that the red he had seen on the cart wasn't paint, and that he was back at the knacker's drop.

The sack came off with a handful of his hair. This time he was at the bottom of the drop where, during the day, the knacker waited for sheared sheep to fall and break their legs, the easier to kill and butcher. There was no knacker now and no sheep, though the floor was ridged with crusts of accumulated fat and gore. A pair of butcher's blocks stood at the side, red as altars. Lanterns hung on meat hooks. On the walls, ancient whitewash was barely visible through layers of black and new sprays of pink.

Bill Jaxon stripped to a silk scarf and brass-toed clogs. Blair recognized Albert Smallbone. He could tell that four others were miners by the masks of coal dust on their faces, and a man with a brush moustache he remembered as the stableman from the Hannay Mine, the man he had helped with the pony. They tore off his clothes, ripping his shirt so that buttons sprayed the floor. As they knocked him on his back and dragged off his trousers, he wished the miners wore real masks, which would have meant they worried about being identified. They didn't seem to think this was a problem.

'Tha've a dark face neow, like oos.' Bill gave his words the full local twist. Dark from the sack's gunpowder, not coal, though, Blair knew.

Bill made a muscular dancer prancing in anticipation. Pulled upright, Blair felt small and naked, daubed with blood from the cart and floor. The men forced a pair of clogs on his feet and pushed the clasps shut.

'Ah'll keep an eye for constables,' the stableman said and ran off.

Bill said, 'See what 'appens when tha messes with a Wigan girl? Tha wants t'be a Wigan lad, tha mun learn t'purr.' He told Smallbone, 'Pull t'cork.'

Smallbone drew the gag from Blair's mouth and held it high. Other men pushed his head forward while Bill looped his scarf around Blair's neck and tightened it until their foreheads touched.

Blair said, 'I could have let you drown.'

'Your mistake.'

Smallbone snapped the rag down and Bill kicked Blair twice before he had a chance to move. Each leg was numb and bloody. He sank to his knees in stupefaction.

'Need a hand?' Bill asked.

When Blair reached up, Bill hit him and Blair felt his nose split. Blood sprayed his chest. Two seconds, he thought, and he already looked like a sheep who had taken the high dive.

He pushed himself up. The problem was that as his clogs broke the crust of the floor they skated clumsily on the sheep fat underneath. Bill, on the other hand, moved with sinuous ease. He spread his arms, retied his scarf around his neck, feinted and, as Blair slipped, tapped him lightly on the centre of his forehead, slowly spun and kicked savagely at the same place, but Blair had rolled away.

'You're not going to stop this?' Blair asked the miners, but they pushed him back towards Bill, ringed around him like dogs in a pack.

Bill had the strut of a champion, the glory of a white body on a red floor, raking his long black hair with his hands. A massive torso pivoting on a pinched waist, with the smile of a man who was turning sport to art. He merely leaned and Blair backed away and fell.

'Need a hand?' Bill asked again.

Blair rose unsteadily on his own. Bill rushed him, lifted him clear of the floor and carried him into a wall.

Blair was crushed, his arms caught on the other side of the bigger man's back. He pulled Bill's head back by the hair, butted him and twisted free.

Miners blocked the door by the cart. Blair looked up at the edge of the drop, where he had stood before with Charlotte, and where the stableman now stood. A scream would have to rise like a siren over the drop and above the pens to reach the houses around.

Bill shook his head and rolled his shoulders, showing no more than a blush on his brow.

'Have you noticed something?' Smallbone asked Blair.

'What's that?'

'You're not worried about Maypole any more.'

Bill approached almost on the toes of his clogs while Blair slid sideways in retreat. Bill feinted as if to scoop up Blair's front leg and as Blair leaned back, he took a second, longer stride forward and kicked Blair on the inside of the thigh, continued moving in, and with the other clog kicked Blair in the small of the back. Blair stepped in and hit him square on the mouth. It was as ineffective as punching a man armed with swords. Bill kicked him in the middle of the chest and he rolled against the wall.

Cats 'purr'. What did that have to do with kicking? Blair wondered. Or killing somebody with brass-tipped wooden shoes? He found himself standing up again, using the wall. He was as red now as if he had been skinned. He ducked and Bill kicked a white hole in the plaster. When Blair tried to tackle him, Bill skipped aside, tripped him and kicked him on the side of the head. Blair was still rolling, or the blow would have pushed his brains out of his ear.

'That's enough, Bill,' one of the miners said.

Smallbone said, 'Bill's not through.'

Bill's clog tagged Blair's chin – not squarely, but enough for him to find a tooth loose under his tongue. Buttons, teeth – he was coming undone like a rag doll. He was dizzy, while Bill was spinning like a whirling dervish. Another kick and Blair found himself against the opposite wall. He got up again. It seemed to be his role in the drama. A kick in the ribs propelled him halfway across the floor and into a butcher block. A cleaver would be handy now, he thought. He crawled up the block and held on.

'Are tha goin' t'kill him?' someone asked.

'He's still standing,' Bill said.

If that was the issue, Blair thought, he was willing to lie down. Before he could, Bill gracefully leaped through the air and kicked him so hard he felt he had been shot from a cannon. He folded over. Bill kicked out his knees from behind. Well, I'm down now, he thought.

It didn't matter. As he curled up, Bill kicked his side, his arm, his leg. This was the way iron was forged when it was cold, by pounding. Blair trembled and it wasn't from cold.

'Constable's coomin'!' the stableman shouted from above.

Not fast enough. Bill tore open Blair's knapsack.

'No,' Blair said weakly.

Bill unwrapped the telescope and swung it against the wall. As the brass tube bent, broken glass poured out like sand. He tossed the tube aside and gave Blair another kick in the head.

What Blair knew next was that the lanterns had gone. He lay without moving until he was sure he was alone in the dark. He didn't feel for damage. He didn't particularly want to know. Some of him was numb. He wished it all was.

It would have been simpler to push him off the drop. He remembered his mother falling from the ship. In retrospect the waves seemed warm and restful, certainly softer than the knacker's floor.

He told himself that if he could reach a wall, he could find the door, and if he could find a door, he could reach the street. But the effort of lifting his head made it swim, and his last conscious act was not swallowing the tooth in his mouth.

Water woke him. The stableman had returned with a lantern, bucket and sheets.

'There was no constable coomin', you know, but Bill was going to kick thi inside out. In fact, I think he did.'

Were those his own hands, Blair thought, so red and amphibious? He washed them with the last water in the bucket before he put his fingers in his mouth, found the empty socket and pushed the tooth back in.

The stableman towelled him with the sheets. 'You can go t'constable but it won't do thi any good. We'll all stick up for Bill and you were messin' with his girl, he says.'

'Rose?' Blair tried to speak without moving his jaw.

'Who else?'

The lightest touch on flesh felt like the edge of a blade. What Blair waited for was the more pointed response of a fractured arm or rib moving in separate directions.

'Your head looks lahk a meat pie.'

Blair grunted with nausea, agreement and lack of surprise.

'Ah washed the coal dust out of the cuts as best Ah could so you won't look like a miner for the rest of your life, but you'll want t'get up sewed up and on a train as fast as you can. Bill won't rest until you're gone. Ah've kept your clothes as neat as Ah could and saved your hat and shoes and pack. Ah'm truly sorry about the telescope. Can you stand?'

Blair stood and passed out.

When he woke again, he was in the cart. He was dressed and the cart was rolling, so that was progress. He held the slits of his eyes open to see a lamp pass overhead.

The stableman was pushing the cart by himself. He looked in and asked, 'Is there anything else I can do for thi, Mr Blair? Something Ah can get?'

Blair muttered, 'Macaroni.'

'Maca—? Oh, Ah get it. Macaroni. Lahk in Africa. That's a good one, Mr Blair. We're almost there. Ah'll get thi to thy room, don't worry.'

The stableman had made a bed of sheets, but the jostling of the cart made Blair feel as if he were being rolled directly over cobblestones. He struggled to lift his head. 'Maypole?'

'No one knows. Forget him. Ah'll tell thi, Mr Blair, Ah'll miss thi more.'

Chapter Twenty-Five

He heard someone say,

> *'For oft, when on my couch I lie*
> *In vacant or in pensive mood,*
> *They flash upon that inward eye*
> *Which is the bliss of solitude;*
> *And then my heart with pleasure fills,*
> *And dances with the daffodils.'*

It was better than last rites.

His eyes were swollen shut, his limbs distant and unresponsive. If he raised his head, he was nauseated from a swelling on the brain. He wheezed through a nose that had been broken at leisure and reset in haste, and slept profoundly or couldn't sleep for more than a minute before the work of breathing or the prick of a stitch summoned his attention. When he heard miners walk to work in the morning, he dreamed of clogs and winced, as if his head were a cobblestone.

Tea and laudanum were forced through his lips. Laudanum was liquid opium, and the images flowed through his mind, a great unravelling of memory. One moment he was in bed in Wigan, the next stretched at his ease on a red hill in Africa, and the next burrowed for safety's sake as deep underground as he could go.

A miner in uniform climbed down into Blair's pit, took off a brass helmet to protect its ostrich plumes and tentatively touched the wall.

'Can you hear me? It's Chief Constable Moon. You're living very high, Blair, very high. I've never had a room like this to myself. Look at this wallpaper. Feel the flocking. Soft as a virgin's bum. Am I right, Oliver? Soft as a virgin's bum? The maid wouldn't know, Blair. No more than you.' As he buffed his helmet with his sleeve the plumes turned every move into a flutter. 'Well, I suppose it was a slip on the stairs? An accident? I just want to be sure you aren't shamming, taking the Bishop's money and lolling about in bed with only a broken head and maybe a rib or two. Bad enough you should upset honest working people, accosting women and provoking the men, but when you take advantage of a local girl you can't come tugging the sleeve of the law for protection. The men here protect their own.' He leaned close. 'Fact is, I found it hard to believe you really were the famous explorer, but you certainly look like "Nigger Blair" now.'

Blair saw in his inward eye a field of daffodils with a pit girl walking through them, gathering a bouquet. She was at the crown of a hill; he was at the bottom, blinded by the sun. No matter how much he called, she didn't hear.

Leveret joined him in the hole.

'I don't know if you can hear me, but I wanted to tell you that Charlotte has acquiesced to marrying Rowland. Actually, she agreed the day after you were found in your ... condition. The Bishop is very pleased, in good part thanks to you, and you're free to go as soon as you are able. I have recommended an extra bonus for you and a letter obliging the Bishop to sponsor your return to the Gold Coast. You've earned it.' Leveret knelt on the coal. 'I have a confession. I knew when you came that the Bishop's interest was more in forcing Charlotte's hand than in finding John Maypole. I did hope, though, that you might find him.' Leveret's voice dropped. 'So you got involved with a woman. You're only human.' He added, 'I envy you.'

An ember chimed the hour. He thought of Charlotte's cottage, where a red-headed girl hid in the dark.

Dark was comfortable. He heard in the tunnel not Leveret but someone more familiar, old Blair, of all people, stumbling in a beaver coat and a whisky fog, whistling and offering bits of song.

ROSE

Maintes genz dient que en songes
N'a se fables non et mençonges . . .

He dropped into a chair and let his coat slide, revealing a black front and an ecclesiastical collar. A book of faded red hung in one hand, a lamp in the other. He screwed up the wick and held the light over Blair.

'More poetry. How is your medieval French? Not too good, you say? As good comatose as conscious? Fair enough. I'm told we should read to you to keep your mind alive in case it is alive.' He opened the book. 'Smell that?'

A rose, Blair thought.

'A dried rose,' said old Blair.

A pony fell down the shaft, its white tail and mane snapping like wings, ticking first bricks and then timbers on the way down. The horse's tail trailed out behind.

Old Blair returned. Blair was happy to see him not only back from the dead but trading up, exchanging his moth-eaten fur coat for the crimson-lined cape of a bishop. The old man was anxious. After offering some pleasantries and getting no response, he sat silently in the dark of the tunnel for an hour before pulling his chair nearer. A visitor to the comatose is practically alone and words have a licence they usually lack.

425

'You're right about Rowland. I only hope he breeds a son as fast as possible. Then he can poison himself, for all I care, but he will marry Charlotte first. She has the strength of the Hannay line. It either goes through her or becomes a feeble caricature and we've enough families like that, with heirs too dimwitted to speak to anyone but their nannies, or else as queer as Dick's hatband. Long after Rowland is food for worms, Charlotte will have Hannay Hall to run, like a republic if she wants. Old families have odd problems.' Blair smelled a soft scent of roses again. 'And curious prizes. Remember, last visit I was reading you the *Roman de la Rose*. I hope you weren't expecting the Bible. The *Roman* was the great poem of the age of chivalry.' Blair heard a rustle of pages. 'Once there were hundreds of copies, but we consider ourselves fortunate to have a surviving one that has been in the family for five hundred years. Too bad you can't see the illustration.' Blair imagined a brilliantly painted scene of an amorous couple in a canopied bed framed by flowers of gold leaf that glittered and shifted in the lantern's flame. 'It's allegorical, of course. Decidedly sexual. The poem is set in a garden, but instead of a Tree of Good and Evil, at the centre is a single rosebud that the poet passionately desires. You couldn't write like this now, nor publish it. All the Chubbs and Mrs Smallbones in the land would rise up against it, banish it, burn it. I'll translate as I go, and if you find it excruciatingly dull, lift a hand or bat an eye.'

Blair made a pillow of the coal to listen. It was the sort of antique, endless tale that grew like a concentric garden, and his mind wandered in and out, catching and losing sight of the story. Venus, Cupid, Abstinence played hide-and-seek from hedge to hedge. Narcissus paused by a pool.

> *Ce est li Romanz de la Rose,*
> *Ou l'art d'Amors est tote enclose.*

He tried to use his time in the dark to good effect by going over the day of the fire. He had a new advantage. The pieces of information he had were scattered like the tiles of a half-seen mosaic, and he had tried before to bring a perspective to the little that he knew. Now that his own brain was scattered, he let each small, separate glimpse expand.

He could see Maypole join the miners' early-morning trudge to work. It was black and wet, and the curate was dressed for the pit in clothes borrowed from Jaxon, his inadequate chin hidden in Jaxon's scarf.

They moved over Scholes Bridge through Wigan and, still before dawn, across the fields. Maypole hung back but stayed part of the group, identified as Jaxon by his size and by Jaxon's mate Smallbone walking at his side.

Blair lost them in the lampman's shed. Did Smallbone pick up both men's lamps? Did 'Jaxon' get his own, tucked into a scarf? From the murk of the yard they descended into the black of the shaft. Inside the cage, close bodies smothered the weak nimbi of safety lamps. 'Jaxon' coughed and everyone turned away their faces.

At the pit eye, miners gave George Battie, the under-looker, no more than a wave as they headed for the tunnels. 'Jaxon' and Smallbone were quick to move out of Battie's sight, although once they were in the tunnel, they stopped for 'Jaxon' to set something right with his clogs, while other miners, who might notice that 'Jaxon' was suddenly as clumsy as a curate, went ahead.

Better yet, the damp weather had brought methane out of the coal. Since Battie had prohibited shots until the gas cleared, the fireman and 'Jaxon' had a slack day, hewing coal for lack of their usual labour, but at a slow pace, not exerting themselves enough to strip. They worked at the farthest reach of the coalface where no one could see beyond his lamp for more than a few feet. On this day, Smallbone could have been working with anyone. The real Jaxon came into the yard later and slipped into the winding house in case of problems.

If someone on that coalface had noticed that the Bill Jaxon below was, so to speak, not himself, that his costume or acting had slipped in the dark even for a second, no one on the surface would ever know now that all those men were in their graves. There might be no mystery to Maypole's vanishing at all if so many hadn't vanished with him.

What happened then? He tried to imagine further, but he saw Maypole's journal, and the script of vertical and horizontal lines that filled every page confused his eye. Sentences looked not so much like words as a trellis of spiky canes that even as he watched began to show red buds.

*

Old Blair, as if he understood French, translated in
Hannay's distinct, rolling cadence.

> *'I seized the rose tree by her tender limbs*
> *That are more lithe than any willow bough,*
> *And pulled her close to me with my two hands.*
> *Most gently, that I might avoid the thorns,*
> *I set myself to loosen that sweet bud*
> *That scarcely without shaking could be plucked.*
> *Trembling and sweet vibration shook her limbs;*
> *They were quite uninjured, for I strove*
> *To make no wound, though I could not avoid*
> *Breaking a trifling fissure in the skin.*
>   *'When I dislodged the bud, a little seed*
> *I spilled just in the centre, as I spread*
> *The petals to admire their beauty,*
> *Probing the aromatic flower to its depth.*
> *The consequence of all my play*
> *Was that the bud expanded and enlarged.*
>   *'Of course the rose did remind me of my pledge*
> *And say I was outrageous in demands,*
> *But ne'ertheless she never did forbid*
> *That I should seize and strip and quite deflower*
> *The bloom from off her rosy bower.'*

Blair opened his eyes.

The curtains were closed, framed by light like shadow
in reverse, stirred by a draught. Rain tapped on the
windowsill. Coal shifted in the grate. He sat up carefully,
as if his head might split. A pitcher and basin of water

sat on the night table. Empty chairs were pulled close to the bed and the door to the sitting room was ajar.

He slipped his legs over the edge of the bed. His mouth was dry, his tongue almost adhered to his palate, but there was clarity to his mind, as if a wind had blown away a film of dust. He stood, and, holding on to chair backs for support, hobbled towards the closet. He remembered Livingstone, who thought he wouldn't die as long as he kept moving forwards, which was why he stumbled further and further into the African bush until his porters found him dead, kneeling at his prayers. Blair decided he wasn't going to die quite yet, certainly not by making the mistake of praying.

Facing the closet mirror, he forgot about Livingstone and thought of Lazarus, who was four days dead before being miraculously raised. Which was what Blair looked like in the glass, a little ripe for resurrection. There were too many bruises to catalogue, blotches of aubergine purple, and overall week-old, decaying shades of yellow as if he had died of jaundice or the plague. His ribs wore a patchwork of plasters, and above both ears there were shaved hair and stitches. He turned his head to see. Good needlework. One eyebrow was split, but his nose was human size and the tooth had rerooted, so he was alive.

From the hiding place behind the mirror he took Maypole's journal and opened the book to the small pasteboard photograph of Rose.

'You're awake.' Leveret was rushing in through the sitting-room door. 'And up. Let me help you.'

As Blair slumped against the chair he clutched the

book. 'If you want to help, get me out of here. I have to hole up.'

Leveret caught him and eased him back towards the bed. 'Africa? America? Where do you want to go?'

'Rowland showed me a house.'

The house was a sullen presence in red brick, as if it brooded on its isolation from every other structure in the Hannay grounds. Its driveway connected to a lane deep in weeds. Its hedge neither shielded the front windows from the western wind nor blocked a view of slag heaps. The rooms were empty of furniture. Thanks to Rowland, broken glass covered the floors. Dismal for a normal tenant, perfect for Blair.

Leveret set up a cot in the kitchen. 'I'm afraid you won't be able to do more than heat tea on the firegrate. The former occupants found it too wild and alone, and I can't say that I blame them. You can't grow anything in slag, not even your own vegetables, and without a proper windbreak you get the gales straight off the sea.'

'When's the great wedding?'

'In two weeks. It won't be as grand as the Bishop wished, perhaps, but he is eager to carry out the event as quickly as possible. He will perform the ceremony himself. You know, you're free to go now. I could get you rooms in London or Liverpool, and arrange for a medical man. I know you'll want to get away from Wigan as soon as you get your legs under you.'

As Leveret hurried to the grate to lay sticks and coals,

Blair dropped on the cot's mattress into the smell of mouldy horsehair. 'Who were the former occupants?'

'Actually it was the Rowlands. The Bishop invited them to live in the main house only last year.'

'Up to then he kept them here?'

'Yes. I noticed that there's been some damage recently. I could have a glazier here tomorrow. In fact I could furnish it for you.'

'No. No one but you. Rowland grew up here?'

'Not often. He was away at school most of the time. When he was here, he never got on with his uncle – or with Charlotte.' Leveret stared at flames, reluctant to rise from the grate into a chimney of cold air.

'So we were the cupids.'

Leveret waved smoke aside. 'It takes a while. Inefficient but there's more than enough coal, you don't have to worry about that.'

'How do you feel about it?' Blair asked.

'I despise myself.'

To test his legs, Blair tottered around the hedge to the slag tip and back. The great circle route, he told himself. A regular Magellan.

Inside, he studied maps of Wigan and the Hannay pit, both above and underground. At night he pulled the spring gun to the centre of the kitchen and rigged strings across the doors.

*

Leveret returned to remove Blair's stitches. 'From what I understand, the patient generally gets drunk first. This must hurt like the devil. I brought some "Invalid's Stout". It's what miners dose their children with when they have a cough or influenza. You know, the stitching is so good I almost hate to cut it.'

'Leveret, this is not the time to develop a sense of humour.'

'Well, doesn't it strike you as ironical that having been born in Wigan, you return only to be beaten almost to death?'

'Something that obvious isn't ironical.'

'What is it?'

'Something that stupid? It has to be the hand of God.'

Leveret drew out a thread. 'The Bishop has been asking about you. He wonders when you want to go. He is offering you your old position as his mining engineer and surveyor in the Gold Coast. You won't have to join an expedition in East Africa or worry about the Colonial Office. This is quite a triumph for you.'

'Does Charlotte ask about me?'

'She asks for a report on your health each time I see her. When will you leave?'

'When I'm done.'

Birches crowned the slag white. What birches did that other trees could not was to tolerate the heat that coal in the slag still generated. Not only tolerate but flourish, with delicate branches tipped in green.

Blair waited until dusk, the right condition for reconstruction. He tied a strip of cloth cut from a sheet on to a limb, paced thirty feet and knotted a strip on to another birch, paced another fifty feet and tied a strip to a third tree. The first strip was for the lamp shed, where a line of men stood in the morning gloom. Smallbone was inside, signing for himself and 'Jaxon', who waited outside the door.

The second strip was for the winding house, where Harvey Twiss, alone, oiled the ten-foot rods of the engine as they smoothly churned.

The third strip was for the winding tower and cage shaft, where Smallbone and 'Jaxon' boarded last and faced the wall.

He walked around the three strips of cloth from different points of view. As light failed, wind arrived. The strips shook, and Blair imagined the ground jumping. Black smoke poured out of the furnace shaft and, from the force of the explosion, from the cage shaft. The stokers underground fed coals as fast as they could to keep the furnace fire drawing air. Messengers from Battie arrived.

Standing in the dark among the slag heaps, Blair thought he was starting to see how things had happened. The one individual that a sportsman like Twiss would have allowed into the engine house was his champion, Bill Jaxon. What had these two men said to each other when they felt the blast? Bill's rush through the smoke to the cage spoke of his fear of being found so far from the coalface where he was supposed to be.

Twiss would have feared for his son. Discipline might have been enough to keep the winder in the engine house except for Bill's race to the cage, an example Twiss would have found hard not to imitate as soon as he could wind the cage back to the surface.

Lamps, what about lamps? Twiss had to lift one off a body lying on the main road. Bill Jaxon didn't because he already had the lamp Maypole had paid for; 'passage to another world for the price of a lamp and pick', Maypole had said about his practice in the tunnel. The safety lamps at the hardware store were, except for the numbers scratched on the base, identical to the lamps at the Hannay Pit. Now that the answer fell into place, Blair saw that Jaxon also would have had to bring one because he knew that, in case of problems, he couldn't go to the lamp man.

Smallbone was easier. Battie had mentioned the fireman's habit of nesting in side tunnels whenever he could slip away from work. Since the underlooker had banned shots for the morning because of the presence of gas, Smallbone had all the excuse he needed to leave the coalface and, incidentally, to survive and meet Bill coming the other way. What induced Smallbone to join Bill? He would have followed Jaxon to the moon, Blair thought, and they were miners, not cowards. And, perhaps, they wanted to be the first men on the scene for other reasons.

But why? Why would Bill agree to Maypole's masquerade in the first place? Maypole had no money. Bill had little religion. What persuasion was left then but personal, a mystery when there was no person whom Bill cared about except Rose?

Most of the grounds were a plantation of mature beeches striped with soot and emerald lichen. In the early morning, following his compass, Blair made his way a half-mile to the stable and then along the lane to the lip of the quarry, where he took cover behind a screen of hawthorn and watched the cottage of Charlotte Hannay.

Sun rested on the red tiles of the roof and, minute by minute, slid down the white upper face of the house. Wisps of smoke issued from a chimney. Dragonflies rose from quarry water on iridescent wings, while empty hay-wagons lumbered along the lane. Leveret drove by towards town at a smarter pace. An ice van came from the opposite direction. By nine, sunlight had moved down to the lower storey of the house and spilled into the garden. A boy in a pony cart arrived to open the cottage's stable and exercise a long-legged bay. An old gardener whom Blair recognized from the Home for Women wheeled a wagonful of compost to the green-house at the side of the garden.

In the afternoon the boy returned to lead the horse back into the stable. Alders overhung the quarry; a kingfisher hunched on a branch and studied the water below. By three, shadow had filled the garden and covered the front of the cottage. Full hay-wagons plod-ded back along the lane, slower than before. They had deep-dished wheels that made them waddle. Again Leveret appeared, glanced at the dark windows of the cottage and drove on. Darkness drew midges, which drew bats to the quarry pool.

Charlotte never showed herself. Once or twice he saw candlelight inside, so briefly that he wouldn't have credited his eyes but for the chimney smoke. He watched until well into the night before he hiked back to his own mean lodgings.

The following day he did the same. The routine was similar. A steam tractor drawing a cocked plough rolled by. The boy mucked out the stables and ran the horse on a long lead. The kingfisher returned and pondered the quarry water as before. One difference was that a baker's van stopped to leave a basket on the front step.

At midday the basket was still on the step. In the garden the daffodils nodded taller, brighter heads. In the hawthorns white buds spread by the hour. The horse was a four-legged statue in its enclosure.

The horse turned. At the house, the door opened as a woman emerged nimbly to pick up the baker's basket and slip back in. But she couldn't resist her moment of air, an opportunity to shake out her red hair in the sun, if only for an instant, long enough for Blair to recognize the girl he had seen inside the house a week earlier. Again she wore a silk dress and again she could not resist a treat. Smoke drifted from the kitchen chimney. For tea, he thought, with fresh bread and jam.

The boy came by to take the horse back to its stall.

Shadows swung over the front of the house. Farm wagons plodded along the lane. The sun fell and clouds faded. Midges were succeeded by bats, followed by stars.

Light showed in the parlour, a second in an upstairs room – gas sconces by their yellow cast, not the shaded candle of someone hiding. After a third one lit the downstairs hallway, the front door opened and Charlotte Hannay stepped out with a lantern in hand. She was unmistakably Charlotte, from the dress of semi-mourning to the black lace smothering her forehead. She was Charlotte by her every brusque step and abrupt glance at the garden and the lane. When she crossed into the stable, he heard the horse's throaty chuff of recognition, the way a pet demands grooming from a favourite person.

While she was in the stable, he moved from the quarry down to the lane's stone wall for a better view. When she came out, she walked the length of the garden to the quarry's edge and looked at the water long enough for him to grow nervous for his partner in astronomy; it was safer to contemplate stars than deep water.

The lamp in Charlotte's hand brushed her features with a soft upward light, raising impossibilities.

Chapter Twenty-Six

Although it was opposite Wigan's Market Hall, Hotham's Photographic Studio had the bright colours and curlicued woodwork of a carnival booth. Signs announced 'Hotham's Portraits, From Scientific to Pathetic' and claimed 'Machinery, Buildings, Groups, Children and Animals Our Speciality'. The upstairs window was hung in heavy drapes that suggested the dark required by art. Behind the plate glass at street level were photographs categorized as 'Natural, Comedic, Historic' and framed portraits of gentry and nobility with cards noting 'By Kind Permission'.

Blair had Leveret's carriage and had rolled over every hole on the way, or so his ribs said. He tied the horse and went through the shop door, ringing a bell above it.

'Busy, busy. Look around, look around,' a voice called down the stairs over a wail that sounded like a baby being bathed.

The population of Wigan, perhaps of the whole British Isles, seemed to inhabit the shop's walls, tables and multiplicity of frames. The usual personages gathered in unusually democratic assembly: the Queen, Royal Family, Wellington, Gladstone, plus such regional honorees as a lord mayor, Members of Parliament, local matrons in fancy dress, washed faces in a workshop, prize cows, atmospheric studies of fishermen and nets, London from a balloon, and a locomotive wreathed in garlands at a Hannay pit. An aquiline Disraeli faced a melancholy Lincoln; the preacher Wesley thundered to a music-hall Juliet. In a self-portrait a photographer with spiked moustache and brows smugly held a shutter cord. And everywhere were Wigan pit girls, in individual and group portraits, and in *cartes de visite* the size of playing cards. They posed singly and in pairs with a variety of shovels and sieves, with sooty faces and clean, but always dressed in trademark shawls, heavy shirts, vestigial skirts rolled and sewn out of the way of trousers and clogs. In one or two instances the same model was shown in matched pictures of herself in filthy working garb and cleaned up in a Sunday dress to show that one day out of seven she could be a female.

When the bawling had gone on for five more minutes, Blair climbed the stairs to what looked like the backstage of an opera. Peeling backdrops of Scottish highlands, ancient Rome, the Grand Canal, Trafalgar Square and turbulent seas leaned against one another in the illumination of a whitewashed skylight. Stuffed parrots and silk flowers drooped over file cabinets. Fake banisters, urns, mantels, chairs, rustic stumps and country stiles were arrayed along one wall. Along the other were a black curtain and posing stands that looked partly like calipers, partly like instruments of torture.

The window at the front of the studio was hung with cloths and tapestries, and here the photographer was posing two children, a girl of about ten who leaned against a balustrade as stolidly as an ox against a post, while a baby already half her size screamed and squirmed against the sash that secured it to a chair. A toy monkey on a wand was attached to the camera tripod. The photographer popped out of the camera's cloth to rearrange the girl's arms. He might have waxed his moustache *à la française*, but he sounded Lancashire to the core.

'Gentle curves, dear, gentle curves.'

Sitting to the side, out of the camera's view, was a heavy woman with the glower of a duenna holding something wrapped in bloody paper. The butcher's wife, Blair thought, paying in kind.

'Watch t'monkey, please.' The photographer rushed back to his camera and jiggled the wand. Blair recognized Hotham from the photograph downstairs. Apparently self-portraits were easier; his hair was plastered forward in poetic curves, but he had the white eye of a drowning man. As he ducked under the cloth, the baby thrashed from side to side and howled.

'If we don't like the picture, we don't pay,' the mother said. 'No picture, no pork.'

'Lookit Albert.' The girl smirked as her little brother waved four limbs at once.

Blair lifted his hat and pulled down the scarf that had muffled him to the eyes. His face was shadowed with bruises and stubble, the cut on his brow livid, his hair cropped and the scalp tracked with dried blood where it had been repaired. The girl's mouth formed a mute and anxious 'O'. The baby ceased its noise, rolled forward and gaped. They remained in these positions when the shutter was released.

From under his cloth the photographer said, 'Not quite what I had in mind, but very nice.'

Hotham accommodated Blair as a customer who looked as if he might choose to shatter every frame in the shop.

Blair said, 'You photograph girls.'

Nervously the photographer patted his hair with fingers that smelled of developer and spirit lamp. 'Proper cards, in good taste. Portraits on request.'

'You also sell them.'

'I do *cartes de visite*. Visiting cards, if you will, sir. Very popular, sold at all t'stationers, passed between friends and business associates, collected by connoisseurs.'

'Of women.'

'All sorts. Religious tableaux, the Queen, all the Royals. Divas, celebrities of the stage. Gaiety ladies and ballet dancers, women in tights, very popular with the soldiers.'

'Working women.'

'Match girls, needle girls, fisher girls, iron girls, ladies' maids, milkmaids, whatever pleases your fancy.'

'But your speciality?'

'Pit girls. I should have known what you had in mind. For discriminating gentlemen there is nothing like a Wigan pit girl. Some say trousers on women are a social scandal. All I say is, buy a card and judge for yourself, sir, judge for yourself.'

'Show me.'

Hotham pointed to the different portraits and *cartes* on view. Blair had already studied them, and the photographer sensed his disappointment. 'I have hundreds more. This is the premier pit-girl studio in t'country.'

'I'm interested in a particular one.'

'Give me her name, sir. I know them all.'

'Rose Molyneux?'

A tentative smile. 'Red hair, very pert, classic vixen?'

'Yes.'

The photographer plunged into a counter drawer. 'I have them organized, sir, categorized and alphabetized.'

'She has a friend named Flo.'

'Yes. I even have some of them together. See?'

He stood and placed four *cartes* on the counter. Two were with Flo, Flo grasping a heavy shovel and Rose holding a coal sieve like a tambourine. Two were of Rose alone, one with the shawl pinned coquettishly at her chin, the other with the shawl open and her head tilted in coarse suggestiveness towards the camera.

Except that it wasn't Rose. Not Blair's Rose. It was the girl hiding in Charlotte Hannay's cottage.

Blair produced from his jacket the photograph he had brought. The Rose he knew with a scarf turned into a mantilla that hid half her face. 'Then who is this?'

'Unfortunately I don't know.'

'You took it.' Blair turned to the studio's name in

elaborate scrollwork on the reverse of the card. He didn't mean it as an accusation, though the photographer took a cautionary step back.

'In December, yes. I remember her, but I never got her name. She was remarkable. I think she came in on a dare. The girls do, sometimes. I asked for her name because I did want her back.' Hotham cocked his head at the picture. 'What a tease. She had a flash, you know, a pride. She didn't even tell me what pit she worked at. I showed people the photograph and asked, but with the Christmas trade coming on and all, and then the explosion in January, I forgot about her. Sorry.'

'Did you ever ask the Reverend Maypole?'

'Now that you mention it, I showed him a picture because he did know so many of the girls. He said he didn't know her.'

'That was all he said?'

'Yes, but, you know, he was so taken with the likeness that I gave it to him.'

At the office of the *Wigan Observer* Blair searched through the book *Lancashire Catholics: Obstinate Souls* until he found the reference he was looking for.

During Elizabeth's reign, Wigan was the heart of Catholic resistance, and when the Hannay family was sympathetic to their cause, a veritable rabbit warren of priests not only hid in the 'priest holes' of the Hannay estate but were so bold as to travel through

Hannay mines and hold services in the town itself. The tunnels were an underground highway, with the grandeur of Hannay Hall at one end and the most modest of working-class residences at the other. A burning candle placed in the window summoned faithful communicants to the house where the priest was expected, a beacon of religious courage that comes down to us now only in the names of Roman Alley (since demolished) and Candle Court.

The newspaper editor had been watching Blair from under his visor since he had entered. 'It's Mr Blair, isn't it? You were here two weeks ago?'

'How many Candle Courts are there?'

'Only one.'

'Built by the Hannays?'

'For miners. Some of the oldest houses in Wigan.'

'Still owned by the Hannays?'

'Yes. Remember, you were here with Mr Leveret reading newspapers about the explosion? I want to apologize because I didn't recognize you then. With your own book on the counter? I must have been blind.'

You're speaking to the blind, Blair thought.

From the distance of the alley, Blair kept pace with the miners' march home through the street. It was a Saturday, fun in the offing and a day's rest ahead. Between corners, he followed them by the sound of their clogs, a tide of rocks. The calls of street musicians and sweet vendors joined in. Overhead, doves took flight against the evening.

Mill girls were going home, too, but they made way for the pit girls. He saw Rose and Flo pass under a street lamp. Flo pinned a paper flower to her shawl and danced a jig around the smaller woman.

When Blair lost sight of them he was afraid that they would turn off to a beerhouse or pub. Behind Candle Court, he loitered in the alley until a lamp was lit in Rose's kitchen. Flo looked out of the window – no, admired herself in the glass as she replaced her shawl with a plush hat with velvet flowers. She turned to talk, vanished from sight and returned a minute later to the window, pensively at first, then with increasing interest in her reflection, finally with impatience. She added the paper flower to the garden in her hat and was gone. Blair was at the back door in time to hear the front door open and shut. No one answered his rap, and the back door was locked.

The neighbouring houses sounded like carousels of clog stamping and shouts. He waited for a peak to drive in a windowpane with his elbow. When no one appeared in alarm waving a poker, he unlatched the window and climbed in.

No one had started tea. The parlour was dark, with no candle in the front window to let the faithful know that a priest had come to serve the Eucharist, so he lit his own bull's-eye lamp. He opened the closet and kicked the floor for hollow boards. He hadn't actually seen Rose either enter or leave the house, but he was expanding the parameters of the possible, he thought. Most people, for example, would think it impossible to live in the dark or underground, yet in Wigan half the people did.

There were no false boards in the kitchen, either, but the pantry floor sounded like a drum, and under a hook rug Blair found a trapdoor that opened up to a ladder and released an upwelling of black, brackish air. He quickly went down the rungs and shut the door before anyone in the tunnel could feel a draught, and he aimed his lamp low so that the beam wouldn't carry far.

Laid long before the use of rails and tubs, the tunnel floor was polished from the ancient dragging of sledges weighted with coal. The walls, rock streaked by tracer seams of coal, transmitted distant reports of the life just overhead: the muffled slam of a door, the trotting of a cab against a sibilant background of subterranean water. Timbers propping the ceiling moaned with ancient fatigue. By the time he had paced off a quarter of a mile his compass said that the tunnel ran north-east, towards Hannay Hall. He knew that fresh air must enter along the tunnel or it would have been permeated with gas, and fifty yards on he heard street sounds filtering down from an overhead grate almost overgrown by bushes. After another fifty yards, the tunnel widened into confession stalls and benches carved out of the living rock. A remnant seam of coal was cut into a series of black chapels with crude altars, shadowy crucifixes and the perpetual attendance of black Madonnas carved in bas-relief. Ahead, where the tunnel narrowed again, he saw a lamp. He shielded his own light until the other lamp

447

disappeared at a curve in the tunnel, which allowed him to move faster and chance more noise. He was aware that the person ahead was travelling silently and quickly, familiar with the way. He started running, dodging water that had collected in the middle of the floor. The tunnel dipped and bent to the side as he expected, but when he came around the curve he was confronted by two lamps aimed at him.

Blair's own lamp lit two women very much alike. One was the girl he had seen dressed in silk at Charlotte's house, though now she wore the drab clothes and trousers of a pit girl. The other was Charlotte in her usual ebony silk dress and gloves, but her hair was loose and red and her chin was smudged with coal.

The two were almost identical in features, height and colour, but totally different in expression: the girl from the house regarded Blair with the blank eyes of a rabbit caught in the light of a train, and Charlotte glared at him with pinpoint fury. Otherwise they were images in a distorting mirror that made each woman half of the other.

'It's him. What do we do now?' the girl asked.

Charlotte said, 'If I had a gun I'd shoot him, but I don't.'

Blair said, 'You probably would.'

The girl said, 'He knows.'

Charlotte said, 'Better go home, Rose. Now.'

'This is t'last day, then?' the girl asked.

'Yes.'

Blair made room for the girl to pass in the direction he had come from. As she edged by, he saw the subtle difference of less forehead and more cheek, and watched her fear melt to a pouty anger. 'Bill'll have yer skin,' she said.

'Third time's the charm,' Blair said.

She left him with the ghost of a spiteful glance. 'He'll bury you, too, where t'worms can't reach.'

Rose Molyneux slipped around the curve, and he heard her clogs hurry into the dark. His eyes stayed on Charlotte, waiting for an explanation. She twisted from the beam of his light.

'If that's Rose, who are you? Did I catch you in transition? Were you changing yourself from a flame back into a lump of coal?'

Charlotte said, 'It was all coming to an end anyway. The days were getting lighter.'

The tunnel was cool as a crypt. The steam of her breath was no more ephemeral than she was, Blair thought. 'That's true. I never saw the Rose I knew in the light. Except for the first time, when I was blind drunk.'

She started to go and he grabbed her wrist. It was disorienting for him to talk to a Charlotte with wild red hair and the strength of a pit girl, as if he had hold of two women at the same time.

'You're put out because I fooled you.'

'You did. I preferred *your* Rose Molyneux to the one I just met. More than Charlotte Hannay. How did you do it?'

'It wasn't hard.'

'Tell me. People have been trying to kill me, thanks to your game. I'd like to know.'

'Attitude. I covered my hair, dropped my shoulders, wore gloves so no one would see calluses from working at the pit. And I'm taller in clogs.'

'More than that. Your face.'

'Pinched for Charlotte Hannay, that was all.'

'And the language?'

Charlotte put her hand on her hip and said, 'As if tha knew owt aboot t'way we speighk in Wigan or at t'Home fer Wimmen. Ah've oonly heard it aw me life.' She added in her normal voice, 'I acted.'

'You acted?'

'Yes.'

'And Flo acted?'

'Flo is a pit girl. She was my wet nurse's daughter. We used to come into town together and play Wigan lasses.'

'It was fun?'

'Yes. In masquerades that's what I always was. Not Bo Peep or Marie Antoinette: a pit girl.'

'And the family always had the tunnel from the cottage?'

'My father used it for his visits to Wigan, for his girls and fights when he was young.'

'Does your father know about this charade?'

'No.'

She tried to wrench loose and he pinned her to the wall. In the light, between her flaming hair and mourning dress, she was one woman, then the other.

'How did you find Rose?'

'She came to the Home for Women last year. She was from Manchester and she was pregnant. She'd just started working at the pit. She wasn't on the register at the Home. I couldn't persuade her to stay.'

'You noticed that you looked alike?'

'I was amused by our physical similarities and then I began to think how odd it was we could look so much alike and yet lead such different lives. Then she lost the baby and had a fever and would have lost her place at the pit, so I went in for her. She had no old friends here, the other girls hardly knew her. It wasn't as difficult as I thought it would be. It was just for a day and then for a week and after that we took turns.'

'Rose liked the idea of trading?'

'I put her in my house. She much preferred wearing nice dresses and eating sweets to sorting through coal.'

'What a social revelation. Bill Jaxon's sweet on *her*?'

'Yes.'

'Which was an arrangement I was upsetting, coming to the house in Wigan, but you didn't want to warn me. Why did *you* want to trade and play the pit girl?'

'Aren't you the one who said I was a princess, that I had no idea of real life? Admit it, you were wrong.'

'And that's where Maypole comes in. The poor bastard. That's why he had to be a miner, once he knew about you. I wondered where he got the idea.'

She sank against the wall. 'He came by the pit and saw me.'

'No one else ever recognized you?'

'No one else there knew Charlotte Hannay.'

'Then he had to match you. "My Rose," he wrote. That was you.'

'I'm sorry about John. I tried to talk him out of it. It was only going to be for a day, he said.'

'He went to Bill Jaxon to change places. Bill must have been upset to learn that Maypole had found out, but he was willing to help for love, for *his* Rose, the real Rose Molyneux, so she could go on eating chocolates while you went slumming.'

'It wasn't slumming. It was freedom to have a voice that asked for more than a cup of tea. To have a body that had desires and could satisfy them. Who wore her arms bare and cursed out loud when she felt like it.' She met his eyes. 'Who had a lover.'

'Some fool who knew no one.'

'Better than that.'

'How big a fool was I?' Blair asked. 'How many people knew? Flo, Maypole, Smallbone, Bill?'

'That's all.'

'Does Rowland know he's marrying a pit girl? That will please the new lord of the manor.'

'No.'

'Why *are* you marrying him? Why did you give in?'

'I changed my mind. What do you care? All you want to do is go back to Africa.'

'Not to leave you to him. You think Rowland's only an unpleasant cousin who will make an unpleasant husband. He's not. He's a murderer. I've seen him kill Africans who walked to the right instead of the left. And

452

he's an arsenic addict. I'm half one myself, so I know. He's worse. He's insane. If he gets one glimpse of Rose in you, you're dead.'

'That was acting.'

'Not all of it. I liked the Rose in you. He'll hate it. A shrewish, prunish Charlotte might survive a year or two with him, but you won't.'

'I was pretending with you.'

'It was real. Enough was.'

'What does it matter? I don't have a choice. I'm not really Rose, I'm Charlotte Hannay, who is marrying in two weeks.'

'When you were Rose, you asked me to take you with me to Africa.'

'I remember.'

'I'll take you.'

Someone else seemed to be speaking for him, some other half of himself, because he was as astonished as Charlotte, who caught a hint of his self-surprise.

'You're serious?'

'Yes.' He didn't want to think about it, the subject defied rational thought.

'You liked Rose that much?'

'I was getting to.'

'You liked the girl who drinks gin and pulls you into bed. What about Charlotte, someone who keeps her clothes on and has a functioning brain?'

'She can come, too. I'm offering you an escape.'

'It's the strangest proposition I've ever heard. I'm flattered, Blair. I am.'

'As soon as I collect from your father we can go.'

She scooped hair from her eyes. 'What a pair we'd make.'

'We'd be deadly.'

She looked down the tunnel as if she could glimpse a picture of the future forming in the dark. Blair could almost see it himself, some vision looming closer, dissolving as it came into view.

'I can't.'

'Why not? When you were Rose, you wanted to.'

'That was Rose. I'm a Hannay.'

'Oh, that *is* different.'

'I mean, I have responsibilities. The Home.'

'No, you mean the class difference, education, you having a real name, Rose being a footloose girl from Manchester, and God knows what my real name is. How could you entertain a trip with me when you can lock yourself up in a grand hall with a killer? I must have been joking. Perhaps I was, but I did like your imitation of a woman. It was the best one I've ever seen.'

'You're impossible.'

'I think we both are.'

'Well, we didn't get very far, did we?'

'No.' Blair agreed. He ignored the sadness in her laugh. As far as he was concerned, they were back at that point where every word between them was a stab.

She looked away, this time at nothing. 'What are you going to do?' she asked. 'Disappear?'

'Your men seem to do that. I'll miss the wedding, but I'll leave you a wedding present.'

'What is that?'
'Maypole.'
'Do you know where John is?'
'Let's say I know where to find him.'

Chapter Twenty-Seven

Night seemed to have welled from the shaft of the Hannay Pit and flooded yard, sheds and tower, as if everything up to cloud level was silent and underwater. There was no clamour of railway wagons, no coal tubs ticking to the top of the sorting shed nor rush of coals down sorting screens, no bantering of women, no line of miners murmuring towards the cage. The contrast was a blackness where locomotives sat dead on their rails and the winding tower was an unlit beacon amid a ring of shadows.

A secondary light escaped from the small upper door of the winding house where cables ran to the top of the tower. The cables were still; the cage was below and probably hadn't moved for hours. Inside the winding house, the winder would be staring at the dial of the indicator, or puttering around the great, immobile engine, keeping himself awake by oiling pistons and rods.

Air escaped from the upcast shaft, the draught driven by the pit furnace a mile below. Whether miners worked or not, the fires of the furnace stayed fed or the draught would die and the ventilation of the mine would fail.

There were two furnacemen below, Blair remembered Battie saying, the winder and perhaps a stoker above.

The lamp shed was locked. He returned from the blacksmith's forge with a bar and jemmied the shed door open. He set his knapsack and bull's-eye lamp unlit on the counter and opened the grate of a potbellied stove to a bed of half-dead coals whose glow lit the shelves. In their cages, canaries shifted and fluttered anxiously as he took a can of caulking and a safety lamp.

He walked to the tower platform, pulled the signal rope twice and heard the bell ring inside the winding house for 'Up'. A winder was supposed to stay at his post, not even leaving for a call of nature. At most, the man might glance out of the door at the platform rather than assume the signal was coming from below; Blair doubted it, but he kept his lamp dark and stood behind a leg of the tower as the great wheel overhead began to turn and the cable stirred from the ground.

He waited for the cage to make its mile trip. The furnacemen wouldn't hear it; the roar of a pit furnace covered all other sounds. As soon as the cage rose and came to a stop level with the platform, he jumped on between the tub rails and pulled the signal rope once for 'Down'.

Every descent was a controlled plunge, especially in total darkness. Midway the cage seemed to float and tap against the guide wires, a sensation of flying blind, even while the mind knew it was dropping in a steel cage. As if he ever really knew where he was. He winced. What was the speech he had given Leveret about the method of triangulation and the making of maps? That was the way he had pursued his amateur investigation, except that two of his points, Rose and Charlotte, were the same.

Pressure rose from the soles of his shoes to his knees. Round iron wire stretched as the cage shuddered between the guides and touched down at the pit eye.

There was being underground and there was being alone underground, when there was no distraction from the fact that a million tons of rock stood where the sky should be. The work of hookers and drawers pushing tubs, and farriers and stableboys tending the horses, usually created the illusion that the pit eye, underlooker's shed and stables were merely a subterranean village. Without this activity that reassuring illusion was gone and a person had to accept how far from the rest of the world he was.

A burning safety lamp stood in a pail of sand at the platform. The heat and smell of horses was, as always, overwhelming. He opened his box of matches – illicit in a mine, but who could stop him now? – and lit the safety lamp he had brought from the yard. A flame leaped behind the wire mesh. He shouldered his knapsack and found the central black tunnel called the main road. This was where a conscious choice had to be made to travel fearfully or to set off as if the earth were his.

He had studied the plan of the Hannay Pit so long that a copy was imprinted in his head. A map was everything when walking in a mine. Of course, there was also the simple method of keeping the draught at his back. He kept his head low and found a rhythm that put his feet on every second sleeper of the track. Wooden props creaked more audibly without the workaday sounds of horses and wheels. Timbers settled, dribbling dirt. He raised his safety lamp and the flame lengthened to suggest a hint of methane.

Travelling in a miner's crouch made his strapped ribs feel as if they were rubbing together, but without having to buck the traffic of ponies and tubs he made good time. He moved past refuge holes, side shafts and brattices, the canvas panels that directed air. Past where Battie had found the first two victims of afterdamp the day of the fire. Past where the tunnel plunged to the turnaround where a pony had dropped and trapped ten men on the other side. Into a lower, narrower tunnel another five hundred yards. To the coalface, with its pillars of coal and blacker void where the pillars had been stripped away.

Short-handled picks and shovels lay where they had been left the day before. Blair chose a pick and automatically moved his lamp along the roof, finding a pulse of gas with the flame at a crack or two. Nothing like the gas on the day of the explosion. Then it had been damp and unseasonably warm. As the barometer dropped, gas had seeped out of pillars, roof and shot holes. In the whole length of the tunnel, lamp flames had started to separate from their wicks, all the signs that a fastidious underlooker like Battie needed to ban shots for the day.

Sometimes men were pulled off a gassy stretch of the coal-face, but evacuate the mine? Never. Men swung picks or pushed tubs, boys went on leading ponies, all aware that in a gas-charged atmosphere a single spark could set off methane like a bomb or, after the firedamp turned to afterdamp, smother every one of them. Miners always went on working. After all, a man who came a mile underground had already made certain decisions about safety. Besides, they almost always went home at the end of the day.

Two weeks had passed since Blair's first visit. In that time the coalface had moved backwards in that curious Lancashire system of retreat, leaving a gallery of coal pillars that would slowly collapse under the weight of the earth above. Slowly in the sense of not immediately. Sometimes in a week, sometimes in a year, sometimes seemingly never. When the workings finally did cave in, they did so with a thunderous clap that sent waves of coal dust rolling to the pit eye.

The roof where he and Battie had crawled appeared clear for the first few yards; Blair couldn't see further through the ambient dust. He took a bearing from his compass. Pick in one hand and lamp and compass in the other, he crept forward into the void.

He remembered Maypole's journal entry, 'I will give thee the treasures of darkness and hidden riches of secret places.' When the curate reached the coalface, did he understand how grudgingly the Lord opened the veins of the earth?

As the roof angled down, he went backwards through evolution – from standing, to crouching, to his knees. The knapsack made progress twice as difficult until he removed it and tied it with his jacket to his leg; even so, he could move only by pushing the lamp ahead and following, a one-man train through the rubble. Sections of the roof had fallen in tomblike slabs. At one place he felt no floor at all, so he crawled along an edge to firmer ground, where he wiped his compass to reorient himself. His hands and sleeves were coated in black dust; he breathed it, choked on it, blinked to keep his eyes clear. Everything was warm, coal heated from pressure.

By now Blair was sure he had veered to the right or left, gone too far or hadn't gone far enough. The stones had shifted like a collapsed deck of cards – roof fallen in one place, floor crept up in another. He was sure he had missed what he had come for until his lamp flame seemed to lift its eyes, and through the dust he smelled the aromatic 'rot' of methane.

Within the mesh guard of the lamp, the reddish-orange nub became a taller, yellow flame with ideas, a flame with aspirations. Blair set the lamp where it was. As long as the flame stayed a flame and didn't become a blue-white column, he was on the right side of an ephemeral line. He crawled forward and saw a hastily patched wall of bricks and mortar a yard high and two yards wide. He brushed dirt off a brick to read 'Hannay Brickworks' in embossed letters; they were the same bricks, the same wall that he and Battie had found before.

He hiked himself on his elbow and dragged his knapsack close. As Battie had described it, this was not a blower, merely gas that had accumulated in waste stones and coal behind the bricks. In the intensified light he saw the telltale crack on the upper row of bricks behind which methane, lighter than air, would lurk. Lying on his side, he pulled the can of caulking out of his knapsack. He levered open the lid with his pocket knife and scooped the resinous tar out of the can with the blade of his knife, smeared the crack and lay back to see the effect. If the caulking was 'Good enough for the Royal Navy!', it ought to be good enough for the Hannay Pit.

Slowly the flame of the safety lamp cooled to its usual modest orange. Blair tapped the bottom row of bricks with the tip of the pick. Since methane was lighter than air, explosive gas should be confined to the upper space behind the wall, and it would be safe to remove a bottom brick. Theoretically. Which was why mining was both an art and a science, he told himself, because miners, like artists, died young.

Lying on his side, Blair delivered a more solid tap to the base of the wall. As two bottom bricks separated, he saw his own shadow rise up the wall, and when he looked back at the lamp he saw a flame tall enough to lick the cap. He dropped the pick and pressed himself as deep into rubble as he could. Billows of methane lit softly in shades of blue, floating on the heavier air, lapping under the low roof, enveloping him in liquid light. He lay still. Waving a jacket helped when gas wasn't lit; when it was lit, oxygen fed it. He held his breath to keep fire out of his lungs until the burning gas spread, broke and scattered into imps that slipped into crannies and disappeared.

The flame of his lamp settled again, although the

smell of methane was pungent, as if he had plunged into a swamp. He pulled out the loose bricks and reached inside. His fingers felt around until they found, buried by stones, something that was not a rock. He pulled it out and replaced and caulked the bricks, then rolled closer to the light to examine a charred and twisted safety lamp. The lamp was constructed so that it was impossible, short of disassembling it, to remove the safety gauze, but the gauze was gone, ripped out. He rubbed the lamp base and held it to the light. Scratched into the brass was a number: 091. This was the lamp that 'Jaxon' had signed out on the morning of the explosion. No wonder Smallbone and the real Bill Jaxon had volunteered to make their way back to the coalface, for fear of someone else finding the lamp or any other sign of Maypole. To have to rebrick a wall was a godsend to the two men.

The explosion was clear enough now. After Smallbone had brought Maypole down, he had taken the opportunity to 'lark' in a middle tunnel – his habit, Battie had said – leaving Maypole alone at the darkest end of the coalface when he had never been down a deep pit in his life. What kind of spiritual experience was that? Did he fall to his knees in prayer or did he start to feel the weight of the earth above him, listen to the timbers, sense the air start to thin? He had no friend to guide him as Flo had guided Charlotte, and he would have been warned to stay clear of other miners, so he had neither experience nor companionship as solace. And the miners, had they wondered how oddly 'Jaxon' was acting? But who would have dared question as volatile a character if he felt anti-social?

The first time in a pit, men were often so afraid of their lamp going out that they would wind the wick up until someone shouted 'Turn her down!' Then they would overwind the other way, snuff the flame and be left in the dark. Did Maypole strike a match? Was that what he had done? Or had he yielded to the temptation of setting off a shot by himself? Jaxon had bored holes into the coal the day before. Smallbone's tin box of prepared charges was at Maypole's feet. Had he slipped one of those paper tubes of gunpowder into a hole and experimentally tamped it with his pick instead of a fireman's rod of non-sparking brass?

Then there was such a thing as spontaneous explosion. From methane, from the heat generated in coal as it was crushed, from the combustibility of coal dust in the air. It happened.

But what Blair believed most likely had happened was that a careful, dutiful Maypole had done nothing worse than tap the coalface with his pick, hear the firedamp whistle out, and then instinctively, like the good man he was, run to warn the other men working the coalface. Which, as the Inspector of Mines had said, no experienced miner would have done, because running pressed the flame through the mesh of the safety lump to the very gas a man was trying to escape.

Probably that was what had happened. In his innocence, Maypole had tried to warn the other men, and probably they smelled the gas, saw Maypole running with his lamp towards them and begged him to stop. All it took was one blue tip of flame pressed through the safety gauze. The force that ripped out the gauze and twisted the lamp like toffee put him and no one else at the point of the explosion. Where was the rest of Maypole? There might be parts, atoms of the man, but not enough for worms. It was too deep for worms, anyway, as Rose Molyneux had said.

In his journal Maypole had cited Job. 'I went mourning without the sun. My skin is black upon me, and my bones are burned.' Well, that prediction was true enough and he had taken seventy-six other men with him. And when the heroic rescuers Smallbone and Jaxon found Maypole's lamp they bricked it away for eternity and scratched the same number – 091 – on to the lamp Jaxon had brought, so that the lamp system itself would *prove* that every man had been accounted for.

Blair replaced and caulked the bricks, stuffed the lamp into his knapsack and crawled back through rubble to the coalface. He got to his feet, looking not so much like a miner now, he thought, as a stick of charcoal. He didn't feel vindicated, he felt sad, because in the end he admitted they had shared so much in common.

He staggered to the main road, keeping the welcome draught in his face. After a taste of methane, even foul air was an improvement. He was climbing the incline to the turnaround when the rails began to vibrate underfoot. He thought it might be from a rockfall until he heard a squeal of metal wheels. Out of sight, a train of tubs was moving.

A train was half a ton of slackly chained iron-plate tubs that at first push rolled in a lethargic, uncoordinated way. Blair backtracked and looked for room to let them pass by. He heard the train drop into a straightway, smooth out and gather speed. He wasn't gathering speed himself. Between his strapped ribs and the weight of his knapsack, he stumbled over railway sleepers, outpacing the poor glow of his safety lamp. The rails resonated underfoot. Runaway trains were one of the more common causes of fatalities in pits; with momentum, tubs tended to carry and drag whatever they met. He saw them career around the head of the incline, chains banging, filling the low shaft. He dived into a refuge hole as the lead tub clipped his heel and the train whipped by in the direction of the coalface.

After the reverberation of the tubs receded, he heard a rhythmic scraping, like a knife being sharpened. He looked with one eye from the refuge hole. A figure in a skater's crouch, outlined in yellow, a lamp in one hand and a pick in the other, was sliding sideways on the irons of his clogs down an incline rail.

Blair pulled himself in as Bill Jaxon passed, silk scarf at his neck, his back to the refuge hole. He took one-legged strides and balanced on sparks that faded like a comet burrowing through the ground. Blair felt a burning stab and realized that the only reason he hadn't been seen was that he was lying on his own lamp. He unbent on to the track and patted out the charred circle on his jacket. He was halfway to the cage and could reach it long before Bill could turn around from the coalface. He had just topped the incline, however, when he heard clogs following at an easy lope. Jaxon hadn't gone to the coalface at all. He had just flushed him out.

'Rose told me she met you!' Bill called. 'I want to hear about it!'

There was no chance of outracing Jaxon the remaining distance to the cage, or of hiding. His lamp would lead Bill right to him, yet he couldn't put it out without being blind. He pictured the main road he was on, the back road, and all the short side tunnels that connected the two main tunnels. The next side tunnel was covered by a brattice to keep air flowing straight, and he slipped through it towards the back road.

A moment later he was joined by Bill's voice. 'Good try, but don't you think I know t'pit better than you?'

The back road carried return tracks and spent air to the furnace. An oily wind, directed by more panels of canvas, pushed Blair's back. He pulled panels into the tunnel as he moved to block Bill's view of his lamp. Doing so, he hit his head on a low beam and was so dazed for a moment that he didn't know which way to go. From a wetness welling in his ear he was aware that a scar had opened.

'All you had t'do was leave us be,' Bill called.

Blair moved as best he could while he heard Jaxon smashing the brattices he had left behind. He ducked through a side tunnel back to the main road. Through other side tunnels he heard Bill running parallel on the back road. There was a small advantage in that shoes were quieter than clogs, though an ant could claim the same edge. Within a few steps, Jaxon would be crossing to the main road.

A solitary coal tub stood on the track. Blair put his shoulder to it and pushed it downhill towards the coalface. As he looked over his shoulder, Bill's lamp appeared above him on the main road.

Blair put his lamp into the tub, let it go and ducked to the side. The grade was mild; the tub didn't gather speed, but it didn't stop either. The glow of Blair's safety lamp bounced along the roof. In pursuit, Bill skated down the rail in graceful, burning strides.

In the black, Blair fumbled through a side tunnel to the back road and lit the bull's-eye lamp from his knapsack. The match burned bright and the lamp's narrow beam shot ahead, fuelled by the tinge of methane in the air.

After a hundred feet he dared return to the main road. His feet were heavy as andirons, his lungs wheezing in imitation of punctured bags. The stink of the stables was sweet, though, and the dim lamp in its pail of sand was the candle of a sanctuary. The cage sat waiting at the pit eye.

He heard Bill returning up the main road, furious. How he had caught the tub and returned so fast, Blair didn't understand, but he had. Blair stepped on to the cage and hit the signal rope.

As the cage lifted, Bill ran at full tilt out of the road and raced past the stable stalls. From Jaxon's eyes, Blair saw that he was gauging a leap for the rising cage, at the last moment saw that he would fall short, and instead flew the width of the shaft.

Blair sank to the floor of the cage, cradling his lamp and knapsack on his knees as it rocketed up. Through its open side, the beam lit a blur of damp, undulating stone and even though he knew he was headed for a yard of coal and slag he smelled grass and trees.

As the cage slowed, he pulled himself to his feet. The approach seemed endless. Finally, the cage inched up to a lakelike glimmer of lamps and the touch on his face of a genuine breeze. Locomotives crouched, sphinxes in the yard. The flag on the tower was a crescent moon.

As he stepped on to the platform, Albert Smallbone slipped from a tower leg and hit him with a shovel.

Blair stretched out on his back, the square edge of the shovel pressed under his jaw, Smallbone at the other end.

'Have you ever hunted with ferrets?' Smallbone asked. 'Hardly worth it. Worse than criminals. The ferret chases t'rabbit to the end of a hole and then proceeds t'eat him. Not what you sent him down for. If the leash on him breaks, you have t'start digging with a spade t'save some supper for yourself. Anyway, you're my rabbit now and Bill will be up in a mo.'

The cable was reeling fast. Blair couldn't see how much was left because whenever he shifted Smallbone pressed the shovel blade against his neck. His upended knapsack and its contents were spread around Small-bone's feet.

'The first time you went digging with George Battie, I told Bill you'd be back down pit. He didn't believe me. Bill's not bright, but he's beautiful, an element of nature. Like his Rose. I'm a more thoughtful man, like you, but we have t'appreciate people for what they are.'

Blair grunted to hold up his end of the conversation.

Smallbone said, 'Rose told us what she told you, which wasn't the sort of thing t'say to a suspicious man. Weren't we lucky t'get here when we did? Like I was lucky t'be taking a rest from the coalface when the whole pit went t'hell. You know, people have always struck me as the most fascinating of subjects. Rose is not so persuasive to me, but she has her way with Bill. It's Samson and Delilah. I never would have let Maypole take Bill's place, but she liked her special days in the rich house all to herself, and once Maypole got wind of what was up, she was afraid he'd expose her and Miss Hannay. We didn't do anything wrong. None of us did. All we did was help a preacher get a taste of the real world.'

'He wasn't ready for it,' Blair whispered against the shovel.

'You're right there. All I asked him t'do was sit still while I took a rest. That wasn't too much t'ask, I thought. But now you see our situation. Bill, Rose and me, we've done nothing wrong, but we'd be charged for seventy-six deaths. Not even Mrs Smallbone would pray for me, and, believe me, she prays for everyone. God knows, we tried t'warn you off.'

'Like you warned Silcock?'

'That was a botched job. He leeched on to Harvey after the fire and we couldn't know what Harvey had said in his condition. Nothing as it turns out, I suppose. He didn't drown. No harm done.'

'Twiss?'

'We took him for a walk. In Harvey's grief and such, I think it was a mercy.'

'Bill tried to kill me.'

'Bill's heavy-handed, but the idea people might suppose his Rose and you were intimate was a provocation.'

'And the spring gun?'

'An inhuman device. I hated t'set it, but if nothing else it should have been a message. The truth is, you could have left Wigan any time, and you didn't, and now it's too late.'

The cable made an ascending note. Blair knew that if he called to the winding house, Smallbone would cut him off, and even if he didn't the winder probably wouldn't hear anything over the popping of pistons and valves. So what would it be? A trip to the railway line where he could lay his weary head on a track like Harvey Twiss?

The cage rose to the platform and shook as two clogs stepped off and blocked Blair's view. They were familiar clogs with brass caps that shone like spear points of gold. With them aimed at Blair, Smallbone immediately hit the signal rope and the cage started back down.

'That was a good run,' Bill said.

'Good as a Christian athlete?' Blair remembered his first conversation with Jaxon at the Young Prince.

471

'Almost.'

The winder must wonder why the cage kept going up and down, Blair thought, but it was all the more reason for him not to leave his post.

'You were with Twiss when the gas exploded,' Blair said to Jaxon.

Bill looked at Smallbone, who watched the shaft swallow the cage and said, 'It doesn't matter.'

They weren't going to march to any railway tracks or canal, Blair realized. When the cage hit bottom, they would just drop him in after and he'd be one more casualty of a late-night stroll in Wigan. He saw himself plunging down the shaft. 'I shot an arrow into the air, it fell to earth, I know not where.' Well, he would know.

'What do you think happened?' Blair asked.

'The explosion? My opinion?' Smallbone said. He kept his weight on the shovel and his eye on the descending cable. 'It's all a laugh. The Lord giveth and the Lord taketh away, and he's splitting his sides while he does it.'

Blair looked at the twisted brass that had been a safety lamp. 'Did Maypole know?'

'Maybe; he certainly had a bright light t'see by. The truth is, a miner who thinks he's not working in his own grave s'fool. I knew that of Maypole. I'm surprised t'find out you're one, too.'

He nodded to Bill, who drew back his clog to kick Blair over the edge, but was distracted by someone crossing the dark yard without a lamp.

Smallbone squinted to make the figure out and called, 'Is that Wedge? Battie?'

Charlotte answered, 'I talked to Rose.'

'Get rid of him,' Smallbone told Bill, who kicked Blair over.

Charlotte was in trousers and shirt and carried a long-handled shovel, the kind used for sorting coal. When she hit Smallbone the shovel blade made the sound of a Chinese gong.

Blair had caught a guide rope of steel and tried to climb back up. Smallbone was felled by another blow from Charlotte. She was a blur, wielding the heavy shovel like a two-handed sword. Blair reached from the rope to the platform, where Bill waited for him. Charlotte dug the shovel into Bill's back, and when he didn't budge she threw it at his head, getting his attention. He turned and backhanded her. Blair watched her drop as he crawled on to the boards. He picked up the loose shovel and when Bill turned back to him, he swung it with all his might at Bill's knee, like a man's first chop at a tree. Bill tilted to the side. Blair tossed him the shovel. As Bill caught it with both hands, Blair stepped forward and with his fist hit him at the point where his brows met. Bill stepped back where there was nothing but air and balanced, one foot on the edge. His scarf snapped around him in the downdraught. When he dropped the shovel, it rattled off his foot and moved him another millimetre over the shaft. The shovel chased the cage, the blade singing off stone.

'Ah got thee, Bill, me boy.' Smallbone wrapped his hand on Jaxon's.

Reaching for Smallbone had the effect of tipping Bill

the opposite way. Despite Smallbone's grip, the angle continued to change the wrong way, and Bill's clog slid. The iron he had skated on was moving over the worn wood of the platform edge.

'Fooking Maypole,' Bill said. He added, 'That's it.'

His eyes rolled back and the rest of him followed. He made one stroke with his free arm and fell.

'Jesus,' Smallbone said.

He scraped crabways across the boards and tried to free himself from Bill's grasp, and then he disappeared over the lip too.

Chapter Twenty-Eight

A breeze moved ahead of Blair, making a froth of daisies. He had been on the trail before, so it was easy to follow, even easier when marked by a satin ribbon snatched from a skirt or by the cough of a gun ahead.

Meadows led to higher slopes of sheep separated by rows of black rocks. He wore a Harris-tweed jacket over what felt like new ribs, and he breathed without a twinge air that seemed to buzz with life, as if the opalescent glint of insects in flight was a low field of electricity that charged every object in sight. From time to time he stopped to slip the knapsack off his shoulder and focus his new telescope on a hawk hovering over a tumbledown cairn or a lamb nosing through heather.

He turned the glass to the final hill, where wind combed grass up to a picnic set under clouds as white and still as columns. The oriental carpet of the Hannays was spread out as before. Lady Rowland and Lydia again were dressed as genteel, animated flowers, the mother's ensemble the velvet mauve of an American aster, and the daughter in a lavender dress of crêpe de Chine, her golden hair gathered into a sun hat, the muted colours reflecting the ambiguous state the family now inhabited. The men – Hannay, Rowland, Leveret – were in black.

Drowsy flies crawled over the remains of potted duck, savoury pie, biscuits and stirrup cups of claret. A musk of gunpowder lingered in the air.

At the sight of Blair, Lady Rowland blushed with irritation, and Lydia, like a gilded statue, looked around for a cue.

'The very man,' Rowland said.

Hannay sat up stiffly and shielded his eyes. Blair noticed signs of disrepair on the Bishop, a sugary stubble on the jaw.

'A face to cheer us up. Good. The rest of us are inconsolable, but you, Blair, seem fully recovered. Shaved, healed, in the pink.'

'Better yet, paid,' Blair said. 'Outfitted and on my way back to Africa, thanks to you. I'm sorry about your daughter.'

'It was unexpected.'

Lady Rowland said, 'It was a bitter disappointment.' She didn't sound disappointed. If anything, satisfaction lurked in the corners of her mouth.

Lydia shimmered like flowers, a table arrangement brought out of doors. She asked, 'When are you leaving?'

'Tomorrow. Your uncle has kindly employed me to finish my survey of Gold Coast mines, though I was thinking of staying a while longer to search for my mother's family. She was from here. I'll probably never have another chance.'

'I'm surprised you stayed as long as you did,' Hannay said.

'It's beautiful country.'

'From an old Africa hand, that's a compliment,' Rowland said. 'You have risen from the grave. I heard you stayed in our old house for a week before moving back to the Minorca. You have truly infested the complete environs. Sort of a black cousin.'

'The arsenic's holding out?'

'The pharmacist is a good man. You know him well yourself.'

'One more thing we share.'

'The last thing. How are you on irony?'

'Mother's milk.'

'Chief Constable Moon tells me about a pair of miners who fell down a Hannay shaft two weeks ago in the middle of the night. They were found in the morning when the cage came up. They were dead, mangled from the impact and from hitting walls on the way down, according to the Coroner.'

'What a gruesome story,' Lady Rowland said. 'Why would the Chief Constable bother you with a story like that?'

'He knows my interest in unusual phenomena.'

'Two drunks falling down a well doesn't sound unusual.'

'What's unusual is that two experienced miners could have fallen down a shaft at the very pit where they worked. The same two men were heroes in the explosion at that pit in January. If that isn't irony, what is?'

'Or a moral tale,' Blair said.

'What is the moral?' Lydia sounded lost.

Lady Rowland said, 'That's it, dear, we'll never know. The lives those people lead are so different.'

Rowland wasn't done. 'It was the same night, in fact, that Charlotte disappeared, so we have irony *and* coincidence. Perhaps it's the coincidence we should concentrate on.'

Leveret said, 'There would have to be a connection. Charlotte didn't know the miners, had probably never seen them.'

'She was familiar with pit girls. My uncle is closing the Home for Women at my insistence.'

'If that satisfies you,' Blair said.

'Nothing satisfies me. I have earned fame. I carry a great name; at least I will. But it is as if I have been promised a garden in the centre of which is a tree with a certain apple. All my life I have expected to bite into that apple, and now I am told that the garden is mine but that the apple has been stolen by someone else. My satisfaction has been stolen.'

'You still get the coal,' Blair said.

Hannay said, 'Blair had a fall of his own some weeks ago. I visited him. He was delirious most of the time. His recovery is remarkable.'

'Thank you,' Blair said. It was true, even the malaria had abated. No more brown piss, his water was pure as a mountain spring. 'Perhaps it's the air.'

Lydia said, 'You should take up residence in Wigan.'

'I'm tempted. Quit gold for the homelier pursuit of coal.'

'What precisely do you know about your mother?' she asked.

'Nothing precise. We were sailing to America when she died. She told people on the ship she was from Wigan. She could have been a maid, a mill or shop girl, a pit girl.'

Lady Rowland said, 'There must have been a name on the baggage or something.'

'She didn't have any baggage. If she had any papers, she tore them up or threw them away.'

Rowland said, 'She was in trouble. Or perhaps she didn't want you coming back to bother relatives.'

'That's what I always thought,' Blair said. 'Yet here I am.'

Hannay poured a glass of wine for Blair, who took it but remained standing. The Bishop said, 'You should see Rowland shoot. His aim is extraordinary. He has been decimating the animal population.'

'We went shooting together in Africa. He decimated the population there too.'

'Your health.' Leveret raised his glass to Blair. 'I'm glad you're still here.'

He had said not a word about Blair's visit to the stable or taking a carriage two weeks before when everyone else supposed he was too damaged to rise from bed.

'A curious thing,' Hannay said. 'We always dreaded Charlotte's arrival at the table or at any outing. Now I've come to realize that she was, in fact, the centre of every event. Without her everything seems pointless.'

'Life goes on,' Lady Rowland said.

'But life is not the same.' Hannay watched Rowland open a box of cartridges. 'Nephew, your hands are shaking.'

'It's the malaria,' Lady Rowland said. 'We'll go to London, see the doctors and stay for the season. Rowland will be the most eligible man there. He'll have to run from the women.'

'And vice versa,' Blair said.

'It won't be the same without Charlotte,' Lydia said. 'I was always intimidated by her because she was so intelligent, but I was thrilled by her because I never knew what she would say next.'

'Whatever are you talking about?' Lady Rowland asked. 'Dear, you will have a glorious season of your own, and we won't remember any of this. Even Mr Blair will fade from memory.'

'Did the detectives find anything?' Lydia asked.

'No.' Her mother shot a glance at the gamekeepers and repeated more softly, 'No. Your uncle engaged the best private agency in Manchester. There wasn't a sign. You have to think of the family now.'

'Blair could look,' Lydia said.

'Yes, Blair was such a great success at finding Maypole,' Rowland said. 'Uncle, would you please read the letter that came today?'

The Bishop's eyes stayed fixed on the wall that marked the horizon. His hand fumbled absently for a letter he took from the breast pocket of his coat and handed it to Leveret.

'Go ahead,' Rowland ordered.

Leveret unfolded the paper. He swallowed and read aloud:

My Lord Hannay,

This is by way of both farewell and apology for the concern I have caused you. I claim no excuse for my behaviour; I do, however, have reasons that I wish to explain in hopes you may some day think of me with some understanding and forgiveness. If I disappointed you, I have disappointed myself tenfold. I was not the curate I could be, no more than Wigan was the simple parish I first took it as. It is, in fact, two worlds, a daylit world of servants and carriages, and a separate world that labours underground. As my work went on, I discovered that I could not be curate to both those worlds with an equal heart. At one time, like the Reverend Chubb, I honoured dry scholarship above the friendship of my fellow man. I can say now that there is no prize on earth greater than the good regard of the working men and women of Wigan. The vanity of the Church I will miss for not one moment. Wigan, though, will always be in my heart.

I begin a new ministry of my own tomorrow. Thanks be to God, I will not bear this burden alone, for Charlotte has joined me. I cannot share with you our destination, but please know that we are content as two who are armoured by complete trust in God. Tomorrow the great adventure begins!

With respect and love,

Your humble, obedient, John Maypole.

Leveret looked at the envelope. 'It bears a Bristol postmark from three days ago.'

Blair said, 'I would have sworn Maypole was dead.'

'Not according to that letter,' Rowland said.

'It is John's handwriting,' Leveret said. 'These are his most personal sentiments. I've heard him say some of the same words.'

Rowland said, 'Hundreds of ships have left the port of Bristol in the last three days. They could be anywhere in Europe by now, or playing missionary in any slum in the south of England.'

'Do you think they're married?' Lydia asked.

'Of course they're married,' Lady Rowland said. 'It doesn't matter, your uncle will cut her off. He has to. She spited the family to run off with a madman.'

Blair asked, 'That's all Maypole wrote? Nothing about why he disappeared or where he went?'

'That's all,' Leveret said.

Lydia said, 'We have been waiting for a letter from Reverend Maypole for months, haven't we?'

Lady Rowland said, 'He must have been communicating secretly with Charlotte all that time. We called off the detectives. There's nothing to be gained from finding two runaways.'

Leveret removed his hat as if discovering what a warm lid it was. Pinpoints of blue marked his skin at the hairline. 'Do you think you'll need help in Africa?' he asked.

'No. Sorry.'

'The question is', Rowland said, 'whether Blair was in

on it with Maypole from the start. I saw the way Charlotte looked at him when I came with the gifts for the Royal Society.'

'The monkey gloves?' Blair asked.

'Earnshaw told me how Blair was always after her, turning her against me.'

'She didn't act overly fond of me.'

'You were both acting. You were Maypole's agent all along.'

'Your Grace?' Blair appealed for a rebuttal from the Bishop, but Hannay seemed hardly to be listening.

'You never found out about your mother?' Lydia tried to change the subject.

'No, I suppose not. Maybe I prefer the mystery.'

Rowland said, 'Some mystery. A slut gets pregnant by a shop boy, has the brat, is worn goods, gets with child again, though not by any man thick enough to marry her, begs a ticket to America and ends her short, ugly life on the way. I might be wrong on a detail or two, but I would consider this mystery solved. Don't try to lend her dignity by calling it that.'

Blair counted the two steps it would take to cross the carpet, one in the mustard and one in pie, to reach Rowland, who raised his shotgun and said, 'No palm trees or natives to hide behind now, are there? What do you think of my detective work? I think I finally have you. Your mother was a willing whore, a syphilitic, nameless nobody, the sort of garbage ships throw overboard at sea every day. Is that close enough?'

Blair shrugged. 'You know, I have often said the same

– and worse – for years. Because I was abandoned, whether she could help it, whether she died or not. It helps to hear the words from you because it reminds me how stupid and venomous they are. Especially stupid. Because she was no more than a girl, and when I think about how abandoned she must have been, without a penny after she got her ticket, no baggage, friendless, powerless, fatally ill before she got on board and knowing that she would probably die at sea, I appreciate how much courage it took for her to escape from here. So the one thing I know about my mother is how brave she was, and since I didn't understand that until I came to Wigan, I suppose it was worth the trip.'

He finished his wine and set it down. It felt wonderful not to have every bone an aching worm. The shotgun started to transmit Rowland's tremor and sweat rolled off his face.

'You shoot too much, dear,' Lady Rowland said. 'It makes you feverish.'

Hannay leaned forward with a heavy whisper. 'Rowland, if you ate less arsenic, your hands wouldn't shake. If you were any whiter you could be a snowman, and if you were any more insane you could be the Archbishop of Canterbury. My advice is to marry while you still have the wits not to climb the drapes. Responsibilities come first; madmen are not admitted to the House of Lords. You can go mad once you're in.'

'May I?' Leveret eased the shotgun from Rowland's hands.

'Well, I hate to go,' Blair said.

He slipped the knapsack over his shoulder and started down the path the way he had come. He had gone a hundred yards when he became aware of someone wading through the grass after him. He turned and faced Hannay.

'Your Grace?'

'Thank you, Blair. So rare of you to bow to me in any way. About the letter.'

'Yes?'

Hannay had it in his hand. He unfolded the single page and scanned the lines.

'It's well done. All the Maypole tics and flourishes. The question is, do I believe it?'

'Do you?'

'Not for a moment.'

Blair said nothing. Hannay blinked. In his eyes was salt water. His coat shook in the wind, loose as a sail.

'Not literally,' the Bishop added.

'What does that mean?'

'Not word for word. People sometimes ask me whether to believe in Genesis. Were Earth and the Heavens created in six days? Was Eve fashioned from Adam's rib? Not literally. It's a message, not a fact. The best we can do is try to understand.'

'Do you understand?'

'Yes.' Hannay refolded the page and pressed it flat in his breast pocket.

Blair looked back from the path. Hannay rejoined the picnic and it continued, barely audible from this distance. The scene had re-established the languor of an

English family set between English hills and English clouds, the sky as liquid as a pool.

From the bottom of the hill he looked back again and they were as tiny as figures in a bead of water.

Chapter Twenty-Nine

In the haze of a Liverpool afternoon, the African steamship *Blackland* parted from the North Landing and rode the ebb tide out of the Mersey. Heavy with goods, low in the water, it nudged through the coal barges and ketches of the Long Reach, bearing north to begin with, then bending west and finally south to the open sea.

The *Blackland* was a doughty ark of civilization fat with Manchester cloth, Birmingham buttons, Bibles from Edinburgh and, from Sheffield, pots, pans, nails and saws. From London came *Punch, The Times*, and communiqués from the Colonial Office issuing Imperial orders and franchises, not to mention the mailbags of personal letters that made foreign service bearable. Packed with excelsior in wooden crates were cognac, sherry and trade gin, as well as quinine, opium and citric acid. From the hold wafted the perfume of the palm oil it carried on return trips.

The captain made a bonus on the fuel he conserved, and at best the *Blackland* made eight knots, which seemed none as it fought the oncoming swells of the North Atlantic. At the Bay of Biscay, however, the Canary current would surface and sweep the ship towards Africa. The *Blackland* would visit Madeira, execute a cautious swing around the emirates of the western Sahara, where Europeans had for centuries believed that the sea boiled and the earth ended, and, borne by the warm equatorial current, begin its African calls.

Passengers gathered in the first-class cabin at four for dinner and at seven for tea and on their first night out stayed on deck late before retiring to their cramped berths. Coal soot spread by the engine stack made the ship into a locomotive under the ocean night.

Ahead of the stack, though, the rail was a balustrade for constellations as brilliant as freshly lit fires, familiar stars prized because they would soon be traded for the Southern Cross.

Finally, singly and in groups, the passengers tired and went below. Wesleyan missionaries already praying for Zulu souls. A doctor, not too well himself, dispatched to the smallpox epidemic in Grand Bassam. Salesmen versed in tinware, drugs, gunpowder, soap. A lieutenant headed for Sierra Leone to drill Jamaicans shipped for African duty. A new consul for Axim. Creoles in frock-coats and beaver hats.

And last on deck, bound for the Gold Coast, a mining engineer named Blair and his wife, whom he called Charlotte, except when he called her Rose.